Between Friends

BETWEEN FRIENDS

Audrey Howard

CENTURY

LONDON SYDNEY AUCKLAND JOHANNESBURG

Reprinted 1989

First published in Great Britain in 1988 by
Century Hutchinson Ltd
Brookmount House, 62–65 Chandos Place
London WC2N 4NW

Century Hutchinson South Africa (Pty) Ltd
PO Box 337, Bergvlei, 2012 South Africa

Century Hutchinson Australia Pty Ltd
89–91 Albion Street, Surry Hills,
NSW 2010, Australia

Century Hutchinson New Zealand Ltd
PO Box 40–086, Glenfield, Auckland 10
New Zealand

ISBN 0 7126 2292 6

Printed in Great Britain by
Mackays of Chatham PLC, Chatham, Kent

I would like to dedicate this book, with my dearest love, to my sister and brother-in-law, Wendy and Bob Beverly.

Chapter one

The kitchen door stood wide open and the young girl who came through it paused for a moment in the doorway as the full force of the midday sun struck her. The heat seemed to be sucked down the narrow steps to the basement door of the tall house and she narrowed her eyes in the glare, lifting her left hand to shade them from its brightness. In her right hand she held an iron bucket filmed with coal dust.

'Lord, it's hot!' she exclaimed over her shoulder to someone in the kitchen, then began to climb the worn steps, the bucket held well away from her full, grey cotton skirt and the fresh whiteness of her well-starched apron. When she reached the gate at the top of the area steps she opened it, stopping to lean for a moment or two on the iron railings which surrounded the area, savouring the languorous heat of the sun and the dust-filled peace of the square.

A youth on its far side who was indolently shovelling horse droppings from the cobbled roadway into a bucket straightened up slowly when he saw her and his small eyes gleamed. He turned his head quickly to look about him but apart from himself and several curiously dressed small children who sprawled listlessly on the pavement, their feet in the gutter, the square was deserted.

The sun shone brassily on well-painted window frames and the open doors of the terraced Regency houses which surrounded the square and winked back from polished windows. The houses were elegantly simple though well past their best, once the homes of Liverpool's merchants and men of shipping before they had amassed their wealth five decades ago and moved out to Everton and West Derby and the mansions they had built for themselves there. They were narrow, constructed from the locally produced bricks before the days of mass production, before the days of the railways which had transported them, the façades a warm red, edged at each flat window and arched, ornamental doorway in white.

The youth put down his bucket and stepped lightly across the

7

heap of stinking manure. The small garden in the centre of the square was dry now, the grass a lifeless brown, the marigolds and lavender which had been so lively several weeks ago wilted and parched in the still and withering air. The dessicated leaves of the sycamore trees cast a deep shade about him as he moved across it but the usual assortment of old, pipe-smoking men and mongrel dogs who normally sought its sanctuary were missing today, electing to lounge in the cooler shade of a back yard or a shadowed doorway, too enervated in the dense heat to totter even to the garden's wooden benches.

The girl withdrew a scrap of white linen from a pocket in her apron and delicately wiped the perspiration from her upper lip. She was tall. Though her waist and hips were slender with the child-like shapelessness of adolescence, her breasts were already budding, promising a full roundness, a womanliness to come. Her skin, a rich creamy-white, was revealed by her rolled up sleeves and the buttons she had undone at her throat but it was her hair which immediately drew the eye for it was a shining flame, like copper caught in the sun's rays, a vividly abundant warmth which curled vigorously, riotously about her shapely head.

She began to saunter towards the side of the house, the bucket still held carefully away from the full folds of her skirt. She swayed gracefully, her young body relaxed and dreaming, her skirt swinging from side to side, her left hand twitching the hem away from the pointed toes of her black boots as she had seen the grand ladies do in Dale Street. The house was the end one of a row and when she reached the narrow passage which separated it from its neighbour she turned into it and for several seconds, though she continued to move along its familiar length towards the strip of yard at its rear, she was blinded. It was like stepping into a long dark tunnel, cool and completely shaded from the sun and her eyes narrowed as they adjusted to the sudden change. A thin strip of vivid blue sky divided the high walls which rose on either side of her and she craned her neck to look up to it, still, it appeared, deep in the strange relaxed torpor the heat of the day had induced in her.

She sensed rather than heard his footsteps at her back. Though the old cobbles which lined the passage were of stone, moss and grasses had grown up through them, carpeting the ground, softening the sound of his boots and he was almost upon her when she whirled about.

He stopped at once as she faced him, holding up his hands in a supplicatory manner. He grinned foolishly, moving from one foot to the other, swaying in the fashion of a wrestler looking for a weak spot in an opponent but it seemed the girl was irritated rather than afraid though she swung the bucket defensively nevertheless.

'What do you want, Fancy O'Neill?' she said sharply.

'Nowt really, Meg. I seed yer from across the square an' I thought seein' as 'ow you an' me are friends I'd nip over an' pass the time o' day, like.'

'Friends!' she snorted derisively. 'Since when were you an' me friends, Fancy O'Neill?'

'Now don't be like that, Meggie.' The youth took a step towards her and she moved back, going deeper into the trap he had set for her.

'Like what? You've got no friends! Who'd want to be your "wacker", I'd like to know and what d'you think you're doing following me down this ginnel. You're trespassing, that's what you're doing and if Mr Hemingway was to hear of it you'd be for it so clear off, d'you hear me.'

'Now Meggie.' He moved another step nearer, the size of him effectively blocking out the sultry sunshine which fell about the entry to the passage and as his shadow loomed over her he put out a hand and laid it tentatively on her upper arm, stroking it as though she was a restive mare.

She sprang back and her pale amber eyes flared to blazing gold.

'Don't you touch me, Fancy O'Neill. You put your hand on me again and I'll hit you so hard with this flaming bucket I'll bash your brains in.' Her voice was scornful. 'Not that it'd make much difference since you never use what few you've got. Now get out of me way. Go on, clear off!'

She hissed the last words through clenched teeth and the look of revulsion on her face was so strong it twisted her mouth into a grimace and she gave the appearance of having stepped into something unmentionable. She swung the empty bucket menacingly in her work-strong hand and the echo of its clangour as it hit the wall of the narrow passage rang hollowly upwards. A flock of house martins, disturbed by the noise plunged frantically low over the walls which split the yards at the back of the houses, diving and twisting up again and over the roof to the next street,

9

but the sparrows which pecked fearlessly at the sour soil, used to human commotion, scarcely lifted their beaks.

The girl was clearly becoming angry and her free hand clenched into a fist.

'Let me get by, you filthy beggar. Go on, shift yourself.'

'Aah Meg, I'll not hurt yer. I only want a little kiss. Only one, honest. Go on, yer'll like it, really, just one little kiss. It's not much to ask, is it, seein' as 'ow you an' me's such good friends. What's one little kiss? Yer'll never even miss it!'

The enormous youth who blocked the passage smirked in what he imagined to be an engaging manner and began to move in a crab-like crawl along the wall of the house ready to leap aside should the swinging bucket come too near him. His smile widened to reveal teeth greened with the slime of decaying food. The dirty flesh of his face and the stubble of his unshaven chin was crusted with some inflammation and he scratched it vigorously, drawing nasty matter to the surface.

The girl shuddered and took another step backwards. The youth followed eagerly. 'Come on, Meggie, be nice to Fancy. Give us a kiss.' He plunged one hand into the baggy reaches of his trousers to fondle the bulge which grew there whilst the other continued to scratch the purulence on his jaw.

'Get out of my way or I swear I'll take your eye out with this bucket.' The girl sketched another vicious circle in the air with the heavy iron utensil. Bobbing his matted head the youth only grinned. He had been watching and waiting for this moment for weeks now and the girl's threat was taken lightly. He was big and strong and she was only a little bit of a thing and as soon as he found an opportunity to duck beneath that whirling bucket he would nip in and wrench it from her hand, taking it from her as easily as he would a sweetie from a baby. He might not have another chance like this and he promised himself he would make the most of it. It was not often she came out on her own for Mrs Whitley, the cook-housekeeper, kept her close and them two lads were always knocking about but he'd seen them himself setting off no more than an hour ago. They had been shepherding a large group of emigrants who were to sail on the '*Lacy Osborne*' on the two o'clock tide, helping Mr Lloyd, the shipping agent to see the bravely marching assembly safely stowed away on the steamship, and would not be back for hours!

Fancy O'Neill bunched his muscular shoulders and his voice

dropped to a wheedling whine. 'Come on, Meggie, be a sport. Just a little kiss. You'll enjoy it, honest. Fancy's a good kisser. Ask anyone!'

He smirked ingratiatingly. 'There's no-one watching, Meggie,' he continued, as though that was what held her back. He spoke with all the confidence of one who knows he is physically the stronger but there was still a wary cut to the way in which he scuttled along the wall keeping it to his back as though, despite this advantage he held in some respect the girl's show of spirit. He pushed his face towards her and licked his lips and she recoiled in disgust, moving another step away from the safety of the sun-lit square, from the community which lived in and around it and into the dim, empty danger of the back yard.

Fancy O'Neill's hand left the infection on his chin and went out to her, again in the placatory way of a man attempting to soothe a nervous animal but she jerked away from it and the bucket slashed out and he stumbled hastily backwards. On his face began to grow an expression of peevishness but the girl was still not afraid. She was too outraged to feel fear. Her clear eyes blazed like freshly minted golden sovereigns and the firm flesh of her throat and bare arms became flushed. Her hair appeared to take on a life of its own. It sprang upwards and outwards, blazing in as furious an anger as its owner. A ribbon which had held a thick plait of hair to the back of her head, broke loose and the plait which fell almost to her buttocks began to unravel itself, the bottom half escaping immediately into a mass of springing curl. A soft, twisting strand fell across her face and she blew it upwards impatiently. She took a stance like that of a boxer and the bucket swayed dangerously.

'A kiss, is it?' she shrieked, her dander really up now. 'Kiss *you*? You could stick a knife in me and throw me in the Mersey before I'd kiss a pig like you! You great daft tub of lard! Dear God, have you ever looked at yourself in a mirror, have you, because if you have you'll see why the very idea makes me want to puke! Now get out of me way before I brain you!'

The youth, through whose small mind most of the insults, and even the words themselves had sped by without the smallest understanding, merely grinned and edged a little closer, putting out both hands as though he was about to encircle her waist. They were huge, splay-fingered and the wrists which supported them were thick and hairy. The girl watched with fascinated loathing,

11

balancing the handle of the bucket on the palm of her right hand. It was heavy, used to carry coal from the cellar beneath the house to the kitchen. Coal dust clung to its inside, floating in a shifting black mist as she moved it. It brushed against her smooth white apron and drifted upwards to her nostrils and before she could suppress it or even take another step backwards away from the growing threat of the youth, she sneezed. For a moment, a fraction of a moment as the sneeze shook her she was defenceless. Her eyes closed and in an involuntary gesture she raised her free hand to cover her mouth and nose.

He had her then! Dim-witted he might be, illiterate and slow to understand, or carry out an order, Fancy O'Neill knew an opportunity when it rose up and bit him. In an instant he had the handle of the bucket in his massive grip and the vessel was hurled backwards up the passage before Meg had her hand from her face. Thick arms held her and a face as big and round as the full moon loomed over her and those thick, slimy lips seized upon hers, sucking them into his mouth. She felt his teeth against hers, and his tongue and her stomach rose and churned like the waters of the Mersey in a winter storm.

Holding her easily with one arm, now he had her secure, his other hand was at the open neckline of her bodice, pulling it away from her so that the buttons were torn from it right down to her waist. Only her white, pin-tucked chemise stood between him and the small, ripening mounds of her new young breasts and the sight of her soft flesh so tantalisingly half revealed shattered Fancy O'Neill's control completely. The beast in him surged and his filthy hand fumbled at her whilst his mouth gorged on hers. To do him justice he had meant to do no more than steal a kiss from the lively, haughty young girl whose gaze had always passed over him with as much interest it might a pile of rubbish in the gutter. Had Meg giggled, or acquiesced, or even made light of the matter and treated the incident in the manner in which it was intended it would no doubt have ended there for he was ignorant, harmless and easily managed and though he had taunted her with cat-calls of 'princess' and 'your majesty' as she had gone by him, he had intended no real offence, but the feel and the smell and the taste of the girl whose surging, struggling body moved so maddeningly against his own was more than he could resist. He grunted with pleasure as small pink nipples erupted into his hand and renewed his efforts to keep her wildly avoiding lips beneath his.

12

Still she fought him! Like an infuriated kitten she was, trapped and roughly handled by some large, playful child. She was not afraid. Fancy O'Neill was an object of ridicule amongst the other servants who worked in Great George Square. Half-witted and clumsy, performing the most menial of tasks, his shambling walk and slow-paced thinking had always allowed Meg and the other maidservants to keep well out of his way ever since he had come to work there. He was employed in the yard of the house of a rival shipping company and his leering, foolish expression, his winks and suggestive lip-smacking effrontery had been treated with disdain, or a cutting remark which left him scratching his head in bewilderment and never once had he been considered a threat to the safety of the young maids who worked in the houses about the square.

She felt her bodice tear away and her bare back scraped against the stained roughness of the bricks and she winced as the skin broke open. Fancy's knee was between her legs forcing them apart but she resisted fiercely, trying to free her arms in order to claw at his face. She gagged and her head jerked from side to side for more than anything else it seemed important to avoid that gaping, foetid mouth, the thick, gummy lips and the foul breath of her attacker. Outraged dignity made her strong but though she was brave and fought fearlessly he was relentless in his lust and he began to walk her backwards along the last few yards of shadowed passage to the enclosed yard at the back of the house. As he did so she felt the first knife of terror stab at her. It moved in the pit of her stomach, ripping up into her chest, taking away her breath, moving upwards to her mind, dizzying her and she felt her senses begin to slip away.

Fancy O'Neill was well beyond the stage of knowing who he was or what he did to the young girl who battled so valiantly in his arms nor of considering the punishment which would be his when he was done. The supercilious housemaid from who he had desired at best a kiss, perhaps a smile, had the loveliest feel to her, rounded here and here, soft and pliant and her resistance only made the having of her in his arms the more enjoyable.

They had reached the corner where the passage turned into the yard when she had her mouth free for one last gasping moment. Her throat arched in a long and lovely line as she screamed despairingly.

'*Martin! Tom!*'

The birds, only just recently settled from their initial upset flew off again in a long blurring arc and the air was filled with the sound of their frantically beating wings. As her voice echoed about the high chasm of the passage Fancy was brought back momentarily from the delightfully clutching, soft and sensual world into which her white flesh had spun him and he lifted his head from where his lips had fastened once more on hers. She had gone still now, limp and boneless in his arms and he muttered fretfully for he had been pleased with the fierce movement of her body against his but as she slipped to the hard-baked ground, her white flesh shimmering in the dark shadowed quiet of the yard he smiled for she was easier to manage like this.

Her lifeless face was hidden as he bent over her.

They were larking about as boys will when they are unsupervised, jostling one another, whistling, their caps set at a jaunty angle on their heads, their hands deep in their trouser pockets. They shouted to one another, their voices still not yet certain of their newly acquired manhood, and their smooth young faces were slicked with the sweat of their exertions in the afternoon heat. They had found an old tin can and in the fashion of lads everywhere they had become the idols of their own youthful fantasies and were kicking it backwards and forwards between them, urging one another to 'kick it over here, Tom' and 'to me, mate, to me!'

They had been told to get off home by Mr Lloyd and to look sharp about it. He could manage this unusually small group of emigrants on his own, he told them, now that they were safely assembled on the dock and there was no need for them two to hang around and to tell Mrs Whitley he'd see her about five. They had sauntered at first, the fierce heat sapping even their high spirits, but were they not Liverpool born and bred with the Merseysiders' love of football, and were not Scott and Young, the goal scorers in Everton's glorious winning of the Footballs Association Cup the previous season, their football gods, and the tin can they had found in the gutter became a football and the length of Upper Pitt Street was Goodison Park and in no time at all they turned into Great George Square, flushed and breathless, elbowing each other aside in their attempts to 'score' a last 'goal' through the area gate.

The first boy was tall with the light springing step and grace of a natural athlete. He had a hard fighter's body, well-muscled and wide-shouldered and looked as though he was not unaccustomed to using his fists. His face was strong, and would be handsome with deep brown eyes set in a thick frame of black lashes. His hair was straight and abundant, falling over his broad forehead in a dark mahogany sweep. His mouth was humorous and though he was well-used to life's hardship it appeared he was also well-used to smiling at it! Now it grinned widely showing his slightly crooked white teeth. His skin was an amber brown and glowed with good health. His jaw was stubborn, even now at the age of fourteen, thrusting aggressively as he wrestled to take the 'football' from his companion. The second boy was as tall as the first but slender, rangy, still growing in to his young manhood, all arms and legs and sharp shoulders. His face was cheerful, boyish, uncomplicated as if nothing had ever come to trouble him in his young life, which was not so! His hair was thick and naturally curly, as yellow as the sun and his eyes were a bright and incredible blue, clear and steady and shining at this moment with enormous satisfaction. His mobile lips formed in a silent whistle as his nimble foot hooked the tin can away from his friend and as it flew, true and straight, clattering down the area steps to the 'goal' at the open basement door, the despairing scream, coming from somewhere behind them froze them both to a shocked silence, cutting off his own shout of triumph. They did not recognise what the voice which prickled the backs of their necks and lifted the hair on their scalps, actually shrieked, but they were immediately aware of the stark and absolute terror which echoed in it. They stood, both of them, still in the postures of Scott and Young, 'footballers of the season', but their eyes widened and their heads snapped wildly as they looked first at one another then in the direction from which the cry had come.

'Who the . . .?' one said hesitatingly.

'I dunno . . .' the other replied but they both began to move warily towards the entrance of the shaded passage at the side of the house. They stopped for a moment, confused still, turning in bewilderment to look at one another, not yet sure that the sound they had heard might – perhaps – have been the cry of a seagull, or was it some lass larking about with a lad! Young they were and afraid of appearing foolish which was how they would feel if they blundered into a bit of private 'sparking'!

They were about to turn back for the sound was not repeated when another shrill voice pierced the heavy air, this time from

15

behind them. They whirled again to face this new commotion and a plump little woman, her face as red as the geraniums in her own window bottom heaved herself breathily up the basement steps where the young 'footballer' had just scored his 'goal'. At first she could not speak. Her arms waved in the air and her panting bosom rose dramatically with every wheezing breath but at last she managed a strangulated word.

'Meggie . . .' she said but it was enough.

They were into the passage like two terriers down a rabbit hole, each so set on being first in they were in danger of becoming jammed fast before they had gone a bare yard. Their young minds were confused with pictures their vivid imaginations conjured up and their faces were strained into masks of apprehension for they could not endure it if . . . if . . . They were not even awfully sure of what it was they were afraid but their breath rasped in their throats, both of them, as though they had run all the way from the Pier Head and the darker of the two kept repeating.

'Meggie, Meggie, Meggie . . .'

Fancy O'Neill was just unbuckling the belt which held up his trousers when they fell upon him bearing him backwards, one on each arm until he was plastered against the high, soot-caked wall which divided the yard from its neighbour. He had arranged the half-suffocated, almost senseless young girl on the ground to his own satisfaction, drooling over her half-formed breasts and pure white thighs and though they had done no more than register the indecently exposed innocence of her as they dragged him away, it was a picture which was to remain forever engraved in the minds of the two boys. The woman was no more than a yard or two behind them and she began to moan when she saw the girl for she thought they had come too late. She leaned over her, hastily pulling down her skirt, covering her nakedness with her own plump little body.

'There, chuck, there . . . there . . . I've got you . . .'

She had her on her feet, still reeling and almost insensible and had begun to lead her away, unconcerned with what the lads did to the brute who had . . . My God, she'd see him hang for this . . . he wasn't fit to be let out and what McIvers were thinking of to employ him she couldn't imagine . . . Dear Lord . . . if he'd harmed their Meg . . . of all the girls round here he had to go and pick on . . . My God, if she ever got her hands on him . . . the first thing she'd do when she got their Meggie settled . . . Dear sweet

Lord, please don't let him have ... and her only twelve ... she'd send Emm for the scuffer who patrolled the area of Upper Pitt Street ... By God, she'd have him flogged, she would, aye and stand and watch it, an' all. But first she must get Meggie away, away from the sight and sounds which were beginning to fill the high-walled yard.

Meg came to slowly from the shock into which Fancy O'Neill's hands and mouth and breath and teeth and smell had spun her. She was still half fainting. She could feel the inside of her head reel and whirl about and her stomach ached with a longing to empty its contents in a violently nauseous wave. She could feel herself gathered against a comforting breast and strong arms cradled her. Something – Mrs Whitley's large white apron? – was placed about her and she was conscious of the curtain of her own hair rippling against her face and shoulders. Her back was on fire where the skin had been rubbed off and she could feel a trickle of blood run down it. Her lip was cut and sore where Fancy's rotting teeth had caught it and all she wanted to do was get away from here and be home safe in the comfortable haven of the kitchen.

She heard it then as she began to stumble away in the shelter of Mrs Whitley's arms. It was the sound of flesh on flesh, an impression of substance meeting resisting substance, shattering, breaking, of blood flowing. Something cracked viciously against the wall and a voice cried out. It was a hard sound, bone on brick and yet it was pulpy, ugly and bad ... and frightening! Somehow more frightening than what had happened to her. There was the gabble of a voice, thick and blurred and terror-stricken, the dreadful sound of Fancy O'Neill sniffling for mercy but what was worse, far worse was the remorselessly silent way in which Martin and Tom were beating him to bleeding insensibility. It seemed they could not get enough of it and the realisation of it brought her to a frantic halt. She turned her head to look over her shoulder, pulling away from Mrs Whitley's arms and she cried out in horror at what she saw. Both their faces were crazed with blood lust!

'Come away, chuck, come away in now,' a soothing voice said in her ear. 'The lads'll deal with him. You're safe now. He'll not harm you again or anyone else if I have my way, the sod! I've got you safe, come on, queen.' But still Meg held back from the arms which tried to draw her away up the passage. They were familiar, strong and smelling of all the good and safe things she

17

knew in her life, fresh baked bread, lye soap, freshly ironed cotton, lavender and yet she knew, for some reason she could not yet get quite clear in her mind she must not listen to it.

She almost went. She wanted nothing more than to be petted and shushed and told what a brave girl she was and that Fancy O'Neill was a brute and would be punished for what he had tried to do. She wanted to weep her fear and her outrage. She wanted to be comforted and see the indignation on Mrs Whitley's face and have her back bathed and a cup of hot, sweet tea pressed into her hand and sit by the fire with Emm and Betsy and May and let their sympathy heal her but there was something going on behind her, something bad and violent and destructive. It had to do with Tom and Martin and if she left them and went to the consolation she craved something disastrous would happen, she knew it. Suddenly, she knew it!

They were out of control now, both of them and Martin's hard relentless fists, used only in the disciplined atmosphere of the boys' boxing bouts in which he was successful could kill the youth he was beating and Tom was no better. Though he was a mild-mannered boy, good-natured and easy-going, at this moment he was out of his mind with rage.

'Martin . . . Tom!' she cried, struggling to escape the encompassing arms which held her. Her own teeth snagged on the cut made by Fancy's and the names she spoke were barely intelligible.

'It's alright, lovey, they're seeing to . . .' but it was not alright and Meg knew it. She tore herself from Mrs Whitley's grasp, the apron she had put about her falling from her. Mrs Whitley stared for a horrified moment at her naked breasts, then reached out hurriedly to cover her again but Meg was away. She tried to stop her for she thought she was deranged with fear but Meg Hughes had recovered from her weakness and was concerned with but one thought. Martin and Tom! She did not reason why. Indeed her brain sent messages to her limbs which were acknowledged instinctively, acted upon instinctively and leaving Mrs Whitley with the amazed look of one who thinks she holds in her arms an injured lamb but finds it is the wolf, she ran back up the passage and without further thought leaped on the first back which presented itself to her.

Even then they would not stop but continued to methodically beat Fancy O'Neill to semi-consciousness. They would not be satisfied, it seemed, until he lay dead and bloody at their feet.

Gasping, her strong young arms about Tom's neck, Megan screamed his name, and Martin's, again and again.

'Tom . . . Stop it . . . Stop it. Martin . . . it's alright . . . listen to me . . . I'm alright. He hasn't hurt me . . . stop it . . . you'll kill him . . . stop it, stop it!'

She had hold of Tom's short curly hair, gripping it fiercely, pulling so hard she began to force his head back. His chin jutted to the sky and his throat formed an arc and his fists fell away from Fancy O'Neill and became claws to reach behind him and detach the assailant who was on his back.

'Tom!' she screamed, her wide open mouth close to his ear, 'Tom . . . stop it . . . it's me . . . Meggie . . . please!'

It was as if she had known even before she had leaped upon him that this was the one she must first bring to his senses, that this was the one she *could* bring to his senses. Martin would have flicked her away without a thought, beyond reason in his wild and violent fury, unreachable in his need to punish the youth who had attacked her, but Tom, who was not really a fighter, preferring words to blows, had more self-control. Her hands were on his throat now, bearing him back, choking him and slowly, reluctantly he allowed himself to be drawn away.

'Stop him, Tom . . . for God's sake, stop him or he'll kill him!'

Through the red mist of hot blood, Tom Fraser, shaking uncontrollably, was eased back to sanity and the consciousness of what he was doing and in that moment, as he watched, appalled now, the fists of his erstwhile football companion smash once more into the pulp which was Fancy O'Neill's nose, he became aware of what they were about and in his turn he began to wrestle Martin away, holding his arms, shouting his name in a hoarse voice.

It took a while but the violence was spent now, drained away in the satisfying feel of their young fists on Fancy's flesh and Martin allowed himself to be held, then pulled away until the floundering, disjointed, blubbering heap that was Fancy O'Neill, was free. Face bloody, eyes almost closed, his jaw slightly askew, the youth was up on his feet, sprinting away down the passage with the speed of a greyhound after the hare, blundering past Mrs Whitley as she stood, her hand to her mouth, still in an agonised state of shock. The sound of his boots died away across the square until it was silent but for the harsh breathing of the two boys.

They did not know where to look then nor what to do with their bloody, grazed fists. They trembled, still in the aftermath of the savage emotions neither had before encountered, nor understood! They were young, untried, carelessly ignorant of the ways of the flesh. They had whispered and laughed and nudged one another as they became aware of the opposite sex but they had not the slightest knowledge of how to deal with their own growing sexuality. They were awkward with it, ashamed of the feelings in their own maturing bodies and the sight of their Meg, the girl they had always thought of as their little 'sister', shivering in the heat, her sweet, pink tipped breasts on display for all to see was too much for either of them.

And for Mrs Whitley!

'Dear God in Heaven!' she screeched, her small, gooseberry green eyes agonising over the inordinate amount of white flesh which was immodestly exposed to the young men's carefully averted eyes. 'What are we hanging about here for when that poor girl is in need of attention. You two, get away to the kitchen and see the kettle is on. I shall need some hot water and tell Emm to get my medicine bag out and to look for the salve and those hands of yours will need looking at. Now don't stand about gawping!'

They were away before she had finished speaking, as fiercely glad as Fancy had been to leave the scene of such devastation but more than anything they needed to get away from the sight of their Meg whose sweet, girlish beauty neither had before noticed.

They were missing for several hours that night, and on others. They made no excuse and Mrs Whitley asked for none as though she was quietly understanding of their vulnerably growing manhood and its need of satisfaction. She was quite well aware of what they were about and though she knew they were on a wasted errand she said nothing. The whole Square knew by now that Fancy O'Neill had gone too far in his search for a 'bit of fun', and in the way of a small, close knit community in which each member is vitally, often vicariously concerned in the life of every other, the episode had been discussed in detail. The speculation had raced from kitchen to kitchen and when it reached the one from which Fancy had received his orders, his disappearance had not caused a great deal of surprise. Well, he wouldn't hang about to be abused by the Hemingway lads, would he, they said to one another, not if he had the sense he was born with. Elevenpence

20

halfpenny in the shilling he might be, but he wasn't daft enough to take another beating like the one they had already given him and no doubt he was half way to London by now, or even America, if he knew what was good for him. Ships needed deck hands and would take on anyone with a strong back and a willingness to take orders and he'd be wise to put a stretch of ocean between himself and the hot need of revenge of Martin Hunter and Tom Fraser, they said knowingly.

By the end of the week the incident, and Fancy O'Neill, who was never seen again, was entirely forgotten by everyone bar those who lived in the Hemingway house in Great George Square.

Chapter two

Mrs Whitley could remember the time she first saw them as if it was yesterday. Well, she was not likely to forget, was she? It was but a fortnight since the old Queen had gone to her Maker and the 'three of 'em' were dressed in the dyed black the City of Liverpool considered suitable for mourning, even in its orphans. She herself and all her staff were similarly dressed for Her Majesty had been much loved and respected in the sixty-three years she had ruled them. That was two years ago but the picture the three of 'em had presented would remain with her to the end of her days. They had stood on her clean kitchen step, not exactly clinging to one another for the boys were twelve, and tall, but giving the impression that they did and as she remarked later to Emm, you'd have thought she was about to land the little girl a 'fourpenny one' the way the lads settled themselves protectively about her. She had stood between them, Cook recalled, the top of her comical black bonnet not quite reaching the angle of their thin shoulders and as the door was opened to them they both edged a fraction closer to one another in a manoeuvre to which they seemed well-accustomed so that the girl was almost hidden behind them. They were all dressed in the usual orphanage attire of cast-off clothing but the girl bobbed a curtsey and the boys snatched their cloth caps from their heads and Cook had liked that!

'There's to be three of them, Mrs Whitley,' Mr Lloyd had told her apologetically, though two strong young boys had been all that was asked for. 'You see, this little girl has been with these two lads since she first went there and she's so attached to them . . .'

'A little girl, sir! What am I to do with a little girl?'

She had been considerably put out, imagining a child, no use to anyone, probably crying all day long and not fit to do a hand's turn but she was to be proved wrong for it turned out that Megan Hughes, an orphan since she was five years old at which age both her mother and father had died in the same week of the typhoid was as much a 'beggar' for work as Mrs Whitley herself! And she disliked 'muck' only marginally less! A perfectionist was Agatha Whitley, her former mistress had been fond of saying, and she was enormously mollified to discover she had met another in the ten-year-old child who came – against the cook's wishes – from the orphanage to the emigrant lodging house owned by the 'Hemingway Shipping Line' in Great George Square. Mrs Whitley's kitchen was as spotless as her maids could make it, as was the rest of the house. Nothing would do but their 'best', she was to say to them at least half a dozen times a day and Meg was put through the same rigorous training she herself had undergone at the same age nearly fifty years ago!

And the lads as well! The 'three of 'em', as they were increasingly to be called, had never worked so hard in their lives but they thrived on it. Meg, because she was still only ten years old, attended the local 'council' school in Cornwallis Street, not five minutes walk from the house but before she left in the morning and again when she came home at four o'clock she had her allotted tasks to do, for as Mrs Whitley remarked firmly, she must earn her keep if she was to stay. Under the cook's tutelage she was given the chance to try her hand at one or two of the simpler of Mrs Whitley's dishes and Meg was pleased when she was told she had an aptitude for it and if she was a good girl and kept at it, and given a few years of practice she might make a half-way decent cook!

But for the first few months at the house Meg had done nothing but clean and black-lead grates, lay fires and sweep and dust. It was her job to polish the ebony grates for these must not be neglected or they would rust. Emm showed her how to make 'Brunswick black' which was a mixture of common asphaltum, linseed oil and turpentine and when it was applied with a small painter's brush and left to dry it came up a treat if you buffed with a dry leather! She swept carpets, first sprinkling them with wet tea leaves to lay the dust and give a fragrant smell to the rooms. Every Saturday morning all the rugs were beaten in the back yard and here the boys were allowed to help her for it was a big house and the floor coverings were too numerous and too heavy for a young girl to throw over the clothes line.

They had a bit of fun then, the 'three of 'em', larking about and shrieking with laughter as Martin chased Meg with the carpet beater, darting breathlessly between lines of rugs and he and Tom had furious 'fencing' bouts with two sticks and they invariably came in for a lashing from Mrs Whitley's tongue and the threat that she would send them all packing back to the orphanage and get some replacements who would do a decent hand's turn instead of fooling about and wasting the company's time and good money!

But by then of course they knew the value of Mrs Whitley's warnings and had the measure of how far they could go with her and though they stood still and cast down their eyes, suitably reprimanded, when she was done and had gone indoors with a last admonishing wag of her finger they would giggle and jostle one another just as children everywhere will when left unattended.

Meg had left school when she was twelve years old, bright as a polished russet apple, Mr Lloyd said, pleased that his impulsive gesture of two years ago had turned out so well. She could add a column of figures in her head quicker than any of the other servants could write them down and was a big help to Mrs Whitley whose eyesight was not as good as once it had been in the preparing of the weekly accounts for his inspection. She wrote a good bold hand and was shrewd in her dealings with the local tradesmen.

The boys laboured just as hard, doing, as Meg did, the work of full grown adults. Polishing windows, cleaning the marble tops of the dressers and fireplaces with soda, pumice stone and finely powdered chalk, hauling carpets upstairs and down, whitewashing the walls of the outside privy and laundry. They cleaned and sharpened cutlery, attended to boxes and bellows, cauldrons, cisterns, funnels, flues, hand-mills and oil jars. They polished lamps, copper pans, brassware and plate and, as they grew and became more responsible began to help Mr Lloyd with the actual emigrants who lodged at the house. It was arduous work but the three children were fed on Mrs Whitley's hot-pots and 'scouse', on her steak and kidney pies, on fruit tarts in season with custards, eggs, milk and roly-poly jam puddings and they grew like weeds, upwards and outwards. Their eyes were bright and lively and so were they, shining with good health for hard work harms no-one. Their skins glowed and their hair was glossy and their limbs were straight and strong. Beseeched by Mrs Whitley to taste her delicious tripe and onions, her cowheel and pigs' trotters and currant dumpling the three of them grew six inches in as many months and the boys thin frames began to fill out and put on muscle, particularly Martin who would be a big man when he was full grown. At thirteen the boys were five feet four inches tall and a year later a little under six feet, the two of them! Their voices deepened and broke as they came to that stage of awkward vulnerability in which they developed the inclination to fall over their own feet as they passed into graceless adolescence. Meg, two years younger, would laugh at them, teasing until Martin turned on her pulling the thick plait of her hair until her eyes watered and Tom would patiently separate them though he himself felt like giving their Meg a clip round the earhole at times! He was very conscious of his own fourteen-year-old shortcomings as he approached young manhood and the lively child and her tormenting was more than his growing pains could sometimes endure.

He and Martin bickered over who was to run to the 'Fiddlers Arms' for Mrs Whitley's nightly jug of stout until she threatened to knock their heads together and they could scarcely understand their own snarling hatred of one another which seemed to alternate with their usual careless affection. They would pummel one another ferociously, only to go off arm in arm moments later, one nursing the bloody nose the other had given him and their young minds and bodies, growing and maturing were uncertain of which state they were in between boy and man.

The house was part of a chain linking the old world from which the emigrants came to the 'New World' across the great Atlantic Ocean. Most who sailed with Hemingway's came from Scandinavia, gathering in Gothenburg in Sweden from where they went by steamer to Hull and then by rail to Liverpool where they took ship for New York. Emigrant traffic was a major part of the earning capacity of the passenger liner companies in Liverpool and of the five and a half million men, women and children who had left British shores since 1860, four and three quarter million of them had gone from that great seaport. For two reasons Liverpool was able to deal with this vast flood of humanity – firstly, the port had the tonnage available and secondly it had the railway network which served the city, bringing those millions not only from all over Britain but from other countries as well. Mr Lloyd and his officials would meet them at Central Station and they would march them through the streets, peasant stock for the most part, men, women, youths, girls, babes in arms, silver-haired infants and grey, bald-headed patriarchs, silent and staring, to the welcome of the house in Great George Square. For a few days they would be sheltered and fed, waiting for the sailing of their ship in the steerage accomodation which would be another temporary home until they reached their final destination. They had that stunned look of those who are afraid beyond describing of what they are about to do but are powerless to change their fate, only the children treating the upheaval as a great adventure. They were well-cared for during their stay and their rooms, though small, hardly more than divided cubicles were scrupulously clean and quite comfortable. They ate Mrs Whitley's nourishing food and each batch of emigrants was inspected daily by the doctor from the Medical Committee for the rules regarding the health of the travellers was strict and must be complied with before they were allowed to sail. The house was registered and the conditions under which they lived whilst awaiting passage must be strictly observed.

It had not always been so! Mr Lloyd, whose father and grandfather had both worked in the emigrant trade had tales to tell of the harrowing conditions which had once prevailed. The emigrants had had to provide their own food for the journey and before the weary traveller had ventured more than a yard or so from the transport – often on their own feet – which had carried him to the city he was accosted by 'runners' or 'man-catchers', which, as the name implied snared the unwary and swiftly parted him from what few belongings he had. He was swindled by lodging house keepers, porters, ships chandlers and even those from whom he bought his passage.

Now, twenty to thirty thousand went annually from Liverpool alone, their steerage accomodation costing them two pounds ten shillings a head and in the past fifty years or so the population of the United States of America had quadrupled. They came from Europe, Scandinavia and Ireland, bound for America, Canada and Australia and their temporary presence in Liverpool, most dressed in their native costume added a new interest and colour to the streets of the city.

Meg, Martin and Tom worked amongst them and Meg had become Mrs Whitley's right hand, or so the cook said, for none of the other maids, even the willing Emm had the capacity to understand what was needed in the often ticklish reception of two hundred bewildered foreigners. She was efficient and business-like and yet she had an intuitive understanding of their needs. Her sharp wit and common sense, even at twelve years old quickly had them arranged into the obligatory order of age, sex and marital status for families were kept together and the unmarried

26

men and women were strictly segregated. Tom and Martin took charge of the younger men and would stand no larking about, something neither Mr Lloyd, nor Mrs Whitley would allow amongst the people in their charge. She and Meg attended to the unattached women and to the families, and order, and propriety reigned!

Meg might have lived in the house all her life, so well did she take to the task of caring for the perplexed and exhausted travellers. Her enthusiasm and pleasure in her new life flourished and as she grew so did her beauty. The skin of her neck and face was flawless with no more than a hint of colour in it apart from the dozen or so golden freckles which dusted her nose. Her eyes glowed with the richness of a topaz and her hair became even more vivid with the shine of her health.

Martin was the 'handy' one of the two boys. A 'wonder' he was, Mrs Whitley said with 'that there machinery', or indeed anything which came apart and could be put together again. He was neat fingered, showing an aptitude from an early age with kitchen appliances such as the knife sharpener, the mechanical workings of the insides of the household clocks, the mangle in the laundry which had a tendency to become jammed, the workings of the flue and the hot-plate and indeed any gadget or apparatus which needed oiling, cleaning, repairing or a part replaced. They had only to be put in his hands and he seemed to sense what was needed and to know exactly how to put it right.

Now Tom, he was different! Though his parentage was not known since he had been an inmate, like Martin, at the orphanage, from birth, it seemed evident from his appearance that one of the young travellers from Scandinavia, on his way to the new world had persuaded some pretty maid to succumb to his fair-haired charm! Like the Vikings of old Tom was tall and golden-skinned with a short cap of curls the colour of wheat. His eyes were the vivid sea-blue of the waters of the Norwegian Fjords and his slow, easy-going smile was already beginning to turn the heads of the parlour maids in the Square. He was even tempered, quick to laugh, unhurried with an infectious good humour which would allow no-one to be cross with him for long. Mr Lloyd said he had a head on his shoulders and if he could conquer his natural inclination towards unruffled indolence, his tendency to live only for today, would make a good steward, or even an agent in the company's service like himself.

They were each as different from one another as the carriage is from the horse which pulls it and yet they fitted together, the three of them, forged in the years of their young childhood into a strong, unbreakable triangle. Children then, but suddenly, with the incident of Fancy O'Neill, they were grown up!

The hot weather ended the following day with a storm of such magnitude, and with rain which fell so heavily and for so long it flooded the coal cellar and Martin Hunter and Tom Fraser had no time to consider their new conception of Megan Hughes as they worked furiously to keep the storm water from invading Mrs Whitley's kitchen. They barely had time to notice Meg as she huddled in the corner of the hearth and had they done so it was doubtful they would have plucked up the nerve to speak to her! Just at the moment and possibly for the next few days, or even weeks the sight of her would embarrass them to awkward silence for they were still only boys at heart, without the delicate perception to know how to deal with her shocked female humiliation at Fancy O'Neill's hands. She had become an unknown quantity, one of the beings whom, during the past months, as they matured, they had eyed and whistled after and whispered about. They were boys and yet *not* boys. Young men and yet *not* and their Meggie had suddenly and in the most devastating way, become a woman and they simply could not cope with it!

Their Meggie was just a kid. A teasing girl fresh from school with a ribbon on the end of her plait, a youngster in an apron who drove them mad at times with her constant chatter, her wayward determination to be in on everything they did in their masculine world, her ruthless and spirited certainty that she should know their every thought! She was a bloody nuisance at times, as younger sisters are. She worked with them, shared their table and many of their jaunts into town but more and more, as Martin went down to the boys' gymnasium where he was part of the boxing fraternity, as Tom pursued his interest in football and his idols at Everton, Meg had been left behind in the female world, which was only right! She was, after all, only a kid and were they not now young men?

Fancy O'Neill altered all that in half an hour and they did not know, in their youthful innocence how to address this woman who had come among them!

Meg remained in the kitchen for several days, still in a state of shock, trembling about the place and recoiling at any sudden

28

noise, under the sympathetic guidance of the other women, avoiding Tom and Martin as assiduously as they avoided her. She had noticed their quickly averted eyes and the asperity with which they fled the kitchen claiming that they must be about their duties or the house might fall down around their very ears and at first she had been relieved. She had been led away from the shadowed passage, sick and in pain, shivering again violently once she had been certain that the danger to Martin and Tom was over and that Fancy was gone, and Mrs Whitley had kept them away as she bathed Meg in the hip bath before the kitchen fire. Cook had seemed to understand Meg's need to feel clean again and even her thick curly hair and her white scalp had been scrubbed vigorously in her effort to erase every last contact with Fancy O'Neill. Mrs Whitley had soothed her back with ointment and Meg had cried a little in the consoling comfort of the kind arms for it had been a nasty experience and for a day or so she had enjoyed being fragile and pampered, scarcely noticing that the boys excluded themselves from it.

When she did she began to wonder why? They had been so brave and *manly*, so *fierce* in her defence as she had been in theirs when it seemed they would kill the youth who had attacked her. But why did they not now come and ask her how she did? And why were they so busy all the time even when the floods went down and the usual evening companionship round the kitchen table was able to be resumed? Why did they go up to their bed so early, or take themselves off for a walk and why did they appear, so blatantly, not to want to be with her any more? It was not because of what Fancy O'Neill had done to her, surely. It had not been her fault! She had not asked for it! Were they going to avoid her forever, not speaking, not looking at her, acting as if she wasn't there for the most part? She was too upset to bring up the subject herself but surely, if they loved her, and she knew they did, should they not now be . . . be . . . enquiring after her . . . her health? Always in the past they had stood together, protecting one another. Was she now to be ignored because of something for which she could not be blamed?

Sulkily she watched them go out early that evening, saying they felt like a walk and declaring their intention of strolling down to Sefton Street and along to Dingle Point. The storm had cleared the air and the early September evening was soft, the pale perse blue of the sky turning to oyster and peach over the silvered waters of the river. The sun was setting, dipping towards the western horizon, silhouetting the cranes, the black funnels of the great ships at berth and stitching like lacework against the sky the rigging of sailing ships which could still be seen, delicate as fireflies amongst the elephantine steamships. The rain had laid the hot dust of August and the parched grasses had recovered and everywhere a bit of green grew, it thrived, and late geraniums and begonias bloomed in the garden in the Square.

It was pleasant on Sefton Street. The air was sharp as it came off the river, smelling of all the aromas with which she had grown up. Salt, tar, the fumes from ships' funnels and the tantalising fragrance which drifted from the holds of ships just berthed. Gulls floated serenely on the currents of air above her, scattering as a train clattered on the overhead railway which ran to Toxteth Dock goods station. There were couples about, courting she supposed, walking sedately side by side, eyes shyly cast down, not speaking some of them and she wondered idly why they did it for it seemed so unexciting!

She walked the length of Sefton Street beyond Harrington Dock and the red house which had once been the Dockmaster's until she came to Dingle Point, and as she did so the curve of the red orb of the sun fell beyond the horizon and a star or two pricked the softly darkening sky. Among the strolling couples, and the rather more than she would have liked *gentlemen* on their own there was no sign of Martin and Tom! Damn them, they must have lied about where they were going! They were most likely at this very minute in some pub propping up the bar pretending to be young men about town, quaffing ale, no doubt and getting 'bevvied' and thinking themselves to be great fellows indeed! In the 'Fiddlers', she'd be bound and yet, would they go there where they were known for the landlord, who was acquainted with Mrs Whitley would be bound to tell her. So where the dickens had they got to, the beggars! Just wait until she found them, she'd give them what for, trailing her all the way out here, and she'd be certain to get the rough side of Mrs Whitley's tongue for leaving home without permission! But still, it was worth it just to get out of the house. She drew the salty air deeply into her lungs, throwing back her head to stare into the darkening sky. It was the first time she had been out since . . . since Fancy, and the small diversion had restored her own confidence in herself and her ability to go about on her own again. She sighed contentedly.

She was turning back, idling along the dock side, admiring the way the sky had turned to an exquisite shade of pink at its far edge as the last of the sun's glow draped itself behind the roof of the Custom House, which stood out above the other buildings near the Pier Head when she saw them coming towards her and she began to smile a welcome since she admitted, only to herself, mind, that she had not cared too much for the idea of walking past those ruffians outside the 'Fiddlers'. They didn't frighten her, not really, for it was but a step to home but their often little understood remarks made her uneasy.

For an incredible moment she was convinced they were both going to hit her as they drew near and she cowered instinctively, bewildered by their white, straining faces, raising her arm as though to fend off a blow. Martin's hand gripped it with vicious fingers just above the elbow and she winced. Even in the dusk she could see the flare of his hot brown eyes.

'Where the bloody hell d'you think you're going?' he hissed, putting his face so close to hers their noses actually touched. His breath washed against hers smelling of beer and she reared away, affronted by the words he spoke, but triumphant just the same. They *had* been for a 'bevvy' and just let Mrs Whitley find out and she'd skin them alive. They were only fourteen and though tall as grown men, far too young to be drinking and if they thought she was going to be intimidated by their strange aggression they were mistaken!

But her self-satisfied smugness was shattered in amazement as Tom took her other arm and the pair of them, scarcely able to speak so strung up with some deep emotion were they, began to shake her, one on each arm and her head tumbled backwards and forwards and her boater fell foolishly over her face and a man who was passing by with a young lady hesitated.

'Where the hell d'you think you're off to?' Martin repeated, his voice snarling in his throat and his fingers bit deep into her arm. He towered over her threateningly and again she shrank away from him. She had never seen him in such a rage. He could lose his temper if goaded beyond a certain point, as she could. They were alike in this and she could understand it in him but he was savage now, in a passion so great his face was flushed with it, red and furious.

'And at this time of night, an' all!' Tom shouted, his voice overlapping Martin's. 'Don't you realise what sort of men there are about?'

'You daft beggar! Have you no bloody sense at all?'

'You're just asking for trouble.'

'. . . and if we hadn't gone home early and found Mrs Whitley having bloody hysterics . . .'

She tried to pull away but it seemed they were incapable of letting go of her, now she was safely in their grasp and each word they spoke was accompanied by a shake and a violent drag on her arm and her hat fell off completely and the man who had stopped to stare began to walk slowly, warily towards them. After all, his expression seemed to say, there *were* two of *them* and only himself to see to them, should it be needed.

Her eyes were wide, a deep tawny amber in her white face. Her mouth opened in a round grimace of protest and she began to dig her heels in an attempt to back away from them.

'What the heck d'you think you two are doing? Have you gone mad or something?' she gasped.

'It's you who are mad, lady, and if I had my way I'd take a stick to you.'

'Tom!' Her heart began to thud in her chest and she was not really certain whether it was with fear or anger. They were both incensed about something. She had never seen them so wild, particularly Tom who was ordinarily as mild and easy going as an early day in summer, but now his face had become suffused with perilous blood and his vivid blue eyes were narrowed and quite dangerous.

'Don't Tom me, you silly cow. If we hadn't got here when we did God knows who might have got at you! Have you so soon forgotten that sod . . .' He glared about him, quite beside himself in his outrage and she turned too, sweeping the broad promenade with bewildered eyes as though expecting to see, as he apparently did, hordes of dangerous madmen encircling them.

'What's got into you, Tom? I was only . . .'

'Excuse me, miss, but can I . . . er . . . are you in any . . .?'

They all three turned to stare at the intruder. The young man teetered bravely on the balls of his feet, ready to dart away should either of the two bully boys who were still dragging at the pretty girl take some action which he might find alarming and at his back his companion grasped her parasol, fiercely determined to protect him if he should need it and the three youngsters glared

32

madly, as though to say who did he think *he* was, butting in on a private quarrel.

'And what's it to you, mate?' Martin's voice was loudly aggressive.

The young man, to his credit, stood his ground.

'This young lady is . . .'

'Nothing to do with you, so push off!' Martin, unable to contain the harsh, frightening dread which had gripped him since Mrs Whitley, half out of her mind over the disappearance of their Meggie had screamed at them to '. . . run, run lads and find her 'cos if that Fancy's got her again . . .' turned now on this new provocation and was as ready to beat the living daylights out of him as any of the bastards who he had been convinced had taken their Meg. Brown eyes glowered, and so did gold and the blue of Tom's paled to an icy azure and the valiant young man stepped hastily back from them.

'But you and this . . . this lad have no rights to be molesting this lass and if you don't give over I shall fetch a policeman.'

Meg stood in the midst of the mad medley of angry voices and hot-blooded, threatening gestures and her young mind began at last to make some sense of the situation. She recalled other times, times at the orphanage when these two had bristled up to others in her defence. They had been boys then and not as strong as they now were. Less menacing but just as willing to knock senseless anyone who made a move they did not care for and now they were the same. She became still, standing passively, her arm still gripped in Tom's savage grasp. He was no longer glaring at her but had turned, like Martin, his demented attention on the poor uncertain chap who had done no more than attempt to halt what he had seen as two young lads interfering with a defenceless girl. The young man had taken a chance and brave he was too, standing up like that to the strange and yet understood – now – animosity of Martin and Tom.

'It's alright,' she said quietly to him, 'these are friends of mine.' She smiled gratefully and he was mesmerised by her sudden sweet beauty and the soft golden light which had come to take the place of the anger in her eyes. The young lady who accompanied him became snappish as she saw it.

'Well, we weren't to know, were we?' she said huffily, taking her young man's arm possessively. 'Funny friends if you ask me. Come on, Arthur, let's get on and leave them to it!'

'Thank you!' Meg said again and Arthur could not resist a last peep over his shoulder as his companion marched him away.

When they had gone Meg gently eased her arm from Tom's slackening grip. She bent down and picked up her boater, spending a moment or two arranging it on the crown of her springing curls, replacing the hat pin which had come loose, giving them all time to gather their reeling, embarrassed senses. Giving Martin and Tom time to return from the fear-ridden, treacherous unpredictability into which their concern for her had flung them. They watched her moodily, shuffling about with an awkward, uncoordinated lack of grace, their usually lounging bodies tensed, even now, to coiled springs, their hands clenched at their sides, longing still it seemed to lash out at somebody, anybody, allowing the pent up fury of their young, scarcely understood emotion to drain away. Their eyes still gleamed and their glowering expressions had not yet dissipated but she could see that they had lost that mindless need to shout and bluster and hit out at her.

In her youthful – sudden – wisdom she did the only thing she could think of. She laughed!

'Well, poor Arthur!' Her voice was gleeful. 'Did you ever see such a face on that girl of his? I bet she's giving him what for right now. Can you just imagine it?' She adopted a high, falsetto voice and lifted her nose in the air. 'Really, Arthur, I just can't understand why you have to get yourself into such predicaments. That girl was obviously well able to look after herself and you have to go sticking your nose in where it's not wanted. Fancy making such a fool of yourself and what's more to the point, of me. I'm never going to walk out with you again and as for that kiss I promised you, well you can just go and walk in the water till your hat floats . . .'

She watched as they relaxed and the beginnings of a smile curled each young mouth. 'I was mortified . . . mortified I tell you . . .' she went on, still imitating Arthur's young lady and Tom began to grin and he lifted his hand to settle his cap more comfortably on his mop of fair curls. Martin shoved his hands in his pockets, his dark eyes narrowing in a reluctant smile, his white teeth gleaming in the fast falling dark.

'Poor devil!' he said, quite amiable now. 'I bet he's right under her thumb.'

'But it took a bit of nerve, Martin. You've got to give him that.' Meg began to saunter along the promenade in the direction of the blossoming lights of the city. 'I mean, you two must have been a bit of a sight scowling at the poor blighter and yet he still came. And it was two to one!'

'Yes . . . well . . . I suppose so!' They fell in on either side of her. 'But you know the whole thing was . . .' Martin hesitated, wiser now than he had been ten minutes ago.

'My fault, I know.'

'You shouldn't have come out by yourself, our Meg,' Tom said quietly, 'not after last week.' He could speak of it almost normally now, the catharsis of the set-to with poor Arthur purging him of his guilty embarrassment.

'I know, but you two had gone off and left me . . .'

'. . . and you can't stand being left out of anything, can you?'

She put her arm through each of theirs and they strode out together and their laughter was high and pleased. The lights from the overhead railway shone on their youthful faces, picking out the glowing satisfaction in their eyes and they began to run, too full of well-being and spirited energy to merely walk and the strong bond of their shared affection and loyalty to one another bound them as it had always done.

Chapter three

'I'm off now, Mrs Whitley.'

'Right lad and don't you be late home or you'll feel the back of me hand! When I say ten o'clock I mean it, d'you hear me, Martin Hunter, so don't you come sneaking in at half past. Big as you are I can still give you a clout, so think on!'

'I will, Mrs Whitley.'

'And don't let none of those hooligans be giving you no black eyes or a broken nose, neither. You know I don't like you to get hurt.'

'Aah, Mrs Whitley . . .'

'Don't you pull your lip at me, lad. It's not good for the house to have one of the servants going about with the countenance of a pugilist and I won't have it. Why you took up with it I'll never know, but there, I suppose boys will be boys and at least you do your fighting in the boxing ring and not on the streets . . .'

Martin Hunter, aware of the grinning face of Tom Fraser at his back, stood impatiently first on one foot, then the other, waiting for the moment when he could reasonably hope to escape Mrs Whitley's regular homily on the nastiness of 'fisticuffs', as she called it, and of those who indulged in it. Though Mr Lloyd had given his permission for the lad to spend his evening off at the young men's sporting club in Renshaw Street, and the gymnasium which was part of it, and of course Mrs Whitley must bow to the agent's higher position in the Hemingway Company, she made no bones about the fact that she would have preferred their Martin to have taken up a less belligerent interest! He and Tom went as often as they could manage to watch their football team, Everton, the 'toffee men', whenever they played at home and that was a good, working man's preoccupation with sport in her opinion, but this 'bashing' another poor chap's face to pulp that Martin appeared to relish was beyond her.

'I don't bash anyone's face to pulp, Mrs Whitley,' he explained patiently. 'The lads I spar with are as big as me, bigger sometimes and there's a trainer to see we do it according to the rules.'

'I don't care! It's brutal and undignified.' Nevertheless she had to admit to herself it certainly had helped to build up the lad's shoulders and back. She'd not missed the looks the maidservants in the square gave him as he effortlessly heaved the sacks of coal potatoes down the back cellar steps and his springing step and swift and graceful stride brought an appreciative gleam to many a pert young eye. He had had his fifteenth birthday at Christmas and his voice had deepened even more. He had put on another two inches in height and two pounds in weight, the last he was ever to gain as he became the full grown man he was to be. Broad, tall, straight, with a narrow waist, flat belly, slender hips and long, well-muscled legs which carried him round the boxing ring with the grace and speed of a young leopard. He had drawn ahead of Tom in the past few months, she recognised, and the fair-haired lad appeared to be still a young boy beside the maturing Martin.

'I'll be off then, Mrs Whitley,' he said now, reaching hopefully for his cap and muffler and she shook herself from her reverie, nodding her head irritably and waving him away with an impatient hand. The room was warm, the temperature outside a little below freezing but if he must go, daft as she thought it, her attitude said, he might as well be off. It was the quiet season from November to March in the migration of those who moved from the old world to the new and the house, in this month of January, was empty and silent. He had done his chores and there was no reason for her to hold him back.

At the door he turned, looking back to the table, bathed in the golden glow from the lamp which stood in its centre. The light fell on the bent heads of Meg and Tom as they pored over the books they were reading. They sat companionably side by side on the bench, shoulders almost touching, oblivious it seemed, to anything, to anyone, even himself and a strange and elusive sensation fluttered in his chest. It touched him briefly but even before he could grasp it or even realise its existence, it was gone. He stamped his feet impatiently and his young, eager manliness carried him half way up the area steps but, surprising himself he found himself retracing his steps to the kitchen door he had just slammed urgently behind him.

They all four lifted their heads enquiringly to look at him, Mrs

Whitley, Emm, Tom and Meg and he was himself quite amazed to hear his own voice speak.

'Why don't you come with me to the gym, Tom?' it said, his mouth seeming to form the words of its own accord. 'A bit of boxing would put some muscle on you.'

'You what...?' Tom was clearly bewildered. Though they were as close as brothers with a long record of friendship stretching right through their childhood they were in no way alike in their interests and it was the first time Martin had ever suggested that Tom accompany him to the sporting club.

'You heard! Come and do a bit of sparring with me. It'll build you up, put some muscle on you like I said.'

'What do I want more muscle on me for?' Tom asked laughingly. 'I'm quite satisfied with what I've got, thanks.'

'Come off it! You're like a long drink of water! I can nearly see through you! All skin and bone and nothing to hold it together. A couple of months working out in the gym'll build you up...'

'You mean if I came with you and bashed hell out of some poor sod...'

'You watch your mouth, Tom Fraser,' Mrs Whitley tutted angrily.

'...I could look like you?' Tom finished.

'What's wrong with that? It's exercise that does it.' Martin flexed a muscle in his arm, glancing at Meg but she merely lowered her eyes to her book, losing interest in his and Tom's argument and he scowled, still young enough to feel the insult of her girlish disdain in his own manly pursuits. Nevertheless he persisted, quite perplexed by his own sudden determination to have Tom go with him.

'Come on. It'd do you good, a bit of exercise...'

But Mrs Whitley had had enough of Martin standing there with the back door wide open letting all the lovely warm air out 'Never mind a bit of exercise, Martin Hunter. If Tom wants a bit of exercise, or you an' all for that matter, you can run round to the "Fiddlers" and fetch me a jug of stout.' Her voice was sharp. 'Is that enough exercise for you because if it isn't I'll soon find you some. Now shut that door and be off with you before I change me mind!'

Half way along Duke Street, his puzzled mind still deliberating on what on earth had possessed him to invite Tom to come with him to the sporting club when he knew perfectly well Tom disliked

38

any kind of violent exertion unless he was watching it, he found his footsteps had turned him in a direction which would take him *away* from the club. Though he had been filled with the need to work off his frustration – at what? his baffled mind asked – he knew he was making, not for the boxing ring where he could fulfill that need but to somewhere else. To somewhere he went whenever he could find the time and the opportunity and the *privacy* he seemed to need for it. He had told no-one about it, not even those who were closer to him than the family he had never known and he had asked himself why frequently, for in all things but this he and Meg and Tom had shared their hopes and fears, their triumphs and disappointments. This part of his life was perhaps the most important; the most precious; the most vulnerable to the scorn of others and he had been unusually secretive about it. That must be it, he reasoned with himself. That must be why. Because it was so fragile it could not be exposed to the gaze of even Meg and Tom. Not yet!

Turning out of Whitechapel into Victoria Street he heard his own footsteps quicken eagerly and his mind flew ahead, dashing forward to meet the excitement which always flooded him when he allowed it its way. There were shops on either side of the street. Shops of all kinds, but not grand like those in Dale Street or Bold Street. These were small, run down, crammed with all the commodities needed and purchased by the working man and his family. A butcher, the blinds drawn and nothing but the sign in the window to proclaim its business. A grocer, a greengrocer, a fish merchant, a cheese and butter shop and the inevitable pawnbroker! At the far end, on the corner, appearing to stand apart from its companions in its shining splendour was a double-fronted shop which declared itself to be 'Hale's Modern Bicycle Emporium' and beneath this splendid title were printed the words 'Albert Hale, prop.'

Martin's footsteps slowed and the gas lamplight which shone from the evenly but distantly spaced lampholders along the street picked out the soft, almost lover-like gleam in his eyes. He turned to look into the dim window, a light from the back of the shop evidently shining from Mr Albert Hale's own living quarters, outlining the silhouettes of the bicycles which were crammed there. He put out his hand, placing his fingers gently against the glass which separated them from him, then rubbed at the glaze of frost which coated it. He breathed on the window, rubbing again, this time with his coat sleeve, peering reverently through the small hole his breath had cleared.

For several minutes he stood there, gazing in dream-like fashion at the machines, his head on one side as though considering which one to choose for himself, then with an eager squaring of his shoulders he moved to the arched doorway and tapped gently on the door.

They were about the kitchen table on a bitterly cold evening at the end of January when Martin cleared his throat and as though at a signal they all raised their heads to look enquiringly at him. The room was slow and peaceful, the people in it lounging about in that last reluctant awareness that they should make a move and get to their beds. The fire was dying away to slumbering rosy embers, a tendril of pale grey smoke drifting from the falling ash to escape up the blackened chimney. The kitchen was lambent with pale gold and rose tinted reflections from the last flickering flames in the fireplace and the end of the day indolence gave the figures who lolled about a strange grace.

Emm was there curled up on a tuffet, her spindly legs to the coals for she felt the chill in her almost fleshless bones. Mrs Whitley dozed in the 'best' chair, as was her due, proclaiming at intervals that she really *must* get up them stairs but making no effort to do so.

'Can I have a word, Mrs Whitley?' Martin said gruffly and she turned, surprised, for could he not always have a word if he wanted and without asking her permission.

'You what?'

'I want to ask you something before I discuss it with Mr Lloyd.'

'Oh yes!'

Tom and Meg looked from one face to the other, then at each other, blue eyes asking amber what on earth this was all about. Meg raised her eyebrows and shrugged. She had been sewing, absorbed in the fine tucking she was putting in a new muslin blouse she intended for the spring days to come. The lamplight touched her hair and the glow of it gilded her white skin to cream and put tawny shadows across her shoulders, following the sweet curve of her breasts but Martin was looking at Mrs Whitley and Tom at Martin and neither noticed. She had returned to being 'their Meggie', the tomboy sister they were so used to, the confrontation with Fancy O'Neill buried deeply, firmly, in the pit of their

40

minds where it could do them no harm, and her growing, maturing loveliness escaped their casual young men's interest. Her hair was piled on top of her head, more to keep it out of her way when she was working than to follow fashion, but loosely so that there was a soft fullness around her face. Springing curls escaped to lie about her forehead, above her ears and on the smooth skin at the nape of her neck.

'Yes!' Martin stood up abruptly and began to pace the room and they all watched him, waiting expectantly.

'Well!' Mrs Whitley said impatiently.

'Well . . .'

'Oh for pity' sake, lad, get on with it!'

He turned decisively. Looking her full in the face in the manner of one who is to sink or swim on his next words, he spoke jerkily.

'I want to go to night school!'

Mrs Whitley blinked, then sat up slowly straightening her back, crossing her plump arms beneath her thrusting bosom.

'Do you indeed? And who is to pay for it, may I ask, *and*, more to the point, how are you to find the time. You have work to do at night and . . .'

'The classes cost nothing, Mrs Whitley. It's the Collegiate Institute in Shaw Street. It was built to provide an education for the commercial, trading and working classes of Liverpool,' he said, parrot fashion as though he had repeated the words over and over again. 'I shall learn mechanical engineering and draughtsmanship. Twice a week and I'll do my work still, never fear but at some other time . . . if you don't mind . . .' he added hastily.

Meg could contain herself no longer. 'What sort of classes are those, Martin? What does it mean . . . er . . . mechanical engine . . . and what was it . . . draughtsman something or other . . .?' Her voice was excited and her face glowed with the wonder of it all but Mrs Whitley made short work of *her*!

'Never you mind, miss! This is nothing to do with you!' She turned again, her fat cheeks wobbling in outrage but before she could make short work of *him* too, Martin moved across the kitchen and in a way which was as simple as that of a child about to say its prayers, knelt down before her and took her hands in his. She would have shaken him off but he calmed her with a curiously adult dignity, forcing her to look into his face.

'I'm speaking to you first, Mrs Whitley because the work I do affects you as much as Mr Lloyd but when I have your permission

41

I mean to put it to him. I promise you it won't interfere with what I do here. I shall make some adjustments . . .'

'Adjustments!' How grown up he is suddenly, Mrs Whitley had time to consider – then she was captured again by the simple conviction in his voice.

'I want to be an engineer, you see, Mrs Whitley and I can't do it if I don't learn how!'

The room was silent. They could not have been more dumbfounded had he said he was to take the train to London to be a guest of his Majesty the King. An engineer, their collective minds considered, barely aware even of what that was! They had all heard of men with such titles who built bridges and railways and so on but what was that to do with their Martin? He was an odd-job boy, for goodness' sake and would no doubt, if he worked conscientiously for Mr Lloyd, one day be a steward, and agent, or even, God willing, a manager, but an *engineer*!

'I've not had much schooling,' Martin continued, his voice falling strongly into the stunned quiet his announcement had created. 'I can read and write and do sums but there's more to it than that. You know how . . . how good I am with machinery. I can mend things, I always have done. I don't know how, or why I can do it. When I was eight years old I took Matron's watch to pieces when she said it wouldn't go and when I put it together again . . . it went! You've seen me mend things, haven't you?'

Mrs Whitley nodded, hypnotised by his quiet certainty.

'Well, I can do it with anything. Mr Hale said . . .'

'Mr Hale?'

'Yes, I've been meaning to tell you . . .'

'Tell me what?' Mrs Whitley drew back suspiciously but Meg, Tom and Emm leaned closer, mesmerised by this incredible scene they were witnessing. Martin continued to kneel at Mrs Whitley's feet, speaking to them all really, but his eyes never left the cook's face and she felt the power in him and knew there would be no stopping him, ever! Whatever he did, now or in the future, he would not be stopped!

'He has the bicycle shop at the corner of Victoria Street. I've been helping him out . . .'

'. . . and you never told us!' Meg was affronted but again Mrs Whitley turned on her sharply, telling her to hold her tongue.

'Go on, lad, helping him out?'

'In my own time, Mrs Whitley. Instead of going to the sporting club ... whenever I had an hour free ... I met him at the club, Mr Hale I mean ... he plays billiards there and when I told him about ...'

'What, lad?'

'That I liked ... loved machinery ... bicycles ... the internal combustion engine ...'

'The internal ...!' Mrs Whitley could only gasp on the unfamiliar words.

'Yes ... the horseless carriage, you know ... you've seen them in town ...' Martin shook her hands impatiently.

'God save us all!'

'Well, he said I could give him a hand in his shop and I did and he said I was wasted here.'

'Wasted! Now see here, young man!'

'... and that I could go to night school and learn it properly. I've got a knack, he said. It's coming, he said ...'

'What is?'

'The motor car, not just for them with money but for us all and so I want to be in on it, Mrs Whitley, by God I do. It's 1903 and before this decade is over we shall see the roads crammed with them. There's already more than eight thousand of them! Think of that, Mrs Whitley!' His voice was filled with awe, 'and the speed they go now that the Motor Car Act has been passed ... twenty miles an hour, can you imagine it?'

Mrs Whitley couldn't, not having the slightest conception of what he was talking about and neither could Emm but Tom and Meg, as enthusiastic as the young are about anything which might bring excitement and colour into their lives, became flushed with Martin's own triumph and they jostled with one another to hear the better.

'They have to have a registration number now,' Martin explained eagerly, 'so that those who break the law can be identified and prosecuted ...'

'Prosecuted.' Mrs Whitley said feebly.

'It's not just a hobby any more, you see, like sailing or ... or such like. It used to be a toy for the well-to-do but not any more. Oh no! Everyone will have one some day but before they can someone has to get the design perfected ...'

'Perfected ...' Meg breathed reverently.

'... so that they can be turned out cheaply ...'

'D'you mean chaps like you and me will be able to have one?' Tom's expression was disbelieving.

'Oh yes, and all the . . .'

'But what about the roads? Will there be enough room on them for everyone?'

'That will come, with time . . .'

'Yes, but who's going to make all these motor cars . . .'

Meg's eyes gazed wonderingly at Martin and in the midst of his jubilant elation he found himself staring in quite the most fascinated manner at the moist curve of her open pink mouth. She had licked her lips with her little tongue leaving them shining and . . . and . . .

He cleared his throat and tore his gaze away.

'We are!' His voice sounded strangely husky.

'We? Who's we?'

'Well, me for one!'

'What do you know about it?' Tom's voice was derisive and Mrs Whitley snorted as though in agreement. He was but a lad, her expression said with a lad's big ideas and if he didn't give over and get down to the job he had he might find himself without one altogether. But Martin Hunter had not yet finished.

'I know a lot! I can read, can't I, and Mr Hale takes all the latest magazines. It's ten years now since it began so I've got to be quick . . .'

'Tell us about it, Martin, please . . .' Meg's voice was humble, paying homage to his masculine knowledge and he lifted his head arrogantly.

'You wouldn't know what I was talking about, for God's sake!'

'Try us, go on, please.'

They listened carefully, caught up in his own excitement, turning their heads and straining towards him as he explained the difference between steam and the internal combustion engine, talking incomprehensively about fly wheels and crankshafts and horsepower and valves until their eyes began to glaze. It was too technical for them, Martin could see that so he told them of the days, told to *him* by Mr Hale, not too long ago when Timothy Osborne (a gentleman of much power and wealth in Liverpool, related to their own Mr Hemingway) was one of the first to own an 'infernal machine' as they were then called and had caused a sensation in Dale Street by driving his vehicle at the speed of two miles an hour which was all that had then been allowed, the machine manned, as the law demanded, by three persons one of whom walked ahead carrying a red flag of warning! Horses had reared and ladies fainted and men had laughed. Yes, men had laughed but not now! Not when every man with the slightest conception of what internal combustion would one day mean to the world, men like himself, were about to launch it in the shape of the motor car and ... yes ... the flying machine, on the unsuspecting world! Every detail of motoring, it's past and it's future was of the utmost importance to him and although Martin Hunter knew he was barely scratching the surface as yet he was quick to see the possibility of the new ideas and his shrewd intelligence, more vital than the slower thinking Tom, had grasped and marvelled at what it would mean to their future.

Those who owned carriages and rode horses could see no purpose in the 'automobile' for had not the railway opened up the country to anyone who cared to travel, providing he had the price of a ticket! They were hostile to the idea of the motor car. Where the railway line went so did people, freight, workers moving from one destination to another so what possible use was a motor car? The roads were not made for them, they said, roads meant only for the horse and carriage, for pedestrians and cyclists. Crops were ruined by the dust the machines raised and even washing hung out to dry in one's own garden was spoiled! Dangerous, horrid, odious things, frightening everyone within a mile of them! That was the general opinion of most folk, including Mrs Whitley who had been no nearer to one of them than to the wild animals she believed they resembled, but already Germany and France, Italy and America were manufacturing them, taking the lead and surely, young Martin agonised, Britain – and himself – must soon catch up. And only by *learning* could he do it. Learning how to do it. Learning how to design and *make* the machines he loved, and to do that he must go back to school!

He fell back on his heels and his dreaming eyes stared off into the far corners of the kitchen, to the far corners of the universe or wherever it was he must go to find whatever it was he sought, then he sat upright again and his face was bright, young, hopeful, boyish again.

'Can I go, Mrs Whitley, can I?'

Chapter four

The city and port in which Megan Hughes, Martin Hunter and Tom Fraser lived was a flourishing one. It was a city of contrasts as the great merchants whose fortunes had been amassed by their forefathers in the early part of the previous century looked out from the splendour of their homes on Everton Brow across what had once been meadowland and marsh to the teeming streets, the bursting tenements of those not quite so fortunate; across the bustling dockyards and warehouses and the landing stages to the busy, swaggering river. It was a bustling highway filled with a constant shouting and hooting and whistling and banging and the lovely dancing sight of eager craft as it swept in a silvered ribbon down to the sea which had brought the city it's wealth.

But the three young people who idled along the length of Renshaw Street cared nothing at the moment for this. Today was Shrove Tuesday and they had been given an afternoon off! It was not often that they were able to get out together for Mrs Whitley could not spare all three at once, but it was nearly spring and the influx of emigrants which lasted all through the summer months had not yet begun in earnest.

The sun sparkled on her shining copper pans, the polished crockery and the gleaming floor tiles of her kitchen and acknowledging that Meg, bless her had put the sparkle there, that Martin and Tom had done all their chores and Cook was only making work for them to do, she shoo-ed them away, ordering them to 'be off and be quick about it before I change me mind!'

They had needed no second bidding, stopping only to grab their caps and Meg's straw boater and like the youngsters they still were despite their fine proportions, had kicked their heels to the corner of the square, their youthful, excited voices beseeching one another to decide on how they should solve the delightful problem of what to do with this precious, unexpected holiday! Should they take the ferry across the water to Wallesey and have a walk along the domed and glittering pier which delicately pierced the river? Or to New Brighton to climb it's sky scraping, lattice work tower? Perhaps a stroll along the great stretch of the white sea promenade which threaded its way up the coast to Egremont? Would it be a brisk pace down the Marine Parade to see the splendid liners at berth, or Bold Street with it's elegant shops selling rare fabrics from every corner of the world and where the wealthy and fashionable, the ladies, the carriages and fine horses which pulled them moved in superior respectability?

They looked at one another with shining eyes!

'Well, go on then, make your minds up.' Tom grinned amiably at the other two, carelessly willing as usual to do whatever they chose.

'I don't care as long as we go somewhere.' Meg executed a little jig, enjoying the feel of her brand new alpaca skirt swishing importantly about her ankles. 'Where do you want to go, Martin?'

'Well . . .'

'Yes?'

'I've been wanting to . . .'

'Yes?'

'Well, you know I've been going to the bicycle shop for the last . . .'

'Oh no!' Meg whirled about, walking backwards in order to look into Martin's face, completely forgetting her new, grown up state. She was thirteen now and quite the young lady, she believed, but at times her fledgling sophistication deserted her. 'Not that place again. Not on a lovely day like this! Every time we have some time to spare all you want to do is go and look at the damn bicycles and talk to that old man. Not today, Martin, please. The sun's shining and . . .'

'Alright then, I'll go alone . . . only there was . . . I wanted to show you something but if you're not interested . . .' Martin's face became truculent but there was an expression in his eyes which made Tom put a warning hand on Meg's arm. She tried to shake it off but he held on to her, still watching Martin's face, his own guarded.

'Shut up, our Meg, just for once. Was there something . . . special you wanted to see, Martin?' he said carefully, but Meg turned away, flouncing along in front of them and Tom clicked his tongue impatiently.

'Give over, Meg. If Martin wants to have a word or two with Mr Hale we can spare half an hour, surely and before that we go we can slip up and watch the fun at Lime Street. Go on! What d'you say?'

Meg turned again her face alive with excitement. 'Oh can we, Tom?' She looked at Martin. 'Can we, Martin, can we? Just for an hour, then we'll go to the bicycle shop. There'll be music and dancing and games . . . oh please, please . . .'

They were all smiling, discord averted, as they crossed the junction of Ranelagh Place, picking their way through the crowds at Lime Street Railway Station. As they did so the customary sport which took place every year on this day had just begun. In imminent danger of being run down by the horse drawn trams which travelled the length of Lime Street in a placid amble to the Pier Head where the route terminated, hundreds of the city's working class had gathered to watch the traditional sport which obliged young boys with their arms bound to catch a furious cock with either their legs, their feet or their mouths! The cocks darted about the area paced off, squawking with rage and terror. The boys fell and shouted in pain, the whole a meleé of bloodthirsty excitement and hysteria as bets were laid upon which scruffy urchin would catch the most birds or, as was more likely, would last the longer without a broken limb!

In another cruel arena, men, and a few women too, were attempting the dreadful, competitive pastime of eating as much scalding hot porridge, kept boiling in a cauldron on an open fire, as was possible without taking the skin from their lips or the roof of their mouths! It was excruciating work and those who took part were the poor who had not eaten that day!

The familiar adenoidal accent of Liverpool in which Ireland and Wales is mixed swirled about the great crowd as the spectators shouted on their favourite or poured scorn upon an opponent.

'Gerrit in yer mouth, our Frankie, never mind bluddy feathers . . .'

'Not like tha', yer daft bugger! Kick it . . . kick it!'

'Gerrup, yer daft sod! Yer'll do nowt sittin' on yer bum . . .'

'Go on, Doll, gerrit down yer! It's norras 'ot as yer old man on a . . .'

Shrieks of ribald laughter, grunts of pain, the high, wheeling cackle of the gulls which hung above the city and the river. Ships' sirens, hooters, the crash of enormous hooves on cobblestones as the huge Clydesdales thundered by. Street musicians, fiddlers, a penny whistler, an organ grinder, a hurdy-gurdy man and all toting for farthings, aware as they did so there would be small pickings in this crowd unless they were fortunate enough to find a group of middle class young men out on a spree!

The three youngsters stopped to watch for, cruel though part of it was, the rich tapestry of northern humour and enjoyment, drew their excited curiosity. Meg did not like the cock-baiting nor the sight of the poor little boys with bloody knees and noses but the rollicking music of the organ grinder and the piercing sweetness with which the penny whistler played his tune made her want to stop and tap her feet and let the fresh spring breeze blow against her flushed face.

She turned to look for Tom. He had stopped to watch two men who danced a lively hornpipe to the tune of the penny whistle and his face was animated and his foot rapped out an enthusiastic accompaniment to the rhythm. He clapped his hands and those about him, especially the women, eyed him appreciatively and began to do the same. He was easy, natural, unrestrained and they responded to him with the gregariousness of those who have been friends for years.

A woman, old enough to be his granny nudged him, grinning gaptoothed and in a second he had her in his strong arms, jigging her round the centre of the growing crowd to the cordial delight of those about him.

'Oh Lord, will you look at him now?' Martin snorted impatiently, eager to be off to the bicycle shop and the masculine companionship and guidance of Mr Hale, resentful of anything which kept him from the evergrowing obsession which was the hub of his life. He never stopped talking about it to anyone who would listen, even Emm, as though the strict leash he had kept on his tongue for so long, now it was slipped, would not allow him to be still. Meg and Tom were patient and tried to show an interest but they barely understood half of what he tried to explain to them. His enthusiasm flowed from him with all the fervency of an undammed river, in full spate now it was free, heady and exhilarating, dashing headlong from it's source across the shining rocks and boulders of his mind, flinging its ebullience into the air like spray from the water and carrying with it the message of his hope and excitement. His warm brown face would be charged with colour at his cheekbones and his deep, toffee brown eyes would become rich and glowing. He was intoxicated with his own dream, carried away with an uncontrollable passion which had him on a course of bewitchment in his almost, at times, senseless state of joy. It cascaded from him endlessly and in such a deluge Mrs Whitley asked him irritably if he could 'find summat else to talk about for she was sick of it, really she was!'

He spent three evenings a week, with Mr Lloyd's permission, at the Collegiate in Shaw Street where he was taught the basics of mechanical engineering and draughtsmanship and as many hours as he could manage in the Royal Institution in Colquitt Street. The late William Brown, one of its founders, had believed in the development of the young mind, and the building housed a library, a lecture room where interesting speakers might be heard propounding on the subject most dear to Martin Hunter's mind, and a laboratory.

He found he was not the only young man in Liverpool to believe, not just in the ascendancy of the horseless carriage but of the flying machine! He began to spend every penny he could save on the motoring magazine, *The Autocar* and was quite astounded to learn that steam propulsion which he had thought peculiar only to the railway train and the iron steamships on the river, had been in use in several countries for more than a century, particularly in the big, agricultural engines, but the very first motor car which moved falteringly under its own power was undoubtedly that invented by a German, Carl Benz in 1885! Martin had seen picture slides of it, shown by an enthusiastic lecturer and had been enchanted to be amongst men with the same passion as himself. He was shown pictures of the first passenger carrying vehicle. Spindly wire wheels, one at the front, two at the back and with *electrical* ignition! It was like a tricycle with a seat wide enough for two with the engine at the back, all horizontal wheels, chains, belts and bright, canister-like receptacles, one of which held petrol, the other water.

He hung about many of the small workshops which had sprung up in Liverpool to service the bicycles which crowded the roads, earning Mrs Whitley's wrath when he arrived late back from an errand she had sent him on. These were the only places available to the new motor cars should they go mechanically wrong, which happened quite frequently and by a 'suck it and see' method, the men who worked there, men who could by no stretch of the imagination be given the title of 'mechanic' for which Martin strived, learned the intricacies of the new machines, and Martin learned with them! He was not allowed to do more than watch, mind, for these were expensive vehicles put into their hands by their wealthy owners and a boy of his years could not expect to be allowed to do more than peek over their shoulders as they worked!

He read everything that had been written on the 'internal combustion' engine, haunting the reading room at the Institution whenever he had the time, poring over the accounts of the inventors and their inventions, from Germany, France and America. Gottleib Daimler, Edouard Sarazin, Emile Levassor, who it was said had shaped the present motor car, putting the engine in front of the driver with a 'bonnet' over it and the gearbox behind, and of his partner, René Panhard! There was Armand Peugot, a simple ironmonger and bicycle manufacturer, and in America, the Duryea brothers and their gas powered 'buggy', Alexander Winton who, in 1899 had managed an average speed of seventeen miles an hour between Cleveland and New York, a distance of eight hundred miles in eleven days, and Frederick William Lanchester, one of the Englishmen who were already producing a commercial automobile in this country!

They were his heroes now and those of his football days, his *young* days, were forgotten and he could not wait to become one of them though how this was to be done was not yet clear to him. But he would and he said so frequently until, exasperated, Tom asked him how?

'I don't know,' Martin shrugged carelessly, 'but I will, don't you fret.' His voice was confident, arrogant with the certainty of youth. 'I understand them, Tom. They speak to me.' He was not ashamed to say the words which sounded fanciful and made Tom smile. 'They do! I've always known how the steam engine works. Times I've been down to Lime Street railway station and watched them get up steam, I could damn near do it myself and when I go to Mr Hale's repair shop – he's tackling a few motor cars now, did I tell you? – and see him stripping down an internal combustion engine I can put the thing back together quicker than he can. He stands there scratching his head, wondering what the hell to do with it but *I know*. Don't ask me how but I do and he says I've ... I've got a ... a feeling ...'

Martin was serious with an intensity within him which often irritated his two companions but today, in the carefree joyousness which infected Meg and Tom he forgot, for the moment, his own passionate concern with the future and he and Meg began to push

51

their way back through the good natured crowd. Several others had taken courage from Tom's camaraderie and were stepping out beside him. He saw Martin and Meg and lifted his hand to wave and on his face was an expression, laughing, which said quite plainly he had not the slightest notion of how he came to be in this situation, but *they* knew, for it was Tom's nature to hold out the hand of good-fellowship and his gift to have it taken! He grinned, his mouth stretching over his white teeth. He looked down in to the face of the grandmother and said something to her, then placing her, cackling joyously into another's arms, walked purposefully towards Meg. He stopped in front of her.

'Meggie?' he said airily, questioningly, holding out his arms. She did not hesitate but moved into them delightedly and in a moment they were whirling about the growing circle of admirers for indeed they made a handsome sight, her bright loveliness sharpened by his own golden good looks.

Feet stamping, hands clapping, men whistling, the sun brilliant in the pale washed blue of the spring sky and as they galloped by with more enthusiasm than grace for the third time, Martin, the bicycle shop forgotten in the unexpected pleasure of the moment, threw out a hand and grasped Meg's arm and turning her about plucked her from Tom's vigorous clasp.

'My turn now, Meggie!' he shouted above the din and his strong arm held her to him and his big workman's hand, rough and brown and still stained with the deep grained oil with which they were everlastingly occupied, took hers and in a mad echo of a lively reel they jostled their way round and round the circle.

Tom, never one to hang back and wait his turn had found a pretty, flower bonneted young girl to partner him in the music and the amiable, hail-fellow-well-met atmosphere instilled into the assembly gathered momentum and smile was returned with smile and lovers exchanged a kiss or two under cover of the joyous dance.

Martin's arm tightened about Meg and his long legs carried her even more rapidly through the sun-dappled crowd and his eyes beamed glowingly into hers and she was conscious only of how happy she felt and how wonderful the day was. She threw back her head and her boater fell to her shoulder blades held on by the ribbon beneath her chin beating in rhythm to the lively tune. The sunshine enveloped her and her vivid hair blazed in it. More than a few male glances fell about her as she danced by for though she was only thirteen she looked several years older. She was tall and as the months passed her breasts had ripened, rounded and thrusting. Her slender hips curved from a waist fined to a handswidth and she had long, shapely legs beneath the smooth alpaca of her new skirt. Her clear skin and eyes and the firm flesh of her throat were as glossy and magnificent as though she had been just newly polished with a chamois leather!

Martin had become aware of the interest her young beauty aroused in the other men's eyes as they watched but when one young man, bolder than the rest stepped out of the crowd, tapping on his shoulder and smiling admiringly at Meg he was quite taken aback and allowed himself to be elbowed aside. He stood indecisively, astonished by the strength of his own anger, then, in the space of thirty seconds his brown eyes darkened almost to black and his fierce eyebrows swooped over his nose in a frown. Something in the way the young man had placed his large hand on Meg's back offended him, he did not know exactly why and before the laughing Meg and her new partner had gone more than a yard or two the young man found himself pulled sharply away from her. He almost fell over backwards and Meg lurched, unsupported, against another couple.

' 'Ere mate, what's up wi' you?' the young man said, his smile slipping somewhat but still good-natured for he was not yet aware of the dangerous change in Martin's mood.

'Nowt, *mate*, just find someone else to lark about with.' Martin's face was tense and quiet and those around him slowed and began to move back in anticipation. They liked nothing better than a good laugh, a good sing-song, beer glasses at the ready, or a good fight and were eager to be part of all three!

'Now listen ere, you! I meant no 'arm to the young lady and . . .'

'Right then, clear off!'

'What's up wi' you . . .?'

'Just clear off!'

The young man was becoming angry. He *had* meant no harm to Meg, nor disrespect. She was a pretty girl and besides it *was* Shrove Tuesday, a holiday and every man was dancing with anyone he could get his arms around!

Tom, the one who had begun it all, though he still gazed admiringly into the bright, upturned face of his partner, began to sense the changing mood of the crowd at his back and when the penny whistler suddenly stopped his whistling, he glanced about him uncertainly. He was just in time to see Martin duck beneath a smart, left-handed swing from some burly chap with bright red hair and he groaned despairingly. Nevertheless he placed his disappointed partner carefully amongst her friends and elbowed his way towards Martin and Meg, smiling politely and murmuring his thanks to all who moved out of his way. He shrugged his shoulders at the horrified Meg then threw himself into the fray, having not the slightest idea of what it was about. He did not care for fighting and was not, like Martin, handy with his fists but he was willing if needs be to stand beside his friend; to defend what was theirs, whatever that might turn out to be! In a few seconds both he and Martin had disappeared beneath a melée of bobbing cloth-capped heads and flailing fists for the young man who had so offended Martin had not come alone!

The uproar became more turbulent and noisy as those on its perimeter were persuaded to become involved and women danced about its edge, encouraging a sweetheart, a husband, to 'gerron wi' it', all interest abandoned in the cock-chasing boys and the porridge-consuming competitors. The fiddler and the penny whistler looked at one another resignedly and shrugged for they knew it was hopeless to try to tempt to their entertainment those who were enjoying themselves in the vastly more amusing pastime of fisticuffs. The 'Liverpool kiss' dropped a few, noses erupted with blood and it was only a question of time before the 'scuffers' arrived.

Meg was pushed further and further back from the centre of the crowd as excited women elbowed her aside to get a better view. Her temper showed in her heightened colour and the blaze of the golden light in her eyes. She was furious! She'd never forgive Martin, never! What on earth had got into him picking a fight with that chap and him only asking for an innocent bit of a dance with hundreds watching! It didn't take much to ignite Martin's temper, true, but the chap had done nothing and would you look at Tom, usually so mild and inoffensive, happy-go-lucky even and the last man on earth to pick a fight, throwing punches like he was 'Gentleman' Jim Corbett himself!

She turned away and stamped her foot in frustration, almost in tears. This had promised to be such a lovely day, unexpected and therefore the more exciting and now those two great daft lumps had spoiled it for her! Martin had hinted at a surprise at Mr Hale's though what it could be in the smelly old bicycle shop she could not imagine. This small diversion, before it had erupted into the rumpus it had become, had been lovely, dancing in the sunshine amidst the good fellowship of the holiday crowd and now it was ruined. They'd probably end up in gaol, the pair of them and she'd have to go home and report to Mrs Whitley that two of her servants had been arrested for brawling in the streets!

A hand clutched her arm and she spun about, ready to give what for to whoever it was had the temerity to interfere with her, so short was her temper but a lively voice told her to 'Look sharp, Meggie, before they miss us.' and Martin's laughing brown eyes and glowing face were there and she was pulled along at such speed she was in danger of falling.

'Tom,' she gasped.

'I'm here,' a voice cried from her other side and Tom's hand gripped her left arm and as she began to laugh, her feet scarce touching the ground as they bore her along, they laughed with her.

From behind the noise of the fighting multitude died away, pierced by the sharp shrillness of police whistles. The culprits continued to run, Meg clinging to her boater and the length of her skirt which threatened to trip her up until they turned into St John's Lane.

'Oh for God's sake stop!' she beseeched. 'I've a stitch in my side that's cutting through me and I'll lose my hat in a minute. Let me go, the pair of you!'

They all three slowed down and shrugging her arms from their grasp Meg adjusted her straw boater and pushed back the crop of curls which had become loosened in the mad flight, tucking them carelessly under her hat. Her face had become stern though her eyes could not rid themselves of the laughter. She felt she should be cross with them both for hadn't they spoiled her lovely dance but they leaned against the wall, blowing on their grazed knuckles and grinned at her and she could not stop her mouth from forming into a wide smile. Martin had a cut lip and as his grin deepened he winced, putting his hand to it ruefully. Tom's eye looked suspiciously swollen and there was no doubt he would have a 'shiner' which he would have to explain to Mrs Whitley in the morning but who cared, his expression said. He had acquitted himself well beside the more skilful fists of his friend and he was pleased with himself. He was enjoying this day, this moment and with Tom's outlook on life that was all that mattered!

'Will you look at the two of you! Cook'll skin you when she sees the state of your good jackets!'

'No she won't, Meggie. I shall tell her she's lovely and give her a kiss and she'll forgive us like she always does.' Tom's engaging smile was perfectly confident for he knew what he said was true.

'Don't you be too sure me old cock sparrer.' Martin fingered the tear in the sleeve of his jacket. 'This cost Mr Lloyd good money and you know how she says we've to look smart and she can't keep up with us growing so fast.'

'Oh stop worrying! You're like an old woman going on about your damn coat. Meg'll sew it up for you, won't you chuck? You'll sew poor old Martin's coat up for him, won't you . . . ?'

Tom began to dance round Martin, sparring and jabbing playfully with his big-jointed fists, evidently still enjoying his new found prowess and Meg could see that Martin, not yet steady after the fight in which they had just been involved would not take much to inflame again. Hastily she intervened.

'Oh come on you two, don't spoil a perfectly good day any further. It's bad enough when you fight other people. If you're going to start on each other I'm off!'

She began to walk away, her tall figure swaying slightly in the graceful, girlish manner she was developing as she matured and the two youths were suddenly, strangely, quite diverted. Her hips swung from side to side below her slender waist and her head was held proudly, the plain straw boater clinging desperately to the tumbled mass of her effervescent hair. For a moment they might have been watching a stranger, a pretty girl who had caught their eye, then she turned and grinned and she was only their Meg again!

They followed her, falling into step, one on either side as they had always done! Tall houses built a century ago leaned on each side of the road. A tram ran alongside of them, the driver clucking affectionately to the horse which pulled it and a hansom cab reined in behind, the cabbie cursing as he attempted to overtake the tram. The tram driver looked over his shoulder and grinned amiably and mouthed a word or two of 'Liverpoolese' and the cabbie shook his fist.

The air smelled good – a mixture of sea freshness pungent with the sharpness of tar from the rigging of the sailing vessels which were still to be seen tied up beside those of steam. A strange miscellany of aromas in which could be recognised coffee beans,

Indian tea, citrus fruits, nutmeg, camphor and the sharp new tang of timber. All the perfumes which assail the nostrils – for the most part unnoticed – of those who live beside the great highway of water which brought them there. There would be life down there at the dockside, just as there had been in the vital enthusiasm of the crowd they had just left behind and Meg loved it, and this city in which she had been born.

They turned into Victoria Street and half way down came to Mr Hale's shop, the 'Modern Bicycle Emporium' which was Martin's Mecca and the start of his dream, and at the door, smiling in welcoming anticipation was Albert Hale.

Like all men who love something with a passion beyond all others he was always eager also to discuss his obsession with a fellow devotee, and also the finer points of the advancing technology, and Meg and Tom would have to wait patiently until Martin had inspected each nut and bolt of every last one of the latest models in the shop, and the wonder of the 'Vauxhall' motor car belonging to one of Liverpool's wealthy, it's engine stripped down for a minor repair in Mr Hale's back yard!

In the dim light which struggled from the street they could make out the silent, skeletal frames of the bicycles which were Mr Hale's main livelihood. Some were on racks above their heads, ranged along the walls in strange, threadlike shapes, their narrow structures resembling the delicate vertebrae of dozens of spiders. They were everywhere, propped against walls, leaning against one another, heaped and piled, some of them upside down and others still in the crates in which they had travelled. On shelves were saddle bags and saddles, bells and lamps and along the wall, ranged in orderly rows hung knapsacks, capes, maps and every conceivable aid which the cyclist might require.

It had become familiar to Tom and Meg during the past few months for they had been here several times with Martin as he 'mucked about' as they tolerantly called it, in the element he loved. They had spent hours watching and idly listening as Martin discussed with Mr Hale the merits of the 'Napier' versus the 'Vauxhall' and the chances of the former in the 'Gordon Bennett Cup' in July. It was an enigma to them both still for they had not yet got over their bewilderment at Martin's passion for these weird contraptions but they were willing to be part of it, as they had always been part of Martin's life.

Threading their way through the muddle, led by Mr Hale they

passed beyond the curtained alcove which led from the shop and into another room which looked as though some playfully destructive hand had taken a score of bicycles and torn them apart, flinging the pieces in joyous abandon to every corner of the room. There were wheels and frames, pedals and handlebars, saddles and mudguards and all lying about like the pieces of a giant jig-saw puzzle waiting to be put together. Here again Tom and Meg were on familiar ground for it was in this workshop that Mr Hale kept his 'spares', the pieces he used to construct or repair a machine. On more than one occasion Tom had been ordered to shuffle them about in search of a decent spoke or brake as Martin helped Mr Hale to fit up some contrivance he was re-building.

'How's it going then, Mr Hale?' Martin asked politely, though his eyes shone with excitement.

'Fine lad, just fine. All ready then, are yer?'

'Aye ... if you are!'

'Oh aye. I said a week or two and ... well, come and see fer yerself!'

Meg and Tom looked at one another and pulled a face, mystified by this cryptic exchange, then followed the retreating backs of Mr Hale and Martin, stepping over the explosion of bicycle parts which barred their way.

'Come through then, you two,' Martin called over his shoulder.

Another door was opened in what seemed the endless depths of the shop and what was evidently Mr Hale's living quarters until they came at last into a back yard. In one corner, draped lovingly with a tarpaulin was the shape of what Meg and Tom understood to be the wonder of the 'Vauxhall' motor car, not apparently to be revealed to their amateur and therefore heretic gaze and they were directed to the furthest corner. Here again were a myriad pieces of what had once been bicycles, from the old 'ordinary', the 'pennyfarthing' and the 'boneshaker', all discarded now for they were rusted and rotting away, but standing in their midst, shining and proud and leaning against one another in companionable equanimity was a tandem, it's two leather seats polished to the shine of a horse chestnut, and a bicycle!

'Now then!' said Mr Hale, 'will these do yer?' His face was fondly indulgent as though he showed off two beloved children. 'I 'ad to put a couple of extra coats of paint on them mudguards after you left, Martin. Well, they'd bin rusting out 'ere for months, but they turned out right well. What d'yer think to 'em?'

Martin appeared to have lost his voice and Meg and Tom were beyond speaking anyway so Mr Hale went on comfortably.

'Not bad, eh, considerin' not one piece belongs to another. I reckon there must be at least fifty machines in them two, if yer don't count the spokes! Now get on 'em, the three of you and let me see what you make of 'em!'

Chapter five

They were never off them dratted machines Mrs Whitley grumbled and what about the scullery steps and them windows hadn't been polished for two days and would you look at the state of the kitchen floor, she said, but secretly she was as proud of her three as if they had been of her own conceiving and was heard to boast quite openly to neighbouring servants of the vast distances they covered on their 'machines'! Still, it did no harm to let them know where their place was and so she did, quite volubly, endlessly pointing out the slow deterioration of her 'standards' and her disapproval of it! It was as if the very house was falling in ruins about their ears as Meg and Tom and Martin spent every spare minute, very often as late as nine o'clock in the evening as the spring days drew out, 'messing about' on their bicycles. On most days they got no further than the end of the street which led into the Square, or even just once round the Square itself but they took to it like a duckling will take to its element, the water and for the first few weeks whenever they were free might be seen speeding about the surrounding streets of Great George Square.

But as the season for travellers began to reach it's peak they had no time during the day to even think of their new passion. It was only at night when Meg was tucked up beside Emm that she could read the books she took from the lending library, searching for anything which would give her information on what was, now that she had the means to be about it, her consuming interest. Travel! It had seized her, hypnotised her like the flashing wheels of the bicycles and her young mind yearned endlessly towards it. Travel! That was it!

Of course those with money and time enough already moved about the country and across the channel to see what was on the other side but now, with the advent of the breath-taking machines Martin had devised for them with the sweat of his own endeavours in helping out Mr Hale in his workshop and yard, they were to be part of it! The idea overwhelmed her with it's spellbinding possibilities and she fell asleep to dream about it.

She would never forget that first day they set out on a *real* ride!

It was almost the end of May and the last boatload of emigrants had been disposed of for the next week as Meg and Tom and Martin pedalled away, turning to wave as though they were royalty, Mrs Whitley observed proudly when they had swung round the corner. Of course by then they had cycled several times to Sefton Park in the lengthening evenings to travel sedately round and round the cricket pitch and review ground on the paths which formed a figure eight and though it had given them practice in handling their machines they had not really *seen* anything, Meg complained.

Stanley Park was better because it was further away and there were lots of intriguing paths to cycle along when they got there but then those who were out for an evening stroll often took exception to Martin and Tom who, in the manner of high spirited youth would race against one another, Martin's legs forcing Meg's to go faster and faster as she clung to the handlebars behind him, and the walkers objected to being forced from the path on to the grass verge and when the park-keeper told them angrily 'Tweren't made fer the likes of them great nasty machines,' they gave up!

But before Mrs Whitley would let them go for a whole day there were bedrooms to be cleaned in readiness for the next batch of travellers, tables and floors to be scrubbed, furniture to be polished and mats to be taken up and beaten. The 'masters machine', the one used for sharpening knives must be taken apart and oiled – Martin's job, the lamps cleaned and trimmed – Tom's, and the brassware on them polished with a mixture of oil and rottenstone made into a paste.

And the laundry! Fires in the boiler to be lit, sheets to be soaked in water and soda, rinsed, rubbed and rinsed again and that was before they even began the starching! Not until the bed linen was alabaster white was it hung, snapping in the breeze, on the lines which stretched between the walls of the rear yard. Next, when it was dry it was the turn of the flat iron. It was back breaking work but Meg was used to it after three years and her routine, worked out and practised upon until it was second nature to her, cut out hours of unnecessary labour.

When the great day arrived the whole Square came out to watch as they rode round and round the railinged gardens, ringing

61

their bicycle bells smartly. They were masters of balance by now and were swooping and diving like sea-birds, tearing along to the enthusiastic encouragement of every emigrant who was temporarily housed by the many shipping lines in the area. Everywhere there were men and women, many of them dressed in rough homespun, sturdy and made to last, dark-coloured shawls about the fair plaits and coronets of hair of the women, the men in furry caps, top boots and leathern waistcoats and the excitement and noise as support was shouted in half a dozen different languages was as joyful as anything Meg had ever known. Those who were here for merely a moment formed an alliance with their hosts in the delight of the lovely young girl and her two stalwart escorts, plunging in a mad dance of youth on their startlingly modern machines.

Meg was a joy to behold. Her straw boater was whipped away in the stiff breeze, retrieved and held by a shy Swedish lad who did not know what to do with it, nor the smile she bestowed upon him as she took it from his hand. Her copper hair flew out behind her as the pins which held it scattered and were lost. Men cheered and whistled for her breasts were clearly defined beneath the fine cotton of her shirt as she strained at the handlebars in an effort to keep up with Martin's flying legs and Mrs Whitley, as she told Emm in the privacy of the kitchen later, quite literally did not know where to look and swore to have a word with her when she got home!

It was barely seven-thirty in the morning. Maidservants clustered on the small bow-fronted wrought iron balconies on the first floor of each house and at each area entrance, waving dust rags and admiring Martin's broad shoulders, laughing as Tom bowed to them as he pedalled by. The park was green, freshly mowed and the last of the late daffodils were a brilliant dash of gold lining the pathway which surrounded it.

Meg had taken to heart the list put out by the 'Cyclist Touring Club', which she hoped one day to join and though she had not the money to buy and wear the 'rationals' or cycling dress for ladies recommended by the club – and should she have it was doubtful Mrs Whitley would have allowed *knickerbockers* – nevertheless she was sensibly dressed in the mandatory straw boater, a cool blouse and full skirt, a pair of fine cotton gloves and felt herself to be the epitome of what the 'lady cyclist' should be. Martin and Tom wore knee breeches and stockings, an open necked shirt and an old jacket, their caps perched jauntily at the back of their heads.

They turned left into Upper Pitt Street and headed in the direction of the Pier Head. They had considered which might be the best route to take on this, their first 'proper' ride and had decided on the Wirral Peninsula. They were to go across the Mersey on the ferry and strike out for Shotwick which was acknowledged as the Wirral's oldest and most secluded village containing a lovely old manor, the Cyclist Touring Club list stated, and which Meg was determined to see. She wished longingly that she possessed one of those photographic cameras so that she might take pictures to keep forever but you couldn't have everything, could you? and at least she was lucky enough to get there! Mrs Whitley had never been further than Bootle village on a day trip and that wasn't even across the water!

They manoeuvered through traffic so thick and bustling in the streets of Liverpool which led down to the docks they were in distinct danger of being run down but they loved every thrill-packed minute of it! They were perfectly matched, the three of them, holding their heads high, riding with alert and easy carriage in the saddle and Meg's grace, her neat ankle and daintily turned elbow drew admiring male glances at every corner. As she got on and off the tandem she did so with a tiny skip which delighted those who watched.

The river was wind ruffled as they took the ferry to the other side. It smelled of tar and salt. The gulls' cries were harsh yet jubilant and the high, hazed early summer sky seemed to go on forever until it met the glistening smoothness of the water. The sun warmed Meg's cheek and touched her back as they were put down on the pier at Rock Ferry and without thinking she undid the tiny buttons at her throat, unaware of the sudden stillness which affected the two young men as brown and blue eyes studied, as if for the first time the startling white smoothness of her skin. It was just as she had imagined it. It was her dream, the one she had studied each night since they had brought the bicycles home. The blue sky, the lark which swept the curve of it bursting his heart with song, the smells of the grass, of woodsmoke, the sharp but not unpleasant acidity of animal manure, the flowers, the sea and the ecstatic thrill to come of speeding like the very bird above her head along deserted, dusty lanes. A pulse beat in the soft curve of her neck and the two boys stared at it but her eyes were drawn along the pier to the lane they would take and their strange absorption, their curiously silent appraisal of her went unnoticed.

'Look,' she cried, 'look at the cottages,' and obediently they both turned, the moment gone as they followed her pointing finger. 'What lovely gardens they have. I've never seen flowers like that before. I wonder what they're called and where d'you think that lane leads to?'

'Only one way to find out, Meggie,' Tom answered cheerfully and began to push his bicycle along the wooden pier, his boots spilling echoes down to the water beneath.

They took the road through the village and turned left beyond a farm and meadowland in which cows raised their heads as Martin rang the bell on his handlebars and a couple of men working in a field turned to wave. They sped along a quiet lane until they were out in open countryside with nothing on either side but tall, blackthorn hedges and fields awash with wild flowers. The pedals flashed in the sunshine and the spokes of the wheels made shadowed patterns in the dust. It was warm and the boys stopped to take off their jackets and Tom said this was the life, wasn't it? and didn't you have to be quick to see everything? It all went by so rapidly it was gone before you had time to take it in and could they get off again, please and have a look at that sailing ship which was making its way up the river. He could feel his circulation quicken and his energies seemed to have become awakened and a feeling of such physical satisfaction came over him he threatened to sing but Martin begged him not to since they didn't want it to rain, did they? Their laughter was high and pealing in the almost hysterical pleasure they had found and the wheels went faster and faster until they blurred and Meg felt as though she was flying, she said.

They met no traffic beyond a milk cart, it's driver startled out of his drowsing contemplation of his horse's ears by their swift descent upon him and a fruiterer's van which almost ran into a hedge for the driver was of the opinion he had the lane to himself and the sudden appearance of the lightly skimming, attractive young people who seemed to have grown wheels made him pull violently on the reins!

When they reached Parkgate with its disorderly row of cottages looking out over the estuary of the River Dee they were singing the bicycle song made famous by the music hall performer, Lottie Collins.

64

'Ta ra ra boom de ay,
Ta ra ra boom de ay,
Ta ra ra boom de ay,
Ta ra ra boom de ay,' and Meg knew she had never been happier in her life!

The sun had turned her skin to rose and that of the boys to a golden brown when they arrived back at the ferry. She had lost her ladylike white gloves and her sleeves were rolled up to the elbow. Her hair was carelessly tied with a strand of couch grass and both Tom and Martin had a crown of buttercups and daisies in their windblown hair

They were quiet as they stood in the bow of the ferryboat, reluctant to break the magical enchantment of the last moments of the day, reluctant to have it ended. Their shoulders touched in that instinctive way which had grown up with them though they were not consciously aware of it and when Martin finally spoke the other two turned dreaming faces towards him.

'How about going the other way?' he murmured thoughtfully. 'We've got a good hour before dark. We could ride down to the Jericho shore and have a paddle.'

Instantly alert the other two agreed enthusiastically and within half an hour they were giggling and splashing each other, chasing the lengthening shadows across the hard packed sand of the shoreline on their side of the river.

They grew quiet again as night began to creep across the water and they walked in silence, side by side, their bare feet slapping through the tiny pools that had formed as the tide dropped.

They came to the boat house, almost hidden amongst the stand of very old trees which leaned outwards to the beach, and across the smooth stretch of lawn which sloped away from the river they could see a fine house and lights beginning to illuminate its windows.

'Electric!' Martin said with awe and the others were silent for none of them had ever seen an electric light.

There was a roaring, snarling, rattling sound which grew louder and louder and Meg drew back uncertainly, reaching for Tom's hand but Martin stepped forward, climbing up the small incline until he stood amongst the trees, staring mesmerised across the lawn at the monster which had drawn up to the door of the house.

'What is it?' Meg whispered fearfully though of course she knew for had they not seen more than a dozen or so about the streets of Liverpool. It was just that the first time you came across one in the flesh, so to speak, it was a frightful shock.

'It's only a motor car,' Tom whispered back.

'*Only a motor car!*' Martin's voice was coldly scathing. 'It's not only a bloody motor car you fool. It's a "Rolls-Royce" three and a half litre V8! A six cylinder . . . Oh Sweet Jesus!'

'Martin . . .'

'Where are you going, you daft sod . . .' Tom's voice was agonised and Meg put out a hand as though to hold Martin back but it was too late!

'Dear God . . . He's going to get caught if he goes any nearer,' she whispered frantically.

But Martin Hunter was no longer of their world, nor indeed any world at all for he was in his dream, the one he dwelled in whenever his young mind was not occupied with cleaning knives and peeling spuds and polishing lamps and fetching coal. He moved with wary masculine grace towards the magnificent motor car. It's driver had climbed out and gone inside the house and the faint click of the cooling engine could be heard in the quiet, darkening twilight.

The sun had fallen behind the grey smudge of the far shore across the river but the last light of the evening illuminated the machine. It glimmered like a precious jewel on a dark stretch of velvet, the lights from the house glowing on its polished surface.

It was truly the most beautiful thing Martin Hunter had ever seen! He stood before it, bewitched and when he put out his hand to it he might have been about to caress a beloved woman. His fingers touched the shining bonnet then moved to the high mudguard, trailing lingeringly across the smooth surface.

'God help us,' whispered Tom, 'he's going to get in the bloody thing!' He and Meg watched with the fascination of total horror as Martin Hunter stepped for the first time into a motor car and though it was almost dark by now they saw the flash of his white teeth as he smiled!

For the time being at least they must be satisfied with their bicycles, Martin said as though sooner or later a motor car would be delivered to the front door of the house, and truth to tell Tom and Meg *were* satisfied and during that summer and autumn they rode as often as they could together, going further and further afield as their confidence grew but it seemed that Martin, having seen and actually *sat* in the sheer intoxication and joy of an automobile could be satisfied with nothing else. He took to spending much of his spare time reading more and more books, making intricately drawn plans of what appeared to be boxes on wheels, and what he swore was an 'internal combustion engine' though the other two could make neither head nor tail of it, and when he was not at his 'drawing board' as he grandly called it in the room he shared with Tom, he was at the bicycle shop with Mr Hale. Meg and Tom shared the tandem now, whilst the bicycle, except when Martin rode it to Victoria Street, leaned forlornly against the cellar wall.

Meg was fourteen in September and the childish loveliness of her which had blossomed into the beauty of a young girl began to be something else. She grew even taller and acquired that indefinable quality given to very few women which men admire but which has very little to do with her looks. It was sensual and at the same time innocent! An earthiness and yet a delicate softness which spoke of promised pleasures of the flesh when she was fully matured. Her back was straight and graceful. She had a strong white neck upon which her head was set proudly and she drew admiring glances wherever she went. Mrs Whitley often wondered where she got it from, that haughty look of a young queen. Perhaps it was something to do with her Welsh heritage, she thought, knowing nothing of them from across the two rivers except that they could sing! And Meg did that too, carolling all over the house from morning till night, cheerful as a sparrow but far more exotic!

She was lively, full of fun and liked nothing better than a good laugh and Cook had noticed lately how the eyes, one pair brown, the other blue, of the two young men had begun unconsciously to follow her swaying, graceful figure as she moved about the kitchen. They did not realise they were doing it, she could see that for they both had a dreaming quality about them which did not at that moment contain more than an appreciation of Meg's quick wit, her bright eyes and flashing good humour. She was their 'little sister' and they were devoted to her and it showed in their protective manner but there was something else there now!

Meg was quick tempered but on the whole good-natured and tolerant and her affectionate approach to her companions held no more than that of a sister to two much loved brothers. She fussed them and nagged them, treating each one with the same fondness and irritation, scolding them if they went out in the wet without a coat like a mother with two irresponsible children and praising them where she considered praise was due!

She became weary sometimes of Martin's everlasting preoccupation with motor cars, especially as it often interfered with what were really the loveliest outings, or would have been if Martin had come along! It was not that she was uninterested in the exciting possibilities she was keenly aware would undoubtedly make a difference to all their lives but she did wish sometimes he was not so ... so *obsessed* was the only word she could find to describe him and the subject which filled his mind week in and week out! She had to admit that she was herself fascinated with the thought of travelling about, seeing the country, the world even (for Meg had no limits when it came to daydreaming) in one of the smart and increasingly reliable machines which were appearing more and more on the roads of Liverpool and the surrounding countryside. They were a nuisance at times when they thundered past them on a country road, lifting the dust in a whirlwind about their heads, settling it on their clothes and skin and causing a cloud through which they could barely see, but imagine being *up there*, actually on the high seat able to look over hedges to the fields of wild flowers beyond, and beyond that to the very horizon!

Martin would cheer wildly when one rattled past them, waving his cap and standing up on the pedals of the machine, causing no end of problems with balance but still, as she watched the automobile veer madly down the lane she admitted to herself that she wouldn't mind changing places with those who rode in it!

And the speed at which they went! Twenty miles an hour! It meant you could get about so much more quickly and arrive at places the bicycle could not reach in a day. Meg meant to travel, to see people and places she had read about in her books and yet that was only part of it! She not only liked the idea of having a look at other parts of the world, she wanted in some way to share in the change Martin, and through him she herself, sensed was coming, because of the motor car! Not only would she hope to share the exciting fascination of their countries, their people would come and see hers!

Holidays! Travel! Movement! Would not this marvellous machine of Martin's, when it became readily available have the effect of shifting people, ordinary people like herself who had scarce moved from their own fireside in a lifetime to seek out and discover what was at the end of the road, the limit of their village or town, or even beyond the shoreline of the country in which they lived?

Martin said so and though she was often in discord with him in so many matters, in this they were in agreement. Her brain would seethe sometimes as she lay in the darkness next to the supine Emm whose only anxiety was the keeping of her share of the blankets which covered them both. Her thoughts would try to regulate themselves into coherence. Somewhere in the future was her own fate. Martin was so sure of his and already was setting about it with the possessed certainty which Meg wished she could emulate. She admired him for it and envied him too and wished she could go back to school, evening classes, to learn something, but what? That was the trouble! She didn't know what it was she wanted to do. She was perfectly happy doing just what she did. She loved seeing to the comfort of the weary travellers who crept over her threshold and nothing gave her more pleasure than to watch their care-worn frightened faces relax and grow peaceful as she shepherded them to their alloted place in the house, or put before them some tasty dish she herself might have prepared.

But where would that lead, she began to ask herself? Did she want to be a kitchen maid, or even cook at an emigrant house until the end of her days? Finish up like Mrs Whitley complacently toasting her toes at what would never be her own fireside? How was she to see the rest of the world from the kitchens of a house just like this one and if she left it, what would she do? She was well aware that Martin would be off soon for he would never be satisfied with the job he had now. A repair shop somewhere in Liverpool, she imagined, where he could tinker to his heart's content with his blessed machines and he would get a good job once he had the necessary qualifications. Not that he couldn't do it now, given the chance, but he needed a bit of paper to show folk, he said and besides, there was the designing of motor cars which he intended as soon as he was able and he needed his 'certificate', whatever that was, in order to do that!

It was at the end of September when it happened!

It had been a lovely day. A Sunday and quiet at the house and with Cook's blessing they had taken a few of her pasties, the three of 'em and set off just before noon. They had got no send off today! They had become a familiar sight by now to those who lived in the Square and those few emigrants who still remained

69

after the sailing of the *Lacy Rose III* and *Girl Sophie II* of the Hemingway Line the day before, were out seeing the sights of Liverpool before they too sailed away to their new life.

Meg almost fell from the tandem as Tom, who was sharing it with her that day, stopped pedalling, for when his feet slowed so did hers and, her balance suddenly interfered with, she jerked at the handlebars to steady herself, causing further disturbance.

Martin had come to an abrupt halt ahead of them and they almost ran into his back and for a chaotic moment it seemed they would all crash into the bonnet of the amazing machine which stood forlornly slewed across the junction of the lanes. It was bright, polished, a beautiful gleaming blue and from its surface the sun winked back at them, dazzling, blinding. The hard top was black, the bonnet was raised and all they could see of the man who had his head buried in the depths of it was the seat of his trousers! It was a Rolls Royce Silver Ghost, and Meg heard Martin whisper the name in a soft, hushed tone.

Like a man who has entered a church and walks reverently towards the altar he simply left the bicycle to crash against Tom and Meg and began the short journey from where they stood, to the motor car! A few steps only, but for him a journey from one life to another. His head was held high and his hands clenched at his sides and on his face was a look of exalted joy!

When he reached the vehicle and it's driver who seemed momentarily oblivious to everything but what was under the bonnet, Martin cleared his throat politely. Instantly the man withdrew his head, looked at the spanner in his hand then turned and almost as though he knew that here was a man who could be trusted with his expensive machine, said simply, 'I don't know one bloody nut from another!'

Martin smiled. The man was a gentleman, despite his inadvertent oath, that was apparent, not just from the way he spoke and the clothes he wore but from the simple fact that he owned a motor car at all for only those of wealth and position could afford to do so! He was in his sixties but spry, with a pleasantly humorous face, high-coloured as though used to an open air life. He wore what was then described as a 'motoring' outfit though as yet none had really been designed for the pastime of driving about in the 'infernal' machine was considered to be merely a passing phase. A double-breasted reefer jacket buttoned high with a small turn down collar, wind cuffs with straps, trousers of twill, a yachting cap and gloves.

'I might be able to help, sir,' Martin said respectfully, but not humbly for was he not suddenly in charge? This man might be one of the ruling class of Liverpool but it was Martin's knowledge that this man needed and at this precise moment that put Martin in authority over *him*.

'Are you a mechanic then?' the gentleman asked.

'Not yet sir, but I know a bit about motor cars.'

Tom and Meg stood, mesmerised and frozen to the spot on which they had come to a confused halt, the bicycles every which way about them. They turned to gawp at one another, mouths slack, then looked back at Martin who now had *his* head under the bonnet.

'Mmm,' they heard him say. 'I see it has six cylinders . . . three and half litres . . . the one which won the Isle of Man TT this year . . . what a marque . . .'

'Yes, I was there . . .'

Martin lifted his head and turned eagerly to the old gentleman. 'Really sir . . . *really*!'

'Yes, it was a splendid race I might tell you . . .'

They might have been alone, two acolytes glorying in the worship of their own particular god and for quite ten minutes they spoke in words of such an extremely detailed and technical nature Tom and Meg began to wonder if they had blundered into a foreign country and were listening to a language neither had heard before.

'. . . automatic lubrication . . .'

'. . . three speed epicyclic gearbox . . .'

'. . . preselection of the two lower gears . . .'

Their faces were animated in their shared enthusiasm '. . . but this isn't getting your engine fixed is it, sir,' Martin said at last, 'so if I might borrow your spanner . . .' He held out his hand, oil covered now and the old gentleman put the tool trustingly into it.

'Aah!' the two who watched in silent awe heard Martin say, '. . . there's where the trouble is, sir. Can you see, just there.'

The old gentleman obligingly looked where Martin's finger pointed saying politely. 'I really had no idea . . .' and 'how very interesting . . .' and 'well, I'm blowed . . .'

Martin turned peremptorily to Tom at one stage and ordered

him to leave the bicycles and give the starting handle a crank. He had to show him what to do, of course, for Tom stood there uncertainly, staring at the thing which had been thrust in his hand, not sure which end of the vehicle he should approach and when he had 'cranked' and still nothing happened and he had fallen back winded on to the grass verge, Martin begged the bemused gentleman to check 'that the petrol cock on the feed pipe from the petrol tank to the carburettor was on!'

'Er . . . where exactly is . . .'

Martin sighed, then remembered that he was dealing with not only someone who knew *nothing* about the motor car he drove but was one of Liverpool's most influential residents and therefore must be treated with respect.

He spoke politely. 'Never mind, sir. Tom and I will see to it.'

He moved about the vehicle with all the aplomb of the Hon. Charles Stewart Rolls himself, one of it's designers, and Tom sidled after him, impressed beyond measure and, if he were honest, not a little fascinated by this marvellous invention which he was seeing at close quarters for the first time.

'D'you know what the hell you're doing?' he whispered at a critical moment and was silenced by Martin's withering expression!

With nothing to do the elderly gentleman sauntered across the sunny lane to Meg.

'As I can be of little help here perhaps you would allow me to relieve you of one of those machines, young lady?' he said courteously. 'And I think it would, at this stage, be only polite to introduce myself. Robert Hemingway at your service, miss.' He bowed gallantly, taking the tandem from her and wheeling it some yards away where he let it fall against the bank, carelessly crushing harebells and golden rod which grew in profusion there. Meg, her face glowing with heightened colour did the same with Martin's machine then stood awkwardly, not quite sure what to do next or even how to address this cultured being who stood casually beside her.

'Are you from about here?' he asked her smilingly.

'Liverpool . . . sir . . .'

'Liverpool! And do you cycle this far very often?'

'Oh no sir! Only when we get time off.'

'I see, and where do you work, Miss . . . er . . . Miss . . .?'

'Meg, sir, Megan Hughes.'

72

'Miss Hughes.' He tipped his yachting cap in a courtly fashion and Meg was enchanted. 'And what is the name of my saviour over there?' He waved a hand in Martin's direction.

'Oh, that's Martin, sir. Martin Hunter.'

'He evidently knows a lot about motor cars, Miss Hughes.'

'Oh yes, sir!' It was said proudly as though part of it was her doing.

'Is he employed in a mechanical capacity?'

'He's odd job man, sir, but he can mend anything! Anything at all!' Meg's eyes beamed into those of the elderly gentleman's and this time *he* was enchanted for with the sun filtering through her copper curls she looked exceedingly pretty. Old enough to be her grandfather he might be but that did not mean he could not appreciate beauty when he saw it.

'*Odd job man!*' he protested. 'And where, pray, does he work, for wherever it is he is wasted!'

Meg glanced away diffidently for she knew by now who this man was and felt in some way he ought to know *her*. Hadn't she and Tom and Martin worked in his employ for the past four years and yet ...

'What is it, Miss Hughes?'

'Well sir, by rights you should call me Meg, sir!'

'Oh, and why is that?'

'Well ... I ... we work for *you*, sir. The three of us!'

'You do?' He looked quite disbelieving as if to say he would certainly have remembered at least two of this remarkable trio if he had come across them before!

'Yes sir, Mr Hemingway, in Great George Square at the emigrant house. I'm a maid and Martin and Tom are ...'

'Odd job boys!' He finished her sentence his eyes crinkling in a friendly way but in them was a speculative and strange expression. 'Well, I'll be blowed.' he added slowly.

'Yes sir!' She smiled shyly.

'And where did he get his knowledge of motor cars, this Martin Hunter?'

'From books and Mr Hale at the bicycle shop lets him mess about there and he goes to night school ...'

'From books ...!'

'Yes sir. He's very clever with his fingers, is Martin.'

'I can see that, and a very enterprising young man from what you tell me.'

73

A thoughtful expression settled itself about Mr Hemingway's face and he fingered his moustache as he watched Martin tightening something or other beneath the bonnet.

'Give it another turn with the starting handle, Tom,' Martin called and this time, as sweetly as the thrush which sang in the hedgerow beside the lane the engine burst into life and so did the motor car, shuddering gently like a horse which is eager to be away to the starting line.

Mr Hemingway took Meg's arm, handing her across the narrow lane as though she were a grand lady until they stood beside the vehicle. His face, ruddy and gleaming like a polished cider apple smiled in delight and he reached to Martin and took his hand, shaking it enthusiastically.

'Well done, young man! Well done, indeed. I don't know what I should have done had you not come along. There cannot be a repair shop within miles.' He looked up and down the empty lane. 'It was foolish of me to come out alone but my chauffeur – well, he goes by the name of chauffeur but he is a most reluctant one – was occupied with a defect in my wife's carriage, which he much prefers to the machine anyway and I wanted to test the engine on this ... this beauty.' He looked worshipfully at the splendid motor car and went on as though he was speaking to himself. 'A damned coachman he is and will be nothing more even though I had him taught to drive when I myself learned but his first love is the horse and I must say ...' He shook himself from his meandering as though suddenly aware that he had an audience who, politely, was listening to his every word.

He smiled warmly. 'Still it was a stroke of luck for me when you came by. I would like to thank you in some way ...'

Martin smiled deprecatingly but his eyes burned a hot, velvety brown as though the joy which consumed him was blazing throughout his body. His face was streaked with oil and he had deposited a fair amount from his hand to that of Mr Hemingway but the old gentleman seemed not to mind.

'This young lady tells me that you are in my employ, Hunter ... is it ...?'

'Your employ?'

'Yes. I am Robert Hemingway. I own the emigrant house in Great George Square.' He nodded and smiled at Meg.

Martin's face was a study of mixed emotions. His eager youthfulness to be about what he loved best in the world was overlaid with the polite regard one must show to one's employer, but there was something else, something instantly recognized by the old gentleman for he had seen a few such in the world of the shipping magnates, and some in his own family. It was, quite simply an utter belief in the rightness of what Martin Hunter meant to be! He knew who he was and where he was going and though he had been temporarily bemused by the realisation of who he was addressing, Robert Hemingway recognised that this boy was not overawed by him for he knew his own worth!

'Indeed sir, we did not know ... We have worked there for four years now ... Tom as well ... he helps me ...' Creditably he included Tom who stood quietly beside him. He *had* helped and it was only fair he should be acknowledged, his gesture seemed to say.

'Of course,' Mr Hemingway said smoothly, giving Tom his due but it was evident that Martin was the one who interested him.

'I believe you have had no training, Hunter, in the mechanics of the motor car, bar the attending of evening classes?'

'No sir.'

'And that you picked up most of what you know from books?'

'Well ...'

They stood for a moment, two pairs of eyes regarding what was evidently a shared love of the sweetly purring machine. Martin's hand rose involuntarily and with the tenderness of a mother, stroked the quivering bonnet. Robert Hemingway did not miss the movement, nor the expression in the young man's eyes. He cleared his throat and Martin looked at him, his soul exposed and yearning in his eyes.

'Well, I must be off or my wife will think I have had an accident. She hates this contraption, as she calls it. You know what women are.' He smiled and Martin smiled back as though the two of them shared something unique. Climbing into his motor car Robert Hemingway put it into gear, raised his cap to Meg and with a cheery wave, moved off, turning the corner with a triumphant flourish. They could hear the noisy sound of the engine for several minutes in the peace-filled quiet of the country road, then, as it died away, the trill of the thrush, silenced by the commotion, was taken up again.

'Well!' said Tom, his eyes a wide and brilliant blue in his tanned face. 'What d'you think of that then?'

'What?' asked Martin absently, still staring towards the corner where the automobile had disappeared.

'Us talking to the great man himself! Wait till we tell Mrs Whitley. She'll never believe us.' He grinned engagingly at Meg and she grinned back but Martin silenced them.

'Never mind him! Did you see that engine? Did you? And it was me that got it going! *Me*!'

His expression glowed with an enchantment so rare and lovely it lit his face and eyes to a strange beauty and Meg felt her heart shift painfully in her chest. The sensation was strange and uncomfortable and she put her hand to her breast in alarm but Martin was not yet finished. He began a slow shuffle, his feet moving in a tapping rhythm in the dust then with a shout of abandoned joy he raised the thrush from its perch and his arms lifted and his fingers snapped and he could not contain the emotions which filled him. Taking her in his arms he began to whirl her round and round until she could not breathe and their laughter rose up, high as the thrush and Tom watched and laughed with them.

The note came that evening. It said simply that Martin Hunter was to present himself at 'Silverdale' the home of Robert Hemingway first thing the next morning!

Chapter six

'Wait there, boy,' the high-nosed, black-suited man said and Martin did as he was told, standing quietly in the spacious square hallway where he was put. He looked about him. His eyes marvellously clear and sharp, wandered from one lovely object to another but he did not fidget and his hands were relaxed at his side, one loosely holding his cap. Only his mouth gave way his inner excitement and it was fixed in a determined line, almost grim, though the curled corners showed it's inclination to laughter.

In the centre of the hall was a round, silkwood table, polished so lovingly over the years the reflection of the copper bowl in its centre was as detailed as if it stood on a mirror. In the bowl were roses, pink and scarlet, a vivid fusion of colour to light up the softness of the gently shaded room. Against the walls stood delicate little chairs upholstered in green velvet and a grandfather clock ticked in a stately fashion standing between the two arches which split the rear of the hall and through one of which Martin had just come from the kitchens.

There were wall sconces which had once held candles, now artfully made over to illuminate the hall with electric light and at the back of the room, beyond the arches, long and symmetrical were Georgian windows curtained in green velvet. Paintings lined the walls and Martin's eyes flickered across them. Though he was not interested in such things it did not take an expert to see they were family portraits for each face had same similarity to its neighbour. He studied them, moving his gaze round the walls from the two he deduced must be the first Hemingways by the style of their dress until he came to the last. It was of a girl with silver gilt hair and eyes the same colour, like moonlight on a stretch of smooth water. Her expression was bold and yet charming. There was strength in the beautiful face which still retained a feminine softness, an intelligence, and yet an impertinence which Martin found endearing. He liked her whoever she was and he found himself returning her impish smile.

There was a soft click and the door through which the butler had disappeared, opened and a gloved finger beckoned imperiously.

'The master will see you now.'

Across a vast expanse of deep pile carpet, miles of it and all cluttered with tables and spindly gilt chairs, what-nots, glass-fronted cupboards, tall sideboards and rosewood sofas and what seemed to Martin to be hundreds of ornaments, bric à brac, crystal, ivory, and in the centre of the room standing just in front of the elaborate fireplace was an elephant's foot! What the hell can that be for, he remembered asking himself wildly as he set off across the room, following the stiff, sure-footed back of the man who knew the way, placing his feet where the butler put his! It was like a minefield and he stepped hastily through it, glad to be on the other side!

Through another set of doors and this time Martin was moment-arily brought to a standstill for the sight which met his eyes was truly enchanting! This was where the roses in the hallway had come from and wouldn't their Meggie have given her eye teeth to get a look at this, was his barely coherent thought. It was like a garden brought indoors and housing the most exotic plants Martin had ever seen, plants he was certain had never grown in the stark unpredictability of the North! The floor was of some polished wood all set in a beautiful pattern, glossed until you could see your face in it and the walls were *entirely* of glass. He lifted his head and his eyes strayed over the exquisite moulding of the roof, high domed and glass ceilinged and the man who led him in flicked his fingers irritably as though to say he was not here to stand and stare. Martin followed him past white painted wrought iron tables and wicker chairs heaped with bright cushions, pots in a pleasing brick colour and all erupting with vivid plants and above his head, brushing his hair with their trailing leaves were hanging baskets of flowers. There were fluted pedestals on which stood small statuettes, singing birds in cages, plants and more plants, so many Martin was quite bemused and there, in the very centre, lifting his face to the rays of the sun was the old gentleman whose motor car Martin had so recently rescued!

He was sitting in a comfortable chair, his eyes closed in that light, half dozing which is the habit of the old. His head was wreathed in tobacco smoke from a cigar which hung from his relaxed fingers and the tiny, bird-like woman who sat beside him waved her hand in the air to disperse it, fruitlessly, her expression said as though the gesture was so habitual she hardly knew she did it!

The butler cleared his throat and the old gentleman opened his eyes and they both turned, the woman to stare with interest, but the old gentleman sprang up as though Martin were an honoured guest and must be treated with the greatest respect.

'Martin Hunter, sir.' The butler uttered his name as though it was something quite offensive but his merry faced master cared nought for that and moved forward, holding out his hand agreeably.

'Hunter! How punctual and how very good of you to call!'

Martin was quite non-plussed for was he not this man's employee and what else was he to do if his master called except run hastily to his side, but he was not yet aware of the special qualities of naïve friendliness and old world gallantry which Robert Hemingway had possessed since he was a boy. Not in his sixties as Martin had originally thought but seventy-three now, he was the younger son of the great Charles Hemingway himself, once one of Liverpool's greatest shipowners and the brother of the famous, some said *infamous*, Lacy Osborne, a shipping magnate in her own right. Robert had inherited his elder brother's share of the shipping line and also this house, on his brother's death. He was himself retired, the business run now by *his* son, another Charles.

He was in his last years and there would not be many more, he was the first to admit and in them he had discovered a passion for the motor car. His wife said indulgently that he was in his dotage, his second childhood and she washed her hands of his foolishness. They had been married for over forty years and in that time his tranquil and kindly outlook on life had led them through a contented and uneventful marriage.

'Is this the young man, then, Mr Hemingway?' she said, studying Martin from the tips of his well-polished boots to the arrogant set of his dark head. He was well turned out, neat and clean, but his thick, straight hair fell in a defiant tumble across his broad forehead. He had cycled from Great George Square, speeding as fast as the pedals would go round to get to Silverdale by 'first thing'! He was not sure when exactly that might be so best be on the safe side and at half past eight he had knocked on the kitchen door, snatching his cap from his head as he did so.

'Good God, man, Master's not even up yet!' he was told by a pert kitchen maid. She eyed him appreciatively though, liking the

79

set of his broad shoulders and the brown depths of his long lashed eyes. His young body was firm and hard and straight and yet already it had a kind of indolent grace which signalled his complete masculinity and his own knowledge of it, and what's more, it's impact on the opposite sex. His eyes warmed her, admiring her rounded prettiness and despite his errand, or perhaps because of it and the importance of this moment, his amber skin seemed to glow with life. He smiled and the corners of his mouth lifted and the maid caught her breath, quite enthralled by the curving delight it promised. His teeth gleamed for a moment between his lips and his expression seemed to say if only he had the time what pleasures they could share, then an elderly woman had called sharply, enquiring who was at the door and the maid stepped back regretfully.

He sat where he was told and ate gratefully the bacon 'butty' pushed roughly but amiably into his hand and watched the early morning preparation for the running of Silverdale swirl smoothly into action. There seemed to be more servants here than there were in all of the houses in Great George Square put together and all under the direction of a black-gowned woman he had first thought to be the mistress.

And the snotty-nosed chap who ran *her* was, it appeared, the butler and a more miserable bugger he had yet to meet, he secretly told himself. He watched as the man reduced same poor little skivvy to tears and longed to get up and defend her as he would their Meggie but as soon as the butler and the housekeeper left the kitchen to enjoy their own breakfast, the atmosphere relaxed and it was almost like being at home. Someone whistled and there was laughter and the young maid who had let him in sidled up to him saucily, asking questions about why the master wanted him. He answered truthfully that he did not know. He said nothing of his hopes!

'Well then, Hunter,' Mr Hemingway said genially, rubbing his hands together with every sign of satisfaction and looking him up and down as his wife had done. 'Now this is Mrs Hemingway . . .'

'Ma'am.' Martin inclined his head respectfully but looked directly at Alice Hemingway as he did so and old as she was she could not help responding to the attractiveness of his smile. There was no boldness in it, not for her, since Martin knew his place but it had a boyish charm she was quick to recognise as a woman and she smiled back.

'... and this is Martin Hunter, my dear. He's the young man who got me going yesterday. D'you remember me telling you?'

He sat down but did not motion Martin to do the same. Martin stood quietly and waited. 'Martin Hunter?' Mrs Hemingway murmured. 'Oh yes, and where do you come from then Martin Hunter?'

'From Great George Square, ma'am,' he replied politely.

'Ah yes, my husband told me that. You work as ... as boot-boy, is that it?'

'No, no, Mrs Hemingway ... I told you, he's odd job man ...'

'Is there a difference, dear?'

Robert Hemingway sighed and looked at Martin.

'Well yes, I think so, my dear and I'm sure Hunter would say so. Not many boots to clean at an emigrant lodging house, eeh, Hunter?' He laughed and winked and slapped his thigh and Martin warmed to him. 'Not part of your duties at all, I'd say?'

'No sir.'

'Well, I don't see why not,' Mrs Hemingway interjected, then stood up suddenly and made a little sideways sortie to a springing growth of Bougainvillaea with dark green leaves and flowers of cerise, scarlet and deep pink. With a tiny pair of pruning shears which she took from a deep pocket in her morning gown she delicately removed a leaf, dropping it carefully into the same pocket.

Her husband watched her fondly as though they had all the time in the world.

Martin waited patiently.

'I meant where did he come from before that, Mr Hemingway?' she went on as she returned to her chair.

The old gentleman turned smilingly to Martin.

'Hunter?' he questioned.

'I was in the orphanage, sir, until I was twelve.'

'The orphanage, oh dear, oh dear, dear!'

Mrs Hemingway stared at him, then sighed deeply, shaking her head at the apparent wickedness of the world.

Mr Hemingway waited for a moment politely, to see if she had anything else to say, then returned his attention to Martin.

'Now then, where was I?' he said briskly.

'If you don't know then I am sure we don't, do we Hunter?' Mrs Hemingway smiled engagingly.

Martin was just beginning to think the two delightful but

dotty old people had forgotten what it was Mr Hemingway had summoned him for when the old gentleman leaned forward and said abruptly.

'And are you content with that, Hunter?'

'I beg your pardon, sir?'

'Does your work give you satisfaction?'

'Well . . . I'm not . . . unhappy, sir, but . . .'

'Yes?'

'Well . . . I . . .'

'There is something else you would rather be doing?'

'Yes sir!'

'And what is that?'

'Motor cars, sir!'

'I thought so.' The old man leaned back in his chair satisfied.

'Sir?'

'Six-thirty tomorrow morning then, Hunter. I'll arrange for someone to replace you at the emigrant house. Report to Andrew. He'll show you the ropes for a few days and then we'll get down to it. Once you've the hang of the steering you'll have no difficulty. It's just a question of practice. Of course my son and I will have your progress monitored but I'm perfectly certain there will be no problems. A chappie we know has been to a few races in his day. France, Germany, Italy, America so he can recognise a decent driver when he sees one. He raced in the 'Gordon Bennett' last year in Ireland and came second so he knows what he's about. And your knowledge of engines will give you an enormous advantage. We've been keen to get in on it for a few years now, ever since it began but of course, we're both too old.'

He chuckled and his wife raised her eyebrows and rolled her eyes heavenwards. '. . . so we decided the only thing to do was to get our own man,' he continued. 'Put him through his paces in the Isle of Man, or perhaps Ireland and then see what he can do against the Americans at Daytona Beach.'

He leaned forward, apparently unaware of the rigidity and death-white face of his guest.

'I was impressed by your confidence and expertise yesterday, young man and it seemed to me you have a natural flair for the motor car. It's new yet in terms of years but we've watched it grow, my son and I and we've learned to spot a man who's as keen as we are and who knows what he's about and it appeared to me that you are just such a man. A bit young but that's to the

82

good. You have time to learn and your enthusiasm will see you win, I'm positive and that's what we want, a winner . . .!'

He stopped suddenly.

'What's the matter, Hunter? Have I said . . . my dear chap, you look quite . . . see, Mrs Hemingway, ring the bell and get Ferguson to fetch a brandy. I think the poor fellow's about to swoon . . .'

He didn't quite know how he cycled the half mile along the meandering driveway from the house to the gates which led into Aigburth Road. He had to contain his jubilation until he got there for it would not do for the gardeners who worked about the lawns and flower beds to think he had lost his wits but the moment he was out of earshot of the gatekeeper's lodge he put his feet on the handlebars of the machine, raised his arms in the air and yelled his joy to the meadowlark which hung above him in the sky. A thrush which was feeding on the berries of a rowan tree beyond the hedge flew wildly for cover and a flock of sheep, browsing the fields of Jericho Farm scattered, their heads up and wildly bobbing but he was not even aware of them, nor of the open-mouthed astonishment of those he passed on the country road.

He'd done it! He'd done it! He'd done it! Oh dear Lord, at last he was to work with the thing he loved best in the world, at what he knew best, at what he was best at. The skill he possessed was to be used and in a way that even he had scarcely dreamed of! He was to start tomorrow morning with Mr Hemingway and when he had learned to drive – and that wouldn't take him long, ·best part of five minutes, he reckoned – they were going to try him out as a *racing driver*. He, Martin Hunter, was going to be tested against men like S. F. Edge and Charles Jarrott, go to France, Germany and when he was ready, to Daytona Beach in America to race against the great Barney Oldfield!

Mr Hemingway had explained, when Martin had recovered somewhat from his first paralysing shock that he must be prepared to work in other capacities around the garages in which were housed the Hemingways' growing fleet of automobiles. He was to look after them, keep them maintained to the highest peak of perfection an internal combustion engine can achieve, but whilst he was doing this he was to be taken to any track which was available to him and given a chance to show if he was capable of joining that select few who were simply called 'the fastest men on earth'!

He would need plenty of practice but that would be no problem, Mr Hemingway said with the enthusiasm of a boy. He and Charles – his son, he explained – were keen to match their new machine against the best the racing world had to offer and if Martin lived up to expectations he did not see why they should not have a good chance of winning a race or two! Show the world what the Lancastrians were made of! It wasn't only great ships that came out of Liverpool, eh Hunter?

To the Hemingways, both father and son, it was a hobby, a pastime new and thrilling but to Martin it was his life's dream and not to be taken lightly, as they did. This was the opportunity he had been waiting for, striving for! The start of the work he had been cast on this earth to do and by God he was ready to start doing it! He'd show them! He'd not let them down! He'd win every bloody race they put him in! He'd make the name of Hemingway as famous in the motoring world as it was in the sphere of shipping and with it would rise the name of *Hunter*!

Oh dear God . . . dear sweet Jesus . . . *it had begun!*

Meg thought she would swoon with the excitement of it all at first! Martin was like a candle . . . no . . . one of those new exciting *electric* lights which were beginning to appear in all the smart shops and the homes of the wealthy. Brilliant, unable to stop talking, unable to sit down or even stand still, he lit up the kitchen with his magnetic presence and Mrs Whitley said she was all of a 'do-dah' and she'd have to have a sip of stout to steady her and would Martin be a good lad and slip round to the 'Fiddlers' . . .

It was then, as she mentioned the 'Fiddlers', without warning she began to weep and the three of them became as still as animals which scent a trap and are helpless to avoid it. Was it not at this precise moment, years ago, that they had first set eyes on the weeping woman and in such a manner and tone of voice she had sent a young and defiantly brave Martin for that first jug of stout and now, now it was ending and Mrs Whitley's tears said she did not know how she was to do without them! The first was to be off and soon it would be the other two and she was heartbroken. They had not thought, any of them, as they exulted over Martin's good fortune, that this was the moment when the 'three of 'em' were to become two, then perhaps only one as they all went their separate ways. Mrs Whitley's grief struck at their elation, crumbling it to fragments as their young hearts considered it. All these years, their eyes said to one another and did we ever think the day would come when we would have to part and could they bear it, they silently asked each other?

Emm stared from one to the other, her face which had shrieked its joy with the rest, slipping into bewilderment for where, suddenly, had it gone? One minute high jinks and laughter, the next, tears!

Martin moved jerkily, his eyes tearing themselves away from those of Meg and Tom. He reached in a fumbling fashion for the door knob, awkward and anxious to regain the high euphoria of moments ago, resentful suddenly that it should have been taken from him. He was young and unable yet to cope with his emotions and his instinct was to run, to run away from what he could not easily manage.

'Right, Mrs Whitley, I'll not be a minute.' His voice was deep, unconcerned he would have them believe, doing its best to be normal but his eyes were strangely blurred as though something dimmed their usual soft and depthless brown.

'Alright, lad and don't you get lost,' Tom said, trying to make a joke, his voice only a fraction from cracking. '. . . and make sure you get the right change, now.'

Meg put her hand to her mouth, covering it with shaking fingers for were they not the very words Mrs Whitley had used so many, many times in the last four years and now she could not bear to hear them spoken for were they not the symbol of their united lives and was it not to end with this last night together!

'Oh don't . . . don't, Tom . . . don't joke, please . . . it's the last . . .'

'Now then, Meggie . . .!' Martin moved forward as though her distress had released some maturity in him, some strong and protective emotion which would not allow him to turn away as he had intended. 'Don't say that! I'll not have it! Bloody hell, it's only up the road . . . to start with, anyway and later . . . I'll be home as often . . .'

'Of course you will! Of course you bloody will!' Tom was quite overcome and could do no more than repeat the same words over and over again, moving in his turn towards Meg but she turned away and began to carefully re-arrange the crockery which was set out for their meal, moving the salt and pepper a little closer to the centre of the table, smoothing the white cloth though it was unwrinkled, straightening the already straight cutlery.

85

'I know, I know! Take no notice of me,' she said, but her voice trembled as she bent her head, her spirit oppressed and joyless.

'Nor me, lad!' Mrs Whitley heaved herself to her feet, wiping her eyes on her apron. 'Daft beggars we are! Why, you'll be in and out of this kitchen all the time, I'll be bound. Sick to death of you we'll be, eeh, Meggie?'

Meg felt the silent, waiting presence of Martin at her back. She knew she must say something to bring back to him the rejoicing which was his due. She must not spoil for him what was the greatest day of his life with her own sorrow and squaring her shoulders she took the first step on the path which was to lead her from the careless selfishness which is the mark of the young to the hard won generosity that comes with maturity.

'Not half!' she managed. 'He'll be up here after those pasties of yours if for nothing else!'

'Which reminds me,' Cook said, cheering up at the thought of food. 'I'd best get a few in the oven for you take with you.'

'Mrs Whitley!' Martin was laughing now, immensely relieved the tears had stopped for like most men he had not the slightest notion of how to deal with them. 'They will feed me up there, you know!'

'Not like the grub you're used to, my lad,' Mrs Whitley said firmly. 'You're still growing and you need feeding up. Now promise me if you get hungry you'll come home for a bit of decent food . . . promise . . .?'

Home!

Martin moved across the kitchen. Mrs Whitley had her back to him, busy as a bee as her silent tears fell again into the bowl in which she was ready to prepare the pastry for the meat pasties for her lad. Gently, his action as loving as a son with his mother, he put his arms about her, turning her until her trembling cap fitted beneath his chin.

'I promise faithfully I'll be home every chance I get.' He hugged the plump little woman awkwardly in his young man's arms but his eyes were on Meg as he spoke.

The rest had gone to bed, Mrs Whitley hiccoughing her way up the stairs on her last glass of stout for she had felt the need for a bit extra that night 'to make her sleep' she said.

They sat together before the dying fire and no-one spoke. Tom lounged as he always did, long legs sprawled out before him, hands deep in his pockets, his eyes half closed as he stared into the fire. It was as though he saw pictures in its brightness, pictures of something serious for his usual light-hearted expression was missing and his young face was sombre with his own heavy thoughts.

Meg sat on the rug, her back against the chair in which Martin slouched. He watched her as her hand idly played with a strand of her own bright copper hair, twisting it in a glowing curl about her finger. It sprang to life beneath her hand and his heart moved painfully with the sadness of this moment.

The last time! In the midst of his great joy he could think of nothing else and the pain of leaving these two who had been like an extension of his own mind and growing body for what seemed to be all of his life, was almost more than he could bear. He could not recall when he had been without them! They had not consciously been aware of the bond which had tied them inextricably together, at least not to put into words but it had been there just the same. It was no good telling himself that this was what he had wanted to do since he had first seen the strange and wonderful invention called the 'horseless carriage', now that the time had come to leave them, and he knew it would be for good, his bewildered heart ached with it!

He had thrilled them all with the splendour of Mr Hemingway's hallway and the picture of the lovely silver-haired girl whose portrait hung upon it's wall, the Victorian grandeur of the drawing-room and the incredible loveliness of the glass room filled with flowers. He had seen Meg's eyes glow with wonder and longing, and Tom's widen at the incredible idea that Mr Robert and Mr Charles Hemingway owned not one motor car but three, one a racer, and had gratified Mrs Whitley with his assurance that the kitchen at Silverdale was not a patch on her own! He had tried in his way to let them see the wonder of the life he would be living and to reassure them that in every way he could he would share it with *them*! No, he should not be sad for this was the next, inevitable step towards his future and both Tom and Meg knew it and accepted it, or would when they became used to his absence but that step would take him away from them and that was hard!

The 'three of 'em' were to be split up at last!

Meg turned and put her bent arm across his knee. Resting her chin upon it she looked up at him, her eyes so lost and depthless he felt the incredible need to lift her up into his arms and hold her close and pet her back to the blithe young girl she usually was.

'What is it?' he said gruffly, his young manhood once again in jeopardy.

'Will we still go for rides, Martin?' she said. 'You an' me an' Tom? When you're home, I mean?'

'Of course we will, you daft beggar,' relieved that it was to be no more than that. 'I'll take the bicycle and you and Tom keep the tandem. Every chance we'll go off somewhere, won't we, mate?' He winked at Tom and as he had intended, hoped, she brightened and sat up, smiling.

He smiled himself, a man suddenly, with a man's fate before him but before he went he must ensure that what he had begun over nine years ago still went on.

'And you behave yourself, lady, or I'll know the reason why when I come home!' He looked across at Tom and his expression said quite clearly that his words meant something else entirely and that they were directed not at herself, but at Tom. Their Meg was placed in *his* care from now on.

Tom nodded briefly, understanding!

Chapter seven

They missed him, of course they did, they said a dozen times a day and how on earth was Tom to manage all the lifting and carrying he and Martin had done between them; and that dratted clock, the one Martin had put right years ago and which had ticked away merrily ever since, had suddenly decided to stop and who was to mend it now? It was the same with the mangle which inexplicably refused to turn its rollers, jammed it seemed to eternal inactivity, and poor Meg, forced to hand wring the dozens of heavy cotton sheets was close to tears as the skin of her hands cracked and broke open in the icy chill of the wash-house.

Tom did his best. Mr Lloyd had thought enough of him to give him a rise in pay when Martin went saying that Tom was to consider himself the agent's deputy and that when he was absent Tom was in charge. *In charge*! Promotion, and what's more he was to have a lad under him when one could be found but somehow the wondrous pride of it seemed to evaporate before he really got to grips with it in the atmosphere of sudden and constant bickering which arose between himself and, of all people, Meg! They just could not agree on anything from who should eat the last piece of Mrs Whitley's summer pudding to the choice of where they go on a bicycle outing. Tom's once bright and cheerful face became moody as the weeks wore on and Meg developed what Mrs Whitley called a look of the 'mulligrubs' with a most uncharacteristic peevishness about her which set them all on edge. Her temper, always volatile, was even more menacing in the many flaring quarrels which erupted between herself and Tom over nothing at all.

The last straw came one day when he and Meg were about to take a short spin on the tandem up to Aigburth Hall and back one bright frosted Sunday afternoon. Their route would take them along Aigburth Road and past the gates to the Silverdale estate and with a bit of luck they might see Martin, they said. They were themselves again that day, in affectionate harmony and eager to be away together on a jaunt, teasing one another, joking with Mrs Whitley on the prospect of one of her kidney and mushroom casseroles on their return.

They were to get no further than Upper Pitt Street and as they hobbled home, Tom dragging the crippled tandem on which the chain had broken, Meg clutching the grazed elbow she had suffered as she was flung from the machine, Mrs Whitley could hear their high, angry voices coming from the Square even in their cosy nook by the chimney corner. Meg's face was crimson with temper as she burst into the kitchen and her eyes glared furiously into Tom's. She had snatched her boater from her head, crushing it between frenzied hands and her bright hair sparked about her head and fell dramatically over her forehead. She pushed it back impatiently as she continued to heap recriminations on Tom's head, tossing her own as he met her fury with his.

Emm and Mrs Whitley sat, appalled and speechless, their mouths open, their eyes wide as saucers as the frustrated rancour of the two young people filled every corner of the room. Their expressions said they could not really believe what they saw and heard and for a bewildering, *stunned* moment they were frozen, unable to move or even utter a remonstrance. Emm, never one to say much at the best of times, a silently cheerful little presence scuttling busily about the place, looked as though tears were imminent but Mrs Whitley's face had begun to turn a truculent puce and her eyes narrowed, their gooseberry green depths turning pale as her own temper rose to the surface. She stood up abruptly and reached for the wooden baking spoon, her symbol of authority, or so the gesture implied and Emm shrank back since she was convinced Cook was wild enough to lay it about the shoulders of the threatening couple who were bridling up to one another so dangerously. She had never seen them like this and her bewildered, frightened mind – for surely they had lost theirs – considered what it was that had brought them to such a ferment. Their Meggie had a hot temper and could you wonder with that hair of hers but Tom was so amiable, sweet tempered, as free and easy as the breezes which blew off the river and just as carefree. Would you have believed he could snarl in such black anger, that his blue eyes could burn that bright and snapping blue? He was what Emm secretly called a 'laughing boy', unembittered by his sad start in life. Though she did not know the word, if she had she would have described him as uncomplicated, peaceable, patient, always the one to pour oil on the troubled waters stirred up by the other two. As he went about his work he gave the appearance of someone who will stroll idly, blithely through life, a whistle on his lips, perfectly content to let the world go by whilst he stood back to admire its passing!

Now he looked as though he wanted nothing more, indeed could hardly restrain himself from striking their Meg with all the force he could muster and if Mrs Whitley didn't act quickly Emm could see him doing it. But Mrs Whitley was in control of herself and the situation by now! She'd never, in all her years in service, seen such a commotion between two members of her own staff and she'd had one or two volatile maidservants in her charge over the years and though as yet she had not got fully to grips with what was going on between these two it was beginning to infiltrate into her astute mind what the trouble was.

She grasped Meg's upstretched arm in the strong grip which had stood her in good stead when she herself had been a young skivvy, and thundering in her best, her most authoritative tone to 'give over, the pair of you or I'll crack your heads together' she hauled Meg a foot or two away from the fierce, knife-edged anger of Tom Fraser. She pushed her short, full-bodied superiority – was she not the mistress here? – between them, glaring from one turbulent face to the other, placing a hand firmly on each heaving chest and in the midst of the savage, inexplicable defiance which flared in her kitchen she found herself understanding at last!

It was as though a triangle, a shape which will stand confidently on any of its three sides had suddenly been deprived of one of them and the two remaining are left, unstable, unbalanced and bewildered by the strange and confusing lack of equilibrium. They had been three for so long, a perfect immutable relationship which had nurtured each of them. They were different in temperament, wondrously unique and yet they had made one perfect whole and now, for the moment, until they could accept and re-build themselves the two who were left could not function properly nor deal with the complexity of it. They had been left behind. Martin, who had been the natural leader had gone ahead and in the void his going had left, Tom and Meg were turning on one another. They did not understand why they did it, they only knew that the turmoil inside them was set fiercely free; the unhappiness, the emptiness was filled only when they were quarreling with one another. They glared with narrowed eyes but there

91

was an uncertainty about them, a bewilderment which seemed to ask hesitantly how they had come to be in this predicament and were relieved when she set them each to some task.

When they had left the kitchen Emm and Mrs Whitley sat knee to knee before the roaring fire, the second or was it the third up of tea in their hands. Mrs Whitley spoke thoughtfully.

'We'll have to watch them two for a while, Emm,' she said.

Emm nodded understandingly.

'I'd no idea they'd missed him that much, had you?'

Emm shook her head and sighed.

'Where shall we go then?' Meg asked the next week as they wheeled the repaired tandem across the pavement. They were disappointed that Martin, when asked in a hurried note to Silverdale, was not able to come, but they had begun to accept now that he had a new life, a job in which they had no part and could not always take time off when they did.

'How about Chester?' Tom asked airily.

'Tom! You devil!' She smiled, her good humour quite restored. 'You'll be saying London or Edinburgh next!'

'Hey, steady on Meg Hughes!' They smiled into each other's eyes and on a crisp, sparkling, clear December day, when the earth seemed to lie quiet in that last moment before finally settling to sleep for the winter, when the air was sharp and still, Meg and Tom set off together.

The houses and the factories and the quiet Sunday streets of Liverpool fell away and Meg's spirits rose, the familiar feeling of joy which cycling, or being on the move, always gave her, filling her veins and flooding her fast beating heart.

They did not speak as they sped along the empty country lanes from Toxteth and on through Garston and Hale to Warrington. It was cold but the exercise put warmth in their limbs and a flush of rose in Meg's cream cheeks and as Tom turned she grinned with that infectious good humour which was peculiarly hers. Her eyes glowed and Tom winked at her to let her see he was as happy as she was to be out on the road, the mad rush of the machine's wheels skimming across the ground and the satisfying feeling of blood surging through bodies young and eager and glad to be alive!

At Warrington they turned west and with the estuary on their right hand they cycled on until they reached Frodsham. At the

'Bears Paw', an old sandstone inn with lovely mullioned windows, and a favourite stopping place on their rides, they cycled through the gabled archway and into the courtyard to drink hot coffee and eat home baked bread, hot from the oven, with strong cheese and pickled onions.

They sat for fifteen minutes on a drystone wall and let the pale sun warm their faces. Meg leaned comfortably against Tom's shoulder, inhaling the clean smell of him and the fresh country aroma of the fruit of the dogrose which grew in profusion at their back. Two black and white magpies fluttered arrogantly close to Tom's lounging legs and bold finches fed on the berries behind them and Meg was reluctant to leave. She felt peaceful here with Tom. His arm was strong and hard beneath her cheek and she liked the way his hair caught the sun and turned to a cap of gold on his well shaped skull.

'Come on, daydreamer,' he said and his blue eyes were no less bright than the periwinkle which grew on summer days in the meadow on the far side of the lane.

They rode into the Delamere forest just before one o'clock and the tall conifers planted, Meg had heard, by the Crown in 1818 closed in about them. The sunshine made a torch creating shadows and lighting the pines to splendour. They stood still and quiet in perfect solitude and peace and Meg felt it enter her heart. She took Tom's hand trustingly, as she had always done, when they alighted from the tandem to walk between the tall, straight trunks and a soft bed of pine needles moved beneath their feet. He turned to smile and gripped her hand more tightly as they climbed the slight incline which came out at last on the upland crest of the New Pale and the view to the south and west took their breath away, as it always did no matter how many times they saw it. There were forest meres and tiny lakes, studded like jewels on a bed of dark green velvet and the pale, pale blue of the winter sky surrounded them, almost close enough for them to touch.

They stood for half an hour, leaning against one another, speaking only now and then to point out something of beauty but Tom said they must get on for the days were short now and they had promised Mrs Whitley they would be home before dark.

They had just pedalled furiously through Lower Hargrave when they came upon it. They still had fifteen miles to go, another three hours Tom reckoned and he was urging her on and they were both laughing. She saw it first and stopped pedalling at once

93

and Tom looked back in annoyance bringing the machine to a tumbling halt as his feet hit the ground.

'Look Tom,' she said and her hand lifted to point.

'What?' he asked, seeing nothing but what appeared to be a farm building about to fall down into a forest of weeds. A tree grew before it, thirty or forty feet high, the top of it level with the roof of the building. It had a dense, rounded crown and its trunk was gnarled, sinister and furrowed, the roots standing in the exact centre of the overgrown garden. It was covered in a glorious mass of bright red berries.

'What?' he repeated, his eyes going beyond it to the stand of trees at its back. Was it something there she looked at, his astonished expression asked?

'The house! It's ... it's lovely, isn't it, Tom?' she whispered reverently.

'What house?' Surely she could not mean the laughable monstrosity before them?

'That one.'

'What? That one there?'

'Mmm.'

'Lovely! But it's falling down!'

'No, oh no!' She stepped away from the tandem. Her face was absorbed and her eyes were looking far away into some shadow world of her own and Tom was curiously reminded of Martin, he could not say why!

She pushed at the old gate and stepped on to the overgrown path, brushing aside the faded sentries of delphinium, phlox, lupin and lavender. Tom followed her, as he had once followed Martin into Mr Hale's Bicycle Emporium, mesmerised by her stillness and the bemused expression on her face.

'Look at the lovely bricks, Tom,' she breathed. 'They're hand made. You can tell by the size.'

'What about it?' he said but she did not answer. She was at the small, mullioned windows and she rubbed her hand across the filthy glass to peer inside but there was nothing to see as far as Tom was concerned, only darkness and muck and bits of old, broken furniture.

'Oh Tom!' she whispered again and Tom was quite spellbound by her for she really looked as though she had stepped into another world! He didn't know whether to laugh or jeer, for really, she looked very peculiar! And you never knew with Meg how she would react.

A climbing plant grew up to the roof, unrecognisable for there was not a leaf on it and for a horrid moment he thought she was about to attempt to scale up it for she seemed intent on looking into even the upstairs windows! There were two massive chimneys, one at each end of the building and a porched doorway in its centre. A sign, half buried under the weight of a creeping convolvulus said it was for sale or rent and as she read it Meg Hughes turned to smile her lovely but quite unreadable smile at Tom.

Chapter eight

Though it was cold Martin had removed his old jacket and the woollen pullover he wore for what he called 'mucky' jobs and had rolled up the sleeves of his shirt. It was March and a stiff breeze blew across the river and up the sloping lawns which led to the terraces surrounding the house but in the yard at the back where the motor cars stood it was sheltered and the sun had some warmth in it.

He worked in perfect harmony with the machine he had just driven from the garage and though he was doing no more than the routine work of cleaning it, a job usually performed by one of the grooms, leaving himself to the more important task of maintaining it's engine, he did so with all the loving tenderness a mother might lavish on a new born infant. He even crooned what could be described as a lullaby as the wash leather moved steadily across the shining surface of the bonnet. Back and forth his arm swept. Where the sun had caught it the skin was already brown, the fine dark hairs upon it, soft as swansdown curling to the knuckles of his hand. He was long-boned, hard muscled and his back had broadened in the months he had been at Silverdale. As he bent over the machine the flesh beneath his thin shirt rippled, hard and lean. His narrow waist lengthened with the movement and the tight breeches he wore clung to his hips and strong thighs and clearly revealed the small hollow which was carved out of each slim buttock. His legs were long and shapely in their leather knee boots and were in perfect proportion to his tall frame. His deep brown eyes glowed with health, with the content of a man well pleased with his world and his strong, uncompromising young mouth turned up at each corner in the most appealing manner. The sun caught his hair, turning the darkness to polished chestnut.

He was a beautiful young man! And yet his beauty was completely and absolutely male with an earthiness about it which was instantly appealing to women. There was no softness in the

96

smooth, almost delicate amber of the skin about his face and neck. It was taut and hard and where the buttons of his shirt had been undone to reveal his chest, a fine layer of dark hair curled crisply reaching almost to the hollow at the base of his throat. Though his body was pliable with youth and bounteous health it had a challenging toughness and durability, a set to the way he stood and moved which matched the tenacity of his facial expression. He walked with a tensile spring to his step, light and buoyant, his movements as graceful and fluid as a young roebuck. He was put together with the precision and symmetry, the balance and proportions of a thoroughbred and if his charm had given rise to the belief amongst the young menservants of the household that he was 'soft' and fair game for the tomfoolery and pranks to which newcomers are subjected, his hard fists had soon shown them they were sadly mistaken. He allowed no-one to take liberties with Martin Hunter and he smiled agreeably as he told them so!

He was bare-headed and his thick hair fell upon his forehead and over his ears and he pushed it roughly back with a strong, capable hand. It was the hand of an artist, slender and fine and yet it had a strong, workmanlike appearance, well used to manual employment.

'Goodbye Dolly, I must leave you,
    Though it breaks my heart to go . . .' he sang more loudly, his voice forced into a ragged tempo as it moved in rhythm with his arm. He scowled, then breathed heavily on a small blemish which spoiled the perfection of the elegant radiator, rubbing it energetically with the cloth. His breath wreathed about his head, wisping away to nothing in the clear, almost springlike air. He moved round the vehicle, touching it gently here and there. The bright brass of the horn and twin headlights, the gleaming, polished glass of the windscreen, and the shining bonnet, the smooth, supple leather of the seat where *he* sat, running a possessive lingering hand up and over the curved perfection of the mudguard.

'Do you know how beautiful you are?' he said out loud, then looked round hurriedly to see if there was anyone about to hear Mr Hemingway's racing driver, chauffeur and mechanic talking to a motor car! There was no-one there, only a couple of yellow retrievers lolling in the sunshine at his back, their tongues hanging from their panting mouths in the warmth. A kitten, intent on capturing some invisible quarry it stalked by the garage door leaped frivolously into the air and two hens which had apparently lost their way from the stable yard pecked viciously at the cobblestones in their vexation.

He smiled at his own foolishness and stood back until he could see his reflection in the magnificent, polished surface of the bonnet. She *was* a beauty and it was not just skin deep either. Beneath the bonnet was a superb engine, the best in the world he reckoned, flexible and smooth running, making the motor car easy to handle. The steering and clutch were light and the great speeds she could reach were attained with none of the vibration which was an affliction suffered by many of today's vehicles. It was almost completely silent when it ran and Mr Robert and himself were unanimous in their belief that she was really quite the most noble of man's creations!

He turned away, still smiling for though he loved the splendid motor car dearly, as one would love a child of his own body, the one which held his complete devotion, the one which would surely have been his secret favourite should he have *had* children, was not standing in *this* yard!

As though some image had created itself in his mind his expression altered to one of almost besotted adoration and of it's own volition his gaze turned towards a building on the other side of the cobbled yard. His eyes narrowed and a warm dreaming shone there and without thought his booted feet turned him away from the vehicle he had just polished and he began to saunter in the direction of the closed door. He'd just take a peep, he told himself, that was all. Just make sure she was covered up and well protected against the frost which still might come down at night.

There was no-one about. Andrew had gone off to the stable yard to see to his beloved horses. Martin found it hard to understand how anyone could prefer a dumb animal and the slow carriage it pulled to a real, live motor car but then Andrew was of another generation and set in his ways and he was used to horses. He had been employed by Mr Hemingway for many years and still drove and cared for Mrs Hemingway's carriage horses. Motor cars were new and for the young, like himself, or the young at heart, like Mr Hemingway!

Now there was a man Martin could admire. Seventy if he was a day and he loved motor cars and this, the 'Silver Ghost' Rolls-Royce, with the same passion as Martin, *and* the splendid machine they had been working on for months now and which drew Martin to it like a cat to a saucer of cream! Mr Charles Hemingway was not such an enthusiast as was his father, being more concerned with the prestige the beautiful machines brought his family, the éclat and glory in motoring circles the vehicles might give him, rather than a love for the actual automobiles themselves.

His step was light and joyful and before he knew it he was across the yard and had the door to the old tack room opened. He stood for several minutes, just looking, just standing and breathing in the smell of oil and leather, drugged by the deep sense of belonging to, of being possessed by what was there. The sheeted shape was long and low but he made no move to uncover it, no move to draw nearer to whatever it was there that held him in it's spell. The sun fell about him, casting his shadow across the sheet and he felt the thrill go through him as though in anticipation of what was beneath it and the meaning it would have in his life.

Turning slowly away he closed the door and as he did so his mind slipped back to the day he had, for the first time, sat behind the wheel of Mr Charles' old Vauxhall. He had thought he would faint right away, like a young maiden at her first dance. His heart had thudded in his throat and he could not answer Andrew's curt questions nor explain to the ex-groom that he had no need to show him what to do. He had been born with the knowledge! Andrew had been quite short with him as Martin drove them steadily down the drive turning into Aigburth Road with the panache of a Louis Chevrolet, the famous driver of the Buick racer, saying he had been told that the new 'lad' had never driven a motor car before and he'd be obliged if his time was not wasted again!

He smiled at the memory, then, after returning the Rolls Royce to its splendid garage, made over from what had been stables, he began to walk in the direction of the house. The kitchen door opened on a familiar scene of intense activity as Martin entered. Mrs Glynn, the cook, fluttered frantically about her oven, lifting the lids of each pan which simmered there, her manner that of someone convinced nothing would be right if she herself did not personally see to it. Two kitchen maids hovered at her elbow, acolytes attending the high priestess and she threw sharp commands at them over her shoulder which they scurried to obey.

A saddle of lamb was lifted from the oven and Martin's mouth watered as the lovely smell tantalised his nose. One of the maids basted it, pouring the sizzling fat in which the juices of the meat mingled, over the nicely browning joint. Another chopped mint

99

leaves, sprinkling them with sugar ready for the sauce and a third tossed a green salad in which were radish, cucumber and tomatoes, all grown under glass during the winter at the far side of the vegetable garden.

'See! You, Lizzie, stop gawping and get on with them egg whites. They've to be frothy, girl, frothy I said, standing up in peaks when you lift the fork! Not like that! The pulp of the apples is to be mixed in it and it'll look a right mess in that runny stuff you're about! Elbow grease, my girl, ever heard of it? Now get on with it at once. Mr Charles is right partial to my 'apple snow' and I'll not serve that concoction you're fiddling with. See, give it me!'

The girl was elbowed aside and the irritated monologue continued, interrupted by frequent asides to this or that maid on the preparation of some dish which was to appear on the luncheon table of the Hemingway family. Martin grinned for she reminded him of Mrs Whitley, all bark and no bite and he wondered if all those in charge of a kitchen were the same. It made him feel quite homesick as he listened to Mrs Glynn bullying the girls around her and the faces of those he had left in Great George Square spun for moment in his mind, then he shook off the feeling for it did no good to look back! He peered round the kitchen to see if either Ferguson or Mrs Stewart, the housekeeper was about and when he saw they were missing he sidled up to the cook and as once he had with Mrs Whitley grinned endearingly.

'Any chance of a cuppa, Mrs Glynn? I've been out in that cold yard since cock-crow and I'm frozen to the marrow. Feel my hands. See, they're like ice!'

He cupped her flushed cheeks between his strong brown fingers smiling down with his deliberately seductive eyes into her harassed face, his head on one side and the cook's distracted expression gave way to one of indulgence for like Mrs Whitley before her she could not resist him and despite her high state of tension she smiled.

'Oh give over, Martin. Can't you see I'm run off me feet here. I've no time to be making pots of tea for the likes of you. It's nearly one o'clock and the mint sauce not even done . . .'

She gave him a nudge with her elbow and he pretended to wince, staggering about in a charade of agony, rolling his eyes towards the roomful of young maid servants who all stopped whatever they were doing to watch and giggle.

100

'Dammit Mrs Glynn, you should have gone in the wrestling ring. With a move like that you'd have been champion in no time. I think you've broken my ribs!' He clapped his hands to his chest and sat down in Cook's own special chair before the fire. 'Oh dear, oh dear, there's only one thing to be done. A cup of tea's the only thing . . .'

'Oh for God's sake, give him a cup, Jess, before he has us all in tears . . .' but Mrs Glynn was laughing as loud as the rest. There was no doubt about it he was a charmer, this lad, with a grin on him that'd melt the stoniest heart. He could wind all the girls round his little finger with those eyes of his and she'd have to watch him for there was not one of them'd say 'no' if they were to be asked.

And his wit could fetch a smile even to the sour face of Mrs Stewart! Not Mr Ferguson, mind but then he was a chap and could see nothing special in Hunter, Mr Hemingway's protegée, and if he was to come in now the lad would be out quicker than a wink. But he had something the girls liked, that was for sure.

The bustle and tumult progressed about Martin, each servant busy with his or her allotted task. There seemed to be a never ending whirl of activities to be accomplished and he often wondered at the hurly burly as he remembered how Meg and Mrs Whitley between them had completely catered for the appetites of over a hundred hungry men and women and children at a time. Here there were four if the children, Mr Robert's grandchildren, were not included! Four adults and there must be twenty-four indoor servants to see to their needs! Housekeeper, butler, cook, footmen, kitchen maids, parlour, upper and under house maids, chamber maids, ladies maid, valet, laundry, dairy and nursery maid and all to attend to four adults and three children!

And that did not account for the outside servants! Gardeners, coachmen, grooms, stableboys, and back at Great George Square there was only Tom!

He leaned back comfortably in Mrs Glynn's chair and lifted his booted feet to the fender, stretching his legs as he drank his tea. The young maids eddied about him, their full white aprons brushing against his legs as they leaned to this or that in the cupboards on either side of the fireplace.

'Excuse me Martin . . .'

'Sorry Martin, can I just get the . . .'

He smiled, not displeased by the attention he was receiving and was gazing up into the fire-glowed cheeks and bright, knowing blue eyes of the under parlour maid who had no rights to be there anyway, contemplating the possibility of snatching a moment or two with her later, when Mrs Glynn's ferocious hissing brought him to his feet. He had only time to hide the cup, straighten his jacket and smooth his vigorous hair when Ferguson was upon him. The little maid had melted away somewhere for which Martin fervently thanked the Good Lord.

'Aah Hunter, there you are,' Ferguson said coolly, his eyes studying Martin with an intensity which told of his yearning to find some fault, *any* fault, even if it was only a crooked tie, for it vexed the butler that he had no control over this young whipper-snapper who had been brought into the household by his master. The trouble was he had no specific place here. He was neither servant nor guest. His work was under no-one's control and he was answerable to no-one but Mr Hemingway. It irked Ferguson for he would dearly have loved to put him in his place, if only one could be found for him!

'The master wants to see you immediately.' His voice came out from somewhere at the back of his neck and his mouth sneered in a most peculiar way when he spoke. Martin made a mental note to tell them of it at home. It would make them laugh when he impersonated Ferguson's 'posh' voice.

'Get on then,' the butler continued irritably, 'and go straight to the drawing room. No loitering about.'

Clenching his jaw ominously, offended by the implication that he would dawdle about, 'spying' on the activities of those beyond the kitchen door, Martin ran swiftly up the steps which led to the splendour of the hall which he had first seen over a year ago.

He knocked on the drawing room door and a cheerful voice told him to come in. He would never forget that moment, never. He could remember his own hand, brown and no matter how he scrubbed it, ingrained with the oil and grease with which he was constantly in contact, reaching for the door handle, turning it and the door opening inwards.

Mr Hemingway was there. Mr Robert, called that even now to distinguish him from his son who was Mr Charles, and Mr Charles himself, standing, men-like, shoulder to shoulder with their coat-tails to the blazing fire.

He was conscious of his own careful feet across the remembered expanse of carpet and the elephant's foot which seemed to spring from nowhere to trip him. There were ladies seated on the rosewood sofa. They were drinking from delicate crystal glasses and he distinctly recalled hearing Mr Charles asking his wife, young Mrs Hemingway she was, though she was a lady well past forty, if she would care for another sherry.

Mr Robert's wife smiled at him as he moved towards her, her face placidly kind.

'Well Hunter,' she said vaguely.

Mr Robert turned as his wife spoke and his air of excitement communicated itself to Martin and even before the twinkling eyes had told him that this was no ordinary gathering, he knew that some moment had arrived that was to be crucial to his future. For the past six months they had been preparing on the specially built track Mr Robert had had constructed at the edge of the estate, preparing not just himself, but the machine which stood in glory in the tack room off the stable yard and now, surely, *now* . . .!

Mr Robert studied him and for a second they were alone together in their shared love of what they were about to do, then . . .

'Well, Hunter?'

'Yes, sir?'

'Are you ready?'

'Oh yes sir!' *I've been ready since the day I was born*!

'Good boy! Our passage is booked and we are to sail on the *Alexandrina* in a fortnight's time. It's the fourth annual race on Ormond-Daytona Beach.'

'Yes sir.' His voice was reverential.

'There will be some good racing men there, Hunter. The best, but in these last months you have shown yourself to be a natural driver and a keen competitor, the two most essential aptitudes needed in motor racing. So . . . we're going to give it a try.' He grinned delightedly and his face was like that of a child who is to be given a treat the likes of which he can scarcely believe. 'What d'you say, lad? D'you think America is ready for us?'

'If it's not, *we're* ready for it, sir!'

He had rung the bell at the front door for he wanted to impress on them that this was no ordinary visit such as he made on his day off and he would always remember that moment when Meg opened the door to him. Her eyes had widened incredulously, for what was their Martin doing on the *front* step, she seemed to be saying, then they had gone beyond him to the magnificence of the gleaming machine which stood at the kerb.

'What . . .' She appeared to be incapable of speech and her hand went to her mouth.

'Can I come in, Meg, or are you going to stand there like a tailor's dummy for the rest of the day?' He was delighted by her reaction and he swaggered slightly as he brushed past her, tipping the peak of his smart chauffeur's cap to a more jaunty angle.

He thought she was going to swoon from the sheer joy of it and indeed was quite prepared to catch her as she did for their Meggie was growing into a very pretty girl and Martin Hunter, the darling of Mrs Glynn's kitchen had quite an eye for a pretty girl! It was the word 'spin' which did it. He had asked her if she would care to sample one quite airily, as though well used to taking such things and indeed thought nothing of them, so sophisticated had he become!

Spin! That's exactly what she was in, she declared and as for Mrs Whitley who was invited too, she positively refused to get within ten yards of the dratted thing, convinced it would explode or run away, dragging her with it! She allowed herself to be persuaded to peek from behind her net curtains at the kitchen window but the wild notion of not only climbing up the area steps to look at the thing at close quarters but going for a *ride* in it gave her 'palpitation of the pluck' she cried and if Meg was willing to risk life and limb in it that was her affair but there was nothing on God's green earth that would make Agatha Whitley climb up and perch herself on that high seat and go at the mad speed of twenty miles an hour! *Nothing*!

But Meg could and *would*! Tom had gone on an errand for Mr Lloyd, she said, and would not be back until later but she'd go like a shot if Mrs Whitley would allow it! Give her a minute to get her hat and coat, and how on earth had he managed it, and was he sure it was alright with Mr Hemingway, she didn't want Martin to lose his fine job and 'Oh Lord' . . . goggles . . . she must wear *goggles*!

'It's alright with Mr Hemingway, Meg, honest. This is Mr Charles' car, his old Vauxhall and he said I could take it out for the afternoon.'

It didn't look old to Meg. It looked brand new, in fact, shining there in the sunshine. It was like a golden beam of sunlight itself, all yellow with bright brass lamps and even the spokes of the wheels gleaming like daffodils. There were two black leather seats side by side and when she climbed up she could smell the lovely smell of them and they were warm from the rays of the sun.

She saw Cook's white face at the window, drawn there by her dread, her eyes staring and her hand to her mouth. In Cook's mind it was possible for a man to go about in one of those dreadful things – just! Men understood such intricate contrivances but surely to God this was the last she would see of their Meggie for no woman could survive such an ordeal!

But their youthful faces were so alike, so full of sparkle and zest Mrs Whitley was quite overcome and retired to her chair with Emm at her heels.

'Them two' was all she could say, quite tearfully, but Emm knew what she meant!

Martin rotated the starting handle.

'Is the hand brake on, our Meg?' he shouted cheerfully, for he had explained a hundred times to her the workings of the handbrake.

'Which one's that?' Her reply was fearful for what did she know of what seemed like a dozen gauges, dials, knobs and levers.

'Never mind.' He ran smartly round to the driver's side and peered inside the machine, just beside the steering wheel.

'Yes, it's on. We don't want to run away, do we, not on your first trip!'

'Oh no!' Her eyes were huge and brilliant with excitement.

'Now then, see this switch on the dashboard?'

'Yes,' she breathed and Martin was quite bewitched with the way she hung on his every word. It was not often he had Meg's undivided and admiring attention. She liked the limelight too much herself!

'Well, I'm going to give the crank a few turns and I want you to move it – it's called the magneto switch – to the "on" position, see?'

'Yes,' she breathed again.

'We don't want to flood the carburettor, do we?'

'Oh no, Martin.'

They were off at last and Martin honked the horn and went round the square a few times until everyone came out to see what the commotion was about, just as they had when the 'three of 'em' had set off on their bicycles. Meg sat perfectly still, one hand on the side of the open motor car, the other on Martin's arm. The wind blew in her face and the movement, the speed at which they went took her breath away, but never in all her life had she experienced such ... such rapture. She had thought the bicycles to be the pinnacle of all her young dreams, the means by which she would fulfill them but this ... this was like ... like being a bird, she thought. Far distant and apart from the people who crawled along the pavement on either side of them. Through her goggles she peered at them pityingly and felt the smooth shudder of the engine beneath her reach the very heart of her and fill it with joy. She was not cold for there was a certain amount of heat coming from the engine, and from what Martin explained was the gearbox at the back.

Martin turned to grin at her, his teeth incredibly white in his amber tinted face. 'What d'you think then?' he shouted into the wind.

She was unable to speak but through the eyepiece of the goggles he saw her wide eyes glow with an emotion which he knew was the one he experienced whenever he was in or about the machines he loved, and suddenly he felt that curious sensation in his chest which she had awakened in him several times in the past. He turned again to study her, narrowly missing a horse and carriage, the irate driver of which shook his fist at him. He had not really noticed before except in the most casual way but she really had become extraordinarily pretty, sitting there with her hair which the sun had turned to fire, snatched out of its pins and blowing in curly tendrils about her ears and neck. Her mouth was parted in an enchanted smile and her eyes were that familiar deep and golden brown he had known since childhood, the colour they turned when she was excited. She was looking about her and then at him as if he were the King himself, as though he had just presented her with the most wonderful gift she had ever had, and he found he *liked* the sensation.

She pressed his arm and he felt a small thrill of masculine pride for everywhere they went people turned to look and it gave a chap a big kick, not just to be driving a motor car which was a rare thing in itself but to have a pretty girl by his side as he did it! The more he looked at her the prettier he realised she was but what on earth had got in to him, he thought. She was only their Meg, his little 'sister' and a damned nuisance at times, still she did look grand sitting there beside him!

They drove out of Liverpool towards Aigburth and on to

Garston through villages which sprang to life as they clattered through. They turned away from the river at Garston thundering along the open country road which was bordered with high banks of marigolds and cowslip. They were stopped several times by animals. Farmers were unused to motor cars on what they considered the natural footpath from farmyard to field, and a herd of cows was one of the most common hazards the motorist must deal with. The animals jostled one another to get a better look at this peculiar device in their midst until Meg became alarmed and begged Martin to drive on but the look on the cowherd's face was enough to assure him they would be ill-advised to do so until the animals had passed by!

At the junction where Rose Lane ran into Allerton Lane they came to Beechwood, a favourite place for their cycling excursions though as Meg declared admiringly it took a lot longer to get there on the tandem. Martin stopped the motor car on a grass verge.

'We'll let her cool off here, Meggie,' he said importantly, 'then we'll have to make our way back, I'm sorry to say.'

'Don't be sorry, Martin. It's been the most wonderful, wonderful afternoon and such a lovely surprise.'

'I thought *you'd* like it,' he said and then wondered why he had. He was having some strange thoughts today but somehow he was immensely pleased with *her* pleasure!

They sauntered across the grass verge and into the shade beneath the trees. The path was insubstantial, obviously not much used and on either side as far as the eye could see was a hazed, floating mist of bluebells. They were dense beneath every tree, clustering about Meg's skirt and she drew in her breath in delight. The sun shone through almost transparent leaves, sparking green splashes where it touched, shading them to a darker green on the lower branches. Forest birds hovered above the dazzling carpet of blue and green and an early bumble bee jostled clumsily about the lovely swathe of wild flowers.

There was birdsong though neither Meg nor Martin could identify them for they were city dwellers and could scarce tell a pigeon from a gull, but the notes were sweet and there was an air of expectancy, of hushed calm as though the day waited for something exciting which was about to happen.

'It's funny without Tom,' Meg said abruptly and for a reason

Martin could not understand he felt a twinge of annoyance and he frowned.

They had turned now, walking slowly back in the direction of the automobile and they both were silent. Meg sensed the change in Martin, his sudden withdrawal from her but for the life of her she could not understand why. He was strange sometimes. One moment he would be laughing, teasing, talking up a head of steam about the seventy-four things which interested him and in which she was expected to take an undivided interest, the next he was off in some daydream in which no-one was allowed to follow. She could sense the tension in him now, the build up to something he wanted to say, or do, but was not sure about. He would tell her when he was ready.

They were about to climb up into the motor. Meg was an old hand now she felt and she confidently adjusted her goggles before putting her foot on the high step but again Martin's manner drew her gaze to him. He was looking at her, almost sadly and yet his eyes were glowing with a deep brown excitement and his mouth twisted on what could have been a smile or a tightening of pain.

'What is it, Martin?' Her voice was low.

'Well, I wasn't going to tell you . . . not yet . . .'

'Go on, I won't tell anyone if it's a secret.'

'No . . . it's not that . . . it's just . . . well . . .'

'Oh for God's sake, Martin, tell me.'

With a shout which raised the birds from the trees and the cows from their buttercups he yelled: 'I'm going to America, Meggie.' His face was ecstatic and caught up in his rapture, Meg began to jump about like an excited child.

'When, when?' she pleaded to know and taking his hands in hers she began a dance in the dusty lane, and it was several minutes before he could speak coherently.

'I'm going to race, can you believe it? I'm going to race the "Hemingway Flyer"!'

'The Hemingway Flyer!'

'Yes, in Florida, America . . .'

'. . . America . . .'

'Can you believe it?' His voice was hushed now, almost humble in the wonder of it.

'Oh Martin . . .!'

Chapter nine

They were sitting one on either side of the pantingly hot fire with Emm on her low tuffet between them when the front door bell rang.

Meg and Tom and Emm had eaten the steak and kidney pie Meg had cooked earlier that day, relishing the delicious taste which, thanks to Mrs Whitley who had taught her how, she put into all the dishes she cooked. She was as clever and imaginative cook, as once Mrs Whitley had been and she had at her disposal hundreds of recipes, all written in Cook's neat, childish hand in her recipe book and which she now passed on to Meg as she did less and less in 'her' kitchen. They would stand her in good stead, she said, when Meg took up a position in her own kitchen in some grand household for to Mrs Whitley this was the summit to which Meg might aspire.

The pastry crust on the pie had fallen apart when Meg cut into it, crumbling beneath the knife and the steaming aroma, so succulent it flooded the mouth with saliva, rose in a savoury swirl about the kitchen and even to Mrs Whitley's room where she lay. 'I think I could eat a bit of that, love,' she said, and did! The meat bubbled gently in the thick, juicy gravy which was a rich wholesome brown and was just the thing for a winter's night such as this, Tom said, his mouth full. They had a heaped pile of fluffy mashed potatoes and cabbage, boiled and chopped with butter and pepper and all eaten in the glowing comfort of the kitchen, then washed down with enormous mugs of hot, sweet tea, even Mrs Whitley!

Mrs Whitley, over sixty now and ready, in Mr Lloyd's sad opinion, for retirement though he was too soft-hearted to tell her so as yet, was in her bed, put there by the bronchitis which came more and more frequently to plague her ageing chest. Each winter it filled her lungs with phlegm so thick she could scarce get her breath. Each one cut her like a knife she confessed to Meg and Emm, for they could be trusted to keep it to themselves, but she'd

109

be up and about in a day or two, she said optimistically. A sip of Meg's broth, Cook's own recipe of course, and a good coal fire in her bedroom for the cold air was a devil on her chest, and she'd be as right as rain, she assured them, and Mr Lloyd pretended to believe her. If it weren't for Meg, he fully understood, Mrs Whitley would not have managed for as long as she had and if he could arrange it and she could hold on for a year or two until the girl was seventeen and old enough for the position, he meant to approach Mr Hemingway with the idea of putting Megan Hughes in as housekeeper. She was a good, capable girl, young yet but a year or two would remedy that.

When the peal of the doorbell sounded through the house they were all in that state of torpor which a full belly and warm feet, a comfortable chair and the knowledge that all the chores are done, brings about. Meg was almost asleep and both Tom and Emm were at the unashamedly snoring stage!

'Who the hell's that?' Tom mumbled thickly as he staggered from his chair. His expression was comical and he turned to stare first at Meg, then Emm as though they might know. It was almost nine o'clock and the snow outside was inches deep. It had drifted in places to the depth of a foot or more and earlier when Tom had looked out on the area steps they no longer had shape but had formed into a smooth incline.

Meg rose from her chair with Emm as close behind her as she could get as Tom left the kitchen. She peeped from the window at the side of the door. All she could see was white and more white and just before the front entrance to the house the bottom half of the wheels of a hansom cab.

A hansom cab!

The only people to ride in a hansom cab were the doctor or Mr Lloyd and it was unlikely that either would call at this time of night and in the middle of a blizzard!

She had never before seen the man who entered the kitchen ahead of the anxious Tom but with that instinctive reasoning which floods the mind in the space of the tick of a clock she was immediately aware that she did not trust him. He brought something with him that night into the homely kitchen and though she did not understand what it was, she was to look back later and recall that sixth sense which is given to all the animal species and it told her that this man was bad and that he would bring badness with him. She did not formulate the thought coherently for there were many images and feelings crowding her senses but inside the confused workings of her mind was the stealthy, unbidden reflection that their lives would change from this moment.

The man bowed in a derisory manner towards her as if to say he knew she was not a lady but *he* was a gentleman. He did not bow for her sake, it seemed to say, but for his own. He had removed his top hat and held it in his hand. Snow had gathered in its brim on his short journey from the cab to the door and he shook it a time or two to remove the few remaining flakes. They looked at one another and for some strange reason Meg felt her heart beat in her breast, its tempo quickening and she knew it was dread which moved it but what was there to dread? What did this man mean to her that he should set up such a violent reaction of strange foreboding?

Her eyes stared into his. His were insolent and cold and as she watched warily they fell with exaggerated interest to her breast as though he was well aware that he was rude but what did it matter? What did she matter?

They both waited for Tom to speak.

'Megan, this is Mr Harris. He's come from . . . er . . . I'm sorry sir. I didn't quite catch . . .'

The stranger continued to stare at Meg's breast as he said contemptuously – to the underling one supposed – 'I am from Hemingway's. The shipping line which owns this house.'

'Of course.' Tom was calm but his bewilderment showed in his slight awkwardness. He moved instinctively closer to Meg. It was evident she was not the only one to distrust this stranger!

'I have come on a painful mission,' Mr Harris continued silkily. 'If I may be seated . . .?'

Emm had slipped quietly into the shadows, like a small animal which scents danger from a bigger, and as Harris turned to look for a chair he saw the outline of her crouched figure against the glow of the lamp.

'Who the devil is that?' he said sharply, clearly alarmed.

'It's only Emm, sir.' Tom's voice was defensive. 'She'll not harm you. She's timid with those she doesn't know.'

The man was clearly displeased that Tom had taken his alarm for fear and he spoke spitefully.

'I can assure you she'll do *me* no harm, boy, but need she lurk in the corner like that. Come out woman where you can be seen. Stupid creature!'

Emm crept out from her hiding place and sidled behind Meg and the man watched her with his lip curled distastefully then moved towards the chair before the fire. Meg and Tom, with Emm clinging to Meg's apron, moved hastily out of his way, almost tripping over the rug which lay at their feet. Mr Harris smiled and began to remove his topcoat holding it in one hand as he waited for one of them to take it. Tom sprang forward, crushing the long Chesterfield into an awkward bundle and earning a frown from Mr Harris.

'Please, it is wet. Would you be so kind as to hang it up at once.'

'Of course. I'm sorry.' Tom hung the coat over the back of a chair and with the clumsiness which he had not shown since he was fifteen, stumbled over to a chair by the table and was about to sit down when another frown from their visitor jerked him upwards. It said clearly that the 'underling' did not sit in the presence of his superior. Meg continued to hover to the side of the fireplace, hampered by Emm's desperate clutching, waiting numbly for Mr Harris to go on. It must be something to do with Martin, it must. Why else was this man here? He was from Hemingway's, the ones who employed Martin and presumably had been sent with some message ... bad news ... Oh Lord ... not an accident ... Oh Lord ... please ...!

Mr Harris' eyes narrowed, running over her insolently and Meg felt a shudder touch her shoulder blades, then rise to the nape of her neck.

'And you are ...?'

'Megan Hughes, sir.' Her mouth was stiff and the words sounded stilted.

'And where is Mrs Whitley? Is she not here this evening?'

The feeling of mistrust and dread grew in Meg's heart and she felt the pulse in her throat quicken and flutter. It must be Martin! Why else would Mr Harris ask for Mrs Whitley? He must have had an accident. The racing car ... a tyre blow-out. Martin had explained to her what could happen if this happened at great speed ... Oh God ... please ... not Martin. But who was this man and what else could he want with them? To turn out on such a night must point to something of an urgent nature but what could it be? She wished he would hurry up and get it over with, whatever it was he had come for! She didn't like him and she didn't like the sensation of disquiet he aroused in her and which shivered her flesh. There was bad news coming and this man was bringing it and more to the point he relished the telling of it for he was prolonging it for as long as he could.

But he had asked for Mrs Whitley and was waiting for an answer.

'Mrs Whitley is in bed, Mr Harris.' Her voice was polite, no more.

'Already!'

The word implied astonishment as though the cook should have been at some task in the service of the company, but he smiled, just like a cat which is about to paw the mouse.

'She's not well,' Meg answered challengingly as if to dare Mr Harris to question it but Mr Harris only continued to smile pleasantly.

'I'm sorry to hear it,' he replied. No-one spoke for a minute as Mr Harris regarded the two young people. Emm might not have existed. He tapped his lips with his clasped fingers and again appraised Meg's young breast as though considering when might be the most convenient time to savour its delights but this time Tom noticed where his cruel gaze lingered and his young mouth tightened ominously.

'Still,' Mr Harris continued, 'I must speak to her. Will you be good enough to ask her to get dressed and come down here immediately.' He looked from Meg to Tom and there was malice in his expression.

Meg gasped and for a moment was speechless. The idea of waking the sick old woman who lay in her bed, exhausted by the bouts of coughing which shook her was too ridiculous to be even considered but clearly this man was waiting for an answer.

She stepped forward, dragging Emm with her, lifting her chin in a gesture Tom instantly recognised and inwardly he groaned. He knew she was going to 'go' for Mr Harris and her straightforward manner would not please this man, of that he was certain. He himself felt like smashing his fist into the smiling mouth but that was not the way to treat an official of the company, particularly if he was Tom's superior! He was a sod, Tom could see that but Meg would only make things worse if she spoke up. She might be able to treat others with the sharp side of her tongue but not this chap. Every man in his place would be his rule and they were servants and himself above them. He was the kind who liked a toady, someone who was servile and fawning and though Tom had no intention of being either it was best to keep your distance from a man such as this for he obviously had a great opinion of his own importance.

Before Meg could speak Tom insinuated himself between her and Mr Harris. They both looked at him in surprise.

'The doctor gave orders that Mrs Whitley was not to be disturbed, Mr Harris sir. He left her a draught not more than an hour since and she's asleep. It's her chest you see. She can hardly breathe. Perhaps you could come back in the . . .'

Tom's voice was steady and he appeared completely unruffled, his tall frame almost indolent as he leaned between Meg and Mr Harris, but the man interrupted coldly.

'Thank you Fraser but that will not be possible. I would like to see Mrs Whitley now for myself! For all I know the woman might not be sick at all but lying in a drunken stupor . . .'

His unfeeling rudeness and the contemptuous implication that they were all liars was unforgivable. 'You can see my point, I hope?' His manner said it would be all the same if they did not. 'I must be sure that . . . er . . . Mrs Whitley is *really* ill before I impart my news for she is the one to whom I must address it. I cannot tell just any Tom, Dick or Harry who happen to be about.'

Meg flared to life like a Roman Candle, the touch-paper of which has just been lit. Her face flamed in the firelight, scarlet with anger and her eyes flashed tawny sparks which boded ill for Mr Harris or indeed anyone who called Cook a drunkard and Tom and herself a liar. Mrs Whitley was not a young woman and all day she had been wracked with the most terrible, tearing fits of coughing. Her chest rattled in her effort to take a decent breath without plunging a knife in it, clogged with the rottenness which came every winter. The damp air off the river seemed to penetrate the very bones of her and as she got older only the milder, dryer days of spring and summer brought relief. No-one was going to blacken Mrs Whitley in Meg's hearing, not while she'd got breath in her body and a tongue in her head. Mr Lloyd would hear of this. He knew Cook's worth and would make short shrift of this devil, whoever he was. Her fears for Martin were overlooked in her fury.

'You can tell me and Tom, Mr Harris, for you're going nowhere near Mrs Whitley,' she announced imperiously. 'I said she was poorly and so she is and that will have to be good enough. We can pass on any message you want to give her.'

'Is that so, Megan?' It was said smilingly and Meg had time to wonder that a man could smile so much and yet be so completely without humour! 'Well, we shall see about that! I must say I am inclined to believe you for I have been informed Mrs Whitley is a woman to be trusted but you see your insolence is not something I am prepared to suffer. I'm afraid you will have to learn that I do not like to be opposed, particularly by one who is merely a housemaid herself!' His hot eye devoured her waist and hip. 'If you and I are to get on we shall . . .'

'I don't give a damn whether you and I get on or not,' Meg shouted and Tom winced. 'Mrs Whitley is not to be disturbed and if you make a move towards that door I shall . . .' Meg's rage was white hot and Tom was appalled. He had seen her in a temper many and many a time but never like this. She did not suffer fools lightly and said so stormily, but her hot temper quickly cooled and she never bore a grudge towards those at whom it had been directed.

But this was something else and Tom was afraid for her. He thought she would strike Mr Harris and quickly he stepped forward to take her arm for if she lifted it there was no doubt in his mind that Harris would strike back.

'Meg, Mr Harris is not going to hurt Mrs Whitley. He has a message to give her and he must be allowed to do so. It will only take a minute. Isn't that right, Mr Harris?' He turned his head reasonably to Harris, holding Meg's arm protectively but she flung him off, standing on tiptoe to glare over his shoulder, her eyes glittering into those of Benjamin Harris.

'He's not going to see Mrs Whitley, Tom.' Her loyalty to the cook was supreme. 'If he wakes her up after the days she's had I'll not forgive him, nor you!'

Her voice was like granite, hard and coarse and her eyes turned incredibly from pale amber to a still, treacle darkness. She gripped Tom's shoulders as he tried to force her back into the chair from which he had himself risen only fifteen minutes ago and the pair of them fell into it heavily.

Harris rose lazily, again like a cat which moves against its prey and Emm whimpered in her throat, cowering back into the safety of the shadowed corner. He was tall and thin, with narrow shoulders. Everything about him was narrow. His face might have been considered attractive for it was finely drawn with a well-shaped mouth and nose but his features were set in a tapering

115

triangle which gave him the look of a fox. His eyes were grey, colourless, set close together as though there was not enough room for them to be otherwise. It was a face without expression or warmth, a face of aridity showing only contempt for those he considered beneath him.

'I shall go up now,' he said casually. 'Don't bother to come with me. Tell me where it is and I shall find my way.'

With a smoothly smiling backward glance Benjamin Harris moved towards the door.

'You leave Mrs Whitley alone,' Meg shrieked. Tom was holding her tightly, his face as white and set as her own as they struggled to get out of the chair. In their eagerness they impeded rather than helped one another. Tom clasped her lovingly and stroked her back as he tried to soothe her.

'Don't lovey, don't,' he murmured. 'She'll be alright. There's nothing he can do to her.'

'He can frighten her, Tom. Let me go please. Let me go with him. I can't let her be looked at by a stranger. I'll behave myself, honest Tom. Please let me go. Come with me if you want but don't let her wake to a stranger's face. She'll be frightened out of her wits. Please Tom, she's been like a Mam to us. Don't let him do this to her!'

Tom's eyes were soft with understanding but his mouth was grim. He was not much more than a boy and this was a man's thing and he was not sure how to deal with it. He had been ordered to stay where he was by a man of some importance in the shipping line and if he disobeyed he supposed he was in danger of losing his job but Meg was right and he did not hesitate.

Together he and Meg were out of the kitchen and into the long, narrow passage which ran the full length of the house from the front door to the kitchen. It was like stepping into a freezing, numbing stretch of icy water. The warmth of the kitchen lapped from the door behind them, leaking into the hallway but it had no effect on the temperature. Upstairs Meg could hear footsteps echoing on the carpetless stairs at the top of the house and without a moment's hesitation she flung herself to the bottom of the stairs, Tom right behind her!

'I'm here, Meggie,' he said encouragingly and she turned for a second to look into his familiar face. She felt a surge of loving gratitude but without stopping she galloped up the stairs holding

116

her long skirt so high Tom caught a glimpse of the garters which held up her black stockings.

Benjamin Harris was in Mrs Whitley's bedroom standing before the blazing fire, his hands lifting the tail of his coat to allow the warmth to his thin buttocks. The soft glow of the flames peached the walls and ceiling and cast an almost healthy glow on Mrs Whitley's pale, sleeping face.

A sudden squall of wind peppered the tightly closed windows with hard pellets of snow and as if suddenly aware that she was no longer alone the woman in the bed stirred. She turned from her side to her back and immediately, as the new position disturbed the thick phlegm which choked her lungs, she began to cough violently. She struggled to push aside the warm covering which Meg had tucked neatly about her and in an instant Meg was by her side. Tom moved to the far side of the bed and as gently as Meg, lifted the distressed woman to a sitting position.

Slowly the coughing spell began to subside. Mrs Whitley did not appear to notice the tall threatening figure before the fire, but tried to smile, nodding her head and patting the hands of the two who helped her but still she could not get her breath to speak.

'It's alright, Mrs Whitley, we've got you, just take your time. Me and Tom have got you.' Meg murmured soothingly to her as the woman eased herself back on the pillows which Tom had plumped up for her

'That's better,' she wheezed at last, taking shallow, painful breaths. 'That's it, thanks Tom. Will ... you ... pass ... me medicine. It's ...' She panted a little and beads of perspiration dewed her flushed face, '... on the dresser.'

She pointed vaguely, her hand a mere wisp of white flesh and transparent bone and as she turned her head she saw Benjamin Harris. He had remained perfectly still during her coughing bout but as she started convulsively at the sight of him he took a step forward and bowed, his arrogant smile as hard as the buckshot of snow which bombarded the window.

'Good evening, Mrs Whitley. I do beg your pardon for intruding in this ungentlemanly fashion but I have same rather sad news to impart to you. I would not ordinarily invade a lady's room in this manner but Megan here said you were unwell and could not be brought down so I was forced to come to you!'

He smiled his fox's smile and the bright feverish colour drained from Mrs Whitley's face, leaving it damp and leaden grey. Her

117

eyes stared in fearful bewilderment and her hands clasped those of Meg and Tom as she drew further back in her nest of pillows.

'I must say you seem extremely comfortable here,' Mr Harris continued. He looked about him musingly, his expression implying that he had never quite seen anything like it in his life. 'Your room is warmer than my own at the club and I see you are eating well, too!' He slyly indicated the dainty tray on which the remains of the steak and kidney pie lay, and a half eaten egg custard Meg had made to tempt Mrs Whitley's capricious appetite. 'Did . . . er . . . Mr Lloyd give his permission for this . . . luxury in which you appear to live or were you constrained to take it upon yourself to . . .'

Meg turned on him, her eyes flashing like beacons in her rosy face.

'She's ill, Mr Harris. You can see that for yourself. The doctor said she was to have eggs and . . .'

'At whose expense, Megan?'

'Pardon!'

'It appears the shipping line is paying to keep its servants in considerable comfort!' He turned to look at the fireplace. 'This fire alone is worth a week's wages to many a poor labourer and this room is very fine! Very fine indeed! Well, we shall have to see about that later.' He became brisk. 'I must be about what it is I came for.' He rocked slightly on his heels and affected a peculiarly chilling smile. 'I'm afraid one of our company's servants has had a little accident. The snow and ice, you know. It really is dreadful underfoot. Apparently a Clydesdale lost its footing in Chapel Street. Its hooves could not find purchase on the hill and as it went down it took its partner and the dray they pulled. Beer barrels, I believe, which of course rolled down the hill and . . . well . . . poor Mr Lloyd was in their path and . . .'

Mrs Whitley began to moan and her head fell back limply on to her pillows. Harris shrugged and an unreadable expression moved across his face and lifted the line of his thin cut lips. There was, apparently, worse to come!

'I happened to be in the office with Mr Hemingway when the news came and I thought, as I am to take his place, I would come and tell you of it at once.' He paused. 'Edward Lloyd is dead, you see, and I am to be the new agent for this house!'

He looked round at the three ashen-faced figures and his teeth showed exactly like those of a wolf as he smiled.

Chapter ten

Meg and Tom attended Mr Lloyd's funeral in the company of the new agent, who represented the Hemingway shipping line, and though Meg was anxious to get back to Mrs Whitley who had worsened in the last few days, Benjamin Harris refused to allow them to leave the graveside until the last spadeful of earth was patted into place on the grave. He spoke at length in false sympathy to the widow, eliciting a remark later to her daughters on his understanding kindness and how lucky dear Edward's employees were to have someone of such benevolence following in his footsteps, and only when the last mourner had gone did he finally turn to the two who waited resentfully, indicating that they might go ahead of him to the hansom cab which waited.

Benjamin Harris was a widower. His wife, five years older than he had left him childless but with a comfortable income to augment the salary he earned as an official with the 'Hemingway Shipping Line'. It was not quite enough to enable him to live in the manner which he would have liked, nor was his salary, but combined they gave him the means to maintain the standard of living which he considered suitable for someone of his station.

He was the youngest son of a parson and had been given a good classical education but little else besides an overwhelming sense of his own superiority. He was brought up in the sanctimonious atmosphere of the parsonage for the first eighteen years of his life since his father had not the resources to send all his sons to a good school, hedged about with pious observances on the sanctity of the cardinal virtues and the proper fear of God. Submissiveness, humility, respect for one's own chastity and the exaltation of prayer! These had been drummed into the boy and his many brothers and sisters since his father's views on celibacy did not extend to himself – from the moment he was able stand on his infant feet in church. He had repressed all feelings bar those of bitter resentment at the world which had consigned him to this life without the means or education to escape it but when he was eighteen a miraculous thing occurred!

An old school friend of his father came to visit the parsonage, a Mr Robert Hemingway, a shipowner and a wealthy and influential man in his home town of Liverpool. In a moment of expansive volubility Mr Hemingway had disclosed to those at table that he was about to employ a man to assist one of his agents in the matter of the emigrant trade which flourished in the city and before his father's astonished gaze, young Benjamin had sprung from his seat and offered himself for the post. Of course his father had refused it, saying it was no position for a gentleman but Benjamin persisted and during the whole of Mr Hemingway's visit took every opportunity to show himself to his best advantage.

'If you can persuade your father the job is yours, my boy,' Mr Hemingway said as he was handed in to his carriage by the young man, fully expecting never to see him again. Benjamin made no effort to convince his father. He had lived with him for eighteen years and knew the futility of attempting to change the man to a view which differed from his own but three weeks later, his possessions packed neatly in a carpet bag of which he was immensely ashamed, he caught the train to Liverpool, presenting himself at Mr Hemingway's place of business.

He did not do well! Though he was charming and could mix with the society which was Robert Hemingway's, as his employee he was not invited to, and those with whom he worked were not considered the 'right sort' by young Benjamin. When one called him 'Ben' in a friendly fashion Benjamin was most rude to him and he was ignored from that day by all levels of class. His courteous civility was not required when dealing with rough peasants who did not understand what he said anyway and he was short-tempered in his dealings with them. He was not liked! His contempt for those he considered beneath him was poorly concealed and he was cold-shouldered not only by those with whom he wished to be friendly, but by those he did not!

When he had been in Liverpool for two years he met the daughter of a moderately wealthy trader. The father, a widower, owned a brewery, a modestly luxurious villa in Sefton Park, and Matilda was his only child. She and Benjamin were married when he was twenty-one and Matilda twenty-six and from then on his life improved, for Matilda doted on her young husband. She was eternally grateful to him for selecting her as his wife and when, three years later her father died they lived together in his house, now hers and entertained the lesser gentry of the district.

Matilda was passive in their marriage bed, averting her face until he had finished whatever it was he did to her twice a week and so Benjamin took up again the pretty waitress he had met one night at the Music Hall and set her up in rooms and whenever he could get away from Matilda the waitress allowed him to act out the many perverted fantasies he had dreamed of as a repressed youth.

Ten years after he had married her Matilda died quite suddenly and all that she had came to Benjamin. He sold the small villa and joined a good club in town where he kept a room, alternating between there and his 'love nest' in Granby Street and passed the days – and nights – pleasantly enough.

He had never worked his way up as Mr Hemingway would have liked for he made no effort to. Perhaps Matilda's cushioning inheritance had taken away any ambition he might have had, or perhaps it was all too demeaning to compete with men who were not of the same class as himself. Whatever excuse he made when he and Mr Hemingway met, the old gentleman, because of his schoolboy relationship with the 'boy's' father, made no attempt to get rid of him as he would another and when Edward Lloyd died even found himself offering the position to Benjamin Harris. He was often to wonder why!

The new regime began immediately after the funeral since a new intake of emigrants was to arrive the following day. Mr Harris had waited until Betsy and May, who were sisters, had trudged through the snow from Banastre Street. They had scurried hastily to put their package of clothing in the tiny room they were to share, conscious of Mr Harris' impatient eye upon them, before placing themselves beside Megan, Emm and Tom as Mr Harris began what he called the 'new routine'.

'I shall begin with the need for economy,' he said grimly, and his eye fell directly on Meg. 'I have noticed that the indiscriminate use of coal and other commodities which belong to Hemingway's is taken for granted by certain members of the staff and it will stop immediately! This room will be kept warm by the kitchen range where the cooking is done and a fire will be lit each day in the communal room used by the emigrants *but that is all*. We are given an allowance on which to run this establishment and it cannot be used for the servants' own comfort.'

Meg's eyes were upon the square of drugget which lay before the fire – the small fire which burned in the grate. She was afraid to look into the face of the tall man who was now her master for if he should see the expression of pure hatred in her eyes there was no doubt in her mind he would make her pay for it. There were a hundred ways in which he could punish her for her very evident loathing of him. Small ways which are known to a man who employs others and over whom he has complete command. The servants were all in his power, almost as though they were slaves, for employment was hard to come by in this city of the workless! Because of it she and Tom, Betsy and May and Emm must take the long killing hours. Mr Lloyd had always taken on extra staff, casual girls to scrub and polish when the house was busy and even *then* they had worked a fourteen hour day, but the harmony of those who work in conditions of human kindness, almost like that of a family made up for the hard work. But it was evident Harris was about to take immediate advantage of the situation in which those who are employed are forced to put up with anything rather than lose the job they have! Because of it they must accept the cruelly small wage, the contempt and malice of the man whose menials they were. She would dearly love to tell Harris what to do with the buckets of coal, the bowls of milk and eggs he begrudged poor Cook. When Mrs Whitley was herself again, her 'winter chest' relieved by the warming breezes and the soft approach of spring, Meg would see to it that she and Tom and Emm found fresh work and somewhere for Mrs Whitley to end her days in peace. They could not work for this man, that was certain but whilst Cook was ill they could not leave. As she stood by Mr Lloyd's grave she had made a vow for she knew the kindly gentleman had thought the world of Mrs Whitley, and would turn over in his grave if he knew of her present dilemma. It was he who had given Meg her chance and in repayment Meg would look after the old cook for as long as she was able. If Harris sacked her – and if he did Tom would go with her – Mrs Whitley would be left alone, probably to die. It would not be for long, she consoled herself, just until spring! Surely she could put up with this bastard for a few short months? Martin would come home and then the 'three of 'em' would find a solution to this plague which had befallen them!

She kept her eyes cast down but the hateful scene which had taken place only that morning in Mrs Whitley's bedroom flamed still in Meg's enraged mind. He had hung over the end of the bed and spoken of the tasks which needed to be done, as though the other servants neglected them! Of the emigrants who were expected shortly, and who was to do the cooking if Mrs Whitley continued to keep to her bed? His attitude seemed to imply that the poor woman lolled there for her own pleasure, eating chocolates and grapes, no doubt, whilst his back was turned!

'I will do Mrs Whitley's work as well as my own,' Meg had said through gritted teeth, determined to keep faith with the pledge she had made to Mr Lloyd's lowering coffin.

'I see! Am I to suppose from that remark that you have time to spare from your own duties?'

'No sir.' She bit her lips to prevent them forming the words of furious temper which longed to pour from them. 'I am willing to work longer hours, that is what I meant.'

'Just as you like,' he said carelessly, 'but make sure it is done to the standard I require.'

'Yes sir.' She breathed a sigh of relief but it appeared he had not yet finished. 'And then there is the question of this room!'

'This room?' She was genuinely puzzled.

'It could be let to a *paying* tenant.'

'A paying . . .!'

'Unless Mrs Whitley cares to pay for her board and lodgings!'

Mrs Whitley began to cough as the breath of fear caught in her throat.

'Oh sir . . . oh sir . . .' she moaned, the liquid in her lungs shifting thickly. 'Please . . . I can get up sir . . . I'll manage . . .'

'Indeed you will not, Cook. In your condition!' Meg was plainly horrified by the very idea, bending to soothe the distress Harris had thrust upon the sick woman. 'I'll do your work as well as my own until you're fit so don't you fret. Tom and Emm'll help me.' She held the frightened woman's hand, patting it reassuringly but Harris only smiled his wolf's smile and said gently. 'We shall see.'

He moved towards the door. His face distorted in a grimace of distaste as another bout of phlegmy coughing attacked Mrs Whitley, then he turned as though in afterthought. 'Oh, and there must be no more coal brought up here, Megan. See to it, will you please? Hemingway's can hardly be expected to warm the room of every servant. If Mrs Whitley has a fire then they will all

123

want one. This is not a charitable institution, you know. I am accountable to Mr Hemingway for every penny which is spent and if I make him no profit . . .'

Before he could finish his sentence Meg leaped away from the bed and Cook's desperate, clutching hand.

'But you can't keep a sick woman up here in a cold room,' she gasped. 'The doctor says she's to be kept in a constant, warm temperature. The cold air makes her cough. It irritates her lungs and she can't stop it. This room's at the top of the house. It's like ice without a bit of a fire. You can't leave her in a cold room . . .'

'Can I not?' His voice was dangerous.

'Oh please sir, you can see how she is. She needs to be kept warm and . . .'

'Then she must come down to the kitchen. She could perhaps do something useful to earn her keep. Something at which she can sit . . .?'

'She's not strong enough.' Meg's voice was explosive. Cook was not *really* her responsibility. She was not even a relative but Meg's fierce loyalty and challenging defence of those she considered oppressed made her unable to back down. She was trying desperately to control her own runaway temper since she was just beginning to realise that he had the upper hand; that he was the master and she the servant and that should she displease him he would have not only her but Cook as well out on the pavement in the snow. She was nothing but a skivvy to him and there were a hundred others who would clamour to take her place.

Biting the inside of her lip to stop the heedless, maddened words pouring from them Meg breathed deeply before she spoke. She was not afraid of him. Not yet and not as she had been in that first moment of meeting when her subconscious mind had given her that strange warning of what was to come. She was only sixteen but she was strong, physically and in her will and on her own she was a match for any man, this one included, she thought contemptuously, but there was Mrs Whitley cowering in her bed and where was she to go if Harris turned them out. If Meg defied Harris as she longed to do, all of them would suffer. She was caught in a trap, a trap made for her by her own stubborn allegiance to those she loved. She could not see Mrs Whitley flung willy-nilly into the street, nor freeze to death in this room.

Her eyes narrowed to gleaming amber slits and her jaw was rigid as she spoke.

'I'll pay for the coal myself,' she hissed.

'Yourself! In what way?' His eyes flickered over her salaciously and Meg felt herself prickle nastily inside her clothes. God, she had time to think, if Tom or Martin were to hear this bloody conversation they'd half kill this bugger for there was no mistaking what he meant.

'I'll pay for it out of my wages,' she replied coldly, her young face set into a mould of strangely mature dignity. There was hauteur in her manner as she went on. 'I'll buy it by the bucket from the coal man and Tom will bring it up. I trust you will allow me to use Hemingway's bucket!'

She was pleased to see the expression of mortification twist his thin features but it passed in a moment as though he was reluctant to allow her to see she had flicked him on the raw.

'From your wages?' He managed a smile.

'Yes.'

'And who is to pay the doctor's bills?'

Meg looked round wildly, her disdain shattered now but the satisfied look of triumph on Harris' face and the terror of the woman in the bed stiffened her resolve again. She tightened her soft lips and her eyes were steady and filled with contempt.

'I will pay them myself!'

'From your wages?'

'Yes!'

'And how much do you expect to receive?'

She suspected a trap and hesitated, confusion and a fearful dread holding her tongue. She was like an animal in a cage looking for a way out. As soon as she thought she had found it the door was slammed in her face. He was up to something, she knew it. Some scheme which made him almost purr with pleasure, but what?

'I ... don't ... I'm not sure ...' Her voice had lost its arrogance now.

The man looked down at his immaculate shirt front, the one which Meg had ironed only the night before and flicked away an imaginary spot. He cleared his throat nastily before he spoke.

'I have decided to review the servants' wages,' he said. 'Mr Hemingway has discussed with me economies which must be made. The emigrant trade is in the doldrums somewhat and Mr Hemingway feels that a budget must be worked out in order that the house may be kept open and the servants of it retain their jobs. A reckoning will be made and kept to and I intend to see to it immediately. But you will hear all about my plans when I speak to you and the other servants later in the day.'

He became brisk as though the day was wasting and time to stand idly and chat with servants could not be spared.

'Oh . . . and perhaps you would be good enough to remove that bucket of coal to the cellar at once. It *is* Hemingway's coal, is it not? Yes? I thought so, but by all means use the bucket when you purchase your own coal. I'm sure Mr Hemingway would have no objection to *that*!'

Meg stood in the line of frightened servants and listened to Benjamin Harris as he spoke at length on the matter of the economies he and Mr Hemingway had worked out whilst upstairs Mrs Whitley shivered in her rapidly cooling room – they could hear her cough even beyond the closed door of the kitchen – waiting on the moment Tom could be spared to run to the coal merchant for some coal.

It seemed that the economies their new master considered urgent were the cutting down on the amount and quality of food provided for the emigrants, the increase in the hours the servants must work in order to do away with the necessity to employ others, and the cutting of their own wages!

'. . . and so your wages will be halved in order to ensure that we keep within the strict budget set us by Mr Hemingway. I shall buy the provisions and keep the accounts myself.'

They stood before him as he warmed to his theme and his buttocks at the kitchen fire. 'Oh, and Fraser . . .' He turned smilingly to Tom. 'I'm afraid it's back to boot-boy for you unless you would care to try for something elsewhere?' He waited a moment, looking smoothly into Tom's wooden face. 'No! You will stay on as odd job boy?'

Tom nodded his head briefly, his jaw clenched and Meg felt her heart flinch in pain for him. He was doing this for her, and for Mrs Whitley. If he was alone he would no more take these insults, this demeaning of his pride in his work than she would. He would be off, cap slung to the back of his head, giving to Harris no more than a contemptuous gesture, knowing that somewhere there was work, *any work*, to be had for a young, well set-up lad such as he. He had been so proud of his promotion and the trust put in him by Mr Lloyd but he was not the man to let

126

another treat him as Harris did. There were men, men who had families to feed who would think themselves lucky to work for more than fourteen hours a day and take home the meagre portion Harris offered and Tom knew it, but he would not leave her and Mrs Whitley, nor those who needed him now.

But Benjamin Harris had not yet done with Tom.

'Of course I must deduct more than a few shillings a week from you Fraser. An odd job boy does not earn ten shillings a week, or anything like it, does he, especially if he is given board and food!'

Tom said nothing and Meg began to feel that familiar flare of temper grow in her. Why didn't he stand up for himself, the fool. They were all to have their wages halved and only God knew what Tom would end up with. When he was a boy of twelve he had earned three shillings a week, so what was he to have now. The same? He was a man, almost nineteen and had been held in high esteem by Mr Lloyd. She knew, for she had heard him say what a conscientious worker Tom was and trustworthy too.

'You do credit to those who raised you, Tom,' she had heard the elderly gentleman say a dozen times.

Meg felt that familiar surge of rage which had got her into trouble so often before. It seemed it did no good to tell yourself you must be silent when you had a will such as hers but she must, she must. It was hard, listening to the way he spoke to Tom but what else were they to do but submit?

Yet years of defending the underdog, of challenging the injustices she found around her had given her an almost instant reflex for 'sticking up' for those she considered badly done by and her determination to hold her tongue seemed impossible. Her mouth opened of its own accord!

'You can't do that, Mr Harris,' it said.

Benjamin Harris turned his head in a leisurely fashion and in his cold eye something stirred. His face was expressionless and his usual smile was missing. Behind the smooth blankness of his face his crisp brain, that which was accounting the money he was saving here and about to put in his own pocket, was becoming stimulated by a feeling he had never before encountered. Here was a girl, a child really though she had the glorious figure of a woman, who seemed to think she was the champion of all those about her from the old crone upstairs to these dolts who trembled before him and said nothing in their own defence. He found her fighting spirit excited him. He had never met it before but with

127

her head thrown back, her hair tumbling in a profusion of glossy, angry curls about her brow and her eyes flashing thunderbolts he thought he might just enjoy breaking that same spirit which, though it angered him might give his work an added zest! The girl could be the most aggravating creature in the way she challenged his every move and statement but ... well ... one could hardly ignore that heaving bosom!

His eyes narrowed with anticipated enjoyment!

'Yes Megan, you have something to say?'

'Tom has been here for five years and Mr Lloyd always said what a good worker he was. He told him he was to work with Mrs Whitley in the running of the house and that he was to try his hand at the accounts ...'

Harris shook his head as though in sudden understanding of where the money was going but Meg wouldn't let it pass.

'... and Mr Lloyd always checked them and found them correct.' Her face was indomitable in her anger.

'So! What is the point you wish to make, Megan?'

'Well, you can't just make him odd job boy again and give him a few bob a week ...'

'And why not?'

'Well, it's not fair. He's worth more than that.'

They both looked towards Tom and Meg was infuriated anew by his silence. She knew he was as angry as herself by Harris' heartless treatment of Mrs Whitley and had said so in the privacy of the kitchen but he had advised caution for the time being, saying they must not dash headlong into open rebellion. This man was not one to take kindly to having his authority questioned. Though he said Mr Hemingway was behind all this it seemed hard to believe from what Martin had told them of the old gentleman, so best wait and see which way the wind blew before going off half-cocked, as he put it. But it was hard for Meg to accept. Why didn't Tom speak up? Martin would have! He wouldn't let this chap walk all over him as Tom was doing.

'Say nothing, Meg, for God's sake,' Tom had pleaded. 'I know you. You'll open that big mouth of yours and we'll all be without a job. Let's get Cook better and the winter over and then we'll see.'

She knew he was right but it was hard. *Hard*! *It was impossible*!

She turned back hotly to Harris. 'He can't be expected to live on less than he got as a young lad, Mr Harris. It's not right!'

'Then if he cannot manage on the wage I am offering he must look elsewhere!'

Tom's voice was soft but the words seemed to have the greatest difficulty in leaving his closed jaw. Nevertheless he said them.

'Thank you sir. I'll manage.'

Meg looked at him bewildered by his servility. *She* wouldn't put up with it if she were a man. If it wasn't for Mrs Whitley she'd be away looking for another job right now. She wouldn't stay here to be treated like dirt by this devil. He was bad and bad things would come from him. No, she'd get a room and knock on doors until she'd found something. Why, she could take up a position as housekeeper right this minute with the training Cook had given her. There wasn't anything she didn't know about running an establishment which catered to the needs of the traveller ... and Tom ... he could do ...

Her furious thoughts were interrupted by Harris' velvet voice.

'You have something to say, Megan?'

'Yes, I have. These people are ...'

'Cannot these people speak for themselves? Do they always need you to take up for them?'

Meg looked along the line of petrified servants. Frightened and puzzled they were for they were not completely sure why they were so afraid. Only Betsy, who had more 'go' in her than the others was aware of what was happening and when you are well past thirty and with no knowledge but how to scrub a floor and light a fire, anything was better than nothing! The other two women, with eyes like saucers, stared ahead of them numbly.

'Of course they can, can't you? Tom, Betsy, May. Tell Mr Harris you're not willing to have your wages cut. Go on, stand up to him. Don't let him push you around.'

But Betsy only clamped her mouth shut even tighter, throwing Meg a grim look, then, as though driven to it, not by Harris but by her said, 'Be quiet, Meg. You don't know what yer talkin' about so just be quiet!'

'A wise woman ... er ... Betsy ... isn't it? A bird in the hand, eeh?'

'Yes sir,' Betsy stared directly in front of her.

'But Betsy ...!' Still Meg would not give in.

'Be still, Meggie, for God's sake be still!' Tom's voice was like ice!

Meg fell silent, defeated at last as she fought back the surprising tears. Why had Tom not stood up for her as she had for him? He was always the first to jump to her defence, even against those who bore her no real grudge, yet here was this devil treating them as though they had no more rights than beasts in a field and Tom was letting him do it!

She listened apathetically as Harris propounded on his plans for the future of the house. He meant to make it the most efficient, well-run house in the company, he said. He thought they would manage very well with Megan doing the cooking, implying that if she did not she had only to pack her bags and those of the sick cook and go elsewhere and by mid-afternoon he would have a replacement. There was only a small consignment – that was the word he used to describe the men, women and children who were to be in his care, as though they were merely so many pieces of baggage! He was certain Betsy and May – he smiled winningly at the two sisters who bobbed a curtsey apiece – could manage for now, with Fraser's help. He was not sure of ... *her* ... he deliberated, looking at Emm who had been struck dumb since his arrival and gave the appearance of being mentally incompetent because of it, but they would see. She could work for her board and might be useful.

He dismissed them with a peremptory nod and made his way to the room he was preparing for himself on the first floor. It was a large room at the front, the best in the house, once used as a dormitory for the young, umarried girls who lodged there before embarking. He had decided it would do very well as a bedroom and study in which he might do his accounts he said, but it must be redecorated and furnished to his taste! He would stay at his club for the time being, he told them and they had looked at one another, not even sure what a club was! He would come in each day though to supervise the running of the house in Great George Square.

He did not tell them at what time, that way they would never be sure when they might find him looking over their shoulder!

130

Chapter eleven

They did not see a great deal of Martin that year. Their leisure time was so curtailed that even when he was home they could not get out to meet him more than a couple of times during the spring and summer, and then never together. Liverpool was celebrating its 700th anniversary of the granting of its first charter by King John, that year and the feeling in the air was one of great excitement and jubilation, though as Tom said sourly to Meg, there would be little jubilation going on in Great George Square! An era of great prosperity and development was taking place, Mr Harris told the servants pompously, including the extra four he had been compelled to take on as the house filled each week with a couple of hundred emigrants, and they must all work harder to ensure that it continued. He had taken it into his head, when they were almost prostrate with exhaustion at the end of each long day, to call them together to 'educate them about what was going on in this great city', he said and despite the fact that they were all of them wanting nothing more than to get to their beds, kept them standing, women in front, men behind, whilst he – sitting, naturally – 'improved their minds with topics of the day'. He even read the newspapers to them, relishing his complete mastery of them and liking, one supposed, the sound of his own well-bred voice and though they were all Liverpool born and bred, knowing every ship which sailed from the port, felt bound to recount the news of the Cunard's two crack liners, the *Lusitania* and the first *Mauritania* when they left for their maiden voyage.

Still thousands of emigrants from Central Europe, Scandinavia and Ireland, bound for the United States of America, Canada and Australia, poured into the city. Those who remained for more than a day or so were encouraged to take a tour of the city, to marvel at its flourishing splendour, to view the many passenger liners and cargo ships which jostled for a berth and to stare, awe-struck, on the occasion of the grand opening of the new Cotton Exchange in Old Hall Street. They strolled the length of Lord

131

Street, admiring its well-groomed traffic and glittering shops. They frequented the cheap cafés in Whitechapel and stared entranced into the shop windows of the clothiers and bootmakers for none were finer in the world. There was Stanley Street, noisy, narrow, sunless, filled with floats and lorries and carters and a red flow of horse drawn post office vans to the General Post Office Building. Bold Street, intimate, elegant, alive with fashionable ladies gliding across its wooden pavements, no electric cars nor sandwichmen allowed to disturb their peace and quiet, and Brunswick Street, its complete opposite, exclusively masculine with its banks and brokers, merchants and clerks.

And at the end of the day they came back to Great George Square. As many as 250 of them and Meg and Tom, Betsy, May, Emm and Mrs Whitley as she recovered from her winter cough were there to coax them into the large dining room, helped by the 'casual' maids and the young boy who was 'under' Tom. There they were fed, silently, efficiently, quickly! There was perfect harmony and order! Mr Harris insisted upon it and if they ate bread and margarine and endless and repetitious bowls of 'scouse' in which the cheapest cuts of meat, 'scrag-end', carrots and potatoes were cooked instead of the delicious and nourishing broths, casseroles, tripe and onion and cow heel which Mrs Whitley had once given them, what did it matter, what did *they* matter and did they know any better, he asked contemptuously, since they were the dregs, coming from the gutters of Europe!

The servants spent every hour of every day in the constant cleaning of passages and stairs and bedrooms, looking constantly, nervously over their shoulders for one never knew when he might come stealthily upon them, smiling his stoat's smile as though to catch them taking a 'breather', an enjoyment he most definitely did not allow! The oppressive, unspoken threats, of what they did not really know, frayed their nerves to shreds and yet when they whispered about it in the frail warmth of the kitchen at night, what did he actually do? Nothing they could put a finger on. He was exacting in his passion for cleanliness but then so was Mrs Whitley! He did not shout, nor clout an ear as many a man in a position of authority had been known to do but the strangeness of his eyes, the foreboding, even threatening air of stillness which hung about him was enough to bring Emm to silent and unexplained tears. They would drip into her bucket of water which Mr Harris insisted must be changed for every square yard of floor

132

she scrubbed – a daunting task when water must be heated on the open fire, then carried sometimes from cellar to attic – and wonder why, dwelling tearfully on the happy days of Mr Lloyd. She was overworked, that she understood, without the extra help Mr Lloyd used to hire to carry out the rough work in the summer, and underpaid with her already small wage cut by a shilling a week, but she was not cruelly treated.

She had never heard the words, despotic, oppressive but the tyrant who was now her master was both these and the happy balance of hard work but unworried composure she had known with Mrs Whitley under Mr Lloyd's authority and benevolent rule was gone forever!

Christmas had passed them by without notice bar Meg's fervent and daily surging prayer to some faceless, nameless deity that she might be given the strength to hold her clacking tongue until Mrs Whitley was sufficiently recovered for them all to look for other employment. She still had the bold courage and undiminished ardour which had been knocked out of poor Emm by years of uncomplaining servitude and the 'crying shame', as Meg forcefully put it when Harris was absent, of servants, particularly poor Tom, compelled to work twice as hard for almost half the money, was more than she could abide!

'Please Meg, keep your trap shut!' Betsy would beg of her. 'If me an' May lose these jobs it's back ter me Mam's an' if yer could see the way we're jammed in there yer'd not begrudge us this, even with 'im over us!'

Betsy was quite frantic in her pleading, afraid it seemed that Mr Harris might throw her and May out along with Meg if he was crossed. It was alright for Megan Hughes to go ranting on about injustices and the inexcusability – whatever that might mean – of taking advantage of those not able to defend themselves against exploitation – whatever *that* might mean – but she and May were a part of a tortuous family working arrangement in which every member was involved, from her Dad who got employment when he could at casual dock labouring to the youngest who was a road crossing sweeper! Take away two parts of that arrangement and the whole would fall apart and no longer function!

So Meg kept her trap shut! Like Betsy and May and Tom she had no option to do otherwise. There was the frailty of Mrs Whitley to protect and the vulnerability of simple Emm to be considered. Already Meg's savings were dwindling away and the anguish of parting with what was to be the start of a new life for them all was cruelly heart-breaking. When she could she sneaked a few lumps of 'Hemingway' coal into the bucket kindly lent to her by Mr Harris, carefully re-arranging the black heaps in the cellar so that Mr Harris would not notice.

But those weeks of waiting seemed beset with perils. He would follow her about the house, standing in doorways, arms carelessly folded, watching her as she changed beds, polished floors, baked bread and ironed sheets. She would feel a compelling urge to turn, to stand, hands on hips and demand cuttingly what the devil he thought he was doing? Didn't he trust her to perform properly the work she had been doing for five years, she wanted to say, but her will would force her to silence for she knew he waited only for a chance to rouse her to temper and impassioned resentment. His insolent regard, amused, mocking, touched the back of her bare neck and she would feel the instinct to flinch. He appeared to derive enormous pleasure from her obvious discomfiture and she longed to slap his narrow, sallow textured face if only to see his arrogant smile knocked away in rage. That she could bear, for she could meet it with her own!

But she knew she must not!

When she worked in the kitchen, doing the cooking which was now an added and accepted part of her duties besides those for which she was employed, he would stroll in and sit at the table, not saying a word and his eyes would slide about her figure and her rosy, inflamed face as though daring her to object. She would stare defiantly, her mettlesome spirit hungering to set about him with a frying pan but, control clasped tightly to the inner vision of her future, of all their lives, she kept still and silent.

The only pleasure, the only brief but joyful moments in the drab uniformity of Meg and Tom's hard life was the news they had of Martin's success. He had done well in the Irish trials, mastering the dread Ballinslaughter Hill Climb in the 'Hemingway flyer' and was fast gaining a reputation as an 'up and coming' young racing driver. In an early encounter at South Harting he had been involved in a challenge match, amongst others, with the formidable lady driver, Miss Levitt, whose christian name appeared to be unknown, owing perhaps to the gentlemen racing drivers aversion to her impertinence in daring to breach their

134

strictly male preserve, and he had gone on to win a prize at the 'Gordon Bennett' at Hamburg!

His first 'outing', of course, had been at Ormond-Daytona Beach in Florida where he had met and raced against the great Fred H. Marriott, Louis Ross, Vincenzo Lancia and Victor Hemery. He had seen Marriott become the first man to go faster than two miles a minute that day, he told Meg in a letter. The annual speed tournament in January had produced clear skies, bright sunshine and a large crowd on the dunes, to watch the petrol motor cars break the flying mile record. The surf washing the Atlantic coast at Ormond-Daytona Beach left hard ripples in the sand when the wind was blowing from the east as it was that day, and though Fred Marriott was determined to beat his own record of the year before, it was young Martin Hunter in the 'Hemingway flyer' who was first over the winning line and the grand photograph of himself and Mr Robert Hemingway holding the cup between them proved it! He raced in France; in the Isle of Man 'Tourist Trophy'; at the Ardennes Circuit and behind the Hon. C. S. Rolls as he made his record run from Monte Carlo to London. Now he was to take part in the first ever meet at the newly opened track at a place called Brooklands, he wrote to Meg and would tell her and Tom all about it when he was home.

The summer dragged on and only Mrs Whitley's improved health made it bearable. Though she was far from capable of doing the work she had once done she was at least able to direct Meg and Emm to the gigantic task of catering for the hundreds who passed through the house as the emigrant trade reached its peak. She was experienced in preparing and cooking food in the enormous amounts needed, and with the help of the extra girls and by the sheer back breaking, teeth-gritting feat of working eighteen hours a day, they managed to get through, longing only for September and the slow easing of trade.

When they could find the time Meg and Tom had gone to one emigrant house after another, knocking on back kitchen doors, enquiring if servants were needed, and even to boarding houses which catered for the itinerant workers who passed through the city.

'What can you do?' they were asked, their strong young bodies and healthy appearance finding approval.

'I can cook and clean and Tom can do anything he is asked,'

Meg answered confidently, speaking for them both as usual. '. . . and Mrs Whitley can cook as well and Emm is willing . . .'

'Mrs Whitley . . . Emm . . .'

'Well, there are four of us looking for work . . .'

'*Four* of you!'

'Yes, but we're all good workers . . .'

'Now look here young lady, I might be able to fit you and the lad in. You look as if you could do a day's scrubbing, and the lad could be . . .'

'Scrubbing?'

'Only casual, of course . . .'

'But what about Mrs Whitley, and Emm?'

'I know nowt about Mrs Whats-er-name and I'm only willing to take you two on because of the rush. Now do you want it or not 'cause there's others do if you don't!'

'But . . .'

It was the same wherever they went and as the long, hot days eased into the cooler days of autumn they were faced with the dreadful spectre of spending another winter under the authority of Benjamin Harris. Meg renewed her efforts, even trying to find separate employment for them all but no employer was willing to take on an elderly cook, sight unseen and a skivvy whose age and mental ability seemed uncertain, though she and Tom could have been placed a dozen times.

It was November when the first invidious, clammy fogs began to drift along the Mersey wall, aiming, Mrs Whitley declared painfully, straight for her old chest. By the end of the month she could scarcely breathe and only the relief of 'Friars' Balsam', melted in a bowl of hot water and inhaled beneath the folds of a towel which she placed over her head, relieved her a fraction.

Meg was frantic. It was to be a repetition of last winter, she said worriedly to Tom and how the dickens were they to manage the coal for Mrs Whitley's bedroom if she had to take to her bed again. She shivered now before the meagre fire in the kitchen, begging Meg not to 'let on to him' that she was badly, praying that he would not catch her, sweating and white-faced, sitting about 'wasting his and the company's good time' when she should be about the task of preparing his dinner.

'He'll put me off for sure this time, our Meg,' she wept, her thin face haggard. There would be no doctor, she realised that for how were they to manage his fee from the small wage they were paid

136

by Hemingway's and from which they could save nothing now. There had been new winter boots and a second-hand overcoat from Paddy's Market for Tom who had grown six inches in as many months, though God only knew how, she said tiredly on the 'bloody awful' food they now ate, making no apologies for her own swearing!

On the first of January she collapsed at Mr Harris' feet when he summoned her to his study to make an accounting for the month of December. As Tom and Meg almost carried her from the room, his nostrils were dilated in distaste as he told them he could no longer pay the wages of a woman who could not even keep her feet before her employer, let alone do her work as she should!

It was the next day when he called Meg into his study. Tom had repainted it during the summer and new, floor length curtains had been put to the windows, a rich, plum velvet. A fire crackled pleasingly in the well-shined black-leaded grate – no economy here Meg thought bitterly – and before it was a round table upon which Harris did his accounts. There were a pair of comfortable leather chairs, brought by him from the house he had once shared with Matilda, a desk against the dark, heavily papered wall, a sofa of haircloth and rosewood and all warmly set on a patterned Brussels carpet. There were ornaments of silver and cut crystal and bronze, a sepia photograph of Harris and his Matilda on their wedding day in a silver frame and on the wall above the fireplace, Landseer's 'Monarch of the Glen' looked down loftily on the scene beneath his fine nose.

In the corner of the large room, standing next to a massive mahogany cupboard in which Mr Harris' entire splendid wardrobe hung, was a double bed partially hidden behind a Chinese screen, installed there for the night when he was disinclined for the charms of the barmaid. All very warm and comfortable . . . and threatening!

Meg stood just inside the door. She did not often come to this room for it was the job of Betsy and May to do the cleaning here, he had told them, whilst Meg saw to the kitchen and the cooking, and Tom, of course, was set about any lowly task Mr Harris could devise for him. The other girls, taken on for a few weeks when the 'rush' was on, had, naturally, been turned off when it was over.

'What's it about?' she asked Betsy when the maid told her

breathlessly the master wanted to see her immediately in his study. 'An' yer to put on yer best dress,' Betsy added.

'What for?' she asked, instantly on the alert.

'How do I know?' Betsy retorted. 'He don't tell me what goes on in his head,' but there was a strange gleam in her eye.

'What can it be, d'you think, Tom?' Meg asked anxiously.

'God knows, lovey! Probably wants us to *pay* him for the privilege of working at Hemingway's!'

Tom Fraser was badly disturbed by his own inability to find a decent job, a safe refuge for his 'womenfolk'. He felt it strongly, his young manhood strained to the limits and his bitterness showed in his inclination to be sharp where once he had been ruffled by nothing more serious than Everton's failure to score a goal on a Saturday afternoon. He did his best to relieve Meg's burden of extra work which was put on her by Mrs Whitley's illness but the constant undermining of his own carefree belief that life was good, filled with hard work but good nevertheless, had been severely tested. He detested Benjamin Harris, a feeling he did not relish for it was not in his nature to be vindictive. He watched Meg leave the kitchen, clearly nervous, and his mouth clenched into a straight, tight line for he would have given his right arm to take the worry from her and he knew he could not do so. The feeling of frustration did not sit sweetly in his young breast!

'Come in,' Harris called when she knocked on his door. She did so.

'Close the door behind you.' He was standing before the fire in much the same pose he had affected when he had first entered Cook's bedroom on the night he had arrived. His coat-tails were lifted to warm his buttocks and he stood with his legs apart, his hands behind his back. His cool gaze rested on her face as she closed the door obediently behind her. Her heart banged in her chest and her mouth had mysteriously dried up!

How did she know? She asked herself the question later and she could not answer it but every female instinct in her, every sense and pulse told her why she was here and she was deathly afraid.

His brutal gaze fell to her breast and he smiled, running his tongue round his lips. His hands beneath his coat seemed to move in some strange way and he rocked back and forth in a manner which implied all manner of dreadful things.

'Come here, Megan.' His voice was no more than a thread of sound in the soft comfort of the room.

'Betsy said you wanted to see me.' Her's was loud, a barrage of noise to form a defence of sorts. 'What is it, sir?'

'Come here by the fire,' he repeated.

'I'm alright here, thank you sir but if you please I must be getting back to the kitchen in a minute. I've left some pies in the oven and Betsy won't . . .'

'Never mind the pies, Megan. I want you to come here. I have something to discuss with you and we can hardly carry on a conversation shouting across a room, can we?'

Suddenly Meg's spine stiffened and she lifted her chin. What the hell was she so scared of? Trembling here by the door as though Harris was about to leap on her and throw her to the floor. Tom was only a few yards away, and Betsy and May and if he so much as laid a finger on her she'd scream so bloody loud half the Square would be bashing at the door in a minute. Even Constable O'Shea who patrolled Upper Pitt Street regularly as clockwork would hear her once she got going.

'What is it, Mr Harris?' she said tartly. 'If I leave those pies for more than ten minutes they'll be burned to a crisp.'

'How is Mrs Whitley today, Megan?' Benjamin Harris' voice was like velvet and the sudden reversal, the abrupt departure from the 'discussion' which Meg had supposed to concern the usual economies threw her off balance.

'Mrs Whitley . . .?' she faltered.

'Mmm. She is still . . . unwell, is she not?'

What to say! Dear God what was she to say? Confirm to him that Mrs Whitley was still 'lingering' as he put it, in her bed or pretend that the cook was up and about, doing her duty, busy in the kitchen? But then she had just admitted, inadvertently, she realised now that she herself was making pies and that there was no-one but Betsy to supervise them. They had all, somehow . . . Dear Lord . . . managed to keep up the pretence that Mrs Whitley was about somewhere whenever he had come into the kitchen. The poor woman was terrified that he would send her packing if he discovered she was unable to fulfill her duties, as he most certainly would and yet here he was asking after her as though there was nothing but concern for her in his heart. She felt her's begin to thump erratically in her chest and she swallowed the lump which had formed at the back of her throat.

139

'Well . . .' the word she spoke was no more than a despairing breath on her lips.

His voice was silky with menace. 'I have heard her cough in the night, even from down here. I wonder does she perhaps disturb the other servants, as she does myself? Keep them from their sleep? If they do not rest, if I do not rest, we cannot do our work properly, would you not agree, Megan?'

He smiled and his hands moved more quickly beneath his coat. 'Would she not perhaps be better served with her own relatives, d'you think?'

'She has no family, sir.' Meg's voice had become lifeless, hopeless.

'Oh dear, then I can see no alternative but the poor house . . .?' The statement which was not really a statement but a query, was spoken sadly.

'Mr Harris . . . sir!' Desperation overcame Meg and her eyes blazed, '. . . she is sixty-two! She has been here for twenty years.'

'It is her home, you are saying?'

'Oh yes sir, it is.'

'Quite so, quite so, but then . . . dead wood, you know the saying, Megan?'

'Dead wood, sir?'

'Yes, I'm afraid so and then there is the question of the . . . other one . . .'

'Emm . . .?' Meg's voice faltered and the glow of outrage drained away and despair took its place.

'Yes. She really is quite . . . useless, as is Mrs Whitley. I need strong, willing persons . . .'

'Emm is strong and very willing. She works all hours God sends, sir, really. I know she is not . . . she is . . . nervous, perhaps and a bit slow too . . . but she is the best worker we have and will work until she drops, sir!'

Harris seemed to consider this though his expression made games of it.

'So! You are saying she and Mrs Whitley would not want to leave.'

'Of course not!' The words were said bravely, defiantly, hopelessly!

'You would not want them to leave?'

Meg drew a shuddering breath and the pulse in the hollow of her throat beat a frantic tattoo. Though he had not said a word which could, if it had been overheard by another be construed as threatening, there was no doubt now of what he had in his mind. She was an innocent girl but she was not simple. It was all there in his manner, in the way his eyes glowed hotly about her trembling figure and she was in such mortal terror she could no longer speak. She knew finally there was no comfort to be had in calming herself with vigorous thoughts of fighting and screaming if this man should touch her. He did not mean to force her. He had no need, had he? She was to go to him willingly. He had only to speak softly of Cook, of Emm, to consider out loud the possibility of getting rid of 'dead wood' and the struggle was over before she had a chance to fight. What a fool she had been. A naive fool who had come to the butcher's block with all the ignorance of a sheep which is to have its throat cut. She had believed in her own strength and courage and had despised this man, thinking she could treat him with disdain, with contempt until the time came when she and Tom would find – miraculously now she realised – a new place for them all away from this man. He could level a pistol at her head, raise a sword or an axe and she would spit in his face but he was telling her that if she did not submit to . . . to whatever his foul mind had prepared for her, he would fling not only Emm from the house, but the frail old woman who was ill upstairs with as much compunction he would a basket of unwanted kittens. She and Tom would survive. They would find other employment for they were young and strong but Mrs Whitley and Emm? Would they?

Still she tried to outface him. Her lion heart pumped hot blood through her body and her trembling limbs struggled to gain strength from it. Her face was the colour of pipe-clay. Her eyes were the deep yellow of a cat which is cornered but she stiffened her back and lifted her head challengingly.

'Now Megan, let us not be unreasonable,' he said softly. 'I merely wish you and I to be . . . friends. It is not too much to ask of you, is it, and it would mean so much to Mrs Whitley and the other one. I am good to those who . . . please me, Megan. I believe you to be fond of the old woman, and of course, any good fortune *you* might gain from your . . . friendship with me, would encompass those of whom you are fond. A rise in your wages could be used to make your companion's life more comfortable, you do see that, do you not, Megan. There would be no need for you to tell the others of our little . . . arrangement if you did not wish it since I can see where it might make it awkward for you. The other servants ... well ... they need not know. When I am in need of ... companionship I will come to your room and we will ... well, I am sure you know what we will do, my dear. You are a very pretty girl, Megan and I would find it most enjoyable to ...'

Here he began to speak words of such obscenity, such odious, scarcely understood grossness, Megan felt her mind begin to slip away to escape the filth with which he smilingly coated her. The images he evoked were so terrible she felt herself to be already violated and her young innocence hid her mercifully away from it in the only way it knew how. Megan Hughes turned off completely then. She stared numbly into Harris' pale, pale grey eyes and from across the room the vileness in them and in the looseness of his mouth did not even penetrate the numbness of her terror-stricken brain.

'... you shall naturally have another room, nearer to mine, so if you would like to go into Liverpool and choose some ... some pretty things, for your new room and for yourself ... underwear ... lace ... you know what I would like, I'm sure. All women know how to please a gentleman, do they not Megan and I'm certain you are no exception. Would you not like that, Megan? To have nice things ...?'

Her head had drooped as his words hung over her. Her face was in shadow and her long lashes hid her eyes.

'Look at me, Megan.' His voice was blurred and hoarse with his lust. 'Look at me.' Her hands trembled against the smooth whiteness of her apron, clutching at each other, but when she raised her eyes to his the expression in them made him recoil. In them was the venom of a snake before it strikes, the hatred of a lioness as she defends her cubs from the hunter, the loathing of a woman who will kill to avenge a wrong done her. Though her face was waxen, with no colour nor life and her mouth was soft, trembling, vulnerable as that of a child her eyes were on fire, hot and smouldering with malevolence, a passion of loathing so great he fully expected her to spring for his throat.

His exultation soared and he could scarce keep his hands from her now, this very minute. God, it was going to be marvellous taming this magnificent child, he rejoiced. The barmaid had long since lost her charm. Those of the working class who had taken her place, for Benjamin Harris had a liking for those who were socially inferior to himself, had not always been willing to cater to his own predilection in the ways of pleasing his body but this

142

one, she would be formidable! She would have no choice! Her eyes told him she knew that as they looked at him balefully but they said she would fight, fight him every step of the way nevertheless! His humbling of her would give him the greatest satisfaction he had ever known with a woman, but she must be absolutely certain that he meant every word he had said to her.

'The night air is sharp at this time of the year, Megan and the food in the poor house quite inferior. It would not sustain a woman in good health, let alone one who is . . . vulnerable!'

He watched as she became as lifeless as the porcelain figurine on his mantelshelf. 'Now, my dear, you may return to your duties but remember what I have said. I will leave you some money to buy yourself some . . . pretties.' The word was said with a lecherous, almost inhuman smile, like that of a fox which lifts its muzzle to take its prey. 'I am to be away tomorrow and have some business to which I must attend later today, but when I return on Friday I shall expect to find you in . . . well, I leave it to you to choose a suitable room.'

He smiled, waving her away peremptorily, the master dismissing the maid.

Quietly she turned and left the room.

Chapter twelve

'Has he gone?'

'Aye. Across to the wolds for a few days, he said, wherever that is and I hope he falls and breaks his bloody neck because I don't think I can take much more of this, our Meg. If he calls me "boy" once more I'll bash his flamin' face in, gospel, our kid, or wring his neck and then I'll swing for him. Jesus only knows how we're going to get through the rest of this winter with Mrs Whitley like she is. He'll kill her, Meg, you realise that, don't you? Surely to God it can't be true what he says about old Hemingway and all these economies he's on about. I can't believe that decent old chap we met with Martin could be so cold-hearted that he'd begrudge an old woman, someone who's worked hard in his employ, honest as the day is long, a bit of a fire in her room when she's ill! It just goes to show! Much always wants more and I suppose that's why he's living where *he* is and the likes of us are here! What I can't understand is why Martin thinks the world of him like he does. Surely he wouldn't work for someone as bloody minded as Harris makes him out to be? Martin's got a bloody good head on his . . .'

'You'd better watch your language, Tom. You know Mrs Whitley doesn't like it.'

'I can't help it, Meg. He's enough to make a saint swear. D'you know, if he wasn't away with Martin I'd go up there and demand to see him . . .'

'Who?'

'Hemingway, of course. It's not right, Meg and if Martin was here he'd say the same, you know he would. I wonder when they get back?' Tom pushed his hand distractedly through his hair, forcing the short golden curls to stand on end. 'What the hell can they find to do with them damn racing cars, anyway? You'd think they'd get sick to death of dashing from one bloody place to another. Irish trials, hill climbs, Scottish trials, Brooklands track, Pately Bridge, bloody places I've never even heard of.'

144

'Well, Mr Hemingway is pleased they've won so many events, Martin says, so I expect...'

'I dunno...' Tom interrupted her irritably, his hands thrust deep in his pockets as though to release them they might do someone some damage, 'it makes you wonder what grown men find so fascinating about racing one motor car against another. I can see no sense nor purpose in it myself. Aah well...' he sighed resignedly, '... each to his own, I suppose!'

He began to mix up the paste with which he cleaned the brass base of the lamps, his face set in lines of puzzled ill-humour. The fierce look of concentration, the hunted air of a fox as the hounds close in, the almost visible tension which swept Meg about the room like a broom being wielded by some demented hand seemed not to be noticed as he spat and polished, muttering as he did so under his breath.

'You got any money, Tom?' The abrupt question made him jump and he dropped the glass bowl of the lamp on to the chenille covered table.

'*Money?*'

'Yes, for God's sake! You know what money is, don't you?'

'There's no need to snap my head off, Meg. I was only...'

Meg sighed and turning on the rug before the kitchen fire sank slowly to her knees. Her face was rosy from the dancing flames but beneath the soft colour there was strain and her mouth was set in a rigid line. The light danced in her eyes giving them an almost merry sparkle but there was a dispirited droop to her strong shoulders and a faint shake in her hands as she held them out to the warmth.

'I'm sorry, Tom. I know you haven't got any, it's just that...'

Tom got up from the table and moved across the kitchen until he stood beside her. He sat down on the stool where Emm usually perched herself to warm her thin shanks and leaned forward. He took Meg's hand, holding it with such gentleness it might have been a wounded bird. It trembled in his and he bent to look softly into her face. His eyes were filled with the light of his loving concern and she nearly gave in then. The sweetness, the inherent goodness of this boy for that was what he was compared to her own brutal introduction to the foulness of man's perversion, swept away all the fragile half-formed plans she had devised during the night to gain their freedom and which now she was bitterly aware were no more than a child's fairy tale. Tom's gaze almost cracked the thin casing of armour she had gathered about herself to protect what was the pure essence of Megan Hughes and she despaired then, for how was she to shoulder alone the enormity of this ghastly burden? Try as she might, twist and turn and duck as her mind had done in the bed she still shared with Emm, she was fettered as closely to Benjamin Harris as if they were joined by iron shackles. She could walk away! She and Tom could walk away and be free to pick and choose from the work which was available to those who are young and strong and experienced. They could put Mrs Whitley and Emm into the Poor House. There would be a pallet for them there to sleep on, with a thin blanket and a bowl of something each day to sustain life but how could *she* be sustained, how could Megan Hughes live on and be free if she allowed it. And she could not share her burden! She could not find relief by pouring out her fear, her horror and shame to Mrs Whitley or to Tom.

Tom! She held his hand and leaned her head against his shoulder. He smelled . . . clean. His shirt had the fragrance of fresh ironing, his hair and skin of the coal tar soap he used and his breath was as sweet as that of a child. He was sound and wholesome. He was strong and he would protect her with his life and that was why she dare not tell him for there was no doubt in her mind that if she did his rage would be the killing rage of a *quiet* man, the rare and terrible anger of those who do not come to it easily. He would simply beat Benjamin Harris with his untrained fists until the violence had been spent and they would be worse off than they were now. Mrs Whitley would still be at death's door. Poor simple Emm would be without a job and bereft of the prospect of another and the winter weather as fierce as a hungry wolf at the door. Tom would no doubt be in prison and herself . . . Dear God . . . where would *she* be without them all? If only it were summer again. If only they had been able to get a new place during the *past* summer. If only Martin was home . . . and Mr Hemingway. Surely, *surely* the old man would listen to her if she were to tell him of what Harris was after. Surely he would *believe* her . . . Oh dear Lord, she was so frightened . . . so frightened . . . she couldn't think properly she was so frightened.

'What is it, lovey? What's happened?' Tom put his big hand clumsily to her bright hair.

'It's . . . no, really . . . it's just . . . well. I wish we could . . .'

'What? What is it?'

146

'If we could just get away from here...'

Tom stroked her hair gently and his face was sad. Sad with the helplessness of a young man who longs to protect and provide for his family but who knows it is beyond him. And yet there was a fierce resolution in his eyes which struggled with his sorrow, asking was he not a young man and strong and would not his youth and his strength prevail in the end. If they could just scrape through this winter they would find something, somewhere, someone who would take them all in. By God, he'd tramp the streets every hour he had free until he'd found them a resting place. Perhaps he could manage a cycle ride out to some of the farms which were scattered about the countryside. They needed labourers and maids and skivvies just as they did in town, didn't they? and the three of them, if they worked hard, could support Mrs Whitley. Maybe they could get a cottage, a 'tied' cottage they called them, which were rented for a nominal charge, he had heard, to those who worked the land or in the kitchens of the farmhouse. They would find *something*, of course they would. Or they could even go to another town. He was a real 'Dicky Sam', the name given to a man born within a mile of the Mersey wall and he loved his native town of Liverpool but he'd go anywhere, *anywhere* to get work and take that strange and dreadful look from their Meg's face.

With the eternal optimism of youth he turned Meg's face to his, smiling into it, determined to instil his own hopes for the coming spring into *her*.

'We will, love, we will, I promise you. As soon as Cook perks up and can get out of her bed we'll look for another place. We'll get her and Emm fixed up right as rain. Just give it a couple of months. We've stuck it so far, Meggie. Another couple of months won't be so bad.'

A couple of months! Dear God, it would be too late in a couple of months. By then she'd be Harris'... she would be... She could find no word to describe it except the one by which all such women are called and her heart turned to stone within her at the sound of it in her head and she knew unequivocally that she could not do it. She could not. *She could not!*

Tom had moved away now, returning to the cleaning of the lamps for if he didn't have them, and the hundred and one other jobs Harris had instructed him to 'see to', finished by the time he got back he'd be out on his ear, he said. He felt quite cheerful now, his own thoughts relieving his mind somewhat. Harris was to be away until Friday so they would have the dread sense of his presence removed for a while. They could relax a bit. Meg could have a rest and be easier in her mind without *him* breathing down her neck and Mrs Whitley could have a bit of good grub inside her for a change. He turned to grin endearingly at Meg, the words of comfort already forming on his lips but they never got there. Instead he stared, bewildered, his mouth open and gaping.

'Hey, what d'you think you're doing?' he managed at last.

Meg was still kneeling before the kitchen fire. She turned to look up at him, her own expression unreadable but in her eyes was a light of battle, changing them from the pale dusted amber of a moment ago to a glittering transparency as deep and warm as golden honey. She had picked up the shovel and in her other hand was the brass poker which it was Tom's job to polish. Her face was flushed now as though from some inner fire and a strand of curly hair fell across her forehead. She pushed it away with the back of her hand and the poker waved wildly in the air, then she grinned but there was no warmth in it.

'What does it look like?'

'He'll have a bloody fit when he finds out!'

'He'll not find out! He's gone, hasn't he and you can move the coal to look as though there's no more been used than there should be. He'll never know, Tom and we might as well make Cook comfortable while we can. Damn him, Tom! Damn him to hell and back and if he walked in this kitchen now I'd tell him so!'

Tom was surprised by the vehemence in her voice but his eyes crinkled into a deep, delighted smile and in an instant he was the merry, engaging young man he had been before Benjamin Harris had come to torment them. Meg was slowly drawing several live coals from the brightly blazing fire, transferring them onto the shovel. They glowed hotly, the smoke from them stinging her eyes. When she was satisfied they were secure she stood up, turning away from the fire.

'Put some more coal on, Tom, so that it can build up again, will you? We're going to have us the best potato hot-pot we've eaten in months and while you're at it, make us a decent cup of tea. I'll just run up to Mrs Whitley's room with these. It'll not take long to get a fire going up there and his bloody lordship can walk in the river 'til his hat floats for all I care!' She seemed to be injected with some strange emotion which Tom did not recognise as

148

hysteria and though it made him uneasy he was pleased to see her more lively.

They smiled triumphantly at one another. Tom lifted the coal scuttle and selecting several small pieces from it made up the fire until it glowed cheerfully and its warmth spread out into the kitchen. They both turned guiltily as the door opened but it was only Emm.

'Is she settled, Emm?' Meg's voice softened as she spoke to the little skivvy. Emm nodded her head, her eyes darting anxiously from one corner of the kitchen to the other as though she fully expected the hated agent to materialise, something on the lines of the devil, from the very floor. She knew he was gone. Had not she and Meggie seen the cab Tom had called disappear round the corner into Upper Pitt Street with him in it, but his ghostly presence seemed to hang relentlessly about the place even when he was absent.

'Run up with these then whilst Tom fills the buckets, will you? You know how to do it, don't you? Here's some kindling and a few twists of paper and I've put a bit of sugar in a bowl so that if it doesn't catch right away you can throw a bit on. Now you're sure you can manage all that?' Emm nodded again, taking the shovel in one hand and the small fire basket, stuffed with small pieces of wood and paper, in the other. 'I'm just going to warm up this bit of broth for her then I'll follow you up. Tell her I'm going to make us a nice "tater" hot-pot. That'll cheer her up.'

Tom was in the cellar when he heard the screams. For fifteen minutes he had filled coal scuttles, one for the kitchen, one for Mrs Whitley's bedroom and another for Mr Harris' study for his master would insist on the comfort of a decent fire when he returned at the end of the week and he might as well see to it now. He had shovelled a great heap from one corner of the underground room to another for no reason at all other than it gave him an excuse to work off some of his youthful frustration. And he supposed guilt played a part in it too, for he felt he should have been able to find some safe and homely place for himself and their Meggie before now. And he would an' all, even with the added burden of Mrs Whitley and Emm, he told himself stoutly.

The screams lifted the hairs on the back of his neck and he felt the skin prickle all over his body. He turned, disorientated by the suddenness of it, by the violent confusion which blasted its way into his mind and in the fearful dread which came to replace it he fell over the coal scuttles which someone – surely not himself – had placed directly behind him, cracking his elbow agonisingly on the stone floor as he went down.

'Jesus . . . oh Jesus . . .' he whispered and for a dreadful moment he was back in the past on that day when Fancy O'Neill had dragged Meggie . . . *Meggie* . . . Oh dear Lord, into the back yard of this very house. In his memory's eye he saw clearly the white flesh of her and her innocent female vulnerability which Fancy had been about to despoil and a great anguish exploded in him. It hit him with such force he almost fell again, reeling towards the steps which led to the yard.

It was that bastard! That creeping, evil bastard who had come to take their peace from them and now, whilst Tom's back was turned for a moment, imagining Harris had gone from the house, he had come to viciously brutalise their Meggie. Tom had seen the way he looked at her, his eyes on her breasts and . . .

'Meg!' he shouted, his long, hard muscled legs carrying him up the cellar steps three at a time and into the yard. He flung himself across it and along the passage which, three years ago, he and Martin had fought to be first down to get at Fancy O'Neill. It could have been no more than a minute, two at the most from the time he first heard the distant scream to the moment he flung open the front door of the house but the fire, already darting along panelled, dry stick walls, greeted the vast volume of air he brought in with crackling glee, feeding on it greedily. It blasted out to meet him and he threw up his hands to protect his face, stepping back instinctively for though the heart and the soul willingly would dare the agony, the flesh will not.

'Meggie . . . Meggie . . .!' he screamed and the red-flecked heat jumped into his open mouth joyously and his throat was on fire with it and in the midst of the horror he had time to consider in the detached corner of his mind which stood off and watched that this was his fault. *His fault,* for beneath the stairs which led up to the first floor was the drum of lamp-oil which had been delivered only an hour since.

'I'll take it down to the cellar in a minute,' he had shouted to Meg, then stood back, gritting his teeth resentfully as Mr Harris sauntered by him casting him with that look of contempt he reserved for those he considered beneath him.

'Call me a cab, boy!' he had said to him and Tom had run to

the corner and whistled one up, then gone directly to the kitchen to pour out his rancour on Meg. His dangerous hatred of Harris had emptied his mind of all else and beneath the stairs, just waiting for the first spark to ignite it was the element which had furnaced the embers dropped from the shovel. *Emm?* ... was it Emm ... or ... dear sweet God ... not ... not Meggie! Was she even now engulfed by the flames which were devouring the hallway and the staircase from the front door right the way down the passage to ... to ...

He shaded his eyes against the heat and glare, oblivious now to the agony of the skin shrivelling from his hands and beyond the dancing, curling, roaring flames he could see the open doorway which led into the kitchen and even before his mind had digested the information his instinct had him racing back towards the area steps, down them in one leap and through the basement door which he did not merely open but almost knocked from it's hinges in his terror.

The kitchen was empty ... Meggie, where are you? But through the door which opened into the hallway came the growing roar of the flames and the kitchen was turned to orange and rose and gold with the reflection of them. As he leaped across it he heard the scream again, fainter now and weaker and his heart banged unmercifully against his chest, bucking and kicking in it's effort to make him move faster.

'Meggie ...!' He did not even know he was shouting her name as he crashed through the kitchen door and into the hallway. The flames reached for him but he eluded their embrace, springing away from them as they consumed the doorway through which he had just come. The stairs were there, a long incline edged at each side with licking, creeping fire, the walls smoking, the wallpaper blackened with smoke and beginning to crackle. It seemed he had reached the top safely for he was on the first floor landing but it was empty and the conflagration was at his back and the smoke, black and pitiless was pressing down on him.

On his belly, his face hugging the linoleum which lined the stairs to the second floor he crawled towards her for where else would she be but with Mrs Whitley, with Emm, guarding them, willing to give her young life to protect their old ones.

'Meggie ...' he croaked, his throat parched, scorched, and he began to feel himself suffocate then for the flames and the smoke were moving faster than he was. He could not see now, only feel

151

the shape of each stair tread and the smooth texture of the linoleum which was considered good enough for the servants to walk upon. He reached blindly forward, his hands clinging to whatever they could and suddenly he was at the top and the three doors, all closed, of the bedrooms, wavered in his vision then one opened and strong hands gripped his, lifting him, leading him forwards. A door banged quickly behind him and the blessed relief of Mrs Whitley's room which the fire had not yet reached, bathed him in its coolness.

'Meggie . . .?'

'I'm here, Tom and . . . and Mrs Whitley.'

'Emm . . .?'

'I don't know, Tom!' He could not see her face but he heard her begin to weep dementedly.

He turned again. 'I'll go . . . and look . . .' but the flames howled their defiance on the other side of the door and from the bed someone moaned and the smoke edged its way through the cracks about the bedroom door and the roaring, triumphant as a beast about to close in on its prey, filled his ears.

'Emm . . . oh Emm . . .!'

'Our Father which art in Heaven . . .' Mrs Whitley said quietly from the bed and as she did so Tom's agonised vision cleared. The tiny dormer window was tight shut against the cold for the doctor had said Mrs Whitley's diseased lungs could not stand it but they must take their chances with it now!

'Come on, our Meg. Don't stand there wingeing.' He knew he must be brutal to get them both on the move. 'Get Mrs Whitley's coat on her . . . anything warm whilst I open this window . . .'

'Tom . . . Emm . . .?'

'There's nothing we can do for Emm, lass. No doubt she's . . . she's in one of the bedrooms . . . there's windows there too, you know and not so far to . . . to jump. Come on now . . . good girl . . . get Mrs Whitley wrapped up . . .'

Brave she had been in the rescuing of Tom but now her fine spirit was diminished in her agony over Emm and she wrung her hands and tears coated her paper white cheeks.

'But Cook can't get out that way, Tom . . .'

'It's the only way, lovey. If we can get her on to the roof . . . across to next door there's a chance we . . .'

'She's too old, Tom . . .'

'D'you want to leave her here to burn then, Meggie!'

The bedroom door was smoking badly now and tiny fingers of golden flame were slithering insidiously about the frame. The coolness Tom had so gratefully acknowledged was suddenly becoming warmer, much warmer and from beneath the rug which lay upon the worn floorboards a fine trickle of wisping smoke rose gently into the room. Mrs Whitley began to cough, her face crimson and beaded with sweat, then suddenly, as her old heart protested, it turned a dull, leaden white. She leaned back against the iron frame of the bedhead and Tom knew that they had a minute, no more, perhaps only seconds to get her out for unless she could help them, lifting herself as best she could there was no way he and Meg might carry her through the tiny window and up on to the sloping, hoar-frosted roof.

When he opened it a jumble of crazy sounds came through the window; harsh cries, screams, the jangle of a bell but the worst noise was at his back for the draught from the window caused the flames about the bedroom door to break out into a full-throated roar of approval as they were given fresh quantities of air to fuel them.

'Meggie . . . for God's sake . . .'

'I'm coming . . .'

'. . . Thy Kingdom come. Thy will be done on earth as it . . .'

Mrs Whitley was deep in shock now and the words she spoke, dredged from some corner of her mind which had carried her back to her days at Sunday school were mingled with her black and tearing cough. There was a smudge of blood at the corner of her mouth but she allowed them to lift her bodily, clumsily, forcing her through the tiny window, doing as Tom bid her like a child, obeying his hoarse commands with the automatic reflex of her younger days. She sat quietly, blindly on the narrow ledge, her old, mottled legs dangling pitifully from beneath her nightgown, high above the square, not even glancing down at the sea of faces which stared up at her now in horrified silence. The fire engine was slewed at an angle across the front of the house next door and men were feverishly working hand pumps. Tom was quite astonished to see them. Surely not enough time had gone by since he had heard the first scream, Emm's scream, to allow the man on the high tower in the centre of Liverpool whose job it was to indicate in which district the fire lay, to pass the message to the firemen and for them to gallop the distance from town to reach them? It had seemed merely minutes but he realised

153

that considerable time – how long? – had passed for the fire to claim such a hold.

The wheels on which the fire hose was attached were being drawn close to their own front door but he could not see what was happening since the angle of the steep roof and the broad gutters cut off his view. The horses which had pulled the engine had been returned to the entrance of the Square but even from where he clung he could see the frightened whites of their eyes. Ladders were being jockeyed into position but the smoke was billowing in great black swathes across the Square and it was as if he and Meg and Mrs Whitley sat above dense clouds, thick as blankets, scorching, suffocating, acrid and slowly taking the linings from their tortured lungs. He could hear the shattering of glass and in one terrifying moment the horizontal cornice which crowned the building blundered past them with a devastating crash and fell into the street and there was a hoarse cry from beneath them. The house was slowly falling apart, the fire eating away at it's supports and, tormented by fear and anxiety, Tom Fraser's young courage began to crumble for how was he to get an old woman deep in shock and near to death, he was convinced, and a young girl whose terror was so great she could do no more now than cling to him, and to the sparking window ledge, away from this danger to the safety of the next roof. The slates were wet now, the frost which had coated them melted away by the heat. It was steep and he was but one pair of hands, one pair of arms to bear two frail women across the horrifying slope.

'Tom! Tom ... for God's sake, man ... over here ... quick ... Tom, over here to your right! We've got a rope ... Tom! Damnation, Tom, turn your bloody head ...!'

The voice was sharp, forceful, confident and yet soft with the passionate certainty that was so familiar and both Meg and Tom turned their heads instinctively; turned their frozen, stunned minds towards the source of it. It was as if new life, vigorous and filled with the sureness that *now* all would be right brought them back from the depth of the black hell into which their fear had forced them. *Martin was here!* Martin had come, not to save them but to give them the strength to save themselves and of course they could do it! Of course they could!

'Chuck it over, Martin,' Tom said urgently, but steady now and unquestioning in his belief that though it would be difficult, well nigh impossible really, he and Martin and Meg could do it!

Mrs Whitley was the first to go, the rope securely about her waist, Tom holding one end, Martin the other, her eyes fixed trustingly, *aware* now, on Martin, creeping like some ancient old cat, her hands like claws scrabbling for purchase on the tiles and Martin's voice never stopped, hypnotising her into believing that she was perfectly able to do it until her old hand touched his own, young and strong and she was pulled to safety and borne away by the firemen who crouched at Martin's shoulder.

Meg was next, faster and more nimble than Mrs Whitley and Martin's surprising tears were wet on her cheek as he held her for a brief moment before she was passed in her turn to the waiting firemen. The crowd was quite amazed as they watched the two young men, high on the rooftop for all to see, cling together for a desperate second before the firemen pulled them urgently apart. This was no time to be embracing like a couple of schoolgirls, their manner seemed to say, not with the whole bloody lot about to go any minute!

Chapter thirteen

'You shall stay here, Megan, and Fraser as well for as long as you care to. Mrs Stewart assures me there is plenty of work in the kitchen and Fraser ... well ... I'm certain something can be found for you outside as soon as your hands are healed. Whatever you feel will suit your capabilities. Martin tells me you have no mechanical leaning so I assume you will not care to be involved with the motors ... no? ... then there is the garden or the stables and Ramsden is always in need of someone in the carpenter's shop ...'

The room was warm, the lamp lit and casting a cosy glow about the plain white walls of the room in which they all stood. It threw its flickering golden shadows over the patchwork quilt on the bed and reflected in the shine of beeswax on the chest of drawers against the wall. It turned the meticulously starched and ironed smoothness of the linen runner which was placed upon it to protect its surface to a delicate butter yellow. The curtains, fresh and also stiff with starch were drawn against the night and the fire spluttered pleasingly in the grate but there was an air of tension, an unease which rested strangely on the still figures of two of the company and cast deep shadows about their young faces. There were flowers in a bowl on the table along with the lamp, and a bible, and on the wall was an embroidered and framed text which beseeched the Good Lord to 'Bless this House'. A rag rug lay on the superbly polished linoleum and over all was a pleasant smell which spoke of carbolic and blacklead, duster and dust pan, a fastidious attention to the removal of dirt and yet the frivolity of the massed blooms in the bowl softened the sparseness with their fragrance.

'... so you see there is work for both of you should you want it. Mrs Whitley will have one of the estate cottages and will be properly cared for until she regains her strength and if you decide to take up my offer of employment you may visit her whenever

your duties allow it. She should have retired last year when ...
but that is another matter.'

The speaker smiled serenely at the old lady in the bed and she
nodded her head agreeably, willing it seemed to be placed anywhere that was warm and where she could have the 'three of 'em'
to come and see her.

'Of course if you would prefer to make your own arrangements,'
he continued, 'I will not stand in your way and would give you
a reference but I do feel you would be best served staying here
for a week or two before you begin to look around. Perhaps you
might want to work in town.' Robert Hemingway smiled genially.
'I know how young people are. They like to be where there is
some life, a bit of fun, eh? It is very quiet out here at Silverdale.
A long way to the bright lights of Liverpool and I know you are
both accustomed to working in the hustle and bustle that is there
but ... well ... you have both had a nasty shock. Fraser's hands
are quite badly burned and he will be unable to do much for a
while so you see ...'

'Did they find Emm?' The bald question grated painfully from
Meg's throat, cutting through Mr Hemingway's kind words and
he stopped speaking immediately, confused and obviously distressed. He was doing his best to smooth the grievous path these
two youngsters must tread and had not meant to speak of the fire
until they were both somewhat recovered from the blow of it. He
had hoped to occupy their stunned minds with the future, the
certainty that they were not to worry themselves with it for he
would look after them. If he reassured them on the subject of
employment which he knew to preoccupy most of the working
class today, or indeed any day, might they not perhaps feel happier
in their minds, sleep more easily in the warm and comfortable
beds he was having prepared for them. He had dearly hoped no
question would be asked, at least tonight, about the maid who
had unhappily perished in the blaze, but it had been and he must
answer it.

He cleared his throat, playing for time to find the right, the
most comforting words.

'Emm?' he said tentatively and his manner gave the impression
that he had not the slightest notion of who that might be. It was
not the right attitude to take with Megan Hughes. Not at that
precise moment. For the best part of the past two hours Meg could
not have said really what had gone on for she had retreated badly

157

into shock when she had been brought down from the roof, Emm's screams still lingering in her ears. She had followed directions given her by sympathetic young maids, allowing herself to be divested of her foul smelling, charred clothing, to be immersed, quite naked and in front of strangers in a bath in a *bathroom* which, had she been in her right mind would have filled her with wondering delight. She could barely recall having her wet hair towelled and brushed and a soothing salve laid on the burns she could not remember receiving, nor the tranquillising concoction made up by Mrs Glynn, the cook at Silverdale, consisting mainly of honey which had been poured down her scorched, unresisting throat. She had presumably been dressed again for she was wearing clothes she had never seen before but she had not regained her senseless mind until she had been led by the hand into this room and seen Mrs Whitley propped up in the snow white comfort of the bed. She was sipping a honey, glycerine and lemon potion prepared by the same Mrs Glynn, for her chest she explained, and what a blessing it had proved to be for she had felt better immediately, unaware that it contained a liberal dose of her master's best Scotch whiskey. Already she was beginning to doze, the dreadful experience fading into a merciful and alcoholic mist.

Meg stood menacingly beside her, protectively one might even say and Mr Hemingway was quite dismayed by the grim expression on her pretty young face. Her eyes were flat, lifeless and narrowed but in their depths was a tiny flame which seemed to grow fiercer with every moment.

'Yes, Emm,' she repeated. 'She works for you, Mr Hemingway and she works hard but I don't suppose you give a damn about that, do you? She was just another pair of hands used to keep your business running, to make *you* a profit. She is nothing but a skivvy, not quite "all there" as *he* used to say and not even worth the trouble of asking after. *Have* you asked after her, Mr Hemingway? Have you taken the trouble to concern yourself as to her whereabouts, because if you haven't, well I will . . . I'm . . . she's our friend . . . mine and Mrs Whitley's.' Her face began to quiver and her mouth stretched on her savage pain and anger and the tears welled to her eyes. '. . . she's a . . . she's been my friend for a long time . . .' Her agitation grew and in the bed Mrs Whitley tried to sit up and her own face began to work. She tried to lift her hand to Meg but the sight of it, bandaged from finger tips to elbow for they had all sustained burns in their climb to safety, appeared to confuse her, as though, for the moment she could not quite recall where she was or how she came to be here.

'Meg,' she quavered. Instantly Meg turned to her, kneeling at her side, her face a vivid and truculent scarlet and her arms reached out for the old woman.

'It's alright, Mrs Whitley. Don't be frightened. I'll not let him hurt you. I just want to find out where our Emm is and then we'll be off.' Her voice was quite demented and in truth it would not have taken more than a gentle push to send Meg Hughes over the line which divides hysteria from self-control.

'Off?'

'Yes, I'm not staying here with this . . . this . . .' She turned, squaring up to Robert Hemingway like a furious she-cat who will defend her young or die of it, and, about to place a soothing hand on the child's shoulder for surely she had lost her mind and who could blame her, the old gentleman stepped back hastily, afraid that her raking fingers might have his very eyes out.

'It was all your fault, you and that devil you put in charge of us,' she shouted. 'He ought to be . . . to be . . .' She could think of no fate bad enough for Benjamin Harris to suffer, '. . . and I hope he rots in hell. I only wish he'd been in the house. I'd have pushed him into the flames myself . . . oh Dear God . . .'

She began to weep inconsolably since, of course, as she had really known all along, she had begun to accept that Emm was *not* hiding somewhere, nor in another room being cossetted and if she was not *here*, with them, where else could she be but in the fire? She bent her head and laid her face against Mrs Whitley's shoulder and the old lady put up her bandaged hand to the still damp tangle of her hair, stroking it with infinite tenderness as Meg sobbed and Robert Hemingway was overwhelmed by the deep attachment which appeared to thrive between them.

He cleared his throat, looking round helplessly and from the shadows where the lamp light did not reach, two figures stepped forward hesitantly, both, it seemed as non-plussed as himself. He put out his hand appealingly to one of them and instantly Tom moved to Meg. He placed his hands on her shoulders and sensing a friend she allowed herself to be lifted to her feet. Turning her he tucked her into the curve of his arms and oblivious now to the others he stroked her hair and held her close, whispering her name until at last she began to calm. She looked up into his face, her own awash with her tears.

'Tell him, Tom,' she implored him. 'Tell him what he made us do. Go on . . .' but it seemed she could not contain herself, now that she knew that Emm was really gone. She could not wait for Tom to gather his thoughts for her own were alive and throbbing and longing to be released like a boil about to be lanced, needing to expel the evil and noxious matter which lay beneath.

'What did *you* get out of it, Mr Hemingway? A few extra quid a week? Was it worth it? Was it worth it to let that . . . that bastard . . .' She heard a gasp from the shadows in the corner where she sensed someone else stood but she was not deterred.

'. . . treat us so inhumanely, especially Mrs Whitley. She's given a lifetime of loyal service in one house and another, *and* in this company which *you* own. She was really too old to work and poorly and she couldn't pay the rent Harris demanded . . .'

'Rent . . .?' She heard Mr Hemingway draw in his breath sharply on the word but again her own emotions carried her on. She *had* to get this out or it would destroy her. 'She's got nothing now, not even the few bob she'd saved for her old age. *He* took it all . . . for coal . . . and then he took what *we* had, me an' Tom an' Emm.' Her face contorted and her voice was high and Robert Hemingway fell back, appalled by it all for never, in all his uneventful, protected life had he ever seen such pain and anger. '. . . and now Emm's dead . . . in the fire. *Economies!* That's what he said they were. Cruel . . . he was a cruel man . . . they were all afraid of him . . . afraid . . . long hours . . . low wages . . . poor food . . .' Her voice became a frantic mumble and they all strained to hear as Meg re-lived those dreadful months under Benjamin Harris' rule.

Robert Hemingway's old face was expressionless as he felt the guilt and anger enter his heart. The shame of what he had allowed . . . yes, allowed, to be done to this child was unbearable. He should have realised it, he saw that now. The strange unease the son of his old school friend had awakened in him should have been recognised. Even yet he did not know why he had put the man in charge of the house in Great George Square. Simply because he had been there when the news of Lloyd's death had come in, he supposed. Benjamin Harris was not good with people. He did not know how to deal with them for he considered anyone not born to his own station in life to have been put where they were in order to serve him! But he had begged for the chance, as he had done earlier in his career and weakly now, he realised,

160

Robert Hemingway had given in! If it had not been for a fluke – a chance error in the arrangements for an Automobile Trial in Caerphilly in Wales which Martin was to enter – they would not have been home at Silverdale at all and there was no doubt in his mind that the three people before him would have died in the fire because of it. He had seen the way Martin had rallied the other two youngsters, brought them from the terror-stricken trance they had been in. A mistake in the date, his own fault, and they had realised they would be too late for the trials so instead they had motored to Liverpool. A day or so with his Alice, he had thought fondly and a chance for Martin to go over the flyers' engine and then on to the 1,000 miles trial at the Eleanor Cross, Northampton.

They had barely had time to stretch their cramped muscles for they had driven for six hours non-stop that day on roads that were, in many cases not much better than cart-tracks when Ferguson had run, *run* from the house, delighted it seemed to be the bearer of the bad news, just come over the recently installed telephone that there was a fire – 'Bad, sir, very bad,' the butler had said with the vicarious pleasure of the onlooker, at Great George Square.

It was a miracle, Mrs Whitley had insisted as Alice Hemingway had comforted her. A miracle which had brought their Martin to them at that precise moment since, like Robert Hemingway she was of the opinion that only he could have fused the crumbling defences of the other two. 'Yes, yes, his friends from birth, almost,' she rattled, still herself in a bad state of shock, Mrs Glynn's potion not yet having taken effect. It was he who had instilled into them the stalwart resolution which had saved them, she babbled. Without him they would have perished, she insisted, coughing up her old lungs to danger point. Tom had been courageous as a lion, she said, clinging to Alice Hemingway's soothing hands, but thank the Good Lord for sending them their Martin. Only He up in Heaven knew how close they had been . . . she could hardly bear to think of it. But the potion took hold then and she relaxed against the pillows kind Mrs Hemingway plumped up with her own lady's hands!

'. . . and he treated Tom like a dog . . .!'

'Hush, Meggie, it doesn't matter now.' Tom tried to soothe Meg, tried to lead her away from the memories which would not rest but she was fixed on the dreadful route which had led, inexorably, she knew that now, to that last foul scene, the air thick with Benjamin Harris' lust, and she could not be stopped. Her eyes had gone strangely out of focus and her voice had sunk to a whisper and they all leaned forward, straining to hear what she said.

'. . . like a dog . . . a dog . . . and I was to be . . .'

Suddenly, as though in realisation of what she had been about to disclose she shuddered so violently it shook her from head to foot. She stepped back from Tom's restraining hands and put up her own to her face, scrubbing at it, then pushed them through her hair distractedly.

'He was bad . . .' she muttered, 'bad.'

Robert Hemingway put out his hand, his own horror gripping him fiercely for though he was unworldly, an old fashioned and courtly gentleman, he sensed there was something more to what this young girl wept over. Certainly her mind had suffered a tremendous shock and her body was in pain, burned about the hands. She grieved for her friend and was outraged by what Harris and through Harris, what she imagined he himself had done to her, to all the servants, but there was something she was holding back and he meant to get to the bottom of it.

He turned swiftly, agile as a man half his age and with the certainty of someone who is used to being obeyed, spoke crisply to the two young men.

'Martin.'

'Yes sir.'

'Take Fraser over to the stable block and get him settled in with you. Tell one of the footmen to help with a truckle bed . . . Fraser is unable at the moment. Then see that he is comfortable.' He turned to Tom.

'Fraser.'

'Yes sir.'

'I think it best that we postpone this talk until tomorrow. I am going to put Megan in here with Mrs Whitley. They will be company for one another. You understand?'

'Yes sir, thank you.' Tom looked relieved. Meg and Cook would do better together in this big, unfamiliar place if they were allowed to share a room. He was afraid Meg might have nightmares but with Mrs Whitley to watch over her and with Meg having the task of looking after Cook, they would be a comfort for one another.

'When you have all had a good night's rest we will talk again.

162

Perhaps in a day or two.' Robert Hemingway smiled kindly and Tom felt himself drawn to him. He could scarcely credit that they had believed that this genial, gentle old gentleman could be the ogre Harris had made him out to be. They should have known really. The bad times had started *with* Benjamin Harris. Before that, though they had worked hard they had been fairly treated, decently fed and clothed and their wages had been no less than the average domestic servant was paid. It had been *him* who had done it, that . . . that devil, but Tom was no longer concerned for had not Mr Hemingway told them they were to be given work here. His family was to be provided for at last. He turned to direct a last reassuring smile at their Meggie but her head was bowed and her riotous hair hung over her face and she did not see him go.

The door had closed behind them when Robert Hemingway turned again to Meg. 'Now then, my dear.' He spoke softly, deceptively mild as though what she said made no difference one way or the other. 'Would you like to tell me the rest. They are gone now and there is no-one to hear but myself and Mrs Whitley.'

There were two police constables standing before the blackened ruin of what had once been the Hemingway Shipping Line emigrant house in Great George Square and as the cab turned the corner from Upper Pitt Street Benjamin Harris' face fell slackly into grey-white folds, and it was possible to imagine how he would look when he was dead. His mouth opened in consternation and though the cabbie had jumped down from his box and opened the door, his own face bewildered, Harris sat for several moments, frozen to the leather seat.

The two constables moved forward as he stepped on to the soot-stained pavement, but neither spoke. Their very silence had an air of menace about it and Harris felt a slight sense of unease at their presence.

He looked up at the sky where once the high roof had been and then to the houses on either side, damaged and empty for they were considered unsafe, but still standing and his face was quite dazed.

'That'll be a shilling, sir.' The cab driver held out his hand, plucking at Harris' sleeve for the gentleman looked quite mazed and could you wonder? 'Great George Square,' he had said in that disdainful way the gentry have at times, when he had climbed

163

into the cab at Lime Street Railway station and now it appeared that his destination, this house, had been burned to the ground in his absence.

He climbed back on to his box wondering what the 'scuffers' were after, hesitating a moment or two for there was nothing an inhabitant of Liverpool liked better then a bit of scandal but the constable lifted his hand and indicated quite rudely that he was to move on.

When he had gone they both turned to Benjamin Harris, one on either side of him somehow, as he gazed in stupefaction at the space where the house had been.

'Excuse me sir,' the first constable said politely. 'Could I have your name, if you please?'

'What?' Benjamin Harris looked at him, his shock turning now to outrage for the two constables appeared to be almost *jostling* him and Benjamin Harris had not been jostled since last he had been in a schoolboy tussle with his own brothers.

'Your name, sir, if you don't mind.'

'My name! What the devil has that to do with you.' He was clearly displeased, then he turned again to stare at the pile of rubble which was all that was left of the house, his displeasure swamped by his curiosity. 'What on earth happened here,' he said, his silver grey eyes wide and staring.

'There has been a fire, sir.'

'I can see that, you fool, but how did it happen?'

'Now then, sir, there is no need to be rude. You asked me what happened and I told you. Now, if you will give me your name we can all go about our rightful business.' Though he spoke in the adenoidal tone of those born in Liverpool, there was still a trace of County Limerick in his lilting voice. The constable, Constable O'Shea who had known them all at Great George Square and was perfectly well aware of who this splendid gentleman was, though of course *he* did not recognise the likes of a common policeman, kept a perfectly straight face despite the fact that he did not care to be called a fool.

'Rightful business! Do you know who I am?'

'That is what we are trying to find out, sir.'

'I am Benjamin Harris and I am in charge . . . I was in charge of this house!'

'Thank you, sir, then I'd be obliged if you'd come along with me and Constable Jackson here. They want a word with you at the station, sir, if you'd be so kind.'

'At the station!'

'Aye sir.'

'What the devil for?'

'Aah well, that I wouldn't be knowing, sir. I've just been sent along to escort you, like. Me an' Constable Jackson.'

'The devil you have! Well, you can just escort one another back again. If anyone in the police force, no matter what rank wishes to see me he can call on me at my club. Here, I'll give you a card. Now, if one of you can run to the end of the square and whistle me up a cab I'll be on my way.'

'Aah . . . no sir. I think not.'

Benjamin Harris' face had become a dangerous shade of coppery yellow with high and ugly spots of vermilion on each cheekbone and his eyes narrowed to slits of pure, acid rage. He straightened ominously giving Constable O'Shea the full benefit of his savage, scarcely controlled fury but the policeman had come to grips with wills more obdurate than that of Benjamin Harris. Liverpool Saturday night where Scot clashed with Irish and both with those of Welsh ancestry, settling old racial scores, had taught him how to deal with the most recalcitrant and he was quite unmoved.

'Goddammit to hell!' Harris' voice was no less than a full-throated snarl. 'Do you seriously believe I had anything to do with this?' He swept his arm in a furious circle in the direction of the burnt-out house. 'I was away with . . . with a friend and can account for every moment of my time. Good God, constable, do I look like a man who sets fires?' He was almost beside himself in his venom and Constable Jackson put out a restraining hand for it seemed to him that the gentleman was about to strike Constable O'Shea. Instantly Harris turned, knocking it away, his face so livid, his white-lipped anger so intense, the two constables leaped together to hold him, one on each of his arms, in an iron lock from which he could make no further threatening move. No-one impeded the law in the carrying out of its duties, not when Constable O'Shea and Constable Jackson were in charge. They were quite sorry when the apprehended man ceased to struggle for it would have given them both an inordinate amount of pleasure to put the handcuffs on him!

Chapter fourteen

Tom was made up with it, he said constantly. He had never
worked in the open before unless you could count lugging buckets
of coal from the back yard to the kitchen or the tramp he and
Martin had taken with the emigrants to the dockside. He liked
the simple and unhurried pace of the work in the gardens, geared
as it was to the slow change of the seasons. Silverdale was set in
a splendid twenty or so acres of parkland bordered by a stand of
trees. It ran down to the River Mersey in a series of terraces,
lawns and ornamental gardens laced with shaded gravel paths,
and a stream divided it, clear and slow moving over smooth stones.
A stout wooden bridge crossed the running water and further
down were stepping stones, slippery with moss.

There was a small lake, a summer house, vegetable gardens at
the rear and glasshouses in which grew summer fruits all the year
round. All this had to be meticulously nurtured under the guidance
of the head gardener, a silent and dour man named Atkinson but
he and Tom formed a laconic yet equable relationship, sparing
of words and based mainly on Tom's willingness to do any job,
mucky or not, that was put to him. He worked about the stable
yard in the evenings – trying his hand at everything, he said –
and even laboured on the home farm during the sowing. He
discovered quite amazingly that he liked animals, never having
had anything to do with them before, and could spend an hour
leaning on the gate of the pig pen watching the patient sow with
her young ones, or lending a hand in the grooming of the fine
carriage horses, but most of all Tom liked the earth and all that
grew in it!

'But you're still doing all the odd jobs nobody else wants, just
like me,' Meg wailed, 'and where's that going to lead you?'

'Does it have to lead anywhere?' Tom asked mildly enough but
Meg only pulled a face as though in despair at his lack of ambition.
She didn't like it at Silverdale, she said, just as often as Tom voiced
his delight in it, but Mrs Whitley was settled at last, her cough

was better and she was in seventh heaven in her small cottage, her only sadness the fate of poor Emm.

'She'd have loved this,' she remarked every time Meg had half an hour to call on her which was not as often as the old lady would have liked. But Meg was done no favours under Mrs Stewart's charge even if she was considered, like Martin, to be something of a favourite of the old gentleman. All through that spring and summer she worked hard from six-thirty in the morning when she brushed up the kitchen range, lit the fire and cleared away the ashes before she was allowed to put on the kettle for that first cup of welcome tea, until after the family had dined at eight in the evening when she was then free until bedtime. She scrubbed floors and scoured tables and cleaned pots and pans and endless dishes and cutlery and windows. She helped anyone who needed a hand, taking orders from those she considered beneath her in the hierarchy of the servants' hall, maid of all work with no particular duties but to be where she was most needed in the kitchen. The house above stairs was an enigma to her. She rarely saw Tom, for Mrs Stewart allowed no fraternising between her girls and the men outside, and it was only when they could slip away at the same time to Mrs Whitley's cottage they managed to meet.

Martin might have been a member of the family, or some privileged friend of Mr Hemingway for all they saw of *him*, away most of the time, or so it seemed, on inexplicable journeys concerned with the world of motoring, and when he did return he and the old gentleman spent all their time shut up in the vast garages and workshops Mr Hemingway had devised from the stables. Tinkering, he said vaguely when he was asked, and sharp with her when she was persistent, telling her it was part of his job and to get on with *hers!* She complained bitterly to Tom whenever she got the chance.

'I'm just a skivvy, Tom, at everyone's beck and call and neither you nor Martin seem to care! Even the damn scullery maid orders me about. I've no-one to talk to now, with you outside, Martin off God knows where all the time and Mrs Whitley out here.'

She badly missed the family atmosphere which had prevailed in Great George Square, the sense of belonging to one close unit, each part of that unit helping another and the impersonal regimentation of the Silverdale kitchens irked her. She missed the freedom she now realised she had been allowed, when Mr Lloyd had been in charge of them, the camaraderie of Tom and Martin and she resented the loss of the feeling of self-worth Mrs Whitley had unconsciously given her. She had been an important member in the running of the emigrant house, even at fifteen. She had made decisions, particularly when Mrs Whitley had been poorly. She had done most of the cooking, trying her hand at and being amazingly successful with Cook's quite epicurean dishes and now she had been demoted to being *less* than the scullery maid!

They were sitting round the plain deal table which had come from the Silverdale attics along with all the other bits and pieces which furnished Mrs Whitley's new home. A cheerful fire blazed in the grate of the tiny kitchen-cum-parlour (despite the warmth of the day for Cook delighted in her freedom to use as much coal as she cared to) and on it was one of her lamb stews and a kettle whispering steam, and in the small oven beside it was bread baking and an apple turnover and all for her three, whichever one of them could get over to see her. She missed them sorely, she said, and Emm too, tears coming to her eyes, but there, she was lucky to have this little place and Mr and Mrs Hemingway were saints, saints, that's all she could call them! She had a cosy kitchen all of her own, a snug bedroom above it with mullioned windows looking out on a bit of garden and them lovely trees but she did wish ... Here she would sigh, content enough, well fed, warm and cared for but it would have been perfect if only Emm ...!

'I'm worth more than this, Cook, and you know it.' Meg turned passionately to Mrs Whitley who nodded in agreement, her sad reflection on the death of poor Emm pushed to the back of her mind for the moment.

'D'you know what she had me doing this morning, do you?' Meg's face was crimson in her indignation.

'No lass, what?'

'Scrubbing out the dairy if you please whilst that fat lump they call the dairy maid scoured the milk pails! *Me*, scrubbing dairy floors when I could cook a meal for a hundred people *and* better than that there Mrs Glynn! D'you know what she does, Mrs Whitley? She tastes the soup with a spoon then puts the spoon back in the pan! Can you imagine it and when she does braised leg of mutton she doesn't put any parsley in it like we do and she doesn't use the juices to glaze it neither! She throws them away! You never saw such waste in your life and when I asked her if I

168

could just show her what we do, she told me to mind my own business and get back to the mop-bucket!'

Privately Mrs Whitley sympathised with the cook in the Silverdale kitchens for she herself would have said the same to any maid who had tried to tell *her* what to do in her own kitchen, but she said nothing for she knew Meg was fretting badly in those first months for the old happy days, for Tom and Martin, and for herself and Emm. She'd settle soon. She'd have to, but best not agitate her further by telling her she *was* in the wrong.

'She's reckoned to be the best cook in these parts,' Meg continued, 'or so she'd have you believe but she's not a patch on you, nor me either for that matter,' with the supreme confidence of youth! 'And that Mrs Stewart! I was only crossing the yard to see if I could catch Tom to tell him I was coming up here this afternoon or to ask one of the stable lads to give him a message when she screams from the kitchen door . . .'

'Oh give over, our Meg! She wasn't screaming. She only called your name and asked you . . .'

Meg turned sharply to Tom who was just about to take a bite from a thick wedge of the hot apple turnover, and her eyes narrowed ominously. Her expression was truculent for she was in the mood for an argument with him, with *anybody*. What she needed was to pour out her grievances, her sad remembrance of the past, of Emm, of her own inability to settle in this strange place, her unrest and dissatisfaction with the work she was doing. What did she want to do, she wondered? She did not really know, but Tom's interference in her need to exorcise it in Mrs Whitley's sympathetic ear and his defence of the despised housekeeper made her even more wild.

'She screamed, Tom Fraser, she said coldly, 'and asked what I thought I was doing giggling in the yard with a stable lad! *Me*, giggling with a stable lad indeed when all I was doing was asking him where you were and the poor beggar got what for from Andrew just for stopping when I called him . . .'

'Well you know the rules, Meggie. We're not allowed to hobnob with the maids during working hours . . .'

'Bloody hell, there's a difference . . .'

'Megan! Your language if you please.'

'Sorry, Mrs Whitley, but there's a difference between passing on a simple message and "hob-nobbing" as Tom calls it. Are we to walk about with our mouths shut all the time?'

169

'You can talk to each other, just like we can.'

Meg, unused to the company of other girls, as young and younger than herself and unable to understand the need in a big household for the keeping of strict discipline, snorted derisively. She had held, in her own opinion a position of some authority and trust at Great George Square and could see no necessity for the strict watch kept on the maids and menservants at Silverdale. Besides which she was accustomed to the far more interesting conversation of young men like Tom and Martin and the adult guidance and affection of Mrs Whitley. Even Emm had been better than this lot! At least she had *listened* which was more than could be said for her present working companions. Giggle and whisper was all they seemed to do in her scornful view and though she liked a good laugh herself there was no-one with the same sense of fun she had shared with Tom and Martin and not one of them could have done what *she* had done at the emigrant house!

'You'll soon get used to it, Meggie, you see. We've been lucky falling on our feet like this.' Mrs Whitley's voice was soothing. She worried about these two at times for she knew they still grieved badly for Emm and it was hard to convince Tom that the fire had *not* been his fault. She had watched Meg, and Martin, try to persuade him that it had been an accident. No-one would ever know how it really started. Emm, distracted by God alone knew what, must have gone into one of the bedrooms, still carrying the fatal shovel of coals for her charred body had been found next to a bedroom window on the first floor, just above the stairs, the stairs beneath which the lamp oil had been put, and forgotten! Tom had been distraught but Meg, herself carrying a burden of guilt at having been the one to suggest that Emm should carry the coals, something they had often done in the past, had shared his sorrow with him, and their young minds had finally been able to accept it.

She put out a hand to Meg but the girl stood up abruptly, moving away to look out of the small window. The trees were beginning to show a haze of gold and bronze and copper and at the foot of each trunk wild fuschia grew profusely, their bright red bells delicately nodding in the sun and the slight breeze which moved them. Across the drive and near the entrance gates to the estate the lodge-keeper's wife came from her small house, a child clinging to her skirts and she turned to lift him into her arms, giving him a resounding kiss before sending him into the garden at the back. An untidy terrier amiably allowed himself to be dragged with the child and Meg could see the two of them rolling happily together in the carpet of harebells which covered it.

'Have a bit of turnover, lovey, before Tom eats it up. See, I walked down to the home farm this morning and begged a bit of cream from the farmer's wife. Well, I made her a fruit cake, she says she's no good with anything fancy and her Jack does love fruit cake so it was a fair exchange. Will I pour a bit on for you?'

Meg turned and looked at the kindly old woman who was doing her best to console her. Mrs Whitley's face had filled out in the seven or eight months they had been here and was rosy now in her improved health. Her cough had gone and she had put on weight. It seemed she was not averse to a 'walk' to the farm and had apparently become friendly with those about her and her days were pleasantly filled, calm, untroubled as was her due. It was time she retired. Mr Lloyd, poor chap, had said so – not to Mrs Whitley, mind – a dozen times and now her last days would be comfortable. She, Meg had no right to be snivelling like some spoiled child when Mrs Whitley, Martin, *and* Tom had fallen so happily into the order of their new lives and if she could just be given some *specific* job to do, like the housemaids for instance, or a parlourmaid, with a decent uniform to wear instead of the skivvy's outfit she was forced into she might settle to it. If she could take some pride in *her own* job with a *proper* place in the household instead of being at everyone's beck and call she'd feel better, she was sure. It was not that she was afraid of hard work. God, nobody had worked harder from the age of six or seven than she had, and she took great pride in her own conscientious industry but it was galling to have to watch servants doing work she could do far better and in half the time.

'Don't fret, lass.' Mrs Whitley's face was anxious for she hated to see one of her three down in the dumps. 'Give it a bit longer and you'll settle in. You know there's only one way to get on in a big house like this and that's to do your work, willingly, and keep on the right side of those above you. You'll make your mark, lass, and be out of that kitchen before you realise it! I know what I'm talking about, Meg. I worked just like you, running here and there after everyone . . .'

'But I can do so much *more* than skivvying, Mrs Whitley.' Meg's face was mutinous.

'I know that, but you'll get nowhere if you're . . . sullen.'

'*Sullen!* I'm not sullen!'

'You want to look in the mirror, our Meg.' Tom stood up and reached for his cap. 'You've got a face on you like the back of a tramp steamer.' He was impatient to be off to the more important concerns of the stable where one of Mr Robert's beautiful mares was about to foal, an event he had never yet witnessed and which he had been told was little short of a miracle and not to be missed. He grew tired of Meg's discontent at times and could hardly understand it in view of the wonder of their new lives. Why, he couldn't have found a better place for himself if he had been given the choice, and he had never been happier and he knew Martin felt the same. Now if Meg would just knuckle down to a bit of discipline and watch her tongue she would soon be in the good graces of both Mrs Stewart, who was not a bad old stick, *and* Mrs Glynn who was old, nearly as old as Mrs Whitley and ready for retirement! Get on their good side and their Meg could be in line to take her place.

'I have not, have I, Mrs Whitley?' Meg was incensed.

'You don't look contented, Meg and that's a fact and if you get on the wrong side of that Mrs Stewart you'll spend the rest of your days on your knees in the scullery. Smile lovey! You've got a lovely smile and say "Yes please" and "No, thank you" and bob a curtsey and before long you'll be made up to parlour maid . . .'

'I've a good mind to have a word with the old gentleman!'

Tom whirled, his hand on the latch of the door which he had been just about to open. His preoccupied expression was quite suddenly wiped away and his face was stern and his smiling mouth had tightened into a remorseless line. Not much of a one for anger, unless goaded, when it erupted from him it was all the more challenging. He took a step towards her as she stood with her back to the window, ready to give her a sharp piece of his mind, for had not the old gentleman already done more than enough for them? As he moved in her direction the sunshine touched her hair, shining through the tumbled curls, outlining her head in a halo of burnished gold. Her face was in shadow but her eyes glowed a pale amber and Tom felt something start to move inside him, as if his heart had come loose and for an alarming moment he could not speak, only stare wordlessly at this beautiful girl he had known all his life. Her face was defiant, her lips clamped wilfully across her white teeth, her eyebrows dipped in a furious frown as she waited impatiently for what he had to say but

172

suddenly he could not speak and for the life of him he did not know why!

'Well,' she said, hazardously, 'what have you got to say, then? You mean to give me a piece of your mind, I can see it in your face so let's have it.'

'No . . . no . . . it's . . .' Tom put a hand to his own bright curls, pushing his fingers through them and Meg stared at him curiously.

'Well, Tom Fraser?'

'Don't do it, Meg.' At last he could get his tongue round the words though his heart was still thumping in his chest. 'If you speak to the old man he'll think we're ungrateful.' He was finding it easier now and he had time to wonder at his own foolishness. 'Give it another month or two. Do as Mrs Whitley says and make yourself pleasant to those above you. It'll work out, gospel, our kid.' His face lost its look of sternness, the inherent gentleness of his nature unable to withstand her misery. 'You'll find your place, just like I have, and Martin. Come on, our Meg, give us a smile and next week, if we can get an afternoon off together I'll take you into Liverpool to see Madame Tussaud's. You know you've been wanting to go. What d'you say?'

He grinned engagingly and was rewarded by a lessening of the fierce scowl on Meg's face. Her lips curved reluctantly into a faint smile and her eyes lost the hard look of amber and became a soft shade of honey. The stiffness in her posture drained away and she let out her breath on a sigh. Moving away from the window she sat down opposite Mrs Whitley, her knees to the fire. She turned again to look at Tom, then answered his grin with her own.

'Oh go on then, don't stand there scowin'. Go and get back to this work you love so much,' but it was said good-naturedly. She became serious again and her face assumed a look of youthful maturity. 'I suppose you're right and I suppose I've got to try my best to get used to it. What else can I do but work so damned hard they'll not be able to get along without me and before you know it I'll have Mrs Stewart's job from her *and* before you say a word I could do it an' all. Now go on, you daft lump. Go and do whatever it is that's so important. I'll have another half an hour with Cook. I'm not due back yet and they're not getting me in that kitchen a minute before my time's up!'

It was a longer route than by the driveway which led from the gates up to the house but Meg felt the need to be completely alone for a few minutes more and so she crossed the gravelled stretch in front of Mrs Whitley's cottage and entered the closely standing trees of the spinney opposite. A straight, wide path divided the wood, thick and crisp with the early leaves from the autumn falling and it was quiet, still as the pale blue sky above her head. A blackbird sang somewhere and her skirt brushed against the dry and crackling stalks of bracken which lined the path but these were the only sounds to be heard and she felt the peace of it slip smoothly into her heart. Tom was right and so was Mrs Whitley, and she should be thankful that they were all settled so safely. The house in which she had lived for six years of her life was only a shell now and there was nothing there but the ghost of poor Emm who had died in it. You should not keep looking back to what had been, regretting its passing but must make the most of what had been given in its place and look to what the future would hold. Tom was happy here but then Tom would be happy anywhere as long as he was surrounded by people he liked and who liked him. He was popular with the maids, smiling his cheeky smile and promising God knows what with those blue eyes of his and even the manservants trusted him for it was in his nature to be reliable, good humoured and hardworking. She knew she herself was restless and irritable, still haunted by the fire and what had gone before it but that would pass with time and she would find whatever it was she searched for and be at peace with all those around her.

She had seen nothing of the old gentleman except for an infrequent glimpse of him in the stable yard which was in clear view of the back kitchen window. He and Martin would be deep in absorbed conversation, their expressions rapt, their manner serious as they studied, or poked and prodded whatever it was beneath the bonnets of the various motor cars which were grouped there. It seemed that now he had fulfilled his obligation in the placing of herself, Tom and Mrs Whitley in sheltered and decent employment he need no longer concern himself with them and there was nothing more, surely, he could do? He had been kind on the night of the fire, sensitive to her bruised, *violated* emotions and she would never forget it. At one point in the evening, when Tom and Martin had gone and she and Mrs Whitley had been left alone with him she had found herself, surprisingly, held in his arms as she wept. He had comforted her most understandingly and several times during that night of troubled sleep she had been aware of a gentle hand on her feverish brow and a quiet word soothing her back to rest.

Several days later she had gone to his study, alone, and for an hour they had talked and she had finally understood, and believed him when he explained to her, that the misery they had suffered under Benjamin Harris had been done to them without his knowledge. He had even apologised to her, just as though she was of his own class and not merely a servant in his home, and told her seriously that she was to come to him at any time if she should have a problem.

She had had none, not really, beyond her strange inability to settle down and make a home in this beautiful house. She shared a room under the eaves with Lizzie, another kitchen-maid, but then she was used to that for had not she and Emm shared not only a room but a *bed* for six years. Here she had her own, small, scrupulously clean and warm, and the bedroom, though sparsely furnished, was comfortable. Lizzie, inclined to chatter endlessly, was willing to be friendly and there was always as much good, often what Mrs Whitley would have called *fancy* food as she could eat on the table.

She took a deep breath of sharp country air, glancing about her appreciatively as she sauntered along the path which would bring her out at the back of the house. It really was a pretty day. Harebells dominated her senses with their superb purple colour and scabious and bramble bushes, heavy with fruit. She picked a fat blackberry and popped it in her mouth savouring its ripe, sun-filled taste. She would come this way on her next visit and fill a basket for Mrs Whitley and they would have a pie, straight from the oven, hot and with the thick cream which came from the home farm. She smiled.

Chestnut trees rested shoulder to shoulder with aspen and the broad oak which had stood when Liverpool had been granted its charter by King John.

She blinked and shied nervously for he startled her badly as he stepped out from behind a thick trunk and the sun shining through the leaves silhouetted him against the green of a holly bush and he looked like a cloaked spirit which had risen from the ground it stands on. She became quite still, unmoving, when she saw who it was, like a young animal which senses a trap and she was deathly afraid. Though there were a dozen men labouring within

175

earshot she felt the pulse beat painfully in her throat and her terror grew.

'Well Megan,' he said softly, 'here we are at last, you and I, though our respective positions in life are somewhat altered, wouldn't you say? You are well, I trust?'

'What d'you want?' She almost called him 'sir', the habit of six years in service hard to break. Her voice was icy and though she feared him dreadfully, it was steady.

'Now Megan! Is that the way to speak to an old ... friend?' His smile was lazy but as Benjamin Harris ran his speculative eyes about the maturing roundness of her body, his expression was thick with venom.

Her breath was rapid in her throat but she managed a defiant answer.

'We're not friends and never ... never will be!' The memory of their last encounter was vivid in her mind and she felt a violent need to vomit as her stomach churned but she gathered herself to control it. The words he had spoken to her then, obscene and filthy, rang still in her ears and she wanted to run, to lift up her skirts and take to her heels and leap along the path which led to the house and safety but he stood in her way. She glanced behind her, weighing her chances of darting back the way she had come but he put up a hand. Though he did not touch her it was as though he had her fast in its grip.

'I shouldn't if I were you, Megan. That way only leads to the old woman and she cannot defend you.'

She could feel the crazed beating of her heart in her breast and it seemed to her it would bang its way up into her throat and choke her. She could feel the fast, erratic lift of the material of her blouse as it tried to tear its way out through her chest and she could quite definitely feel the urging of her bladder to let go its contents as he took a step towards her.

He smiled and shook his head almost playfully. She could not speak. She could not have screamed had she been given the chance for her mouth was as dry as the shrivelling autumn leaves beneath her feet.

'So, you have settled in here, have you, my dear, you and that idiot kitchen boy, and the old woman too. Oh yes, I have seen her in her cottage parlour, nursing her black cat before her fire like a witch! You should tell her to draw her curtains at night,

176

Megan, and lock her door for who knows who could be lurking about in these woods.' He laughed softly.

She made a tiny sound in her throat and her pale creamy skin took on a tinge of yellow. Her eyes were wide and unblinking and only her hands moved as they plucked at her skirt.

'Yes, very comfortable, all of you, here at Silverdale with old man Hemingway to look after you.' He seemed to swell with some emotion she could not recognise and though he appeared to be even thinner than the last time she had seen him, his face became bloated and suffused with a dangerously violent colour. 'Oh yes, Robert Hemingway takes care of those to whom he feels a sense of responsibility, be it friendly or hostile.' His lips bared across his teeth. 'He is quite a clever man, you know. Unfortunately I discovered that fact when it was too late, but enough of that, my dear. Tell me how you have fared since we last met. Are you kitchenmaid, or perhaps you have attained the exalted position of under-parlourmaid by now? I am sure you are destined for great things, a pretty and dedicated girl like yourself and strangely, you owe it all to me, Megan. Did you know that?' His teeth glinted again between his lips.

She found her voice at last. It sounded piteously faint in the straining rictus of her mouth but she got it out somehow.

'I don't owe you anything.'

'Come Megan, surely . . .'

'I owe you nothing and if you don't get out of my way I'll . . .'

'Oh but you do, you see. You owe me my job, my career, my position, my good name, even my very character.'

'Your . . .?'

'Do you know where I have been for the past six months, Megan?' He seemed to grow taller and thinner as he loomed menacingly over her and she shrank away from him. 'Do you, Megan, do you?'

She stared at him, a rabbit hypnotised, paralysed by the stoat.

'Answer me, dammit,' and she jumped and tears came to her eyes for she was but a young and terrified girl.

'No!'

It seemed to satisfy him and he smiled and into his eyes came a strange expression in which was mixed hatred, a deep and terrible malevolence and yet a kind of pleasure as if at some private memory.

'Well I will tell you. I will tell you where I have been and what

177

has been done to me then I will tell you what is to happen to you. Are you listening?'

She nodded and the tears slipped helplessly down her cheeks.

'I have been in prison, Megan. You did not know that, did you? Yes, I have been in Walton Gaol at the pleasure of His Majesty. Six months they gave me.' His voice was bizarre, a chant of rhythmic plaining which gave him the appearance of a child repeating some lesson it has learned and repeats by rote, spoken again and again until it is word perfect, with no perception of its meaning and yet Benjamin Harris knew exactly what he was speaking of and what it had done to him. Singular he had been before but now he was deranged without the power to reason. It seemed to imply, as he *meant* it to imply that he was no longer in control of his own actions and therefore could not be blamed for them for had they not been forced upon him by a great wrong. A great wrong done him by . . . by . . . by . . .!

'I was arrested on the day I returned to Liverpool, Megan. The charge was fraud. Can you believe it? The pennies and halfpennies and farthings I had availed myself of, the few guineas I saved were made into a trumped-up charge of fraud. He came to see me in my cell.' His face became quite mad then and his eyes flickered strangely in their sockets and a fleck of white frothed at the corner of his lips. 'Have you ever seen the inside of a prison cell, Megan? No? Well, it is not a place I would care to remain in for long. Six months . . . mixing with the foul dregs of the gutters of Liverpool . . . Dear God . . . I thought I should not survive . . . but I digress . . .' His face was sweating and his pallor was quite dreadful now. 'Yes . . . but Robert Hemingway came to call whilst I lay on my pallet in the cell I shared with three others. They were cleared out naturally, whilst the great man and I discussed what should be done with me. It seemed, you see, I had deeply offended him by attempting the violation . . . yes, that was the word he used . . . the violation of an innocent child.' He turned to bare his teeth at her again. 'Yourself Megan, none other, but as he did not wish *you* to be troubled further he was going to see that I was put away on some charge. He knew the judge, of course. They all help one another, those of the same class and he is a well-known, respected gentleman in Liverpool, is he not? But despite this they could not give me more than six months though Hemingway intimated that he would like me put away for good. Six months, six months of hard labour, Megan, but whilst I was there I met one or two quite interesting characters. I made it my business to become friends with them, knowing that one day they could be of use to me. And that day will come, Megan, because make no mistake, I mean to have compensation. Indeed I do.'

He smiled as though they were discussing no more than the state of the weather. 'And it will serve no purpose to tell your friends of this meeting, nor Robert Hemingway, he continued in silken tones, 'since they will never find me. I am a member of the criminal fraternity now, and they take care of their own. I can vanish just as quietly as I appeared today whereas you, and they, are easily found. You may not see me for weeks, Megan my dear, or even months but hear this and mark it for the truth, *you will see me again.* You have offended me, dear girl, most grievously, by informing on me and those who offend Benjamin Harris do so at great risk to themselves.' He grinned wolfishly, 'So keep looking over your shoulder, my dear for if you should be careless who knows what might happen and one day I *will* be there, believe me! No-one crosses me, Megan, no-one! You will learn that, by God you will, and that boot boy, too!'

Megan stood before him, her beauty illuminated by the sunlight. Tawny hair, golden glinted eyes, her skin as fine and flawless as bone china. Her lips were as pale as her skin, completely bloodless and on her young face was the lifeless expression of one who is to be put to the torture. So she had not escaped him after all. The *pleasure* he had told her was in store for her was to be hers just as he had described it. She was to be . . . whatever he *wanted* her to be. Not yet, he said. Not here but it would come when he was ready. When he had played with her for as long as it gave him satisfaction, then he would . . . he would . . .

Suddenly, as he smiled his quite deranged smile she felt something rise within her, up and up until it exploded and she raised her clenched fists, her mouth snarling in its rage. She sprang away from him to stand like a warrior queen, determined to defend herself, or die. Her heart was still bounding in her breast, bursting to break out of the flesh and bone and muscle which held it, but in the centre of her demented terror, her horrified revulsion, the core of outrage which would not let her submit patiently to his demands grew and grew until it swamped all other feelings, even those which warned her to step lightly with this madman who could destroy not only her, but Tom and Mrs Whitley too. He was an object of loathing and if he put a finger on her she would

179

kill him. She was strong and his confinement in prison had obviously weakened him. She had only to reach for a branch, an old piece of wood and he would retreat from her rage like the vicious bully he was. Before she let him touch her she would swing for him. By God, she would.

'You lay a finger on me and I'll kill you,' she hissed.

His lips stretched in his thin smile, then suddenly he began to laugh quite merrily and he even went as far as to slap his leg as though he had never heard such a good joke for years. He stamped his foot and almost did a jig, so great was his mirth.

'Oh dear ... oh dear, dear ... oh Megan, you surely did not think I ... my word, you really thought I meant to avail myself of your splendid body, did you not? You believed that I am to ... carry out the arrangement I had in mind for us at Great George Square!' His expression changed so rapidly she took a step backwards in horror. The laughter vanished and a vicious snarl took its place and his voice grated like two rusted nails rubbing together. 'By God, girl, did you think it was to be so easy, did you? I don't want your flesh, not now. I lost my taste for ... for it when I was incarcerated with hundreds of men for six months. No, you can rest easy on that score, Megan. Your virginity, if you still have it, is quite safe. It is not that I no longer admire your quite obvious charms, Megan, but they are of no further interest to me. It is your ... your future that concerns me and the enjoyment of being able to ... control it, so to speak. The thought of it gave me courage and the strength to bear what I had to, in prison, Megan and I wish to savour the anticipation for as long as it pleases me. By jove, it could go on forever you know, or until I consider you have paid your ... dues, so watch out for me, Megan. I shall always be there!'

He raised his hat to her most politely, smiling as he did so then, just as mysteriously as he had come, was gone.

For a long time she stared at the space where he had been, the trembling in her limbs spreading and spreading until she shook like the aspen tree beside her, then in a graceful, boneless sinking she fell to the ground and wept.

Chapter fifteen

Mrs Stewart began to speak of promotion to housemaid! The autumn days, the fine, warm autumn peculiar sometimes to England with pale, fragile blue skies, gentle and easy on those who worked indoors and out, went on and on. An Indian summer they were calling it, thankful to put off the coming of winter for as long as possible. The rain, when it came, fell most obligingly during the night, soft and refreshing on the gardens, drying again each sweet morning on the velvet lawns and beading the perfect, carefully tended head of each flower in the garden with clear, diamond drops. The servants were more tranquil, inclined to treat one another amiably, with less of the quarreling which is bound to flare up amongst so many of differing natures who live in close proximity to each other. They were allowed marginally more freedom of movement by the stately, watchful Mrs Stewart, mellowed it seemed by the light tempered days and aware of the imprisoning months to come. They were given permission to walk in pairs of the same sex at the back of the house, unseen naturally, by the family, when their work was completed.

'You may take the evening air with the other girls, Megan,' Mrs Stewart told her, 'providing you do not wander to the front of the house, or perhaps you might care to slip over to see Mrs Whitley for half an hour,' she said graciously. Really the girl had improved beyond recognition during the past weeks, becoming as biddable as Mrs Stewart liked her girls to be, running to do as she was told with a willingness which mystified the housekeeper in view of her first inclination to argue over every order she was given. It seemed, suddenly, all that was now behind her and really, there was no need for the girl to hang about the kitchens in her free time as she did, barely stepping more than a yard or so from the back kitchen door. She was no longer disposed to engage Tom Fraser in conversation whenever she felt like it, Mrs Stewart had noticed and because of it she was quite persuasive in her effort to tempt Megan to leave the cleaning of the silver, which was not her job anyway, and get out and enjoy the lovely evening while she could. It would not last forever, she said, and was quite bewildered when Meg declined politely.

'I was there on Sunday with Tom, thank you Mrs Stewart and I believe Mrs Whitley has made arrangements to entertain Jack Tabner and his wife from the home farm. They are to take supper with her, she told me.'

Made arrangements! Take supper! The girl was quick there was no doubt about it. Already she was picking up the phrases she had heard her betters use and there was an air of ... well, Mrs Stewart could only call it *refinement* about her that had not been there six months ago. She would get on if she minded her manners and that sharp tongue of hers for she had the intelligence and the shrewd mind which was needed in service to take a girl to the top of her profession.

'She has made friends then, Megan?'

'Oh yes ma'am.' Meg's serious young face, thinner suddenly than Mrs Stewart remembered it, wondering why she had failed to notice it before, softened and she let her vigorously polishing hands rest for a moment on the green baize cloth which was spread out on the table in the butler's pantry in which the plate was stored and cleaned. Hartshorn power was mixed into a thick paste with cold water – an old fashioned method but very effective – which was smeared lightly over the plate with a piece of soft rag then left to dry. When this was done a soft plate brush was used to clean it off, then the plate was polished with a dry leather. The job was performed by one of the footmen directly under the supervision of Mr Ferguson, the butler but Mr Ferguson was in Liverpool at this particular time it being his day off and William, the footman had been only too pleased to take up Meg's offer to clean the plate. Mr Ferguson would not have allowed it and Mrs Stewart was uneasy somehow over Meg's insistence that she was perfectly willing to do it for surely a young girl should be eager to be off into the fading sweetness of the evening with the other maidservants. It didn't seem quite ... natural when one remembered how restless the girl had once been.

'And she is happy in her cottage?'

'Oh yes Mrs Stewart. She loves it there. She's always got someone or other dropping in to taste her macaroons or ratafias.' The slightly strained expression left Meg's face and she smiled up at Mrs Stewart and the housekeeper was startled by the golden beauty of the girl's eyes. She wore the rough cotton dress of a kitchen-maid, a coarse apron protecting it and her glorious copper hair was dragged back from her creamy face and stuffed into a plain white cap. It was as though she was deliberately quenching her own warm spirit, presenting to the household only her facility to work hard and long, to show only her strength and containment and sudden strange reserve. Her hands were still now, one holding an enormous silver soup ladle, the other the leather with which she had been polishing it.

'She's a good cook, Mrs Stewart and I think she misses having no-one to prepare meals for. She's always making cakes and biscuits and giving them to anyone who knocks on her door and word soon gets round, especially amongst the children of the estate workers. She can't get used to the idea that Martin and Tom and I are well fed and she's always baking pies and scones for us to bring back.'

Mrs Stewart smiled. 'Well, why don't you run across there now, Megan,' she persisted, surprising even herself. 'It's a lovely evening and would take you no more than five minutes if you went through the spinney.'

Instantly the smiling warmth in Meg's face slipped away and she took up her leather and began again to energetically polish the ladle.

'No, really, thank you, Mrs Stewart. As I said she has guests and I did promise William I would do this silver.'

The next month, a couple of days before her sixteenth birthday Megan Hughes was told that in view of her exemplary behaviour; her conscientious application to her duties and the trust Mrs Stewart felt could now be placed in her she was to be 'made up' to housemaid, a big step for her and one not popular with the kitchen-maids who had been passed over. She was to be put in the charge of Ethel, the upper housemaid at Silverdale for five years now and who had herself worked her way up from scullery-maid to her present post. She would be given three months trial to see how she 'shaped' herself, she was told. Perfect order and cleanliness must be her object, Mrs Stewart said. Her duties would be numerous and the comfort of the family must be her main concern. Grates must be polished and the utensils for this job would be kept in her own housemaid's box and she would see to the lighting of the fires, along with Jenny and Rose, in all the downstairs rooms.

At last she had her *own* position, her *own* duties and her *own* utensils with which to perform them and they would be no-ones responsibility but hers! Megan was jubilant!

She was to start with the dusting of the furniture, sweeping the carpets, the stairs, the polishing of windows, all the dozens of rooms, large and small; drawing-room, dining-room, study, the library with its thousands of books, breakfast room, sitting-room, hallways and the great square entrance which made up the ground floor of Silverdale. The bedrooms and magnificent modern bathrooms on the first and second floors of the Hemingway home were cared for by the chambermaids and on no account was Megan to wander into their domain. She was to wear a lavender cotton uniform with a white starched apron, white cap and ribbons and if one of the family should come upon her at her work she was to bob her curtsey and vanish immediately into the nearest hiding place, taking herself out of their sight until it should be convenient to return. When they rang she was to answer the bell and make up the fire and fetch fresh coals if they should be needed.

Megan would always remember her first sight of the luxurious elegance and comfort of the house in which Robert Hemingway and his family lived. Nothing had prepared her for it. The sheer beauty of gilt framed mirrors and sparkling chandeliers! Carved mahogany and gleaming silkwood and deep velvet! Marble fire-places and huge bay windows overlooking the glory of the gardens, the balustraded terraces, the flights of stone steps and deep green lawns with not a chimney or roof, not even another human being to interrupt the splendid view down to the river.

There were clocks in ormolu and enamel pot-pourri vases of Sèvres and Meissen and Coalport, though at that time she did not knew their names. Chairs and sofas and delicate spindle-legged tables and portraits of handsome men and beautiful ladies. Crystal lamps and porcelain figurines, heavy flowered curtains and miles and miles of carpet so thick and exquisite Meg was afraid to walk on them.

She was led lastly into what Ethel called the 'winter garden' and Meg saw with her own eyes the loveliness of the 'glass room' which Martin had tried to describe to them.

'This floor's to be cleaned and polished every day but you're not to touch the plants,' Ethel said in her forthright manner, 'or

Mrs Hemingway'll have your hide, not to mention old Atkinson. It's what you call 'parquet' – Ethel pronounced it par*ket* – flooring and Mrs Stewart likes to see her face in it.'

Ethel was brisk, matter of fact, accustomed it seemed to the handsome proportions and breathtaking beauty as she showed Megan from room to room on that first morning. It was barely six-thirty for all the cleaning must be completed before the family breakfasted, Meg was told. She was not allowed to stand and stare as her spellbound senses demanded but must be on her knees at once before the drawing room grate, removing the ashes from yesterday's fire and laying and lighting today's. The hearth must be swept and polished before moving on to the next, working in perfect unison with Jenny and Rose who were employed in dusting, polishing and sweeping the carpets. Ethel 'did' the ornaments in her privileged capacity as head housemaid.

She did well, Mrs Stewart told her. She was neat and quick and self-effacing. She moved about her new sphere with the instinctive grace and care of someone who loves fine things and her work, hard as it was, became a joy to her. She took pride in the high shine she put on rosewood and mahogany loo tables, on chiffoniers and card tables and pedestal and celleret sideboards, the names of which she had never known until she began to care for them. Her hands were gentle and dexterous as they cleaned the soft apple green, the biscuit and wedgwood blue and madder of the plaster relief which adorned the high and beautiful ceilings, all set about with scrolls, wreaths, fan tracery, medallions and festoons of leaves and flowers, and *her* windows sparkled like crystal when she had done. To handle the exquisite Wedgwood urns – when Ethel allowed it – the white biscuit porcelain, the Meissen bowls which were scattered so carelessly about the drawing-room delighted her and she took enormous care in dusting and replacing them, not perhaps exactly where they had been, but where Megan Hughes thought they looked best! No-one seemed to notice, least of all Ethel who was glad to have the services of such a good worker, she said.

'I'm going to try you in the drawing-room, Megan,' Mrs Stewart said when her three months was up, for really the girl was wasted in merely cleaning. She was a credit to her training and with her restrained comeliness, her immaculate appearance and neat efficiency she knew that Mrs Hemingway would be pleased to have Megan about her. 'Just serving tea to start with in the drawing-room or the winter garden. You will have a black silk dress and a white frilled apron and cap. Agnes will show you what to do. Speak when you are spoken to and not before. The mistress will ring for tea at four. The tray will be prepared by the kitchen staff but you will hand it round to the company after the mistress has poured the tea or coffee, and Agnes will pass round the cakes and biscuits. You will be parlourmaid, Megan. Do you think you can manage that?'

'Yes Mrs Stewart.'

'Good girl.'

Megan moved through that winter with the passive and yet vigilant watchfulness that her meeting with Benjamin Harris had produced in her. Though she had challenged his authority over her then, defying him bravely she was not absolutely certain that if she should encounter him again as he had promised, she would be able to do it again. She could tell Mr Hemingway, she supposed, which had been her first instinct when she had recovered from the fright he had given her, but then she had done that the last time and look where that had got her! She was more in danger now than she had been then for Harris' stay in prison had turned his mind to revenge and she, or Tom, were to be his targets. She would tell Tom and Martin, she decided but each time she made up her mind to it Harris' face would come between her and her intentions, his dreadfully cold and glinting grey eyes which told her he meant everything he had said and the words he had spoken would ring in her head, repeating over and over again his threat against Tom. In his capacity as gardener and general handyman about the Silverdale estate Tom often worked alone and far from the house and it would be a simple matter for a couple of the 'criminal fraternity' Harris had talked about to slip into the woods and catch him, cripple him! And there was Mrs Whitley to consider. She lived alone in her cottage down by the gate and though the lodge keeper and his wife were within shouting distance she was old and frail and just the sight of Harris could kill her. Her only protection, it seemed to Meg, was silence and the immediate safety of the house. And yet, was it rational to believe it would happen?

She lay awake in the night and dwelled on the menace of it, a hundred times telling herself that it had been an idle threat, something Harris had brooded over during his months in prison, then, in a fit of rancour, taken it into his head to blame her for

186

it. Bitter and resentful at what had been done to him he had waylaid her, the one he believed was the cause of it, in the spinney, but now, surely, he would be long gone from the district, the incident, if not forgotten, at least one he was no longer obsessed with. But dare she take the chance? Dare she?

She would toss about on her narrow bed at night, shifting from the certainty that he had left Liverpool where his past would haunt him, gone to greener pastures, she was positive, to the dreadful doubt that he hung about the estate waiting just for her! They would not let her rest, the misgivings crowding to her mind the moment she put her head on the pillow. They would not allow her to go far from the house and yard alone. She longed to beg Tom to be careful – about what, he would ask – and they separated her not only from her young, fellow maidservants but from Tom himself. The girls with whom she worked had accepted her as 'stuck-up', unapproachable, a good worker, mind and always willing to give a helping hand to anyone who was behind but not someone to have a laugh or a 'natter' with to make the deadly routine of the day pass more quickly. They let her alone, some of them resentful at her rapid promotion from scullery-maid to the drawing-room of Mrs Hemingway herself, and envious – now that her growing beauty was fully revealed by the stark black and white simplicity of her 'afternoon' uniform – of the attention she received from the men servants!

She was not aware of it. She did her work well and was recognised by Alice Hemingway who made a note to speak to her husband about it when he came home. That winter he and Hunter had spent most of their time in America where, on the long straight stretch of smooth sand at Ormond-Daytona Beach, Florida, Fred H. Marriott in his Stanley steam car which looked rather like a canoe with wire wheels had made a new flying record of 127.57 miles per hour, outstripping the great names of racing, Hémèry, Lancia and Satori in their petrol driven motor cars! Mr Robert had set his heart on his protegée and the sleek-lined 'flyer', beating this record but though Martin and his machine spent many hours of each day skimming the miles of straight course in practice he could not better the record.

They had raced at Grosse Point horse-racing track in Detroit and in the American Grand Prix at Savannah and the 'Hemingway Flyer' had acquitted itself well and the blighted hopes at Ormond-Daytona Beach had been somewhat made up for. As Mr

Robert said, Martin was young yet, a novice but just let that dare-devil Marriott wait a year or two and young Martin Hunter would make mincemeat of him!

They attended the Paris Motor Show before returning to England, 'to see the opposition', Mr Robert said, tapping the side of his nose slyly and were impressed by the vast multitude of European and American motor cars assembled there. They rubbed shoulders with the élite of the motoring world. Vanderbilt, Rolls, Royce, Marriott and the great S. F. Edge, famous for his twenty-four hour record on the newly opened Brooklands Track. There were more than a few minor royalty of Europe present since the growing world of the motor car and the racing of one machine against another, the gaining of 'speed' records which was their obsessive goal, was fascinating to many others beside the Heming-ways and young Martin Hunter.

They had returned home at the end of February, ready, they said, to tackle the French Grand Prix on the Dieppe Circuit, the Tourist Trophy in the Isle of Man, a speed meeting which was to be held on the promenade at Blackpool, the Welsh and Irish Trials and the Ironbridge Hill Climb. Robert Hemingway described it all to his Alice and was barely interested, listening with only half an ear as she pronounced on the great success of 'that child' he had brought into their house last year and, his attention taken up entirely with the latest edition of the motoring magazine *The Autocar* which he had missed whilst he had been abroad, an odd word here and there was all he heard.

'. . . and she really is most diligent, Mr Hemingway. Her movements are so neat and graceful with none of the nervous clumsiness usually shown in a new parlourmaid. Her manners are perfect and her appearance is delightful. Mrs Stewart cannot speak highly enough of her. She says she is sensible too, and can be trusted to do any job she is asked without supervision.'

'Really, that is most gratifying.'

'. . . and the young man also . . .'

'How splendid.'

They were sitting companionably together, their wicker chairs side by side in the humid warmth of the late Lucinda Hemingway's winter garden. A 'tunnel of flowers' it had been described as and so it was and the old couple sat at its far end. Alice gazed out serenely at the glory of the early daffodils which blazed in her garden clustering about every tree trunk, and wildly carpeting the lawn; at hyacinth, anemone and crocus, lining every path with a riot of colour as far as the eye could see. Men laboured diligently at each bed, weeding and hoeing. A path of crazy paving led away from the door of the winter garden, not straight and purposeful, but meandering gracefully through the flower beds towards the lawns which stretched to the stand of trees and beside it a tall, bright-haired young man was bending to something on the path.

'Look! There he is now.'

'Who dear?'

'The young man I was speaking of.'

'Which young man is that, Mrs Hemingway?' Robert and Alice were of the generation which never, except in the privacy of their bedroom, addressed one another by their Christian name.

Alice Hemingway sighed resignedly.

'The young man who was involved with Megan in the fire at the emigrant house. You remember him! He worked as boot boy and then . . .'

'Oh yes . . . John . . . or was it Jack . . .?'

'Tom, I think. Atkinson tells me he has a real feel for the garden.'

As they watched, their old faces nodding in gentle interest over the quite ordinary pursuits of their gardener, Alice and Robert Hemingway were surprised when the young man rose slowly to his full height, glanced furtively about him and with the definite air of someone who is up to something he shouldn't, darted swiftly into the stand of trees.

'What's up with our Meg, Mrs Whitley? Has she said anything to you? I just can't make her out these last few months. Every time I speak to her she jumps a foot in the bloody air – sorry Mrs Whitley – and all she seems to care about is the colour of the curtains in the sitting-room and the charming arrangement – her words, not mine – of the ornaments. She's got nothing else in her head and when I *do* get her on her own, which is difficult, that's all she seems to want to talk about. She won't even come over here unless I practically drag her!'

Tom paced the small crowded room which had become the centre of Agatha Whitley's contented world in the year she had lived on the Silverdale estate and his tall, rangy restlessness made it appear even smaller and more cluttered. Mrs Whitley watched him anxiously, turning every now and again as if to consult the other occupant of the snug kitchen, her face, plump and rosy in the glow from the fire, begging for understanding.

'She seems alright to me.' Martin spoke with the lazy indolence of one who is convinced the whole conversation and its contents was a storm in a teacup. 'Keen to get on, I'll grant you but what's wrong with that. Mrs Stewart told me the mistress has got her eye on her and you know what that means in a house that size. Even old Ferguson can't fault her. In fact I'd have said she's fallen on her feet has our Meg, as we *all* have . . .'

'You've been away too long, Martin, that's your trouble and you're so taken up with them machines you can see no further than what goes on under their damned bonnets. Can you not remember how lively she was? Jesus – sorry Mrs Whitley – it's only been just over a year! She used to drive us all barmy with her joking and her everlasting poking her nose into everybody's affairs. Questions! She never stopped and if she thought there was a day out in the offing she'd never let up until she was included . . .'

Mrs Whitley nodded her head sagely. 'It's true, Martin.'

'. . . and now all she has to say is what lovely carpets there are in the drawing-room . . .'

'Well, it's true . . .'

'That's not the bloody point and you know it. She refuses to come into town with me on her day out and that's not like her . . .'

'She's growing up, that's all. She's sixteen and girls are funny at that age. Besides she feels she has a position of responsibility she told me and . . .'

'Balls!'

'*Tom*! I'll not have language like that in my house . . .'

'I'm sorry, Mrs Whitley but he makes me so wild. If he can't see the change in her then he must be blind! Still, what can you expect? All he ever thinks about, cares about, talks about is motor cars and circuits and speed and chaps with names we've never even heard of and *we're* supposed to be interested but when you ask him to discuss something important like our Meg he . . .'

The lounging length of Martin Hunter rose unhurriedly from the depths of Mrs Whitley's best armchair, the one in which only she usually sat. His sun-browned face, warmed by hundreds of hours in the fierce sunshine of Florida was deceptively mild but his eyes had darkened to the deep colour of treacle and the muscles in his jaw clenched ominously. He was smartly, even 'nattily'

190

dressed in what was known as a 'lounge suit', the very latest in fashion with broad shoulders which needed no padding on his well muscled frame. He might have been taken for one of the Hemingway's select circle of acquaintances and not, as he really was, a servant, since he mixed with the cosmopolitan and wealthy assembly into which his situation as Robert Hemingway's skilled racing driver and favoured protegée had placed him. There was beginning to be a certain polish about him, a style, a confidence he had always had but which was now to do with his growing knowledge of good hotels, fine food and wine, the conversation and company of those whose education had been gained not only at the public schools most had attended but in the privilege and birthright of their class. He was almost nineteen years old but looked older, his maturity far outstripping the boyish, unfledged youthfulness of Tom. Side by side it was difficult to remember that they had grown up together and had been tutored in the same rough school of life. If Martin was the almost complete confirmation of young manhood, Tom was a rough draft, an outline of what one day he would finally become!

They faced up to one another now, exactly the same height but where Martin was powerfully built, the strength and breadth of his arms and shoulders developed in the constant wrestling with the steering wheel of the 'Hemingway flyer' and the boxing bouts he had fought as a boy, Tom was still slender, rangy, with the awkwardness of boyhood which he had not yet outgrown. He worked as a manual labourer and though, as Mrs Glynn put it, he ate like a horse, his body took on no weight. But his increasing strength of character, not yet completely formed and more than likely to break into helpless, youthful laughter on the slightest provocation, showed now in the truculent face he thrust into Martin's. He was artless, unsophisticated, candid but he would not back down from anything in which he believed and now he believed there was something troubling their Meg and could hardly contain his outrage that Martin, *their* Martin who had always been the first to defend her could not see it too. Martin might be some big-shot with his growing reputation as an up and coming young racing driver but it seemed his continued absence from Liverpool, and the lives that Tom and Meg led meant he was slowly becoming cut off from the world of his two childhood companions.

'Look here, lad,' Martin said now, quite softly but very dangerous. 'Are you saying I care nothing for Meg any more because if you are you had better be prepared to back your statement up with more than just words . . .'

'*You* look here, *lad*! Don't you come the high and mighty panjandrum with me. You've been across the bloody ocean and played about with them motor cars of yours and might have sat down to dine with the bloody Emperor of China for all I know but don't you tell me you give a damn about the change in our Meg. Your head might be filled with . . . with crankshafts and . . . and whatever it is you fiddle with all day long but I'd like to give you credit for seeing what's under your bloody nose! Trouble is I can't! You're too full of what you've done to be concerned with her. Damnation Martin! Just because she sat and listened to your tales of all the wonders of *your* life doesn't mean she's the same girl. Can't you see it? I agree she's fallen on her feet and I agree she's made a good impression on Mrs Stewart and the Hemingways an' all but . . . but she's not the same girl she was!'

They had eased away from one another in a gradual lessening of tension as Martin recognised the distress in Tom, and Mrs Whitley took her hand away from her mouth when she had held it in appalled horror. *Her* lads fighting and over something as important as their Meg who, she had been made aware herself, had altered these last few months. She was as concerned, as caring of Mrs Whitley's comfort and happiness as she had always been, coming, she said, as often as she could to visit her but she was *not* the same and Tom was right. Some lovely sparkle in her seemed to have been quenched. The irrepressible mischief, the warm readiness to take an interest in everything about her had gone and a young lady, serious and concerned, it seemed only with her own future career had emerged. She was to 'get on' in the Hemingway household, Mrs Whitley could see that. Two promotions already and the mistress' eye on her. Head parlourmaid next, perhaps Cook, if she was allowed to show what she could do or even the exalted position of housekeeper, the highest peak she could attain in Agatha Whitley's opinion!

Tom turned away slouching to peer out of the window across to the gatekeeper's lodge which stood on the opposite side of the long, curved gravelled driveway. His young face was set in moody lines, a far remove from its usual engaging openness but he appeared to have backed away from his confrontation with Martin.

'I'll have to go,' he muttered. 'I only slipped away while Mr Atkinson's back was turned for a minute and if I don't get back before he misses me he'll have my job. Jenny said you'd told her you were coming over here so I thought . . .'

He turned, his face earnest and pleading. 'Have a word with her, will you Martin? See if you can get it out of her what's bothering her, if anything is.' He looked confused now, uncertain, longing to be told *he* was wrong. 'Perhaps you can see better than me, being away an' all. Happen she is growing up and that's all it is but she might talk to you, tell you what's in her mind. I get no chance now what with me working outside and her indoors. The only time I get to see her is if I catch her here with Mrs Whitley and then she's always in a dash, she says, doesn't she, Mrs Whitley?' He turned his worried gaze to the old lady who nodded in agreement.

'It's true, Martin. I know you're to be off again soon. Scotland, is it? Oh my!' Her face was suffused with pride in this, her cleverest chick, her expression said, who travelled about the world as though it was no more concern than a trip to the corner shop but her eyes were anxious, clouded from their usual bright gooseberry green alertness to the haze of old age and her worry over their Meg whose well-being she cared about more than anything in this world. The lads were lads and could see to themselves but Meg was nought but a lass and needed someone to look out for her. 'Get her to go to town with you. Take her to the Music Hall and give her a laugh, there's a good lad. She needs taking out of herself and perhaps if she was to get away from Silverdale – d'you know she's not been off the grounds since I can't remember when – she'd open up and tell you what's in her mind. Dear Lord, I can remember the day when she *never* stopped talking, always at you with what she was going to do and with her nose in everything that didn't concern her and look at her now. Scarce a word for anyone and then it's all to do with her work!'

Mrs Whitley's eyes welled at the fond remembrance of the past and Martin knelt at her feet as he had done so often before. Then he had been begging for a favour, an outing perhaps or an hour off to slip down to Mr Hales to see his beloved machines. Now he did it to comfort, smiling his warm, affectionate smile into her tremulous face. He sighed inwardly for he had made arrangements to entertain and *be* entertained by a certain pretty young housemaid who was vastly impressed, not only with his masculine charms but his elevated position in Mr Hemingway's home. He had meant to dine her at the 'Adelphi' and then, when she was soft and sighing, completely enraptured as most women usually were in his increasingly experienced hands there was a certain room, above the garage, the one which was kept just for himself when he was home and in which ... aah well! There would be other nights and other pretty young women...!

Chapter sixteen

They made a striking couple, very young that was obvious and the girl was wide-eyed with wonder as though she was bemused by the splendour of it but they were well dressed, both of them and not out of place.

The Adelphi Hotel, 'the Delly' in the idiom of the native Liverpuddlian, was the most prestigious, the most well-appointed, the most elegant hotel outside of London with a staff of over 200 to serve the 250 rooms, including private rooms, parlours, sitting-rooms and apartments, the prices for which could be as high – with food and wine and any delicacy a guest might care to order – as one hundred pounds a day! There were two chefs, one English, one French and thirty cooks, specialists most of them in the making of pastry, entrées and sauces, four bookkeepers, a housekeeper, a linen-keeper and eighteen porters.

The building was extensive, magnificent, with a restaurant which could cater for some 120 persons at one sitting, the cost, again, high for a meal. Five guineas it could amount to and that was without wine! Many of the items were wired from Paris; the strawberries, for instance which were that night on the menu, and asparagus since the untold visitors from many parts of the world who sailed in and out of the great seaport on her luxurious passenger liners, the sportsmen, the aristocracy, royalty – for had not certain members of the Royal family stayed there when visiting or passing through Liverpool – princes of foreign royal households, ambassadors from Washington, all the well-to-do who stayed in the fine hotel, demanded, simply, the best!

'Your table is ready, sir,' the maître d'hôtel told Martin, his face smooth and expressionless, well used it appeared to serving young men such as he and the very young but lovely girl who accompanied him. The gentleman, one supposed, was quite at home in the glittering white and gold and ruby splendour of the Drawing Room, the decorations of which were a replica of those of a similar room in the Pétit Trianon, Versailles, as he and his ·

195

companion drank a pale sherry before dining but the young lady stared about her quite openly, her strange golden eyes drinking in every costly, elegant, comfortable detail.

She was very simply dressed, the head waiter noted in a floor length one-piece dress of pale cream chiffon over cream satin. The neckline was scooped out quite demurely as befitted her age and the sleeves were short. It had an overtunic of the same material which reached to her knees, the very *latest* fashion and just below her softly rounded breast was a narrow sash of gold satin. He would have been quite amazed to learn, had he been told, that she had made it herself, the cost with the tiny pearl buttons which flowed in a line down the curve of her back, a mere two and eleven pence halfpenny, the material a roll end from Paddy's Market! Bon Marché sold it – the one from which she had copied it – for forty-nine shillings and sixpence! She wore no jewellery and needed none to enhance her young, undimmed loveliness.

Her escort wore a dinner jacket, double-breasted and unbuttoned, ready made, the head waiter could tell for had not he served the best dressed gentlemen of the world in his restaurant and knew the difference, but immaculate and looking quite splendid on his well-proportioned athlete's body.

They stood up and the young man gallantly offered the girl his arm.

'Megan,' he said softly and she put her hand in it. They followed the important, black-suited figure of the maître d'hôtel, moving past darting, crimson coated porters and attendants in the hall, sauntering visitors come to see and be seen in their Paris gowns and glittering jewels, suave gentlemen and soignée ladies on their way from one exotic place to another and glad to find a 'decent' place to stay en route. The wealthy of Liverpool who, now that it was fashionable to eat out, as they did in London, rather than entertain in their own homes, had been driven in their new motor cars, leaving them in the care of their chauffeurs whilst they dined. They were floating, like fairy spirits, or so it seemed to Meg, up and down the handsome grand staircase, the lovely colour of the carpets, the furnishings, the drifting gowns of the elegant ladies all heightened by the miracle of the electric lights which gleamed everywhere.

The first Adelphi Hotel was opened in 1826, a squat, three-storeyed building in the Georgian style of architecture. It was situated in a charming residential thoroughfare, at the foot of

Mount Pleasant, which led to the Botanic Gardens and the open countryside beyond. The great writer Charles Dickens had stayed there en route to America and was reputed to have said of the dinner he was served that it was 'undeniably perfect'! The history of the hotel during the Victorian era might be said to be the history of Liverpool itself for as commerce and shipping increased so did the fortunes of the hotel. The railway adjacent to it, also helped to account for its unbroken record of popularity and prosperity and in 1876, to meet the ever-widening circle of its clientele the hotel was entirely rebuilt. Its magnificence was undisputed. Five storeys high with a splendid pillared entrance, its arched windows looked out on Ranelagh Place with all the superiority of a king's palace.

Meg gasped quite audibly as she and Martin entered the restaurant. She could not have said later what exquisite pastel colours had been used to pick out the delicate carvings of acanthus leaves and garlands on the walls and high ceiling. She could not have described the richness of the light fittings and chandeliers, the sumptuous elegance of plate and silverware glittering on snow white damask cloth and napery. She had been introduced now to the luxury of the Hemingway home 'above stairs' and the extraordinarily beautiful, but to the family, everyday objects which crowded it but the sight of gracefully arranged, daintily set tables, decorated with flowers which had been put on display by the hand of an artist; the velvet, round-backed chairs on which gloriously gowned ladies and immaculately tailored gentleman were seated, temporarily stunned her. Everywhere was glitter and colour and movement and the murmur of well bred voices. There was the subdued chink of silver on porcelain and over all lay the delicious aroma of the finest French cuisine.

'This way, sir,' the waiter said politely for though he was not certain of the young lady, the young gentleman appeared to be at his ease and it did no harm, in fact it was the policy of the hotel, to show courtesy to those it served whatever their apparent station in life.

They were seated, a pleasant table for two beside a draped window which overlooked the lights and night life of Ranelagh Place before Megan could bring herself to speak. The head waiter had moved away, bowing his head and at the same time summoning another waiter with a barely perceptible movement of his gloved hand. She watched him weave his way between the tables, stopping to speak to one seated person and another, his smiling face begging to be told how he might make their stay more enjoyable and as he did so she began to laugh.

'Now what?' Martin leaned forward, beginning to smile for really she did look a 'corker' as the new language of 'slang' put it.

'Who does he remind you of?'

Martin turned to peer at the retreating back of the maître d'hôtel, then looked into her own impish face.

'Ferguson!' They both spoke laughingly together and those about them, both men and women turned to stare reprovingly, at the youthful high spirits of the young lady and her escort.

They had sampled the hors d'oeuvres, Meg encouraged by Martin who said airily he had tried them in Savannah and found them nothing to write home about and certainly not a patch on Meg's own oyster patties but you had to try everything once, didn't she agree? She did, most seriously, pleased with his remark about her own cooking and when they moved on to the consommé julienne, she considered Mrs Whitley's thick pea a lot more substantial! They tried whitebait and grouse and bombe Leslie – who was Leslie, did Martin think? – pétits fours, strawberries and a dish with peaches in it which was delicious, coffee and, at Martin's insistence a liquer.

She was *quite* relaxed by then, the sherry, the glass of wine Martin had pressed on her and the liquer combining to make her pleasantly light-headed, voluble though not loudly so, flushed with laughter and utterly beautiful. Martin could not take his eyes from her!

It had taken all his powers of persuasion to make her go with him. She had been suspicious, for Jenny, the pretty young housemaid with whom she worked at times had talked of nothing else, almost hysterical with excitement, of the wonder of her evening out with Martin; of what she would wear at the Adelphi – *The Adelphi*! just think of it – of how handsome Martin was and what a man of the world he was, and how witty he was and did Meg think she should do her hair this way or that, and if Mrs Stewart should find out she would lose her job for the servants were not allowed to 'walk out' with another member of staff! She was to meet him at the gates, she said, where he would pick her up in the Vauxhall, *her* in a motor car, she said wildly and Meg thought she was about to swoon with the sheer joy of it!

She was in tears an hour later, her outing to the Adelphi with Martin postponed, she said. He was to go on an errand into town on Mr Hemingway's behalf, she said, wiping her nose forlornly on her sleeve her bright blue eyes dulled with misery, her hopes in ashes one supposed, for Martin was off to Scotland in the morning and a good-looking chap like him would have the girls after him like bees to honey and now her chance was lost.

'I've booked us a table at the Adelphi for tonight, Meg,' he said carelessly when another hour had gone by, knowing nothing of poor pretty Jenny's confidences to Meg, catching her as she slipped out of the kitchen to fetch a silver soup tureen from the footman's pantry and was quite put out when Meg turned to stare at him in amazement.

'You've what?'

'I thought you might like to have a night out before I go off to Scotland so I've booked a table at the Adelphi. Put your best frock on and you and me'll "do the town" as they say in the States!'

'Oh do they indeed? And what do they call it when you ask one girl to go out with you and then let her down for another, telling lies into the bargain about errands to be done for your employer?'

'Pardon?'

'You heard.'

'I don't know what . . .'

'Oh yes you do! I've had nothing but Martin this and Martin that from Jenny since the minute you got back. Now she's in tears because you've *suddenly* got to go into town for Mr Hemingway. What's going on then, our Martin?'

Martin looked abashed then grinned audaciously. In the four years since he had started work for Robert Hemingway, first as his mechanic/chauffeur and then as that special and quite astonishing creature, a motor car racing driver, he had become a complete man. Young still in years, his experiences, on and off the racing track had changed him considerably. Behind the wheel of his racing car he was a machine to match the one he drove. Steady eyes and hands and nerves, and the power to make split second decisions had induced in him a belief in himself which showed in his easy carriage, his relaxed and quite unthinking air of authority. The danger, the likelihood of injury or even death, though it was part of his life did not signify for he was young, immortal and this belief gave him a dash, an élan which set him apart from other men. He had always been an attractive boy and youth with abundant charm for the ladies which had made seduction not only comfortably easy but enjoyable for himself and his partner. He never made the mistake of taking this style he had for granted treating each new love with a sensitivity and pleasure which, when the relationship ended left no bitterness on either side, rather a memory of excitement and sweetness. He had learned from these brief encounters and built upon them and his liking for, his genuine admiration of pretty women was apparent in his treatment of them. He was polished, easy with himself and yet not self-complacent, an adult and yet boyishly engaging. His virility was beyond question. It showed in his confident manner, his vibrant and often audacious wit and the agreeable but very positive approach he took with every woman he found attractive. He was headstrong and proud, sometimes arrogant for he had achieved so much and wanted more, not only in the world of motor cars but also from the women that world had put in his way. But his brown face would smile and his brown eyes glow warmly in admiration and when his lips curled in that certain way they had, they lifted the corners of his mouth into what each woman was sure was the beginning of a laughing kiss meant irresistibly for her.

Now Martin put his slender, workmanlike hands, still ingrained with the oil from the engine of the Hemingway flyer (which had arrived only that morning by ship from New York) about Meg's waist and began to whirl her around the confines of the small pantry in a fair imitation of a waltz but she would have none of it.

'Give over, Martin! Let go of me at once!' She was stiff with offended outrage and her hands slapped at his. 'What the hell d'you think you're doing? If Mr Ferguson catches us he'll have *my* job for sure. And what are *you* doing in the house? You know how particular he is about inside and outside servants . . .'

'I'm not "outside", Meggie.' His grin was endearing as though he was perfectly certain she would forgive him as Mr Ferguson would forgive him, for could he be resisted!

'So what are you, pray?' she asked, then, as though realising she was being diverted from her original complaint she pushed him away and, raising her hands to her hair in the age old gesture of a woman seriously displeased with the pranks of the man who

200

had disarranged her she moved huffily away from him, intent, one assumed, on returning immediately to her duties.

'Oh come on, Meg, don't be mad at me. I know I told Jenny I would take her but ... well ...' His deep brown eyes softened and melted and despite herself, *surprising* herself, Meg hesitated, drawn back to him into the cool dimness of the pantry. 'You see ... you'll think I'm daft but ...'

'What ...?'

'I had this idea ...'

'What ...?' She took another step towards him her curiosity, always impossible to repress getting the better of her.

'Everywhere I've gone I've always been with Mr Hemingway. Good hotels, restaurants, and he's taken charge, naturally, after all he was paying and I am his employee. Wherever we stay it's always the best. Oh, I know I don't have the standard of room he has but I often eat with him and I've watched him and listened to him go through the menu with the waiter. I've seen him study the wine list and decide what to drink with what and I made up my mind ...'

'What, Martin?' She was quite absorbed as he had intended.

'... that it was time I did it. Just walk into some posh place, demand the best table and be exactly like he is. Like they all are! Order what I fancy and if I don't like the way it's cooked, send it back to the kitchens just as I've seen him do! Why not? I've got the money to do it now, not often but I can see no reason why I ... we ... shouldn't do it now and again do you?'

His face was absolutely certain of it and his eyes glowed into hers with all the unhesitating conviction which his months of travel with Robert Hemingway and his own complete and undisputed confidence in himself had given to him. He lifted his chin arrogantly then something in him, perhaps for the last time, remembered that he was a boy who had no past, no name bar the one given him at the orphanage where he had been abandoned as a baby, and the expression on his face became curiously vulnerable, shy almost, and he put out both hands, taking one of hers between them.

'Share it with me, Meg, this first time. I'd rather be with someone I know, someone who knows me, knows what I've been and where I've come from. Someone who knows what I've achieved and where I'm going. You understand, Meggie, you always have. You'll know what it means to me, without being impressed, or overawed as Jenny would be. She's alright, good fun and all that but . . .'

Meg shifted impatiently, not knowing why the mention of Jenny and her talent for 'fun' should irritate her but Martin saw it and hastily took another tack, quite well aware that no woman wishes to hear the qualities of another.

'. . . but she's not such good company as you and it'd be the first time for us both. An experience we've never had, never even dreamed of when we were at Great George Square! Imagine us dining at the "Delly" all dressed up in our Sunday best letting the rest of 'em see what orphanage kids can do when they've a mind to, what d'you say?'

'Well . . .' but he knew she was willing, had known long before she did that his power of inducement, well tested and practised upon would win her round for didn't it always, with *all* women! Besides, was he not doing as Mrs Whitley and Tom had asked him to do? Had they not begged him to find out what was going on in Meg's secret mind these past months. Why she had become the compliant, unfathomable, seemingly tireless workhorse who, besides the passion for work on which she had always thrived, bore no resemblance to the light-hearted Megan Hughes they had once known.

Her face had come alive with excitement and she leaned towards him in the most delightful way and he could smell some fragrance about her which he did not recognise but found extremely pleasing. Her eyes, as he had seen them do a thousand times when she was happy changed to a flashing, golden warmth and her soft pink mouth, full and moist, parted on a sigh.

'The "Delly"! Lord, I can't believe it! You and me and Tom at the "Delly"! D'you really mean it, Martin, because if this is one of your daft jokes I'll not forgive you. You're not having me on, are you? D'you mean it, gospel, our kid?'

Jenny was forgotten. She was nothing to do with Meg and Martin and Tom who were a separate, complete unit, set apart from the rest of the servants, the household, the rest of the world even, by the circumstance of their close upbringing!

Martin's face became uncertain and he opened his mouth to protest for there had been no thought in his mind of taking Tom with them to dine at the Adelphi. He did not stop to wonder why, nor even to question his own objection, he only knew that the image of dining alone in the opulence of the best restaurant in the

202

north of England with this amazingly radiant creature appealed to the masculine in him. The predatory male though God alone knew why for was she not only 'their Meggie'? She was gazing at him with the rapture of a child who has been granted a peep into a fairy grotto and it filled him with a strange but quite gratifying piquancy. Tom was a good fellow and they had been friends, brothers even for a long time and Martin would defend him with his life if it was needed but on this one occasion, this one evening he felt the desire to have Meg to himself. To talk to her and tell her of his plans since there was no-one more interested – was there? – than Meg. He wanted to find out – didn't he? – what *she* was up to, did *she* have hopes for the future since he knew that of the two of them she was more ambitious, more like himself than Tom. Tom was . . . was settled, happy as a pig in muck in the very job he was doing. He would have nothing to say that he hadn't said a dozen times before on the benefit of a steady job and a place to put your feet up with people you liked about you. Careless and carefree was Tom and he'd think nowt a pound to the Adelphi, or so Martin told himself. Besides, he'd not have a decent suit let alone a dinner jacket!

But how to say this to Meg without making her think he was deserting Tom, the Tom who had never yet been left out of any of their excursions, at least not deliberately but Meg saved him the dilemma of it by clapping her hand to her head.

'Oh, I forgot! He told me he had to go over to the home farm. I can't remember what for but he'd promised Jack Tabner . . .'

'Oh, what a shame, but never mind, Meggie. He can come next time for there will *be* a next time, don't you fret. We'll make a pact that when I'm home we'll all go to the "Delly" for a slap-up meal, on me of course,' he finished magnanimously.

They lingered, as seemed to be the way of those about them, over their coffee. The lights were soft and the diners, mellowed perhaps by the magnificence of the food they had eaten and the fine wine they had drunk talked quietly. The laughter was muted, the waiters hovered attentively, unobtrusively, ready, should they be needed to pour another cup of coffee, to light a cigar. They were easy with one another, their long association as children and through their adolescence giving them the unruffled facility to talk, or not; to laugh together over half-forgotten memories, to be unhurried, companionable, to listen.

'And your designing, Martin?' Meg said at last, her tawny eyes dreaming through the candlelight into his. 'What of that? Will you spend more time on it or are you to go on racing?'

Her world away from this one with Martin was momentarily forgotten, her anxious dread of Benjamin Harris, her unease for Tom's safety, her absurd – she was certain of it – belief that Harris might harm them both, were all put aside in the wonder of these incredible hours Martin had created for her. It was enchantment, a magical span of time cut out of the routine of the days and weeks of her life, polished and glittering and unique and she meant to remember it, cherish it, to put it away carefully with her other few, lovely memories. Like the bicycle ride to the Wirral Peninsula and Tom with buttercups in his hair; the first birthday she had spent in Great George Square when Mrs Whitley had made her a birthday cake with eleven candles on the iced perfection of its top, the first she had ever had; the Shrove Tuesday fun at Lime Street station! Not many yet but she would have more, many more, she knew she would. When she had drawn together all the threads of the ideas she had been weaving for the past few months in her active mind. She might present a submissive, obedient face to those for whom she laboured but behind it her brain was not docile, nor stagnant and when the time came, she would be ready with them.

She watched Martin's face change at her question. The ease in it altered and formed into an ambiguous hesitation, not of purpose for that would never vary, but of direction of that purpose. In just that fraction of a second it was all there to see but Meg was not yet mature enough to read it.

He sighed pensively, leaning back into his chair and a shadow blurred his face to a gypsy-like darkness. 'I love racing, Meg, I really do! You have no idea of the . . . the feeling you get when you know you are moving faster than man has ever moved before. Not just the thrill of it but the knowledge that it's *you* who is in control of the machine which is moving you at such speed. That it is your skill . . . and daring, I suppose, that is the source of it. We are unique, you know,' it was said without arrogance, or even pride, just a statement of fact, 'those of us who race. Not many can do it. Not many have the guts to do it,' he smiled, 'or the sheer bloody madness, but . . . well . . . I don't know how to describe it. It . . . it gets into your blood and before you know it you can't seem to do without it. It distracts you from what you really want to do . . .'

'Build your own motor car?'

'Yes! You have no conception Meggie, no man has who hasn't done it, even Mr Robert, of the . . . the intoxication, the sensation, Jesus, and then when it's over and you've won . . . they go wild, those who come to watch you. They treat you like a god . . . wanting to . . . to touch you and . . . give you things . . . presents. It's hard to remember sometimes that this isn't really what I set out to do. I thought it would be a step towards it. A means of getting into motoring, making money, making a start on my own ideas, and it has been. I'm very grateful to Mr Robert, believe me but somehow I've been side-tracked, led down another route . . .'

He made an impatient gesture with his hands and shrugged his broad shoulders. His face was pensive, irritable almost. 'I've got to make up my mind to it. I've got to convince Mr Robert that though it's very enjoyable, great fun really, especially for him because it's his *hobby*, it's to be *my* work. I'll have to be quick, Meg. The trouble is there are so many in it now. America, Italy, France, Germany and here. So many new, *good* designs. Ten years ago, when it was just beginning . . . if I'd been old enough then . . .'

'But surely you can't mean that there's no room for you . . .'

'No . . . it's not that but . . .'

'Well what then?'

Meg looked bewildered. All her life she had listened to this young man who sat across the table from her agitating the very air about him with his determination to 'be in on it' in the world of motoring. He had worked towards nothing else. He had lived, breathed, eaten, drunk and dreamed about the automobile and it's potential to change the world, his potential to change the world and now he seemed to be saying he was – surely not? – having doubts! *Was* that what he was saying? She couldn't believe it! Dear Lord, Martin would not be Martin without his head beneath the bonnet of a motor car, his hands covered in grease, a spanner in one and whatever tool mechanics used for whatever it was they *did*, in the other, his face serious and stern in the business of maintaining, cleaning, *building* the machines he loved!

He leaned across the table and took her hands in his and his face was rapt and she felt herself drawn closer, a magnet compelled to another, her own will submerged by his. His voice was soft as he spoke.

'I've got an idea for a new racing car. She's a machine with formidable power with a capacity of ten and a half litres. She

205

could travel comfortably at under twenty miles an hour in top gear and pull away while the engine is still turning over at a little over a thousand revs per minute.' Whatever is he talking about, Meg had time to wonder wildly when he was off again.

'She'll have disc wheels, a radiator cowl and a stream-lined body which will give her the advantage of tremendous speed. The "Darracq" we've been racing, the one we call "Hemingway flyer", is superb and she's won us a few trophies but I want to design and race my *own* car . . .'

'Well, why shouldn't you, Martin?' Meg hung on his every word in the most gratifying way but Martin's young, joyous face became solemn, scowling almost and he sighed heavily. Leaning back in his chair he looked down at the table and began to fiddle with the silver spoon in the saucer of his coffee cup. His left hand was pushed deep in his trouser pocket and he gave the impression of a small boy, truculent and slouching, who could not get his own way.

'Money! that's why, Megan, bloody money!'

'But Mr Hemingway . . .'

'Needs a lot of persuading! He loves racing and he's as proud as punch when the "Flyer" wins but he can't see any reason to design a car of our own. It would take time, you see, time we could spend racing and that's what he hasn't got! The season starts soon and he wants to be there, wherever there's a race, flags flying and him hopping up and down like some elderly small boy. Oh, I can see his point but I'm not in my seventies! I'm nineteen with my life before me and I'm going to make my mark on it. I've got to persuade him, Meg, I've just got to but whatever I say he just puts me off. And then there's flying!'

'Lord save us all . . .'

'Have you heard of the Wright brothers, Meggie?'

'No, I can't say I have . . .'

'No, you wouldn't! Not many have . . . it's so new really . . .'

'What is?'

'Flying!'

'Flying?'

She was hypnotised, her eyes unblinkingly held by the power of his.

'It's five years now since they flew their aircraft, a controlled flight, you understand, in North Carolina, but it's still young, flying I mean. It's only this year that the first recognised flight was made in this country and that was by an American! Orville Wright took his first passenger up last week, Meggie, and they covered almost two and a half miles in three minutes and forty seconds. A passenger, a paying passenger. Can you not see where it will lead? Dear Sweet Lord, the potential is overwhelming! Passengers, freight, going . . . well . . . all over the world!'

'*Martin . . .!*'

He squeezed her hands until they turned white and his excitement was a living thing. 'I love the motor car, Meg. I always have and at first I couldn't understand why it was I had been . . . diverted, first by racing and now by the idea of flying. Then I realised that the two are really the same in a way. It's not the automobile, nor the airplane but the engine, the movement, the structure!'

He stopped suddenly, aware that around him people were beginning to turn their heads, to stare in astonishment at the young man who was raising his voice so unusually. He had been carried on the cresting wave of his own joy in the discovery of his purpose in life.

He looked superb that evening in his black dinner jacket which was now increasingly fashionable, replacing the tailcoat. It had wide, pointed, double breasted lapels and beneath it he wore a white piqué waistcoat, a white pintucked shirt and a black bow tie. The trousers, without turnups and decorated down the outside seam of the leg with a row of black braid, matched his jacket. He had bought the outfit ready made, the jacket costing him 1.15.6d and the trousers 1.13.11d. Both fitted as though they had been made for him. When he leaned towards Meg the muscles across his back and shoulders were clearly outlined beneath the smoothness of the twilled worsted and as he stood when Meg left the table it was noticed that he had exceedingly shapely calves! Though he was with an extremely pretty girl – and not a few ladies envied her – numerous pairs of feminine eyes glanced slyly in his direction, watching his mobile, smiling mouth, his firm brown skin warmed in the candlelight and the movement of his long fingered hands as he caressed the brandy glass he held. His masculine vitality coursed just beneath his skin, restrained by the occasion and his surroundings but it was very evident in the narrowed depths of his brown eyes, in the graceful indolence of his long, hard body, in the tumble of his thick brown hair which he flicked carelessly back from his forehead that in different circumstances and, those who watched him covertly were certain, with a different partner, Martin Hunter would be a superb lover. They could not have said exactly why, though he was a remarkably attractive young man, but in that inexplicable way some men – and women – have, an excitement which is completely of the flesh, he seemed to tell every woman how it would be for them – with him!

'I'm going to fly, Meggie,' he whispered. 'That's what I'm going to do. Find out what holds it up! What makes it lift itself into the air. I know about engines and construction so what's to stop me from finding about that too?' He leaned further forward until his nose was almost in the fluttering flame of the candle and Meg's eyes reflected the dancing glow in their depths and for a breathless moment Martin's attention was diverted from his own bewitchment and he found himself wondering ... wondering ... what was it that he wondered about ...?

'What is it, Martin?' she breathed, breaking his oddly confusing thoughts and putting them back together.

'In January we were in California. We'd gone to a circuit there, a race meeting but in the evening Mr Hemingway had to see someone. I can't remember what it was ... or who ... so I was on my own. There was an aeroplane meeting organised by the Aero Club of California at a place called Dominguez Field in Los Angeles.'

He paused and the whole room seemed to hold its breath, waiting one supposed, on the stupendous confidence he was about to divulge.

'I went, Meg. I went to see what it was all about and that was it! I was ... enchanted!' He looked shame-faced for it was such an absurd word for a grown man to use then his face cleared and he lifted his head, his expression perilous as though daring anyone, *anyone* to laugh.

'I'm going to design that racing car, Meggie, *and* build her and I'm going to make Mr Robert see what a glory she will be! But first I'm going to get him up in an airplane because after racing a motor car I believe flying must be the nearest thing to ... to ...' He could find no word to describe what he was feeling. He was a young man, articulate, confident, more and more at ease with those he lived and worked beside but now he was speechless, mindless almost at the need which was in him and he could do no more than stare across the table through the candle's flame into Meg's wide, brilliant eyes and in them he saw her positive understanding, her absolute belief that he would do it!

He relaxed, the tension draining out of him, his dreams resting peacefully now within him, the sureness that he would bring them to life strengthened by this girl who knew him so well and who had always, *always* believed in him. He wondered why it was she had the ability to bring him such release and he also wondered, smiling inwardly, how Jenny would have reacted if he had poured out his heart to her as he had just done with Meg!

'Megan Hughes,' he said and his strong face was quite gentle now and the affection he felt for her shone in his eyes. 'Megan Hughes . . .' He shook his head, smiling.

She smiled too. 'What now?'

'You're a sight for sore eyes, d'you know that, our Meg and although you've not said much except "oh Martin" . . .' he began to laugh, '. . . you make me feel there's nothing in this world I can't do!'

'There isn't, Martin.' Her face was quite serious.

'And you, Meggie? What are *you* going to do?' He leaned towards her and his commanding face, so often concerned only with what Martin Hunter wanted, was genuinely concerned for her. 'Will you stay at Silverdale and become housekeeper and have all the servants running after you, shaking in their boots at the sound of your voice?'

'Oh no!'

'You sound very certain.'

'I am!'

'Go on then. Tell me what great plans you've got . . .'

'Don't laugh, Martin. I didn't laugh at you.'

Instantly he was contrite and he reached across the table for her hand but she was offended now and drew back.

'I'm sorry, Meg. Don't pull away. I meant no harm and I wasn't laughing at you. It's been such a . . . a grand evening. I feel good, Meggie and when I feel good I smile and say daft things. *You* know that!'

She relaxed, flattered somehow by what he said and she put her hand back in his, then grinned and he knew he was forgiven.

They talked easily for another half hour, forgetting the time and when they remembered it in the bustle of attending to the bill, of running hand in hand to the Vauxhall, of starting her up

209

and singing all the way back to Silverdale, Martin completely overlooked Meg's failure to answer his question.

Chapter seventeen

It was two weeks before her seventeenth birthday when she finally made up her mind to speak to Mr Hemingway. They were home again, he and Martin from God only knew where this time, somewhere up north doing trials in readiness for the French Grand Prix she had heard, but if she did not look sharp Mr Hemingway, who was to be home for three days only would be gone again and her opportunity missed. She did not know why she did not consider Mrs Hemingway. Perhaps it was the old lady's vague though kindly manner, her quaint state of always appearing to be in another world, an unworldly world in which she would not have the slightest idea on advising Meg how to go about it.

Young Mr Hemingway, Mr Charles Hemingway – who had never been as interested as his father, nor did he have the time, he said, to chase about the world in the pursuit of the thrill of racing – was a distant figure in Meg's world, seen only at the dinner table where she served, aloof and somewhat forbidding, and his wife, young Mrs Hemingway was the same. There was often talk, respectful naturally, in the kitchen, on the difference between father and son and the two Mrs Hemingways, but then the old gentleman was retired and had time for a chat and a joke with his servants and Mr Charles was concerned, as head of a vast shipping empire, with its daily running and could not be expected to do the same. So Megan waited, knowing instinctively that it was the old gentleman she should speak to. The months had gone by, the months in which her fear of Benjamin Harris, when he had made no further attempt to interfere in her life, had dwindled. It was a year since that day in the spinney and she let out her breath thankfully on the realisation that he really was gone, finally, from her life. She had seen Mrs Whitley housed and content. She had watched Tom settle like a dog in the sunshine, turning about a time or two but finding his place at last and Martin, well, she had no part in his life, in the making of it, nor in the defending of what he had already made of it. Her actions made no impression, had no influence on his and whatever she did, wherever she went, his work would continue just as it had for the past three years.

She was free!

'Come in, Megan, come in,' Mr Hemingway said when she knocked on his study door, beckoning to her to stand before him by the side of the enormous fire which burned in the hearth. He had a cigar and a glass of whiskey on the table at his left hand. He had eaten a splendid dinner which she herself had helped to serve and he was in the mood, if it was in his power, to dispense largesse to anyone who asked it of him.

'Ferguson tells me you wish to speak to me.'

Ferguson had been most put out when she had asked his permission to have a word with the master, quite furious when she had told him it was a private matter and she would prefer a private interview!

'I can speak for you, girl, if you will tell me what it is about.' His lofty disdain was very evident for was she not merely a parlourmaid and clearly, his expression seemed to say, would be better served if she were to confide in him and let him negotiate for her. Perhaps she was of the opinion she might get a rise in pay, or better conditions, promotion even, if she spoke personally to the master. Ferguson liked to know exactly what went on, not just in the household he ran but in the minds of those whose manipulator he was and Meg's defiance of him rankled.

'Thank you, Mr Ferguson,' Meg said, her expression stubborn, 'but I must speak to Mr Hemingway myself.'

She did not fidget, nor show signs of nervousness but stood quietly before him, pretty as a picture Robert Hemingway thought in her simple black and white maid's outfit. The fire's glow and the soft electric lamplight burnished her hair to the brightness of copper. It was pulled back and up severely, a huge chignon held at the crown of her head with neat, unobtrusive combs but here and there a vagrant curl had escaped to drift to the nape of her neck and over her ears. Her cap – how did it stay on that thick and springing mass, he thought? – was frilled and most becoming and in the gentle light he could see the rose flush in her creamy skin at the cheekbone and the brilliant, excited glow in her eyes, the only sign she showed of her emotion.

'Now then, Megan, what can I do for you? You have no

complaints, I trust.' His eyes twinkled merrily for he had not forgotten her heated defence of Mrs Whitley over a year ago.

'Oh none, sir. I have been most . . . most comfortable here.'

'Comfortable Megan? Not happy?'

She would not lie but neither did she want to appear ungrateful.

'My time here has been most useful, sir and it is you I have to thank for it but now I have to move on . . .'

'Move on, Megan! What on earth do you mean? You have a home here with us, surely? Mrs Stewart, so my wife tells me, speaks most highly of you and it is clear you have a future before you. Like Hunter you are a hard worker but you also have a quick mind, as he does and the two qualities combined will enable you to reach a good position in the household . . .'

'Thank you, sir,' she interrupted politely, 'but that's not what I want!'

'What *do* you want, Megan?' His old face was quite astounded. He was of the generation in which the female sex had two choices. To be married and bear children, supported by a husband, or to go into service. Of course in the industrial areas there were women who worked in factories and mills but not nice little things like Megan who was as well mannered and decently brought up, in a different way of course, as his own wife. She and Hunter and that other lad – what was his name? – were a credit to the orphanage and to old Mrs Whitley who had continued their training and he had thought all three to be decently settled! Now, here was Megan wanting to be off and Hunter, for the past month or two pestering him – could you credit it – for flying lessons of all things, and a year in which to design and build his *own* racing car! He did not expect fulsome thanks for what he had done for the three of them, far from it for they had all turned out to be keen, conscientious workers. He had derived enormous pleasure from Hunter's enthusiasm and talent for racing the motor car and from his quite extraordinary ability to be good company when they were alone together on their travels, which was often. He had turned out well and was fast becoming quite the young *gentleman* but Robert Hemingway was not entirely certain he wished to be involved with the hair-raising and extremely unstable pastime of flying!

But Megan was standing here, obviously eager to tell him what *she* now needed and he supposed he must listen.

'Well?' he said gently.

'I have thought about this for a long time, Mr Hemingway. I

213

have not considered it lightly, nor on impulse.' She had evidently rehearsed what she would say to him carefully. 'I dare say I could manage it without you for I am not without a tongue in my head and I am certain I could convince whoever is in charge to consider me. Despite this I would be grateful if you would give me a "character" and perhaps use your influence to help me. I wish to apply for a position at the Adelphi Hotel, you see. I wish to go into the hotel business, Mr Hemingway, sir, that is what I wish to do!' Her young face was in deadly earnest and Robert Hemingway suppressed the desire to smile. The hotel business! What on earth was she talking about? She would do exactly there what she did here with no higher expectation than housekeeper and under much more stringent control. There would be no 'family' atmosphere as there was in this house. She would work hard and long, starting as she had done here, he supposed, as kitchen maid. He had no real knowledge himself of the running of an hotel but he imagined it would be not much different from a large house so why on earth did she want to move?

'Why Megan?' he said. 'What can it offer you that we cannot?'

'I want to own my own hotel, sir. One day!' Her face was very serious.

Dear God, substitute the word 'hotel' for that of 'motor car' and it might be Hunter speaking. Were the two of them in league? Had they got together and dreamed up this preposterous nonsense between them of motor cars and hotels and going into business on their own account, flying high on their youthful enthusiasm, or were they, perhaps, two of the most extraordinary youngsters he had ever had the fortune – or was it misfortune? – to come across? He didn't know, really, he only knew that the child was looking at him trustingly, quite certain that he would not smile, nor frown but would take her at face value, believing, that she was quite, quite serious. After all his own sister, the well-known, still active Mrs James Osborne, Lacy Hemingway that was, had made her way in a world filled with male scepticism of the female ability to do anything other than breed their sons!

'It has been in my mind for a long time, sir, but I did not know where to start ... that is until I was taken ... well, sir, I dined at the Adelphi some time ago...' Like Mrs Stewart, Robert Hemingway marvelled at Megan Hughes' choice of words, her phrasing for she sounded like no parlourmaid *he* had ever spoken with. '... and it was then that it came to me that the only way

214

to begin was at the beginning. In other words, at the bottom, sir. I was brought up in the hotel trade, in a manner of speaking . . .'

'You were!' The old gentleman was quite astounded.

'Oh yes sir. What else could you call the house at Great George Square, if not an hotel. Oh, not in the same class as the Adelphi . . .' She smiled infectiously, '. . . but what we did in Great George Square is exactly what is done in any hotel. We had guests who must be made comfortable. They had clean beds to sleep in and good food to eat and were treated courteously. I know that is a very simple way of putting it, Mr Hemingway, but can you tell me I am wrong. They did not eat hors d'oeuvres or paté or pétits fours but what they did eat was well cooked and presented. They did not sleep between silk sheets or walk on velvet carpets but they were warm and comfortable and clean. And I liked them, sir, and they liked me.' It was said simply with no intention to boast. 'I got on well with them though I could speak no more than a few words of their language. It gave me a good feeling to see them made . . . tranquil and at ease and to know that I had given that to them. But at the same time I am a good . . . a good housekeeper, sir. I can budget. I know how to . . . what's the word . . . balance comfort with profit, combine the two, if you know what I mean. So you see, sir, Great George Square, the Adelphi Hotel, the travellers' needs are always the same, whatever their class. And now, since I have worked here at Silverdale I have seen what . . . if you will pardon my frankness . . . what luxury is! I have seen the food that is cooked and served to those who would stay at an hotel like the Adelphi. I have discussed wines with Mr Ferguson . . .'

'Ferguson! Good God . . .' Robert Hemingway's mouth fell open.

'Yes sir. Now I realise I have a lot to learn but what I am saying is I already know a lot. And I know that I want to be a hotelier!'

He was silent for so long Megan thought he had dozed off in the way the elderly have. His face was in shadow and she could not see the sharp interest in his eyes.

'Sir,' she said tentatively.

'Yes, Megan. I am still here. Now tell me just what you want of me?'

'I want a job at the Adelphi Hotel, Mr Hemingway.'

'I see, and what position would you like?' He smiled good

215

humouredly for it crossed his mind that if she said manager, and got it, she would have tackled it with the enthusiasm of César Ritz, the genius who ran Europe's finest hotel, named after him, in London, but Meg was needing none of his light manner. This was her start. This was to be the first step on the ladder she would climb and she did not intend to have jokes made about it. Mr Hemingway had been very good to her, to all of them, more than good really, for there were not many gentlemen who would have taken the trouble he had with three refugees as she and Tom and Mrs Whitley had been. He had eased her own way that night, through the pain and despair Benjamin Harris had inflicted on her, sharing the dead weight which draped her shoulders and had tried, in his anger at what she had gone through, to punish the culprit. He had done his best. He had given her an arm to lean on and a fresh start when she had rested, but now she wanted him to do this one last thing for her. After that she would make it on her own.

'I don't care what I do, Mr Hemingway, as long as it gives me a chance to get on. All I want is a job there, any job and I'll show whoever is in charge what I'm made of. A reference is what I want sir, and perhaps a word from you. The word of an important gentleman does nobody any harm, Mr Hemingway.' She dimpled and dropped her eyelashes demurely and Robert Hemingway was made fully aware that Megan Hughes was not averse to resorting to a bit of flattery if it got her what she wanted. She knew how to work, to work hard and to learn from it. She was skilled in the art of how to get on with those above her. She had a good head on her shoulders and knew how to use it and by God she deserved a helping hand. His Alice would be sorry to see her go for a good servant such as Megan was hard to come by but really, it would be interesting to see how far she could get.

She started on the first of October. A kitchen-maid, the housekeeper said, sniffing, for it had got round that the new girl had been spoken for by one of Liverpool's most influential gentlemen and what might that mean, they all wondered. She was pretty enough and when she arrived at the staff entrance on that first day she was smartly dressed in a dove grey skirt and jacket with a white ruffled jabot at her neck. Her hat was large and fashionable with a drooping brim and a white tulle rose pinned to the side. Completely unsuitable Megan knew for a kitchen-maid but she

216

was Megan Hughes and this was the way she liked to dress – they were not to know she had made the outfit herself from a remnant bought at St Johns Market – and she was damned if she would arrive at her new job looking like a little brown mouse just to suit others. Start as you mean to go on, Mrs Whitley always said and that was what she was doing. Elegant she looked in a way they could not understand for surely – she could see it in their manner – if she was the fancy piece of a rich gentleman of the city she would hardly be working as a skivvy in the kitchen of the 'Delly'.

Within five minutes she was out of her lovely costume which was hung away carefully in the cubicle she was to share with another maid and, draped in a cap and apron three sizes too large for her, was on her knees scrubbing, a position she was to maintain for the next six weeks. She was polite, willing and self-effacing and if she went off to meet her 'paramour' those about her could never determine when, for she seemed to be in ten places at the same time, helping someone or other, forever asking questions and her room mate swore she spent the whole of each night in heavy and exhausted sleep!

'Now then, Megan,' the housekeeper in charge of the first floor said to her as she swept by one morning. Meg was on her knees, up to her elbows in a bucket of hot water in which caustic soda formed a large part and her mind was concerned mainly with the problem of how she was ever to restore her hands and forearms to some semblance of the white softness they had known as Mrs Hemingway's parlourmaid. Then she had worn gloves. Gloves to polish and clean and dry the beautiful bone china and lead crystal glasses and at night she had applied the sweet smelling salve made up for her by Mrs Hemingway's own personal maid with whom she had been on friendly terms for those who waited personally on the mistress could not appear with red and chapped hands.

'Come along to my office, Megan, quickly girl,' the housekeeper said, continuing on her way past the open-mouthed kitchen maid. 'See ... Nellie ...' She summoned a gawky girl who had been about to slip off for a cup of tea and who stood riveted in the doorway. '... finish this floor and look sharp about it. Now follow me Megan ... oh, and remove that cap and apron first, if you please.'

She was not asked to sit down nor did the housekeeper waste time.

'I believe you have worked as housemaid and parlourmaid, Megan,' she said crisply.

'Yes ma'am.' Megan knew better than to answer with more than the absolute minimum words necessary.

'For how long?'

'A year, ma'am.'

'Then why are you on your knees on the kitchen floor, if you please?'

'I was put there, ma'am.'

'So I see. Well in future you will work under my supervision. I shall give you a week to show me what you can do and if you do not suit you will be back at your scrubbing pail.'

'Yes ma'am, thank you.' She hesitated, breaking a cardinal rule which said never speak unless spoken to and then only with the shortest possible answer. There was no time in the busy, one might say hectic day in the life of an hotel such as this for idle chatter.

'Yes Megan? You wish to say something?' The housekeeper looked imperiously at Meg, her manner implying she would do much better if she didn't.

'May I ask . . .'

'Yes?'

'Did . . . did Mr Hemingway get me this promotion. There are girls in the kitchen who have been here much longer than I have and who work just as hard so if it was the old gentleman's influence . . . well, I'd rather not have it. I want to get on on my own merits . . .'

'*I beg your pardon!*' The housekeeper seemed to swell up like a toad and her already florid face turned to magenta.

'I said . . .'

'I heard what you said, young lady and I should advise you to keep remarks such as that to yourself if you wish to get on in this establishment. Nobody, *nobody* is promoted to my floor except on merit, d'you hear. If King Edward himself recommended you I should ignore him. Oh yes, I heard that you . . . shall we say . . . applied for the job of kitchen-maid through the auspices of a certain gentleman but that had nothing to do with me nor did it affect my judgement when I chose you over the others, I might add, for the position as underchambermaid. I heard of your previous experience and I have watched you work, Megan and I liked what I saw and that is why you are to come out of the kitchen. It will not make you popular with your fellow servants but it strikes me you will not let that worry you. Now report to the head chambermaid at the cleaning station on the first floor, by the back stairs, if you please, and she will instruct you in your duties.'

It was almost like being back at Silverdale. She was careful, tender even with the beautiful rooms which came into her care, and, as it became known that she was to be trusted, with the exquisite pieces of fine porcelain, the crystal and jade with which the upper reaches of the hotel were crammed. And she was quick! She could look at a job – had she not used the same method at Great George Square and at Silverdale – assess it thoroughly, be it cleaning a grate, changing a bed or polishing the windows of which there were a great many, and within minutes have her cleaning routine worked out and the time that was saved put to good use in another task. Her capacity to work at twice the speed of the other maids and twice as thoroughly brought her no friendships as the housekeeper had foretold but it did bring her to the attention of the head housekeeper! Her organisational abilities, her enormous capacity for work and the efficient and speedy way in which it was performed were noticed and commented upon and she was told that if she continued as she had begun there was a strong chance she might be promoted again.

'The chambermaid on the second floor is to be married, Megan and will leave us at the end of the month. I shall be sorry to see you go from my floor but I believe in rewarding good service.' The housekeeper nodded approvingly, well pleased with her own good judgement in putting forward this girl. In six months she had become what it took most a year or more to achieve, *and* on her own merit. Those in the kitchen who had been passed over muttered of favouritism but in their hearts they knew this was not so. Megan Hughes had got where she had, only chambermaid yet, but at least a rung or two up the ladder, on hard work and determination and nothing else.

But it was in her spare time that Meg learned the most. She did not need to be taught how to clean a carpet, to make a bed or polish a delicate ornament. When the time came her own good taste and what she had seen here, and at Silverdale would guide her in the way to furnish and decorate a room. What she wanted to know was how to *run* a hotel. A luxury hotel! How to manage the hundreds of tasks the man at the top managed. And to do that she must know what every single employee did as well! She was already a competent, imaginative cook for had not Mrs Whitley, one of the best herself, told her so. She had Mrs Whitley's recipes and had turned out a score of delicious meals at Great George Square, but French *haute cuisine*, as prepared by Monsieur Rénard and the other chefs in the kitchens, that was another matter.

And then there were the wines, the running of the grill room, the restaurant, the work of a waiter, the maître d'hôtel, the meaning of 'table d'hote', 'a la carte', the purchase of delicacies from all over the world, the arranging of balls and banquets, and of people! The accounts, the auditing, bills, receipts, the work done by receptionists, the board of directors, cellar men, electricians, engineers and the dozens of men and women who kept the hotel running smoothly without effort, or so it must seem to it's guests!

She knew she had a knack for it. A flair! She knew she had the capacity to work for nineteen hours in every twenty-four. She was obsessed with it, knowing instinctively that it was right for her, as Martin knew that the world of the motor car, of the flying machine was his, but before she moved on she must acquire the technical knowledge, as *he* had, to carry it out.

It became known in the months that followed that Megan Hughes was willingly at the beck and call of everyone who might need a helping hand and in return she demanded no more than the knowledge that was in their heads, cramming into her own receptive mind like a sponge soaking up water. She forced herself on with fierce, hungry resolution so that when the opportunity should occur she would be ready for it, preparing for the day she was convinced would come. She picked up, by listening and watching others in the kitchen and in every corner of the hotel where people worked, everything they themselves had learned or been taught, working every spare moment of the day and night. She made herself manage on three or four hours of sleep a night and the twenty remaining were spent in learning.

By helping everybody she helped herself. She learned to understand others and what interested them and made them speak of it. She learned kitchen administration for what working area will *work* if it is not efficiently managed and the people within it properly organised? She picked the brains of the wine waiters and the engineer in the boiler room. She became on the friendliest terms with the meat buyer, the meat carver, the head floor waiter, the French, the Italian, the Viennese chefs, the pastry chef, the entrée chef, the soup chef moving from crowded rooms bustling with industry to one in which a man laboured in solitary delicacy! Bakeries, cakeries, still rooms, they became as familiar to her as the tiny cubicle in which she took a few hours sleep each night.

She worked herself to a slender shadow and Tom said she looked like a bloody scarecrow and what the hell did she think she was doing to herself but she took no notice. She meant to learn how to run this great hotel with one hand tied behind her back if needs be, she told him blithely, and blindfolded into the bargain!

Chapter eighteen

It seemed the three of them could do no wrong now and Mrs Whitley grew dewy-eyed with proud emotion each time she spoke of them, which was often, to everyone who called to see her. Of course, their Martin had been a success for a long time now in his chosen profession, travelling the world alongside of Mr Robert and mixing quite naturally with the gentry and, she whispered confidentially, it was rumoured he had even spoken to His Majesty who it was well known took a great interest in motor cars and had not a few of his own! Martin had his very own motor car himself now, bought with the money he earned as one of Britain's foremost young racing drivers, a golden boy, Mrs Whitley had heard him described as in the newspapers, to match the golden era, driving round Liverpool when he was home, quite the man about town in his dashing little Austin two seater motor car. It was a glossy green, decorated with a trim of gold with bright brass lamps, a luggage rack to take the growing number of suitcases which held his fashionable wardrobe and a leather hood which he put up only when it rained. He had offered to take her for a 'spin' in it, she told one and all, not boasting exactly but pleased as punch just the same! She had declined, naturally, for she was past the age when she cared to hazard herself as their Meg did, in one of those wicked machines. He had told her privately that he had won Mr Robert many thousands of pounds in prize money and – she could not keep this to herself for he was the only person she had ever known to have done it – had finally persuaded Mr Robert to allow him to fly! Yes, John Tabner and his wife might well stare open-mouthed, she told them, for she had done the same when she had heard. He had flown solo, which meant, she explained kindly, that he had gone up completely alone in what he called a 'box-kite', only last month. He had received his official Aero Club Certificate and if they didn't believe her she'd ask him to show it to them the next time he was home. There was a belief that the motor car was a rich man's toy and

222

the aeroplane a young man's folly and what did she think of that, John Tabner asked her tartly but Agatha Whitley knew her boy was neither rich, nor foolish so she soon had *him* in his place!

Now their Tom, though not quite so ... so remarkable in his advance as Martin, had made good progress in the employment of the Hemingway family and was well nigh indispensable to old Mr Atkinson who, it seemed, could do nothing without his young assistant beside him. Well, you only had to see their Tom directing the other lads in the planting to know who was really in charge of the gardens. The old gardener was past his best but no-one commented upon it in Tom's presence for he was a kind lad and let the old man think he still ran the place. Tom was interested in new methods, she told her visitors sagely, not knowing exactly what they were, but you could see the results of the books he read on the subject in the splendid rows of pure, creamy cauliflowers, the sweet green cabbage, the shapely, plump marrow, French beans, potatoes and artichokes which lay like shining ribbons across the dark earth of the vegetable garden. The Hemingway's and their servants had never seen such fine asparagus and cour- gettes on their dinner table; old Mrs Hemingway had said so personally in the hearing of their Tom who had told her himself. He tended apple trees, damson and plum and had brought her the fruit of them for the very pie her visitors were eating! He had become quite an expert, Mr Atkinson had said on the growing of the exotic such as passion fruit – had they ever heard of it ... no ... well neither had she until Tom brought her some – fig, melon and mango. He had an aptitude for it. Well, she'd always known he was a patient sort of a lad and that's what you needed in his job, but he had a head on his shoulders and he'd be head gardener one day, she said, you mark my words.

And then there was Meggie! Was there ever a girl like her? Work! She could polish and clean a whole floor before you could say Birkenhead ferry and, if Mrs Whitley was any judge, would end up Head Housekeeper before she was twenty! She had her own floor now as head chambermaid and her only there eighteen months. There was no doubt about it, a girl could get on these days if she put her mind to it, *and* without creating a fuss like that Mrs Pankhurst and her two daughters who were playing havoc with life up in London, so she'd heard. Breaking windows and setting fire to schools and railway stations. They'd slashed a picture or two in the public art galleries and dropped burning rags

223

through the slits of letter boxes so that decent folk were deprived of their rightful mail but they'd get nowhere with that sort of nonsense. Gentlemen didn't like unfeminine behaviour, she could have told them that and could you wonder they got themselves arrested? Thank God their Meggie had no time for it, sensible lass that she was and had made a good start in her own career without the help of universal franchise, whatever that might be!

Yes, there was a lightness of heart in Mrs Whitley's ramblings on the endlessly interesting subject of 'her three', just as there was in the whole of the country. Though there was misery and poverty endured in the cottages and dwelling places of the working class for unemployment was rife that year, high spirits marked the era of King Edward the seventh for he had given his people a unity and a pride in themselves which, though the nation had been wealthy then, had not existed during the reign of his mother. He loved ceremony. He was gracious and charming and his passion for pageantry resulted in parades and processions, bringing life and colour to a people who had just moved from the prim, widowed puritanism of Queen Victoria. He liked State occasions with all their pomp, giving a show to those who had none. He moved about the country, letting all those about him know where he was and what he was up to and he was much loved by those he ruled. He liked the theatre, opera and the music hall and he encouraged the nation to do the same.

Yes, there was an air of enthusiasm and hope in the air. They were a generation standing on the threshold of a new era and Mrs Whitley's 'three' were to be amongst them.

The previous summer, just after she had begun working at the Adelphi Hotel, Meg had bought a cheap, second-hand bicycle from Mr Hale. He had let her have it for next to nothing since he still remembered the days when he and 'that lad', spoken with wistfulness in his voice, had worked side by side on the old tandem. He had shaken his head wonderingly when she called at the shop, saying he should have known the lad had something special about him, even then, tickled to death to have been a part of it. She could see it gave him immense pleasure to talk of his protégé's exploits, 'and if he should be up this way sometimes I'd be right glad to have a chin-wag with him,' he said. Aye, he could sort her out a cycle right enough. He had one this very minute which would suit, hardly used for the young lady who had owned it had been bought a motor car for her twenty-first birthday by her doting father and no longer needed the cycle. Would she like to see it, he said, and perhaps a cup of tea might be welcome.

Overwhelmed at the notion of a 'young lady' being bought, and driving a motor car, even in these enlightened days, Meg could only nod and allow herself to be led through the familiar clutter of 'Hale's Modern Bicycle Emporium'.

Each Sunday afternoon she was free from two o'clock until six and clad in her sensible skirt and jacket, leaving her 'best' dove grey behind, her straw boater firmly pinned to her errant hair, she would cycle down to the Pier Head and, putting the machine in the guard's van, board the overhead electric railway to Otterspool. From there it was but a few minutes cycle ride to Silverdale and by two-thirty she would be sprawled before Mrs Whitley's pantingly hot fire, a cup of tea in one hand and a coconut macaroon in the other. If the weather was warm they would sit in the tiny square of garden at the back of the cottage beneath the canopied shade of an old Cedar of Lebanon whilst the fat bees bumbled, heavy laden, about the borders of crimson poppies and the daisy starred grass. The sun streamed in benevolent warmth through the branches of the trees and Mrs Whitley's black cat hummed contentedly on her lap and Meg would feel the tension of her hectic week slip away. Her active mind and aching muscles, pushed to the limits of their endurance in her effort to cram three years' learning into one and a half, would become hushed and languorous and Mrs Whitley's voice would fade away to a pleasant drone. She needed this moment of complete inanimation to recharge the energy she used in the week as the old lady brought her up to date on the innocent gossip up at the house. What Mrs Glynn had said to Mrs Stewart when the housekeeper had criticised the cook's excellent paradise pudding! How it was rumoured that Mr Ferguson had a 'friend' in Liverpool and what could it mean, did Meg think? Mrs Hemingway's increasing quaintness and Mr Hemingway's everlasting kindness and patience with her and the score of quite unremarkable happenings which made up Mrs Whitley's contented life.

'... and of course when Martin said to me that he meant to take part I said he was quite barmy, which you would, wouldn't you? and where was he to get a flying machine I said and d'you know what he said? Well, you could have knocked me down with a feather. I'll make one, he said, proud as a peacock. Well, you know what he's like! If it moves or makes a noise our Martin will put wheels on it, or in this case, wings. It's only forty odd miles to Blackpool, Mrs Whitley, he says, and I mean to show the old gentleman . . .'

The words drifted about Meg's head, their humming refrain blending in a pleasant melody with those of the bees and the sharper call of the birds. A sentence here and there penetrated her cocoon of inertia and it might be said that her brain had almost come to a halt until, from the drift of trifling verbiage the words began to sharpen and make sense, to run cogently and she opened her eyes and sat up slowly.

'What did you say, Cook?'

'Pardon?' Mrs Whitley was clearly confused for she had said a lot of things.

'About Blackpool and . . .'

'I thought you were listening.'

'I was, but I missed the bit about . . .'

'What?'

'About the flying machine . . . and Martin.'

'Well, he can tell you himself because here he is!'

He stood at the fence, his tall, broad-shouldered figure casually dressed in pale grey flannels, immaculately pressed and a long sleeved polo neck sweater in a shade of blue which accentuated the sun bronzed flush of his face. He was grinning and his warm brown eyes did not waver as they ran audaciously over her own reclining figure for though she was their Meggie, she was still a bloody attractive woman, they seemed to say. He pushed open the small gate and sauntered up the narrow path, his hands thrust deep in his trouser pockets.

'Well, well, look who's here and pretty as a picture, if I may say so though why you wear that drab grey I'll never know. You should be in green or a vivid blue with that hair of yours, our Meggie.' His eyebrows tilted and the corners of his mouth turned in an ironic smile and Meg felt the small glow of pleasure his first words had induced in her, dash away in irritation for she knew he was right. If she had known she was to see him she would have put on a smarter outfit. She had a new one in a beautiful shade of apple green but it was so lovely she was reluctant to wear it on her bicycle for fear she might spoil it . . . But why should she care what Martin thought? Her own confusion made her sharp.

'Well, I can hardly wear my ball gown and diamond tiara on the bicycle, can I, though I would have done so if I had known you were to be here, my lord. After all, mixing with the posh and the privileged as you do all the time, you must expect it. But I'll know next time!'

'Now then Meggie. Don't get your dander up though I must admit you look a treat with those eyes of yours flashing like golden guineas. My word, but it's a little tiger cub when it gets going . . .'

'You're the one who gets me going, Martin Hunter.'

But the day was so pretty and so was Meg and Martin's admiring eyes told her so and she felt quite inordinately pleased with herself somehow so she grinned to let him know there was no ill-feeling.

'Now, what was it I was to tell you? I heard Mrs Whitley say . . .'

'I was telling her what you said about that aeroplane meeting in Blackpool next week, Martin and . . .'

'Ah-ha! and I suppose she wants to come with me?'

He grinned even more widely and Mrs Whitley regarded him fondly for had you ever seen such a charmer? Those lovely brown eyes of his and those strong white teeth and that air of knowing quite definitely that he was irresistible.

Meg straightened her long, supple back and her face became alight with excitement. Her eyes were as bright and glowing as Mr Hemingway's new electric lamps and she put her hands together like a child in prayer. She had become more controlled during the months she had worked at the Adelphi, for in her position as head chambermaid on her floor she had duties which called for a clear head, an organised mind and the need to appear calm and unruffled in the most trying circumstances. The young maids who it was her responsibility to direct and supervise must be able to turn to her in the sure certainty that Miss Hughes could deal with any problem which might trouble them and she did! But beneath it all was still hidden the star-flash, joyously fun-loving Meggie Hughes who had liked, nothing better than an unexpected outing, a good laugh and the company of her child-hood companions.

'D'you mean it, Martin?' Her voice was a reverent whisper. She had heard Martin enthuse, as who had not, on the marvel of Samuel Cody who only this year had flown an aeroplane from Laffans Plain to Danger Hill in Hampshire, a distance of just over a mile, the first man to do so in this country. Two months later, in July, the *Daily Mail* had offered prize money of 1,000 for the first pilot of any nationality to fly across the English channel. Martin had been in an agony of frustration since, if he had been able to get his hands on an aircraft, he said, he could have won it, certain in his youthful arrogance that even Louis Blériot, the Frenchman who had triumphed would not have done so had Martin been in on it! And in all this exciting time Meg Hughes had yet to *see* an aeroplane.

'If you can get the day off,' Martin said lazily.

'It's my monthly day off on Thursday.'

'You're on, then, our kid!'

'Can Tom come?'

'My God, you'll want to take the whole damn kitchen staff next. I have only got a two seater, you know,' but he was laughing indulgently for really she looked quite the prettiest thing he had seen for a long time. He met many attractive young ladies wherever he went, some of them from wealthy, good class families. They were all of them excited by what he did, for he had found there was something almost sexual in their response to the thrill of seeing him court death or maiming on the race track. They would cluster round him and the other drivers when the race was over, their smooth, well-bred young faces flushed, their breath quickened, their eyes wide and shining and promising all manner of delights. Most were strictly chaperoned by father or brother, but some who were married and did no more than accompany a husband, an enthusiast of the sport, to the track, were seldom reluctant to indulge in a flirtation and some to go even further! He was successful with women despite his youth for though he was single-minded about his career and would let nothing stand in his way, he had a masculine charm which allowed him the company, not just of the ladies with whom he mixed but their menfolk who respected his courage and clever mind.

He smiled his compelling smile, then turned to wink at Mrs Whitley. 'Are you sure you don't want to come as well? You can sit on Tom's knee, oh and don't forget those oyster patties of yours. Motoring, not to mention flying, gives you a good appetite!'

'Oh Martin!' she gasped, then, relieved, '. . . you great daft thing!' when she realised that he was only joking.

Blackpool! Mecca of the Lancashire holiday maker, it was called. Compressed like the fingers in a glove in the small motor car the three of them left Liverpool at six-thirty and at a spanking speed of twenty miles an hour which was all that was allowed, made for Ormskirk which they reached by seven-thirty. Another hour and they were through Preston and on round the coastal road through the villages of Freckleton, Lytham, the smart little seaside holiday town of St Annes-on-Sea and on to the outskirts of Blackpool and the Lancashire Aero Club where the meet was to be held.

'My God, I've never seen so many people,' Tom gasped, 'not even in Liverpool on a Shrove Tuesday. Where the hell have they all come from?'

'All over the place. There are excursion trains from at least a dozen places in Lancashire alone and then that doesn't account for those who have come in their own motor cars and on motor cycles. They have been preparing for this for months, you know, Tom. It's the first air meet in the country and this aviation ground has been built especially for it. Members from Aero clubs all over Europe have come, bringing their machines, and I heard you can't get a bed to sleep in if you were willing to pay a fiver a night.'

'But where are you going to leave the motor? There isn't an inch of space to spare,' Meg was looking about her, her head turning wildly from side to side for there was so much to see she was afraid she might miss some of it. There were more motor cars than she had ever seen in her life, jammed bonnet to tail along the road into the town, most illuminated in some splendid way and all the streets were decorated just as though royalty was expected. Indeed it had been hoped that His Majesty might honour the town with his presence but unfortunately he had been unable to attend.

'Look, oh look up there.' Meg pointed excitedly and taking his eyes from the road for a moment Martin, and Tom looked up to where Meg's quivering finger pointed. 'What are they, Martin? Oh will you look . . .?'

'They're hot air balloons, Meggie. There's one on each of the three main roads into the town to direct motorists on the most direct route to travel.'

'And look up there . . . on the tower . . .' Meg stood up, nearly losing her balance in her wild exhilaration, for indeed the air was tense with a strange intoxication which was infectious and had Tom not held on to her it seemed certain she would climb up on the bonnet in order to get a better view. She looked quite glorious and each young man found his eyes wandering constantly to the

229

special glowing beauty of her face. She wore a simple tailored costume of apple green cloth with a narrow skirt and a close fitting long 'Russian' jacket which had buttons of a darker green down the sleeves. The skirt just touched the arch of her foot and was also buttoned down one side. Her cream straw boater had apple green velvet ribbons two inches wide round the crown, tied in a flat bow at the back and the ends fell down her back to her shoulder blades.

'Where? Where d'you mean?' Tom was filled with the same heady stimulation which was turning Meg's eyes to the brilliance of burnished gold and his gaze followed hers to the breathtaking top of the great lattice work tower which dominated the centre of the town.

'There . . . those flags . . . what do they mean, d'you think?'

'What colour are they?' Martin shouted, his own breath beginning to quicken in his chest for the splendid day, the joy of the crowd, the delight and elation which seemed to have captured this enormous seething mass of people was growing in him. He was, of course, well used to the excitement, the tension of the race track but this was like nothing he had ever experienced.

'They're red.' Meg shaded her eyes against the sun. 'Yes . . . red!'

'That means someone's up.'

'Up? What d'you mean . . . up?'

'Someone is already flying.'

'Oh my God . . . where . . . where?'

She swivelled round in the car, her eyes searching the heavens for her first sight of a magical flying machine but there were only serene blue skies, the only thing in flight a solitary seagull floating over the promenade.

'Oh Martin . . . hurry, hurry . . . we don't want to miss it. Oh Lord, what if it should all be over before we get there. Can't you find somewhere to leave the motor so that we can get there quickly.' Her voice shrieked over the sound of the vehicle's engine, the shouts and laughter of the crowd and the brass band which was marching to meet them down the promenade.

'I've got to find this place I saw advertised in *The Autocar*. It's some chap with a garage and a large plot of ground which he's renting. There are parking spaces for over a thousand motor cars and motor cycles. It's not far now and then we'll catch a tram back along the promenade to the meet.'

Meg swore when the day was over she really did not believe they could ever, ever have a better one, which was sad really for one did not like to think the peak of one's life had been achieved, then she laughed and kissed Mrs Whitley's cheek since she was young and did not believe it.

There were huge hangars ... sheds, she explained kindly when Mrs Whitley looked mystified in which were housed at least fifty airplanes ... well, a dozen and standing about, having their photographs taken with such notable personages as Lord Lonsdale who had opened the Air Meet, and Lord Derby, were the aviators, Alliott V. Roe, Henry Farman, Rene Fournier and many others.

'And guess who else I saw, Mrs Whitley, go on, guess, and I swear he smiled at me.'

'Well, he would, a pretty girl like you,' Mrs Whitley said fondly, 'but go on, tell me for I'm sure I can't imagine.' She was quite captivated for it was almost as good as being there herself.

'*Grand Duke Michael*, that's who!'

'Eeh, well I never!' Mrs Whitley was not awfully sure who he might be but he sounded splendid.

'He's the cousin of the Czar of Russia!'

'*No!*'

'Yes, could you believe it? There were special stands built which could seat 250 spectators each and special boxes for folk with money. Guess how much to sit in one. Go on.'

'Eeh Meggie ...'

'Twenty-five guineas for the week!'

'Never!'

'... and there was a dining-room with a band playing and one lad told me there were thirty-six of them, lads I mean, including himself who had been brought all the way from Manchester just to organise the selling of the programmes. Can you imagine it! It cost us two bob to sit in the enclosure and when we went to get something to eat ... well, Cook, you and I would have been out of our depth, I can tell you. They had quartered 300 sheep on just that one day, with 300 of beef and a 1000 hams just to make up into sandwiches. There were eleven marquees ...'

'No ...!'

'Yes, it's the honest truth and the chap in the bar told Martin when he went to get us a drink that they sold 500 hogshead of beer, 36,000 *dozen* bottles of stout and 600 cases of whiskey *each day*!'

231

It had been a wondrous day, the summit of which had been when the first airplane was towed out across the field ready for take off. It was Mr Henry Farman's bi-plane, looking to Meg no more than a wooden crate on which a child might have stuck two flimsy wings. It began to move and she held her breath and her hand clung to Martin's and the flush of her cheeks and the glow in her eyes was quite beautiful. She felt the exhilaration flow through her veins as the machine gathered speed and she watched in total fascination the caressing separation of wheels and soil as the aircraft imperceptibly took wing. Its stately progress through the open air, had about it a grandeur she could not put into words, forging gracefully ahead into sheer space with nothing to hold it up until it was majestically aloft and *flying*! Away it went, disappearing into the pale blue sky above Lytham and for twenty minutes the crowd was almost completely silent, as one would be in church until at last the beat of the engine was heard and the airplane came back into sight. As it approached the field the aviator shut off his engine and was obviously about to attempt to bring the plane down from over the club house into the middle of the ground. As soon as he turned off his engine the machine stopped absolutely still and began to drop vertically and somewhere a woman's voice cried out, the only sound to be heard, but for the wind, in the whole of that vast crowd. Suddenly, with a sound like thunder the engine was switched on again and the machine veered up and to the left, lurching, as Tom put it later, like Kelly's drunken dog, and after a terrific swerve in which the machine was in danger of landing on the spectators' enclosure, indeed Meg swore she could see the aviator's face, landed sweetly at the far end of the field.

As it came to a halt Meg Hughes had tears on her face!

Records were broken that day in the art of aviation. They flew to the staggering height of over 1,000 feet into the air and as far as forty-eight miles, and at the frightening speed of forty-seven miles an hour and when Henry Farman claimed the first prize for speed *and* distance of £2,400 the roar of the crowd could be heard in Southport, they said.

At the end of the day, with the black flag fluttering on the top of Blackpool Tower to indicate that there would be no more flying due to the gusting breeze which had sprung up, the three of them followed the crowd along the promenade until they came to Church Street and Parkers Restaurant where they ate fish and chips and peas, with a sticky bun to follow before going on to the Palace Theatre to see Miss Amelia Bingham, 'the American Ellen Terry', as she was billed, and 'Coram, the great ventriloquist. They sat, just like royalty, Tom said, in a box which cost one whole guinea!

They walked back along the promenade under darkening skies, Meg in the middle, her arms through those of the other two and they talked of what they had seen that day and Martin was on fire to get started on it, he really was, he said for though he had not managed a flight he had heard one chap asking another, a Mr Compton-Paterson of the Liverpool Motor House, if he might order one of his machines and Mr Compton-Paterson had replied that normally he could give a very quick delivery but that he had had so many orders from the Aerial Rendezvous, deliveries might now be delayed. He was heard to say he turned out his machines at a very competitive figure of £500!

'£500! My God, what an industry it will be in a few years . . .'

Meg was certain she would take to flying too, and really, when Martin had his own machine he must promise that she would be his first, his very *first* passenger . . .

'Well, I dunno,' Tom remarked amiably, scratching his head and grinning. Everyone's to be off doing something but me. Our Meg's to be head cook and bottlewasher at the Delly, that is after she's flown in Martin's aeroplane which he is to build after he has put every man and his wife on the road in a motor car whilst all I do is watch the bloody grass grow on the Silverdale lawn!'

It was said without rancour, since, if the truth were told, of the three of them Tom might be said to be the most content. He strived for nothing since he had what he wanted. His pleasant face was just visible in the dusky light and it had a strength and a stillness, a simplicity which spoke not of lack of intelligence but of peace of mind. He was that rare being, a complete man, lacking nothing he needed, needing nothing he lacked. He did not dwell on the fashionable but simple elegance with which their Meg had begun to dress beyond telling her she looked a 'real treat'. He was not especially impressed with Martin's 'nippy' little sports car, nor his 'natty' pale grey flannels, worn without braces, since to Tom nothing had changed between them. It was doubtful he noticed that both Meg and Martin were leaving him behind, the reason being that when they were with him they were just as they had always been.

233

Mrs Whitley's 'the three of 'em'.

Those on the road on that lovely autumn evening, cyclists, pedestrians and the growing mass of motor cars turned to stare, open-mouthed as the three attractive young people in the speeding, southbound Austin motor car flashed by them and the song they roared floated for several moments on the disturbed air they left behind,

'Ta ra ra boom de ay,
Ta ra ra boom de ay,
Ta ra ra boom de ay,
Ta ra ra boom de ay!'

Chapter nineteen

For the past week or so the Adelphi Hotel had been at its busiest. Numbers of sportsmen had daily and nightly crowded its corridors, its suites and its parlours. Everywhere in the extensive and magnificent building there was a rush of life, and business. It was one of the busiest days of the busiest weeks of the year for the 'Waterloo' coursing fever was at its height.

There were all kinds and conditions of gentlemen to be seen in the entrance hall with only one topic of conversation and that was dogs and should a gambler have listened carefully he might have picked up a tip for the winner of the Waterloo Cup which was to be run that day. There were sportsmen aristocratic, democratic, plebian and any other kind you cared to mention though these might have had some trouble with the law should they have been spotted. There was the well-to-do gentleman of leisure, the home spun moderate man who just this one time of the year ventured a bet, the 'owning' gentleman, the 'laying' gentleman and the 'backing' gentleman, all mixed together in the common love of gambling, especially on the 'dogs'. Tall hats mixed with low hats and slouched hats and evidently they all had plenty of money in their pockets for they moved about the elegance of the hotel as only gentlemen of means can do.

Mr Willmer, the manager had been at his best for was that not the mark of a good hotelier, he who rises to the occasion and produces perfection under the most trying of circumstances. There were at least an extra hundred guests on top of those who stayed at the hotel on a regular basis, and he and his staff had been on duty each day from six in the morning until two of the following day. The number of calls and callers in this one single day had been above 200 and he had dealt with at least double that number in telegrams, letters, telephone calls and applications from callers wishing to book a room.

Forty-five passengers, Americans from two of the Atlantic liners had arrived only that morning and were, it seemed, everyone of them, crowding the entrance hall surrounded by an enormous weight of luggage. There were hatboxes, suitcases, vanity cases all stacked and waiting to be taken up in the lift to the private suites which awaited them. Outside on the road porters were wrestling with straps which secured boxes and trunks to the back of hansom cabs and one or two of the new taxi-cabs which plied between town and the pier head, vying with one another to catch the Americans for they were known as good 'tippers'.

A well-dressed gentleman moved through the melée with the high-nosed arrogance of one who is not a little put out by the restless activity which surrounded him. His face wore an expression which spoke plainly of his contempt for the mass of humanity, all speaking at once, or so it seemed, and intent on capturing the services of the receptionists, the porters, the crimson coated attendants or indeed anyone who would listen.

The gentleman was incredibly thin. His back was arrow straight and he walked with the boldness of a man who is in complete command of himself and his destiny and is quite, quite sure that when *he* snapped his fingers those put there to serve him would jump to it! He wore a single breasted Chesterfield overcoat of fancy black cashmere woven with a faint self-colour stripe. It had a fly front and four silk basket buttons. It was lined with black silk which continued on to the front of the lapels to form a facing. In his hand he carried a black silk top-hat. His hair was smoothly brushed, a silvery grey and liberally applied with pomade, and his eyes were the same colour.

Without hesitation and in a way which surprised those about him for they had really no intention of making way for anyone, he cut a path through the crowd until he stood directly in front of the reception desk. The attractive young woman who worked there, about to attend to a querulous, extremely tired American gentleman, just docked that morning and who wanted to be taken immediately to his suite he declared, found herself drawn quite strangely to the newcomer and before she knew it she was asking him if she might help him.

'I have a suite booked,' he said. No more.

'Yes sir, and your name?'

'Here is my card.'

She took it nervously for really the gentleman was very . . . very forceful. She glanced at it and then at the register on the desk, then she smiled.

'Aah yes sir, here it is, Mr . . .'

He cut her short abruptly. 'My luggage is in a hansom cab outside. Have it brought to my room. Is that the key? Thank you,' and before she could speak another word he had taken it from her and was making his way towards the lift. As he left, the hubbub which had died at his appearance, broke out again and the young receptionist forgot him as she was swamped again by the demands of the guests.

Meg had gone down to the basement that evening for only the second time in eighteen months for of all the working areas in the hotel in which she had hung about since starting work at the Adelphi, the cellar which contained the hotel's famous turtles was the one she liked the least. Large steam-heated tanks contained up to 250 live turtles at a time and from these inexhaustible reservoirs turtle soup was sent all over the country, and even to Europe and America. At the height of the trade, an industry in itself and one very profitable to the hotel, more than fifty quarts of soup a day were sent out, much of it to London dealers who then directed it further afield. The situation was ironic for the turtle caught in the Gulf of Mexico was transported to Liverpool, turned into soup at the Adelphi and then returned to the New World! The reptiles often became tame enough to take the heart of a lettuce from an attendant's hand whilst waiting for that same hand to decapitate it. Meg hated it. It was the one aspect of the hotel trade she abhorred, swearing that as she had no intention of serving turtle soup on any menu in her establishment she had no need of experience in the preparing of it, but a message had been left in the kitchens that she was to go there immediately.

'What for?'

'How do I know? Perhaps Mr Willmer wants to show you his tame turtle.' There was much ribald laughter which Meg ignored for she was well used to the broad humour which was directed at her own determination to 'get on'. The other girls were jealous of her success and of her looks and the men frustrated in their efforts to get their hands on what they considered she flaunted and so they taunted her whenever they could, for the most part good naturedly for despite her 'standoffishness' she was always willing to give a helping hand to anyone in need of it.

She took the lift down to the basement, surprised to find it so deserted. She could hear a telephone ringing somewhere and someone must have answered it for it stopped and there was absolute quiet. The light was dim for it was late evening and the bustle of the day was over. Those who had laboured had gone and the few who were on night duty were off somewhere in one of the dozens of small kitchens which honeycombed the basement. She trod softly through interminable passages, corridors, cellars and underground apartments, passing through empty kitchens which in the daytime would be crowded with chefs in spruce white linen caps and overalls, cooks and assistants, meeting no-one, hoping she was going in the right direction for the last time she had come down here she had been accompanied by Mr Willmer, the manager. Even he had heard of her thirst for knowledge and who amongst us can resist airing what we know? It was cold here for there were ice-chests filled with meat, game, poultry and fish, and she shivered suddenly and for some strange reason her heart missed a beat.

'Mr Willmer,' she called and her flesh began to tingle and crawl and she hesitated. The thought of being down here alone with all those slow swimming, quite obscene – in her opinion – creatures in their tanks was giving her the creeps and if whoever it was who had sent for her – who the devil could it be? – did not show himself soon, she was off and he could whistle!

It was almost a repeat of the scene of two years ago for he stepped out from behind something, she could not have said what it was, like a genie appearing from a puff of smoke. This time the light was behind him, outlining his overcoated figure and his shadow fell across her, touching her with its cold presence and she began to shiver more violently. She could not see his face for it was in darkness but of course she knew who it was at once. Only his eyes were visible as they gleamed like star pricks in the dark. Like rats' eyes will. They were cold and grey and narrowed and Meg felt the wash of despair flow over her, wondering as he walked towards her why she had been so naive as to imagine he had given up, gone to some other place and forgotten her. Men like Benjamin Harris did not forget, nor forgive an insult, an offence, an injury, real or imagined and though it was nearly two years since she had seen him he acted as though it was merely yesterday.

'Well Megan, we meet again as I promised.' His face was in the light now and his fox's smile widened but he made no move to touch her. It would do him no good, she realised to create a scene here on the premises of Liverpool's most renowned hotel. She was quite safe from physical assault – wasn't she? – whilst they were here, even in the depths of the basement since it was too close to where staff worked who might come upon them in the course of their duties. Her thoughts were wild and frightened, darting like captive birds from one question to another. Where had he been these two years? What had he been doing? ... The criminal fraternity, was that how he lived? His clothes he ... looked as immaculate as any of the dozens of gentlemen who stayed here and why ... why was he here? And why, *why* had he not come back to intimidate her ... and Tom ... until now?

It seemed he read her mind.

'It has been longer than I intended, Megan,' he went on, 'since I have been away. On business, shall we say, here and there, wherever there was a profit to be made, but I never forgot you, my dear and at the first opportunity which presented itself I came hurrying back to see you. I was distressed at first that we should be parted for so long, and then the delicious thought occurred to me that perhaps it was better this way. You had hoped I had gone, had you not, Megan? For good, I mean. You had begun to believe you were not to see me again, were you not? You were doing well, you and Fraser, and the old woman was spending her declining years in well deserved comfort and your world was shaping up very nicely, was it not? You had forgotten about me! I had dropped out of your life completely so how ... titillating, it seemed to me, to leave it awhile! Give you a few months of believing all was well with your world, and then ... pouff!' he made a movement with his hands like that of a magician producing a rabbit from a hat, '... here I was back again. Yes, I liked the idea Megan. It seemed most appropriate. My word, it really is a most civilised way in which to collect what is owed one.'

He smiled with silken menace.

'Have you nothing to say, Megan? Nothing to say in greeting of an old friend? No! Then may I add that you have grown quite delightfully since last we met. One wonders where the time goes. You have become ... a woman, my dear, and a most attractive one. But then you were a very pretty girl!' He eyed her superb figure, gloating on the curve of her magnificent breast, her slender waist and the thrust of her curved hips. She was nearly nineteen and had reached her full maturity, tall, full-bodied and strong, five feet nine of superb womanhood and she carried herself and her height with a natural, quite instinctive grace.

'And how is Fraser?' he continued, not, it seemed, expecting her to speak. 'Well, I trust, and getting on in his ... career! Gardener's boy now, I believe.' His lips curled in a sneer, 'And most suited for it, I suspect, whereas you...' Again his eyes crawled over her, '... are going from strength to strength. Oh yes, I have my informants, my dear. I keep up to date with all the news of Liverpool. I am here now and again, of course, for I would not wish to lose touch, shall we say, with my friends. You understand?' His smile was as cold as his eyes and Meg shivered again.

Instantly he was full of false contrition. 'You are cold, Megan? Now why is that? I find it quite comfortable here in the humidity which houses these handsome creatures. They are enormously interesting, don't you think, and yet ... stupid! They allow themselves to be caught, to be fed and even ... petted, I hear, before being led to the executioner's block. Strange is it not?'

He made no move to touch her and yet in her imagination she felt his dreadful hand make contact with her face and neck and linger at her breast and she felt the horrified scream rise in her throat and he saw it begin.

'Don't do it, Megan. Make no sound for if you should alert the staff and bring them here you might be inordinately sorry. I got in here so easily and I wish to get out the same way but ... if I do not, my friends who are waiting will know the reason why. I am a guest here, Megan, did you not know? Of course you did not since I am not on your floor. Oh yes, I know just where you work, my dear. I could have summoned you to my suite but I did not wish to draw attention to our relationship so I had a message left for us to meet here. Naturally it was worded so that it gave the impression one of those in charge wished to see you. More suitable, I thought and such a marvellous atmosphere down here. Do you not like it, Megan? The smell of ... what is it, do you think? A strange smell ... a smell of death ... yes ... for that is what takes place here, would you not agree?' He smiled charmingly and Meg knew that if he should put a hand on her she would be unable to move to stop him. She was probably stronger, even heavier than he, for he was as thin as a garden rake but his eyes hypnotised her and her limbs would be frozen until he released her. She could hear the hiss of steam from the tanks up ahead and a curious bubbling sound and her head felt strangely heavy as though it was stuffed with bricks.

'Well Megan, what shall we do now, you and I? We are alone here and there is no-one to hear us if we are quiet about it. Now what shall it be, my dear . . . ?'

He cocked his head suddenly, turning it in a listening attitude and though she heard nothing for she was deaf as well as paralysed, he began to move away, treading backwards softly.

'It seems we are not to become better acquainted just yet, my dear, for I do believe there is someone about. What a pity! Never mind, you could come to my room later. I have some friends who have confessed to me they find you quite . . . delectable. We were about to have a party, a celebration for we have just concluded a most successful business deal. Highly illegal, naturally but very lucrative.' He smiled slyly. 'I confide in you since I am quite convinced of your . . . loyalty. But I must go, Megan before our trysting place is discovered. We must keep our . . . friendship a secret, must we not? Au revoir then, Megan, until later, and I hope by then you will have found your tongue. My friends do like to be entertained!'

The cellar man who found her was most concerned, telling her sternly she should not be here alone at this time of night, and yes, the damp heat and the smell of the turtles could sometimes be quite overpowering and enough to make even a strong man swoon, as she had done, and to take his arm as he guided her to the lift.

She crept along the passage to her room and her feet made a swishing sound on the oilcloth for she found she could not lift them to step out. For an hour she sat on her bed, deep in shock and she could utter no sound.

'What am I to do?' she whispered at last and a pulse beat painfully in her head. She stood up and groped her way to the tiny dormer window of the room which was her's and stared sightlessly at the lights of Liverpool and felt a terrible desire to laugh creep up her throat from her chest. She did not know why for God knew there was nothing humorous to be found in the sickness and terror which swamped her but hysteria rose in her, choking her, shaking her body from head to foot.

'How long?' she muttered. 'How long can I go on with this?' She turned and walked on unsteady legs to the low chair and sat down. She bent her head to her knees and the dread and panic

241

which had been held at bay by shock flooded her body and she
thought she would drown in it as it reached her lungs making it
difficult for her to breathe. What was she to do? Dear Christ, what
was she to do? She could not go on with her life in the certain
knowledge that at every turn, at each moment she felt herself to
be drawing near to her goal, *he* would be there to pull her down.
Her goal! Her dreams! They had begun with the plans *she* had
conceived. They had thrived with the energy *she* had created,
strung from her weary bone and muscle when they cried for rest
but she had forced herself onwards and she was almost there. An
hour ago she had been filled with jubilation, ready to take on the
world for she was almost there, almost there and now it had been
blown away as though by a capricious breeze and had slipped
from her grasp.

It was then that the merciful curtain fell about her and she
slumped sideways behind it.

It was six-thirty the next morning when they knocked on her
door and Miss O'Hara was most put out when she could not open
it.

'Megan, open this door at once! Do you not realise the time?
The maids on your floor are hovering about like marionettes
without you to tell them what to do. Megan!' She rattled the door
handle, clearly becoming more angry by the minute,'. . . what on
earth have you got on the other side of this door? I cannot open
it. Are you ill, girl, answer me.'

Had it been anyone but Megan Hughes there was no doubt
Miss O'Hara would have given her no chance at all to explain
this dreadful event, for an unreported absence with no warning
was the most heinous crime to be committed in an industry which
relied completely on the trustworthiness of its staff. Guests must
be fed and kept warm and comfortable for after all that was what
they paid for, and if they were not they would simply take their
business elsewhere! Megan Hughes was the most reliable member
of Miss O'Hara's team and not once had she been known to be a
minute late in reporting for her duties. She took no time off to
which she was not entitled and indeed, often stayed on to work
when her shift was finished. She was never ill, or if she was she
did not complain of it. Now, like a bolt from the blue, she had
simply not turned up for work!

There was a scratching from the other side of the door and it
opened a crack and Miss O'Hara fell back from the apparition

which swayed there. If she had not known better she would have said Megan Hughes was suffering from a hangover! Her face was grey, quite shapeless really as though the flesh had slipped somewhat and her eyes had sunk an inch or two into her skull, deep and dusty and blank. Her hair fell in tattered swathes about her face just as though she had pushed her hands through it time and time again.

'Megan . . . my God . . . what is the matter with you, girl?'

Megan Hughes could remember nothing of the night which had just passed. She recalled *his* face, of course since it would haunt her until the day she died, and the words he had spoken to her, and the ride in the lift with the solicitous cellar man and her own pathetic gratitude when, concerned about her, he offered to take her to her bedroom door, for really Miss Hughes, who everyone knew for the sprightliest of girls, had seemed quite out of her mind about something. She had groped her way inside and the rest was shut away somewhere in her head for she could not remember straining every muscle in her back, as she must have done, to shift the heavy dresser across the door and even then her fear had driven her to push the bed behind it for that was where it lay, barring Miss O'Hara's entrance.

'Megan, my dear . . . are you ill? You look dreadful.' The housekeeper managed to push her way through the small space between the door and the frame, then turned to stare in astonishment at the dresser and the bed, all askew behind it.

'What . . . Megan . . . dear God, girl, have you taken leave of your senses? What on earth is going on here . . .'

She looked wildly at the younger woman, her own face quite appalled by the expression on Meg's for she stood there like a whipped child and for a moment Miss O'Hara was hard pushed to remember that this was the girl she herself had picked from the floor beside her scrubbing pail and groomed . . . yes, that was the word . . . groomed for the position she now held.

'What is it, Megan?' Her voice had become stern and she folded her arms forbiddingly over her ample bosom. 'Has someone been . . . forcing their attentions on you? Why are you barricaded in here, girl, tell me at once. If one of the men has been . . . has made advances then I wish to know about it.' Not for one minute did it occur to her to suspect a *guest*! 'My God, lass, have you seen yourself in the mirror? Now then, his name, if you please and I shall see what's to be done . . .'

243

'No . . .'

'No! Do you mean there is no-one, or are you protecting his name? Come Megan. I mean to get to the bottom of this.' Miss O'Hara sniffed and lifted her head imperiously. If there was anyone intimidating this young woman she wanted to know about it. She was a good girl and besides she did not want to lose the best worker she had ever known, and if her manner was anything to go by that was just what was about to happen. Megan Hughes looked as though she was about to disintegrate beneath some burden which she could not carry alone.

'Come Megan, answer me at once. What's to do here?'

Sympathy would have finished Megan Hughes just at that moment. If Mrs Whitley had come upon her, opened her arms and called her name, Megan would have walked into them, wailing her fear and her despair and would never have been the same again. She wanted nothing more, and would gladly have curled up on the old cook's knee, if she had been allowed, and wept like a child. Like the child she wanted to be again, but Eveline O'Hara was *not* Mrs Whitley and would allow none of *that*, her expression said. Good honest advice she would give, if asked, and sensible support but no pampering of *her* work force. If there was trouble she would deal with it. Megan Hughes looked as though she was at the end of her tether but if she was about to hang herself with it then the housekeeper did not intend to stand and watch it. Get her back on her feet was her remedy in the only way she knew how. Hard work, perhaps a cup of tea first and in the satisfaction of doing a good day's work this girl would recover. She was certain of it for Megan Hughes was made of strong fibre, her expression said so. It stiffened Meg's spine and she straightened her drooping shoulders. She put up a faintly trembling hand to her dishevelled hair and brushed it back.

'No Miss O'Hara, there's nothing like that,' and the housekeeper knew she was lying but admired her for it just the same. She would shoulder this trouble alone then! 'I have a . . . I have not been well in the night. I did not want to be . . . disturbed.' She stared at her superior quite defiantly and dared her to contradict her and the housekeeper watched her as she quite visibly pulled the damaged threads of her self-control about her. Something had badly frightened this young woman and she was determined to keep it to herself apparently but Eveline O'Hara meant to find out what it was. She would get nothing from her now. Question

244

her and she might be spun off into whatever dread had held her in the night but leave it awhile, watch her and perhaps she would give it away herself. There were a number of menservants, young and self-opinionated who would gladly give Megan Hughes a tumble. The only thing that disturbed her was the absolute certainty that, should one of them have tried it, Megan would have put him in his place before he had so much as given her the time of day! It really was a mystery!

'I'll ... I'll have a wash, Miss O'Hara,' Megan was saying, '. . . and get changed and be down in ten minutes.'

'Good girl.' The housekeeper nodded her approval. 'And, well, it might be a good idea if you, well why don't you take tomorrow off? Go and have a chat with your friends. Now, ten minutes, no more and in the meantime I'll get your girls on the move. God knows what they'd do with themselves if left alone. Sit and drink tea, I shouldn't wonder, imagining themselves to be duchesses!'

Chapter twenty

The large crowd held its breath as the great sleek monster roared its snarling anger. It sounded quite amazingly like a wounded beast, hurt beyond endurance but still lethally dangerous as it surged dramatically close to the lip of the banked track. It would go over, they were convinced, leaping up into the air, hurtling beyond its own seeming ability to fly but when the driver of the sleek-nosed motor car pulled it skilfully back on to its true path, the soft sighing from more than a thousand throats could almost be heard over the ferocious sound of the racing cars' engines.

It was 1910. Since 1907, when it was built, Brooklands had been the Mecca for all driving and flying enthusiasts. It was created in the private grounds of the home of a gentleman named H. F. Locke-King, built by private enterprise and was the world's first real motor course.

Apart from racing it was meant to provide a ground for the testing of motor cars since the speed limit on the public roads was twenty miles an hour and the police were enthusiastic in their enforcing of the law.

The first 'meet' was run like a horse race with the drivers dressed in 'silks' in the colours of their choice like jockeys and it was not until later that numbers were used to differentiate between drivers. There was a clubhouse and the 'Brooklands Automobile Racing Club' was formed, together with a flying club for those who were daring enough to try it! Those who were members were wealthy and of the upper and middle classes. 'The right crowd and no crowding' was their slogan and it was seriously meant for the club was very exclusive. The facilities were outstanding and those who manufactured automobiles were inordinately glad of them to test the speed and durability of their inventions. Anyone might compete in the races and a side-valve 'Morgan' had as good a chance to win as a super-charged Bentley for there were many handicap events. There were neat enclosures, white-painted rails and wooden seats from which spectators might cheer on their particular favourite. It was just like a racecourse and the broad sweep of the two and three quarter miles of banked concrete oval gave a marvellous sense of space.

The cars were a blur as they attempted to accelerate beyond the impossible speeds they ware aiming for but the one the crowd watched, the one it hissed through its clenched teeth over; missed its heartbeat over, drew in its breath over would not be overtaken, surging ahead, doing yet another dauntless circuit of the track. He was fearless, they said to one another, or quite, quite mad, depending on one's point of view. Just look at the lion-hearted way he ventured his machine, and himself to the very edge of the track, risking time and time again being forced over the top of the banked track by the other machines as he overtook them. It made one's hair stand on end, really it did, the risks he took and not one of them would change places with him, no, not for a gold clock but by God it was exciting seeing him go!

It was the Whitsun meet. Whit Monday and the holiday crowds had come for miles, some in their own motor cars, those who had the money and daring to purchase and drive one, many on motor cycles, charabancs, outings from as far away as London for the sport of motor racing was fast becoming a national favourite, not just among those who loved the machines but with those who thought of it in the same category as horse racing, but more exciting! They had moved about the paddock, staring in awe at Lord Lonsdale in his Mercedes, Malcolm Campbell in his now famous 'Bluebird' and at men whose names were fast becoming household. Selwyn Edge. Montague Napier. Percy Lambert. They had rubbed shoulders with two of Brookland's most celebrated sons, Dario Resta and Kenneth Lee Guinness, admiring the dashing way in which they wore their caps with the peaks at the back, their white silk scarves and the goggles each man adjusted carelessly as he climbed into the driving seat of his open, pitifully vulnerable racing car. They were narrow, those dangerously roaring machines, their frames made of pressed steel with a flimsy covering to streamline them into the shape which might gain them a precious second in the records they strived for. They had wire wheels and not a lot in the way of suspension but the crowd loved them, and the men who drove them!

The one they encouraged, silently at first then with increasing enthusiasm as he catapulted ahead of the other cars, had caught the crowd's fancy from the start. He was tall, broad-shouldered and very handsome. He had grinned, his white teeth flashing in his brown face and waved his hand carelessly to the crowd as he climbed into his machine. A young lady very blonde and dashing in a hobble skirt, tight and tubular, the very pinnacle of fashion and in a brilliant shade of cerise kissed him full on the mouth for everyone to see, quite shocking really but all part of the day's excitement! They were not of the ordinary, these men and their women too, one supposed, who dared their lives and their young, unmarked bodies in the pursuit of speed. They, like those who entertained the public in other ways, in the theatre, the music hall and in the new, strangely flickering, moving pictures which were thrown on to a screen, as in the drama *The Great Train Robbery*, and which were now fascinating a growing audience, were of another world, came from another world where such things were commonplace, where they were allowed because of their difference to the rest of humanity, a tolerant license to display whatever emotion they cared to in public.

The crowd had become still again now, silent and deliciously afraid for surely no man was supposed to go so fast, nor so dangerously. His machine was merely a streak of yellow and chrome and the head of the handsome young man was seen to shake quite madly on his shoulders with the force of the movement and speed. His cap was long gone!

It was all over really before any of the crowd could grasp it. One moment their eyes were struggling to keep the bright yellow flash in view, waiting impatiently for it to circle the two and three quarter miles of track, and in the next women were screaming, their hands to their mouths, men were shouting hoarsely, all clutching at one another in a curiously thrilled state of horror as the machine appeared to leap into the air, all four wheels completely leaving the track, slammed onto its side where it landed, slithered along the concrete track and finally, slowly it seemed to those who watched, turned over and over and over, at each turn loosing some part of itself, a wheel, a piece of jagged metal hurtling into the cars which followed it, some careening into the members' enclosure which stood close to the banking.

It came to rest at last, its three remaining wheels spinning madly in the air and beneath it the handsome young driver lay still and in the distance could be heard the wail of the ambulance.

He was alive, Mr Hemingway told them, and a miracle it was

too, but he was badly injured and would have to remain in the hospital at Weybridge for several weeks. They would bring him home to Silverdale to recuperate, naturally but it would be a long while – he did not voice the awful words, 'if ever' – before he would race again. Martin's left leg was fractured, four of his ribs were cracked, his pelvis and hip bone were 'suspect', whatever that might mean and his face was cut somewhat but he was strong, a young and healthy man and would heal quickly, the doctor assured him. There was nothing anyone could do. Mr Hemingway would be going back by train to 'have a look at the boy' in the next few days, he said and really, they were not to worry themselves. It was an excellent hospital, the surgeon was a splendid chap and Martin was having the best possible care.

But they did worry. She and Tom and Mrs Whitley spent the whole of the following Sunday afternoon telling each other that their Martin had a constitution as strong as a horse – look at the way he had fought in the boxing ring. He had always been 'bobbish', Mrs Whitley said, never ailing a day, begging for reassurance from the other two, secretly picturing her lad with his strong, straight leg all smashed up and his lovely looks gone forever! He would be as right as rain, hale and hearty and as good as new before the month of May was out, they hastened to tell one another as they gathered about the table. They smiled and pretended to tuck in to beef and dumplings and Mrs Whitley's baked almond pudding into which she had poured a whole glass of sherry in the hope it would lift their anxious spirit, but they could not avoid catching one another's worried glance nor keep up the pretence there was nothing wrong and that this was their normal Sunday visit.

It was three weeks before the doctor at the hospital in Weybridge would allow Martin to come home and then it was only because Robert Hemingway had reassured him that 'the boy' would have a trained nurse in charge of him at all times, his own personal physician would look him over every day and that the facilities at the Liverpool Infirmary were excellent and should an emergency crop up, God forbid, they would be freely available to a man such as himself. An ambulance was to take Martin to the railway station at Weybridge. A private carriage was to be put at his disposal on the train. He would travel with the nurse who was to be in charge of him and in short, nothing, *nothing* was too good for the young man who had brought such joy, such reward, such acclaim to bless an old man's declining years! Though he might never race the Hemingway flyer again, or even her successor which would no doubt be built from her ashes, Martin Hunter was not to be discarded like some worn out tool which has lost its use but would be looked after until he, or Robert Hemingway, or perhaps both of them had decided where his future lay.

They were all there at the front door of Silverdale to meet the ambulance as it drew carefully up the long, gravelled drive, even Mrs Whitley, tearful and hardly daring to look for if her lad should be horribly scarred how on earth would she be able to endure it? He and the other two were the closest she had ever known to children of her own. He had helped to save her life at great risk to his own on the day of the fire. She had guided him through his boyhood, taken pride in his achievements, even clouted him a time or two and been driven to distraction by his passion for motor cars but when it came to 'aye lads aye', he, perhaps more than Meg and Tom, was the darling of her heart.

His face grinned up at her from the whiteness of his pillow as he lay on the stretcher but for an anguished moment all she could see was the neat bandage which shrouded one side of it, fastened securely beneath his chin and across the top of his head. It was only a degree or so paler than the colour of his skin and where, her old heart pleaded, beneath the pallor of his weakness, was the Martin she remembered? Then he called her name and held out his hand to her, and to Meg, and his grin became wider and they all crowded round him for was he not a hero? With a hand in each of theirs he was carried indoors and the pleas of the nurse to 'stand away from her patient, if you would be so kind, and be careful of the doors, and to mind the cast on his leg' ignored by one and all. Mr Ferguson was quite put out for it seemed the servants cared not a jot or tittle for him at that moment and as Tom remarked later, he looked as though he was about to have a bloody fit he was in such a tantrum. Tom should not have been there really for his place was in the garden. At least the indoor staff had some excuse to mill about in the wide hallway but Mr Hemingway was like an old hen with a chick and didn't seem to mind what anyone was doing as he supervised the stowing away of it in a comfortable nest! Martin was placed in a small, sunny room on the ground floor at the back of the house, a smaller one adjoining it, once a footman's pantry, made over for the nurse. A coal fire crackled in welcome in the grate and Mrs Hemingway had instructed flowers and books to be placed on the window sill for his pleasure and at last, one by one, after speaking a word to him or merely patting the shoulder of the returning hero, the servants had dribbled away, called to their duties by a peevish Mr Ferguson. Even Tom was reluctantly drawn back to the hoeing he had been about when the ambulance had arrived. Mrs Whitley had clung to Martin's hand for as long as the nurse would let her, exclaiming woefully at the heavy cast on his leg and the thinness of his 'poor face', but cheering up immensely at the thought of the egg custards she could now get into him, the kidney omelettes, light enough but nutritious for an invalid, the dumplings as he grew stronger and the good vegetable soups she would carry over to the house and which could be guaranteed to get him on his feet again and his manly strength returned.

Only Meg, with two whole hours before she need return to the hotel, remained, the nurse giving reluctant permission for it, glad herself to have someone sensible to watch over her patient whilst she recovered from the long train journey with a cup of tea and the bite to eat offered beside Mrs Glynn's kitchen fire.

'Well, our Meg.' Martin looked tired now, somewhat drawn about the eyes, his mouth formed, after all its smiling into a thin line of pain.

'Well, our Martin.' She leaned her elbows on the neatly folded bedspread which lay across his chest and smiled affectionately into his eyes. She could see he was ready, after all the excitement, to be left alone to sleep for a while but the weeks of worry, of wondering how he *really* was plus her own private anxiety had been long and hard on them all and she needed a moment or two to reassure herself that he was not irreparably damaged. Though they had been told he would mend with time and might not even have the limp which had at first been envisaged, she was not completely certain, not just yet awhile that what the doctor had said was true. She needed to see for herself; look at him for a few minutes longer; study his face and listen to his voice. She would know then. She was not quite certain what she would know or how she could be sure her instincts would not lie but something curious inside her, something she had carried with her since those first days at the orphanage and which had fused her and Tom and Martin into one unit, would tell her. She would know!

'How is it, then?' she asked softly.

251

'Alright now, Meggie, now I'm home,' but when he said 'home' she knew he meant with her, with her and Tom.

'You'll mend now, Martin.' Though it was spoken as a question, it was really a statement of fact.

'That I will, our Meggie.'

'What will you do then?' She held his hand lovingly between hers and he watched the firelight play warmly in the curly tendrils of her hair which she had pulled carelessly back with a bright green velvet ribbon, her usual trim and proper 'housekeeper' self left behind at the hotel. Her eyes were as soft and golden as the sunlight which struck the yellow daisies in the bowl on the dresser and an excited flush of colour stained her cheek. Her hands were warm and softly soothing as they folded about his own. Her lips curved in a smile and the light enhanced her shoulders so that they gleamed beneath the sheer clinging material of her white muslin blouse. Like most of her clothes she had made it herself, knowing instinctively what suited her and it was soft, feminine, quite simple with an embroidered panel down the front. The sleeves were long and close fitting and it had what was known as a 'Medici' frill about the neck. It fastened down the back and was tucked neatly inside a straight, tubular skirt made of a pale grey face cloth. She looked lovely. She was looking at him questioningly and speaking his name, smiling, her lips parted a little to reveal her white teeth and the tip of her tongue. She shook the hand she was holding, leaning closer towards him.

'What is it?' she asked softly. 'You are miles away. Where have you gone? Off into the future I'll be bound, deciding which motor car you will design first and how you will spend the enormous amount of money you are going to make. Will it be a grand house in Aigburth or perhaps one of those lovely villas you talk about in the South of France? Will you invite us to stay with you when you get there or will you be too grand for the likes of us by then? Mixing with dukes and princes, and princesses too, I shouldn't wonder. Eating caviar and drinking champagne from ladies' slippers and getting up to all the tricks we read about in the newspapers. Won't it be wonderful, Martin, when you are rich and famous and I will be able to tell my grandchildren that I once boxed the ears of one of the most important gentlemen in the world!'

She spoke laughingly in the soft, well modulated voice she had acquired quite without realising it from the wealthy and privileged persons she served. It was smooth, rich, quiet, the nasal sing-song of her native Liverpool virtually eliminated. It still had the slight inclination to rise at the end of each sentence but it was by this alone that her background could be detected. His was the same. Though neither spoke of it they both recognised that they had changed beyond imagining. They were both of them a different person, a world away from the gauche young girl and boy who had worked in the immigrant house in Great George Square.

He managed a full and impudent grin. 'Listen Mrs Woman,' using an old Liverpool expression, 'I'm tired and I'll get little rest if you don't stop your gabble. I'm tired, Meggie. I'm not the man I was, our kid but give me a few days and you and I and Tom will be off on those old bicycles again. What d'you say?'

She leaned towards him eagerly, pleased to see the smile, aware of the effort it had taken him as she had always been aware since they were children of his every strength and weakness. His eyelids were drooping and though he did not complain she knew his leg ached naggingly for the pain was etched in the lines of his face and his pallor beneath the bandage had worsened. She wanted to talk with him softly, to return them both to the happy moments they had shared with Tom in the days at Great George Square. The bicycles, he had said! They were a symbol of those lovely days, the sunshine gleaming on chrome and the flash of pedals, the smell of leather saddles, and oil on the chain and the sound of three young people laughing. She wanted to tell him that though they were older now, two grown men and a woman, they would always be a part of one another as the twirling wheels took to the road again. He was wounded now, like a magnificent eagle which has been brought out of the skies but he would soar again one day when his injuries were healed. They had not the keen excitement he knew as a racing driver, but the days they had spent in companionship, and would again on their machines had a magic which was unique to the three of them, a special mixture of peace, content and intense pleasure which, when they were returned to would help to mend him, to make him fly as an eagle again for that was what he was truly meant to do. She longed to lay her head on the pillow beside his, to comfort him with these bright and lovely thoughts but already he was slipping away into the deep, pain-free sleep he needed. She tucked his hands gently beneath the sheet and smoothed it across his chest. For a moment longer she continued to watch his face, her own drawn into a

253

worried frown. He looked so pale, his dark eyebrows and thick curling lashes stood out against the whiteness of his skin and she felt her heart move in anguish for if anything happened to him . . .

Suddenly his mouth curled in a smile. He did not open his eyes as he spoke but the humour was rich in his voice.

'Go away, Meggie. I'm not going to die, only sleep!' and everything was alright again and she smiled too as she tiptoed from the room.

She did not ask Ferguson this time for she was no longer under his control. She simply ran down the broad staircase, ignoring the rule that the back stairs were for servants, and knocked at the study door as she had before. It was over two years since that day and she had changed from a green girl to a woman, a woman who was quite determined on her path and she would not deviate from it now. She had been confident then that she could do it alone. She had contained within herself the arrogance of youth, the belief that her own strength was enough. She would need to ask for nothing else from anyone, she had told herself, believing it, but now she was here again, for the past few weeks had shown her there was a kind of strength in admitting to weakness provided one took steps to safeguard it and the only way to do that was to ask for help. She must either give in to the inevitable, submit to the demands of the brute who was blackmailing her – it could be called nothing else – or fight him. And she could not fight him alone!

She had become even more unapproachable at the hotel in the weeks following her encounter with Benjamin Harris, allowing no-one access to her own private thoughts, indeed it was difficult to get a word out of her unless it concerned the running of her floor. Harris had booked out the next day, she had found out, making discreet enquiries of the receptionist, and when the girl's back was turned it had been an easy matter to memorise the address he had written in the register. It was a club in London!

It seemed to those who worked for her that her obsession to be the best, to know and learn, and assimilate what she learned of the detailed minutiae of the hotel trade was driving her at such speed she would surely crash for no-one could continue as she did without coming a cropper. Even Miss O'Hara was heard to tell her to 'take a breather' if you please! When she was not working no-one knew where she got to for she simply disappeared and even the housekeeper, still trying to determine what had happened to her on that strange night several weeks back, did not know where she might be found. Secretive was the word they applied to her. She was rarely to be found in her own room and when she was it took her five minutes to open the damn door!

'Who is it?' she would call and until she had recognised to her own satisfaction the identity of the caller she would open the door to no-one! It was a matter for intense speculation what she did in there but whatever it was she did it alone!

Meg was aware they discussed her, those who worked for her, but it escaped their notice entirely that whenever Miss Hughes moved about the rooms and hallways on her floor she was never alone. She always had some young maid under instruction, or she accompanied one or other of the experienced chambermaids about their duties, letting them see, they imagined, muttering to one another, that she had her eye on them at all times.

They did not know of her nightmares! No-one did and she knew that the haunted pallor of her face was put down to overwork by Mrs Whitley and Tom. It did no good to comment, she had heard Mrs Whitley say in an aside to him, for he would only get his head snapped off as she had done!

She had agonised over it during the long nights, afraid still but no longer paralysed by it as she had been at first. She had not just herself to consider. If she had perhaps she might have chosen a different course, but Tom, and Mrs Whitley must be protected. It was a gamble, a risk she did not like since he had told her he had 'friends' but she had lived in this shadow for long enough and the risk must be taken.

'Come in,' the old gentleman said in answer to her positive knock.

He looked surprised to see her for they had discussed Martin's condition and the surgeon's optimistic prognosis and what more was there to be said? The boy was recovering and would be well cared for and when the time came ... well ... there were plans to be made and no need for worry.

'Yes Megan?' he said, noticing for the first time how slender she had become and how pale. She had always been what he would describe as 'bonny', robust and bursting with good health and vitality. Now she looked quite ... quite drained. And yet there was a certain lift to her head, unbowed it was, and a defiant set to her shoulders. Her mouth was grimly clenched, stern for one so young and her jaw jutted but her eyes were wary, unsettled, and moist with some curious emotion.

'What is it, Megan?' he said gently for he had become fond of this strong, sweet young woman.

Her answer rendered him speechless.

'I want Benjamin Harris arrested, Mr Hemingway, on the grounds of threatening behaviour and attempted blackmail.' She lifted her head even further and glared at him in a way which suggested *he* might be the one who was being accused but her eyes appealed to him desperately, begging for his help.

'Dear God ... Megan!' he managed to gasp, then fell back in his chair as though she had pushed him.

'And if it's convenient I would be glad if Mrs Whitley could be moved into the house until he is behind bars!'

'Dear God in Heaven ...'

'And there is one other thing I would like to discuss with you!'

Chapter twenty-one

It was September before they were settled but Meg did not worry
for the threat which had hung over her for so long had been
removed. Or more correctly put where it could no longer harm
her, or Tom and Mrs Whitley. The trial had lasted a week and
she had given her evidence in a clear decisive voice and though
he had been drawn from the dock when he was sentenced, swearing
vengeance, it seemed she was no longer afraid of Benjamin Harris.
There were witnesses, not as articulate as herself, in the shape of
Betsy and May who were quite overawed but willing, nevertheless
to speak for her, and Tom and Mrs Whitley, the latter in tears
and gaining immediate sympathy. Clever as he had thought
himself, the young receptionist at the Adelphi remembered Mr
Harris, she said, and without prompting spoke of his interest in
the housekeeper on the first floor and even the cellarman could
vouch for Miss Hughes' terror on the night in question, he said.
Miss O'Hara enjoyed her spell in the witness box, glad at last to
have got to the bottom of it all for she did like things *tidy*!

But it was Mr Hemingway's interest, and influence, Meg was
in no doubt of it, which gave credence to her own charge. He
made a grand witness and the counsel for the defence could not
pierce his evidence, nor, in fact, find the men Harris claimed
could give him an alibi!

Tom and Martin, white-faced and stiff with repressed and
violent rage had been reluctant to bother with a trial when they
had been told, begging Mr Hemingway to leave it to them, their
intention quite clear.

'And will you murder him, then?' the old gentleman asked
quietly.

No, they said just give him the hiding of his life, obviously
relishing the idea.

'And when he recovers? What of Megan then? No lads, best
leave this to the law.'

She continued to work at the Adelphi during the summer

months, afraid she might miss some important facet of the hotel trade, something she had not picked from its already clean carcass. She was perfectly well aware that already she was capable of running the hotel herself now but though Mr Hemingway had pleaded with her to come back to Silverdale during the trial, afraid of the pressure on her already stretched reserve, and, if he were honest, of the 'friends' Harris had threatened her with, she resisted. She was at peace at last and it showed in her firm tread and the brightness of her eyes. She knew where she was going now and those who worked with her could not get over the change in her, really they couldn't. Sorry she was leaving, they said for under all that stiffness and her resolute demand for the best they could give, she had turned out to be a right good laugh!

It was mid-summer when they found it, her and Tom.

She had caught no more than a glimpse or two of Martin recently. It seemed almost every time she rode out to Silverdale she was told he was sleeping, away up to the infirmary for an examination, taking exercise for his leg which was healing nicely, or lately, gone for a 'spin' with the old gentleman in the splendour of his latest Rolls Royce motor car!

'I see less of you now that you're home than I did when you were racing,' she called lightly as she finally found him one day sitting in the mellow sunshine of the stable yard. The sky was blue and empty but for a few high clouds which looked like tufts of windblown wool and the shadows fell across the cobbles, dark and well defined. It was warm and Martin wore no coat. He had pushed up the sleeves of his shirt and his arms were brown again from the hours he had spent during his convalescence sitting in the summer sun. He could walk quite easily now, only needing one of Mr Hemingway's walking sticks to steady himself and the slightly limping gait he had suffered at first was entirely gone. He had placed a bucket upside down on the cobbles, resting his outstretched leg on it and his back was against the sun-warmed red brick of the old stable wall along which a bench had been put.

Two yellow retrievers lolled at his knee, older now but still the ones who had been his companions in the days when he had been occupied with the task the boy he now watched was about. His hand fondled each domed head in turn. The sun glossed the dogs' coats to golden silk and their plumed tails moved lazily.

Three motor cars stood in the the centre of the yard. There was Mr Charles Hemingway's 'old' Vauxhall, the lovely daffodil yellow of it as perfect as the day Meg had taken her first motor car ride in it. His new Vauxhall, the 'Prince Henry', named after the German trials in which the model took part, stood beside it. It was the palest silvery grey, dazzling in its distinctive beauty and next to it, perhaps the most matchless of the three was the 'Silver Ghost', a monument to the brilliance of its designer, Charles Rolls who had died in an air crash only that year.

In that moment, as she walked across the yard towards Martin, Meg found she could understand his love for these magnificent machines. They were sleek, glossy, pure in line and colour and yet the marvel of them did not end there for not only were they as well favoured as a lovely woman, as majestic and fine as a thoroughbred horse, they worked as hard and were as useful to man as any mechanical thing he had ever invented. Many would not as yet agree with her, saying they were no more than a toy but the day would soon come when they would be indispensable. The sun caught their bright surface, bewitching the senses and Meg found herself as mesmerised as Martin appeared to be.

The boy with the wash-leather which he was using to buff up the already gleaming bonnet of the Rolls-Royce, hesitated as he saw her approach, glancing anxiously at Martin not certain whether he was to stay or go. His gaze was reverent, worshipping almost as he turned it on this dare-devil of the racing track who had started his illustrious career as he himself was doing, by cleaning the Hemingway collection of superb motor cars. His hero nodded, indicating that he was to take himself off and the lad scuttled away, looking back as he turned the corner to stare in envy at the glorious young lady who was crossing the yard towards the seated man and he heard her laugh ring out in quite the most lovely way, and he wondered who she was as he made his youthful and bedazzled way back to the garage.

Meg stood with her hands on her hips for a moment, then lifted an arm to push her fingers impatiently through the windblown mass of her hair. Her cream boater was in the basket at the front of her bicycle which she had left propped by the fence and the ribbon which fastened her hair to the nape of her neck had come loose. Her hair fell about her shoulders and down the length of her back, the ends forming ringlets of bright copper. She had undone the top three buttons of her cream blouse and pushed up the long sleeves and she looked like a gypsy girl, careless and vitally alive with the sun brushing her pale cheeks to gold and lighting a flame in her eyes. They snapped joyously for she had enjoyed the vigorous bicycle ride from town, scorning the train on such a beautiful day, and there was a tiny smudge of oil on her chin where she had touched it after inspecting her bicycle chain as instructed to do by the cycling club before each ride.

'Can I sit down then,' she asked laughingly, 'or is this a private wake? You look as though you'd lost a quid and found a tanner. What's the matter? Won't Mr Hemingway let you play with his motor car today?' Her eyes gleamed wickedly as she teased him, then, becoming concerned suddenly, she leaned towards him, casting a shadow over his dark, sun bronzed face, '. . . or is your leg hurting you? You really shouldn't come so far from the house, you know, not until it is stronger. Mrs Whitley told me that you had walked over to see her this morning and that must be nearly a mile there and back. Why don't you take more care, Martin, and use the sense God gave you, for heaven's sake!' Her anxiety made her sharp. 'You try to do too much and it's . . .'

'Oh for God's sake, Meg, leave me be. You're like an old hen fussing over it's one bloody chick! Nag, nag, nag . . .'

'*Nag!* I never damn well see you to nag, Martin Hunter. Ever since the trial you've been like that character in the book, what's he called . . . The Elusive Pimpernel, always off somewhere doing some damn fool thing that can't be any help to that leg of yours.' She stepped away from him, the laughter of a minute ago swept away by outrage. 'Each time I come over you're either away in the motor car with the old gentleman or having something done to you. I seem to spend my every afternoon off cycling over here to see you and when I arrive they tell me you're not here!'

'Well Tom is, and Mrs Whitley.'

'I know that but it's you I come to see.'

'Why?'

The question surprised them both and Martin could have bitten his tongue. The look of anger in Meg's face changed to one of amazement and she took another step away from him. Her mouth dropped open and her eyes began to flash their warning of danger, and he saw her hands clench into fists just as though she would like nothing better than to land him one. He wished he could take the word back for it sounded so ungracious and he knew he had hurt her deeply. He swallowed hastily, then managed a grin, impudent and careless, putting his hand to his brow to shade his eyes from the sunlight.

'Why? Why, you daft happorth? Because you should be out enjoying yourself not hanging about here with me and Tom and Mrs Whitley on your day off, that's why!'

'But . . . but you're my family.'

'I know, but you must have . . . friends, surely, at the hotel?'

'You know I haven't. When did I have time to be gadding about?' but he saw her relax and a wide smile lifted the corners of her mouth and with a great relieved sigh she sat down on the bench beside him, her shoulder touching his in the companionable way it had always done.

'You're quiet all of a sudden.' Her voice fell into the sun-drenched torpor of the warm afternoon.

'Sorry, our kid, I was miles away.'

'Where were you?'

He laughed. 'Guess.' He leaned forward to stroke the retriever's long back.

'Thinking about the future, I shouldn't wonder.' Her face took on contemplative expression. 'It's strange how it's changing for all of us. All at the same time, I mean. Your accident, the trial and now we're all off on a different road. Tom and I know what ours is to be but you, Martin? I know you've been waiting to see what Mr Hemingway was going to do, now that you can't race for him . . .' She stopped and put her hand to her mouth guiltily but he turned and smiled at her.

'Meg, it's alright. Don't think you can't say it. I know I can't race but the reason isn't my leg. I told you three years ago I'd been sidetracked from what I really wanted to do. I meant to start designing then but somehow . . .' He gazed over the fields which lay to the north of Silverdale and his eyes narrowed as though he stared at some bright memory. His hand still fondled the dogs' heads and Meg found herself watching them intently, her mind quite distracted from what he was saying but he turned again to her and she looked up from them.

'I don't want to race any more, Meggie. I've got a bit of money, saved it all these years. Mr Robert was generous, and now I'm going to do what I always planned I would do. I'm only twenty-two. I've years ahead of me and Mr Hemingway has accepted it at last. We're going to find a new lad to train up to race. I'll help him for if I'm honest I still love the thrill of the race-track but this time it will be *my* machine that will race on it. It's all up here . . .' He tapped his forehead and his eyes glowed warmly, his strangeness gone now. 'All those ideas I had years ago. I've still got the plans and designs, most of them hare-brained, I realise that now, that I used to put on paper at Great George Square, remember, but since then I've seen the *real thing* and how they perform and I know I can better them. We've got to replace the Hemingway flyer and while I've been hanging about with this damned leg I've had time to think and do some new designs – just outlines really – and with Mr Robert's backing and some of my own cash . . . well . . . we'll be *partners*, Meggie! I'm going to build it in this stable block. We're going to turn it into a machine shop . . . get the equipment . . .'

He looked about him and his breath had quickened in his throat and chest, and Meg saw the old Martin and rejoiced. She took his hand quite naturally between hers and held it lovingly, feeling it warm and strong, the brown flesh hard against hers.

'Martin!' Her voice was a whisper of velvet and her lips curved softly on his name and her happiness for him shone in her eyes but he almost snatched his hand away. He stood up and stamped the foot of his injured leg.

'Damn leg! It goes to sleep if I keep it still for long,' he said and she was quite bewildered by the harshness which had come to change his voice. 'Anyway,' he said, 'I must get off now. I forgot to tell you, I'm moving back into my old room over the stable this week so Jenny is coming over to give it a clean . . .'

At once Meg's face clouded over and her eyes flashed and the mutionous set of her lips said he had offended her though neither knew why.

'Jenny! That empty headed little baggage. Why can't I clean . . .?'

'Now Megan, give over. There's nothing wrong with Jenny, or her cleaning and there's no need for you to . . .'

'Don't be daft, Martin Hunter. That girl has been longing to get into your . . .'

'Yes? My what?'

'You know what I mean.' Her face was a bright pink. She was standing up now and they squared up to one another in the old familiar way, only at ease it seemed when they were fighting, the strange and awkward tension which had suddenly sprung up between them dispersed in the ritual of a quarrel.

'No, I don't know what you mean. She's a decent girl . . .'

'Oh is she? Then why does she sneak up to the summer house with all and sundry every night when Mrs Stewart's not looking?'

'How the hell do you know that? Can you see Silverdale from the Delly then?'

'I've been told, that's how!'

'Oh yes, and by who, because whoever he is he's a liar!'

'Tom's no liar.'

'Tom! D'you mean Tom's been gossiping like some old woman or perhaps he's one of the "all and sundry" Jenny is supposed to be meeting in the summer house.'

'Oh don't be daft!'

'What's daft about it? Why shouldn't Tom fancy her? She's a pretty girl.'

'Pretty! Jenny?'

Suddenly it was as though someone had stepped between them, someone who told them scornfully that they were making fools of themselves for it seemed to occur to them simultaneously that they were spitting like wild-cats over something which neither particularly cared about. Jenny meant nothing to Martin and Meg knew it, and even if she did, her sensible mind questioned, what was it to her? And why were they attacking one another with such venom?

'What's up with you two? Not scrapping again I hope. Not on a lovely day like this!'

Into the strange instability their hot tempers had caused Tom's cheerful voice fell like cool water over a fevered brow. It laid itself calmly about them, steadying their curiously beating hearts, bringing them back as it had always done from the brink of the explosion into which their warring natures flung them and they both turned eagerly, relieved to escape it.

He stood at the gate, his elbows on the top bar, his face split into a wide, engaging grin. He had pushed his cap to the back of his curly head. His collarless shirt was open at the neck and he wore a red spotted neckerchief about his throat. He had on cord trousers held up by braces and big, sturdy boots for he often worked in mud and for a moment, an unkind moment she realised later, Meg had the thought that he only needed a straw in his mouth to complete the picture.

'Now then,' he said sternly, 'what's this all about?' but his vivid blue eyes twinkled and the fine skin about them drew into the

263

faint lines which were forming as he narrowed them against the sun. His skin was smooth and clear and very brown and his teeth were white against his well cut lips.

'Nowt!' said Martin, scowling, reverting to the vernacular of his childhood, but already his eyes had cleared and the strong, angry line of his mouth had relaxed. His expression was beginning to shape into one of affection for the man who had always stood as a buffer between his own resolute nature and that of Meg, and the long length of his body leaned against the wall as the tension drained from it.

Meg began to laugh then, Tom's presence putting the quarrel in it's true perspective. She threw back her head and her hair flowed like a living cape of copper flame almost to her buttocks. She put up both her hands, searching for the errant ribbon to secure it and both young men found themselves staring at her with the total fascination of the male for the sensual beauty of a woman, each unaware of the other's quite frozen, quite sudden stillness. Her breasts thrust themselves boldly against the cotton stuff of her blouse and the shape of her nipples were clearly defined.

'Oh, take no notice, Tom,' she said arching her back to reach the ribbon. 'It's only me and Martin up to our usual tricks. No offence meant and none taken, eeh lad?' She was tying the ribbon into a bow, dragging back the heavy springing coils of her hair and when she turned to Martin, grinning widely he was watching, not her as he had been only a moment ago but the retriever who still leaned companionably against his leg. The second dog had ambled across the yard to Tom and both men were suddenly occupied, quite frantically absorbed it seemed, in the smooth coat of the two animals.

Tom opened the gate and walked slowly across the yard, the dog at his heels, his hands deep in his trouser pockets. He turned to the three motor cars, looking for all the world as though no other thought but their splendour was on his mind. He ran his finger along the bonnet of the old Vauxhall.

'I always liked this the best,' he mused. 'Nice colour!'

Martin snorted, then began to laugh.

'Nice colour! Bloody hell, Tom Fraser, you sound like a woman! Trust you to like a motor car because of its colour.' His face was soft in his fondness for his friend and the awkward, strange moment was over.

'Why not? There's nowt wrong with liking the colour. I know nothing about motor cars, lad, you know that, but I know what colours I like and I like yellow!'

They were all laughing now, even the dogs seeming to smile in the pleasure of the day. The tension was completely gone. The air they breathed was sweet and uncomplicated. Birds sang as birds will and the benevolence of sunshine and youth and friendship, of trust and shared memories drew them together in the familiar pattern of their childhood.

'Nice day for a ride,' Tom continued, squinting into the sun. He turned his back on the automobile, leaning against it, and looked amiably at Martin, then away again, his smile easy. 'Up through Garston and Hale and Frodsham. A pint at the "Bear's Paw", perhaps a walk through the forest.' He sighed pensively though his eyes were glinting with mischief. 'We might even get as far as . . .!'

He winked at Meg and she held her breath for it was like old times. She could see Martin as he had been all those years ago, his head studiously bent over a book or something he was drawing, his face creased in a frown of concentration, irritated beyond measure by Tom's teasing, by her own sharp and not always good humoured efforts to pry him from his seriousness. She could remember how furious he would be as they both attempted to cajole him into coming on some jaunt, to ride out with them and have some fun, to leave his books behind and to get out of his stuffy attic room where his 'drawing board' held him fast. He would be aggravated to the limits of his endurance, threatening violence to them both but little by little Tom would have him trying hard to control the unwilling smile at the corners of his mouth, the twitch of his lips and the broad grin which would involuntarily split his face. It had not always worked for Martin's direct path to the future which was to be his had not been allowed to be strewn with the foolish, the flippant, the frivolous diversions of youth but today . . . well today was a holiday, surely, made for a jaunt, a spin, an escape from the routine, the mundane!

Martin was grinning widely.

'What are you up to, lad? You're not actually telling me you *want* to take a drive in one of these "bloody machines"! I believe that's what you've called them a time or two. Or are you suggesting we take turns on Meg's bicycle? How about you pedal, Meg on the handlebars and me on the back mudguard with my leg stuck out. We might get as far as the gate or even . . .'

'I've got an afternoon off.' Tom pulled his cap round until the peak was at the back. 'I always fancied myself taking a spin round that motor track you and the old gentleman built. It looks simple enough. It must be if you can do it!'

'You're joking, of course!' Martin could hardly speak through the laughter. '*You* at the wheel of a motor car!'

'Why not? I've cranked the bloody thing often enough. It's time I had a turn of the wheel. You tell me which way to steer it and . . .'

'Oh go on, Martin! Let him and can I have a go as well!?'

They both turned to look at her, their faces a picture of masculine amazement. Tom *had* been joking. One day, he supposed, he might take to driving a motor car. Martin had predicted that every working man would own one, one day. But somehow, though Martin said so and Tom believed him, he could not quite see himself actually *doing* it. Give him a bicycle any day of the week. It was good enough and practical enough to carry him the short distances *he* wanted to travel. Safe, economical and sure to arrive, perhaps slowly, nevertheless, but it did get there, just like himself! But their Meggie! Driving a motor car! A woman behind the wheel! There had been the curious and strangely unfeminine – in masculine eyes – woman or two who had taken to it though both Martin and Tom did not care to consider it, but their Meg! It was unthinkable, laughable!

But Meg was not laughing. Her face was quite serious. She had grown up with these two young men, dragging along, often unwanted, at their heels as they went about their entirely male pursuits. They had accepted her for the most part for had she not been an adjunct of their growing up, sharing its hardships as well as its joys but there were limits, after all to what a woman can do, the expression on their faces told her. But in her own mind she was Megan Hughes, Miss Hughes of the Adelphi Hotel, a person of some importance, worthwhile and certainly well able to cope with the mysteries of driving a motor car. If she could run successfully, a hotel floor and the staff who worked on it, she could as a matter of course, drive a motor car and come what may, she intended to!

Tom had been spellbound when Martin got out his own small Austin two seater from the garage. He sat apprehensively on the luggage rack behind the hood which had been folded neatly away and clung for dear life to the rail which surrounded it, his long legs tucked up beneath his chin. On his face was an expression which said quite clearly he expected to be flung off at any minute since Megan Hughes could not be persuaded to keep to the regulation twenty miles an hour the law allowed!

'Slow down, Meggie,' he heard Martin bellowing, his mouth close to her ear but she seemed deaf to his pleas in the wondrous delight which filled her; brimmed from her every pore and made her eyes glow to match the gold of the sun itself. Her boater had been tossed carelessly backwards to Tom with a shouted injunction to 'Hold this, will you Tom,' and her hair was alive about her head in a riot of windblown, shining curls and on her face, though he could not see it, was an expression of pure unadulterated joy.

Martin had explained patiently the intricacies of the gears, the ignition, the starting handle and the correct way to steer and brake the machine. He had not liked it, not at all and would have much preferred to have been teaching Tom who, though he knew nothing of motor cars was at least a man! His attitude had said quite plainly that though he was taking the trouble to show her how to do it, he doubted very much whether they would ever pull away from the stable door, let alone the yard. He had been quite confounded, even uneasy that a woman should have taken to it so easily, when Meg started the engine at the first turn of the ignition. He was even more astounded when she let out the clutch exactly as he had told her and the motor car jerked to an erratic but nevertheless definite start.

'Careful Meg.' His hands reached instinctively to the steering wheel, certain she would run his much loved little car into the stable yard gate.

'Get off, Martin,' she shrieked at him. 'I can do it,' and with a face as white as paper and eyes blazing with the brilliance of sunshine on water, she did, steering the car neatly between the gateway and on to the wide gravelled drive which led to the front of the house.

'Jesus, Meg . . . Dear God, take it easy,' he gasped as she changed gear with a jerk which nearly had Tom off the back. Faces appeared in windows and a couple of men working in the garden lifted their heads to stare in open-mouthed amazement as she jerked and banged and coughed and hiccupped her way along the driveway from the house to the gates.

267

She was smiling as she steered the machine between the ornate gate posts and even, to Martin's complete horror, took her hand off the wheel to wave nonchalantly at Mrs Whitley who came to her cottage door to stare, not awfully sure she could believe what her old eyes had just seen.

'Keep both your bloody hands on the wheel, for God's sake,' Martin roared but she only turned to grin at him, speechless with excitement.

'Keep your bloody eyes on the road,' he roared again and at the back Tom closed his eyes and tried to remember a few lines of a prayer he had been taught as a child.

They were in Garston, just passing St Michael's Church when she began to sing and Tom opened his eyes then, turning to stare over his shoulder. Martin was still sitting with the air of a man being taken to his own execution, but the high colour had flooded Meg's face and on it was an expression of utter and complete satisfaction. He could see her hands on the steering wheel and he realised she was gloriously happy, relaxed and perfectly in control.

'By God, Martin, she's not bad, is she?' he shouted admiringly above the noise of the engine. 'You'll have to watch out or she'll be borrowing this thing to take Mrs Whitley for a spin.' He then began to roar with laughter at the expression on Martin's face. Tom was delighted with Meg's prowess, proud as punch to see the confident way in which she manoeuvred the little car along the narrow country lanes which had not been designed for the automobile but for the peaceful passage of cows and horses. He was not the slightest bit put out that she had mastered the controls so well, having no inclination himself to take part in the supposedly masculine pastime of motoring.

They had reached the outskirts of Warrington and Martin insisted, absolutely insisted, he said, on taking over from her since there was far too much traffic for a beginner to manage. Horse-drawn drays and waggons, carriages and omnibuses, alongside the growing number of motor cars which were increasingly to be seen.

They stopped at Stretton for a cup of tea and when they resumed their journey she begged to be allowed another 'go' since it was quiet here and if she didn't practise how was she to ever become an experienced driver, she said, as they bowled along towards Lower Hargrave.

'An experienced driver?' Martin's face was a study in bewilderment.

'Yes. I can't get the hang of it in one day, can I, and if I'm to be any good at it I've got to practise. It's like anything else . . .'

'Practise!' Martin looked at her as if he had never heard such lunacy.

'Of course!' Meg was becoming exasperated and she pressed her foot down a little harder on the accelerator, thrilled with the way the motor car surged forward.

'Just a minute, lady. What the hell d'you think you're doing?' Martin's voice was becoming quite dangerous for though he had allowed her to drive, teaching her, however reluctantly, with a quiet patience not usual in him, he was not prepared to be taken over, so to speak, in the way which Meg seemed to find increasingly easy these days. She was used to giving orders now and having them obeyed. She had loved every moment of the last couple of hours and was well pleased with herself in her new capacity as 'lady driver' and could see no reason why she should not continue.

'Just slow down a minute, if you don't mind . . .'

'What for? There's nothing on the road and I . . .'

'Slow down, Meg! Take your foot off that accelerator and put it on the brake and then get . . .'

'Oh come on, Martin, don't be such a wet blanket. I'm perfectly able to drive now and well you know it.'

And so he did! She was a natural driver, the car running as sweetly as though he himself was at the wheel but his strange male ego, that which had been brought up to believe that women were unable to equal a man in almost every aspect of life, could not admit it to her. For weeks now, ever since he had been brought home from Weybridge on a stretcher he had been careful with her, avoiding her if he was honest for he could make neither top nor tail of the strange emotions she awakened in him. When he had heard of what Benjamin Harris had tried to do to her he would have killed him if the law had not got to him first. His own rage had frightened him, though he had not even told Tom who had shared his anger. She was exactly the same as she had always been now, despite the terror she had been through but he felt awkward with her, vulnerable to her sharp and often wicked wit which once he would have answered with his own. She was smart, clever, beautiful, good at what she did and she knew it, and he

269

wanted her to be soft, soft as she had been on the day he had returned.

Now Meg's panache, her almost careless handling of his smart little car infuriated him and he wanted nothing more than to see her *out* from behind the wheel and in the passenger seat where she belonged!

'Stop this car at once!' His voice was expressionless and Tom turned to look at him in surprise. There was nothing he himself would have liked better than for the bloody car to be stopped. The skin of his buttocks was bruised, he was sure, from long contact with the luggage rack but there was something in Martin's voice he did not like. He himself could see nothing wrong with Meg's handling of the machine and indeed after the first bone-shaking half hour he had relaxed considerably and if he had had a cushion to sit on would have enjoyed the day immensely for he knew just where Meg was heading. Meg continued her smooth journey along the empty lane to Lower Hargrave and the pretty village of Great Merrydown beyond, just as though Martin had not spoken and Tom felt rather than saw the sudden tightening of his body. Nevertheless he was almost thrown off the back of the automobile as it came to a screeching, jerking standstill, slewing across the lane to end with its front wheels hanging perilously over a ditch.

Meg turned haughtily in her seat.

'I don't know why you did that, Martin Hunter, since I was going to stop anyway. Look.' She lifted her hand to point and Tom smiled for she had always had a strong sense of the dramatic.

They both looked obediently and Tom waited, smiling.

'What is it?' Martin asked the very same question he himself had asked all those years ago.

'Its our place.'

'Your . . . ?'

Martin was bewildered, his anger forgotten as he looked at the tumbledown building surrounded by what seemed acres of overgrown wilderness. 'You don't mean to tell me that this is the place you and Tom have . . .'

'Yes! Isn't it absolutely beautiful?'

Martin watched as Meg climbed down from the vehicle and with the air of one who has come home, began to walk towards the old farmhouse.

Chapter twenty-two

'If you will sign here, Mr Fraser and you too, Miss Hughes, and also here, if you please, the property is yours.'

Tom stared, quite mesmerised, at the solicitor and though Meg acknowledged that the man was a pompous ass and enough to make you squirm, he knew what he was about in the world of the law. He had been recommended by Mr Hemingway as the man she needed to negotiate the details of the purchase of the farmhouse on Merrydown Hill and though it was only three months since the day they had rediscovered it, it would, in a moment legally belong to herself and Tom. The property was to be in their joint names, of course. She had insisted upon it. The old gentleman, Mr Hemingway, unimpressed by Tom's easy-going, and in his eyes, quite careless manner on the subject of business, which after all, this was to be, had been hesitant, saying might it not be more realistic if the property was put completely in Megan's competent hands, and name! He was thinking of the loan the bank had made her, on his surety, naturally, and having absolute faith in her ability to repay it had had no hesitation in backing her – particularly when he had been made aware of the sum she had saved in her three years at the Adelphi which was to be added to it! Not that the one hundred guineas she had asked the bank for had constituted a *risk* but he did not want the girl brought down by an unreliable partner and if the business was in her name only she was safe. Fraser was a hard-working young man. He had proved his worth in the years he had been at Silverdale but was he the kind of chap who could 'make a go' in the world of commerce? Robert Hemingway had his doubts.

Still, she would not be moved and grudgingly, admiring her loyalty, he had agreed to Fraser's name on the documents.

Surreptitiously Meg put her toe against Tom's foot and gave it a gentle nudge and when he turned to look at her she nodded to let him know it was alright and that he should go ahead with the signing. They were together in this, her shining eyes said, as they had always been and what was there to fear? He grinned, then winked as though to say the whole thing was really a great joke anyway and picking up the pen signed his name to the document which made he and Meg the new owners of the farmhouse.

It had taken all of Meg's formidable will and the desperation of her belief in what she did to persuade him to it! What did he want with an *inn*, he said bewilderment written all over his boyish face, when he had a perfectly good job, one which he thoroughly enjoyed and, more to the point, he was good at. He liked the outdoor life and the satisfaction of watching what *he* had planted, grow and mature and be enjoyed by those for whom he worked. He loved the animals he worked with. He liked the feel of a bit of wood in his hands and the way he had learned, under the guidance of Bob, the carpenter employed on the estate, how to use a hammer, a saw and all the other tools he was allowed to tinker with. He was no good with figures, he pleaded with Meg, and had no head for business and besides, he and Jess . . .

Like all those with an uncomplicated and facile nature he could be stubborn but he was no match for Megan Hughes in the end! She had all the answers to his every argument. They were to be the perfect team, she told him. In fact, she could not do it alone for without him she would be working, as it were, with only one hand. He was to be the other, the hand which would be employed with all the manual jobs *her* hand could not manage.

'Dear God, Tom, have you any idea what it would cost me to buy fresh vegetables if we don't grow our own? Fruit? Eggs? Milk? Cheese? Butter? With our own kitchen garden, fruit trees, greenhouse and with a cow, a couple of pigs, hens, we could be completely self-supporting and within a year be showing a healthy profit. I need a man I can trust in the bar, when it opens and someone to supervise the men who will do the repairs. I can't be everywhere, Tom. I shall have the financial arrangements to see to, staff to organise, the renovation of the inside of the inn for I mean to take in guests as well as do meals and . . .'

'Confound it, Meggie, don't go so bloody fast. I have to have time to think . . .'

'What is there to think about? Either you want to do this with me or you don't!'

'It's not as easy as that. There are other things to consider besides you.'

'I appreciate that, Tom, and I realise how much you enjoy

doing what you do at Silverdale but you can still work at exactly the same thing at the inn, only you will be working for yourself!'

'I don't see how . . .'

'Because we'll be partners! It will belong to *us*. You and me, and every penny we make will be ours.'

'But I can't just up and leave the Hemingways after all . . .'

'Why not? He has a dozen men to do what you've been doing. Not as well, I give you that . . .' She grinned but he was not to be distracted.

'And what about . . .'

'What, for God's sake? *What*? Give me one good reason why you should stay at Silverdale. Go on!'

'It's a steady job, Meg. One I like and which I can stay in for the rest of my life.'

'Good God, Tom Fraser! You're twenty-two years old and all you want is *safety*!'

'Now look here, Megan, there's nothing wrong with liking a bit of security. I might want to get married . . .'

'Married! Who to?'

'Well, me an' Jess have . . .'

'Bring her with you. She can work in the kitchens, or the bar . . .'

'Here, hold on! I didn't say I was going to . . .'

'Well, stop making excuses then. Listen Tom, listen to me.' Her voice became soft and she took his hand between hers. She looked up into his face with all the earnest entreaty of a child who longs to be allowed this special, special favour. From his chair in the corner of Mrs Whitley's kitchen where he sat, his mending leg resting on a stool, Martin Hunter felt his heart go out to his life-long friend for how, how was he to withstand the enchantment of Meggie Hughes when she had set her heart on something? She was absolutely glorious, irresistible and he could see Tom's determination begin to falter. Tom really did not want to leave Silverdale. He was completely happy here. It was his place and he was entirely suited to it but then, knowing his nature as he did, would he not be just as satisfied doing exactly what he did here, in the place Meg had marked out for him? She was the driving force. She would guide the business, and Tom with it, along the path of success, for she would *be* successful. There was no doubt about that but Tom was afraid to gamble what he already had on an uncertain future.

273

'Tom,' Meg was saying and both Martin and Mrs Whitley held their breath. 'Tom, please come with me. Come and help me in this. I can't do it alone, Tom. I need you, please Tom, please.' Her eyes swam with unshed tears and Martin watched as Tom's open face, so expressive that every emotion showed there, became uncertain, soft with his fondness for her. As Martin turned away his eyes met Mrs Whitley's.

He stood up abruptly, his gaze fleeing from the understanding he saw in her face and the stool crashed to the floor and the tabby cat which had curled itself in its own tail on the hearthrug before the fire sprang to its feet, spitting in fright.

'I must be off,' he said harshly. 'I can't stop here listening to you two bickering about your bloody future. I've my own to see to!' He reached for the stick which he still leaned on when he was tired and for a dreadful moment he felt as though he was about to fall.

'Martin?' Mrs Whitley's voice was anxious and the other two looked at her curiously for she sounded so odd but Martin Hunter turned back to her, smiling now, then leaned to kiss her soft wrinkled cheek.

'Cheerio Cook,' he said, his voice and manner quite normal, his eyes smiling imperturbably and she wondered why she had been so suddenly wary for there was nothing there but his affection for herself.

The farmhouse, as Meg had always thought of it, had, it turned out, once been a coaching inn, it's custom destroyed in the early years by the coming of the railway, and she had been delighted to find when she and Tom had been shown round by the agent who was acting on behalf of the owner, that the front room into which they stepped directly from the overgrown garden, was actually a snug bar-room with an enormous fireplace at one end and a counter at the other. The floor was flagged, covered by a layer of filth inches deep for the place had been empty for six years, and cobwebs were laid like lace from one end of the room to the other, drifting in a haze about her head and touching her face with soft insistence.

Behind the counter a door led to a cold room and then into a huge kitchen with an alcove at one end in which was placed a fire-grate and on either side of the grate were huge ovens. There were wooden seats built in beside them underneath which were cupboards. The beams overhead in each room were black and at least a foot thick and in the centre of the kitchen was a deal table so large it had evidently been abandoned as it could not be heaved through the doorway.

There were long, stone-flagged passages with tiny rooms off them and several larger ones, the biggest of which would serve admirably as a dining-room. A narrow stone spiral staircase, the steps of which were worn in the centre led to the upstairs landing. Again there were meandering passages off which led bedrooms, large and small, all dark and gloomy for the windows were mullioned and incredibly dirty.

Tom wandered behind her, opening cupboards and looking inside for signs of damp and rotten wood, well able to recognise it now with his new expertise learned from the carpenter at Silverdale. He ran his hands appraisingly across crumbling floor-boards and flaking plaster, window sills and door frames, whistling to himself, absorbed, now he had made up his mind to it, in the consideration of how much it would take, in time and money, to get this old place fit for human habitation. It had been occupied by nothing but field mice and roosting birds in the chimney, and it was for that reason they had got it for such a low sum but would the restoring of it, in the long run, make it an expensive purchase? Meg had said not and that they could make a go of it and if hard work and determination were the factors needed to do it, then by God Tom Fraser agreed with her.

They stayed with a certain Mrs Annie Hardcastle in the village of Great Merrydown during those last weeks before the inn opened, supervising the work which was being done. She was glad to have them, she said, for she was a widow with one child, a son with a crippled leg four inches shorter than the sound one. Born like it, just after her Bert went in the South African wars, Annie Hardcastle said, wanting no sympathy, and no-one could tell her why, but she loved her Will for he was all she had and he loved her. He did odd jobs about the village, and they managed but she was always glad of a bit extra. She had a small house two doors down from the village store, convenient to the inn. She had taken in lodgers for thirty-six years now, ever since she had become a widow. Casual farm workers, migrants who came and went with the seasons, sleeping in her clean rooms and eating her plain nourishing food. She was pleased, though slightly mystified, to be paid the good money she received from the young couple who had been spilled, with their boxes, on to her doorstep from the shining motor car which, it turned out, though not driven by him, belonged to no less a personage than Mr Robert Hemingway. It was a name known even out here in Great Merrydown and though she was uncertain of their relationship to the great man she was not unduly concerned. Live and let live, was Annie Hardcastle's motto, and besides, she took a great liking to Miss Hughes and Mr Fraser and wished them the best of luck in their undertaking. They had a lot of pluck, the two of them restoring that old tumbledown place on Merrydown Hill and by God they would need it.

They employed two men to help Mr Fraser with the repairing of the crumbling woodwork, replacing the tiles on the roof, replastering the walls and putting in new window frames. He was a real handyman and Zack Entwistle – one of the two men taken on and a distant relative of Annie's, as were most of the folk hereabout – was fulsome in his praise and his awe at the amount of work the young 'maister' could get through.

'We can't keep up wi' 'im, me an' Albert,' he remarked repeatedly to anyone who would listen and it was true, but Meg and Tom were determined that by the spring of next year they would be ready for their first 'guests' and before that exciting day there was much to be done. The walls were whitewashed until they gleamed and the floors scrubbed a dozen times until the beautiful red of the flags glowed softly in the sunlight which streamed through the sparkling windows.

'Eeh, Miss Hughes, it looks a fair treat,' Annie breathed for really who could have believed that such a transformation could take place. Megan Hughes was a girl after Annie's own heart and if there was anything else she could do to help her, she said, she had only to say the word.

'Just call me Meg, please,' she was told, and she did and with Edie Marshall, another relative of hers from over Lower Hargrave way and always glad to earn a bob or two, the three of them had made a right good job of it and if she said it herself you could eat your dinner off them floors!

Meg had been down to Northwich, and on a cold but sunny day at the beginning of November, a dray the size of a small house drew up the steep hill between the double row of sturdy, stone built cottages, past the staring women and children and dogs, to the top of Great Merrydown village street. Annie Hardcastle was there with Edie on that day, putting the finishing touches to the tiny bedroom which Mr Fraser – call me Tom, for God's sake – had finished painting only that morning. He had papered the walls with the loveliest wallpaper, all pink rosebuds and tender green leaves on white. The curtains were a thick white muslin, lined in pink cotton and Annie Hardcastle would have been happy to settle in it herself, it was so pretty. It was to be Meg's room, Tom had said fondly, for she had never had anything really nice of her own in her life and it was time she did!

The horses which pulled the dray were breathing heavily when they arrived at the top of Merrydown Hill. They stopped outside the inn gladly, 'whoa-ed' to a lumbering halt by the carter who enquired cheerfully if they wanted a hand with this lot? 'This lot' proved to be strong oak furniture, settles, beds, tables, chairs, a dresser and all in need of a good dusting and waxing with Annie's special polish, but built to last and as good stuff as Annie had ever seen. There were boxes filled to overflowing with copper pots and pans and crockery, bedding rugs and even a picture or two, and she heard Edie whisper to Zack who seemed to have become more or less a permanent fixture about the place even though the work was all done, that there must be a bit of 'brass' to pay for all this lot!

'Will you stay and help, Mrs Hardcastle? I would be so relieved if you could. I am hoping to have my first visitors by Easter and there is still so much to be done, and Zack . . .' Meg Hughes turned her brilliant tawny smile on the old man who blinked like a dazzled schoolboy and snatched his cap from his head, '. . . perhaps if you have no other commitments in the future you could make a start on the garden with Tom. It is somewhat overgrown . . .' She smiled at the understatement for indeed the garden was like a wilderness and would need a great deal of work to bring it to the situation Megan Hughes envisaged. 'I intend to do cream teas when the weather permits and of course a gentleman may bring his beer outside from the bar if he has a mind to. Perhaps a bench or two, what d'you think, so that those who wish may sit in the sunshine. The garden has a pleasant outlook.'

The old man hardly gave her time to finish speaking before he had picked up his spade and had begun to attack the weeds as though the first customer was to arrive that very afternoon.

Edie moved restlessly. What about her, her manner seemed to say but Meg had not forgotten her. She was a good worker and would be useful when they were busy, as Meg fully expected to be. She could get on without supervision which was a great asset when the director of this tiny empire needed to be in two dozen places at the same time! There were ten bedrooms to be cleaned each day when the first guests arrived, and a kitchen the size of a football pitch besides the other downstairs rooms, and she herself would be busy with the cooking, the baking, the managing and accounting of every penny made and spent, the planning and running of the venture and would have little time for anything else.

'I was wondering, Edie ... I was wondering if you would consider working full time? This is a big place and I will need someone who can be trusted to keep it as I like it.'

Edie preened and her face was rosy with pleasure and Annie Hardcastle, shrewd with the native wit of the Northcountry woman and a good judge of character was aware that this girl – for she was really no more – would go far. She knew how to treat people, to give them a feeling of self-worth. She had a way with them which brought out their best. She was a hard taskmaster but she was fair and when a job was well done she told you so! But she had a control which was strange in one so young as though something in her past had given her the need for self-discipline. She was often sharp-tongued and her eyes were keen in the search for any infringement of her rules, and if she was quick to praise she was also quick to remonstrate for her standards were high.

And look what she had done with this place! A couple of months ago it had been no more than a ramshackle dilapidated old building, almost a shell really, ready to fall in on itself with age and disuse, but she had seen its potential, found a 'backer', as she put it to Annie Hardcastle, though Annie was not entirely certain what that meant, got on her knees with a bucket and scrubbing brush, an occupation she was well used to, she cheerfully said and turned the place into a little palace. The paintwork was white and shining against the rosy bricks, the windows winking in the sunshine, pretty chintz curtains, clean and fresh fluttering at each one and the spotless rooms waiting only for the furniture to be moved in.

They were alone on that last night before Meg and Tom were to move in. Tom had gone up to the inn to check on something or other and they sat, the two women over a companionable cup of tea before clearing the table of the remains of their supper.

'I'd like to wish you good luck, Meg but I know luck has nothing to do with it. Bloody hard work – and that's swearing – guts and determination, are what you've put in that place, you and Tom, but there's just one thing you seem to have overlooked, lass.'

Meg sat down again slowly and her face took on a certain hauteur.

'Oh, and what's that?'

'Don't put on that hoity-toity look with me, miss, for I'm old enough to be your grandmother ... well, nearly ...' She smiled grimly.

Meg smiled too, and reached for Annie Hardcastle's hand though she was well aware that Annie would not care for it. Not one to put much credence on great demonstrations of affection, except perhaps with her handicapped lad, Annie shook it off irritably and began to shuffle the supper dishes about in a haphazard way and Meg knew something serious was troubling her.

'What is it, Mrs Hardcastle? What have I done wrong?'

'Nowt yet, leastways, I don't think so.'

'Well, what is it?'

'It's ... well ... have you thought what folks are going to make of you and that lad up there all alone?'

'Pardon.'

'You heard me, Meg Hughes.'

'I know I did but I'm not sure I understood you.'

'Come off it, lass! You're a young and bonny lass. He's a young and bonny lad and you're not related! Neither are you wed. What d'you think folk are going to say to you living up there all alone ...'

'We're not alone. Edie is going to live in. She says it's too far each day from Lower Hargrave so ...'

'It won't do. She's nowt but a servant!'

'Now look here, Mrs Hardcastle ...'

'No, you look here, young lady. I've lived here all me life and I know these people, high station and low, and there's not one will give their custom to your establishment when it becomes known that the owners are living over the brush!'

'Over the ...! Mrs Hardcastle ...!'

'It's true, Meg. I know we are in the twentieth century now and that times are changing but there's some things never change and sin is one of them.'

'*Sin!*'

'Oh lass, I know there's nowt going on and so does Edie and Zack but the rest of them don't and they'll not come. The parson won't like it and he'll have summat to say, not outright but you can be sure he'll make his feelings quite clear. Now, you'll do well up there, you and Tom, but there's something that's got to be faced. Either you and Tom get wed or he must sleep elsewhere!'

Tom didn't like it, not one bit and said so forcefully each night when he set off down the hill to his lodgings with Annie.

'This is bloody ridiculous! Paying out good money for a room when there are a dozen here all empty and it's damned cold setting off on a winter's night to walk a bloody mile . . .'

'It's not a mile and you know it . . .'

'And Annie's place is like a bloody ice house it's so cold. Them sheets on the bed are frozen together, I'll swear . . .'

'Ask her to put a hot water bottle in.'

'It's alright for you. You're not the one who has to leave the warmth and tramp down . . . and besides, do we have to live our lives to suit other people? We've got Edie here, surely that's enough to satisfy the conventions?'

'Tom, we've talked this over a dozen times. Do you want us to fail before we've even got started. If there's talk they won't give us their business, you know that. Perhaps the working man will come for his pint but I want the others . . . the . . . the gentry, if you like, when the time comes, and if there's a whiff of scandal attached to this place they simply won't come. It all has to be seen to be completely above board, you know that!'

He did, of course and on the night he pulled his first pint from the barrel which was placed in the cold-room behind the bar he was pleased with the grand way in which it ran into the tankard. It was brown and clear and the head on it was of just the right depth and consistency and he found it gave him inordinate pleasure to watch the man who had ordered it place his bushy moustache into the foam and drink deeply.

The man reached into his pocket but before he could put his pence on the counter a cheerful voice from the doorway which led into the cold-room stopped him.

'No sir. Put your money away. It's on the house!'

Tom turned, speechless and quite astounded for if they were to make a profit from this place they couldn't be chucking their money away on free beer but Meg stepped forward and, putting her arm through his, smiled warmly at the gratified customer.

'You are our first customer, Mr ... er ...?'

'Jack Thwaites, missis.'

'Mr Thwaites. My partner and I would be honoured if you would drink a toast with us, to this new venture of ours. Each man who comes in here for the next week will have his first drink on the house. We would be happy to begin with you.'

'Well, that's right generous of yer, missis! Yer good health.' He nodded and lifted his foaming glass again. 'I'm only sorry I didn't order a rum!' His eyes twinkled above the rim of his glass and Meg laughed.

'You shall have one, Mr Thwaites, but don't let on to the others or we will be bankrupt by the end of the week.'

'Not you, lass! With you behind that counter you'll not be short of custom.' Suddenly aware that he did not know the exact relationship of this woman to the chap standing beside her, he realised it would not do to chaff her as one would any ordinary bar-maid. Jack Thwaites buried his nose in his pint pot. But as Tom turned away to pour him a measure of rum, he winked at Meg to show he meant no disrespect and was tickled to death when she winked back!

The door behind him opened somewhat hesitantly and Jack Thwaites turned to see who had come in, leaning on the counter in that relaxed way of a man who is at his ease in his local hostelry. Two young men, obviously farm labourers from their rough but decent clothing moved slowly into the room, looking about them in astonishment at the bright flagged floor, the fresh white walls, the sturdy, polished farm furniture. There were deep, cushioned chairs covered in dark, hardwearing fabric, a long refectory table, black and handsome around which were eight ladderback chairs with rush seats. Stools of elmwood stood against one wall but not along the counter for Meg had been told that men liked nothing better than to stand at a bar, and lamplight gleamed on copper and brass and horse leathers which hung about the fireplace.

A settle carved in yew was placed beside a gigantic log fire and a couple of tabby cats purred on the rug before it. A large yellow dog wandered about, nudging knees and smiling, and thinking he belonged to Jack Thwaites, Meg allowed it.

The room was grand, grand without being overwhelming, for these were working class men and they wanted nothing fancy. Clean, homely, bright and welcoming and not far from the likes

281

of their own farm kitchens but with something added which they were at a loss to understand but which they found to their liking.

'Come away in, lads,' Jack Thwaites called with the bonhomie of the landlord himself, the pint of beer and generous tot of rum filling him with conviviality. '. . . and the first drink's on the house!'

Meg moved forward, leaning her arms and deep breast on the counter top, smiling at the two young men with the friendliness and innocent trust with which she had treated the travellers in Great George Square. She asked their names and where they came from and evinced such interest in their ordinary lives that they tripped on their own tongues in their eagerness to tell her.

More men came in, quite taken aback by the warmth and laughter and the friendly greeting they received from the good-looking young woman behind the bar and the cheerful chap beside her, but with one satisfying, free drink inside them it was easy to buy another. Though they had come merely to look at the new place, curious about the charms of the inn, news of which Annie Hardcastle had spread about, they found themselves still there when time was called. Though they may at first have considered it a bit 'posh' for their taste, Miss Hughes did not seem concerned when Arnie Whittaker spilled a pint of best bitter on her lovely polished table, nor when she saw the mud trekked in by George Anderson, come straight from the fields where his cows had turned the track to liquid manure, and when Bert Taylor sang a song in which they all joined, slightly saucy, raising the roof with the noise, she stood behind the counter and banged a pint tankard in rhythm on it, her face flushed and laughing.

There was good grub for those who wanted it. Pickled eggs and onions. Cheddar cheese and home baked bread. Pork pies so tasty Bert Taylor took one home for his missus to taste, and pease pudding and faggots!

There was only one thing missing, Jack Thwaites told Tom when he took his leave, first one in, last out!

'And what is that, Mr Thwaites?' Tom asked, grinning amiably, for he had thoroughly enjoyed his first night working for himself!

'A dart board and dominoes,' Mr Thwaites replied.

'You shall have them,' Tom laughed, 'on your next visit to "The Hawthorne Tree".'

'The what?' Mr Thwaites was clearly mystified.

' "The Hawthorne Tree", Mr Thwaites,' Meg cut in graciously. 'That is the name of the inn.'

'Well, I never did,' he grinned, 'and mine's Jack!'

No-one knew how it began, of course. Perhaps a dying coal fell from the fire though Tom swore he had stirred the hearth until the flames were almost out, or was it a fag-end thrown carelessly by one of the cheerful revellers as he downed his last pint in the bar-room? How could they be sure, they asked one another? They only knew that had it not been for the dog which, unaccountably, was still about the place and whose frantic barking had brought them all tumbling, fearful and wide-eyed from their beds, they would have been burnt to a crisp, the lot of them, Edie said. Not another bloody fire, Tom was shouting as he scrambled up the hill, which, only an hour since he had gone down and Meg was fretful over the mess her well-placed bucket of water had caused on her new rug. Her heart had recovered from its desperate tattoo of remembered fear and though the blaze had done no more than singe her curtains and scorch the smooth white paint Tom had just completed it was a nasty thing to have happened on their very first night.

' 'Tis an omen,' Zack remarked ominously, peering at the last wisps of smoke like an old raven with a portent of doom to deliver but Meg would have none of it.

'Nonsense Zack! It was nothing but a live coal from the fire and if the guard had been put up as it should have been this would never have happened!'

Tom jumped to his own defence as Meg glared at him.

'I put the guard up. It was the last thing I did before I locked the door.' He glared back at her, his face suffused with the blood of indignant rage.

'Well how did it start then, tell me that?'

'Some drunken fool throwing a fag-end in the corner, I shouldn't wonder . . .'

'Which corner I'd like to know for the fire started here by the curtains . . .'

'Well, if that's the case then it couldn't have been an ember from the fire either!'

Meg turned to look at the spot where she had thrown the bucket of water, her lips pursed reflectively and the fight went out of her.

'You're right, Tom ... that's strange ... but then ... what caused it?'

'Nay lass, I don't know. Perhaps a spark from the fire flew over the top of the guard.'

'The guard? You're sure you put it up?'

'I did, our Meg, honest.'

'When I found it it was lying on it's side ...'

'Perhaps the dog knocked it over when ...'

Meg's face cleared and the split second feather of premonition which brushed her spine was gone before she had time to register its existence.

She smiled in relief then sighed heavily. 'That must be it, Tom, but we'll have to be more careful. If it hadn't been for the dog's barking God knows what might have happened. I wonder where he came from? I thought he belonged to one of the customers but anyway, thank the Lord he decided to stay on, whoever he belongs to!'

Chapter twenty-three

The thunder roared across the garden and up over the rooftop of the building and Edie rushed to close the windows, convinced a storm was upon them and she did not want her freshly washed nets ruined. It was early in the year yet for the summer thunderstorms which could brew up in these parts, raging down in the valleys and over the high peaks, but best be sure!

She had never seen anything like the dreadful scarlet apparition which stood snarling, just like some beast about to attack its prey, outside the front door of the inn and she could feel the very floor move beneath her feet with its noise and movement. It would tumble the old foundations of the building, she was convinced, and them none too stable after all these years, and bring the walls down about their ears. She put out a trembling hand to Miss Hughes who was behind her supervising the placing of fresh linen in the bedrooms, imploring her voicelessly to witness this dreadful monster which had come upon them.

'What is it, Edie?'

But Edie couldn't answer for in truth she did not know!

'For heaven's sake, Edie!' Meg's voice was tart for she had just sent on their way twenty-three young cyclists, members of the Leicestershire Cycling Club who were on a tour of the northern beauty spots, and their youthful enthusiasm and high spirits in the dining-room and snug last night where even the young ladies had ventured a glass of cider, had worn them all to a frazzle. Annie Hardcastle who had offered her help had declared she didn't know what the world was coming to, she really didn't, and what were their families thinking of, she asked, allowing young girls the freedom to ride about – in *knickerbockers* if you please – as readily as gentlemen and they all needed their bottoms smacked in her opinion! But there, she sighed, these folk were Meg's bread and butter and she supposed they must be prepared to make sacrifices to earn it. One might have been forgiven for believing that it was *she* who owned the inn, and made the sacrifice!

Meg moved across the bedroom and stood beside Edie. Twitching aside the newly washed nets she craned her neck to see who it was who had driven up to her front door for if Edie had not recognised the sound of a motor car, Meg had, and she did not want her freshly mown lawn spoiled by tyre tracks. Some of her clientele, the younger ones, had little respect for the property of those who served them and who were, consequently inferior to them, they believed!

The garden was a delight and a credit to the man who had created it, bursting with the life Tom Fraser had implanted there. The wild grasses and overrun flower beds had all been scythed to manageable proportions, then dug over again and again during the winter months. Every weed and nettle and strangling acre of convolvulus had been ruthlessly destroyed, and in the right season the lawn had been laid stretching from the gravel path about the building right down to the boundaries at the front and at each side of the inn. When the land was cleared a small stream had been discovered running across the bottom of the garden, gurgling and splashing most obligingly as the rubbish which choked it was removed. There was a high hedge of blackthorne and the huge hawthorne tree itself from which Meg had named the inn. Tom had planted 'country' flowers, many of them wild. Field-rose and meadowsweet, bellflower, campion and marsh marigold by the stream, blue and pink and yellow spreading in a multi-coloured carpet beneath the tree. Nearer to the house, edging the lawn in a more formal fashion was phlox and zinnia, begonia and dahlia and against the house wall itself the fragrant violet-blue beauty of the wisteria which had, over the decades, grown up to the roof top.

A gravelled pathway, wide enough to accomodate the motor cars Meg expected, led from the open front gate along the side of the house and round the inn to the back yard, cobbled and sensible, where the vehicles might be parked. There were stables which would eventually be made over into garages but along the walls which surrounded the yard Tom had planted climbers, rose, honeysuckle, clematis so that even here was beauty and fragrance. Beyond the cluster of stone built stables lay Tom's 'working' garden in which there were row upon row of vegetables, fruit trees and a greenhouse, large and humid in which he was trying his hand at grape growing. There was a cow in a small pasture discreetly out of sight behind a stand of trees and a pen with pigs in it and round the stable yard, pecking restlessly at the cobbles, a dozen hens.

The man in the motor car switched off the engine then climbed down and stood for a moment or two looking round him and stretching like a cat in the sun. His arms reached high over his head, then out from his shoulders and he arched his back and moved his head from side to side on his neck. He pushed his hands deep into his pockets and sauntered a short distance from the motor car and stared out over the golden, sun-wrapped serenity of the garden, breathing deeply, then he turned on his heel and as if sensing that he was being watched looked up at the open window.

Martin Hunter was twenty-three years old, tall and straight with a beautifully proportioned body which bore no visible signs of the injuries he had sustained on the race track at Brooklands. Only his cheek still had the indentation left by his scar and it was very appealing for it lifted the corner of his mouth in a wry half-smile. His face was strong with the uncompromising determination which had made him a success on the racing circuits of the world but his manner, the way he stood, though still bearing a certain impudence, gave the impression that he was quieter now, mature and somewhat older than his years since he was, for the first time in his life, his *own* man!

Edie was shocked when, as he looked up to where Miss Hughes stood framed in the window he winked, actually winked, and then blew a kiss, bold as you please, but then the sight of Miss Hughes tumbling over herself to get to the bedroom door and the sound of her excited squealing – Edie could think of no other word to describe it – took all thought from her head. Miss Hughes was just like a big kid promised a treat, and here it was, her manner said, and Edie watched breathlessly as she flew out from beneath the porch at the front door and flung herself into the chap's arms!

'Oh Martin,' she was crying, her face all aglow in that particular way it had and her eyes like candles in the dark, and then she was laughing and calling for Tom and for several minutes the three of them, Miss Hughes, Mr Tom and the stranger formed an awkward circle, arms about one another in a comical shuffle of joy.

'Why haven't you been up . . .?'

'It's grand to see you, lad . . .'

'You look so well, what . . .'

287

'We hoped you'd be over before this . . .'
'. . . might have telephoned . . .'
'How's your leg . . .?'
'Not one word in all this time . . .'
'I know . . .'
'How's Cook? She was . . .'
'. . . this place . . . what a bloody difference!'
'How long can you stay . . .'
'My God, you both must have worked like demons . . .'
'Sit down and tell us about . . .'
'Must be at least nine months . . .'
'. . . should have brought Mrs Whitley . . .'
'*Cook*! In a motor car . . .'

Edie was quite spellbound as the three of them all talked at once, sentences overlapping, the men pounding one another on the shoulder and back in the way men do to show their masculine affection; Miss Hughes clinging to the newcomer's arm and looking up at him in a way Edie had never thought to see her employer do, and her with half the men in the district in love with her!

At last they turned and Megan Hughes and Tom Fraser began to walk slowly round the motor car which stood at the front door and on their faces grew a look of awe. Meg put out a wondering hand and stroked the shining bonnet then turned to Martin, her eyes wide with the marvel of it.

'Is it . . . is it yours, Martin, the one you have always . . .?' She could not finish.

'Yes,' he answered simply.

She turned back to the machine. 'Your very own . . .'

'She's called the "Huntress".'

'Of course . . .'

Tom shook his head, lost for words since this was the moment, the longed for, fought for, dreamed of moment which had been the irresistible destination of Martin Hunter ever since he had knelt beside Mr Hale at the Modern Bicycle Emporium and put a spanner to a nut for the first time. Then, as a boy of thirteen or fourteen years, he had had no conception of what he was to do, of what he was to become, of how his life was to change, of where that meeting with Albert Hale in the snooker room of the gymnasium was to lead him, but here it was, part of his destiny already fulfilled, it seemed, in the glory of the racing car which stood before them. It had long and lovely lines, sleek and shining and simple, with none of the awkward contours and ugly corners of those to be seen at race meets up and down the country and in it was clearly expressed the brilliance of the mind of the man who had started out in an orphanage. He had done this, brought forth this beautiful creature from his own rough beginning. Taught to read and write and cypher, no more, at the orphanage, he had educated himself until he was able to put on paper the dashing, daring ideas which had teamed in his head and this, this perfect machine was the result.

'If she goes as well as she looks.' Tom's words were quietly spoken.

'She does!'

'Oh Martin . . .' Tears slipped down Meg's face and she took Martin's hand in hers, placing the back of it against her wet cheek.

'Damnation, Martin . . .' Tom's voice was rough and his own eyes were suspiciously bright and he reached for Martin's other hand and began to pump it vigorously and all three were, in that special moment together, beyond words. They continued to stand, shoulder touching shoulder, smiling first at the racing car, then at each other until at last Martin managed a laugh, choked with emotion but a laugh nevertheless.

'Come on, you two, now you've seen what I've been up to, show me what the pair of you have been doing this winter.'

Edie watched as they turned away, walking arm in arm down the length of the garden to the shade of the great hawthorne tree with the bubbling stream flowing beneath it and where Meg had set out garden furniture of white wicker with pretty flowered cushions. It was here that she intended the ladies would be seated, those who would be driven over in their carriages, or even in their motor cars to take tea and idle away their carefree afternoons in one another's refined company. It was empty for though it was June and the day was as warm and lovely as only an English June day can be, the ladies had not yet come!

'What'll it be, Martin?' she heard Mr Tom call out. 'How about a beer or is it too soon in the day?'

'No, a beer would be fine, lad.'

Edie had too much to do in the increasingly successful little inn, or hotel, as Miss Hughes like it to be called now, to stand and listen to the conversation between her employers and the stranger – dearly as she would have loved to since it would have been something to tell their Annie when she saw her on her next day off. She visited her cousin whenever she could, and often gave her a hand with her 'gentleman boarders'. Annie had her hands full at this time of the year as the casual labourers who were her customers crowded her small establishment. There was no conflict between her and Miss Hughes for as Annie liked to say Meg's clientele – Meg had 'clientele', Annie had 'customers' – did not interfere with Annie's!

Edie moved reluctantly towards the kitchen, passing Mr Tom on the way back with two foaming tankards of beer and a lemonade for Meg in his hands.

'Tell us about it, Martin,' she heard him say as he made his way down the garden, then she shut the kitchen door for the girls who worked there were all agog at the arrival of the handsome stranger and his fearsome machine and it was *her* job, in the absence of Miss Hughes to keep them at it!

It was at Meg he looked throughout the whole recital of his life since they had last seen him, never taking his eyes from hers, and as his glowed, so did hers and as his flashed, hers did the same and when his softened with some mysterious emotion, she seemed to feel it too for was there anyone, *anyone* who understood him and his dreams as Meggie did?

'You know I always meant to build my own motor car?' he said, his beer forgotten. She nodded and somehow her hands slipped across the table between them and into his. 'I had the use of the tack room. It was converted into a machine shop. There's electricity and . . .'

Tom Fraser was as overjoyed as Meg. Martin had come to see them after nine months without a word, not even by the challenging and complicated telephone system which Meg had insisted on having installed. They had been a time or two to Silverdale to see Mrs Whitley but each time Martin had been off somewhere, doing trials or some such and they had not seen him. Nine months doing some wonderful thing in the world of motor cars, the mysteries of which were now about to be revealed to himself and Meg. Martin and the old gentleman had gone into business together and from the look of it they had met with some success. But there was some strange undercurrent involving the two of them, Martin and Meg, carrying them this way and that and for some reason he found himself drifting to one side, excluded,

290

forgotten and he sat back in his chair, quietly sipping his beer, watching them and a strange and disquieting emotion grew within him. What that emotion was he could not have said for was he not here, sharing the happiness with Meg and Martin, the friends he had loved for all of his life. The two people who had shared with him, *their* lives. He was content with Meg and the new life they had created together at 'Hawthornes'. He worked in the gardens during the day beside Zack, tending the bounteous growth of his vegetables, his apple and plum trees, his strawberries, raspberries, peaches, damsons, grapes and mushrooms and all destined for the delicious dishes which Meg was to put before her 'clientele'. And all created and worked by himself. He knew his own worth. He was comfortable. He was, though he was not aware of it, possessed of enormous patience; there was an air of serenity about him as he went about the slow and peaceful task of weeding, of hoeing, his attitude one of a man in tune with the earth which supports him. He smoked a pipe and wore a cap and a working man's jacket with a pullover beneath it. His face was bronzed by the thousands of hours he had spent in the open air and his eyes were clear, untroubled, a bright pansy blue and shining with health. They were surrounded by a fine tracery of lines, put there by the sun as he narrowed them against its glare, and by his own tendency to easy laughter. He moved, seemingly without purpose, through the hours and days of his life, doing, he realised, the very work for which he was best suited. He worked hard, though he did not give the appearance of it with his careless, indolent way of moving. He took a simple, uncomplicated pleasure in the company of the working man he served in his bar at night and should he have been asked about it, he would have replied that his world was just as it should be.

Tom was an endearing, likeable young man, completely at his ease in the company of the more sophisticated, more worldly Meg and Martin, seeing no difference in either of them from the two spirited youngsters with whom he had grown up. Now, suddenly, as he watched Meg's hands held so *lovingly* in Martin's, he felt a dreadful need to knock them apart, to have Meg sit away from Martin and to have that expression, whatever it was, wiped off Martin's face!

'I'm sorry,' he was saying, 'that I've not been up to see you but we've been up to our eyes in it, Meg. I've just not had a second to spare. I should have telephoned, I knew you'd had one put in,

291

Cook told me, but . . . you understand, don't you?' His eyes begged for forgiveness and Tom watched Meg's become lustrous with warmth and again that hostile feeling arose in him.

'We're going to try her out on all the major race tracks in the country,' Martin was saying, 'There's to be a rally, the first Monte Carlo Rally and another in America. The "Indianapolis 500" it's to be called, and then we're going for the "Lightning Long" at Brooklands, and the "Long Handicap" if she does well . . .'

He lifted his head with the pride of a young prince and squeezed her hands ardently and waited for her to speak, to give thanks for this gift he brought to lay at her feet. She shook her head, quiet now, moving from the excited young girl of a moment ago to the maturity Martin could see was starting her on her *own* course. She was different, controlled and perfectly capable of ordering this business, this hotel and managing *the* people who worked for her and looked to her for guidance. She would follow him, in her chosen profession and travel, as he had done, a long way from the world of the three youngsters who had larked about at Great George Square. The subtle change in his own relationship with Mr Robert had deeply satisfied him. They were no longer employer and employee. They were man and man working in partnership, a partnership assumed on the completion of Martin's design. That was *his* and Mr Robert accorded him the respect which was due to him as a professional man. He had two young men working under him – young men from the engineering college he himself had attended – and they were to travel with him wherever he and his machine went, together with a third young man who was training to race Martin's car. They were all under his directorship. He was the master now and he gave orders to them with a positive authority for only he knew what they were about.

He turned then to smile at Tom. His friend had been silent for the past half hour and Martin was quite bewildered by the awkward expression which had fixed itself on Tom's face. He was looking at Martin for all the world as though he cared nought for Martin's success and yet only a while ago he had been as genuinely enthusiastic as Meg. His tankard was gripped fiercely in his hand and though it was empty he placed it to his lips and pretended to drink.

Martin's smile deepened. 'What's up, me old scouser?'

'Nowt.' Tom's voice was sharp. It was now, when he was put

beside Martin that the gulf which had grown between them was most apparent. Tom's casual flannels and open-necked, collarless shirt were haphazard, appearing as though they had been thrown on that morning, the first thing that came to his hand. He liked what were called 'peg-top' trousers, comfortable, with a loose waistband and braces, wide thighs and knees and tapering at the bottom of the leg. He could tuck them into the tops of his boots he said and they were practical for the job he did. His cap was pushed to the back of his head to reveal the short crop of his golden curls.

But it was not just in the way they dressed that the two young men differed. Tom had not changed from the easy going good-natured lad he had always been. The new position he had acquired as the proprietor of a country inn, as he still thought of it, had in no way brought him a sense of his own importance. He had not gained the urbanity Martin had, nor his discriminating taste for the good things in life. In their different ways they had become men, and in their different ways they were going about the business of *being* men, and as Meg looked at Martin she quite failed to see the expression which clouded Tom's boyish face, and was quite amazed when he put his arm tightly about her to walk up the slope of the lawn to Martin's beautiful motor car, but Martin did and a truth was born between them that day. It was something which both momentarily recognised but neither would admit to, since after all, they were brothers but Megan Hughes stood between them, not as she had always done, to be protected and watched over, to be kept safe from other men, but amazingly, from one another! It was over in that brief fraction of a second and, startled, they smiled warily, then nodded, two young animals not awfully sure what the other was up to.

When Martin drove away he did so with the insolent swagger of a man who knows exactly his own worth, borne up by the absolute certainty that he and his automobile were, without doubt, the finest on the road. Edie viewed their combined magnificence from the safety of the porch and sniffed. Racing car, indeed! All flash and glitter in *her* eyes and so was *he* and not to be put in the same class as Mr Tom who was a grand lad. She had heard Miss Hughes plead with the handsome strutting chap to stop for a taste of her steak and kidney pie, telling him that it had only this moment come from the oven and that there were fresh strawberries grown by Tom and cream from their own cow but he only laughed and kissed her cheek.

'Martin has things to do, Meg,' Edie heard Mr Tom say quietly and knew quite positively that he was glad when Martin said he really must go but he would be back as soon as he was able, perhaps after the racing at Brooklands, whatever that was!

The sunshine wrapped about the couple who stood in front of the porch, falling in a warm curtain of gold and as the monster roared away Edie thought what a lovely couple they made. It filtered through the open doorway and into the wide passage, softly touching the polished red of the quarry tiled floor and lapped gently in a receding wave at the white-washed walls. Copper glow was picked out from the warming pans which hung there, buffed to brightness each day by herself, and a magnificent profusion of Mr Tom's early roses, flaming in crimson and scarlet, burned in an enormous copper jug on a low table at the foot of the stairs.

She watched them come in and as Mr Tom sauntered off, whistling cheerfully now – to the back of the house to have a last look at his lettuces before it began to rain as he was certain it would – she hoped that the chap would stay away for really Miss Hughes and Mr Tom were better off without him and certainly did not need the disturbing influence he seemed to bring!

Chapter twenty-four

It was after midnight and Meg stared sightlessly towards the half drawn curtains which fluttered at the open bedroom window and beyond to the summer darkness and wondered what it was that had awakened her. She turned her head on the pillow and listened but the sound did not repeat itself. Perhaps the dog had moved against something in his restless wandering in the dark, disturbing an ornament on a table or the brush which hung beside the fireplace in the kitchen, or was it the echo of the barking of the dog fox in the spinney which had awakened her?

She shifted fretfully, pushing aside the sheets which snarled about her, lifting and straightening them, then settled herself to sleep again but her body was disturbed now, alive with the vividness of the half forgotten dream from which she had awakened. She could scarcely remember it, but Martin had been in it and his warm presence was still with her in a strange and distracting way and it left her ... well, she could only call it ... tingling and subject to rhythmic spasms of some half remembered feeling she had no name for, but which was unnerving and decidedly uncomfortable.

She punched her pillow violently, turning to lie flat on her stomach, tossing her mind feverishly back and forth between tomorrow's menus and yesterday's takings, to the problems of where she would accommodate the three young American cyclists – they had descended upon her that afternoon with the wild enthusiasm of their nationality declaring they must have a room, even to share, for three nights and were at this moment on camp beds in the attic directly above her!

Perhaps it was this which had rendered her so restive. The American accent was quite distinctive and Martin had picked it up slightly when he was in their country, and she had learned to recognise it from the many young people who toured the country, some, as they artlessly confided, searching for their roots!

She tossed her thick plait of hair away from her shoulders. It

295

was heavy and hot as it unwound itself about the pillow and she muttered irritably, swearing she would have it cut off. She turned again, rolling to the edge of the bed, flinging her arms across her closed eyes. She wished she could sleep again. They had been frantically busy since Easter and the inn was now filled with tourists, young people, like the three Americans, mostly men who were cycling from one end of the country to the other, intent it seemed on missing nothing from the craggy cliffs of Cornwall, the soft downs of Devon, the grandeur of the Cotswolds and nor-thwards through the Derbyshire peakland, the Yorkshire Moors and gaily on to 'do' Scotland! Anywhere a bit of lovely countryside presented itself or a place of historical interest caught their imagination, they went. They poured in hordes, not only from other countries as far away as America, but from every town and city in Britain where a young man or woman might afford the price of a bicycle! From nearer home, Manchester, Bolton, Wigan, St Helens, Liverpool and Stoke-on-Trent on a day's outing, moving on to Chester or North Wales.

'The Hawthorne Tree' was now on the 'Cyclist Touring Club's' list as suitable accommodation for its members and was a favourite stopping off place. The inn was packed out every single night of the week, the farmers, their labourers, cottagers, woodworkers from the forest area, men from the local saw-mill and those who worked in rural jobs in the vicinity, dropped into the 'Hawthorne' for a pint or two. Meg's food had become well known for its tasty goodness and cheapness and many of the men who were single ate their evening meal there regularly. The nearest public house was over in the next village of Little Davenport, only a mile or two as the crow flies and though these men had been prepared to leg it over there a couple of nights a week there was no need now they had their own local. It had not been just luck on Meg's part that she had picked a village which did not enjoy its own public house, and she gave thanks that it was doing even better than she had hoped for, but though these men were the bread and butter of her business she was after the jam to go on it!

The cyclists and the hikers came. They sat in the 'snug' or the public bar, or if the weather allowed it, on benches in the lovely gardens Tom and Zack had created from the wilderness and drank beer and shandy and cider and ate heaped platesful of her roast meats, steak and kidney pie, veal pasties, cheese, pickles and Whitstable oysters which were inexpensive and tasty, before 'pushing on'. If they had come far then they would stay the night, lovingly bedding down their machines as though they were thoroughbreds, in the stables at the rear of the inn.

Meg sat up and sighed tremulously. It was no good. Her mind was as active as a hive of hornets stirred up with a stick! Easing herself from the bed, on edge and restive – that energy which had always been her's keeping her from sleep even after eighteen hours on her feet – she moved to the window and sitting down on the padded seat Tom had made for her, she looked out into the impenetrable darkness that was the countryside at night. Not a light showed anywhere for those who must be up at dawn did not spend the hours allotted for sleep in any other activity! She could hear the faint echo of Edie's snores from the far reaches of the attic bedroom she slept in and the creak of a camp bed above her as one of the travellers turned in his sleep.

She sighed again and rested her head against the leaded panes of glass. She wished she could rest. She had so much to do, so much to plan in her mind but though her body was weary her thoughts would not let it rest. She stirred awkwardly, then stood up, stretching her arms above her head. She would go downstairs and look at the accounts and tomorrow's menus. That would stop her mind from wandering about in useless circles which led nowhere. It was what she and Tom were doing, and would do in the future which must concern her now. They lived amiably side by side and she knew he was a contented man. He enjoyed what he did at the inn each day. He had no responsibilities for Meg dealt with everything from the ordering of the beer and spirits, the food which she herself prepared to the payment of the bills and the servants' wages. She told him when to open the bars and when to close them, when another barrel was needed and even, since she had compared his clothes to those of Martin, what he should wear in his position as the owner of a successful hotel!

And he liked being the owner. The men who frequented the inn looked up to him, affording him the respect given a man who works for himself. He got on well with his customers as he had done with the men he had once worked with at Silverdale, since it had always been in his nature to like his fellow men and to have that good fellowship returned.

She herself helped to bring in the men who drank there since she was not blind to her own attractions, nor the looks which the men gave her when she laughed with them. A hungry look, it was, as though they would like nothing better than to get to know Tom Fraser's partner more intimately. The field was open to all comers, they knew that, for Tom himself seemed not to be interested, though there were those who were convinced and said so to the others, that he had a certain look about him which said a man should take care in his hearing when he was speaking to Megan Hughes! Her magnificence was like the splendour and warmth of the sun to the men who drank in the low-ceilinged rooms and her superb body was a constant lure to them. But the strange thing was, they said, she appeared to have no conception of her own beauty, which was a kind of beauty in itself, nor the effect she had on them, but they treated her respectfully and brought her their custom again and again and that was all Meg cared about.

She and Tom made a good team since he knew the men's admiration and banter meant nothing to her. Indeed he took part in it and the atmosphere was convivial to those who were their customers in the bar. They had been successful in what they did. It was almost eighteen months since they had begun and in the first year they had made a clear profit of over £500 and already this year they had doubled that and the loan from the bank was completely repaid. The inn was theirs and the deeds to prove it lay safely locked away in a tin box in her desk. She had even made one or two investments, under the guidance of Mr Chancellor, the shrewd bank manager Mr Hemingway had recommended, in the world of stocks and shares. Tom had been stunned beyond speech by Meg's boldness, longing, she was sure to put their profit in a sock and keep it under the mattress, and could not understand that these small enterprises in which Meg invested could bring them further dividends.

'But Mr Fraser,' Mr Chancellor had protested, when he and Meg had gone to pay the final part of the loan, 'you cannot allow capital to lie about unemployed!'

Capital! Unemployed! What in damnation was the man talking about, Tom's expression said and Mr Chancellor, relieved to have one member of the partnership who knew a sovereign from a farthing, turned again thankfully to Miss Hughes whose bright intelligence and quick grasping mind knew exactly what Mr Chancellor meant. She was eager to take his advice which was most gratifying and learned quickly. She read the newspapers he told her would be of interest to her in business, those dealing with finance and when she turned her deep amber gaze on him as she stood up to shake his hand and thank him for his help, he was quite bowled over by the disparity between the two partners. A nice enough chap with a most personable disposition but Miss Hughes was so attentive where one could only say he fidgeted. She was level-headed and far sighted but he seemed as merry and careless of their money as a ten year old, saying cheerfully that it was for spending, wasn't it!

The inn was silent. Meg cocked her head to listen as the faint bark of the dog fox sounded from across the fields towards Three House Farm. It would be after Jack Thwaites' hens again. Downstairs she heard the yellow dog stir and knew he would be at the back door, nose to the doorstep as he tried to sniff out the scent of his old enemy. He gave a small warning growl and she smiled. He would not bark unless the fox, or indeed any intruder came within the inn's yard, but he could not resist letting whoever was out there know he was to be reckoned with. An intruder himself, wandering in one day soon after they had moved into the inn, he had settled down as if he had as much right to be there as they did and he guarded his territory zealously.

Meg crossed the room and slipped quietly through the open doorway and down the stairs. The dog was there to greet her, his delight showing in his thrusting nose and pluming tail.

'Good boy, good old boy,' she said quietly and fondled his head as he followed her down the long passage to the small room which she used as an office. She sat down at the desk and reached across to light the lamp. It reflected in the dark square of the window beside her own pale face and she stared at it pensively for a moment or two then, her thoughts beginning to drift again she reached hastily for a ledger which was placed to the right-hand side of the desk. She opened it, flicking through it until she came to the last written page. She ran a practised eye down the long, neat columns of figures, her lips murmuring wordlessly as she added and subtracted. There was not one mistake, not one erasure nor incorrect total and Meg admired the perfection of it, remembering the hours she had spent in the company of the bookkeeper at the 'Adelphi'. She checked the amounts at the bottom of the page, making a swift calculation in her head and smiled.

How well they had done! Eighteen months and their success had exceeded far beyond what she had hoped for. It seemed everything she did, every innovation she carried out – bar one –

had brought them good fortune. Her goal had been an efficient, profit making concern in which she and Tom might find a niche and she had succeeded. Her own skill in the hotel trade had not surprised her. She was good at it. She had always known it. She had a felicitous knack of being able to judge where and when she should take a gamble but they were not gambles, she came to realise as her achievements grew. It was an instinct which told her what would serve favourably and what would not and except for one instance she found she could rely on it and trust it!

There was the scheme she had thought up of turning the loft of the disused stables into small, spartan but clean rooms in which the overflow of young cyclists and hikers might be accommodated. It had cost money to renovate, good money chucked down the drain in some people's opinion, but it had proved otherwise for the young people were quick to take advantage of the cheaper lodgings and the freedom to be more high-spirited in the rooms away from the main building; and the better rooms in the inn were left for those who desired more comforts and had no wish to cross the stable yard to reach them!

But no matter what she did, no matter how hard she worked at it, despite the word that got round of the elegance of her dining-room which might be hired privately and was furnished in exactly the way the dining-room at Silverdale was furnished, of her bedrooms and drawing-room, of the simple beauty of her secluded garden where one might take tea on a sunny afternoon, *they* did not come. The trade she was aiming at, the class of person for whom she had created it, the clientele for whom she had trained for so long at the Adelphi, to serve, they did not come!

She had spent hours, days, in the company of Annie Hardcastle, scouring second-hand shops, going to sales and auctions in which household furniture of only the very best quality was to be found, purchasing a dining table with pillar and claw ends in the loveliest burnished mahogany with a dozen chairs to match upholstered in pale cream velvet, rosewood side tables to place next to a rosewood sofa where the ladies might take their coffee. Pedestal and slab sideboards and a silver salver to place on it. A Victoria bath for a bedroom, plated candlesticks and sets of ivory-handled knives and forks. Handsome cut crystal and a fine bone china dinner service. A lady's wardrobe and posted bedsteads with velvet curtains, mirrors and dressing glasses and Brussels carpets, all of the finest quality and hand-picked by herself and Annie Hardcastle who knew good stuff when she saw it. They all sat in quite elegant splendour where she and Annie had arranged them in the empty quiet of the rooms she had set apart from the rest of the hotel waiting for the quality guests she had envisaged and who never came!

She let it be known that there was a private dining-room with its own entrance where a gentleman might take his family for Sunday luncheon, or where a small reception might be held in the evening, since her cuisine was of the highest order, without becoming involved with a person who was not of his own class! Dishes such as asparagus soup, crimped salmon, trout à la Genévése, lobster sauce, Charlotte à la Parisienne, compôte of gooseberries, soufflé of rice, vol-au-vent of strawberries and cream, all home produced, naturally, and dozens of other gourmet dishes which she had studied under the greatest chefs in the country, at the Adelphi Hotel to perfect, and which she would prepare with her own hand, were whispered discreetly in ears which might be persuaded to pass them on to those who dined on such dishes, but they did not come!

What had begun as an ordinary inn where a man might have a pint and chat to his cronies had now been transformed into an hotel where the traveller might have a drink in one of its cosy bars, tea in the garden or the delightful tea room, a more substantial meal in the elegant dining-room, or stay the night in one of its comfortable bedrooms.

But they did not come! Oh yes, she was full each night and day from May until October with the young and the enthusiastic cyclists, and motorists now, who wanted an inexpensive holiday and were happy to eat good, plain fare and sleep in a clean, plain bedroom. She made money and worked hard for it but it was not what she wanted and she knew the reason why!

She had wanted both. She had thought in her innocence that they could be kept apart. They did not mix. They *could* not mix and she should have known it. The good folk, plain and outspoken who came to her inn because it was value for money, who liked a laugh and a tart remark, a joke and a wink, would not care to be on their best behaviour in the company of the gentry and the gentry did not wish to be in *their* company at all. The working man occupied her snug and her tap-room, chaps who wanted nothing more than their dominoes and dartboard, their tankards resting comfortably on the plain wooden bar, the air they breathed

301

thick with pipe smoke and they were not to be tampered with. They did not wish to see the 'carriage' trade drifting round to the 'smart side' as they called it good humouredly and Meg knew that once it happened, she would lose *them*.

And the 'smart side' set itself? What of them? Should she persuade them to it, would they wish the well-bred peace of their French cuisine to be interrupted by shouts of ribald laughter as Jack Thwaites told one of his questionable jokes? Would they care to find themselves face to face with George Anderson, smelling of the farm yard through which his cows had just passed, and where his boots had picked up most of what they left behind? And how would they react to the sight of Bert Taylor, legless and cross-eyed, staggering down the drive held up by the solicitous, good-natured arms of his fellow drinkers, only fractionally less drunk than himself? The young people, many of them working class themselves who 'put up' in her 'plain' bedrooms and who rollicked merrily in the loft above the disused stables, thought of it as a 'lark', part of their holiday, their freedom from the routine of their daily life. They ate her good food and cycled off with great vigour, promising to return next year and to recommend her to their peers.

Her own face looked back at her from the black depths of the window. Her hand fell to the dog's head and he sighed as though in sympathy and she became aware, as her thoughts marched dolefully round and round inside her head, that she must face up to the fact that unless she was prepared to change it, it would not change for her. She had a splendid little business here, successful and growing, as word of her hospitality spread, taken by young cyclists and hikers to all parts of the country. Tom was jubilant, proud of her, he said, for it was all her doing and in a way she had pride in herself for it had gone well. Her shrewd brain and quick, far-seeing mind, her sharp business sense had made it what it was – but Tom must not be left out for he did the work of two men, cheerfully, willingly and was clever at what he did. He had left only an hour ago to walk down to Annie Hardcastle's after being on the go for eighteen hours, first in the gardens which were a full time job in themselves, the pasture, the care of the pigs and hens and then, when the bars opened, standing genially pulling pints until closing time. He loved it! These were his kind of people and what she had in mind would have to be hard fought for. She would have to struggle, not only for his agreement but for his support since she could not do it alone. He would see no sense in it, she knew that for Tom had not the restless need to fly higher and higher as she had. Martin would understand since he was the same as she was, striving for that dream they both had, of different worlds certainly, but a compulsion which made them fight tooth and nail in the free for all that was life.

His face swam to rest beside hers on the darkened window pane and she sighed again, more deeply than ever. They had not seen him since last Christmas when she and Tom had gone over to visit Mrs Whitley. He had been busy he said, for the racing car, the 'Huntress' had been enormously successful on the racing circuits of America and Europe and now he was to manufacture a smaller version from the prototype and, eventually, a motor car for the 'family' man for that was where the future lay, as he had always said. He and Mr Robert had taken on new premises for the stables at Silverdale had become too small for their growing concern. He was to design a glider, he said, an idea which had been developing in his head since he himself had learned to fly, perhaps he had told her? and he and the old gentleman were to branch out again and all in all was, as Tom said somewhat sourly, far too busy for the likes of them!

Meg had been quite amazed for it was not like Tom to speak in that way, particularly about their Martin, but both men had been somewhat strained with one another and had looked away when she questioned them, saying they were both working hard and not to mind them for after all it *was* Christmas!

'Anyway,' Martin said, 'you're never in when I telephone.'

Meg's mouth fell open since it was the first time she had heard of a telephone call.

'I'm never in! When did *you* telephone? From what you tell me you're too busy chasing your own tail to get in touch with us.'

'I called a couple of times. That woman of yours said you were out.'

Meg looked doubtful. 'Well, I suppose I might have been but it's funny she didn't tell me.'

He had smiled and his eyes had been soft for her and she thought of it now and wished with all her heart he was here so that she could talk to him about it, about this choice she had to make, which was silly because there *was* no choice. He would understand and encourage her in this step she meant to take for he would realise, as Tom would not, that it was the only one she *could* take. It was the only one for *her*. If you did not move on, you stood still and in Meg's opinion to stand still was to take a step backwards, but oh Lord, how was she to make Tom understand?

The clock struck twice and as it did so Meg closed the ledger which still lay open in front of her, replacing it carefully where she had found it. She stood up and stretched. The dog watched her as she moved away but did not follow as she walked along the passage towards the stairs. She would sleep now for she had set her active mind to peaceful rest by fixing it on the future and what she meant to have in it!

Chapter twenty-five

She might have proclaimed her intention of buying the crown jewels, the furor it caused and Tom was so astounded for the first time in his life he put his foot down and stated quite categorically that he *was not* having it! No, not at any cost, not even if they were *giving* the bloody things away!

'Why not?' Meg asked genuinely mystified since he had been brought up with them, so to speak.

'*Why*, for God's sake? Why Meg,' he snapped. 'Throwing cash about like a man with no arms and for what? First it was investments and stocks and shares and such, which you know are beyond me but I trusted you and let you have your own way, but this, this is lunacy. A motor car! Sweet Jesus, what next? I've never heard anything like it in my life. What the devil do we want with a motor car? We never go anywhere except into Northwich and there's a perfectly good train service.'

Tom's tall figure, still inclined to awkwardness when he was upset, became quite unco-ordinated and he cracked his elbow sharply on the bar counter, swearing rudely and wincing with the pain of it. He was well aware that Meg liked to have her own way and most of the time she got it. He was also aware that she was usually right for she had a sense for business he did not, but in this he was adamant! A new stove if she wanted one, or a carpet for her sitting-room, but a bloody motor car, never!

Meg's face turned to stone. She wanted this motor car! She needed it. She wanted to get about, to travel to other parts of the country to search out the potential site of another establishment. *An hotel*, though she had not yet broken *that* news to him and she could not do it without transport. She needed to be independent, to be able to get to places, test them out for their accessibility by motor car since she intended catering to the *motor car* trade and how was she to do it if she did not know where one could go? There was no question about it. She must have one.

She made her face smile. 'Tom,' she said, perfectly sure in her mind that he would agree if she explained it to him, for if there was anyone who would back her to the hilt it was Tom. For the past two years he had been her staunch support, her right hand in making the inn what it was. They had shared a companionship, a curious relationship which had baffled the community in which they lived, but firm and true, in step all the way in the manner of how they could better the establishment. They had made it what it was but he must be persuaded that it was time to move on. The inn would continue to be a fine, profitable business and if her approach to the bank for a loan with which to purchase a new hotel, with the inn as security, was successful, she intended to put in a manager. One who would be prepared to work under her own supervision, and it would then continue in its prosperity, but she had gone beyond it now. She wanted more. She wanted bigger! Better! Quality! The wealthy and she wanted a motor car to search out the place where they might be found. She had built up this business, it was hers and would remain so but it was time to move on.

'Let me tell you what I want to do.' Her smile was bright and luminous and she moved across the kitchen to stand before him. 'You see, if . . .' but Tom shook his head.

'No, Meg . . .*no*! We've no need of one. If you want a bicycle I'd not deny you,' he added magnanimously, 'though that bloody hill'd be a killer, no mistake. You could get about on a bicycle, Meg, if you've a mind to, but a motor car, well, I'd have to say no.'

For a second Meg thought she was about to break out in hysterical laughter. A bicycle! To get where she wanted to be on a bloody bicycle. It was utterly ludicrous but something in Tom's expression stopped her. Her own became set in a cast of mutinous obstinacy, and Tom took a step back for he had seen that look before.

'I don't think you heard me properly, Tom,' she said softly. 'I am not asking your permission to buy a motor car. I am *going* to buy a motor car! I have already ordered and paid for it so you see it's too late for argument. I thought you would be with me on this but I can see I was wrong. Nevertheless, I shall have one, whatever you say. Don't you wish to know *why* I want a motor car or to hear my plans for the future, nor how the motor is concerned in it? No! Then you are a fool and I suppose it is useless at the moment to discuss it with you.' She left the room quietly.

No more was said about the matter during the following days and Tom did not ask to be enlightened about Meg's plans for her motor car. The routine of the inn went on and though Tom was stiff and quiet with her, he did his work with as much thoroughness as usual and was even heard to whistle a time or two as though he thought the whole thing was a storm in a teacup and would no doubt blow over given time.

The automobile arrived the next week!

Meg thought she had never seen anything quite so magnificent and from the first moment she sat behind the steering wheel she loved it, just as she had done when she drove Martin's little Austin. She loved it with a passion which was to influence her life and colour her days with the joy and excitement only those with boldness and daring in their blood can know.

It was blue, somewhere between the brightness of a cornflower and the royal richness of a peacock. It had two headlamps, one at the level of the dashboard and the other slightly lower, in front of the bonnet. They were of a gleaming, polished brass. It was a solid little machine, capable of twenty-four miles an hour, reliable and simple to drive.

'Most suitable for a lady, if I might say so, Madam,' Megan was told by the mechanic who delivered it. It was the very latest Austin and had cost her £115. She thought Tom would faint when she told him, for really, the very idea of chucking away £115 – when years ago they would have been hard pressed to find a spare sixpence was quite alien to him. But he had had time to calm down in the last week and was prepared to listen when she drew him into their own small sitting-room and sat him down.

'It's only fair that you should know how and why this money is being spent, Tom, since the inn and it's profits belong to you just as much as to me. The motor is in both our names,' she said for she was always honest with him, 'and I'm sorry that I was so secretive. Well ... not secretive exactly, but just ... careful I wanted to have all my facts and figures secure in my head before I brought you in on it because I know how you worry. Yes, you do, so don't argue but you know you can trust me, don't you? Yes! Well, trust me just once more, Tom and hear me out before you have your say.'

Her gaze was candid and the truth shone from her eyes into Tom's, and he was aware that it did not really matter what she said, should she speak of Timbuktu or Shangri-la, or indeed of any place in the world to which she had a fancy to travel he would go with her. In the motor she had bought which sat now at the front of the inn waiting for the journey to begin, in one of the flimsy butterflies which Martin assured them would soar into the sky, and fly; across the waters of the earth in a canoe if she cared to, she had only to look at him as she was doing now, take his hand as she was doing now, smile at him, speak his name and he would simply stand up and follow her. It did not matter what she was about to reveal. It was of no concern what her plans for them might be, she was his star, the one he knew shone only for him, lighting his life and his heart.

'You see, Tom,' she was saying earnestly, 'I have discovered that in business you just cannot stand still. If you want to get on you have to be prepared to accept change, to move with the times. Do you understand?' Tom nodded his head and drifted in the sweet contemplation of the tawny beauty of her eyes.

'This place has been fine for us. We've made a success of it the two of us, but you see, we've gone as far as we can with it. It will never be anything else but a country pub. A place where the locals will come and have a pint and play dominoes and have a meal of steak and kidney or peas and faggots and I can do more than that, Tom.'

Her steady gaze became unfocused as she regarded some unseen vision way beyond Tom's comprehension. 'This business and the property is ours now, all paid for and with no outstanding debts. I got word today from Mr Chancellor that, with the inn as security and taking into account our record, the bank is willing to lend us the cash to purchase another property. I'm going to put a manager in here, keep it as it is and with you, or me to keep an eye on it, once a month, say, it will continue to make us a fair profit. The "carriage" trade won't come here, Tom and that's what I want. It's what I've trained myself for. The cyclists and hikers and the young people who can afford no better will come here and will keep it as a viable concern. It has been a stepping stone, if you like, leading us to what I'm really after, so you see . . .'

She paused and Tom stared as though hypnotised into her dream-filled eyes.

'There's this house. A lovely house down towards Matlock, Georgian, square with a slate roof and bow windows. It was once a rest house for waggon freight carriers. It has two acres of land with it, a small lake and twelve bedrooms. There are smaller rooms which could be made into bathrooms and even private suites if we had a mind to ... and I have! The estate agent in Northwich showed me a picture of it and a plan of the outlay and it looks exactly the sort of place we want. It would be a hard uphill slog, Tom, but I know we could soon have it as successful as this. I could do all the recipes I learned at the Adelphi, and then perhaps a chef, who knows and it would be ours, Tom, the second business we have started towards a ...'

Meg's face was flushed as she ran out of words. Her eyes were a blaze of excitement as she was carried along on its peaking wave. The vision she had burned into her mind of a lovely, stately, *elegant* hotel where those who were used in their own homes to luxury and comfort, would find it under her roof. Where they would feel themselves to be welcome guests and not paying boarders. It was a dream she had held since her days at the Adelphi. She had sensed their approval of their surroundings then, even though she herself had not created it but she had known how to please those at 'Hawthornes' and she would do it with the new concern. She had her own style and charm, yes, charm and it had brought them back again and again. If she could manage it in a country inn which was all she had to work with then, what might she achieve with a *proper* setting. She knew she could do it. She *knew* she had it in her to be a successful hotelier and she must make Tom see it too. Tom had stood shoulder to shoulder with her, lent her support and encouragement in establishing 'Hawthornes' and he had shared in its success. Now he must do the same with this new venture.

And besides, Meg needed to share her exhilaration with *someone*. She needed to talk about it, to endlessly make plans for the alterations she had in her head for the as yet unseen house. There would be redecorating and the installation of private bathrooms, the engaging of staff, experienced and trained in the hotel trade and those she would train herself and the planning and sheer, bloody size of the whole undertaking. There was the financing to be discussed with Mr Chancellor and the consideration of the repayment of the loan they had agreed, and if she did not get started on it soon she was afraid the lovely dream she had conceived in her head might turn out to be just that, and she would wake up one day in her bed at Great George Square where it had all begun. She knew it was right. She could feel it with some instinct, some sixth sense which had deserted her at Hawthornes in

309

the matter of catering to the gentry. But she would not make that mistake again.

'This might not be the right place for us Tom,' she went on. 'It might be too inaccessible, too big, too small, not suitable for alteration. It might be over-priced, run down and not worth the expenditure and that is why I must go and see it and that is why I need a motor car. I have to know that a motor car can *reach* it, and if it's not what we want then I shall look at other places until I find it.'

She took Tom's big, work-worn hands, wrapping her long, capable fingers about them and looked up into his face. There was something there she did not recognise but there was also agreement and the willingness to trust in her judgement. He would support her his expression said, as he had always done but the reason for it was hidden from her for she did not really wonder *why*!

'D'you see, Tom? D'you see where we're heading?'

'You're a clever woman, d'you know that, Megan Hughes.' The answer surprised her and she stood back to look more closely into his face.

'What does that mean?'

'It means we could be millionaires before we reach twenty-five if we go on at this rate.' He was laughing now and though his hand still held hers, softly caressing the base of her thumb with his, she did not notice for she was too carried away with the joy of it all.

'Hold on, lad. Don't get too enthusiastic! There's a few things to be got out of the way before we start entertaining the aristocracy.'

The journey of fifty miles or so which was to take Meg from Great Merrydown to Matlock must be prepared for with the utmost care and eye for detail, since it was no small feat to embark upon such a momentous undertaking alone. Her motor car was the most up to date and mechanically sound of its day but the expectation of her arrival time in Matlock, or even that she was to arrive at all, could not be taken for granted. She would travel as far as the roads, the weather and the automobile allowed and if necessary put up at some inn on the way.

She was the talk and wonder of the whole open-mouthed community. She was cheered wherever she went for naturally Tom insisted she put in a few days of practice before setting off into what was to him as fearsome as venturing into darkest Africa.

She was dressed for the journey in a long, caped coat, very serviceable and suitable for motoring the advertisement had said, made in navy alpaca. It was double breasted and warm for though it was summer there was no protection from the elements in her little runabout. Her boots were sturdy and knee length and her stockings were made of wool. Her skirt and bodice were comfortable and made to keep out the sharp breeze which was whipped up by the forward movement of the machine and on her head she wore a navy blue toque hat. It covered completely her luxuriant mass of hair and brought into sharp focus the beauty of her high cheek-boned face. Her eyes glowed hotly, the golden brown of a tobacco leaf and her face blazed with excitement. She was absolutely magnificent as she strode from beneath the porch of the inn, pulling on her thick leather gauntlets.

Though it was August the day was bleak. Tom stowed away her luggage and cranked the starting handle for her and when the engine fired she let it turn over for a moment as she had been instructed.

'Now Tom, don't worry,' she said, hugging him to her. 'I'll be back before you know it and Edie is as capable as me in running the kitchen. You see to the bars and keep old Zack in order and look after the dog for me.'

She knew she was talking nonsense, but really he looked as though she was off to the bloody moon and she must say something to take that anxious look from his face. He had put his arms about her, holding her tightly and his face was buried in her neck and she became quite alarmed for what would Edie and Zack and the rest of them think as they stood by the porch to see her off. She pulled herself gently away from him, smiling into his eyes, then turned to Edie.

'Take care of it, Edie,' she whispered, knowing she would understand, 'and don't let Tom brood.'

She turned at the gateway and her heart moved strangely in her breast for he looked so lonely already as though the moment she was out of sight he would not have the slightest notion of what to do with himself.

A flicker of something, unease? dismay? touched her for a moment with cold fingers then the changing of the gears in all their complexity took every bit of her attention and in a moment she was away down Merrydown Hill waving her hand to all those who came to see her away.

311

She reached Macclesfield the first night without incident and caused a sensation when she drew up unperturbed before the porch of the small hotel she had picked from the Cyclist Touring Club's booklet. Though it was on the list and offered reduced terms to its members it *was* rather smart and Meg was pleased with her choice.

She turned every head in the reception area, mostly male for few women as yet frequented hotels such as this and never unaccompanied and the male receptionist was thrown into wild confusion as she turned her brilliant smile on him. She was not the slightest bit put out, nor overawed by the covert looks she received, the chicness of the little hotel, nor her own lack of male protection. Though she knew this would happen everywhere she went she was well prepared for it and in fact was enjoying herself immensely.

'May I help you, madam,' the receptionist stammered looking beyond her in hopeful expectation of some masculine person who might be in charge of this confidently beautiful woman, but sadly none appeared.

'I would like a room please,' Meg said courteously. 'Just for one night. I shall be travelling on to Matlock tomorrow.'

'Matlock?' the man said as though he had never heard of the town which was a mere twenty miles or so away.

'Yes.' Meg waited smilingly.

The man drummed his fingers nervously on the counter and considered sending the delighted boy who carried Meg's bags for the manager, for this hotel had never, in its entire existence been presented with a single, unattached lady as a prospective guest and the clerk was at a loss as to how to proceed. The place was filled with men, commercial travellers and business men on their way north – or south – and how could he place one lone, unchaperoned lady on a floor with a dozen gentlemen?

'Do you *have* a room?' Meg asked smilingly and before he had time to think that here was the perfect solution, there were no rooms available, he had answered that he had.

'May I register then, if you please?' Meg said briskly, removing her leather gauntlets 'and if someone would show me to my room I would like hot water brought up immediately. It is exceedingly dusty driving a motor car and I feel I am covered in grit.'

She signed the register the young man had presented her with, having little choice in the matter it seemed, and he turned in bewilderment, studying the row of keys on the board behind him. Which should it be? His expression was haunted.

'Any will do,' Meg said sweetly, 'as long as the bed is clean and comfortable.'

He selected a key at random and put it into her hand, staring hypnotised into her eyes. It was the beginning of the new century but women just did not travel about alone even so, especially in a motor car of all things! And one as lovely as this was bound to cause a commotion wherever she went. What would it do to his male guests when she entered the dining-room? Could she perhaps be persuaded to eat in her room? A tray? Anything! He agonised again over the question of whether to summon his superior for he longed to have the problem taken from him, but the lady had put the key into the hands of the grinning porter and the two of them were half way up the stairs before he came from his trance.

The hush as Meg stepped gracefully into the dining-room that evening might have been heard in Buxton! Twenty-seven gentlemen froze in various poses of eating as her regal beauty stopped their heartbeats and raced their pulses and twenty-seven minds were seething with what the chances were that this charmer, this magnificent, bounteous specimen of womanhood was available at a price? They did not consider her for a moment to be a lady since, as the clerk at the desk had believed, as indeed all gentlemen of the era believed, no lady travelled alone. She must be an actress or a courtesan of some extravagant kind. They were reluctant to put the name 'whore' to such loveliness.

The waiter was apoplectic, but Meg smiled so graciously and her demeanour was so modest as he guided her to some distant corner table he could not fault her. Her eyes looked neither to the right nor left but directly ahead, her back straight, her bearing proud and she met no man's eager glance. When she was seated and took up the menu her knowledge of the dishes, the wines, and which should be drunk with which, amazed him.

She was dressed simply in an afternoon tea gown of cream silk in a style which was to be called the 'Princess' cut. It was well ahead of fashion hereabouts, without a waist seam, the bodice and skirt cut in one with a gored skirt. The sleeves were long and tight-fitting and the square cut neck-line was modest, but nothing could hide the splendour of Meg's breast nor the lovely slender line of her waist and hips. Her hair, brushed and brushed until it glowed like a tawny candle in the night was dressed full and loose, wide rather than high with a swirl on top, and round her neck was a narrow band of bronze velvet ribbon on which she had pinned the tiny gold locket which had come with her from the orphanage and which had been her mother's.

Not one man in the room could take his eyes from her and many sat long after they had finished their meals fiddling with coffee cups and such in an excuse to stay, but so coolly imperious was her manner that when she rose to leave not one dared approach her.

It took her ten days to pursue every thread which might lead to the perfect house for her new hotel. The one in Matlock which originally had excited her interest had proved too derelict to be a good investment. The amount of money needed to be spent on its renovation made it an impractical proposition. It was lovely, in a magnificent setting looking down into the Derwent valley but she knew it was not what she was looking for since it was remote and its accessibility by automobile was hazardous.

She motored from town to town, through sleepy villages which sprang to life as she clattered through, crawled up defiant hills and spun down into dales with the speed of a swooping bird and she believed she had never loved anything so much as she did the joy of motoring. Her runabout behaved in an exemplary fashion. She followed the list made out for her by the mechanic who had delivered it, each time she started it up, and there was always some curiosity seeker – one who could now boast at work or over the tea table of how he had been personally involved with one of them new-fangled machines – to handle the crank for her.

She had only one fright. She had started down a steep hill with a nasty drop to the side and had her brakes on. At the steepest part, just as she was congratulating herself on her own handling of this tricky manoeuvre for she was travelling above the speed limit, she felt the hand brake lever yield and go up against the stop. Her own heart did the same for she was left with only the foot brake with which to control the descending charge of the vehicle.

Pressing firmly with her foot she held her breath as she guided the motor car along the twisting hill. Harder and harder she pressed and with a sudden soggy crack the lever bent and the brake was fully depressed to the floor.

Away went the motor car down the hill, curves and bends

314

flashing beside and behind it, blurring and blurring, swerving from side to side as it gathered speed. Oh God, oh dear God, keep everyone from my path, she prayed. Carriages, carts, drays, waggons, children and dogs. Keep them away for just ten seconds, Lord until I get this monster under control and to the bottom of the hill, for I swear I will. It will not best me . . . it will not . . .

A corner came up and the motor car jumped round it like a horse swerving to take a fence and ahead, miraculously was a long, straight incline. Down, down she and the machine went until with a quiet apologetic cough it came to a polite standstill.

A passing carter was delighted to give her a lift and to laugh discreetly in masculine fashion at the poor lady motorist stranded upon the highway, and forced to fetch a male mechanic from the nearest repair shop to mend it.

Meg could not believe her ears at first and asked the mechanic to repeat himself. 'I said these brakes have been tampered with, Madame.' His face was quite impassive but he gave the distinct impression that not only did he believe women had no right to be in control of something they clearly did not understand, but that it had been she who had meddled with the brakes, probably doing something no man would ever dream of doing!

'*Tampered with!*' she said incredulously.

'Yes Madame.'

'I haven't the faintest notion of what you mean.'

'I mean, Madame, that someone unqualified has been messing about with the . . .'

'Messing about!'

'Yes Madame. If you'd look at this . . .' The man turned away from her, pointing to the foot brake, ready to explain quite patiently since it was very evident the lady knew nothing at all about the mechanics of the motor car, but Meg came to life like a fire-cracker, almost knocking the man into the road as she elbowed him aside.

'Are you telling me this is not just a faulty . . . er . . . whatsit . . . or a natural break in the . . . in that thing there? That it was done deliberately?' Her voice was full of disbelief.

The mechanic took umbrage. Brushing himself down as though she had actually flung him down into the dust of the road his face became truculent and his mouth was so tight-lipped he could barely speak.

'This . . . see just here . . . look . . .' she looked obediently, '. . . just

315

here ... can you see that mark...' She said she could. 'Well, that's where it was ... well ... cut! I hardly think it was done on purpose but some damn fool ... pardon me Madame ... some idiot has cut clean through the line which ...'

'*Cut through!*'

'Yes, if you'll let me finish ...'

'But no-one would cut it on purpose, surely!'

The man looked slightly mollified for it seemed he was being taken seriously at last. 'Well, you wouldn't think so. Perhaps your mechanic was careless.'

'He seemed a good mechanic and to know what he was about so ...' she stared at the footbrake her expression perplexed, '... so surely he would have noticed if something was wrong?'

'You'd have thought so.' The man scratched his head.

'Why didn't I notice it sooner? If there was a fault, or a ... a break, why didn't it go before. I've done hundreds of miles!'

'P'raps it was only slight. The movement of the brakes over the miles would have worn it away until ...'

'Until?'

'Until it finally snapped!'

The mechanic repaired the fault and went on his way, convinced even further that the day women were let out of the kitchen and the nursery had been a sorry day indeed for mankind and Meg went on *her* way, her mind cluttered with the confusion he had put there. The car was brand new, so how could a fault appear so soon. Perhaps it had been done at the factory, a careless hand fitting together of all the bits and pieces of what was now her motor car. Was there some other fault somewhere? Was it safe to go on, or was it, as seemed more likely, just a small hitch in the otherwise smooth beginning to her career as a motorist.

A whisper of disquiet – what was it – fluttered in her head, urging her to study this event further, to be cautious, but her fast beating, excited heart, eager to get on and complete this adventure told her she was being foolish. She listened to her heart and began to sing, for really, it was over now, an accident and therefore unforeseeable and she had better things to do than worry, like some old maid looking for intruders under the bed, over something which had been beyond her control!

The roads were dusty, used only by horse and carriage, wag-goners, cyclists and pedestrians but Meg did not mind the grit and dust which coated her from head to foot for she travelled in a haze of joyous delight searching for what she wanted.

She found it just above the Dovedale valley, north of Ashbourne. The house was set in beautiful open countryside with magnificent views from every window. It was placed in the centre of three acres of splendid gardens, a stand of oakwood and holly trees carpeted with wood sorrel and wild violet, a fruit orchard, an ornamental pond and to the rear of the house a stable yard and coach houses suitable for conversion to garages.

There was a good road recently macadamised from Macclesfield, from Stoke-on-Trent and Derby and it was easy to reach by motor car. There was fishing, clearly defined riding tracks, walking, both gentle and serious; and the loveliness, the serene calm and music of the River Dove which ran through the gorge beneath was enough to enrapture the eye, the heart, the ear and soul of the most demanding traveller.

Meg sat upon a rocky shoulder of grey granite overlooking the Dove Valley whilst the estate agent fussed with keys back at the house, and contemplated gravely the panoramic stretch of the Derbyshire fells which were to be part of her future. She was taking another great stride into unknown territory, alone, unsupported, relying totally on her own judgement and ability. Tom would work with her, night and day, sweat blood to help her in their venture, but she must be honest with herself and admit that *she* was the mainstay of their lives, that it was Meg Hughes who would breathe life into it, feed it, nurse it and bring it to full maturity with *her* strength. Tom was her dearest friend, with Martin, but his merry disposition had not the cut and thrust which was needed in the world of commerce. He was too readily wary of the unexpected, and unlike herself and Martin, afraid to step off the safe and the secure, into the unknown.

She shaded her eyes against the strong sunlight which flooded the valley then stood up briskly and began to stride purposefully in the direction of her small motor car.

She was singing the old cycling song as she turned into the gateway of 'Hawthornes', joyous as a linnet as she pulled up triumphantly before the front door. She blew the horn as she came to a final halt and lifted her hands to remove the velvet toque. She shook out her hair and ran her hands through it for though she felt gloriously, wonderfully alive, buoyant with success, she was tired. She had driven hundreds of miles alone. She had

317

struggled over roads barely fit for horse and cart and had slept in many a dubious bed but she had come through with flying colours, bringing home the fruits of her endeavour in the shape of the document Tom must sign to make the property theirs.

He was there, just where she had left him, looking as though he had been rooted to the same spot for the whole time she had been away. His eyes were warm and blue as the lovely skies above the Dove Valley and his lips curled and his mouth split into the deep grin which endeared him to everyone who knew him.

'Meggie,' he called, 'oh Jesus, Meggie!'

He lifted his arms to her and even before the engine stopped his hands were beneath her arms, lifting her down to stand before him.

'Dear God, Meggie, if you knew how I've missed you.' She was not quite sure how it happened, and really, neither was he. The days had been empty, long and dreary without her in them, and though he had been busy, they had been as blank as an empty page and now she was here, smiling at him with such joy and . . . and . . . something else shining in her eyes, he was positive, as pleased to see him as he was to have her home.

How tired she was! She realised it now that Tom's strong arms were about her and she leaned gratefully against his body. Long of bone, hard of muscle and achingly familiar it was. Loved, yes, for was he not Tom who had never in all these years let her down, always there to smile and listen and hold her hand; he had never been anything but sweet, gentle, good and when she lifted her face to him it seemed only natural for his lips to rest on hers, and when she found she liked the warm wholesome taste of them, the soft hesitancy of her first kiss, she responded and his moved on hers and became more insistent, parting her lips and their mouths clung, and their arms, and when he raised his head there was glory in his eyes and they stared in wonderment at one another.

'I'll not let you go without me again, Meggie,' he said huskily and remembering her strange sadness in the emptiness of the Derbyshire Peaks she was glad, glad, raising her lips again eagerly to his.

She did not want to go without him, ever again!

Chapter twenty-six

Tom was like a boy at Christmas, his presents around him beneath the tree, some opened and wondered over, others still to be unwrapped and cherished, the joy of anticipation almost more than he could bear but his patience was eternal and he would wait until she was ready, he said ardently. Yes, he agreed with her, they had a lot to see to with the new place an' all and there was time enough for a wedding in the spring and naturally she wanted to enjoy her new status as 'fiancée' for a while. He would get her a ring, glowing with his own ability to purchase one, as soon as they could get into Northwich together, he promised her.

They chaffed him in the snug when they heard the news since he could not keep it to himself, could he, he asked her, and wished him and his betrothed well and he was made up with it. His clear eyes blazed with the blue joy of a field of cornflowers and he swore his face ached with the sheer and endless enchantment of smiling.

He kissed her softly, carefully, whenever they were alone, scarcely able to believe his good fortune, and held her awkwardly for he had no experience with women, against the long, hard length of his restrained body, marvelling on the discovery that after all these years they were to be, not only friends, but husband and wife. He had not yet the courage to say the word 'lovers' for even if she had intimated that she was willing, Tom would not have countenanced it until she had a gold band on her finger. He held her hand and stroked her arm and put a gentle finger to the curve of her cheek. He damped down his masculine longings with hard work, and by God there was enough of that as they prepared to make the move from Great Merrydown to Ashbourne for they were to be off within the month.

They called it 'The Hilltop Hotel' for obvious reasons. 'Hilltops' for short. It was a great upheaval of boxes and cases all piled on to a motor waggon which was to take them the fifty miles or so to Hulton Cross, which was just outside Ashbourne, in one incredible day. It would be a circuitous route going through Holmes

Chapel, Biddulph and up and up into the high peaks of Fenny Bentley and on to Hulton Cross. Tom was anxious, his distrust of anything which could not be coaxed, soothed, and generally eased round perilous bends and up steep hills – as one would a strong and reliable horse pulling a cart – emerging in a tendency to kick the vehicle's tyres and shake his head gloomily.

'What if the thing breaks down on the bloody bit of road by Axe Edge? You know, there's a hell of a drop there and this old rattletrap doesn't look as though it could get from here to Merrydown let alone to Hulton. And those boxes don't look too safe. I'd best get a bit more rope and tie them on more securely. There's the good china in there, Meg, and you'd not be wanting to see it smashed to smithereens. That chap's not got a happorth of sense when it comes to fixing those packing cases so that they balance properly. He might be able to drive the damned waggon but how he can hire himself out as a carter, I don't know!'

Tom's normal state of good-natured, good-tempered harmony with those about him, his cheerful acceptance of Meg's, in his opinion, quite mad determination to give up a successfully growing business for the uncertainty of another, was seriously tested that day. He had been reluctant to leave Silverdale and the security he had found there, the satisfying work he had done and the camaraderie of those with whom he had lived. But the gamble they had taken had paid off handsomely. His savings, and Meg's, with the loan which had been provided by the bank had not been thrown heedlessly away as he had feared but had come back to them a hundredfold. They had turned their investment into a handsome profit, built up a venture of which any man might be proud and he had felt himself to be worthwhile, important and his natural pleasure in their achievement had been enormous. He knew his own limitations but if hard work and honesty were the ingredients needed to make a success, he knew he was endowed with both in abundance.

Now Meg was different. It was not that she lacked honesty or a compulsion for hard work but she was afraid of nothing! She was blessed with the certainty that what they were about to do was entirely right. She had no doubts, no misgivings, having, it seemed, complete faith not only in herself but in *him*! It gave him the courage to step out with her bravely, though he did wish she would curb what to him seemed a quite frightening inclination to make up her mind in the blink of an eye. She appeared to see an opportunity even before he was aware they were looking for one, and had taken advantage of it, twisting it to her liking and wringing every drop of profit from it there was to be had.

Edie Marshall was to go with them since, as she said, what would she do with herself without Miss Hughes, soon to be Mrs Fraser, to work for. She could not get on with the wife of the chap who was to manage 'Hawthornes' for Miss Hughes, though *he* had begged her to stay, saying she would be an enormous help to him in the running of the inn. And so she would but she was used to Miss Hughes' ways and could not learn new ones at her time of life. He was a nice enough fellow and would do well for Miss Hughes, and besides, Miss Hughes said she would be keeping an eye on the place. Well, she would since it belonged to her and Mr Tom now, lock, stock and barrel and she was not one to let a concern of *hers* get run down. She'd be over in that little motor car of hers to see Annie, she said, and the friends she had made in the village and if Edie liked she could come with her on her day off. Well, that had clinched it as far as Edie was concerned and she was looking forward to her new position as 'housekeeper' at the lovely old house, soon to be a hotel, in Derbyshire.

They had been there just a week when Martin arrived. He came out of the October sunshine, stepping between deep, dappled shadows and brightly moving shafts of light to stand just inside the hedge on the newly-scythed lawn and when Meg saw him her heart swooped in a great arch of joy, then, as he walked slowly towards her his face told her he had brought a vast and devastating sadness with him and she shivered. She was wearing a white dress. It was of muslin, light and pretty and simple, floating about her feet on the brick path. Her hair was pulled back carelessly, held by a narrow white ribbon to fall in a curly knot to the middle of her back but strands of it had escaped, as he remembered it had always done, drifting in soft curls about her white neck and ears.

There was a wooden seat against the house and a massed bank of rhododendrons, pink and purple and blood red, the broad leaves green and glossy. They grew behind her, towering above her head in magnificently dying profusion and the whole area around her was bathed in the clear light of the pale midday sun.

'Martin?' Her voice was wary, questioning.

He continued to walk slowly across the rough-cropped grass, his feet making no sound. He did not smile and yet his eyes held a compassionate warmth which told her that whatever it was he was to sadden her with, he was ready, as he had always been, to offer her comfort.

She had been digging with a small trowel as he approached, planting some green thing beneath the rhododendron bushes, plunging the gardening tool energetically into the black soil, pressing in the plant with strong fingers, heedless of the stains on her completely unsuitable gown. A thick rim of dirt had collected beneath her finger nails. She rubbed her hands against the soft fabric of her dress, leaving two black marks, then looked down and pulled a face and Martin knew she was putting off the moment when he would tell her why he was here.

'Not quite the outfit in which to garden, Meggie.' His voice was gentle and filled with some deep emotion.

'No, I didn't mean to start but there were some cuttings . . . Tom was busy . . .' She put a trembling hand to her mouth, 'The day was so lovely . . . warm . . . so warm you can hardly believe it is October already . . .'

Her glance drifted from his to encompass the sunshine falling about the fading beauty of the overgrown flower borders, to the softly moving shadows which the leaves placed across the wide expanse of lawn. The fragrant smell of autumn was everywhere, moving with the timid breeze over great wild swathes of pink ageratum, the lovely deep cream of skimmia and the fresh blue of lobelia. There was mallow, and daphne bushes of yellow and pink and white, and the magnificent gold of a stand of wallflowers, all growing as they had done for months, in complete and glorious abandon, untouched and unseen until now. There was a fire somewhere and the unique smell of burning woodsmoke, symbolic of the ending of summer, rose above the house and up into the pale softness of the sky. Trees stood about, fading but ageless, their leaves beginning to loosen and drift to the ground. Oak and elder and rowan and elm, guarding the boundaries of the property on three sides, the fourth opening out to the splendour of the Valley of Dovedale. He felt light-headed with the enchantment of it and had a moment to consider that this must indeed be the perfect place in which to linger on one's travels and that Meg had chosen well, but he must speak and he could not soften the words, only tell her decently as she deserved.

But of course, she knew, for why else would he be clothed from head to toe in black.

'Meggie.' He put out his hand to her, ready for when she needed it.

'It's ... it's Cook, isn't it?' Her voice was a whisper.

'Yes.'

'When ...?'

'Last night.'

'You were with her?'

'Oh yes. I would have come for you, darling, but there was no time.' The endearment seemed not at all out of place. 'I was going to send the boy, the one who races for me, he is a good lad and reliable on the roads but ... she went before ...' His voice broke and he could not go on and without a word they stepped into one another's arms. He bent his head to rest his cheek against her hair and she pressed her face into the curve of his neck beneath his chin and their bodies strained to be close in their grief for the great lady, for she had been that to them, who had given three children her love and her caring heart and brought them from the dispassionate neutrality of the orphanage to the first home they had known.

'She spoke of you and Tom.' His voice was muffled in the soft mass of her hair and she could feel the sound of it move through the bone and flesh of her and somehow it seemed to soothe her savage pain. It was not the words he spoke but the vibrancy of his voice and the soft, reassuring impression of his breath against her skin and she could feel the relaxed way in which her body settled against his. Her arms held him more tightly to her and his were strong and supporting and though she had begun to weep now, a soft and quiet grieving, she had a great, comforting sense of knowing that she would not fall, could never fall now, with Martin to hold her.

'What did she say?'

'She was proud ... I think she was as proud as if we had been her own ...'

'We were.'

'Yes ... and these last years ... what you gave her ...'

'Not me, Martin ... all of us ...'

'Sweetheart, it was you who had the courage to speak up against Harris ...'

'Don't! Not now.'

'She ... she said ...'

323

'What?' Her tears had wet the collar of his shirt and he could feel the warmth of them against his skin.

'She said she wanted to see you settled. It worried her . . .'

'Me?'

She could hear the emotion in his voice and when he lifted his head she looked up at him wonderingly, her eyes brimming still with tears, and there it was, in his, and he allowed her to see it at last.

'Martin . . .' His name sighed in her throat and through the sadness that was between them came softly stealing the unbeliev-able and breathless awareness of something so overwhelming, so precious, so *right* she was afraid to take it out and study it for fear it might slip through her fingers and be gone again.

'She said that Tom and I were well able to get along since we were men and this is a man's world, Meg, but that you were a woman and needed . . .'

'What, Martin?' She could not tear her eyes away from his and the joy which was beginning to throb through the veins of her body and move to her heart in great bewildering leaps was miraculous and true for it was answered in his.

He smiled. 'She was wrong, of course, but she said you needed someone to look after you.'

'Wrong.'

His eyes were a deep, rich brown and his mouth curled whims-ically and the small scar in the corner deepened.

'You need someone but not to look after you, my Meggie. You need someone to stand beside you, to understand you and allow you to become what your nature intended you to be. You are strong and though you are sad now you will overcome your grief and go on to fulfill whatever dreams you have. As I will. We are alike, you and I and we know each other well because of it.'

They looked at one another, sighing over the simple and obvious perfection of it. She put her cheek against his shirt front and he tightened his arms about her and as he did so Tom Fraser came round the corner of the house.

They did not see him, nor hear his approach across the grass and when the violence of him fell about them with the dreadful force of a stallion which will fight another who covets his mare, they were confounded. Their embrace had in it now, not only the unspoken awareness of what had just happened between them but their quiet grieving for Mrs Whitley. They had not kissed. They stood, not as lovers, but as friends who will comfort one another in any way they can and the sudden intrusion of this wild man who tore them apart so dreadfully flung them both into an unreal world so savage they did nothing but stand instinctively away from it. Martin was the first to recover and he put up an arm to defend her, just as though Tom was an intruder for in truth they could neither of them recognise this stranger.

Martin understood immediately and as he did so reality returned to Megan Hughes as well. She stepped between the two men and her face lost the luminous quality Martin had put there and sadness returned.

'What the bloody hell's going on?' Tom was shouting, ready still to pull her behind him, anywhere that would ensure Martin could not get his hands on her, but she would not have it for this was not the time for it. She spoke the only words which would, at that moment, quench the jealous rage which burned in him.

'Tom, Martin has come to ... oh Tom ... what are we to do ... Mrs Whitley ... died last night. We were grieving for her, Martin and I ... oh Tom, Tom ... she is gone ...' Her face crumpled and she began to weep again and this time it was Tom who put his arms about her, understanding, he thought, the frightening scene he had just witnessed. He wept too as he comforted her and looked apologetically over her shoulder at the man who was his brother.

Later they sat in the small sitting-room which was to be theirs when the hotel opened and ate the omelettes Meg had put before them, none of them hungry, still inclined to silence as the realisation of Mrs Whitley's death was finally accepted. They spoke softly of their days as children in her care and smiled at memories only they and she had shared and the pain eased a little. The funeral was to be at the end of the week, Martin said, at the small church where lately Mrs Whitley had worshipped and which she could see from her parlour window. It seemed she had asked for it, saying it would be but a step from one home to another.

They tried to talk of lighter things 'You look well Meg,' Martin said. 'Being an hotelier agrees with you, it seems, and you too, Tom. Tell me about it.' They were in perfect unison again, their shared past linking them together, as Meg told him about the purchase of the hotel and what she intended for it and Martin watched her approvingly. She had not changed, he could see that.

She was as filled as she had always been with enthusiasm for the task in hand, whether it be setting himself and Tom to rights, baking up an enormous batch of scones for their supper, or just, as she was doing now, speaking of the future. She had matured, not just physically but in her own character for there was an air of confidence about her. Not blazing and defiant as it had once been but a quiet confidence, one that had no need to be shouted about. It gave her a poise, a maturity which in no way detracted from the young, breathtaking beauty of her. His eyes warmed in masculine appreciation of her womanliness but he was slightly tense in Tom's presence for it had been very evident what Tom Fraser had in mind for Megan Hughes.

They brought his motor car from the front gates where he had left it and for ten minutes they stood in the autumn sunshine and admired the machine, just as elegant as his first but much smaller. She was the prototype, he explained, of the newest, low-priced, small engined vehicles he and Mr Robert were to manufacture, and which were to be aimed at the ordinary man who was beginning to feel he had as much right as his so called 'betters', to ride about in a motor car. She was economical to run and could reach the incredible speed of forty miles an hour! They were to have a dozen like her on the roads by Christmas, manufactured in a small factory he and the old gentleman had bought at Camford. They were partners in the venture but he was pretty sure it would all be his very soon for he meant to buy out the old gentleman as soon as he could raise the cash. At the moment he had a half share in it. Well, it was his bloody genius – smiling, trying to put some relief in the sad day – which had made them what they were and already there were enquiries coming in from interested purchasers. He was twenty-five years old and the success he once swore would be his had come. Not just as a racing driver but as the designer and builder of the motor cars he had dreamed of since he had first climbed on to a bicycle and he was not finished yet, he pronounced for he was to push on in another endeavour – one which was almost as dear to him now, as his passion for the motor car. His eyes were clear and steady with that bright light of determination which was as familiar to Meg and Tom as the lamp which had once shone serenely in the centre of the kitchen table at Great George Square.

'This year, 1913 has become known as "The Glorious Year of Flying", did you know, and that's just what it is, by God. Earlier

326

in the year I went over to Monaco for the first "Schnieder Trophy" contest . . . have you heard about it, no . . . few people have. There were only seven entries and I was one of them. It's for seaplanes and I took one up belonging to a friend of Charles Hemingway. He was meant to do it himself but at the last minute he hurt his hand, or lost his nerve, or something. I didn't win it but it gave me an idea of how aircraft are to develop. I haven't flown since I got my Aero Club Certificate but damnation, if I can manage to get a craft of my own, I mean to. I've designed a glider. The government are interested now that the Royal Flying Corps has been founded. There are four squadrons at the moment and they are looking for likely designs.'

He was to build the glider in the hangar at Watkins Field, the ground they had bought at Camford and if he could find the finance, it would be in the air within six months. Mr Hemingway was old now and really no longer concerned with it all. Flying was for the future and the old gentleman had none but he, Martin Hunter, had and it was to be . . .

Tom Fraser watched him, feeling the magnetism of Martin's strong personality pulling Meg into that fascination she had always known, a fascination she had shared in his love of anything mechanical. He himself had been the odd one out in the threesome, since for the life of him he could not seem to capture the taste for clattering along in a noisy contraption, smelly, and going so fast the beauty of the countryside could scarcely be appreciated. A bicycle was so much more satisfying, he had always thought. Quiet, slow, the exercise filling one with a feeling of well-being it was hard to beat. Now, it appeared, even the motor car was not enough for Martin Hunter. He was to take to the skies, had already done so, up there with the birds and where the hell would that lead him, he wondered, except down to earth with a crash, for surely only birds were meant to fly? He recalled the excitement they had shared at Blackpool but on looking back it had not been the aircraft which had filled him with delight, but the crowds, the sunshine, the laughter and the company of Meg and Martin. He had not believed then that it would catch on, this flying about in a thing which seemed scarcely bigger than a moth and he still believed it.

Meg leaned across the table towards Martin, the sadness of the day momentarily put to the back of her mind, as Martin had intended, hanging on to his every word, as Tom had seen her do a hundred, a thousand times and as she did so something sweet inside him cracked and for the second time that day he wanted to strike at Martin Hunter and draw blood. To hurt him badly and take that look of satisfaction from his face and the strange warmth from his eyes which were looking so searchingly into Meg's. He wanted to let him see that he, Tom Fraser, though he might not be able to drive a motor car, or fly an aeroplane, had something special, something unique which Martin Hunter would *never* have.

He broke into their absorption with one another, his voice harsh with his ragged jealousy.

'You haven't told Martin our news yet, Meggie.' He held himself rigidly for suddenly he was aware that the following moments would be, strangely, the most important of his life.

She pulled her gaze almost angrily from Martin and he was dismayed by the expression in it.

'What . . .?' She did not seem to know what he meant.

'You haven't told Martin about you and me.' His eyes softened with his pride and his deep and endless love for her.

'What about you and Meg?' Martin stood up abruptly, his long body threatening, for of course they had no need to tell him. It was there in Tom's wondering face and it was there in the dreadful agony in Meg's eyes and at last he understood his own unease, that sense he had of something hidden and here it was, out in the open and in that moment he was stricken with pain for he had left it too late!

But had he? Meg Hughes was looking at him and Tom at her and the expression in her eyes was puzzling. She seemed bewildered, strained, even guilty and he knew with a certainty that was born of his love for her that it was the look of a woman who is completely unsure of what she did.

'We are to be married, Meg and I!' Tom's voice was rough with possession and Martin wanted to smash his fist into his mouth, the mouth which had just spoken the words.

'*Married*!'

'Yes, aren't we, sweetheart?' He reached across the table and took her surprisingly flaccid hand in his and Martin felt the need, the violent and dangerous need to dash his hand away from Meg for she was his, *his*!

He turned to her, not trusting Tom, it seemed, to tell the truth.

'Meg.' His voice was menacing. 'Is this true?'

'Yes.' Her's was anguished.

'When?' He spoke harshly, the word uneven and Meg shrank away from him.

'Oh . . . soon, eh Meggie! As soon as I can get her to name the day.'

'I see.' That was all before he turned away from them, his face dark, vital and burning with the simple conviction that as long as he had breath in his body Meg Hughes would never belong to any man but himself.

'I'll see you at the funeral,' he said and for a horrified moment they all three realised that they had forgotten Mrs Whitley had died that day!

The tall, middle-aged gentleman was elegantly dressed in the style of a decade ago, suitably formal for the occasion. Frock coat, dark trousers, black waistcoat, silk hat with a black cloth band, black gloves and tie, in strange contrast to the simple folk with whom he stood.

The funeral cortége made its short journey from the tiny cottage just inside the gates of the estate to the church on the other side of the lane and the thirty or so plain folk who lined the route removed their caps or bent their heads and so did he, in respect for the dead woman who was to be laid to rest.

'Poor soul,' the gentleman said piously, 'may she know eternal peace.'

'Aye, a fine lady and a dab hand with a fruit cake.'

'Jack!' The plump woman who stood next to the speaker, nudged him, scandalized.

' 'Tis true, and nowt to be ashamed of.'

The elegant gentleman smiled agreeably.

'Indeed it is true for I have tasted it.'

'You knew her then, sir?'

'Indeed I did. Mrs Whitley and I were old friends. When I heard she had passed on I could do no more than pay my last respects.'

'She was a grand old girl, sir, no mistake.'

'And her . . . the other mourners, the three young people . . .'

'Aye, she thought the world of them three all right.'

There was a pause as they passed through the church gate, then, 'They . . . Megan . . . does not live hereabouts any more?'

'Nay, she went up aways from here.'

'So I believe.'

They had begun to follow the coffin, carried by the two tall young men in black and two others, presumably from the estate where the deceased had lived, up the leaf covered pathway and the splendidly attired gentleman fell into step besides his new acquaintances.

Meg was drifting in some soft, quite painless memory of the days when the old lady they were burying had ruled the three of them, when the face which smiled sympathetically at her from beyond someone's shoulder, sharpened and came into focus. It was a thin face, pallid as though from confinement, and deeply grooved and the eyes which were set in it were a pale, almost colourless grey. It was a long time since she had seen it and yet in that moment, that one split second of recognition, her mind was curiously unsurprised as though it saw nothing remarkable in its re-appearance. Why, it asked quite coolly, had she imagined that it was over, that the man who had terrorised her young life, who had done his best to drag her down to his own depraved level, who had sworn revenge on her as he had been pulled from the dock where *she* had put him, would merely shrug his shoulders and walk away. Twice she had been the instrument, or partly, of his having been imprisoned and yet, in her naivety, once he had been behind bars, she had given no further thought to his words.

'*You will see me again Megan,*' he had said. '*You have offended me and those who offend me do so at great risk to themselves so keep looking over your shoulder for I will be there, believe me!*' And here he was, smiling and raising his hand in greeting like an old friend come to pay his last respects at the loss of another.

She whispered his name, her eyes huge with shock, remembering, the thoughts coming from nowhere, the fire which had started so mysteriously in the bar and the brakes, unaccountably faulty for some reason despite the fact that the motor car had been brand new. Twice she had passed over these occurrences, convincing herself it was no more than coincidence, an accident, a trick of fate, something which could have happened to anyone. The dog had raised the alarm when the fire broke out, another quirk of circumstance for he had wandered in that night belonging, it seemed, to no-one and the man who smiled at her now had not known of his existence. And the brakes! Had they been meant to kill, or just frighten? The latter, she suspected for her tormentor did not intend to give up this enjoyable game of revenge as easily and quickly as that. Dear God, how could she have been so artless, so incredibly foolish, her pounding heart demanded. It got no answer, for Megan Hughes slipped into a world of shadows, and had it not been for Tom and Martin who held her arms, one on either side of her, would have toppled to the ground.

In their concern the two young men did not see the older one slip away behind the trees and when Meg recovered from her surprising faint, he was in his hired hansom cab and half way back to Liverpool.

Chapter twenty-seven

They sat around the small oval dining table in the room Meg had set aside for their own use and the tension in the air was a living thing, snapping and snarling about the heels of the three of them. They had finished the lunch Meg had cooked, a simple meal of clear vegetable soup, fried whiting and one of Mrs Whitley's vanilla creams since the kitchens did not yet allow for anything more exotic, and were sipping coffee. From somewhere beyond the closed door there was the sound of hammering, a voice imploring someone to 'lift it clear, Alf, for God's sake' and the cheerful notes of Marie Lloyd's popular song 'The smartest girl in town' being whistled slightly off key. The yellow dog which had come as a matter of course from 'Hawthornes' lay before the fire, his ears pricked, the movement of his eyes uneasy for he had caught the strange disquiet in the room and he was not awfully sure what to make of it.

The room was not large but there was a lack of clutter in it which gave it the appearance of being bigger than it was. It was on the corner of the house with deep windows on two walls. There were three comfortable armchairs grouped about the fire, covered in a cheerful print of cream and apricot. The carpet was smooth and deep, a plain rich coral and in the corner, placed between the windows was the rosewood dining table with four matching chairs. There were shelves filled with books, flowers and pretty ornaments on the plain, white-painted fireplace and cream curtains fell at each window. It was simple and comfortable, the first room in the house to be completed and all of it done by Tom from Meg's design. He had done as much as he could in the garden until the better weather came, and so he had painted and lovingly restored woodwork, swept the chimney and when the carpet was laid and the furniture moved in, they at least had somewhere to escape the turmoil which lay about them. There were builders and decorators, plumbers and electricians, all combining to tear the place apart and put it together again as Meg

332

wanted it. Tom slept on a camp bed in an attic room which was too high and too small to be considered for alteration though it would eventually house a maidservant and Meg 'managed', she said, as did Edie, in which ever bedroom some workman was not painting, or plumbing, or putting in endless miles of wiring to give them electricity. Each bedroom was to have it's own bathroom and some a private sitting room. The dining-room and drawing-room, the small library, the cocktail bar, the billiard room, the small ballroom and the massive kitchens were to be the very peak of luxury and modern innovation and when it was complete the hotel, already advertising in the 'best' newspapers and periodicals was to be the finest in the north.

It was January. The low sun glittered on the heavy hoar frost which had come in the night, turning great patches of the sloping lawn to the colour and sheen of molten gold. The pines at the far side of the lake were etched, black and white and deepest green against a sky of palest blue, reflected in the absolute stillness of the water. There were small floating islands of frozen ice on the lake on which ducks struggled to keep upright, and just beginning to raise their heads beneath the protection of the trees were folds of exquisite snowdrops and the perky yellow heads of early crocus.

'It seems to me it's a sound investment, Tom.' Meg's hand smoothed a non-existent wrinkle in the damask table cloth. Her face was quite without expression but in her eyes was the clear light of exasperation and the rigid necessity to keep it in check, but her voice was patient.

She had grown thinner during the winter months since Mrs Whitley's funeral and those about her begged her to slow down, to take a rest in the afternoon, have an early night for she worked eighteen to twenty hours in every twenty-four, convinced her loss of weight and appetite, her nervous explosive energy was caused by overwork but she took no-one's advice. She wanted everything to be ready, to be *perfect* by the time the hotel opened at Easter, she said, telling no-one, least of all Tom and Martin of the apparition which had appeared before her at Mrs Whitley's funeral. Had she *really* seen him, she agonised in the sleepless nights, or had her grieving mind conjured him up, dwelling as it had been on the past. He had frightened poor Mrs Whitley until she had been reduced to a nervous shell of her old self, and in the graveyard, beside the old lady's open grave, could not she, Meg, have imagined up the ghost of the man who had almost killed the old lady all those years ago? It would not have been surprising if she had imagined him she reflected later for there had been no sign of him after the funeral and so, for the time being she had decided to keep what she had seen, or thought she had seen, to herself. What good would it do to tell Martin and Tom, or the police? It was no crime to attend a funeral and if she half believed that he had had a hand in the fire and the failure of the brakes, how could she prove it? They would think her demented, obsessed with the man whom she had twice seen put away because of her. Best leave it for now, keep her eyes open, be extra careful and see what happened, had been her decision and in three months she had begun to relax a little and to believe she had imagined the whole thing.

She continued to speak. 'Martin has explained how it will work and though he, naturally will be the major shareholder, we will have 10 per cent and the rest will be sold to the public. It is the only way to raise money, you know that, surely? Such a large sum cannot be found by Martin alone but there will be dozens glad to get in on it. You know yourself, from Martin's accounts, how strong the company is and how much forward business he has on his books in orders and bookings for flying lessons. This is a marvellous opportunity to get hold of the old gentleman's share and if we don't want it, the three of us, he will only let it go to others and Martin will lose control. He has only 45 per cent now and if he, or we, don't acquire at least another 10 per cent he will be outvoted at every board meeting and . . .'

'I know all that, Meg! You've told me a dozen times but bloody hell, we're already in debt up to our eyeballs and the idea of raising a mortgage on "Hawthornes" means we'll owe still more. And those investments we've made have brought us in a good return, haven't they? To sell them now seems to me to be . . .'

'We have to realise the cash, Tom. Tell him Martin.'

She turned to look at Martin. He was lounging quite carelessly in his chair which he had pushed back from the table, his long legs stretched out beside it and crossed at the ankle. He was watching his own hand as it toyed with a fork and the other was shoved deep in his trouser pocket. He wore a superbly cut pair of riding breeches, an affectation really for he had never sat astride a horse in his life, made of fawn corduroy. His knee length boots were highly polished, made from fine, soft leather and his jacket was of excellent cloth, a tweed in a pale shade of chocolate. His thick hair fell over his brown forehead in an untidy, engaging way and now and again he pushed his fingers through it impatiently as though the task he was about was not to his liking. He looked in every way a successful and expensive young gentleman of the privileged class.

'Perhaps Tom would rather not be involved, Meg.' It was a challenge and they were all aware of it. 'He is right, of course. This *is* a gamble . . .'

'Nonsense!' Meg's voice was crisp. 'Oh, I agree, we are to put our money in an untried industry but you have only to look at the growth . . .'

'Don't tell me, tell Tom.' Martin turned to look lazily, smoothly, at Tom and the tension increased for though it was tamped down tight, the awkward and growing conflict, spiky and hurtful, between the two men who had always been brothers, it pushed them ever so gently towards a confrontation, pulsing beneath smooth, masculine skin, slowly stripping away the strong bond which had held them together for twenty years. The fine hair cracks were widening at every encounter, not yet visible, but beginning to spread and undermine the very foundation on which their friendship was built.

The reason for it sat between them.

'Go on, Martin,' she said, 'explain it properly so that we both can understand.'

Martin sighed sadly. He lowered his eyes again to the fork, his love for her hidden and deep, not from her since he was completely certain she had not forgotten the day, three months ago now, when Mrs Whitley had died, nor the unspoken commitment which had bound them together, but from the man who glowered suspiciously at him from across the table. He was well aware that should it have been anybody but himself who had put this business proposition to Tom and Meg, Tom would have grinned and shaken his hand and gone cheerfully back to his vegetable plot leaving the decision and planning and financial arranging to Meg as he had always done but not now, not now! They were no different with one another, not on the surface, and not one word had been said which Tom could take exception to, but he knew, Martin could sense it, that there was some variance, involving Meg, in their relationship. It cut him up in pieces, Martin knew, as it did himself, each time they met and he was beginning to wonder if perhaps it might be better if he looked elsewhere for the financing he needed, but he knew this was a business venture, a gamble perhaps, but it could not lose and he had put it to Meg as a matter of course, knowing she would see it, and wanting to share it with her. She was as astute as he in such matters. She knew him, and his worth and what he had already done and was shrewd enough to realise that there was profit to be had in this infant industry. The motor car and the aeroplane, they were the future of mankind and could not, must not fail!

' "Hunter Automobiles" will form a subsidiary company, "Hunter Aviation" and the first, which is already showing a healthy profit will, as the word implies, subsidise the second. We are turning out a dozen motor cars a week and they are immensely popular. I could sell twice or three times that number, Tom. They are small, medium priced and increasingly easy to handle.' He grinned amiably, determined if he could to take the look of foreboding from Tom's face. 'Why don't you come to the field one day and try one . . . No! Well it's up to you, of course, but really, take my word for it they are here to stay and you will be compelled to it one day. We are to model our production on the ideas of Henry Ford. He's an American whose own aim is to build an automobile sufficiently low priced to sell to the mass market, simple and of good quality, reliable and easy to drive. Roads are improving at an enormous pace and the motor car is no longer considered a capricious toy for the rich. I aim to standardise what I produce, using what is called "mass-production" as Ford is doing but we need the machine work and the tools with which to develop it. But it is the aircraft which is my . . . my own concern now. I am to show mine, if she is ready at "Olympia" in the next show.' His face softened and despite himself Tom felt drawn to that familiar compulsion which drew Martin on and on.

'I'm to call her "Wren",' he said simply.

'Oh Martin, why?' Meg asked smilingly. 'Why "Wren"? It is such an innocuous little bird.'

'Have you not heard the fable of the Wren and the Eagle?'

'Tell me.' She leaned towards him and put her elbows on the table and her eyes were bright, alert and glowing with wonder.

'The legend goes that in the bird world, the bird that mounted the highest in the air should be King. The Eagle laughed and soared majestically above all the others and was about to be acclaimed King when suddenly a trill of sound was heard and the Wren, who had been carried up on the Eagle's back was seen to be fluttering above his head. So the little bird become King of the birds, not through strength but by being the most clever. My "Wren" will be King of the aircraft.'

'Martin, that's lovely!' Delighted she took his hand and held it between her own.

Tom sprang up angrily. He could stand no more and his jealousy showed in his heightened colour and the narrowing of his vivid blue eyes. He strode about the pleasant room, his hands thrust deep in his trouser pockets. Each time he reached the wall, the window or the fireplace he turned about savagely, pushing aside furniture as it got in his way. He did not know what to do to hold it in and Meg could feel the very air strain against the pressure of his tension and she stood up and moved towards him, standing in his way as he made another violent turn about the room.

'Oh for heaven's sake, Tom, sit down and stop pulling your lip like a fractious child. I don't know what's got into you! This is a business arrangement, a financial venture for all of us so why you are taking this preposterous attitude, I can't imagine. Martin is to be our partner. He is short of ready cash and has already reached the limit he can borrow. We can raise it by mortgaging "Hawthornes", which already brings us in a fair profit and you know it is always my contention that an opportunity only presents itself once and you must grab it with both hands when it does. Martin is to run the airfield and motor manufacturing at Camford. We will put up some money and he will do the work. He is a clever man, you know that. His ideas are sound . . .'

'How the hell do you know that?'

'Tom!' Meg was astounded and there was a dangerous movement from the other side of the room as Martin stood up slowly.

'It's true!' Tom was beside himself. 'Your knowledge of the automobile and particularly the airplane, the designing of them and how they work could be put in a teaspoon. He might be . . .'

Martin moved slowly across the soft coral carpet. His face had become charged with a peril, a threatening anger which said he had stood enough. He had allowed so much, but when Tom had the impudence to impute his knowledge of the engine, of the thing he knew best in the world, at which he was best in the world, he would take no more, but Meg stepped between them, her own face explosive in its anger.

'Dammit, Tom! Has he not proved himself over and over again in the past nine years?' Her voice was loud, harsh, demanding his

337

attention. 'Now sit down, both of you. My God, anybody would think you were fourteen again and back at Great George Square. Sit down . . . sit down.'

She wore green. A vivid emerald green and the colour was almost a shock against the flame of her hair. The dress was a plain, tailor made, wool cloth button through, almost in the shape of a tube with a collarless bodice and long narrow sleeves. It clung to her, revealing the startling splendour of her breasts, the rounded curve of her hips and the smallness of her slender waist. The glow from the fire turned her eyes to liquid golden brown and her white skin to cream, and put a rose on each high cheekbone. Her magnificent body, despite the loss of weight was as pliant as it was ten years ago but she was a woman now with a woman's maturity and strength. Tom Fraser contemplated her with the frustrated anger and jealousy of a man who has waited more than long enough for what he wants and is dreadfully afraid he is never to get it.

They had been at 'Hilltops' for three months and almost every week Martin had motored over from Camford to 'see how they were getting on' he remarked casually, 'and to make sure that the standard a gentleman expects in his choice of hotel was being met in their new project'. He would wink at Meg to let her see he was joking and clap Tom on the back and not once had Tom seen him do anything to which a man with a beautiful woman he is about to marry could take exception, but nevertheless he was wary when Martin came and relieved when he left.

Now it seemed that behind his back Meg and Martin had hatched this scheme to buy this bloody airfield from the old gentleman or some such daft plan and what worried him more than anything was *when* for he had been under the impression that the pair of them had never been alone together during the past three months. And if they had managed secretly to put together this . . . this business arrangement they had manoeuvered him into, what else had they been up to whilst they were at it? He was a man. He could recognise admiration in another man's eyes, admiration for a beautiful woman as Meg was and Martin certainly seemed never to be off their doorstep these days. Oh yes, they would say it had been only for the setting up of this business deal, if he should ask them, but perhaps they had set up a more intimate contract, one in which Meg and Martin would be alone, up in one of the many private bedrooms with which the house

338

abounded, or even here ... here on this lovely coral carpet ...
Dear God!

The thought barely had time to whistle through his mind before
he dismissed it since he knew Meggie was the most loyal, honest
and true companion a man could wish to have. She loved him.
They were to marry soon and she certainly would not have agreed
to it if she had not loved him. On the other hand he knew Martin's
reputation with the ladies for as a younger man he had boasted
of it, and the way in which those who came to the racing circuits
flocked about the drivers. But some instinct, all male and born in
the possessive challenge of every animal for his mate warned him
there was some link, not as it had once been in their childhood,
but something else, hidden, deep, perhaps not yet recognised,
between Meg and Martin. He watched them now, breathing
heavily, and they looked back at him. Meg's face was innocent of
anything except her need to persuade him to this thing she was
determined upon and he felt the painful ice about his heart melt
with his love for her. His face softened and he was contrite. Dear
God, what was wrong with him? What the hell was he thinking
about? *His* Meggie? She was his and Martin was his friend, the
best pal a man had ever had and would he try to take from him,
even if he wanted her, the woman Tom was to marry, for God's
sake! Just on a whim, for God's sake! Of course he wouldn't but
he did wish this tension which had built up somehow between the
three of them would go away again for he did not like it. Not
with him and Meg and Martin. It wasn't right. It wasn't *natural*.

Martin eased himself away from the dangerous turmoil which
was growing so insidiously and his own face lost it's menace for
he knew it could not go on, this biting jealousy which was slowly
destroying the strong fabric of his affection for Tom. It was like
the teeth of a mouse, small and vicious, which nibbles and nibbles
until it has torn apart something of immense value. Meg was
wearing a ring now, small, but a diamond nonetheless, pressed
upon her by an ardently resolute Tom, bent on showing everyone
from the joiner who had impudently winked at her one day, to
Martin himself, that she was *his*, his fiancée, the woman he was
to marry and the ring was a symbol of his ownership.

'Well, I'm off,' Martin said carelessly. 'I'll leave you to argue it
out among yourselves. I'll let myself out but telephone me soon
at the field because if ... if Tom's not willing there are others
who are!'

339

When he had gone Tom sighed and his face lost it's look of bitter confusion. He sat down in the chair opposite Meg, jerking irritably as he settled his long, rangy frame into the depths of it, then he leaned forward again as though his body, and his mind could arrange themselves to nothing. He took her hands in his and felt them tremble. Turning them over he dropped a kiss in each palm, rubbing his mouth softly across the cushion of flesh at the base of her thumb.

'Meg, I'm sorry. I don't know what comes over me sometimes. I love you so much, my sweet darling Meg, you understand that, don't you.' His eyes looked into hers and he saw the strong warmth of her feeling for him. 'You and I, we were meant to be together. We are like the two wheels on the bicycle we once rode, d'you remember?'

Meg nodded and her hands clasped his lovingly.

'Rolling along in unison, going at the same steady pace together,' – only because you kept me to it, she had time to think sourly, not allowing me to go at my own speed – surprising herself with the disloyal thought. 'The sad thing is that though each wheel turns on its own the bicycle is useless without both. I am useless without you, sweetheart. Meg, let's get married right away. I don't know what it is that is stopping us, I really don't. I know it's only been six months and that's not long for an engagement but we have nothing to wait for, Meg. You say you want to and yet each time I have pressed you for a date, you put me off. There's always something else to be seen to first, some other priority. I want to ... to have you as a man wants a woman, Meggie. You know what I mean.' His honest, open face was flushed and his eyes were clear and steady, the bright blue of them darkening with the intensity of his feelings. 'Let me love you, Meg! Name the day ... soon ... oh please, Meg, make it soon ...'

His face spasmed in his deep, anguished desire and Meg felt herself sway towards him, to his sweet strength, the deep and quiet strength which had stood by her for so long but something, *something* stopped her as it always did.

'Say you will. Say you will marry me before spring, before Easter, next week, we could get a special licence ... tomorrow!'

He knelt then at her feet and put his arms about her, burying his face in the creamy softness of her throat, his warm lips caressing her skin. She felt her heart bound in her breast for he had never been so bold with her before. He had treated her with a reserved

340

delicacy which spoke of his reverence and love. A long kiss, perhaps, his mouth gentle and smooth on her own. His arms strong and sure about her but his body holding back as though he was afraid he might startle her. Now she touched his thick, tightly curling hair and it fell about her fingers, the brightness of it turned to the colour of a sunflower in the firelight. She smoothed it, comforting him as a woman will a child's distress and she held his head to her as his lips moved down the column of her throat to the fabric of her dress until they rested on the curve of her breast. His hands lifted eagerly to the buttons and they brushed against the skin of her throat . . .

With a jerky movement, one in which she might have been delivered a blow, so sharply did she recoil, she pushed him away and he fell against the armchair from which he had recently risen. His face was flushed, soft with his desire for her but the look in his eyes was dangerous. It was too soon after the dreadful thoughts he had harboured only half an hour ago and they twined themselves inside his head like a nest of vipers and he wanted to strike out and hurt someone as he hurt!

He stood up abruptly. 'What is it, Megan?' he said savagely. 'What is it keeps you from giving yourself to me. You said we would marry last year and yet here we still are, engaged, certainly and you wear my ring to show it, but all we do is talk about it. There is nothing to stop us, nothing, and yet we are still unmarried. We do not have to wait, as other couples do, saving up for our home for we already have one. You have no need to gather a "bottom drawer" as is customary for you already have enough china and linen to sink a ship. We have money and a home and no-one to say we may not do as we please but still we remain apart. You love me. You say you do, but there is something stopping you from making that last, final commitment. What is it, Meg? What is it?'

She did the only thing she knew to keep him from probing her further for in truth she did not want to face the reason herself. She stood up angrily before him.

'Don't you get on your high horse with me, Tom Fraser, or I'll land you one and don't think I couldn't. You don't own me, you know, just because you've put a ring on my finger. We may be partners, living here under the same roof which will no doubt cause talk when the first guests arrive but unless I say so, you keep your hands to yourself. Dammit, just because we're promised in marriage . . .'

'That's just it, Meggie! Promised! That's what we are and you must keep a promise!'

She continued as though he had not spoken, '. . . doesn't give you the right to handle me when and as you like, Tom Fraser.'

She was getting into her stride now, believing in the cause of her own anger which had nothing at all to do with Tom's hands on her, and her face flamed with it, not the outraged modesty she would have him believe in but guilt, guilt and the most dreadful sadness.

Tom took a hesitant step away from her.

'What d'you think I am?' she hissed, 'some chippie you can . . .'

'Meg . . . for Christ's sake . . .' He was appalled.

'. . . fondle whenever you fancy it. I thought you had some respect for me, Tom and were prepared to wait until I was ready, you said.'

'I have . . . Jesus, Meg, I have . . . and I will, you know that . . .'

'No! I don't! What you have just attempted says exactly the opposite'. Her chin jutted ominously and she clenched her fists as though she was quite ready to box his ears for his impudence as she had threatened.

'Oh Lord, Meggie . . . I'm sorry, please . . . you know I adore you. I would never do anything to upset you, you know that. It's just . . . I want you so much and I'm . . . afraid you're so lovely . . . all the men.' Not for the world dare he mention the one man's name of whom he was *really* afraid. 'I've seen the way they look . . . I want us to be married, to be together. I want them all to know you're mine . . . mine . . .'

'So you think if you . . . seduce me I will be!'

'No . . . no Meggie. I wasn't trying to . . . Oh damnation, how the hell did I get myself into this mess?'

When he had gone, swearing he would never touch her again until she wanted it, she sat with her chin in her hands and stared into the fire and gradually her body ceased it's wild trembling, put there not by Tom's masculine embrace but some other emotion she knew must soon come to a conclusion, for it was not to be put aside and left for another time as she had been doing now since the day Cook died. She bent her head and her heart contracted in pain for were not they all to be hurt by whatever course of action she decided, and began to weep. She wept for half an hour, alone and quite inconsolable, then, wiping her eyes and blowing her nose she turned to the table beside her and took the rosewood box which stood there and placed it on her knee. She opened it and began to lift out the papers which were in it. One by one she studied them with the intensity and scrupulous application she had given to each of her small thrusts into the business world, to the transactions she had made and been successful in. They were records of every investment she had been advised on in the past three years, of the property she owned – with Tom – from the first, 'The Hawthorne Tree', 'Hilltops' and the most recent, the shares she had purchased in the small flying field and aircraft manufacturing business near Camford where Martin Hunter was to build his first flying airplane!

Chapter twenty-eight

Tom kept his distance and so did Martin, and during the winter months and on into the spring Meg felt herself settle more comfortably into the belief that after all, she had been, as the saying went, crossing her bridges before she came to them. She was well aware that those bridges would be reached one day for though she held it deeply hidden in her heart and studied it only gently and silently in the quiet of the dark night when she was alone, she recognised the feeling which had been born to herself and Martin. It was nothing to do with the sincere and loving warmth she had always had for Tom, nothing at all, for though that was as deep and endless as life itself, what was between her and Martin *was* life itself and would last as long. He had not spoken of love and neither had she at that moment when they had acknowledged it, since there had been no need for words. Soon it must be faced but for the moment she was occupied from dawn until dusk with the hotel and she was glad that Martin did not come to disturb her composure. Of Benjamin Harris she scarcely thought at all!

Tom was good-humoured, appearing content just to hold her hand when they walked in the slowly burgeoning garden in the late afternoon, believing that all was as it had been before Mrs Whitley's death, his soul at peace as the days drew out. To sit companionably beside her in the fire-lit comfort of their sitting room before they went their separate ways to bed was all he asked of her now. He had been badly frightened by the scene with Martin, relieved that he had not been to see them since, and was glad of the return to the placid waiting he had known when she had first agreed to marry him. She still wore his ring and he did not want to ripple the pond of their shared motivation in making the hotel the best they possibly could. He was absorbed in his garden, the wide vegetable plot at the back of the house, the pastures in which he intended to graze a cow or two. Each evening he sat with Meg and listened to her tell him what they would do at Easter, when the summer came, when the summer ended, at Christmas time and each aspect of the alterations and re-furbishing which was going ahead under her guidance, and he was well satisfied with their accord, their *shared* involvement and the growing hope that, given a month or two and the assurance of the success of the hotel which would certainly follow Meg might be approached again to name 'the day'!

Their financial situation was stable and the renovation of the hotel was costing out within their budget, and the loan they had with the bank. They had been pleased at the continued success of 'The Hawthorne Tree' and the steady income it brought them which was repaying the loan. The shares they had in 'Hunter Automobiles' and 'Hunter Aviation' had already shown a handsome dividend and though Meg knew they walked a financial tightrope at times, robbing Peter to pay Paul, as Mrs Whitley would have put it, they were doing it quite successfully.

It needed only the arrival and approbation of their first guests at Easter to put the seal of success on what she knew had been a gamble. If the hotel failed the whole house of cards would tumble about her ears, she suspected, one venture destroying another as they came apart and she felt the need a hundred times as Easter drew closer to talk to Martin about it. Tom whistled cheerfully about the place, planting and weeding and hoeing, sowing seedlings, pruning fruit trees, digging in his manure and when the weather did not permit it, painting or mending something or other, fixing this or that indoors, his pipe peacefully between his teeth, his head filled with nothing more earth-shattering than whether to plant carrots or onions in the patch beyond the back fence, his confidence in her supreme. She knew if she were to pour into his ears the troubled concern she quite naturally felt about the financial side of their venture he would scratch his head and bite on his pipe before declaring that 'she would find a way, she always had' and go stumping off to the job she had interrupted.

Now with Martin she could talk of the enormous cost of refurbishing the house, the delicacy of drawing from one source to pay another, the dreadful apparition which came to her in the night of being unable to repay the loan, the mortgage, the debts she was accumulating as cash flowed from her hand to that of the builder, the joiner, the plumber and the wages she must soon pay to the staff who were to begin at the end of the month. Chambermaids, waitresses, kitchen-maids and porters, a man to help Tom in the extensive grounds, a mechanic in the garage which had been converted from the stables and on . . . and on . . . and on! It was not that she needed advice, but encouragement, someone to restore to her the strong, resolute, absolute certainty in her own judgement which often quailed beneath the enormous burden she carried. She knew her own skills and once they were employed in the placing of guests in the rooms she knew would please them, in the displaying of her care and attention to the smallest detail of their needs and comfort, in the superb food she would put before them, then she would get down to the task of *doing* it, no longer having the time to *dwell* on it. And Martin would understand this. He had harboured doubts, she knew, in the darkest hours of the night and it was his strength which had overcome them and he could help her, show her the way to do it for sometimes she thought she would go mad with only Tom's cheerful assumption that 'Meg will cope', to bear her up!

'I'm going for a drive,' she told a surprised Tom one afternoon, as she backed her little car out of the garage. 'No, you don't need to come, love. I know you're busy. I'll only go into Ashbourne and back. I feel in need of a new hat or something!'

He laughed. 'That's right, sweetheart, you treat yourself,' he shouted after her, waving his hand, turning away before she had reached the gate at the end of the drive.

She knew where she was going, of course she did, though she had not admitted it to herself, let alone Tom and nothing in the world could have stopped her. She told herself, as she made the turn for Camford, that it was to talk to him, to speak as one business man to another on the difficulties which lay ahead. To ask what he would do to resolve this, or this, or this, and how he would go about that, or that, or that. He had worked with Mr Robert and Mr Charles Hemingway, both astute men in the world of commerce and their shrewdness had been passed on to him in the years he had known them. He had learned from them as she had learned her trade at the Adelphi and he had put what he had learned into practical use, as she had done in a small way at 'The Hawthorne Tree'. She told herself she was merely to consult him on a minor point or two which might prove awkward in the future and ask him how he would go about removing an anxious problem which had cropped up to disturb her. He would listen to her, understand what she was saying and just by doing so give her the support she badly needed at this moment.

He was in his overalls. They were stiff with grease and oil, worn almost threadbare in places, patched in others and evidently much loved by him for why else would he still wear them and she was smiling at this artless, unexpected side to his nature when he turned to look at her. His eyes widened, then filled with his delighted wonder and the depths of his love for her. She watched them darken and the corners of his mouth were tugged upwards in a smile of such joy, her own did the same and she spoke his name though he could not hear her over the noise of the hangar. She saw his lips form her name and began to walk towards him.

Every head in the hangar turned to look at her. She wore a hand-knitted 'sports coat' in saxe blue, hip length, very casual with pockets and tied loosely with a belt, and an ankle length woollen skirt of the same colour. The outfit was warm and comfortable for motoring and on her head was a woollen beret in shades of blue and cream into which she had stuffed her hair. She looked beautiful for the wind had whipped up her colour, and the strange excitement she felt had put a brilliant shine into her eyes.

They all watched as their employer put down the tool with which he was working, wiped his hands on an oily rag and began to walk to meet the lovely young woman who had come in through the hangar doors. The doors stood wide open and the spring sunshine poured in and the men were astounded by the expression on Martin Hunter's face. Mind you, she was extremely pretty and in each man was the thought that he himself would look just like that if she were to smile at him as she was smiling at Martin Hunter. She held out her hands to him and seemed not to mind at all when he clasped them with his own, despite the oil which he transferred to them.

'Meggie,' they heard him say and his voice was certainly not the one they were used to, overbearing for the most part and hazardous in it's intention to make them understand that what he wanted, he got! It was soft, gentle with some emotion which seemed to say that he had waited for this moment for a long time and thanked God that it had at last come.

He drew her by the hand through what appeared to Meg to be heaps of rusted metal and bits of twisted tubing, pieces of engines, rolls of fabric and struts of wood, wheels and cans of oil, strange objects which she could not begin to put a name to and all reminding her poignantly of Mr Hale's workshop in Liverpool and the bicycles which had started it all. There was even the same smell, oil and grease, a strange and pungent burning and an even stranger, sweeter odour with which she was to become familiar, of the substance which appeared to hold together the flimsy little machines Martin built!

'Come into the office and . . . perhaps some tea?' his fascinated mechanics heard him say, turning to stare, open-mouthed at one another for where in the name of God was he to produce tea in this section of the industry which was dedicated to the sole function of producing Martin Hunter's 'Wren' and nothing more? Over in the automobile factory which was situated near to the road in a corner of Watkins Field there was a small canteen and tea could be had from a huge urn during the five minute break Mr Hunter allowed his employees, but here, in the holy of holies where no-one was allowed except those who were working on the aircraft, it would be interesting to see from where he would produce a cup of tea!

'I thought . . . I thought I would come and see . . . how my investment was doing, Martin.' Meg stood where he had placed her by the desk and her breath shivered in her throat in the most awkward way, making it difficult to speak. He had closed the door behind him, leaning against it with his arms folded and should she have wanted to escape his warm regard, or even Martin himself, she could not have done so. The office was of glass so that Martin, when he sat at his desk or his drawing board, could keep an eye on what went on in the workshop, but it worked two ways and Meg was conscious of the eyes which were now on them and she turned away, blushing furiously for surely those men could read exactly what was in her mind. Dear God, why had she not noticed before the smooth amber of Martin's flesh, the shape, the texture, the softness and strength of his lips, the way the light turned his dark hair to chestnut? Though her back was to him she could sense the power in his broad shoulders and in her mind's eye see the shape of the lean muscles in his thigh and the bulge of his calves beneath the tight stretch of his overalls. She could smell the soap, the cigar smoke, the sweat for he had been working since dawn and feel the warm lapping of his eyes on her back, knowing they would be as deep and dark a brown as the hot chocolate Mrs Whitley used to make. She could hear his breathing, realising in her bewilderment that it was as rapid as her own.

'The man . . . he would not let me in . . .' She laughed and her

348

voice sounded shrill in her ears and she pretended to study a poster on the wall which advertised Martin's little family car.

'*Get on the road with a Hunter automobile and be sure of arriving.* Guaranteed delivery within four weeks of order and all for the price of £110.'

'He insisted on driving across the field with me . . . what have you here, state secrets? I left my motor outside the shed . . .'

'Hangar.'

'Pardon.'

'This is a hangar, my darling, and please turn round and face me.'

She turned and their eyes met and their love flowed triumphantly between them and was given and taken with a joyous wonder which was unique and endless, their exchanged glances said.

'You have oil on your cheek, Martin.' She took a step toward him and smiled dazzlingly, putting a hand in her pocket to withdraw a scrap of handkerchief.

'I love you, Megan Hughes. You know it, don't you?'

'Oh yes.'

'Do you love me then?'

'Oh yes, Martin.'

'Say it instead of babbling about oil.'

'I love you, Martin.'

'I want to kiss you.'

'I know . . .'

'But not here.'

'No . . .'

'Where?'

She seemed incapable of thought as she admired the way in which his lips moved across his white teeth and could not bear another moment without feeling them against hers. She was captivated by the slow, sensual drooping of his long lashes across his eyes and as she watched them delightedly, they narrowed with a need she understood at last and she could see the straining of his crossed arms and though he gave the impression of a man lounging casually, carelessly, with no thought in his mind but his attention to a pretty woman she knew he was as tense as herself.

'I don't know . . .' She looked about her and beyond his shoulder to the scattered groups of men, all watching curiously, avidly, some of them, this dalliance between Mr Hunter and his lady visitor and the flush of awkward embarrassment began somewhere behind her knees, working its way up through her body and suddenly she wanted to get away. She wanted their love, their committed acknowledgement of it to be displayed to one another in a place of seclusion, somewhere quiet and tranquil, somewhere they could linger in and sigh over and be certain they would not be disturbed.

'Come to my rooms,' he said urgently.

'Your . . . your rooms?'

'Yes. I have rooms at a house in town. We can be alone . . .'

'But . . .' She lifted a hand to indicate the hangar and the men in it, the gauzy outline of his 'Wren', the benches and machinery and in the far corner, the 'Blériot' in which he gave flying lessons.

'I can leave it . . . for an hour, please Meggie . . .'

An hour! He was asking her to slip away covertly and meet him in his rooms where they would spend an hour . . . an hour . . .

'We can talk, Meggie,' but his burning eyes scorched her face and her breast and his ragged breath tore at something precious inside her and she drew back uncertainly.

'Godammit, Meg, you love me . . . I can see it in your eyes! Do *you* know how long I have loved you, do you? I have watched you and waited for you to recognise your feelings because I knew them for I feel them! All this with Tom, it has to come out sooner or later. I wouldn't have let you go ahead with it, you know that, don't you? I hoped you would see it for yourself . . . he's your *brother*, dammit and you have mistaken what you feel for him as . . . It's not a woman's love for her man, Meg. Face it, my darling! Look at me! That is what you feel for *me*, isn't it?'

He groaned and turned to stare out over the hangar and every man in it was suddenly busy at whatever he was about but he did not notice them. 'I see you standing there, telling me that it's true and I want to leap across the office and put my arms about you and kiss you until you beg me to . . . Is that wrong, Meggie?'

But she had moved another foot away from him, inching along the desk and when he turned back to her, her face no longer had that bemused, familiar look he had seen on a score of other female faces and he knew she had withdrawn from him.

'What is it? What have I said? Is it Tom? You'll have to tell him, you know. You can't keep letting him believe you're going to marry him. It's unfair to us all. The poor sod is besotted with you but . . .'

His face became sad and his voice sighed out of him and he slumped against the door. 'It is Tom, isn't it? And me! I've gone too fast, haven't I? But the sight of you standing in that hangar doorway, the sun shining about you ... and that blue thing you have on. I always said you should wear bright colours...' His voice was soft and Meg wondered at the many facets of this man she loved. He could be fierce, challenging, passionate, a man needing and demanding his woman, sure that he would get her with his wit and charm, and yet he had sensed her withdrawal from an ardour, a sensuality she had no knowledge of. She was ignorant of a man's body, innocent herself and her resistance to the thought of going to his rooms, to the quite premeditated arrangement of herself and him, alone there, had put a barrier between them.

'Meggie, I'm sorry, my love, but I am a man and I cannot apologise for the feeling you arouse in me. I'm not ashamed of it. I love you and I want you! I want you in my bed one day! There, I've said it,' but he grinned wickedly now, impudent and loving, and he saw her begin to smile. 'I really did not mean ... well ... shall we say, my sweet Meg, that when we find the right place and the right moment I shall kiss you and kiss you until you cannot resist me. Now, before I lose any more production I think you must go. But promise me something.' He put out a hand and she moved to it unhesitatingly and put her own in his and her face was soft and quite beautiful in her love for him.

'What Martin?'

'Promise me you will tell Tom as soon as you get home, and another thing. Take that damn silly ring off your finger! I shall get you a ...'

'It's not a damn silly ring. Tom paid a lot of money ...'

'Oh God! don't let's start again, Meg.'

'I'm not, but you should not put Tom down like that. He saved up hard and it took all the money he had ...'

'Oh, I don't doubt it and I'm really not putting him down, sweetheart. I have a strong affection for Tom, you know that but any man is entitled to feel outraged when he sees the woman he loves sporting a ring another fellow gave her. Anyway, that is not the issue here.' He put his hands on her shoulders and held her gently but he had to restrain himself from giving her a thorough shaking for it seemed she must be forever defending Tom Fraser and he really did get tired of it.

351

'No! Then what is?'

'You know exactly what is to be done and you must find the courage to do it, Meggie, or I will!'

He felt her shoulders slump beneath his hands and for a brief moment she allowed him to draw her into his arms. Her own came round his back and she pressed her face against his chest, and the men on the shop floor held their breath as he held her to him, then she stepped away quite briskly. Her eyes were bright with tears for Tom but the strange and lovely joy Martin had roused in her was a promise and he was satisfied.

'Come back to me when you have told him,' he said. 'I'll be waiting for you.'

The low sun shone on the French windows as she drove up the drive towards the house and she stopped half way up it, letting the engine idle as she sat and looked at it. It was a lovely house. The gardens were immaculate now, the slope of the lawn massed with wild daffodils in an undulating carpet of yellow against the green. There was pink campion pressing along the edge of the lake, a willow tree beginning to leaf and at the base of the walls of the house, slashing the grey stone with colour, were hyacinth and narcissus, primrose and anemone. The house was set in grounds of wild beauty, only the area immediately around it tamed so that eventually guests might sit comfortably in the sunshine, or play croquet on the lawns Tom was preparing. The ornamental gardens would be spectacular in their season, a multitude of velvet headed roses in every shade from palest pink to deepest red and all surrounded with a low, clipped box hedge and neat gravelled pathways. There was a conservatory to the side where it would catch the sun and already Tom had magnolia, orchid and gardenia blooming there and a dozen green ferns and even a canary in a cage. There were wicker chairs and tables, a small fountain and a statue or two of cherubs at play.

The sky was high, blue and distant, hazed a little with light cloud but for miles around there was nothing, just high peaks and gentle valleys and the restful peace of the Dovedale Grange. She turned off the engine and slipped down in her seat until her head rested on the back of it, staring up into the tender new leaves of the lime trees which edged the drive. It was so quiet now she could hear the whisper of the breeze in the branches and the high song of a linnet, out of sight in the arch of the sky. She closed her eyes and listened and in her head she could hear the laughter of splendid men and women, dressed in white of course, as they moved about her lawn, and the deferential tones of the maids who set out tables and chairs and dainty trays of sandwiches and cakes and tea. There was movement as horses trotted along the path which led down to the river and the sound of the river itself, and behind the house, out of the sight of the guests, chauffeurs lounged whilst the mechanic filled up the petrol tanks of the dozen elegant motors which stood in the yard.

She herself was waiting in the doorway of the house, always there each time to warmly greet a new arrival, delighted to reassure them that Miss Hughes was not only familiar with their names, where they had come from, where they were going to, but within minutes, any likes or dislikes they might have and which would be catered for during their stay in her exclusive establishment.

And the food, they would ask? It could not be bettered in any of the smartest London hotels or restaurants, she would tell them, and would prove it, and was it any wonder the dining-room was filled each lunchtime and evening, not only with hotel guests but with the local gentry, nobility even, who ate there regularly.

She sighed, then smiled a cat's smile and stretched her limbs and Martin's eyes grinned lazily at her and she could feel the hot blood begin to surge in her veins and her breath grew quick in her throat. Martin ... Martin ... Martin ... *and Tom!* Dear God, how was she to tell him ... Dear God!

There was an irritated honking of a motor car horn from somewhere and she sat up quickly, looking about her for she could have sworn it was close by. She turned and gasped for there was a 'Silver Ghost' Rolls Royce directly behind her, chauffeur driven, the sun striking from its polished surface and brass headlamps and as she stared, her jaw slack, the chauffeur switched off the engine and stepped down from the machine.

'Excuse me, miss,' he said politely, his eyes admiring 'will you be long, only we want to get up to the hotel.'

The hotel. *The hotel!*

'Er ... well ...' Her brain appeared to have been deprived of its usual capacity to function and she continued to sit, half turned in her seat then, as though the new electric light which had been installed in every one of the rooms at 'Hilltops', even the maidservant's attic bedroom, had been switched on, her brain became alive and bounding with joy. The hotel! They were looking for the hotel. Her hotel!

'I am sorry,' she said and her voice took on the warmth and welcome of the professional hotelier. 'I was daydreaming, but please, follow me and I will lead you up to the reception.'

She was exultant! A chauffeur driven Rolls Royce, if you please. She had expected most of their guests would have motor cars when they came, for they were all to be wealthy, though there would naturally still be the occasional carriage, but their very first guests had a Rolls Royce. Surely it was an omen! These were her first guests and they were possessed of a Rolls Royce, the King of motor cars! It must be! It must be an omen!

'Mrs Marrington, how nice to meet you, and Mr Marrington.' Meg moved gracefully towards them as the couple climbed down from their motor car and introduced themselves, extending her hand to the portly little man who was entering the hotel. He walked with all the swagger of a bantam cock, and she was momentarily startled by the appreciative gleam in his pale blue eyes as he looked her up and down before turning to the reception counter. She nodded briskly at Tom who stood as though turned to stone, to get the luggage, and just as though she had been preparing for their arrival for weeks, shepherded the stout and overdressed personage of Mrs Marrington through the foyer.

'Why don't you sit here and I shall bring you some tea, or would you prefer coffee. Perhaps a sandwich. We have smoked salmon, cucumber, pressed and garnished ham. You must be tired after your journey. You have come all the way from . . . Bolton . . . My goodness! What a journey!'

'Nay lass.' Mrs Marrington's florid face beamed, perspiring freely, since, as the day was cool she had put on her new sable collar and she could not bear to be parted from it, even here in the warmth of the hotel. Newly rich was Mrs Marrington and though becoming used to it, she had not yet reached the stage where such things were commonplace to her!

'We stopped over on't way,' she continued chattily for that was how they were in the class from which she had risen. 'Mr Marrington 'ad a bit of business to see to in Manchester. We're in cotton, tha' knows. We put up in a place in Buxton last night. Broke the journey, like.'

She sighed as though in the deepest despair but her face was robustly cheerful and her bright eyes sparkled with humour. 'That

354

lad o' mine can go nowhere wi'out he does a bit o' business, even though we're on us 'olidays.'

As Lancashire as the hot-pot she had used to eat before Albert Marrington made his brass and caring nowt a pound who knew it, Mrs Marrington leaned back in her chair and looked round approvingly at the beautifully furnished, wide hallway which was now the foyer of the hotel, admiring the high polish on the scattered small tables, one at every chair, the electric lamps shaded in pale green silk which stood on them, the deep pile of the dark green and cream patterned carpet and the simple beauty of the fragile, wrought iron staircase which led to the upper floors.

The reception area was what had evidently been a small room off the hall, the wall between knocked down and a wide counter put in. Everything gleamed with beeswax, and flowers made dashes of bright colour on the tables and window sills. The chair in which she sat was of dark green leather and there was a chesterfield to match it on the other side of the open fireplace in which a huge log fire crackled.

There were brass plates on the cream painted walls and copper urns in which dried flowers and grasses had been cleverly arranged, and a painting or two, pretty and easy to understand, of poppies and children and bright meadows. Mrs Marrington thought it 'right cosy', she said to the attentive Miss Hughes and in her opinion it would do very nicely for the few days rest she was bent on for her Albert. She could potter in the lovely garden they had driven through and sit with her knitting in the pleasant glassed winter garden she had noticed, whilst Albert did a bit of fishing in the River Dove.

'You're a bit quiet, lass,' she went on, looking about her as she sipped her tea. 'You *are* open, aren't you?' she said, her voice suddenly anxious, 'only the advertisement in the newspaper said opening shortly and we thought seeing we were in the district – eeh, don't say we've come up all this way for nowt!'

'Of course not, Mrs Marrington. The season is early yet but we are to be open all the year round if the weather allows! We are very pleased to have you, Mr Fraser and I, and you shall have the best suite in the hotel.'

'Aye, we 'eard you 'ad suites just like the Adelphi and the Ritz in London. We've stayed there, tha' knows.' She was visibly proud.

'Indeed, well, I hope you will find "Hilltops" just as comfortable. We are still . . . I do hope you will bear with us . . . having some

355

alterations done but it will not be allowed to interfere with your stay. But perhaps it might be wise if you ate in your room, to avoid inconvenience. You will have a private sitting room, naturally and it will be no trouble to serve you there. Now on the menu tonight there is trout, caught only this morning, of course, lark pudding, breast of veal, rolled and stuffed, fillets of turbot done in cream sauce, lobster salad, fresh strawberries, or, if you and Mr Marrington have any other preference, anything at all, you have only to say so.'

'Nay lass . . .' Mrs Marrington laughed, heaving her round, comfortable body from the armchair, 'that sounds grand, all of it, so why don't I just leave it to you!'

'. . . and of course, champagne!'

'*Champagne*! Nay! I don't think Albert will . . .'

'Compliments of the hotel, naturally.'

Mr and Mrs Marrington had been tucked up in their splendid suite, their eyes hurried past signs of the recent upheaval which had torn the hotel apart for months, their feet treading the luxury of the deep pile carpets, their bodies warmed and cossetted by the central heating and the huge applewood fire in their sitting room, their stomachs filled with Miss Hughes' delicious food, their heads pleasantly reeling from the excellent champagne they had drunk. The chauffeur had been housed and the magnificent Rolls Royce stored lovingly in solitary splendour in the garage. Edie had gone to her bed, devastated by the anxiety of catering, just her and Miss Hughes and Mr Tom, to the demands of their first, unexpected guests, declaring she was 'fair wore out with it all' and how Miss Hughes had managed to dish up that lovely meal and with no warning was a mystery to her and she doubted she'd sleep a wink for thinking about it and had Miss Hughes got a look at the diamond on Mrs Marrington's finger . . .

'Well, Meggie,' Tom said fondly, reaching for her own diamond adorned hand and dropping a kiss into the palm of it. 'How does it feel?'

She held the wonder of it to her like a glittering prize and her face was flushed with triumph. She clasped Tom's hand lovingly for he had been superb, acting just as she had done after the initial shock, as though the Marringtons had been booked weeks ahead. He had been courteous and friendly, changing whilst the Marringtons were involved in signing the register from his 'outdoor' clothes, to his good, dark suit and gleaming white shirt. He had carried bags and served drinks and waited at table as though he had done it all his life and had even accepted the large tip a gratified Mr Marrington had pressed upon him. Meg was proud of him and proud of what they shared and the events earlier in the day might never have happened.

'It's the beginning, Tom,' she said softly. 'They will tell others and the word will get round amongst their wealthy friends and before you know it we will be famous.'

'Aye lass, that we will.'

'Oh Tom, what a wonderful day!'

'Aye, but for one thing.'

'What?'

'You never got your new hat.'

He was quite disappointed when her eyes became suddenly shuttered and she stood up, declaring she was worn out and was off to her bed, since he had thought they would share this special moment for another delightful half hour.

'Goodnight then, sweetheart,' he said, warmly.

'Goodnight Tom.'

'Don't I get a kiss, Meggie?'

She turned back awkwardly and he stood up and took her in his arms and with the new found confidence which his successful day had brought him, kissed her thoroughly, well pleased with himself.

Chapter twenty-nine

It seemed Albert and Nellie Marrington had been most impressed with the service they had received at 'Hilltops' and had spoken of it quite lyrically to several of their friends and, more importantly, Albert, in the course of a business transaction with a gentleman of the manufacturing class, had recommended it to him most volubly.

The telephone rang a week later and a voice enquired of Meg, who answered it, if she could 'put up' a certain Mr Nicholson for a few nights. He was to be on business in the area, he said pleasantly, but his wife and daughter had voiced a desire for a day or two in the country and if Miss Hughes ... yes ... he had heard of her from Mr Marrington, and if she could manage a suite and a single room with bathroom he would be grateful. He was a merchant from Liverpool, in shipping like Robert Hemingway, he said, who also had spoken of her very highly, in trade as both those gentlemen were, but when he and his wife and daughter arrived it was very evident that his wealth was of long standing, as was Robert Hemingway's, for his voice was cultured and his wife certainly a lady and his daughter well educated, well spoken and confident. She was to paint a little, she said, taking her easel down to the river which she had heard from her father, who had heard it from Mr Marrington, was very beautiful and if Miss Hughes could pack her a lunch basket she would be so pleased. If the day remained fine she would not return until evening. Her mother drove into Buxton with her father, or sat in the winter garden with her embroidery, taking tea, served to her by the new, hastily fetched parlourmaid and when they left they had booked a long weekend in August and would certainly tell the Hemingways, the younger Hemingways that is, who were dear friends of theirs, to 'try her out'.

At Easter she had a dozen guests. The weather was blessedly kind and they sat about her lawn and drank in the crisp wine of the clear air and played croquet and the more adventurous even hired a hack or two from a local stable to take them exploring the bridle paths which led across the fells, or motored to Buxton spa to take the famous waters. They sat in her lounge, as it was now fashionable to call it, in sofas deep enough and comfortable enough for the most robust of gentlemen, to take coffee after dinner, or perhaps a cocktail before. There were fragile, round-backed chairs on which a lady might sit to show off her straight posture and the soft curve of her bosom to its best advantage and the colours of the room, flame and gold and white were really as smart as any they had seen anywhere, they told one another.

There was a smaller lounge where the ladies might while away a wet afternoon playing bridge and sipping chocolate or coffee brought specially from France, and choose from a dozen French pastries made by Meg, the art taught her by the pastry chef in the kitchens of the Adelphi.

The men used the billiard room, going there for masculine conversation which bored the ladies, and to smoke their cigars, and in the bedrooms and private sitting rooms were deep, pale carpets, crystal lamps and chandeliers, paintings and delicate furniture, and warmth, always warmth if the day was cool, and discreet service and the comfort to which they were accustomed in their own homes.

It was May when Martin came over, his face cool and quite threatening in his arrogant determination to talk to her and Tom, he said, his meaning quite clear. He would have been over before but a hitch in the planning of the Wren had prevented it. Her heart missed a beat for in five weeks she had scarcely given him a thought in the overwhelming excitement of being, at last, as she had dreamed, the proprietor of a first class, successfully growing hotel and her own mind was amazed that it should be so.

'I waited and you did not come,' he said, 'so I came to you.'

'Please, Martin . . . I have a hotel filled with guests. Not now . . .'

'Then when, Megan?' His voice was dangerous and he gripped her arm painfully. They were in her small sitting-room where she had bundled him – unwillingly, for no-one 'bundled' Martin Hunter anywhere these days – pleading with him for God's sake to keep his voice down since those in the lounge had already begun to turn their heads towards the disturbance in the foyer.

'Can't you see I'm run off my feet.'

'And Tom! Where is he?' His voice had become a snarl for Martin Hunter was curiously afraid of this new thing which had come into her life. He had been so *sure* of her. She loved him, she had told him she loved him and the only thing which stood between them had been Tom but this hotel business had a fascination for her, an obsession which was as strong as his own for the automobile and the airplane and it seemed she was not, now that it was suddenly successful, willing to turn away from it.

'He's in the garden seeing to . . .'

'Then let us go and tell him together!'

'Martin!' She was appalled but even in the midst of the explosive tension which Martin's anger created she could feel her body move, almost as though it had nothing to do with her brain, her strong will, of it's own accord to be near his, excited even more by his masculine jealousy. 'Don't do this to me now. I meant to . . . I was going to . . . but people came and . . . then others and before I was aware of it the hotel was so busy . . . over Easter . . . oh Martin, is it not wonderful . . .?' Her face was flushed now with the joy of it and she wanted to share it with him as he had shared his with her but he was beyond reason and would have none of it.

'You could not do it, then. You were afraid if you told him that you loved me and not him he would have left you in the lurch with no-one to dig your potatoes and milk your cow and that would never do. Is that all he is to you, Meg, for if so he is easily replaced.'

'God in Heaven . . . give me time to . . .'

'How much time does it take to tell a man that you love another, my pet, for I swear I can wait no longer . . .'

He had gone and Tom was not aware that he had even been, and though Edie had seen him swerve up to the front door in his flashy motor car, she said nothing and each week brought fresh guests and though Meg meant to tell Tom, indeed she did mean to, the opportunity seemed always to elude her. Often in the night, though she was tired almost to breaking point, her mind consumed with the need to be chef and book-keeper, charming hostess and every other function she must perform to smooth the way for her chambermaids, her kitchen-maids, her waitresses and porter and barman, her body burned most desperately to arrange itself beside the long, hard length of Martin's and she knew no peace and she determined that tomorrow she would tell Tom. She would go to Martin, she told herself, to his rooms, or anywhere they could be alone and to hell with Tom, to hell with the hotel, to hell with the increasing number of guests who clamoured each week at her door.

At the end of June the hotel was, for the first time, completely full. The weather was perfect that summer. Tom's fruit and vegetables could not wait, it seemed, to fall plumply into his hands and on to the immaculately set out tables in Meg's dining-room. The cows he was grazing in the meadow at the rear of the hotel gave so much milk he had to employ a dairy maid to turn the surplus into butter and cream. Meg surpassed herself each night, turning her lovely rooms luminous with candlelight and crystal, and fragrant with the flowers Tom grew for her, and the superb odours of fine wines and foods that had never been seen outside the Adelphi or the Ritz. Salmon and game and pâtés, sauces and pastries, fondues and soufflés, ices in fancy moulds with nuts and cherries from Tom's trees, and mountains of home-churned cream from Tom's overflowing dairy, and still they continued to come that summer for perhaps they had a premonition, as they say animals do, when disaster is on the way.

It was on a lovely day in July when Martin came again. She tried to keep the encounter light-hearted though her own pulse throbbed like a drum, afraid he might give offence to the several ladies who were sitting beneath her trees taking afternoon tea.

'Now what's up?' she called cheerfully from the open window of the sitting room, just as though they had met only yesterday. His face was quite set though it did not seem that his severity was directed at her. 'Don't tell me the paint's the wrong colour on the bodywork of the motor, or is it that manager of yours? You told me he was an awkward devil and when you meet someone as stubborn as you are there's bound to be sparks.'

'Well, you would know about that, Megan Hughes,' he said quietly and he was not smiling, and her own slipped away from her face as she opened the French windows to let him in. He brushed past her, moving absently into the pool of sunlight which fell across the carpet.

He sighed deeply, then turned to look at her and she felt a feather of disquiet brush her spine.

'What is it, Martin? Something's happened, hasn't it? Something important.' She put out a hand to him and he took it gently between his own and she was frightened for he seemed so ... so sad!

'Where's Tom?'

'He's gone down to Buxton. Some seeds he wanted and one of the guests offered him a lift.'

'He should be here.'

'Why? Dear God . . .'

'Do you remember . . . last month when that Archduke . . . Ferdinand I think his name was . . . yes, that's it . . . when he was shot and killed at Sarajevo?'

'Yes, it was in the newspapers but what . . . ?'

'He was the heir to the Austria-Hungary throne. Well, it appears the chap who murdered him was from Serbia and now Austria have accused the Serbian government of having encouraged the crime. Anyway, they delivered several ultimatums to the Serbian government which have not been fulfilled and the upshot is the Austrians have declared war on Serbia.'

'But what has that to do with us?'

'Don't you see, sweetheart . . .' Even in her increasing dread, caused by Martin's unusual sobriety, the endearment gave her pleasure and she gazed up into his eyes with an intensity which made it hard for him to continue.

'. . . Serbia is bound to appeal to Russia to come to her assistance. They are natural allies and the Germans will come in on the side of Austria-Hungary. France will join *her* ally, Russia and as the whole thing escalates how can we not become involved?'

'Oh Martin, surely not. It has nothing to do with us.'

'No, on the face of it, perhaps not but . . .'

'And why should it involve you, or Tom?'

As she spoke Tom's name it was as though the mention of it had brought his absence from the hotel to their attention and the realisation that for the first time in months they were here alone together without his unspoken reminder to Martin that Meg belonged to *him*.

'Well . . . if there is war . . . there'll be fighting . . .' Martin found he could hardly speak. His thoughts had become scattered and fragmented, thoughts of his 'Wren' and the Royal Flying Corps, his own intention, clear and perfectly formulated in his mind only an hour ago, dissipating as his own breath caught in his throat. He felt his heart buck painfully in his chest. Her eyes were still on him and she seemed bewitched, her attention rapt, wondering, distracted from what he was saying by what she saw in his face.

'Meggie . . .'

'Yes ... I see ... but really ... I cannot think we will go to war ...'

'Perhaps I am being unduly ...'

'I am sure of it ...'

'Of course.'

They had moved a step closer to one another, only a foot or so of space separating them. They spoke the words, their lips forming sentences, answers and questions, their brains functioning automatically at a certain level but they, *they*, Meg and Martin did not speak them, nor hear them for they were fast now in the drifting dream world of the moment, the moment towards which they had been moving since they were children. He had recognised the truth before she did and he felt the desire grow, a desire which was not romantic but a fierce masculine need to put the mark of his love on what belonged to him and he reached out his hands for her. She hesitated, understanding in that last second what he had in mind for her but her eyes still clung to his, speaking, telling him what he wanted to know and he smiled triumphantly. Her face whitened and her lips parted in refusal for her despairing mind registered wildly that she had a hotel filled with guests but her eyes begged him, pleaded with him to go on. They spoke for her, denying the hand she put out to stop him, denying the words which were forming in her dry throat. Her expression was haunted and she felt her heart tear loose and thrash about in her breast but still he smiled, his body almost touching hers now, his manner saying quite clearly that what was Martin Hunter's would never be taken from him. It was there in his face, in the strong brown hands which gripped her shoulders, what he meant to do!

'Martin ... please ...' she whispered, clinging to the last shred of compassion for the man they were to crucify. 'Tom ... he is ... oh, please, don't do it ... the guests. Don't force me ...'

His face was dark and his eyes were fierce with his love.

'As to that, I have no intention of forcing you, my darling, none at all. The moment you ask me to stop, I will. I shall lock the door and no-one will come. I love you you see. I have loved you with all my heart, feeling it grow slowly inside me for many years now. Have you the least notion of how I have agonised over my feelings for you, have you, Megan Hughes? It did not seem ... right, you see. I have anguished on it since the day you sat at my bedside after the crash at Brooklands. Four years, and I have held off, fighting a despairing battle to keep my filthy hands off you, believing that what I felt for my little 'sister' was unhealthy, abnormal, perverted. I had been conditioned, you see, for almost ten years into thinking of you as a child, a young and innocent girl whose protection had been my responsibility. The longing I had to touch you, to put my arms about you and kiss that rich and exciting mouth of yours was the very emotion in other men, the lust I had seen in other men from which I must protect you. I have stayed away from you, taken other women . . . oh yes, even in these last months, do not doubt it for I am a man with a man's needs and I could not wait for you to make up your mind to tell Tom. So, I began to convince myself that what I felt for you was no more than a passing thing. You had grown beautiful, womanly and I was a man and was it not natural for a full-blooded man to desire a beautiful woman? Oh yes, I told myself, young Meg is growing, maturing, gaining confidence in the business world and what were you to me really? One day I said confidently, I will meet a woman who will be more to me than an amusing companion, a lover to soothe and delight me in the night. I would marry when she came along and I would marry well for it does no harm to ally oneself with a family who can give you a push as you claw your way to the top which is where I mean to go. Perhaps a woman with money. Robert Hemingway would know of one and I have kept in touch with him. I have dined with him and his family and you may laugh at this, my darling . . .' His own face grimaced in self-contempt, '. . . had even considered the fifteen year old miss who is his grand-daughter. She was still a child but I could wait.' His voice became soft then and he held her away from him so that she could see into his eyes. 'I held back my emotions, Megan Hughes, those that you aroused in me, concentrating everything I had on my work. But . . .' He lifted his head and his laughter was completely without mirth. '. . . whilst I held my lust in check, virtuously believing I was doing the gentlemanly thing, Tom Fraser had the bloody impudence, the gall, to take what was mine . . . *mine*! Oh, I could convince myself, just, that Megan Hughes was not for me but by God, if I was not to have her, neither was any other man!'

His face was vibrantly alive, the colour in it high and racing beneath the skin. His eyes were almost black, so dark had they become and she could feel and smell and taste the sweetness of his breath as it exploded from between his lips, inches from her own.

'So, my darling, if you are willing, and you have only to say if you are not, I shall hold you in my arms and kiss you and when that splendid virginal body of yours comes *alive*, as I know it will, then *you* shall decide who it is you are to love, and *who* is to love you, but I tell you this, Megan Hughes, Meggie, oh my dearest Meggie, I do not believe it will be Tom Fraser!'

He backed her up to the door and turned the key in the lock, then holding her hands out against it as though she was on a cross, he began to kiss her. Gently at first, a mere brushing of his mouth on hers and when she turned her head desperately away he placed his warm lips beneath the lobe of her ear, kissing and licking until she felt the pit of her stomach begin to warm and throb and melt and her arms struggled, not to escape him but to clutch him to her. They were round his neck and her hands gripped his hair and she began to whimper in her throat. The whimper became a moan. She was a woman who had known no man's touch beyond the loving, almost brotherly hand of Tom Fraser. She was, as Martin said, virginal, but she was no innocent sixteen-year-old. She was a woman, ready for loving these past six years and *she* wanted this as much as Martin.

His hands went to the neckline of her gown and with great deliberation he pulled it from her shoulders and down about her waist and looked in wonder at her glorious, full-nippled breasts. They seemed to spring into his eager hands and he bent his mouth to them and did not stop to ask her if she wished him to go on!

'When will you marry me?' he said an hour later as he lay with his head on her breast and she told him soon, soon, quite bewitched by him but he raised his head to look into her face and they were both sadly aware that they were about to break the steadfast heart of Tom Fraser.

'We'll tell him together, Meg. That's what we should have done months ago.'

'Dear Lord . . . Martin . . .'

'I know, sweetheart, but he has to be told now. You know that.'

'Will you let me . . . I promise this time . . .'

'What, my love?' He bent his head and put his lips to the curve of her silken eyebrow, then brushed back the tangled riot of her hair. They lay on the soft rug, their naked bodies united in the beauty of their love, their bodies *beautiful* in their love, young, supple and thrusting with the strength of it. He was ready again but she held him back, her face strained, its rosy glow gone now in the pain she knew she must inflict on Tom.

'I will tell him, Martin. No, I really will this time . . .' as he reared away in disbelief. 'He will take it better if you're not there to see it.'

His hand was at her waist, fitting the brown strength of his fingers into the soft turned whiteness, urgent again, demanding, refusing to be denied and she lifted her lovely rounded hips and raised her arms to his head as his mouth travelled down the length of her body and Tom was forgotten, forgotten as though he had never existed as Meg Hughes took her second journey to that place of ecstacy into which Martin Hunter led her.

They dressed later, their eyes soft and wondering. His hand cupped her breast before she covered it and lingered on the long white beauty of her leg. She put her face against the brown hardness of his muscled chest and smelled the masculine fragrance of soap and sweat and some indefinable something which was, she knew now, peculiarly her's and Martin's. They whispered and laughed softly, and the busy hotel about them had no being. They were lost in the loveliness of their new love but at last they were as they had been an hour before, but would they ever be that again, their fingers asked as they drew irresistibly together, linking quite naturally in a way which Meg could still not quite believe. This was Martin, her heart exulted, her love, her lover and yet he was Martin her friend, her companion of almost twenty years, familiar, dependable, a part of her life which remained unbroken from the day on which she had put her child's hand in his. It was strange to her, this new relationship with a man who had been one thing and was now another. Strange and wholly delightful and she felt a sudden wave of shyness engulf her and she hung her head before him, like a child with a friendly stranger. He saw it and was enchanted, putting a finger to her chin and lifting it, leaning to kiss her blush away, smoothing her cheek with a hand which trembled for he could not believe even yet that she was wholly, irrevocably *his*!

As though she read the glow of possession in his eyes, the possession of a man for his woman, hers became sad again, dimmed and he knew the reason why.

'Shall I wait?' he said, his hand going to her cheek again for it seemed he could not get enough of touching.

'No . . .'

'I feel we should share it . . .'

'It would be best if . . . he and I were alone. Put yourself in his shoes, Martin. Would you like to have *him* there whilst I told *you*?'

'Aah . . . don't, my love . . .' His face clenched for it was the first time he had actually considered what Tom Fraser was to suffer. And yet if he could change it, would he? If Meg was to ask him to leave, to let her go, would he? If he could spare his friend, if it was in his power to take his pain from him by giving Meg Hughes back to him, would he?

He shook his head sadly and knew he would not.

'When?'

'Tonight.'

'I will come for you tomorrow.'

She turned to look at him then, surprised.

'Come for me! What d'you mean?'

'Well,' he smiled confidently. 'You can hardly stay here with Tom, can you, now that you and I are to be married?'

'But . . . but I live here.'

'Of course you do, my darling. It has been your home. It belongs to you and Tom, but you are to be my wife and will come and live with me in a home you and I will share. As man and wife.'

'But . . . but where?'

'Perhaps you could go and stay with that woman in Great Merrydown? What was her name . . . Annie Hardcastle, until we are married. You don't want a big affair, do you, my darling? A registry office, surely, by special licence for I cannot wait to have you with me all the time. You can wear a white dress, despite the fact that you are no longer the virgin you were this morning . . .' He grinned audaciously, his eyebrows lifting, his tall frame leaning towards her with all the certainty in the world that she would raise her face for his kiss, amenable, compliant, a woman led as was right, by her man's wishes.

'With Annie! In Great Merrydown.' She reared back from him with all the effrontery of a woman who has just been made an indecent proposition. 'How the hell can I run the hotel from a distance of fifty miles? Do you expect me to motor up each day or am I to put a manager in as I did at "The Hawthorne Tree"?'

'But damnation Meg, surely Tom and that woman, what's-her-name, Edie, can cope until you find a buyer?'

She became quite still then and the amazed pique which had coloured her face to crimson began to drain away, leaving it white and stiff, like cement which had hardened. She moved away from him, her body oddly rigid, stiff and painful, or so it seemed, and went to stand at the French window, staring unseeingly at the sun-drenched garden and the guests – they were still there – who sat about in groups or walked beneath the shade of the trees.

'You are saying I am to ... to give up my work, are you, Martin?'

He sensed the withdrawal in her, the sudden widening of a cool gap between them where there had been only warmth and trust and he frowned, straightening defensively from the position of lounging, confident indolence he had taken up at the fireplace.

She turned to face him. 'You are saying that I must sell my hotel, leave it all and come and live with you?'

'You will be my wife!' His voice challenged her to argue with him and an obdurate expression came to harden his face and both of them were aware that they had come to a point – so soon, so soon her agonised heart asked – which was to be vital in their lives. He had, justly, she supposed, assumed that she was to fit immediately into her new role as his wife, the keeper of his house, the mother of his children. There was to be a war, he said, and she had no doubt he would go to it, fight in it and because of it he would want her tucked lovingly away, safe and secure and waiting, waiting until he came home to her. He was a man of many interests, a demanding man and lover. He would be a conventional husband and would expect her to be a conventional wife. Wouldn't he? But perhaps ...?

'Martin ... I cannot just give up "Hilltops" and "The Hawthorne Tree". I cannot abandon them now. Tom and I have worked so hard, with both of them, built them up from nothing. We have put four years of our lives into them. We have made them our lives. I am good at what I do and Tom is learning. He loves the work he does in the gardens, in the bar. Dammit, Martin, you are to take me from him, you cannot mean to take his work as well. He cannot manage it on his own. I can just as easily work here – we could take a house near by, you and I ...' Her face became eager and she began to move across the room towards him but he turned away, staring fixedly into the fireplace.

'Please ... can you not see ... what would I do?'

'You would be my wife! That is what you would do.'

'I can be your wife *and* run the hotel, Martin.'

'I would not wish you to. And it would be too far ...'

'Far from where?'

'From Camford.'

'But we could buy a house somewhere between. Then you could travel to the airfield and I could come up here . . .'

'You would be *my wife*, Megan, not an hotelier or a business-woman but my wife and as such will . . .'

She felt the dread and the anger begin to work in her but still she made a determined effort to control them. This was her life, *her life*, and Tom's, which was being so carelessly dealt with and she could not allow it to be extinguished lightly. Martin was a strong, self-made man, sure of himself, with all the wilful courage which had turned him, in nine years from a raw and callow lad into an increasingly successful motor car manufacturer and soon, when his Wren was complete, he would enter the aircraft industry and no doubt be just as victorious there. At this moment, her body sated with his, with the love he had poured into her during the past hour she would have done anything he asked for her love for him was just as strong. But if she allowed him this she would lose her own identity in his, she would be an adjunct of him, an important, beloved, but quite useless decoration which he would wear proudly, cherish lovingly, protect strongly but never, unless she fought him over it, allow a place of its own. And Tom! Dear Christ! They could not take everything from him. He might not want to stay and work beside her. He might chose to sell his share of the investments he had chanced with her, his half of the inn and this splendid hotel they were beginning to make so successful and she was certain Martin would be glad to find the money to buy him out. He might not care to have her as his partner, instead of the wife he had hoped for and his instinct might, she thought, be to take himself off and start a fresh life, but he must be given the choice!

Martin watched her indecision and his face lost its arrogant expression and his eyes grew soft for he could see her pain. He took a step towards her, then another until they stood but an arm's length apart.

'Meg, please come with me. Come away and marry me. These . . . these moments we have spent together . . . how can I describe what they have meant to me?' His voice was husky, an urgent, desperate whisper. 'Don't deny it has not been the same for you. Your . . . your delight matched mine. We are perfect partners and I cannot live without you beside me. I have waited so long. You are my ... my heart, Meggie, my best beloved ... my only love ... please ... please ...'

His voice broke and he leaned to kiss her, his mouth like velvet against hers. 'Leave this, my darling, leave it for Tom. He will manage ...'

She turned her face away and huge tears began to spill from her eyes, slipping down her face to fall in great patches on the front of her dress.

'Martin ...' Her cry was despairing, 'I cannot just go and leave Tom to do it all alone. He cannot ... a has no business head and Edie can't cook ...'

His face closed up like an iron glove, hard and clenched and he turned violently away from her.

'It seems Tom can do nothing without you beside him and it also seems very clear that Tom's needs come before mine. You will have to choose, lady, and choose quickly for I do not mean to wait any longer.'

'Martin ...!'

'I shall be at the airfield until ...'

'I must have some time ... please Martin ...'

'Time! Take all the time in the world, Megan, but do not expect me to be waiting for you.' His face was cruel, hard, dreadfully so and his words were meant to hurt. 'I was never good at waiting, Megan, nor at playing second best!'

He turned then and strode from the room and she heard the sound of the 'Huntress' as it thundered down the drive and the echo of it beat in her heart and hurt her with a pain she could scarcely contain.

Five days later, Germany, in order to strike at France, an enemy now, from behind, demanded from Belgium the right to march through her territory into France. The Belgian government declined. Despite this Germany marched into Belgium declaring that it was necessary for them to do so and necessity knows no law.

Great Britain's plighted word would certainly lead her to join France and Russia when Belgium was invaded for how could any self-respecting nation remain at peace when another held so low a regard for international obligations? The Belgians tried to resist the German Army but within a month the Germans were at the French border and on the 14th August 1914 Great Britain was at war with Germany sending an expeditionary force of one hundred thousand which took its stand at Mons.

In all that time Martin Hunter had no word from Megan Hughes and when he left Camford for the Royal Flying Corps training camp at Hendon, Middlesex, he made no attempt to let her know.

Chapter thirty

It was the last day in August. Tom Fraser stepped lightly across the polished parquet flooring at the head of the stairs, hesitating a moment before the closed bedroom door. He looked down at his boots, checking to see that he had completely removed all traces of the heavy black soil in which he had been working, for he knew Meg would not greatly care to have it deposited on the carpet which covered the floor. He held a large bunch of roses mixed with lavender and white babies' breath in his hand.

Reassured that his boots were quite clean, he knocked gently on the white painted door panel. He did not want to wake her if she was taking a nap, which she seemed to do quite often these days, complaining when he asked, that she was not sleeping well at the moment.

'It'll be the heat, love, and worry over the war.'

'Probably,' she had answered.

It was mid-afternoon and the hotel was quite silent, just as though all the guests were also napping, pulled down by the excessively warm day. It was close, humid, with big thunder clouds gathered on the horizon, threatening at any moment to tumble across the sky and attack the peaks, to roll across the dales and lash the farms and cottages, and the hotel with treacherous ferocity. Tom would not be sorry if they did for a storm would release some of the springing tension which the heat of the day contained. It would do Meg good as well, if the weather turned cooler for she'd not been looking at all herself lately. It had been like this for weeks now, with heavy skies tinted a strange and sulphorous yellow, pressing down on aching heads, the air almost too hot to breathe and Meg had been pale, listless, quiet as a mouse which was not like her at all. She ate next to nothing, picking at what was put before her, even when she herself had cooked it and scarcely appeared to notice the bickering which went on in the kitchen, the sudden arguments which exploded over the smallest thing, the maids oppressed, as they all were, by the days of endless heat.

There was no answer to his soft knock. She must be sleeping, or perhaps she had gone downstairs again whilst he had been in the garden cutting the flowers for her. He had not seen her as he passed through the kitchen where Edie and the girls had been sitting, stupefied by the heat but she could have gone into the wide reception area, or even into the garden at the front of the hotel.

He was about to turn away, the flowers still held tenderly in his large, working man's hand when he changed his mind. He'd not carry them downstairs again to wilt in the heat, he'd leave them on her bedside table, he decided. She'd not be long, wherever she was and when she came back they would be a nice surprise for her. She loved flowers, did Meg and these would take her out of herself. Cheer her up. He'd been puzzled, he admitted to himself, by her strangeness these last few weeks and was not convinced it was due entirely to the weather. She was vague sometimes, only half listening to what was said to her, giving the impression that she was waiting for something, sitting quietly with her hands folded in her lap as patient as could be. At other times she was restless, pacing about the hotel, peering from windows, striding the boundaries of the hotel grounds and impatient with him when he asked her what was to do. The war was on everyone's mind, of course, and Meg was no exception though she hadn't said much. Well, it was bound to worry her, wasn't it? She was a woman and women are left behind to bear the anxious burden of waiting when their menfolk went off to fight, and then there was the added unease of what was to become of the hotel. They had only just got it on it's feet, so to speak and how was the war to affect it, he asked himself?

Already the manager at 'The Hawthorne Tree' had reported a drop in the takings in the tap room and snug as local men flocked to the recruiting centres to take the King's shilling, though as yet it had not affected the 'other side' where the hikers and cyclists still came and the rooms were filled with enthusiastic young men and liberated young women, still determined to enjoy themselves whilst they could.

'Hilltops' was filled to capacity for it seemed the prosperous and the privileged were also influenced by the onset of hostilities, and every day the telephone rang constantly with enquiries for their luxurious suites as though the nation had gone quite mad in its efforts to take its pleasure whilst it was still available. There appeared to be a feeling amongst many that before long all the diversions of peacetime might be swept away, though Tom could not imagine why, and people seemed desperate to wring every drop of enjoyment from life that there was. They'd settle down soon, Tom thought placidly, when the first shock of going to war had worn off, just like Meg would and if he could persuade her to set their wedding day before ... well ... it had been a year and that was certainly long enough for any man to wait. She was ready for marriage. She had a certain look about her which Tom, inexperienced as he was in the ways of the flesh, could recognise instantly as a male does, the look of a female who needed to be loved. *Physically* loved. He could not explain, even to himself, what it was or how he knew it. It was an aura, a *feeling* of sensuality, though Tom shyly admitted to himself it was not a word he was comfortable with. It had come about her only recently and it made him more restless himself. He felt nervous – a silly word – in her presence, as jumpy as she was and he felt a strong and compulsive need to sweep her into his arms and kiss her until she was breathless. He had never done that with her for despite her love for him and her agreement to marry him, she had held herself from him in a way which would not quite allow it. He supposed it was only right that she should. She was a 'good' girl and should be respected as such but really, he was going to insist she name the day and that it should be soon, especially now.

Quietly he opened the door and stepped inside the bedroom and was immediately wrapped about in a shaft of sunlight, sultry and oppressive which streamed across the carpet from the open window. The curtains were half drawn and except for the bright bar of sunlight, the room was dim and airless.

It was a lovely room and he looked forward to the day he would share it with her. It had a superb view across the lake to the great sweep of the Derbyshire fells and on a fine morning was the first window through which the sun shone. It was simply furnished. A plain carpet in a shade of pale caramel, with walls of the same colour. White woodwork and a velvet chair or two in saxe green. The bed was covered in a cream lace bedspread and the curtains, in silk were a subdued mixture of cream, white and the palest green. There was a small marble fireplace, empty now of a fire but in the hearth stood an enormous pottery jug containing a feathery mass of dried grasses.

He did not see her at first for the room was veiled in the hazy shadows cast by the sun and the half closed curtains. A million floating particles of dust lifted in the movement of air caused by the opening of the door, drifting in the shaft of sunlight and for a moment his eyes were sightless. He narrowed them and his mouth curved in a smile for he could smell her perfume. On the bed was some wisp of something in a pale and lovely blue, with satin ribbons, eternally feminine and he put out his hand to touch it but before he could reach it something caught his attention, some sound, slight and soft and when he turned his head she was there, in the shadows. She was sitting before the dressing table, completely motionless, staring at her own dim reflection in the mirror. In her hand was a brush and her hair hung almost to her waist, vibrant and glowing like a flame. She had on a white cotton wrapper, with lace at the neckline and sleeve, tied with a silk ribbon but its whiteness was no paler than her face, and her eyes, though they seemed to look into the mirror, saw nothing. They were expressionless, blank, pale and lifeless, but worse than anything were the huge tears which slipped, almost of their volition, as though Megan Hughes had no control over them, or even knew of their existence, down her colourless cheeks, falling to stain the cotton of her gown. They simply streamed in an endless flow of sorrow from her eyes.

'Dear God ... Meggie!' Tom's heart bucked, then surged into his throat and he thought he would not be able to speak, or even breathe. With a wild gesture he threw the flowers on to the bed, moving swiftly across the room to her side. When he got there he was not quite certain what he was to do for she looked so ... so terrible he thought for one appalled moment that she could be dead. She *seemed* dead, or so dazed with some dreadful thing she was quite senseless. The hairbrush hung at the end of her arm, held somehow in her flaccid hand, but as he watched, horrified, it dropped with a soft thud to the carpet and lifting both her hands in a sudden movement, she dropped her face into them and began to weep loudly.

'Meggie ... sweetheart ...'

Tom was appalled. He had never seen her in such distress and had not the faintest idea how to deal with it, nor even what had caused it. If he had, perhaps he might have been able to alleviate it. She was vulnerable, as all women are, he supposed, at certain times of the month though he knew nothing about it really, but his Meg had not seemed unduly concerned, and certainly she had never wept broken-heartedly as she was doing now. She was inconsolable, putting her face into her folded arms on the dressing table top and crying as though she was stricken with an unbearable grief.

'Meggie . . . darling . . . what is it, for God's sake?'

But it seemed she could not stop nor even speak though she allowed herself to be drawn into his compassionate embrace and when he kissed the top of her head and begged her to tell him what had upset her, she only cried the more and it was only after ten minutes or so of careful stroking and murmuring that she began to speak incoherently – saying what did *she* care for the doings of crazy men who risked their lives for a dream and weren't all men the same, selfish and uncaring, without a thought for the women who loved them and were forced to wait until that dream was a reality, hearts plunging in fear whilst they played with their dangerous toys like children.

Tom could make no sense of it and did not try but sat her down gently on the bed and held her in his arms and waited until she was calmer before pressing her with the utmost kindness to unburden herself of her problem, to lay it on his broad shoulders, for surely there must be something seriously wrong and wasn't that what he was here for, he asked her lovingly, to take away her worries, if she had any?

But like Martin Hunter, Tom Fraser had only the smallest conception of the depths of Meg Hughes, and the enormity of her strength. Each had but one thought, to protect and care for her, to possess her, unaware that what they saw was only a part of what she was, of what she wanted from them, from anyone. Even Martin who had entered not only her body, but the heart and spirit of her, could not imagine what it was that made her into that unique being, Megan Hughes. Even he, though deep in love with her did not understand her complex and ambitious mind nor the special principle that drove her on. If he had he might have penetrated her resolve, recognised it for what it was, understood it and allowed it to come to fruition and eventual fulfilment.

'I'm sorry, Tom,' she sniffed at last, taking the handkerchief he gave her and blowing her nose vigorously. 'You've found me in one of those moods which sometimes come upon my sex. It's nothing really. The autumn is nearly here and the winter will set in and the snow will come. It will be difficult to get about – remember last winter – and no-one will be staying here and I don't know what I shall do with myself. You can be captured up here on these peaks for months and the very thought makes me shiver.'

She looked out of the window at the great sweep of lawn which the gardener who helped Tom, battled with each day in a never-ending struggle to keep it as smooth as a billiard table, but already the stage was slowly becoming set for the annual change from summer to autumn to winter and she was bereft, it seemed, and inconsolable.

'It's all so . . . so sad, Tom . . . so sad.'

'What is, my darling? Dear God, Meg, this is not like you. I have never seen you so down before. What has happened to make you like this? You are the most optimistic person I have ever known, cheering up others with your high spirits and certainty that everything would be right in the end. Believe me I should not have got through the last four years without your complete faith in what we were doing.'

'Tom . . . I'm sorry, forgive me . . .'

'There's nothing to forgive,' he said smiling, since he did not know what it was she spoke of. 'You have a good cry if you want to.'

'No, I've finished with crying, Tom, for good. I was just giving in to a silly whim.'

She shook herself, like a dog who has been unwillingly immersed in water and smiled brightly. 'In fact, I've made up my mind to get right away for a while. Close the hotel, we've had a hectic season, and have a few days holiday ourselves. What do you say?'

He gasped and his eyes shone with joyful anticipation. He had no idea what was in her mind, perhaps a honeymoon, but if he was to be included in it how could he refuse his expression said, then his face fell and he shook his head.

'I can't do it, Meg.'

'Why not? Oh please, Tom, let's go up to . . .'

'I can't, Meggie, honest . . .'

'But why not, for God's sake? I know the place is full but we can refuse any more bookings for a week and Edie and Albert will keep an eye on the place . . .'

Tom studied Meg with loving, troubled eyes but his heart was heavy for how was he to tell her? He was still the engaging young man who had grown from the cheerful youth and boy, his open, good-humoured face scarcely altered in ten years. The placid country life they had known for years had exactly suited his temperament. He was content in his life now the threat of Martin had been removed. He looked just what he was, a man of the soil, a plain working man in a working man's garb, with a pleasant brown face beneath his cap of bright curls. His eyes were clear and steady in his love for her, blue and reliable as the summer sky. It was a patient face, boyish and yet maturing now, his own confidence, built up layer upon layer by Meg and the work she trusted him with, as enduring as the soil he worked. It was an unlined face for he had nothing with which he was troubled.

But now his eyes were anxious, careful almost for what he had to tell her was going to upset her further and he could not bear to see it in her. But it must be done. He was a man, an Englishman and it must be done.

'What is it, Tom?' She put out a hand to him in sudden fear and on her face was an expression which said she really did not think she could stand any more.

'Meggie . . .'

'What, for God's sake . . . what?'

'I don't know how to tell you, you being so upset an' all, but . . . well, we've all got to do what we think is right, our Meg . . .'

'Please, Tom.' She was beginning to understand what it was he was trying to tell her, he could see it in her tear wet eyes but it did not make it any easier. He had been so filled with pride, with national patriotism, and with the excitement not unlike the fervour of the football supporters with whom he had once mingled. He had queued for hours with them, right along the street and round the corner for the recruiting officer could scarcely cope with the thousands who, like himself, had come to offer themselves to their country, to their King and to the bright, golden chance to be heroes.

Megan began to moan helplessly.

'Oh don't Tom, please . . . don't tell me . . .'

'I'm sorry Meggie . . . really . . .'

'Not you, Tom! I can't stand it if you leave me as well . . .'

He did not notice what she had said after the first word or two. Though he was clearly upset by her grief, and if he were honest, a little gratified, it surely meant they would be married before he

378

set off for France. There was a tilt to his head, a proud lift in his shoulders and the triumphant light of courage in his vivid blue eyes.

'I had to, Meg. There was no other way.' He said it simply. 'The 19th battalion, the "Kings Liverpool Regiment". The third Liverpool "Pals" we are. We're all to stay together, all us "scousers" in a "Pals" battalion. It'll be grand to serve with other chaps from Liverpool, in the same regiment . . . I'm sorry, Meg, really I am, but I've to report tomorrow for training I didn't think it'd be so soon but Albert is a good chap and he can cope and I'll be home soon on leave and . . .' His face became hopeful, warm with his love and the expectation that she surely could not refuse him now, '. . . we can be married before I go, Meg, can't we?'

Tom's eyes shone with patriotic fervour and he almost stood to attention as though already he was on the parade ground beneath his country's flag. 'There are a few weeks training. We've to report to Knowsley . . . but . . . oh Meg, say yes, say we'll be married before I go.'

'Go where, Tom?' It was as if she could not comprehend the enormity of what was happening. Her eyes were bewildered, like those of a lost child and for a moment Tom's bright, excited mind knew doubt and confusion for she seemed racked with a strange emotion. She had been distraught, minutes before, made so, she said, by the dread of what was to happen to the men who had already gone to war. Or that was what her words had implied. 'Selfish and uncaring' were the words she had used, 'crazy men who risked their lives for a dream' but surely she must see that a man had no alternative but to fight for his country, his family, his woman, when the call came. She was upset by it all, justifiably so but she'd come round. They all would, all the women who would wait behind for their men.

'Go where, Tom?' she repeated dully.

'To France, Meg. Where else, but I'll be home by Christmas, you just wait and see.'

He had no idea what war would be like, imagining it to be a grand affair of great marches and even greater battles. He was not even really sure why he was to fight. He knew he was to defend his country in this 'war to end wars' as it was being called and that already a British force was in position, ready to fight, somewhere in France and his only anxiety was that it might all be over before he got there. He dearly wanted Meg to be proud of him.

A few days later he and other members of his company were drilling in the sultry heat of the sports stadium at Knowsley, near Liverpool and the following week they were entrained before dawn for Edinburgh where, under canvas, Tom Fraser and his 'pals' were to be turned into soldiers.

She was in the dining-room, chatting courteously to a guest when she heard the telephone ring in the reception area. She took little notice for it had scarcely stopped now for over four weeks, alive with those who wished to spend a few days in the peace of the Derbyshire countryside before going 'over there'. Parents, moneyed naturally, who desired to share a day or two with a beloved son, young officers with their young wives and even, she suspected, those who were not, and the dining-room was filled with elegantly dressed ladies and immaculately suited gentleman and not a few uniforms that night.

'Excuse me, Miss Hughes, it's for you.' The receptionist, a handsome young man who could have been taken for a guest was reluctant to interrupt the beautifully dressed woman who was his employer but the gentleman on the telephone had been most insistent.

Meg turned, and smiling a polite word of apology, excused herself from the worried mother and proud father of the young lieutenant who was to sail for France the next week.

'Who is it, Andrew?' she said. 'Mr Fraser?'

'It didn't sound like him, Miss Hughes.'

Her mind was still filled with the anxious, tremulously smiling face of the young soldier's mother, a face which said she knew she should be proud of her handsome, eighteen-year-old boy but really she would much rather he stayed at home in the nursery where he belonged and where he would be safe. All over the country, in cottages and mansions, in northern terraces and southern villas, women wore the same expression, not entirely convinced, as their menfolk were, that this was going to be the biggest adventure; that their husbands, city men, bus drivers, clerks, coal miners and teachers were to be off on the greatest 'lark' of their humdrum lives.

'Meg.' The voice at the other end of the line was soft, weary

380

almost and she felt her heart turn over in her breast before it began to pump and beat vigorously, joyfully, lovingly.

'Martin.' She wanted to laugh and cry and shout across the wires of how much she loved him but she kept her voice cool.

'Oh Meggie . . .' It was said sadly, wryly, resignedly.

'Yes Martin?' She had begun to smile, her great golden eyes blazing across the reception counter into the startled gaze of a passing guest.

'You win . . . you win, Meggie!'

'I don't know what you mean, Martin Hunter.'

'Oh yes you damn well do! I can't stand against you, my sweet. If you want to be a business woman, then be one. If you want to run a hotel, or any other bloody venture, then do so. Sweetheart, I can't go on like this. I love you, Meggie. I should have known . . .' She heard him sigh at the other end of the line, 'My God, I should! Ever since you were five-years-old you have made up your own mind and stuck to it. I should have known you wouldn't change now. I was a fool, Meg, the last time . . . oh my darling . . . marry me . . . marry me . . .'

'Yes, Martin.' Her eyes had begun to brim with tears but they were as bright and luminous as the diamonds on the wrists of her guests. Her face was suffused with a joyful, rosy glow and she lifted her head to smile enchantingly, enchanted, at the receptionist.

Martin's voice was ardent in his love for her, and soft.

'Meggie . . .' From somewhere, some female intuition sewed painfully a fine thread of fear in her. 'Meggie, it won't be for a while, sweetheart.'

'Martin?'

'I'm not at the field, Meg.'

'No?'

'No, I'm at Upavon.'

'Where . . . where is that?'

'It's in Wiltshire.'

She knew what he had done, of course, for she loved him and loving him, knew him.

'What . . .?'

'The Royal Flying Corps, Meggie.'

'Yes.'

'I had to, my darling.'

Tom had said that and he was gone, now Martin was saying the same thing and suddenly she was angry, not just with them

381

but with all the men, the stupid, the selfish, the senselessness of all men, men who would kill each other, and for what? Half of them did not know, did not care, they only knew they had to be 'in on it' just as though it was some bloody game they had to play. But Martin was speaking and the love in his voice reached out over the miles from – where was it, Wiltshire – and wrapped itself about her, begging her to understand, begging her to return his love and save it for him until he should return to claim it.

And when would that be, her anguished heart cried.

'Will you . . . come soon, Martin?'

'Aah, no, Meggie, my love. I'm off to France . . .' She felt her body sway and saw the hand of the receptionist as it came out to steady her for her face had drained of every vestige of colour but she clung to the counter and strove to keep her voice calm.

'To France. I didn't know . . . you are to *fly* in France, Martin?'

'Yes . . . I can't speak but I'll write to you, my darling. I should be able to get leave. Bloody hell, Meg, I should have come.' His voice was harsh with his anguish, 'but my damned pride . . . Jesus, Meggie . . . promise me you'll wait for me, promise, my lass.'

'Martin . . .'

'I'll be home soon, sweetheart, promise me.'

'I promise, Martin . . . oh Martin . . .'

'And Meggie . . .'

'Yes?'

'See to the business . . . to Hunter Aviation and Automobiles and the rest. Keep an eye on it, keep it safe until I come home. I've left a document . . . it gives you power of attorney.'

'Martin, I know nothing of motor cars . . . or aeroplanes.'

'Meg, my love . . .'

His voice faded, dying away in a series of crackles and high-pitched whines and though she called his name a dozen times he did not answer.

Chapter thirty-one

She moved about 'Hilltops' as though she had wings on her heels, really she did, and they could hear her singing softly to herself in the back corridors of the hotel as she checked stores and supervised the sorting of linen with Edie, and they marvelled at the change in her. For a month or so she had been another person, not at all the brisk and efficient Miss Hughes with whom they were all so familiar, and though it had been a pleasant change to linger over a cup of tea and a chat, knowing she would not notice, it was good to have her back, at the helm so to speak, dispatching orders and criticism, and praise when it was deserved, and making order out of muddle. The place ran like a Swiss watch, Mr Tom used to say, and the guests had not noticed that slight hiccup between one tick and another during the terrible heat wave for most of them had been too drained themselves to observe it, but by God, you could tell the difference when Miss Hughes was herself again.

It was funny without Mr Tom, though. Such a cheerful, easy chap he had been, not concerned much with the rest of the servants except Albert and the young boy come straight from school to help in the garden. He had been outside for much of the day, making sure there was a plentiful supply of superb vegetables, fruit and flowers for the dining-room tables, milk, butter, cream and eggs, for Miss Hughes insisted on only the best and the freshest to put in the splendid dishes she served at each meal. He ate in the kitchen during the day, sitting with the servants and kept them in stitches over the escapades he and Miss Hughes and a chap he called Martin got up to when they were children and a more likeable chap you couldn't wish to meet. No 'side' to him at all, considering he was part owner of the hotel. Yes, they missed him, but not half as much as Meg Hughes missed him.

It was strange really, she thought to herself, for she and Tom had not seen a lot of each other in the course of their busy day. They shared an early cup of tea and smiled at one another in the kitchen when Tom came in for his 'dinner' at midday. He often helped out in the bar when they were busy in the evening, looking exceptionally smart and very attractive in his good, dark suit and was most pleasant with his guests, speaking, as was his way, in a humorous, engaging manner to which they could not take offence despite his broad northern accent. He would kiss her good-night and make his way to his own small room at the back of the house, spartan, but, as he said, he was soon to share Meg's in his role as her husband, and it was not worth the trouble of 'doing it up'.

Now, it was as though a part of her had been sliced away and sent up north leaving a painful wound which was taking a long while to heal over. She missed Martin devastatingly, but she had not lived with Martin for ten years. He had not been a constant part of her life as Tom had been, and the absence of his physical presence did not leave the terrible hole in her life which Tom's did. She found herself watching for him through the windows, each room she entered her eyes automatically searching across the gardens for his familiar stooping figure, her ears automatically listening for his cheerful, tuneless whistle. He had been beside her since she was five years old, except for her days at the Adelphi and then he had been at Silverdale, not more than half an hour's cycle ride away, not perhaps the pillar of strength she would have liked him to be for he was no businessman, nor had he the capacity to see the fine and dashing future she envisaged for them both. He had lived in the present, not worrying overmuch about tomorrow providing he had a job in his hand, but he had just *been* there, loving her and, if she had asked it of him she knew, dying for her.

He wrote to her from Edinburgh. He was in the infantry, he said. His letters were humorous, describing to her how he and his 'pals' were being put through their paces in a park in full view of the public's ridicule and that his feet, unlike those of his fellow 'soldiers' had not blistered, due no doubt to already being used to wearing heavy duty boots. He was now fully 'accoutred' and equipped, he told her, evidently proud of his use of such novel words, and was 'in line for a stripe', his sargeant had said, so what did she think to that! He could now present arms, drill, was becoming adept at bayonet fighting and bomb throwing and the light-hearted manner in which he wrote of such things showed clearly he really had no intention of actually *doing* any of them, not in *real life*! He loved her and missed her dreadfully, he wrote ardently and worried about her down there alone without him to look after her, and really, Meggie, he must insist on a wedding before he went 'over there'.

But already, though it was not generally known, in that first month of the war, soldiers were dying in their thousands. It was a brutal shock to those who saw them being shipped home, mangled, armless, halves of men, groups of three men with three legs between them, and emergency hospitals were being commissioned with astonishing speed, in schools, mansions and stately homes. Those who lived in the south and east of England were at first confounded, then afraid and finally accustomed to the sound of the guns of Flanders, a good 150 miles away in the Ypres salient. It was a pulsing, thudding sound, more felt than heard and those who suffered it and who had men at the front realised that the sound they heard, day in and day out, might signify the death of their own loved ones!

Posters began to appear on every spare bit of wall, simple, old fashioned and to the point! 'Your King and Country Needs You.' 'A Call to Arms.' 'Rally Round the Flag.' and all ending patriotically with 'God Save The King'. In front windows of shops and terraced houses, in cottages and semi-detached villas there were cards which read 'This House has Sent a Man to Fight for King and Country' or 'Not at Home. A Man from this House is now Serving in the Forces'. Patriotic fervour was high in that first month or two but as the excitement began to wear off, those who had been first to declare their intention of getting in on the great adventure decided they would wait to be fetched and other posters began to appear. The ruins of a Belgian woman asked 'Will you Go or must I?' There were others: 'Is your Conscience Clear?' 'Is anyone Proud of YOU?' and 'Are You Doing your Bit?', and the man in the street still in the garb of a civilian was asked to ponder on how he would answer the question 'Daddy, What did You Do in The Great War?'

Meg moved through those first weeks holding the precious gift of Martin's love to her, taking it out at night to gloat over when she was alone, re-living that last telephone call again and again. The deep, unbreakable love Martin had for her, growing unseen over the years and only now acknowledged was what kept her heart and her step light. The joy which spread in her as she lay in her solitary bed, put the lovely glowing light in her eye and she waited impatiently for his first letter. She was filled with love, overflowing with it and at times she could scarce contain it, inclined to embrace the surprised Edie and put a joyful hand in that of Albert when he brought in her flowers, or presented her with the splendid fruits of Tom's labour. She found herself with a tendency to go back to the days when she and Tom and Martin were children and often, as she sat dreaming by her open window at night she would see a boy with golden buttercups in his hair – was it Martin, or Tom? – or hear the sound of a bicycle bell and the cheerful song they used to sing as they pedalled home. Mrs Whitley was remembered and Emm, but her thoughts would go no further than that for her memories were not all happy. But as she dreamed through those days of waiting she could find no fault with her world for Martin loved her and would be home soon to marry her!

Surprisingly, when the shock of his departure had worn off, she did not worry about him for he was a splendid flyer and was he not in his own 'Wren', the 'King of the birds'? He was behind the lines, not in the dreaded trenches where sadly, British soldiers were dying for their country, how many was not exactly known for the casualty figures were glossed over, but Martin was safe, for two weeks after he left his first letter arrived.

It was ardent! Meg felt her heart quicken and her breath become ragged for he spoke of many things, things concerned with their love and loving and how they would spend his leave which he hoped would be no later than Christmas. He was worried about Tom and how he had taken the news of their impending marriage and through it ran, like warm, sweet honey, his love . . . aah . . . how much he loved her and how well he would show her when he came home.

She sat down immediately to write back to him. She did not speak of Tom Fraser. She had been over to the field, she said – after she had told him of her love and longing – and had had sharp words with Fred Knowsley, the manager, who, it seemed, did not much care to be 'spied on' in Mr Hunter's absence, especially by a woman. He was not much concerned with the fact that Mr Hunter had put her in charge, he said, affronted. He was well able to run the aircraft side of the industry without the – he had not said 'interference' but that was the word he had implied – and Mr Hunter had always had complete faith in his judgement and what his employer was thinking of, putting a lady in charge, he could not imagine. He was a mechanic, after all, just like Mr Hunter and they were building the 'Wren', following faithfully

Mr Hunter's design and had orders from the government as long as your arm and . . . pardon . . . the books? Aah, well, he was not a bookkeeper and had yet to bring the August and September balance up to date but if Miss Hughes cared to look them over . . . yes . . . he would be grateful . . . and the men from the ministry were coming next week . . . yes . . . well really . . . that would be most appreciated for he himself was merely a mechanic! Martin was not to worry, she said for she and Fred, yes she was to call him Fred, had the whole thing tied up and ticking over, waiting on his return. She told him not to give the business a thought for the aircraft side of it was thriving but she said nothing of the slowing down of the production of his little motor car, since the men who were to drive them had all but gone from the streets, serving their country far away. She told him she loved him and missed him and asked him if he thought a small investment or two with their surplus profit might not be a good idea, since there were plenty about in these days of war and would he tell her if he agreed in his next letter and, and, please to come home to her soon for she did not think she could survive much longer without his arms about her and his lips on hers and . . .

The war news was splendid. The 3,000 cinemas in the country, supplied with material by the Department of Information provided a steady flow of propaganda which, while applauding the heroism of the British soldier and deploring the savagery of the German – who it was rumoured, cut off the breasts of nurses and rendered down the corpses of slain British soldiers for fat and tallow – glossed over the true horrors of the fighting and hid the appalling fact that by the end of November the British had suffered almost ninety-thousand casualties. Tom was to go soon, he said, and in his cheerful letters was hidden the vague unease he, and his 'pals' felt, fed by rumours. Nothing he wrote must let her know the anxiety which was beginning to be felt for he did not want to worry her, but the falsely cheerful tone and his repeated demands to be allowed to get over there and get the bloody thing finished rang strangely false now.

Meg had another worry now as the war got into its stride. As men left for the front there was far more work for women to do and opportunities to demonstrate they could do it well. And the wages! £2 a week to work in a munitions factory which was more than double the amount they could hope to earn in service. They flocked to the auxiliary branches of the armed services, they worked on the land, as nurses, clerks and typists and Meg's maidservants, sadly, they told her, for she had been good to them in the short while they had worked for her, felt the need to get in on the bonanza, and, of course, do their bit to aid the war effort!

So there was only Edie, and Jenny Swales, who lived near by and was 'walking out' with a coal miner, a restricted occupation and therefore unlikely to go into the army, the little skivvy, only just fourteen who worked in the kitchen, and Meg, for even the handsome young receptionist had been called to enlist in the service of his country.

Meg had been forced, regretfully, to turn away guests for how could the four of them do what a staff of a dozen and more, had done before the war. She did the cooking still, and Edie and Jenny cleaned and served in the dining-room, doing the work of four, whilst in the kitchen the young maid squared her shoulders and ran like a hare from oven to table to sink in an effort to keep up with Miss Hughes' orders. Half the lovely suites were closed up and the furniture swathed in dust sheets but still Meg sighed through the days for nothing was important now but the safe return of her love. The winter was setting in and Derbyshire was a long way from London, where the young officers on leave from France went and so she waited, and dreamed her dreams contained in her world, indolent and filled with a strange languor.

It was in September that the elderly gentleman appeared, speaking most courteously to Ethel, the young skivvy from the kitchen of 'Hilltops'. It was her afternoon off and she had gone blackberrying that day with her younger brother. They were up the lane which led to Addlestones Farm, their booted feet deep in lady's smock and wood-sorrel, their fingers and lips blue with the juice from the dewed, sun-smelling berries, their baskets already half filled. Alfie was propounding on the nuisance of being so young and considering with Ethel whether the war would last long enough for him to get in it. Did he look sixteen, he begged her to tell him anxiously, his thirteen-year-old frame striving for another inch or two, but Ethel took no notice, the voice of her brother just a constant irritant on the perimeter of her thoughts but when it stopped she was surprised and turned to look at him.

He was standing, awkwardly holding his basket, his eyes on the immaculately turned out gentleman who had appeared – from where, Ethel thought wildly – in the exact centre of the dusty lane. He wore a tweed jacket and well-cut breeches with brightly polished boots. He carried a stout walking stick and on his head was a soft felt hat in tweed with a wide brim. He was the perfect country gentleman and Ethel stared about her, looking for his horse, or his carriage, or even his motor car but there was nothing, only himself.

He smiled and for some reason Alfie moved nearer to his sister.

'I'm sorry, did I startle you,' the gentleman said.

'We were blackberrying,' Ethel replied as though in explanation.

'So I see, and what fine ones they are. Just right for a pie.' There seemed to be no answer to this so neither youngster spoke up.

'I am out for a walk.' The gentleman turned to look about him, studying the rolling hills, the low sheltered valleys, the rippling grasses which stirred in the breeze and the soft, hazed blue of the sky. It had rained in the night and the earth smelled damp and on the bramble bushes, diamond drops glittered where the sun's rays caught them.

'It really is a beautiful day,' he continued affably, 'and just right for a walk but I appear to have missed my turn.' He smiled and again young Alfie seemed inclined to huddle closer to Ethel. 'I am to visit a friend of mine ... Miss Hughes of the "Hilltop Hotel". Perhaps you know her?'

At the mention of her employer's name Ethel's suspicious face broke into a smile and she gave Alfie an irritable shove, her expression asking what the devil he thought he was doing, crowding up to her like a baby, and him wanting to be a soldier!

'Oh aye.'

'You mean you know her?'

'I work for her.'

'Well, imagine that! What a coincidence! In what capacity?'

'Pardon?'

'What do you do at the hotel, Miss ... er ...?'

'Ethel.'

'... er Ethel ...?'

'I work in the kitchen.'

'Indeed. That sounds a very important job.'

Ethel preened. 'Oh aye. Miss Hughes says I'm her right-hand man ... or woman, now that the rest of the servants have gone to fight the Germans.' She became expansive, rounding out her routine, often menial work until it became as important in her fourteen-year-old mind as the cooking done by Miss Hughes. 'Well, I have to be really 'cause there's only Mrs Marshall and Jenny now that Mr Tom's gone . . .'

'Aah . . . Mr Tom!'

'And all the other girls have left to make bombs so I have to do their jobs an' all.'

'My word, you must work hard, particularly with Mr Tom in . . . where has he gone now . . . I have forgotten for the moment.'

'Edinburgh. They're teaching him to be a soldier, Miss Hughes says and then she has to see to the field . . .'

'The . . . field . . . ?'

'Oh yes! Where they make airyplanes, Jenny said . . .'

'Aeroplanes?'

'Yes,' she explained patiently, 'those things what fly in the air.'

'Oh, of course, and why does she do that. One would imagine she has enough to do without . . . seeing to the . . . er . . . aeroplanes.'

Ethel became confidential then, carried away by her own importance, by the thrill of having her own voice listened to by a grown-up, and liking the sound of it herself, and with the delight all those who gossip have in passing on information, usually blown up out of all proportion to the the truth.

'Well, Jenny said that this chap who's a friend of Mr Tom's and Miss Hughes builds them and he's gone . . .'

'Gone! Gone where?'

Ethel blinked and hesitated for it suddenly occurred to her that this man, gentleman or not, was asking an awful lot of questions, but then, as she said later to Alfie, he *was* a friend of Miss Hughes so what harm could there be in chatting to him?

'He's gone to France in his airyplane.'

'Has he now?'

'Yes.'

'Well, that is most interesting and I don't suppose you know where in France?'

'I just told you, France!'

'Of course . . . well, I must be off since I fear it is to rain.'

'Will I show you the way to "Hilltops", sir?' Ethel said, reluctant to part with this gentleman who found her own conversation so fascinating.

'Don't worry, I'll find it . . .'

'But sir . . .'

'Thank you. Good afternoon to you.'

The war was going well, they said, those who knew and the Germans had discovered they could not get through the British Army as easily as they had marched through Belgium. At the first battle of the Marne the German advance was checked by the British Expeditionary Force, and by the French under Marshal Joffre. Not only were they stopped they were forced to retreat across the River Aisne. The Germans' attempt to reach the Channel was similarly thwarted by the first battle of Ypres and the people were jubilant, trying to get their tongues round the strange name with no idea of how familiar it was to become to a nation in which most households were to lose a husband, a father or a son there over the years.

The final attack on Ypres began on 20th October and with the arrival of reinforcements in November, the Germans ceased their attempts to break the line. Both armies dug into their trenches and waited, surely, for the end of the hostilities to be declared.

Letters came from Martin. There was not much doing, he said for there were not many of them to do it! There were in Great Britain at the start of the war only 862 men who held the Royal Aero Club's flying certificate and of those only 55, himself included, were sufficiently advanced to be considered for active service. Despite this they had gone to war with 197 pilots. They earned seven and sixpence a day as officers and got an additional four shillings daily as flying pay.

'We shall be millionaires by the war's end at this rate, swee-theart,' he wrote, 'and well able to afford that diamond ring I promised you by Christmas. I am almost sure of leave then for I will have done three and a half months service and if I am able I shall fly home, so tell old Knowsley to have the runway ready at the airfield. About the investments you mentioned. Do just whatever you think fit, my love. It will be your business as well as mine when we are married and you have become as sharp as any businessman I know, and better!'

She kept his letters beneath her pillow and, smiling at her own foolishness, tied them together with a white satin ribbon as was traditional with love missives, putting them to her face and smelling what she was certain was the fragrance of his cigars on them. She worked hard, as hard as she had ever done, in keeping open a part of her hotel and her health was superb. She seemed to bloom that autumn, her love giving her a gloss and polish, a dancing, sparkling vitality which had the quality of a firework, a shooting star, and yet the delicate wonder of a simple, pink-tipped daisy. The war would be over soon, she believed, for was that not what everyone was saying and perhaps Tom would not even get to France. Martin would be home and together they would face the task of telling Tom how it was between them. It was the only sadness she bore and it was heavy but they would overcome it, the three of them, as they had always done.

The dog began to vomit about midnight. Awakened by the sound of his pitiful howling Meg stumbled down the stairs to the small back room used for storing all the paraphernalia which had not yet had a home found for it and where he slept, afraid he would waken the guests. Perhaps he had scented some intruder, a fox or one of the nocturnal creatures which lived in the woods beyond the boundary of the hotel, on the forage at the dustbins in the yard.

He died with his head in her lap, his eyes, even in his agony, begging her forgiveness for the mess he had made on her carpet. Edie sat with her and when he had gone she helped to lift his heavy body into the cold dawn of the back yard, and beyond to the garden. She would bury him under the branches of the tree where he had liked to lie in the summer, sheltered from the sun's heat, Megan declared, the tears streaming desolately across her drawn cheeks for she had developed a great fondness for him in the four years he had been with them.

'Nay love, Albert will do it. 'Tis too hard for you. The soil is heavy at this time of the year,' Edie protested and drew her away and when Meg went later that morning the dug ground had a sprig of fading heather laid on it and she felt comforted.

It did not occur to her to wonder why he had died and in such obvious pain until mid-afternoon. He had been an elderly dog with grey hairs in his muzzle and she had supposed his time had come, but why had he suffered such agony, she thought? She was preparing the 'Fillet of Veal au Bechamel' which was on the menu for the evening meal. Edie had roasted the fillet the day before and had cut out the middle when it had gone cold. The meat taken out had been minced, mixed with forcemeat and Meg was adding the bechamel preparatory to returning the mixture to the meat, sprinkling the whole with breadcrumbs and clarified butter before browning the dish in the oven to be served hot. Edie was grating breadcrumbs beside her.

'It's strange he died so quickly and without warning,' Meg said and with the words it was as though she had opened a door and allowed in a chink of light. Not enough to see by but sufficient to place an outline around her still quiescent thoughts.

'He were an old dog, lass.'

'I know, but he was fine last night when I let him in, begging as usual for a titbit and lively as a puppy.'

' 'Appen he ate something he shouldn't. A rotten apple or rubbish he picked up in the wood. Them toadstools are reckoned to be poisonous you know.'

'Yes, I know, but he's never eaten them before. Why should he do it now?'

'Nay, I don't know, lass. 'Tweren't as though he was hungry. Not after what he had last night.'

'What d'you mean?'

'I gave him the left-overs from what we cut out of this veal for his supper and by heck, did he enjoy it!'

The door in her mind creaked open further and though she could not as yet make out the clear shape of the horror she knew awaited her, it was there, smirking and obscene and in a moment the full force of it would be upon her. She stepped back from the meat she was stuffing as though it had burnt her fingers.

Edie turned towards her, amazed.

'What's up, lass? What is it? You look as though you've seen a ghost.'

'Oh Edie . . . Dear God . . .' she could do no more than whisper.

'What . . . for God's sake what is it?' Edie was badly frightened by now.

'The veal!'

'The veal! What's up with the veal?'

'Did it come from Mr Talbot?'

'Of course!'

'Can you swear to it?'

'I saw his van meself.'

She telephoned Mr Talbot who was most bewildered, swearing he had delivered no veal to Miss Hughes for at least a fortnight, and what one of his vans was doing up her way yesterday he

393

could not imagine, and he would certainly get to the bottom of it and if one of his men was up to no good . . .

Her face was as colourless and damp as the dough Jenny was kneading and the room and its occupants held their breath in dreadful anticipation for surely she was about to impart something of a quite appalling nature but all she said was, 'Burn that veal, Edie, and I shall personally check every particle of food, and where it came from in future. Do you understand?'

Edie didn't but she did as she was told without question for there were some strange things in her employer's past and they had nothing to do with her, so she shut up Jenny's excited curiosity with a sharp word and told her to mind her own business, which she herself intended to do!

Megan Hughes huddled in her bed that night, listening in her head to his dreadful laughter and thought she would never get warm again.

Chapter thirty-two

The first aircraft to fly over the English Channel in support of the British Army in the field took off from Swingate Downs, near Dover on 13th August 1914. The first British reconnaissance flight over German territory was carried out by a lieutenant and a captain of number four squadron, the Royal Flying Corps, on 19th August 1914 and the first aircraft to be brought down in action was one belonging to number five squadron the Royal Flying Corps, on 22nd August 1914. The aircraft was shot down by rifle fire from troops in Belgium. The first Royal Flying Corps air victory took place on 25th August 1914, when two unarmed aircraft of number two squadron forced a German two seater to land.

On 10th November, two months after he arrived at St Omer, France, Lieutenant Martin Hunter took off in his own aircraft, the 'Wren' to fly over enemy lines. With him was another young airman, in a Blériot monoplane. Their orders were to reconnoitre the enemy's territory and to report back to their Company Commander what they had seen.

The war was young. There was still enthusiasm and a certain feeling that they were boys, playing boy's games, heightened by the fact that they slept in barns, used aircraft as windbreaks, ate in a tent – the mess – all giving the impression that they were almost on holiday and camping. The patrol went out at certain times of the day, depending on orders from wing headquarters and on this particular day the two airmen had been selected for the dawn patrol.

'Good Luck,' they wished one another, shaking hands enthusiastically, two handsome young men in the prime of their manhood, excited, warriors off to war, afraid for they were not fools, but nevertheless willing to go for they were both lovers of the frail aircraft they flew, and firm believers in their contribution in the war they were fighting. There were those who scoffed, asking what possible use these flimsy war birds could have in the destroying of the enemy and so far no-one could answer but at least they could *observe*, it was said.

The two young men were equipped with maps and instruments and told to pin-point the enemy's trenches to a depth of three miles inside their lines, to keep their eyes open for troop movements and anything they thought might be useful, for truthfully, this new war, being only three months old, those in charge were not awfully certain on how to go about it.

The Blériot monoplane was sighted an hour later and those on the ground who watched it land were surprised at the shakiness of it for the man who flew it, though he had been out here only a matter of days, was an experienced pilot who had flown for at least a year back in England.

When the first mechanic reached him, for he made no attempt to leave his aircraft, the young pilot was weeping quite openly, the tears collecting inside his goggles. When he was coaxed to remove them he rubbed his eyes like a child and the oil which covered his face streaked and ran and he looked no more than fifteen.

'Sir?' the mechanic said, at a loss what to do next for his officer seemed close to hysteria. 'Sir, why don't you ... why don't you get down, sir?' He was embarrassed but filled with a strange pity for the young man was distraught.

They got him to the 'mess' and gave him a brandy and his teeth chattered on the glass. The commanding officer was patient for the young pilot was no more than a boy really, straight from his public school, the son of a quite famous father, privileged and, knowing how to fly, one of the first to volunteer for the relatively new Royal Flying Corps.

'He went down!' he was able to say at last. 'We were flying at 500 feet ...'

'Were there guns, Lieutenant?'

'Guns, sir?'

'Firing ... shelling?'

'No sir.'

'Perhaps other aircraft?'

'Aircraft, sir?' The boy was deep in shock.

'Enemy aircraft, boy?'

'No sir, nothing.'

'Then what happened? Why ...?'

'I don't know, sir.' The boy began to weep again for it was his

396

first encounter with tragedy. 'He seemed to . . . to spin, sir. Round and round and then he went into a steep dive. I was shouting to him, sir . . .' The young officer sounded aggrieved as though if only Lieutenant Hunter had listened to him they would not now be in this predicament. 'But he . . . he couldn't hear me. The noise was so dreadful . . . I've never heard . . .'

'No, boy . . . not many of us have . . .'

'Such a dreadful sound, sir . . . and then . . . Oh dear God . . . oh sir . . . he hit the ground and skidded across the field . . .' The boy sobbed uncontrollably and those about him moved restlessly for his anguish was hard to bear. They were all young, inexperienced in the art of the air battles in which they would be asked to take part, and the fine fun of it had suddenly become the grief and shock of their comrade. They had heard of the aircraft which had already been brought down, but they had been from other squadrons and though they had been concerned, of course, it had not touched them personally.

'Go on, my boy, what happened then?' The commanding officer's voice was gentle.

'Sir, oh sir . . .' He might still have been at school, a boy addressing his headmaster. 'It simply . . . exploded, sir.' His voice rose and the officer gripped him by the arms quite forcefully. He must control himself now, his expression said, or he would be of no use to them, to himself or to the man with whom he would fly in future.

'It burst into flames, sir . . . flames . . . Dear God, and the flames were . . . Oh Jesus.'

'And Lieutenant Hunter, boy, did you see him leave the crash?' The officer's voice was urgent.

'No sir . . . oh no sir . . . he was still in it, sir, he was still in it, sir . . . burning.' The boy clawed at his own face, quite unable to bear the pictures his mind conjured up.

'You did not see him . . . after the crash.'

'No . . . I've just told you . . . it was burning.'

'You flew over it . . . flew low enough to . . . to see Lieutenant Hunter?'

'I went down, sir . . .' The young officer had begun to calm himself, though his tears still flowed unchecked across his smooth, boyish cheeks and his eyes stared at the horror he had seen but he was falling into the level of shock which allowed him to endure it. 'I went right down sir . . . to have . . . a look.'

'Good lad, that was brave.'

'. . . but . . . but it was burning . . . against the hedge. There were men . . . soldiers, German I think . . . it was confusing . . .'

'Of course . . .'

'. . . and I could see nothing except . . . except flames and smoke . . . but no-one left the aircraft, sir . . . no-one, no-one.'

The commanding officer stood up painfully. It was the first casualty of his squadron. The first man and craft to go down and it was hard to bear. There would be others, for like the two who had gone out so joyously this morning, and on other mornings, he was perfectly certain that this war would be fought not only on the ground and on the seas, but in the air.

He turned to the mechanic who hovered respectfully at his elbow, the very man, arrived only the day before, who had serviced Lieutenant Hunter's machine before he took off.

'See to him, will you . . . er . . .'

'Johnson, sir.'

'Look after him, Johnson and don't leave him alone until I get back. If he doesn't come out of it we shall have to get the MO, to have a look at him.'

'Leave it to me, sir. I'll keep an eye on him.'

They found the young officer an hour later wandering about the perimeter of the flying field apparently looking for 'Nanny, who would be cross if she saw his dirty face.'

Of the mechanic who had been ordered to keep an eye on him there was no sign and when the commanding officer, suspicious, made enquiries at headquarters of him, it was discovered that the man simply did not exist!

The letter came at the end of November. It was a private letter addressed to Miss M. Hughes, from the commanding officer of the squadron in which Lieutenant Martin Hunter had so briefly, so tragically served. It stated simply that as no record could be found of a relative of Lieutenant Hunter they were forwarding this letter, addressed to her, with this notification. Her name had been on the enclosed envelope which, unfortunately the censor had to open. The officer sympathised with Miss Hughes, regretting his sad duty in reporting Lieutenant Hunter missing, believed killed. She appeared to be the sole beneficiary of the officer's estate in his will, a copy of which was enclosed and she was advised to consult a solicitor as soon as she was able.

Martin's letter was short.

My darling,
  I love you. There is really nothing more to be said but those words. If it had been allowed we would have been lovers, friends, dear and close, trusting, giving to one another the joy of sharing life's pleasures and sorrows, however large, or small. You know me as no other person does and you have the whole of me now, and always. Be happy, my beautiful girl. I cannot believe we shall not meet again for surely it cannot end here. Meg, I love you so.

Martin.

She went into her room and locked the door and drew the curtains in that first moment after reading the letter and sat down on the floor and put her hands over her ears as if the action would prevent her from hearing her world break to pieces around her. She sat like that for a long time and when they came and knocked on her door, asking what they should do about the menus – for Miss Hughes saw to those personally – she did not answer since she did not hear them.

She sat like a marble statue for twelve unmoving hours, her eyes fixed on the emptiness of her life and whispered madly to herself for she was quite out of her mind.

'He was my whole life. What shall I do now?' she asked herself, and her body rocked back and forth in torment.

'Where has he gone?' she moaned. 'The world is so cold without him in it,' but there was no-one there and no-one answered for it was the first time in her life Meg Hughes had been completely alone.

She would have stayed there, dying of it, Annie Hardcastle supposed – had their Edie been made of the stuff which obeys orders and speaks when spoken to and takes no interest in what her employer did as long as she was given her wages at the end of the week – but Edie Marshall remembered Meg Hughes' treatment of her at 'The Hawthorne Tree' and her appreciation, quite openly and delightfully displayed when Edie had worked for her. She remembered Meg Hughes' undeniable pleasure when Edie had promised to come with her to 'Hilltops'.

'Oh thank you, Edie,' she had said, 'it will be reassuring to have someone I can trust in the kitchens,' and she had given her the splendid job of housekeeper which meant Edie did not have the hard, manual work she had done all her life and which she was getting too old to perform and she did not forget those kindnesses. Miss Hughes had been off-colour for a while, out of sorts and peaky, then, just as suddenly, for the space of a month or two she had gone about singing even though Mr Tom had left for the training camp and her face had been rosy and her eyes filled with the loveliest light though Edie could not begin to guess why.

But as she confessed to Annie on the telephone two days after Miss Hughes took to her bed, she didn't like it one bit. Not a sound out of her, she said, though Jenny swore she heard someone moaning in the vicinity of Miss Hughes' bedroom but how much credence one could give to that was anyone's guess for Jenny Swales was known to be of a highly imaginative nature.

'Did anything happen, Edie?' The tinny voice of Annie Hardcastle asked and Edie held the receiver away from her ear since she was not awfully sure of the damage it might do to her. She wouldn't have used the contraption at all but really she was that worried about Miss Hughes. Two days and no-one had seen her, nor heard her voice even, and the post office two doors up from Annie's was very obliging in the matter of telephone calls, bringing anyone from the village to the store in cases of emergency.

'What d'you mean, Annie?'

'Did anything happen to upset her?'

'Not that I know of. Eeh, Annie, I don't know what to do. I've knocked a dozen times a day but there's no answer. If she's not well . . .'

'Has she heard from Mr Tom?'

'No, but she had a letter postmarked in France. Mind you she's had a few of them lately but this looked official . . .'

'I'll be on the next train, Edie.'

Meg lay rigid in her bed and she was aware, somewhere in the drifting waves of agony and mad dashing boulders of the grief which hurled themselves at her, that she would die of it quite soon for the heart of her was gone and it was not in her to live any longer in this world without Martin. She did not sleep except for a light fitful doze from which she came again and again on an anguished cry which escaped from between her bitten lips. Her body hurt all over, even the inside of her mouth and the roots of her hair and she wondered how it was possible to bear such pain and still live.

When morning broke for the second time she rose from her bed and sat for hours in a chair by the window, the chink of daylight which crept through the drawn curtains emphasising the ravages of her face, her untidy snarl of hair, her blank, unwashed sourness and the limp clasping of her soiled hands between which the letter still lay. She slumped on the bed or sat in the chair and stared sightlessly at the drawn curtain and that was all – for Meg Hughes was rapidly sinking into the indifferent, heedless, mindless state of the deranged and there was no-one to stop her until Annie Hardcastle ordered the locked door to be broken down. She stood, appalled for the space of five seconds, staring at Meg's shrunken, wax-like face and plum encircled eyes, gagging on the stale and foetid smell which was captured in the closed and shuttered room, before throwing her not inconsiderable weight across the room to the chair in which Meg sat.

She sent them all away, all those curious and staring strangers who were Megan Hughes' staff, for it had needed the man and the boy to help to shatter the door, and she and Edie lifted her from her chair and stripped her. They bathed her own filth from her and washed her hair and changed her bed, flinging open the window to let in light and fresh air. Edie was sent running to the kitchen, ignoring the questioning eyes of those about her, and she was so upset she told young Jenny Swales who had the impudence to ask after Miss Hughes to mind her own damned business, and she whipped up eggs and sherry in milk.

They put it in her hand and she drank it obediently as she would have done poison if asked, but she did not speak nor raise her eyes beyond the hand which put the glass in hers. She had reacted only when they had tried to take the letter from her, struggling silently, ferociously until it was returned to her when she fell again into her trance-like state and Annie Hardcastle knew she must be brought from the senseless state she was in before it was too late.

'Megan,' she had said quite loudly for several minutes but Megan might have been deaf and mute for all the good it did.

'*Megan Hughes!*' Her voice thundered about the room and escaped from the wide open windows into the gardens where Albert and the boy hovered. The servants, and even the guests now knew there was something very wrong with the elegant Miss Hughes, for an hotel, no matter how well organised, will not run, hitch free, without its leader. Edie Marshall was a splendid housekeeper, hardworking, conscientious and exceedingly efficient but she needed orders, direction, lacking the inventive creativity which Miss Hughes brought to the fine dishes she cooked. There had been several small mishaps, a touch of – well, one could only call it carelessness, a feeling of something, one could not quite put one's finger on it, missing, and where was Miss Hughes, the guests asked, for she surely would put it right?

'*Megan Hughes*.' The voice of Annie Hardcastle could clearly be heard along quiet hallways and in suites where guests held their breath in amazement. It rolled across gardens and down to the lake and they all distinctly heard the slap which Annie administered with all the force she could muster to Megan Hughes' face.

There was silence after that and only Edie heard the muffled, anguished weeping of the woman in Annie Hardcastle's arms, and only she saw the dazed pain of bereavement turn to the awakened agony Megan Hughes suffered in her bitter grieving. When it was done and she was outwardly herself again, only she heard her beg Annie to stay with her.

They were in the pretty sitting-room a few days later. Though she had not as yet been seen by her guests, or even by the staff of the hotel, it had become known that Miss Hughes was herself again, the mysterious illness with which she had been struck down nearly gone and that the high standards on which she insisted, even in these straitened days, would once again be restored.

'I shall need someone, Annie. You know why!'

'Aye lass, I reckon I do, but there's Will. I cannot leave him.'

'Can you not persuade him to come with you? There is more than enough work for both of you. I ... there is so much to be done ... I do not think I can do it alone.' It was said simply and the older woman felt her heart move in compassion. 'I have been in touch ... a solicitor ... he called this morning at my request and he tells me ... the ... the will must be ... we must obtain probate but ... when we do, I must either sell ... or run his business ... Martin's ...' Her voice was ragged and her pale, sad face worked in an effort not to weep again. 'I ... these last months since he went away and I believed we ... would be married. When I knew ...' Her hand trembled and she pressed it firmly against her lips as though to contain the cry of agony which begged to come out. She drew in her breath, fighting to continue. 'I let it ... slip away, Annie. I seemed not to care much anymore ... about the hotel. The war had come and the ... and ... I was

. . . I slipped into a state of . . . merely waiting for him. That's who I became. The woman who waited for Martin Hunter. What did it matter if the servants left to go into factories, or that I had to close so many rooms. I was to be . . . married. I suppose it was because . . . of the way I was . . . but nothing else was important to me. Not the hotel, nor the hard work, nor the sacrifices Tom and I had made to get where we did. I . . . drifted . . . waiting . . . for him and now he is not to come home to me . . . and there is only this left for me to do. The hotel . . . and . . .'

'What will you do, love?' Annie's face was inordinately sad.

'Oh Annie, I cannot sell . . . what he has created. I know nothing of aeroplanes, or indeed motor cars except how to drive one. I might founder, knowing little of how such a business is run but I must try. I . . . I promised him. He has good men, an engineer he trusts. I know nothing of the technical side but if a knowledge of business and finance is any help then I must do the best I can with it. Surely it can be no different from running any other concern. Such as this hotel, for instance? I make and sell a product here and I will try to do the same with Martin's company. I have seen the books and it seems in good heart . . .' Her voice faltered, then became stronger. 'I can only try, Annie, but . . . if you could see your way . . . my God . . . I need your help, Annie, I really do.'

Annie sighed. 'Megan, oh Megan, it's a hard row you are to work and I don't know how you are to do it, lass, but if anyone can do it, it's you. You will have to . . . well, my lass, you can't go on forever and this place takes some looking after, let alone dashing off to Camford all the time . . .'

'That's why I want you to come, Annie. Edie is a superb worker but you . . . you could help me with the cooking and run the hotel . . .'

'You may have no hotel to run, my girl, when they get to know about . . .' She nodded her head in the direction of Meg.

'I understand that, Annie.' It was said with quiet dignity.

'It'll take some swallowing, you know that. I'm . . . well, I've grown fond of you, Megan, but if you weren't as dear to me as my own daughter I'm bound to say I'd feel the same as they will.'

'I know, Annie.'

'I can't approve, lass.'

For the first time in days Meg Hughes smiled. It had not the brilliance nor the humour which had once lit her face, but in it was a strength now, and a quiet joy which said she would manage somehow. There was not acceptance, for Martin Hunter's death could never be accepted, but there was a trust there that she would survive it, and a certainty that, now she had the reason to do so, she would fight to keep it.

'You will come, Annie?'

'Aye, if Will agrees.'

'Thank you.'

'Shall you tell Mr Tom soon?'

'I must.'

'He knows that Mr Hunter is . . .?'

'Yes. I rang his commanding office in Edinburgh. They brought him to the telephone. He is to have compassionate leave. I told them they were brothers.'

'Brothers!'

'Well, they were, Annie. They were brought up as brothers.'

'When will he be home?'

'Tomorrow.'

Chapter thirty-three

He held her in his arms and wept and because she could not bear it she wept again with him and for a long time they simply stood with their arms about one another, grieving for the man, the boy, the friend and protector who had been the cornerstone of the triangle which had formed their lives.

Tom could not speak at first. He sat on her settee in his ill-fitting khaki uniform and held the brandy she pressed into his hand, staring at it with a face in which the expression of loss was etched in deep, painful grooves. He sipped it at regular intervals, not really tasting it, but the warmth of it put some colour into his drawn cheeks and at last he was calm.

He had come down by train from Edinburgh to Stoke-on-Trent and then by a series of frequent changes to Ashbourne, taking a taxi-cab from there to the hotel. He wore a rough pair of service trousers with puttees and enormous heavy boots. His jacket was slightly short for he was a tall man though the buttons were as bright and gleaming as new golden sovereigns. He had removed his peaked cap, and the webbing and ammunition pouches which had been strapped across his chest, and on the floor where he had dropped them was the paraphernalia of war which he must now carry about with him wherever he went. His rifle and tin hat, his haversack and water bottle and the iron rations he must always have about him in case of emergency.

He was exhausted after the long and cumbersome journey he had made, for troops were being hurried here and there as the war gathered impetus and the train schedules were organised solely for the purpose, or so it seemed, of serving Kitchener's 'Call to Arms'. The General had asked at first for 100,000 men, and then, before the end of August, for another 100,000 more and by mid September half a million had been enlisted. The recruitment of another half a million was still going on and they had all to be moved to a place of training before being shipped to France. Tom himself would be off soon, bound by his King's shilling and by his oath. He had been longing for it, for the glory of defending his country alongside his 'pals', and Martin, and now, just as he was about to embark on it, this wonderful adventure, the splendour of it had been torn from him by the death of the man he had loved more than any other, the man he had admired above any other, the man he had called PAL longer than any other.

'I can't believe it,' he said at last. He raised his haggard face, running a trembling hand through the shorn crop of his curls. 'I just can't believe it. Dammit, the bloody war's only been going five minutes and . . .'

'He's not the first to . . . there are already thousands of casualties, Tom, you know that. Edie's cousin's son at a place called Mons, killed on the day after his regiment got there and Jenny's brother was wounded in the same battle . . .'

She stopped, her voice petering out raggedly for though it was sad, the death and wounding of strangers, what was it to do with her? How could she feel the pain as she felt the pain, the agony of knowing she would never see Martin again. Her heart hurt her sorely and constantly and never seemed to ease. 'Remembered most clearly are those who are loved and lost, for the heartache remains.' Where had she read those words, she thought tiredly? She could not recall but they were true. Even now Martin's face was clearly printed before her eyes, on her eyelids when she closed them and though it hurt her desperately to look into his loving brown eyes how could she attempt to push them away, despite the despairing pain they caused? And yet . . .

She sighed heavily, her breath tremulous in her throat but in her eyes there was a softness, a tender candle-flame of hope and it must be heeded. Be recognised and acknowledged and given life.

But before she could speak Tom spoke. He put down the glass he held and took her hand in his. It was gentle, all the love he had for her trembling through his fingers into hers and though his face was strained and filled with sorrow there was resignation there, acceptance and something else which held him steady.

'How . . . how did it happen, Meg? D'you know?'

'Not really. His aircraft crashed . . .' She put her hand to her mouth, '. . . they didn't say how, only that he wouldn't have . . . have known anything about it. Quick, the commanding officer said . . . and merciful . . .'

'Was he . . . was he in the "Wren"?' Tom's face crumpled for they both knew that Martin had loved his little aeroplane more than anything he had ever created and if he had to die, surely that was how he would have wished it?

'Yes ... in the "Wren".'

Tom cleared his throat which threatened to clog up again. His hand carressed her's and his shoulder leaned companionably, as it had always done, touching and warming and comforting her own.

'You know, Meggie,' his voice was sad but stronger now and filled with resolve, 'we can't go on waiting any more, can we, sweetheart? This ... has brought it home to me more than anything that ... that life is ... uncertain now and we mustn't waste what we have. I was going to ask you if we could do it before I go to France. A lot of the men are, but this ... Martin going like he has ... well ...'

She wrenched her hand from his and stood up with a suddenness which startled him. Her face jerked convulsively and she put out her hands in the manner of one who is blind, feeling her way, it seemed, to the window. When she reached it she stared sightlessly across the bare gardens, covered now in layers of dead leaves which the man who had replaced Tom brushed and raked in an effort to keep the lawns tidy. They lay in brown smudged heaps as he placed them ready for burning. The trees were stark and naked and the gracefully shaped branches of the larch trees on the far side of the lake had taken on the crêped, lacy look of winter. Across the lawn drifted the winter smell of wood smoke from the bonfires, lit by the gardener, at the back of the hotel.

'Tom ...'

'What is it, my darling?' His voice was soft, vibrant with his love for her.

'Tom ... dear Tom ... I cannot marry you.'

'Meggie ...' She could almost hear the smile in his voice as though he could not quite believe what he had heard and was in fact, more amused than concerned. She must be thinking of Martin, he seemed to say, afraid that what had happened to him would happen to himself. All women were afraid for their men. It was only natural but it was no reason to delay their marriage. The reverse, he thought, though there were men who could not bear to think they might make some woman a widow, perhaps with a child to bring up alone. But Tom Fraser was not one of them. Nothing was going to happen to him, he would make certain of it!

'I cannot marry you, Tom,' she said again.

'Now Meggie . . .' He stood up and moved to where she leaned against the window. He turned her about to look at him, his hands on her shoulders, his bright blue eyes like speedwells in the brown strength of his face. He had aged somewhat in the last few months, the hard routine of drilling and rifle training, the vague but certain knowledge that he was learning how to kill another man giving him a maturity which showed in the strong and resolute firmness of his mouth. He had always been light-hearted, engaging, quite happy to leave responsibility and all that went with it to the other two but now, with the added sorrow of Martin's death sitting sadly on his weary shoulders, Tom Fraser was a complete man at last.

'You musn't worry, love,' he said gently. 'What happened to Martin won't happen to me. I'll come back to you, sweetheart, I promise you but before I go let me . . . let me love you, Meg. Really love you.' He hung his head almost shyly, then lifted his clear, steadfast eyes to hers. 'You know what I mean, Meg, don't you? I've waited so long now. I want to hold you in my arms before I go and make love to . . .'

'Tom . . . No . . . No . . . Tom . . .' She almost screamed out loud with the horror of it, with the pain and devastation she must heap on him but how could she let him go on? How could she listen to him saying all the words Martin had said to her. They had been beautiful, complete and perfect with Martin. They had melted her heart and brought it love and joy and wooed her body until she had wept in her delight. With Martin they had been right, they had been what she wanted to hear, what she had wanted to *say* and the wonder of them had satisfied her woman's heart and mind and body. They had belonged to her, and to Martin, but not to Tom! Not spoken to her by Tom and in that agonised realisation she at last knew what she had done to him in letting him believe *she* loved him. She *did* love him but not as she had loved, *still* loved Martin.

But she must draw about her the strength to tell him, to take that look from his face, to dam up the love which poured from his eyes and stop the words which hovered, longing to be spoken, on his lips.

'Sit down, Tom.' Her voice was harsh and he stepped warily

away from her, like a boy who has done no wrong but knows he is to be punished for it. But he was not a boy and he had done no wrong and she saw the uncompromising awareness of it come to his eyes and they turned to that vivid, icy blue of his affronted manliness.

'Sit down! Why must I sit down?'

'Because I have something to tell you!'

'And can it not be said face to face?' He was cautious but still insistent that he would not be treated like a child. He was a soldier now and he had just asked the woman he loved to marry him before he went to war, and what was wrong with that, his truculent expression asked.

'Oh Tom . . . Tom . . .' She turned from him, almost weeping. He had no idea, none, of the savage blow she was to deliver and there was no way to soften it. No way to turn the edge of the knife from his sensitive flesh. It must be done quickly, cleanly, cruelly.

'I can find no other way to tell you than plainly.'

'For God's sake get on with it then!'

'I am to have Martin's child.'

The words hung delicately on the air, drifting it seemed, this way and that as Tom Fraser's mind considered them. They made no sense, of course, none at all for Martin Hunter was dead and Megan Hughes belonged to *him*, Tom Fraser so how could she . . . how could she . . . and Martin Hunter was dead . . . was dead . . . was dead . . . and Megan Hughes belonged to . . . to . . . to . . . *Martin Hunter*!

'No . . . oh no . . . no . . . no . . .'

'Tom . . .'

She had taken a step away from him for although she had expected a raging bitterness, the mortification of pain and shock, she had not believed a human face could express such agony of spirit, and she saw her own each day in the mirror! His eyes were glazed with it as though he burned inside his own body. The flames had branded their message into his brain and it repeated, hammer blow after hammer blow, the words which told him that Martin Hunter had, after all, taken what was his. He had seen it in his eyes but not believed it. He had known but had refused to face it and now she had told him the truth of it and over and over again the words struck him and he staggered back from her, like a man who is threatened with a lethal weapon.

409

'Tom . . .' She put out a compassionate hand to him, the hand of a friend for that was all she could ever be to him, but he struck at it blindly, frenziedly, as though he could no longer bear her touch.

'No . . .' His voice was thick in his throat.

'Tom, let me . . .'

'No . . .'

'Tom, I'm sorry!'

'Sorry!'

'We . . .'

'Don't . . . don't tell me.'

'Tom . . .'

'I . . . must go.'

'Go where? Please . . . Tom . . .' She offered him her hand again then withdrew it hurriedly for he was looking at her with such loathing, such terror she began to be afraid.

'Let me . . . won't you . . .?' What could she offer him, her mind agonised, to replace what she had taken from him? What could she say to make him see that what had happened had not been planned, that she and Martin had come together as naturally as the rain falls to the earth. They had loved him, both of them with a deep and enduring strength for he was a part of them, an intrinsic part of their lives, but sadly, there was not . . . there had not been a place for him on the journey she and Martin had begun together and which now would never be finished.

'Tom . . . will you let me talk to you? You have a right to . . .'

'To what, Megan Hughes? I believed I had a right to *you*. You told me you loved me . . .'

'I did . . . I do . . .'

He seemed not to hear. His whole body shook, was charged with an explosive tension which threw him about the room, taking him from one side to the other, knocking him carelessly against furniture and finally bringing him face to face with a wall where he stood, eyes staring tormentedly at the wallpaper.

'. . . all this time I waited. I cannot believe I have been such a fool . . . trusting you . . . and him.'

'We did nothing to harm you Tom, nothing . . . only . . .'

'Nothing! And yet you are to have . . . his . . . his child.'

'Please, oh dear God . . . Tom.' She must try to make him understand that – oh sweet Lord – how could she help him? He hurt so much. She could feel his pain beat against her in waves!

410

If she could explain to him that she and Martin had only once ... Her heart was wounded with the thought ... only once, and her own pain was almost too much to bear ... how could she tell him? It belonged to her and Martin, a sweet, jealously guarded memory and could not be shared, not even to ease Tom's anguish.

With a sudden movement he turned from the wall and without speaking again he stumbled with broken body and heart towards the door.

'Tom ...'

He opened it, his hand on the doorknob like that of a child who has not yet mastered the art of turning it. His face was white and sweating and his chest heaved as though he was about to vomit. She heard him blunder up the hallway, his boots loud and hurtful on the parquet floor, and go down the stairs and her mind had time to consider in that dreadful moment, the effect the sight of him might have on her guests.

He came back the next day. She had spent the night sitting in a chair by her window, watching the moon slip in and out of the silver-edged clouds, watching as it moved across the sky hour after hour, waiting for him to come back. Annie slipped in a time or two, putting a hand on her shoulder comfortingly, standing with her for five minutes, watching the night, sharing her vigil. She brought her tea and without speaking sat and drank a cup with her, then went away again but letting it be known she was about should she be needed.

It was dawn. There was merely a blush of pink on the edge of the hills shading up to yellow and pale, pale blue and though the moon had gone there was a scattering of stars where it had been. She saw him come up the drive, his body dragging in weariness, a dark shadow against the darker bushes. She saw him stand for a moment by the lake, outlined against its breeze ruffled silver, then he turned and when he reached her room he entered without knocking as though in his despair he had no time for such niceties. What were they when put against what he had been through, his attitude said?

'Tom.' Her voice was a whisper in the lightening room.

'The child must have a name.'

'Tom!' She sat up slowly and her heart began to race.

'Are you to make Martin Hunter's child a bastard, Megan Hughes?'

'Tom . . .' It seemed she could say nothing but his name.

'I have been up . . . I did not know where to go . . .'

'Sit down, Tom, or come to the kitchen and I'll make us some tea. There will be no-one there at this . . .'

'I had to think . . .' He stared at a spot directly above her head, his eyes pale and clouded in the faded hue of the dawn light. 'I went up to the top and found a place to . . . I needed to be alone to think it through. I had heard what you had said, about you and Martin . . . and the . . . the child, and though the words . . .'

His voice, which at first had been hesitant, became stronger and more positive.

'I had heard them, those words you spoke, and had been, I thought, destroyed by them. I could not cope with it, you see, so I retreated into . . . into somewhere . . . safe, where they couldn't hurt me. I sat . . . I don't know how long, and watched the night things . . . rabbits, a field mouse and others. I suppose I was so still and quiet they thought I was part of the moor. And I was, I suppose. I am, Megan Hughes! Part of this moor and these hills. I love it up here. I have from the first time we came up together. We made a life. It is our life . . . *my life*. I must go away now . . .' He laughed harshly and the young and eager soldier, the idealist who had thrilled to the concept of patriotism and glory, had gone forever. 'To defend that life. But if I survive I want to come back to it, you see. I want to come back to it! It is as much mine as it is yours and I will not let what you and Martin Hunter have done take it from me . . .'

'Tom, you know I would not turn you out! This is . . .'

'So how are we to manage it then? Our . . . situation has been accepted, just, by those who stay here because it was known we were engaged, that we were soon to be married. Now, before long it will be seen that you are . . . pregnant, that I am away fighting for my country and you will be discredited. No-one will stay in a hotel which is run by a loose woman, for that is what they will call you.'

'Dear God, Tom . . . please . . . you cannot mean what you are . . .' She was distraught but he did not listen to her, indeed he appeared neither to listen to nor be aware of anything but the words he himself spoke.

'This is mine, this hotel and I intend to keep it and if it is left to you it will founder. It will go down, you will go down and I will go down with you. I never thought I could believe that. You

412

were always the strong one, the one who fought for what we would have and whose will held it together. It was you who harried the bank into giving us a loan. It was you who invested what we had, so positive that what I saw as a gamble was really no more than a practical way to make our money grow. You did all these things, but it was *me* who stood beside you, not Martin Hunter. It was me who supported you, who was always there to listen to you, and what I often considered to be your daft ideas. I've worked bloody hard for the best part of my life but never as hard as these last four years and I'm not going to have it chucked away because Martin Hunter couldn't keep his bloody hands off you . . . *and you allowed it!*'

'Tom . . . please . . .'

'Don't "Tom, please" me, Megan, We need each other, you and me. You need a name for your child and I need to know that what I have will still be here when I come home!'

They were married by special licence two days later, and on the same day Corporal Tom Fraser took the train to Edinburgh leaving his lovely wife to drive their motor car back to their hotel from the registry office in Buxton. There were a dozen or so young couples at the railway station, embracing unashamedly, soldiers with wives and sweethearts, boys some of them with their mothers, trying to be brave and there were more than a few curious glances cast on the strangeness of the elegantly dressed young woman who stood so quietly beside the tall soldier. They did not touch, nor even speak though it was seen she wore a wedding ring and whose could it be but his?

The train was stuffed to the luggage racks with soldiers, volunteers dying to get 'over there', anticipating a brisk, spectacular and triumphant campaign, worrying that it might be over before they got to it.

At the last moment, as he climbed into a compartment, Meg put out her hand to him for how could they part like this? The last two days and what had happened this morning were like some dream which, when she woke up would slip away and be forgotten, but this moment was real, Tom's drawn face was real, these soldiers, boys no more, most of them, were real and they were off to something no-one knew anything about and it frightened her. Martin had gone like this, she supposed, and was never to come back, and might not Tom do the same. Dear God . . . to lose both of them! Both her dear childhood companions. She had lost her lover and now, perhaps the only real friend she had in the world.

'Tom . . . take care . . . please . . .'

She put her bare hand on his where it rested on the frame of the open window but he withdrew it hastily, turning away to find a place for his things.

'Tom . . .'

'Goodbye, Meg.'

'Tom . . . oh Tom, will you write?'

'Write?' His face spasmed in pain.

'Please . . .' Her voice was no more than a whisper. The train began to move and at the last moment those about her could see that the strange and beautiful woman was weeping just as despairingly as they.

The official letter came six months later.

Sir/Madame, [The 'Sir' had been crossed out.]

It is my painful duty to inform you that no further news having been received relative to:

(RANK) Lieutenant

(NAME) Martin Hunter

(REGIMENT) Royal Flying Corps

who has been missing since 10.11.14, the Army Council have been regretfully constrained to conclude that he is dead and that his death took place on 10.11.14.

I am to express to you the sympathy of the Army Council with you in your loss.

There were other remarks regarding Lieutenant Hunter's personal effects and a note explaining that as she was the sole beneficiary under the terms of Lieutenant Hunter's will, though they were not related, she had been officially recognised as his next of kin and would therefore be informed when these would be released to her.

It was addressed to Miss M. Hughes but Mrs Tom Fraser opened it and wept, for in her arms she held the two-day-old daughter of Lieutenant Martin Hunter.

Chapter thirty-four

Fred had smiled at first when she told him she wanted to learn to fly.

'Mrs Fraser, really! What on earth do you want to do that for? There's no need for it. Angus can do all the testing that's called for and besides, it's not fitting for a lady to fly!'

'Not fitting! What on earth does that mean, Fred?' She smiled and shook her head and her bright crop of curls stood up about it in a positive halo, Fred thought, or a glowing, flame-coloured dandelion clock, the kind he had blown on as a child. She had had it cut several months ago, to his secret dismay, for really her hair was so beautiful, her crowning glory as they used to say, but she had sworn she was far too busy now, with an hotel, an aircraft industry and the automobile factory to run, and could not spend half her day fiddling about with pins and combs. But then so many young women of the day were having their hair 'bobbed' as it was called, for convenience and for safety's sake since the machinery which many of them worked could be dangerous, and he supposed it was only sensible but he did wish Mrs Fraser had not thought it necessary to do the same. Not that he voiced an opinion, one way or the other for it was nothing to do with him what his employer did and he agreed with her that the demands placed upon her by Martin Hunter's death were heavy, and in his private opinion, more than most women could have borne, but still . . . it was a pity.

He recalled distinctly the emotions she had induced in him on that first day she had come to the airfield after Mr Hunter's death. She had worn dove-grey, a fine woollen coat, long with a full back, belted and with big pockets. It had a draped, cross-over front and a deep collar but though it was roomy it could not hide the swelling curve of her pregnancy. They had heard, of course, that she had married recently, only a few weeks before Christmas and here she was on the second day of January very evidently more than a month gone with child. But it was not Fred Knowsley's concern and in these days of relaxed morality and the high fever of excitement which the war brought about in the young, it no longer surprised him. At least she *was* married!

She had been over before, of course, talking airily of 'carrying on' whilst Mr Hunter was in France and being quite certain that if they all pulled together and continued with what Mr Hunter had begun, knowing absolutely *nothing* of what that might be, they could keep it all intact for him until he came home and if Mr Knowsley would let her have the books she would do the monthly accounts. She had even promised to have a word with the Ministry chaps about a war contract when they came to inspect the factory, all glowing with enthusiasm and some inner beauty which, really, had been a treat to see.

A few weeks later Martin Hunter had been posted missing, believed killed and they had not seen her again until the New Year. She had moved that day through the hangar, the light of her blown out, turning every head as she walked with quiet dignity, a composure which seemed to speak of great pain held rigidly under control. They watched her respectfully, all of them, their heads bowed slightly, their gaze ready to dart away should it meet hers, for they knew by then that Martin Hunter had left everything he had to this woman.

'Mr Knowsley,' she said and held out her hand and he took it gently for it was all there for him to read in her eyes what she had been to Martin Hunter, 'or may I still call you Fred?' she added and for a moment her face was lit by the memory of the smile she once had.

'Please . . . I would be honoured, Miss Hughes . . . oh, I do beg your pardon.'

'That's alright, it is Mrs Fraser now, Fred.'

'Of course,' and he managed to keep his kindly grey eyes from dropping to her waist.

'I was wondering if we might talk, Fred. There is much to be discussed and I shall not be able to get over for much longer . . .'

He was mortified. 'Mrs Fraser, why did you not telephone? I could have come up to the hotel. You should not be on your feet, indeed you should not . . . Please, ma'am . . .' He was a bachelor and unused to such situations and surely she should not be here, under the gaze of these fascinated men who remembered her previous visits, but she was looking about her, still holding his hand.

'I wanted to . . . to have a look, see again what he had done, Fred. You understand?' And indeed he did, instantly, for though he had not married Fred Knowsley had known love, once, and recognised it in this young woman's face, but his own showed only concern and respect.

'Is there somewhere we can talk,' she went on but her eyes had strayed to the office where once, he remembered, she had gone with Martin Hunter, and they became quite haunted and hurriedly, for he could not bear that these staring men should see it, he began to draw her away.

'Come into my office, Mrs Fraser,' he said, 'and I'll send one of the lads for tea. We can talk there,' and she had gone, thankfully, not yet ready to face those two enchanted ghosts.

'Fred . . .' she said as he put her carefully into his own chair.

'Yes Mrs Fraser?'

'I have come to apologise for my behaviour when last I was here . . .'

'Mrs Fraser, I cannot think what you mean.'

'Oh yes. I acted as though I had merely to come in and look around, study the books for an hour and the whole business would run just as it had always done. I was quite insufferable, Fred and I'm sorry. You and . . . and Martin were trained . . . worked hard to come by the knowledge and experience which made you successful and it was presumptuous of me to think I . . . well . . . I had a damned cheek . . . you will know what I am trying to say. I know nothing about Martin's concern, beyond what he told me, but I must learn and I am here to ask if you will teach me?'

'Mrs Fraser, I would gladly do anything in my power, anything at all to keep Mr Hunter's business alive but I cannot think . . .'

'Oh I know, I am a woman and how can a woman do the work of a man, but Fred, I do not mean you to make me into an engineer! I could never be that but then there is no need for I have one in you. You are the engineer and if you will accept the post will become *chief* engineer, for I intend to employ another, and I wish also to offer you the position of manager. No, I do not want thanks. What I want is to know *how* the business works. How the aircraft and the automobiles are found a buyer. What they cost to build and what we can get when we sell what we have made. The technical side of it will be your concern but the business and financial side will be my responsibility. I have a good business head, Fred and can understand many things in the world

417

of commerce that many men cannot but I must know the pounds shillings and pence of the concern, the accounting and costing system, the management of the employees. We can find a designer, a draughtsman, whatever is needed. If there are buyers to be had, customers, then I will find them . . . well, when I am . . . soon, but until then I want you to let me come here and stand beside you, explain to me whilst I am still able . . . to drive my motor and get up here, what makes this factory tick. I want to meet the manager of the motor car factory and he and I will discuss what we are to do with it for no-one, for a while, is going to buy a motor car and so we must find something else to keep the factory running. What can we manufacture *instead* of the motor car? There is so much to learn, Fred and with your help I will learn it. I *can* do it, but I cannot do it alone. Will you help me, Fred?'

'Mrs Fraser, I can understand your enthusiasm but I really don't think I can . . .'

'*I must do it*, Fred!'

'But you are . . .'

'I know . . .' She smiled and Fred was confounded when she placed her hand quite naturally on her swollen stomach, looking down at it with all the love in the world in her eyes, '. . . but I shall have my child in April and there is someone who will look after it whilst I am here so . . . will you help me, Fred . . . please.' Her eyes swam with sudden tears and he felt his throat swell. 'Fred, please say you will help me keep Martin Hunter's dream alive. You see, while *it* lives, so does he!'

As Megan Fraser had predicted, the war effectively brought to a halt the building of the Hunter family motor car but in June she went alone to London and within a week was back at Watkins Field with a government contract in her hand. Her face was rosy and her eyes shone with excitement.

'Well done, Mrs Fraser,' they said, but she laughed and her eyebrows tilted wryly.

'Nay, they were giving them out like sweeties, Fred. Anyone who has a work bench and can turn a lathe or even knock nails in a piece of wood is a Godsend to them for they need men like us to build their machines for them!'

'But what sort of machines, Mrs Fraser,' John Reading asked, for he was the manager at 'Hunter Automobiles' and for the last five months had been watching the steady decline of the factory he ran. Many of the men who had been employed there had gone off to France, like the rest of the country's youth and though there had been a couple of orders for a Hunter family motor car, a residue of those taken before the onset of hostilities, they had been the last and now, what could he do but shut the place down, with Mrs Fraser's consent, naturally, and find himself a position elsewhere.

'Motor bikes, Mr Reading!' She was quite glorious in her triumph.

'Motor bikes?'

'Yes, motor bikes. It seems they are used extensively in France. Couriers, I suppose and some with side cars to ferry about the men who run the war. Oh, I know it seems a step backwards after building a motor car but...' She held her breath, like a child about to divulge a secret and Mr Reading could understand quite readily how she had won the government contract she had on the desk before her, despite her assurance that it had been easy. He leaned forward and so did Fred Knowsley though by now Fred had become used to Mrs Fraser's wild and resolute determination to succeed in this.

'... if we are on time with the delivery and the machines are to their satisfaction, a certain gentleman has promised he can guarantee for us other contracts. Vehicles, lorries, staff cars! The war is voracious, gentlemen, needing not just men, but machines, and sadly, another of those is the ambulance. They are badly needed for it seems they are often ... damaged.' The pictures her words conjured up were too much for her and for several seconds she bent her head, then, '... but if they are to be built, we shall build them and to the best of our abilities!'

Older men were found, those not carried away by the excitement of going to war and within weeks the motor car factory was as busy as it had been under the guidance of Martin Hunter. Meg was elated but her elation was tempered by the realisation that it was not Meg Fraser who had brought it about but the demanding need of the Army for transport for its troops.

Young girls were employed to do many of the jobs which, before the war had been exclusively for men, for they were emancipated now, this generation of women, running garages, driving ambulances and omnibuses, becoming mechanically-minded in all manner of work which had been considered fit only for a man.

419

'Hunter Aviation' was thriving. It was almost a year since the war had started and the Royal Flying Corps was beginning to take on an important role in the hostilities, beyond that of reconnaissance patrols above the enemy lines. The first British bombing raid in direct tactical support of a ground operation had occurred in March, comprising attacks on railways which were bringing up German reinforcements in the Menin and Courtrai areas. Single-seat fighters using machine guns were claiming victories, French certainly, but in June the Royal Flying Corps were similarly armed. Aircraft were being shot out of the skies and the demand for new ones was growing with each month.

Martin Hunter's 'Wren' was only one amongst many and Meg was increasingly aware that, just as she had driven his motor car, now she was ready to fly his aeroplane!

Fred Knowsley looked disapprovingly over the top of his spectacles.

'You know what fitting means,' he said in answer to her laughing question, 'and for a lady to take up an aircraft is not fitting. Oh, I know you are going to tell me that ladies have already done so and they have gained a licence to fly but really, I don't know what the authorities are thinking about, giving pilot's certificates to women.'

'Come on, Fred, you know I can do it.'

'Oh, I've no doubt, *and* kill yourself into the bargain.'

'No, I won't do that. Not if I'm taught by a competent flyer. Angus is good. He must be or Martin would not have trusted him to test the "Wren".'

'Meg . . .' He had by now been persuaded to call her by her Christian name. 'Don't do it, lass. You have . . . responsibilities. You cannot chance your life on a whim.'

'It's not a whim, Fred. I *can* do it, and I want . . . to know what it was that Martin knew. I want to share an experience with him.' She looked into his wise eyes, knowing he knew exactly what she meant.

She wore coveralls, a leather jacket, knee-length leather boots, flying helmet and goggles and around her neck an emerald green silk flying scarf, embroidered with her initial, given to her by Fred Knowsley. He said, if she was determined on it she might as well do it right and wear the scarf all flyers wore to protect their neck against the high altitude cold, and for luck, he said, and she would certainly need her fair share of that!

'We'll do a test flight first, Mrs Fraser.' Angus Munro was a Scot and his manner of speaking was laconic but his keen eyes missed nothing from the polish on her boots to the blaze of excitement in his pupil's eyes.

It was a clear day, cool and windless. The sky was a pale silver grey with a tracery across the arch of it like a child's scribble in charcoal. She could see the wind-sock hanging like an empty stocking from its pole, and from the window of his office Fred Knowsley's anxious face as he watched her walk across the field with Angus. She waved to him and he lifted his hand in a gesture which said quite clearly he never expected to see her again and on an impulse she blew him a kiss. She saw his face split into an unwilling smile and he shook his head as though at a wayward child.

She sat in front of Angus as he began the run down the empty strip towards the hedge which surrounded the field, and for an aching moment she was transported back in time – to a sun-filled day when two young men and a girl had stood amongst thousands of others and watched, their breath fast in their throats, their hands to their mouths, their eyes huge and round with wonder as an aircraft such as this had lifted daintily into the air. The silence had been absolute then, but for the noise of the aircraft's engine, until it had soared, with no more substance than a gull, over their heads, then the crowd had roared and the girl had held the hands of her companions and they had smiled at one another brilliantly and jumped up and down for the sheer joy of it and the day had been perfect!

Oh Martin . . . she had time to cry silently then she felt the ground fall away beneath her and the air lifted her up and up and in that moment she felt the warmth of him near her and his hand was again in her's, and she heard his voice speak of his pride and his love for her and for the first time since she had read his letter which even now, as it always did, rested against her heart, she felt a quiet peace settle about her.

She had five glorious minutes in which to look about her, stars of delight in her eyes behind her goggles, to see the undulating carpet of hills and valleys, the squares of the fields in which miniature cows and horses grazed, tiny houses and tinier people and toy motor cars and waggons travelling on thin ribbons of road, then they were over the moor. The low hills looked blue in the hazed mist in which they floated and for a moment she felt

421

alarm for surely they would be lost then the mist lifted and clear over the wings of the aircraft she could see bare trees and stone walls etched against the horizon, a stretch of green turf and heather, still in bloom in places and so close she felt she could reach out and pick some to take back for Annie. There were grey rocks like gravestones and escarpments of rough sandstone, rough worn paths and a tiny stone hut. Though she had walked on this moor a dozen times she knew she had never before seen it, as a bird sees it, the whole stretched out before her in beauty and peace. She was mesmerised to a kind of trance-like state, still as a bird on a branch as the hawk flies overhead, hardly aware that this was a machine she was in, for she was a bird ... when, without warning there was a stutter from the engine, another, then absolute silence and the aircraft slipped sideways and downwards, turning slightly to jink a little and Meg knew they were in that dreadful condition which pilots most fear. A stall! The engine had stalled and if Angus could not right it the craft would simply fall from the sky. She considered in that moment the irony of it for it seemed both she and Martin were to meet their death in the machine he had designed and though she was not afraid she was saddened for surely there must be some fault in ...

'Don't worry, Mrs Fraser,' a calm voice said in her ear. 'We shall be out of this in a moment. The thing to do is keep your head and remember what has been taught you.'

'Indeed Angus, but supposing it is one's first flight as this is mine.'

'The next time this happens you will be qualified to deal with it, as I am so do not worry.'

'I'm not worried, Angus. Let me know if there is anything I can do to help.'

'No thank you. I think I can manage.'

'This is what is known as a stall, is it not, Angus,' she shouted. The craft slipped further sideways and the wind sang in the struts and Meg resisted the temptation to cling to the sides.

'Aye lassie, but you've nothing to worry about,' and in a moment the engine took up its beat again and soared heavenwards and Megan Fraser had, unknowingly passed her first test!

They flew high and wide that day for an hour and a half and when they landed she could not speak at first but clung to Fred Knowsley's hand and her eyes blazed into his. He wondered if there had ever been another woman like her for he had never known one with the sheer spunk she had.

Going up each day for half an hour at a time she was taught the functions of the simple controls. The rudder bar, the joy stick, the rudder, tail plane and elevator. The ailerons, aileron balance wire and control wire and how each worked and flew the craft. She was allowed to take the controls from Angus and felt the machine respond to her hands and feet for the first time and for ten glorious minutes forgot that Angus Munro was behind her as she flew with Martin Hunter.

She was given demonstrations of straight and level flying, the turn, the misuse of controls in a turn, the action of the controls with the motor cut off, slow flying and glide turns, and finally take-off and landings. Each flight was preceded by half an hour of theory.

She was not a born pilot, as she was a driver of her fast little motor car, but her determination, her pride, tenacity, thoroughness and the stubborness with which she had once tackled Mrs Whitley's kitchen floor at Great George Square, and every challenge since, made her an excellent pupil, Angus told her.

She loved it. The lightest pull on the joy-stick and she was climbing up into the hazy light of the pale winter sky, another and the machine, like a frenzied, fragile butterfly was diving towards the earth, another and the butterfly turned to bank and glide, obeying her, loving her, it seemed as she loved it.

'Simple, isn't it?' Angus said at the end of the second week.

'Indeed,' she answered.

'Take her up then!'

'*Solo!*'

'Indeed!'

And so she did and three weeks after she had begun Meg Fraser was granted her pilot's licence.

Chapter thirty-five

In the spring of 1915 in the battles of Ypres and Neuve-Chappelle, the Germans counter-attacked the British Army with great strength and for a while it was thought they might succeed, through the novel use of poison gas, in getting through to the English Channel.

The gas, launched on a favourable wind at dawn was chlorine! The bulk of it fell on an Algerian division which panicked and took a French division with it but the strange green vapour was no respecter of nationality and a company of the 'King's Liverpool Regiment,' the third Liverpool 'Pals' which was attached to a Lancashire Battalion for trench training got a whiff of it, no more, and one of those who suffered was Corporal Tom Fraser.

At first he felt he was drowning but how could that be for he was on dry land, he agonised, and still the flooding of his lungs continued. His head exploded in pain and his mouth was filled with a raging thirst and instinctively he reached for his water bottle for more than anything in the world he needed to quench it.

A sargeant was running along the trench, knocking men backwards, tearing their water bottles from their hands and his voice could be heard quite distinctly above the barrage of the guns.

'Don't drink, lads . . . for God's sake, don't drink or you'll die . . . don't drink . . . don't drink . . . it will pass . . . get your heads down but don't drink . . .' but some did not hear him and some did not care for the knife edge of pain in their lungs and throat could only be soothed, surely, by a cool drink of water. Those who drank began to cough and a froth of greenish fluid erupted from their stomachs and lungs and they began to fall, insensible, to the ground. The colour of their skins turned slowly, from white, to greenish-black and then to yellow, their tongues protruded from their mouths and their eyes assumed a glassy stare and in this fiendish way they died.

The shells burst round him and Corporal Fraser forced himself to spit and his eyes filled with matter and he could not see, falling down amongst his dead 'Pals' as though he himself was to die and he lay in that trench all day, coughing and gasping with the wounded and the dead, and when they found him they evacuated him by motor field ambulance – on which the name 'Hunter' was written but he did not see it as he was carried to the hospital. He was 'fortunate' to recover, he was told and was returned later, fit for duty, they said, to his regiment as *Sergeant* Fraser for one of those who was not fortunate was the sargeant who had warned the others! It was Tom Fraser's first, but far, far from last brush with violent death.

She was in the new hangar at the field when he came in. She still wore her flying outfit for she had just been up and his eyes passed over her without recognition. She heard him ask if Mrs Fraser was about. He had been told, he said, she was at the airfield and he had thought . . .

She saw Fred Knowsley's dour north countryman's face clamp in an expression of guarded watchfulness for this chap was a stranger. Fred was manager now of 'Hunter Aviation' and this huge hangar, only recently erected to accommodate the growth in the manufacture of Meg Fraser's aircraft, sorely needed in France, was in his charge. How had he got in, his expression asked, for what they did here was part of the war effort and highly secret and not for any Tom, Dick or Harry to cast curious eyes on!

Meg turned jerkily from her machine which the mechanics had just pushed into the hangar and keeping it between herself and the man who had asked for her stumbled on shaking legs towards the small office and changing room in which her clothes hung. Her hand reached out for the door handle and she clung to it as she felt the mist of fading consciousness drift into her head and she thought frantically that for only the second time in her life she was about to faint.

'Meggie.'

He spoke her name softly, and in that particular way she remembered, loving and infinitely patient. She turned, unable to understand her own frightened panic and looked for the first time in fourteen months into the face of Tom Fraser.

'. . . I don't know how he got in, Meg. There's no-one supposed to come in without a pass . . .' Fred Knowsley bristled up to Tom, ready, should it be necessary to manhandle him from the hangar, the field even, though the poor lad looked as though a puff of wind would blow him away. Besides, Fred was not awfully sure he could bring himself to lay an aggressive hand on a soldier. One heard such tales, though how true they were, of what they suffered in the trenches but looking at this one it could readily be believed.

'No Fred, it's alright. This . . . this is my husband.'

Bloody hell! Her husband! Of course he had known she had one. They had all been told at the factory of her soldier husband though no-one had ever seen him. Popped a 'bun in the oven' first, and then married her before going to France, they said, though Fred had his own thoughts on that tale which he kept to himself. This company had not been left in *her* direction for nothing, not in Fred Knowsley's opinion, make what you will of it. Liked Meg Fraser, he did and this business was on its feet again, thanks to her – and the war, but he had seen her face open up like a flower in the sun when she spoke Martin Hunter's name. She did the work of ten men and had even begun to talk of testing the 'Wren II' herself, saying she was as competent as Angus Munro to judge whether an aircraft was workable or not. Angus was keen to get over to France and do his bit as soon as a replacement could be found, and was teaching his employer not only how to fly the machine, but every damn nut and bolt and strut which held it together. She was often to be seen with her head in the engine and oil on her face, determined, it appeared, to follow in every footstep Martin Hunter had once taken.

Fred had gone, clearing his throat awkwardly for really the poor bugger looked dreadful! He just stood there, waiting for orders, or so Fred imagined, his khaki uniform crumpled, the poor quality of his overcoat evident in its creased and sagging coarseness. He had some sort of knapsack attached to his chest with a multitude of strapping. A helmet hung on it, dragging down his already bent shoulders. He wore puttees and a peaked cap, all drab and of a sameness with the thousands of other soldiers who could be seen at railway stations all over the country, but his buttons were bright with polish, and the badge on his cap and his shining boots were like wet black paint.

'Tom,' she said and for a timeless poignant moment they were children again, a lad and a lass working side by side in the cheerful companionship of youth and they smiled at one another in sweet remembrance.

426

'Yes, it's me, Meggie.'

'But what . . . how on earth . . .?'

'I've just come from . . .' His face closed suddenly in that guarded way each soldier fresh from France, or indeed any battlefield of the war assumed, then it opened again and his lips moved across his white teeth in a tired smile. The anger and anguish of their last meeting, and the parting, seemed diminished somehow, made small and unworthy by what had happened to him in between and here he was, take him or leave him, his expression said.

'I was up at . . . at "Hilltops". They said you were here so I came to see you.'

'To *see* me, Tom?'

'It's been a long time, Meggie. I wasn't sure of my welcome.'

'Oh Tom, "Hilltops" is your *home!*' Her eyes shone through her sudden tears and she lifted her hands to him, to the scarred and battered ones he put out to her and as he stood there, quite ready to do whatever she asked of him, go back to France, take himself anywhere from her sight if she commanded it, her heart moved painfully with compassion for him. She had written a dozen letters to him, through the Army Council for she had no idea where he was, and she had assumed they had been sent on to him, and had received her army pay as his wife each week, but he had not written to her. Now he stood like a beaten child before her.

She put out her arms to him and he walked blindly into them.

He had bathed and changed into a pair of his old flannels worn with a woollen jumper for the night was cold, glad to be out of his uniform, she thought, and unwilling to talk of the three stripes which she had admired on his arm.

'Sargeant now, Tom. Such quick promotion. You must be proud.'

'No,' and his eyes turned away from her, rejecting her and she knew then that there were certain areas of Tom Fraser's life that must not be mentioned.

When he came diffidently into her sitting room she had her child in her arms.

Elizabeth Fraser was eight months old with skin like clotted cream and a cap of red gold curls which fluffed about her small skull in exactly the vivid way of her mother's. She was strong and healthy and beautiful, already filled with an enormous sense of her own importance in this household where everybody doted on

427

her and she turned her head from the bright beads which hung about her mother's neck to look, unafraid, at Tom as he entered the room. Her eyes considered him, deep and brown and shaped in that certain way which Tom had seen in only one man. They were luminous, bright and lively, as his had been, inquisitive, willing to be friends, then she smiled showing half a dozen tiny white teeth in an expanse of pink and shining gum. She turned for a moment to her mother as though in delighted wonder at the appearance of this stranger, then put out a plump hand to him.

'This is Beth, Tom . . .' Meg was very evidently unsure of what to do next but the child decided for her. She struggled, her baby voice demanding something of her mother and Meg looked helplessly at Tom.

'She is . . .'

'What . . .?'

'I think she wants to . . .'

' Shall I . . .?'

'If you sit down beside me on the settee.'

'Here?'

And with a delightful and triumphant chortle of glee Beth Fraser, Martin Hunter's daughter clambered from her mother's knee on to that of the man who was to be her father. He held her awkwardly, his big hands round her body and her feet danced on his knee and she put out her hands to clasp his face. She grinned and tossed her small head quite flirtatiously and Tom Fraser saw Martin Hunter's charm and his heart resisted for a moment. This was *his* child, when she should have been Tom's. She was the child who had parted him from her mother and she was Martin Hunter's child, then, suddenly sleepy, the little girl leaned against him and with perfect trust she took Tom Fraser's heart into her own safekeeping.

They ate their simple meal with her at five-thirty in the afternoon since she was put to bed at six-thirty, Meg explained and this hour in her mother's busy day belonged to her. Beth sat in the high chair and spoke continuously to her new friend, her eyes wide and satisfied with him, expecting nothing, demanding nothing of him but his smile and his hand. Meg saw the stiffness leave his shoulders and the strain slip away from his face as he watched her child, Martin's child. He held her again in gentle arms for half an hour before the nursery fire, sitting in peace, the first he had known for over a year. He said nothing much, speaking

428

quietly to the baby, resting his cheek against her lovely bright curls and when it was time to hand her over to Sally Flash, the capable young woman in whose care she was whilst Meg was working, he did so reluctantly.

He and Meg sat on, one on either side of the fire in the nursery, the fresh scent of the soap the nurse had used for the baby, the toys, the small clothes airing at the fender, soothing the sad core of Tom Fraser as nothing else could have done. Life was here, the new life of a child and it laid a balm on the wound which festered and bled inside him.

He seemed unable to talk, now that the child had gone.

'How long have you got, Tom?' Meg said half an hour later.

'A week.' His eyes were shuttered.

'You'll stay here ... I mean ...' She smiled into his face, watching the quiet strength of it and the pain which would never, until this war finished, be gone, and the sense of refuge he had always given her, settled about her. 'I didn't mean that as it sounded, as though you were a guest. The hotel ... I am to close it down until the war ends ... I cannot manage it and run the factories, so there are no visitors, but it belongs to you, if you want it, as much as it does to me. This is my home, and yours too. Beth ... she is ... the servants ... except Annie ... believe she is ... your child, Tom. The eyes ... they never really knew ... well ... she is like me and ... dear God, Tom, don't let me stumble through this by myself. You know what I am saying. Spend Christmas, here in your own home with your family. There, is that plain enough for you?'

She leaned forward and took his hands between her own, glad to feel the relaxed way they closed about hers.

'Tom ... can we speak of it now? It has to be said, lad. We cannot let it ... stand between us, not if we are to ... to make a life. We are husband and wife, Tom, like it or not and Beth is *our* child. She was not fathered by you but ... sweet Jesus, I will not hide his name away as though it was shameful. Martin ... *our* Martin, Tom, yours and mine, for he belonged to us both, is the father of that child you have nursed and ... and he is ... dead, Tom. I have almost accepted it. It is slow in coming but I have ... undertaken it. It is still ... painful and I will not deceive you, I will always love him. Just as *you* will, think what you like. We cannot change it, Tom, nor can we forget it, or *him*. He has left a part of him in Beth. The three of us, remember what Mrs

429

Whitley used to call us? Well, we are still three because Martin lives on in Beth.'

She was weeping now, the tears sliding helplessly down her cheeks on to their linked hands. She bent her head to them, anguished again in her loss and Tom Fraser, who had seen what loss and pain did to a man knew he could no longer blame this woman, or the man she loved.

'Meg.'

'I miss him so much, Tom.'

'Meg, look at me.'

She raised her head and saw his compassion and the love he still had for her and when he stood and took her in his arms she did not resist. She led him to her bedroom and in the depths of her soft bed she loved Tom Fraser, her husband, giving him at last what he needed from her. The rounded curves and hollows of her body soothed and enfolded him. The sweet fragrance of her skin, the feel of life and warmth in her, of complete and undamaged flesh and bone and skin and the love in her eyes which shone just for *him*, bound him to her with strong and tender chains. She had come to terms with her grief, her heartache for the loss of the man she loved. The sweetness, so nearly soured, of this man she held, filled her empty heart and his gentleness and patience gave her something she had never before known. She loved him. She had always loved him and he gave her a peace that night she had thought lost to her when Martin had died. He made love to her, lovingly, slowly, as though he savoured a meal for which he had hungered but never thought to be allowed, exploring her body with hands and mouth and she knew a quiet pleasure when he trembled in her arms as his masculine need came at last to fulfilment.

They spent the five remaining days with their child and in their renewed love and friendship. They took long, rambling walks on the moor Tom loved. He strapped the child on his back and she put her baby fingers in his bright cap of curls and her delighted laughter rose up into the still, winter air and when he lifted her down and cradled her in his arms the bond began to bud and strengthen, even then, between them, and Meg gave thanks. The pale sun and the exercise put colour into his thin face and his eyes became again the vivid blue of his youth as he played with *his* child and his laughter blended with the music of the breeze.

430

Annie cooked him Lancashire hot-pot with dumplings in it, and apple pie and cream from his own orchard and his own cow. She stuffed him with creamy rice pudding and the syllabub Meg had taught her to make, overflowing with chocolate and cream and vanilla. Roast beef and Yorkshire pudding with a mountain of fluffy potatoes and gravy made from the juice of the meats, and every fattening dish she could get into him since he was as thin as a pipe cleaner, she said, and it was her quiet intention to put a few pounds on him before he returned to France.

He spent hours in the garden in silent, peace-drenched solitude, just looking at the things he had planted a hundred years ago before the world had gone mad, touching the rough bark of a tree or the shiny surface of a leaf, drawing in the strength and continuity of the land he loved. He and Will, Annie's son, who had come up from Great Merrydown to take care of it all, and the boy – since Albert was too old now, he complained, for such a big place – sat in almost total speechlessness, sharing a pipe of tobacco, staring out across the garden and beyond to the lovely perfect stillness of the Gorge, and his healing contact with the earth he loved and the quiet strength of the man who watched over it for him while he was away, showed in the relaxed way he could stand, and walk and sit, without constantly looking over his shoulder.

Meg watched him and prayed that the strength in him would continue when he had left this place he loved and which had put it there. They healed *one another* those few days, sharing the small joys of the Christmas festivity, the sweet and simple pleasure of the baby and in their bed at night they renewed the faith and trust that when the time came and the war was ended they would live this life, these few days, again and again and again.

So they said goodbye, kissed and said goodbye and Meg Fraser held her child in her arms that night and prayed that Tom Fraser would come home to her again. To the life she had re-built for them at 'Hilltops'. It was almost a year now since the last frightening episode in which the dog had died and in all that time she had heard no more of, or from, the man she was completely convinced had been behind all the events; the bar-room fire, the failure of the brakes in the motor car and finally the poisoning of the veal and the death of the dog. It seemed too much of a coincidence that all three were unconnected but if he had arranged them all why had he not come forward in some way to let her know of it and to gloat about it. After the dog's death she had been badly frightened and tempted to go to the police but she had no concrete evidence beyond her own suspicions and what could they do anyway, she had agonised? She had nearly told Tom in their new found relationship but he had been so ... so empty ... so frail almost that she had been reluctant to add to the burden his already sagging shoulders carried.

And so, knowing that she must protect the child Martin had left, still a baby and protected in the security of the house but soon to grow into an inquisitive and venturesome child, she turned to the only two people in the world she knew she could trust for there was no doubt she could no longer bear the uncertainty and fear alone.

Chapter thirty-six

Names such as Liége, Mons, Marne, Aisne and Ypres, the Somme and Passchendaele, unheard of before the start of the war were now as familiar as the names of one's own children as battle after battle was fought over ground in which scarce an inch was gained.

The bewildered soldier, as he went out obediently each day to be slaughtered, wondered at the inescapable madness of his superiors, crawling back each time to the same trench he had lived in and died in for over twelve months. Now and again there were 'Big Pushes' and the enemy would be thrown back a few miles but the Germans would then retaliate and the bit of ground won at such cost would be lost again and the 'no mans land' of half a mile between the two opposing armies was re-instated.

Great Britain's first big offensive began on July 1st 1916 at the battle of the Somme and was to last until November. For the first three months the Allied forces pressed on, taking small villages at enormous sacrifice of troops but never succeeding in breaking through the German line. The approach of winter and the exhaustion of the men put an end to the active fighting, and Sargeant Tom Fraser wrote cheerfully to his wife about the sociability of the French people he had met and the loveliness of the weather in that fateful month. He had eaten the tin of apricots she had sent him and found them delicious. He had played cards the night before and won a 'bob or two' but then he was known to be lucky and he was in the best of health. He treasured the photograph she had sent of herself and Beth, he said, and could not get over how the small girl had grown and they were to take care of themselves for he loved them both dearly.

Of the horrors he saw daily he wrote not at all. Of the yellow mass of lyddite shrapnel which burst indiscriminately, taking half a dozen men with it, of blood soaked soldiers in such pain they wept like children, of frightened men, scattered and hurrying and stumbling back towards their own lines, holding in the blood from wounds which leaked and would not stop, of 'Pals' falling to the

433

left and right of him, of tumbling into trenches in which the dead and wounded lay rotting together, of blood and vomit and rats as big as rabbits, of stink-holes and dug-outs and rum-jars which was the soldiers' only comfort, of fearful screams and anguished moans and the terror of men who were obliged to conceal it and went mad in the process. Of shell-shock and trench-foot which swelled the feet to three times their normal size, of lice and dysentry and the sight of a trench when a shell burst in the heart of it, effectively shredding twenty-five men, turning it a brilliant crimson with their blood. Of the mud which captured complete regiments and of men sitting in it, lying in it crying like babies because they could go no further, of British soldiers gasping and choking and dying of the gas which their own leaders sent up.

No, Tom Fraser did not write of this but stored it away inside him where it lay in wait for him. He wrote of skylarks soaring heavenward in the deep blue bowl of the sky, of the pipe of tobacco he had enjoyed and the pleasure of his wife's letters to him, of the comfortable 'billet' he had made for himself and the food parcel he had received, not even able to tell her of how he longed for her, or Beth or the home he loved for his mind could not cope with the memory of it.

But Meg Fraser, and all the other wives and sweethearts and mothers who saw their husbands and lovers and sons come home to ecstatic welcomes, who begged innocently to be told of 'what it was like over there' and who were dismayed by the almost sullen silence with which their questions were received, knew by now that there was something so utterly appalling over there in France their men could not speak of it. These women lived with the dread and fear, the ever present pre-occupation with death or mutilation. Hundreds of thousands of British 'Tommies' were losing their lives, their limbs, their sight and their reason on the battlefields of France and though Tom had remained unscathed as yet, escaping shrapnel and whizz-bangs, bullets and shells, surely, Meg's agonised mind asked, by the law of averages his turn would come.

No, he said in his letters, though she had not asked, he was lucky and even joked about those with whom he served and their efforts to stand beside him when they went over the top, since it followed that as he bore a charmed life, so would those who clustered about him!

The Germans had started bombing raids in 1915, by Zeppelin

or airships, great clumsy monsters which were soon shot out of the sky by the British fighter airplanes, the Hunter 'Wren' amongst them, which went up to get them, but in 1916 the enemy began bombing by airplane causing great confusion and resentment for the British people had never, like those in France, suffered war at first hand. The whole country was blacked out whenever an enemy airplane was sighted and during the raids, over one thousand ordinary British people lost their lives.

The battle of the Somme brought another terror to those at home, a mixture of dread and numbness which was overwhelming, in the daily chronicle of the wastage of young lives which was reported in *The Times*. In it was printed the names of those lost under the headline 'Roll of Honour'. Regiment after regiment was named, seven or eight columns wide, 'killed in action', 'died of wounds', 'wounded', 'seriously wounded' . . . and on and on in unbearable record. In one day, the first of the battle, the British Army lost 19,240 dead and 57,470 wounded and publication of these names was spread over many weeks and was almost too much for the nation to comprehend since they could not believe it had happened. What had become of the great and glorious adventure, the fun, the lark, the expectation that it would all be over by Christmas they asked one another voicelessly, and there was no answer but despair!

But perhaps the greatest living dread was of the telegram! Just the sight of a Post Office boy in the street caused mothers to cry out in agony and apprehension and an unexpected knock on the door was the signal for panic! The poor lad who, as he often said, was not to be blamed for what was contained in the yellow envelope, was hated beyond any other and in the rural areas, should he appear in a country lane or on a dusty footpath, he was often followed by sympathetic women to his place of destination so that they might give comfort to the recipient of his bad news.

It was a Sunday in October and though the factories worked seven days a week she had taken the day off to spend it with her growing daughter. She was often saddened at how much of her childhood she was missing but in her effort to cram the work of two hours into one she was often forced to be at the field for eighteen hours in twenty-four and was acutely reminded of her days at the Adelphi when she had been learning her trade as an hotelier. Then, as now, she had taught herself to manage on a few snatched hours of sleep whenever she could, to catnap in her office over a cup of tea and she had become thin in her continual struggle to keep up with the demands of the war contracts for aircraft, ambulances, motor cycles, staff cars and armoured cars to be shipped to the front.

The past years had been hard on Meg Fraser. As the war escalated the pressure for the manufacture of the small, single seater airplane, like 'Wren II' was growing with every week. Martin's machine was capable of great speed and rapid climbing and her new design made her ideal for air battles. Machine guns were mounted in front and accurately timed to fire between the whirling blades of the propeller.

Hour after hour, round the clock, 'Hunter Aviation' turned out the small machines which the Royal Flying Corps so desperately needed and it was a measure of the advance in the development and manufacture of the aeroplane that the 211 machines they had flying in 1914 had become, by the end of the war, a staggering 25,000, half of which were equipped for fighting and bombing!

Though Meg had men building, testing, working in the drawing-office from Martin's original design, she must somehow keep the whole running, with 'Hunter Automobiles', as one well co-ordinated machine. There were many departments. Metal fitting shops, wood-working, erection and structural testing, each department run by one man, but those men must be organised into a system which had one aim. To produce as many aircraft and automobiles as could be humanly produced in the shortest possible time and it was Meg's job to see that it was done.

She supposed sometimes, when she had the time to consider it that she might now call herself wealthy as the profits poured in and the investments she had made brought her a handsome dividend, but the careless speculation on it was no more than a passing thought. The future, the years which would follow the ending of the war, would inevitably come and what was in them was obscure but what she did now would help to make them secure for the next generation.

Beth was growing so quickly from babyhood, to childhood, so lively and with her enquiring mind and fingers into everything her bright eyes fell upon. She was in the garden at the side of the house 'helping' Will to gather leaves which he would put into piles for burning. As quickly as he raked them she would grab a couple of handsful, carrying them carelessly to the tidy heaps, dropping most on the way, distributing what was left in a casual

436

drift on to Will's neat structure. She was dressed in a scarlet warm knitted jumper and leggings but her head was bare and the mist of rain had put spangles of crystal in her russet curls. She was growing tall and sturdy, good-natured with none of her father's mercurial and arrogant moods, strangely, and Meg often pondered on the irony of it, in temperament more like Tom Fraser than the man who was her natural father. Her charm was evident and she took advantage, as children will, no matter what their nature, of the adoration of her mother, of Will and Annie and Edie, and of Sally Flash who was her nanny, but she was never fretful or peevish when she was not allowed her own way and bore no grudge. She and Meg had that special bond which often exists between a child and a single parent, and though she was so seldom able to get home to be with her child at bedtime, or had already left for the factory before Beth awoke, the little girl, secure and loved by those in whose charge her mother left her, thrived and grew and accepted the absence of the normal family background which Meg longed to give her. She had a photograph of a serious Tom, taken in his uniform which she was enchanted with for it was her very own, bringing it to Meg's knee as they sat before the nursery fire, kissing it tenderly, though she had no clear recollection of her 'Daddy'.

'Say it to me,' she would beg her mother, and drawing her on to her lap, cradling the small and precious body against her own, Meg would slip back in time to the days when three children had stood hand in hand on the doorstep of a house in Great George Square, and speak to her daughter of her 'Daddy' and the child, dozing in the safe cradle of her mother's arms was unaware that the boy her mother spoke of was not the soldier in the photograph.

Tom had been home on leave twice more during the three years they had been married, frightening her with his gaunt, wide-eyed stare as though even here in the peace and utter stillness of the beautiful Derbyshire fells his senses compelled him to search for an unseen enemy over the next hill, to listen for the sniper's bullet, the whizz-bang and the constant dull throb of the barrage which preceded every battle. He was exhausted, stumbling like an old man about the gardens, standing sometimes for more than two hours in one spot, staring at a leaf on a tree, the petal on a flower, the scurry of an ant in the grass, his eyes nailed to the simple beauty, taken so much for granted by those who saw it each day, of the colour and movement of life itself. He was a man apart from other men – sharing only the companionship of those with whom he served and suffered – even from Will who was so like him in his own patient, enduring nature and who would himself, but for his leg, have been in France. Will, usually so taciturn, and shocked immeasurably by Tom's withdrawal from everything around him, attempted to draw him out, to talk about the garden and Tom's plans for it when 'this lot' was over, but Tom merely turned his washed out blue gaze on him as though what Will said made no sense at all. His world, his attitude said, was too far apart from theirs and the gap was unbridgeable, and somehow, though it was ridiculous, Meg knew, it seemed he was ready, after a day or two, to get back to it.

And at night in the merciful compassion of his wife's arms, his strong yet gentle spirit deserted him completely and he wept like a child against her breast, defeated, tormented by his failure to love her. Meg comforted him, held him, loved his body with her own, smothered him with anguished concern telling him that it did not matter that he could not respond, and he left at the end of his leave looking more haunted than when he had come home. Only in the nursery with the child upon his knee, dozing together companionably before the fire did he seem to find peace.

Meg watched Beth now, smiling and shaking her head over the antics of the child. Will picked her up a dozen times, swinging her in a 'twizz', allowing her to ride, squealing with joy in his wheelbarrow, wiping her nose for her on his own white handkerchief, answering patiently every one of her interminable questions. How lucky she was, Meg thought in that moment before the doorbell rang, in having this man who, with his steadfast understanding was keeping Tom's beautiful garden alive for his homecoming and who loved his child and kept her from harm. And Annie! What would she have done without her unquestioning and uncompromising friendship in these years of war. Between them, mother and son, they kept her world together for her while she got through the days and nights of grinding work and the total commitment of her mind and brain and body the war demanded of her.

'There's a chap here to see you, Megan,' Annie said, her hands still busy in her apron, the flour on them testifying to the occupation she had been about before she answered the door. There was only her and Edie now and all the lovely rooms and private suites were carefully shrouded and closed in readiness for

438

the day when the 'Hilltop Hotel' would function again as it should but in the meanwhile there was cooking still to be done and with Edie not much of a hand in the kitchen, except with a frying pan, Annie was baking a tart with the last of the plums from Tom's trees.

'Who is it, Annie?' Meg said, startled since she had heard no motor car engine and who on earth would walk all this way up here, but relieved nevertheless that it was not the dreaded telegram lad.

'Nay lass, don't ask me. He said he wanted to speak to Miss Hughes so . . .' She was not allowed to finish her sentence and in that last moment Meg had time to smile at the affrontery on Annie's honest face at the cheek of the chap who pushed past her, then her own face drained of every vestige of colour and the blood left her brain and the room swayed about her for she recognised him instantly.

'Megan, my dear, how nice to see you after all these years and looking so well too, though I do believe you have lost some weight. What a pity, for really you had the loveliest . . .' He did not finish but his insolent gaze fell pointedly to her breast and as Meg clung frantically to her reeling senses she heard Annie gasp and saw her bristle and her cheeks become a bright scarlet.

'Mrs Fraser . . .?' Annie's voice was questioning and her expression was one which said this chap had best mend his manners for his path was beset with peril if he got on the wrong side of *her*, but Meg had eyes for no-one now but the man who stood in the doorway of her sitting room and did not seem to hear.

'Aah . . . Mrs Fraser now, is it? So you married the boot boy, did you? I suppose it was inevitable in view of your condition. You always were an odd sort of threesome, I thought. Quite . . . unnatural, I would say. Share and share alike was it . . .?'

'Mrs Fraser! Megan . . .' Annie was scandalized. 'May I ask who this . . . this gentleman is for I declare if he says another word I shall be forced to call Will and have him removed. And don't you tell me he's an old friend, like he says because I refuse to believe it . . .'

'Annie, will you leave us . . .?'

'Nay, that I won't!'

'Annie, please . . .'

'Never mind please. I shan't move a step from this room while . . . while he's here, choose how . . .'

Benjamin Harris smiled lazily as his pale grey eyes moved like slugs across Meg's face and body.

'My word, what loyalty you do arouse in your friends, Megan! The pity of it is you choose such *strange* ones!'

'Megan, are you going to allow . . . ?'

Benjamin Harris sighed. 'Must I have this old woman constantly interrupting everything I say, Megan, or can she not do something useful such as bringing us some tea, which is her function in life, one assumes.'

Meg felt the clouded mists begin to clear from her head and though there was a painful mass settled somewhere in the middle of her chest which, if not treated carefully might erupt in a wave of nausea, she was steadier now. Her heart jolted frighteningly, but really, she had nothing to be afraid of since Annie was here, and Will was within earshot and a telephone call would bring the police within minutes. But even while her mind comforted her with these thoughts it cast her back to another occasion when she had conjured up the very same reassurances and the belief that he would never, could never come to terrify her again.

And here he was like a demon summoned from the dark pits of hell, back to haunt her with old fears. She had so much that was precious, her child, vulnerable and defenceless against this man who, in his passion for revenge had followed her for more than seven years and though as yet he had not hurt her physically, he had put the fear of his evil menace in her life, laying it across her like a weight. He had tracked her down like some beast hunting its prey!

'What are you thinking, Megan my dear?' he said silkily. 'I can see behind that pretty face of yours you are wondering what on earth I am to do next and really, I have no idea. Shall I tell you or shall I savour it for a while longer. Shall I tell you what I have *already* done to you besides what you have seen or shall I leave you to . . . to reflect on it. I meant to hurt you, Megan, I told you that years ago but I wished it to be . . . of the mind. Mental torment is often greater than the physical kind, do you not agree? I meant to hurt you, make no mistake, and anyone you happen to . . . care about . . .'

He turned his head suddenly, his gaze going to the window and beyond to the garden. 'What a lovely child, Megan . . . so like her father, whoever he may be . . . so pretty . . . and fragile . . .'

'No . . .'

'Send the woman away.'

'Please leave us, Annie.'

'Meg, I will not leave you alone with this . . .'

'*Annie! for God's sake go!*' Meg's voice rose to a scream and she saw Will Hardcastle raise his head from his raking, his face uncertain, not absolutely sure of what he had heard. 'Stand outside the door, if you must, Annie, but please, if you value my life, do not come in unless I call you.'

They drank the tea Edie was summoned to bring and Benjamin Harris kept up a constant stream of small talk, admiring the cut of her hair, though he did regret the passing of women's femininity which the war had brought about, the cut of her gown which he was sure must have cost a fortune, the setting of her home which he thought must be a very pleasant place in which to spend a holiday, of which he himself often felt in need, and the way in which her business had flourished due, he was certain, to her own shrewd and clever mind. Yes, it must be most satisfying to be so successful and really, did she not agree that success was hard to come by? Take himself, for instance. The bad luck which had dogged his footsteps – here he smiled quite wolfishly at her – had been difficult to overcome but as he was sure she could tell by the way in which he was dressed and the air of affluence those with wealth acquire, no matter how they come by it, he had not gone unrewarded. His own efforts in the business world had often . . . well . . . they had paid him handsomely and of course he was truly blessed in the many friends he had made and the acquaintances he had come by in the course of his travels. They came from all walks of life, from financiers, men of substance in the world of commerce, right down the social scale to one who was no more than a mechanic!

He smiled and Meg Fraser felt the world slip away and a great silence enveloped her and the sensation of nausea which still clotted uncomfortably beneath her rib cage stirred uneasily. She knew quite clearly that he was telling her something, watching for her smallest reaction, enjoying it as a cat enjoys the antics of a defenceless field mouse and in his eyes was a look of such unholy joy she was aware that he had waited for this moment of triumph for many years and that now, at last, it was here. He had done something, which, when she learned of it, or when he was ready to divulge it to her would surely destroy her. But wait Megan . . . wait . . . for I am not ready yet. I have not done with you but

441

when I am you shall know what it is I have achieved, what I have yet to achieve against you.

'Yes. I am fortunate, Megan, in that I am able to bestow small favours on people, who, in their turn, can often help me . . . when I need something doing. Do you find that, my dear?'

'I don't know what you mean.' Her voice was lifeless.

'No, of course you don't but you will one day, Megan, I promise you.'

Her eyes drifted away from him towards the garden where there was goodness, innocence, sweetness, the clean drift of rain clouds, the sound of her child's laughter, but he would not allow her to escape.

'Look at me, Megan,' he said and she obediently turned back to him, a puppet whose strings he pulled. 'I am going to leave you now, my dear, for really, I must not indulge myself for too long or I might tell you my secrets and I have sworn to enjoy them for as long as I am able. It took me a long time, Megan. I had many hours to brood on what you had done to me, and what I might do in return. I thought at the beginning you had ruined me but you merely turned my steps in another direction for which I suppose I should thank you for the rewards were much greater. Nevertheless, you defied me, Megan, but worst of all you *meddled* with my life and I cannot forgive that and so . . . I am meddling in yours! And you have so much more to lose now. The last time we met you were nought but a maidservant. Now you are a successful business woman, wealthy, married, *and with a child*!'

She sprang at him then reaching for his eyes and her fingers turned to claws, and her finger-nails to talons, a snarling she-cat defending her young but though he was nearing middle-age, thin as a rapier, he was just as strong as one and he laughed as he caught her wrists and when Annie burst through the door in a charge like that of an infuriated rhinoceros, he threw Meg at her and his face was malevolent in his hatred.

'Stand away from me, Megan, and tell that woman to do the same,' his hissed, 'or by God, I swear I will . . .'

'*What* . . . for Christ's sake? You will what? What else can you threaten me with?'

'This is not a threat, believe me, just a warning but if you do anything now which displeases me you will wish you had died in that fire with the half-witted skivvy. Step back from me, Megan, and allow me to leave peacefully. Do it now, girl . . . do it now!'

He was smiling as he shrugged himself into his expensive overcoat, reaching for his hat and Annie Hardcastle stood, turned to stone, it seemed, by the sense of great evil which had filled the pleasant room. When he had gone, tipping his hat most courteously towards her and Meg, she led her weeping friend to the settee and held her, crooning a helpless lullaby of comfort above her head.

'What has he done, Annie? Dear God, what has he done?' Meg cried but in truth Annie could not answer, she only knew that the man who had just gone was completely and frighteningly insane.

'Nay lass . . . perhaps when Tom comes home . . .'

Meg lifted her head and her eyes were spangled with wet tears but in them shone a ray of hope.

'Yes . . . oh yes, Annie, you're right. When Tom gets home . . . when this bloody war is done!'

Chapter thirty-seven

It was done at last and at the end of November 1918, Sargeant Tom Fraser, one of the first to do so, came home to his wife and put his trembling hand in hers and gave himself up to the nightmares which had tormented him for the best part of four years, and she finally realised the hope she had held in her heart, that he would share the burden of Benjamin Harris which she had carried about with her for eight weeks was no more than a golden dream.

Though his body was whole, unscathed, just as it had been four years ago despite its dramatic slenderness, Tom Fraser's mind was not. Meg knew, though not at that precise moment, that never again would Tom be the light-hearted, carelessly good-natured, untroubled man he had once been, that though he had gone to war a man, he had come back a frightened child.

He stepped from the crowded troop train at Victoria station, his arm held by a medical orderly, and with hundreds of others who shuffled along the platform with him, going wherever they were led, he recoiled at every sharp noise and seemed confused by everything from her warm embrace to the simple act of stepping into the taxi which was to take them across London to St Pancras station.

She took him straight home by train, holding his clutching hand in both of hers, blind to the sympathetic stares of those who travelled with them. His uniform was stained still with the mud of the last battle he had fought in around Mons, the very place he had begun his war in 1915. It hung about him in empty folds as though he had shrunk inside it and his greatcoat had two holes in the sleeve, neat and round, just below the shoulder.

When she led him, murmuring soothingly towards the first class dining car, desperate to begin to put some decent food into his gaunt frame, he balked at the swaying communicating passage which led from one carriage to the next, staring at the narrow moving floor as though it was about to swallow him up and she was forced to take him back to their own compartment.

'I'm sorry, Meg, I'm sorry,' he kept muttering over and over again, for at least half an hour, agonised it seemed by his own foolishness, and to the dismay of those who shared the crowded compartment, he began to weep inconsolably, then suddenly and just as disconcertingly, fell into a deep and complete silence, almost an unconscious state, though his eyes were wide open and staring.

It was only when Beth, curls bobbing in an undisciplined flame of russet, eyes shining with excitement for her 'Daddy's' return, came running on swift feet down the platform at Derby did he come from his trance and in a way which spoke of his desperation and misery, he swept her into his arms and held her to him in the first natural gesture he had made since Meg took him from the troop train.

'Sweetheart, oh sweetheart,' he cried repeatedly and his tears wet the shoulder of her woollen coat as he buried his face against her soft flesh. Meg thought Beth would be afraid of Tom's emotion for how could her young mind understand the horrors which were in his, but Tom seemed to know that this child must not be made frightened and the slender hold he had on reality told him when to set her down. She put her hand trustingly in his, small, and nestling in his none too clean one and led him along the platform, looking about her in delight to let the ladies and gentlemen know that this was *her* soldier daddy and was he not beautiful and he had come home to *stay*!

He got into the back seat of the Vauxhall, the same model old Mr Hemingway had once owned, the 'Prince Henry' which Meg had bought at the beginning of the war. It was comfortable and roomy, big enough to accommodate an active child, picnic baskets and all the paraphernalia which a family might carry around. Meg had taught Will to drive it since it was convenient on many occasions to have him drive her to the factory and then use the vehicle on errands to Buxton or Ashbourne. When she was tired after a long, exhausting, demanding day at the field she was often glad to have him drive her home and had taken the opportunity many tines to snatch half an hour's sleep in the back seat. Now she sat beside her husband, the child between them. Beth took Tom's hand in hers and watched him unblinkingly with the vivid interest of a child who has something new and novel, touching the sargeant's stripes on his greatcoat, fingering the badge on his cap and telling him seriously of the lovely tea Annie was preparing for them. Her chatter ran smoothly over Tom's shrinking figure and gradually he relaxed a little, his eyes never leaving hers and the need to make conversation – about what? Meg agonised – was dispelled.

Will, with a sad backward look at Meg, put the motor car in gear, accepting, as thousands and thousands were accepting, the stranger who had come home to them. Though Tom had looked through him, his gaze as vacant as a new born child, not seeming to know who he was, Will made no comment but merely drove him carefully home.

Annie was there at the door and though Edie clapped her hand to her mouth and ran silently back to the kitchen as Tom shrank away from her affectionate greeting, overcome with grief at what had been done to Mr Tom, Annie took his hand and without allowing him to stumble or flinch on who she might be, or, when he had remembered her identity, how he could cope with it, she led him into the familiar, fire-warmed beauty of the hall and sat him down on the chesterfield. Meg and Will hovered uncertainly, and Annie held his hands between her own strong ones, murmuring of nothing which needed an answer. In her wisdom she gave him half an hour, with something to hold on to, her hands, whilst his eyes wandered fearfully about the hallway in which once he had whistled cheerfully and grinned endearingly as he welcomed guests to his *his* hotel. Beth sat on the rug before the fire, a row of dolls beside her, chattering tenderly to them all and Meg watched as Tom Fraser began at last to recognise where he was.

'Meg . . .?'

'I'm here, my darling.'

'Oh Meg . . .'

'Yes, sweetheart?'

But it was all he could manage as the tears began again and Beth stood up, disconcerted by the sight of a grown-up crying for she had never seen it before. She touched his knee in sympathy, asking him where he hurt as Mummy did when she herself cried, and when he could not stop crept up on to his knee and put her arms about his neck and kissed him.

That night, in the soft, fire-lit warmth of their room, Meg made no attempt to make love to her husband, nor he to her. He clung to her, holding her gently curving, white-fleshed, eternal femininity to him in a passion of love, but she recognised that it

446

was not the love of a man for his woman but that of a lost and terrified child in the arms of his mother. She held him through that night and the one following and the one following that, as he lived again in the hideous state of terror he had contained within himself for most of the four years he had been in France. The repression of it had been necessary to keep not only himself functioning, but those who fought beside him and who had come to look upon him as the living, breathing proof that there were *some* who could survive it, but it was now no longer needed and, quite simply, for several weeks he went mad with it.

Hour after hour he wept his pain and bewilderment, his face like sweating dough, his eyes staring at some unimaginable shadow in which moved phantoms of those men, who, in their thousands upon thousands had died, horribly mutilated, or what was worse, *lived*, horribly mutilated, whilst he had survived. Why, he asked her, a dozen times a day? Why had he lived without so much as a scratch, he begged her to tell him, when his Liverpool Pals, everyone of them, had fallen, most at the Somme, dying of bullet wounds, of lyddite shrapnel which pierced their tender flesh in a score of places, tearing their limbs from their bodies and even their heads from their necks. They died from the mines on which they innocently trod, from shells which burst indiscriminately above their heads and from the choking gas which infiltrated their almost useless gas masks. It seemed the worst torment to Sargeant Tom Fraser had been the order that on no account must he stop to help his fallen comrade, nor even to bend a knee to see if he was still alive, but must go on, leaving him to die, to suffer, to bleed into the already blood soaked ground of the battlefield.

In his fitful sleep he cried out of bombardment and gas, screaming to someone to 'get your bloody mask on', of salients and tanks and shellfire and wept over the pain another soldier suffered. A rat gnawed his hand one night and on the next he drowned in mud. He babbled endlessly in the dark of the trenches and of the men in them and sometimes seemed to confuse all those he had known and loved in that comradeship which had been born there, as he screamed of shattered bones and blood and torn flesh and fear. He said his head hurt from the shock of the explosions and he felt sick and dizzy and why did she not remove the mountain of rotting men which piled up about him for really the smell was more than he could bear.

Meg never left him. For the first time since she had opened the inn at Great Merrydown, the one in which Tom had so ably partnered her, nearly eight years ago now, she abandoned her work, leaving Fred Knowsley and the other managers to cope without her direction, trusting them to administer the two companies in the best way they could. She was here, on the other end of the telephone, she told them, if they should need her in an emergency, knowing that with the war's end and the resulting cancellation of government contracts, one could easily arise! There would be a lull, naturally, as the need for the machines of war finished but there would be others to take their place and soon, if she was to be as successful in peace as she had in war, she must prepare her organisation for them, but first she must restore Tom to some semblance of normality for unless she did how was she to ever leave him?

He grew stronger physically, fed three, or if she could manage it, four of Annie's wholesome meals each day. Soup made from shin of beef, a knuckle of veal, or a ham shank, thick with vegetables, into which, for good measure she put a 'dollop' of cream, eager to flesh out his bones in any way she could. Barley gruel, easy to digest and tasty to tempt his poor appetite, with a tablespoonful of sherry in it. A cutlet of lamb with mint sauce and Brussels sprouts, grown by Will and fresh from the garden. Egg wine and eel broth and stewed rabbit in milk, chocolate mousse, light and frothy with fresh cream, milky rice pudding and succulent pork pies with pastry which flaked in the mouth.

At first he had refused, pushing away his plate apologetically saying he would 'eat it later and not to throw it out' in a fair imitation of his old self and Meg became frantic as he continued to lose weight. He had been home for three weeks, the doctor shaking his head, wondering, he told Meg, whether it might perhaps be wiser if Mr Fraser was transferred to a hospital he knew of, for soldiers recently returned from the front. There were many like her husband, he said sadly, who had not yet got to grips with civilian life and the problem would not go away, not in weeks, not in years, though he did not say so.

He had wandered away from her that day, in the withdrawn and dream-like manner of a ghost who does not know where to lay itself to rest, haunted by other ghosts which crowded about him, his face sombre and shaded, whatever was in his mind hidden from her. She followed him from room to room, not speaking nor touching him rather as she imagined one would with a sleepwalker.

448

He touched things, a porcelain figurine, the petal on a chrysan-themum, in a bowl which stood on the window sill, the fall of the velvet curtains. He was confused, muttering under his breath and once saying quite clearly, '. . . this is nice, Andy. Shall we take it back to the billet?' tucking a cushion under his arm with a smile of triumph.

He went up the stairs and Meg's heart plunged for in this dreadful show of – dear God, she could only call it derangement – how might he affect her daughter if he should go into the nursery? He was always gentle with her, often vague and not really listening to her chatter, but as loving as he had always been.

'Hello Daddy,' the child said cheerfully as she looked up from the nursery table where she was having her tea. There was bread and butter and a pot of honey, milk and biscuits and fruit. There were toys, balls and dolls, a teddy bear and books and the cheerful crackle of the fire. There was the discreet presence of Sally Flash sitting beside the child, sewing on some small garment. It was lovely, the very heart of Tom's home and in it was the sanity he needed to mend him.

'I'm having my tea, Daddy,' Beth continued, holding up a chocolate biscuit in proof. 'Would you like one?' she said for her mother had taught her politeness was important.

'Why . . . thank you, sweetheart . . . but . . .'

He hovered in the doorway in that hesitant wary way he had, looking about him, one assumed, for German soldiers, or whizz bangs, or worse, his dead and mutilated pals, but there was nothing but the warmth and the blithe and lovely spirit of the child. Her unquestioning love reached out and drew him in.

He ate a biscuit, and when prompted by the little girl, two slices of bread and honey, a glass of milk and an apple. To Beth's everlasting delight he ate most of his meals with her from that day on, though she was not to know the reason why. Whatever she ate so did he. As she tucked in to roast beef and Yorkshire pudding, cut up into small pieces so that she might feed herself, so did Tom Fraser and he was soothed by her joyful pleasure in his company. Her artless babble on the small but momentous happenings in her day did not allow terror into the simple child world of the nursery.

Christmas came and went and when Beth was with him he was quiet, even smiling a little, his weariness of spirit put aside for her sake, holding her hand, walking with her in the garden, looking out from the rough ground beyond the small lake, across to the winter beauty of the snow-capped hills and the meandering path to the Dovedale valley.

He began to put on weight and in the sunshine and clear fresh air in which he had started to spend his days with Beth and Will his face took on a little colour. He became stronger and with Will not far behind, Meg and he and Beth would walk a mile or two, moving across crisp frozen snow in which the little girl threw herself, calling to Daddy to catch her, squealing with laughter as he began, slowly, carefully, hesitantly to play with her. He stood with Meg in a timeless moment of peace to admire the golden sprays of bracken which pushed their way through the snow and the bright thickets of holly, glossy prickly leaves and brilliant berries bright against the white landscape. They sat on one of the drystone walls which cobwebbed the hills and he held her hand and the only habitation was a white-washed cottage and all around there was nothing to hurt him, just peace and silence, the laughter of the child and the healing love of his wife.

Meg began to hope!

He took to following Will about the vegetable garden at the back of the house and finding nothing there to alarm him, turned over a square foot or two of black soil, then sat for an hour with a handful of it clutched painfully to him. Will was wary, keeping an eye on him as he himself continued digging, for what would he do next? What was in his troubled mind as he held the black dirt in his hand, but Tom stood up quite normally, remarking, 'Bit of good soil that, Will,' throwing it back on the garden and brushing his hands together carelessly.

She made her mistake in March. He had been progressing steadily, walking the hills now with Beth sometimes on his shoulders, Will, or Meg always beside him. He was sleeping better, more quietly and his hesitant smile lit his eyes as he helped Will in the garden, or read to Beth, or sat beside Annie in the kitchen as she baked. He helped Edie to polish the windows, delighting her for it was a treat to see him more his old self, she said, telling her that he had cleaned more windows when he was a lad than she'd had hot dinners. Meg was exultant believing that at last she could get back to work.

There were changes coming now in the world of aviation. The new 'Wren', the 'Wren III' she would be, was bigger and to be

450

used not only by the many wealthy men who wished to fly for their own pleasure but for what Meg was convinced, for had it not been Martin's dream, would be the start of air transport as a business. And if that was so, would it not follow that an aircraft which carried freight, could also carry passengers? This business which had, through the war, made her into a successful and wealthy airplane manufacturer was not to die away now that the war was over. They had an embryo 'airline' company and with the bright new designer Fred had found, one who had survived four years in the Royal Flying Corps, at the drawing board and the gigantic new factory which was to be built on the airfield, they would, one day, she was certain, be operating one of the first British 'airline' ventures in the country.

And the motor car! Now that the war was over would not the demand for new designs, light, high-speed engines, the family automobile for the family man which Martin had envisaged, and the racing motor for the racing enthusiast, now be brought down from the shelf where the war had temporarily placed it. Sadly the 'Huntress' still wrapped carefully away at the back of the factory awaiting Martin Hunter's return, was obsolete now, her design, so innovative in 1912, out of date but another could be built, by the right engineer, surely?

Meg, convinced Tom was sufficiently recovered in the three months he had been home, and thinking to stimulate his awakening interest in what had been *her* work, and would be again, put him in the Vauxhall one fine spring day in March, sitting him beside her as she drove cheerfully down the drive and out through the gateway, turning in the direction of Camford.

At first, in the manner of an animal which senses danger, not awfully sure of where the danger lay, but sniffs around warily in the hope of discovering it, Tom allowed himself to be led about the hangar. His hand was shaken by a score of well-wishers for though they did not know him, they were glad to see him, a soldier, back from the trenches and in one piece. Though those who spoke so welcomingly to him, respectfully too for he was the husband of the owner, were disconcerted by his silent, staring face and flaccid hand, they told each other the poor devil had gone through four years of war and could you blame him for being a bit quiet.

Fred walked protectively beside him pointing out what he thought might interest the husband of Megan Fraser, no engineer certainly, but a man and most men were curious about these machines which they had seen in the skies above their heads in France.

It was as they approached the skeleton of an aircraft being erected at the back of the hangar that Tom began to show signs of real distress. Meg, thinking he might be embarrassed should she hold his hand as she had done ever since he had come home, had allowed him to step ahead with Fred but even as she smiled and bent her head to listen to the voice of Peter Dobson, the clever young aircraft designer, above the racket of the bustling hangar, she could see Tom's growing agitation in the rapid jerking of his head and the pitiful sight of his hand reaching out to where he imagined hers might be!

It was the noise of the riveter! Its cheerful chatter echoed about the corner of the hangar as it poured forth its lethal, agonising, fear inspired despair into the damaged mind of Tom Fraser. The man who held it was leaning into what would be the cockpit, directing it into the framework he was putting together and he was whistling as he spilled the machine gun like sound towards the metal.

Meg saw Tom's expression for a second as he turned to look for her. His mouth was open, a black hole of agony in his chalk white face. Deep lines carved his flesh from cheekbone to chin and his eyes were dead as charcoal in the unbearable horror which consumed him. He turned away from her towards the aircraft and the cheerful man who worked there, and even above the tumult of the busy workshop they all heard him scream.

'NO! For God's sake, no! Get down, oh Christ, quickly Andy ... oh Christ ... where are you hit, lad ... *stretcher bearer* ... oh Christ ... Andy ... no, no, lie still ... no ... oh Jesus ... it's ... no, don't move. I know ... I know it hurts, lad ... I know ... its the barbed wire ... its ... you're caught in it but I'll get you out, Andy. Keep your head down ... lie still ... lie still.'

Tom had backed into a corner of the hangar and every man in it felt the skin on the back of his neck prickle in horror and every one of them watched, pityingly, some almost in tears as Tom Fraser re-lived that moment which was, it seemed, the one which had finally driven him to madness.

He sank down on his haunches, his arms about some unseen body, cradling it to him in infinite tenderness, rocking backwards and forwards and from the corner of her eye Meg saw Fred move towards the office. She took a step towards Tom, scarcely able to bear his pain, tears flowing unnoticed across her face, but something told her not to touch him, to let him live out this moment in his broken life.

'Hush now . . . hush lad . . . there . . . I've got you . . . they'll be here soon, no . . . don't cry Andy, yes lad . . . I know it hurts but the stretcher bearer will be . . . no . . . please Andy . . . don't move . . . yes lad . . . your mother's coming in a minute . . . keep still . . . keep still.'

He became quieter then as though the burden in his arms slept for a moment, staring out over the devastation he saw in his mind, then, just when Meg thought she might go to him, gather him up into her compassionate arms he began to struggle, hitting out with clenched fists and drawing back from something, holding the comrade he protected.

'No! No! No! please lads . . . let me stay with him . . . you can't just leave him . . . no, no.' He began to scream helplessly, mindlessly, sobbing and shaking his head and one of the men who watched turned away, moaning.

'*He's still alive, dammit* . . . he's still alive, you bastards . . . Andy . . . Andy . . . I'll not leave you. No . . . no, please lads . . . you can't leave him hanging on this wire . . . see, he's still alive . . . no . . . look . . . let me get him free . . . I'll cut the bloody wire.' Then a subtle change, deeper, deeper until his voice was an angry snarl, 'Kill him then . . . kill him if you won't save him . . . for Christ's sweet sake . . . here . . . you . . . give me that pistol . . . Sir . . . if you won't do it, I will.' A change again, quiet now, peaceful, soothing, 'there, lad . . . there, that's better . . . there . . . no pain now . . . there.'

It was later, as he lay beneath the heavy blanket of drug-induced sleep administered by the doctor Fred had summoned that Meg Fraser finally knew that Tom would never again be the easy going, impishly grinning man who had gone gladly, eagerly to the service of his country. He had come home unmarked but his simple philosophy of good will to his fellow man had been taken from him, and he simply could not function without it. She had thought to heal him with her love, had even believed she was doing so; with the peace and trust and mutual love he shared with her child but now she knew she could not do it alone.

He was seen by a specialist. A man who, with others like him, ministered to the thousands who came back to their families, broken and tormented and who now lived in a world peopled with spectres and Meg was told he must be allowed to live in peace, in the safe and untroubled calm only his family could give him, in his home, in the familiar, *secure* surroundings where there was nothing to frighten him. He was not dangerous, the quiet man told her, merely ... destroyed. His shell remained and a slender thread of what had once been the bright and merry mind of her husband but he must not be confounded by anything more stressful than the drifting by of one peaceful day upon another. And if he was to be left alone, he said, knowing of Mrs Fraser's business enterprises she must employ a man, someone unobtrusive but trained for such things, who would care for Mr Fraser whilst she was away. A strong dependable man. Would she like him to supply one such for her?

'I know of someone who would help me, Dr Carmichael but I'm afraid he is not a trained nurse. He is not young, older than Tom but he is strong ... and kind. Tom is very fond of him ... trusts him. This man has a great affinity with those who are ... hurt. He has ... been hurt himself. He has infinite patience with Tom. Do you think ...?'

'I don't know, Mrs Fraser. I would have to speak with him, assess his character and be convinced he is suitable. When I said "trained" I was thinking of someone who has worked with such men as your husband but many of these are not medically qualified. Many of them were conscientious objectors and worked, not as fighting men but helping those who were wounded. Some of them have remained to care for those who will never recover but if you would like to bring your man to the hospital I will give you my opinion as to his suitability.'

They sat on a bench in the winter sunshine and their breath curled about their heads. They had their backs against the wall of what had been Tom's potting shed. She had brought him out a mug of tea from the kitchen, and one for herself and they sipped it in the serene silence Will Hardcastle seemed able to spin about himself.

A pair of whitethroats had built their nest in the bramble bush at the back of the shed and as Meg had approached he had been standing watching them wing fearlessly back and forth in the sunshine. They had flown away, startled by the sound of her voice but as she and Will sat and talked, the birds came back, reassured by the peace.

A robin slipped from beneath the roots of an old oak tree, burrowing among the campions which grew at its base but seemed unalarmed by the presence of the man and the woman.

'You know why I am here, Will?'

'I can guess, Mrs Fraser.'

'I must get back to work, you see. The factories need someone at their head and there is only myself. I have run them now for four years and though I had hoped . . . well, my first love is the hotel, you know that?'

'Aye! I remember when you first came to "The Hawthorne Tree". They said you couldn't do it, those about. A slip of a lass! Taking that old place and turning it into an inn. They laughed, Mrs Fraser, but I reckon you showed 'em.'

She sighed sadly. 'Yes, I showed them.'

Will shifted on the bench, lifting his crippled leg into a more comfortable position. 'You will again, Mrs Fraser. Happen you could put someone in to see to the airplanes and that, then you could get back to "Hilltops".'

'Perhaps . . . one day but in the meanwhile I cannot let the factories run down. There is so much to be done. This is the era of the machine, Will. The airplane and the automobile and we will see great things in the next ten years. I cannot let what I have been . . . been given . . . slip away!'

Will sipped his tea and watched the robin, saying nothing, letting Meg Fraser talk and his calm acceptance of life, of his own infirmity and the hardships he had shared in his early life with his mother, settled the despair in the woman at his side and gradually the tension eased from her. She felt the sun gently warm her face and listened to the birds call to each other.

'I'll see to him, Mrs Fraser. Don't you fret. You go and do what you must. He'll be safe with me.'

And so he was. In the lovely serenity of the surrounding country-side, the acres of parkland, the gardens, the land behind the house which held the vegetable plot, Tom Fraser found the peace he needed. Meg bought a bit of farmland, twenty acres or so which lay to the rear and side of 'Hilltops' and with a sense of continuity, remembering Tom's love of the animals he had cared for and the land he had tended at Silverdale, told Will to do with it as he liked.

He and Tom, of whom he was in discreet charge, the doctor had told him, explaining what that meant, went off each day to overlook the small herd of cows, the pigs, the hens, the growing kitchen gardens and the paddocks in which Meg intended to put a pony for Beth. Two men just back from France were taken on, to help with the extra work which the added land entailed and often accompanied by the little girl, four years old now, a couple of puppies, young collies which Will had bought from a local farmer, they would form a protective phalanx about the fragile man who was Tom Fraser. Meg thanked God for Will Hardcastle as she watched him, like the Pied Piper himself, moving about the property with a trailing group of children – for what else could she call Tom – and animals at his back.

She watched the dreadful sorrow fade from the closed-up face of her husband in the peaceful routine of his days and even heard him laugh as he tried to milk one of his cows. She was tranquil in the knowledge that the land, the woods, the fields in which he walked, the animals he cared for, the certain surety of the changing seasons would bring a small measure of hope to the man she loved. Hope!

Now, somehow, she must heal herself for she had not gone unscathed in the battle.

Chapter thirty-eight

It was April. Tom was in the garden, his hand protectively in that of Meg's daughter as they watched the playful, excited antics of Will's new puppies, bought to take the place of the old dog whom they had sadly missed, farm dogs of the kind used for sheep and to be trained for work when they were ready, Will said, though of what sort he did not specify. They leaped about the garden chasing shadows and each other and Meg heard Beth laugh and saw her rest her face against Tom's hand. Tom looked down at her and his eyes were in that moment, calm, the haggard look of fear gone in the child's loving acceptance of him.

The wind lifted the peak of his cap and mischievously whipped it away, and for several minutes the child and the puppies were engaged in an exhilarating chase which brought roses to Beth's cheeks and a smile to Tom's face.

The garden was filled with the young growing things of spring. The lawn was a smooth emerald green and the dogs made a frantic eddy of movement on it as they raced round from the back of the house. Tom followed slowly behind, moving with the leisurely step of the country man. He had developed it at Silverdale, ambling at the gait of Atkinson, the gardener, an elderly man with his origins in the soil where crops were planted and harvested in season, where cows calved and mares foaled all in their own good time so what was the sense of hurry. It had embraced Tom, that view on life and now his damaged mind had need of it, was more secure in the ways and pace of what grew in the earth and of the animals he helped Will to tend.

When he had first come home, white-faced and trembling at the least noise, his hand fumbling for hers, often clutching at the very air in his desperate need of something to hold, Meg had remembered how he had once smoked a pipe. She had bought him another one day when she was in Buxton and given it to him, not to smoke as he used to, but just to allow those thin, fluttering hands a focus in their dreadful search for deliverance from terror.

For a week or two he had held it gratefully, clung to it when the trembling began and it had seemed to comfort him, giving him a frail lifeline back to safety.

'Why don't you try some tobacco in it, Tom?' Will had said. 'My old Grandad loved a pipe of baccy. Said it gave him a bit of peace from all the female clacking tongues when he couldn't stand them any more. He reckoned the ladies were none too keen on the smell of pipe smoke and my granny was a right old chatterer so when he'd had enough of her he'd light up that old pipe of his and go off down the garden to his shed and she never followed him there!'

The simple tale had made Tom smile and the next time they went into Ashbourne he asked her hesitantly if she would bring him some tobacco. He had coughed a time or two when he lit it, then smiled.

'I think I've done this before, Meggie,' he said, pleased with himself as though to recapture a *pleasant* memory was a wonderful achievement. The small task of lighting the pipe, of getting it to draw to his satisfaction steadied him on many an occasion when he was struck by what he apologetically called his 'shakes.'

Now smoke wreathed about his head and Meg, as she watched through the sitting room window was suddenly struck by how *elderly* he looked. His back was slightly stooped and his tumbled curly hair had lost that golden vigour of youth and become quite grey and yet he was still only thirty-one. Where did that vital, merry-faced young man go, she thought wearily as her eyes followed his slow progress towards the gate in the high wall which ran at the side of the house. The one with the infectious good humour, the enthusiastic capacity for work, who laughed and gave joy to others, bringing harmony where there had been strife. Who was strong and yet gentle. She could see him now with his bright head thrown back, the arch of his brown throat, the curve of his brown cheek glowing in the sunshine of the back yard in Great George Square. She could feel the swell of his youthful shoulder muscles under her hands as he raced her along on the tandem, his shouted encouragement turning heads along the road. His grin had been lively, his wit not sharp but droll. His bright mind, the width and depth of his compassion, his willingness to listen and simply *be there* for those who needed it. His charm had been endearing and yet he had revealed a quality of endurance which had brought comfort to others, which had brought him

458

and many of his comrades through four years of devastation, only succumbing to the horror of it when his strength was no longer needed. He had given *her* peace in the past and his love for her had been the rock on which she had re-built her life after Martin's death, but *she did not love him in return*! She loved him . . . aah how she loved him for he was Tom and was as dear to her almost as her own child, but her love, *her love* was still somewhere in France, buried in the earth where Martin was. Martin . . . oh my dearest . . . my love . . .

I shall never be free, she thought bleakly. Never be allowed to quicken in the joy of passion again, to be enlivened, stimulated by a mind and spirit as sharp as my own. To lie in the arms of my love, to be loved and sighed over, to whisper in the night, to feel strong and possessive arms about me, to feel the hot kiss of need, the urgency of need . . . dear God . . . the desire . . . a man's strong body . . .

She groaned, deeply ashamed then tapped on the window and when Tom turned, waved to him and was rewarded by the way his face lit up at the sight of her. Beth waited for him at the gate, her hand held out to him with the simplicity of a child, not understanding, nor caring that her father was different from other men. They both looked back to her and waved, and Martin's eyes glowed from his child's face and Meg turned away, a small sound of pain escaping from between her lips, then she stood up abruptly, smoothing the soft camel wool of her skirt about her hips. She had a lot to do this morning if she was to return to work and it did no good to dwell on the past. She had Beth . . . and Tom.

He watched her undress that night and his man's eyes admired her firm, pointed breasts, the slim neatness of her waist and the womanly curve of her hips. They ran down her white, straight back to her rounded buttocks and lingered on the incredible length and shapeliness of her legs but when she turned and saw him looking at her and, astonished, smiled the smokey golden smile of a woman's invitation, his eyes lifted to hers and in them was merely the trusting love, the need, the almost innocent longing to be held, not as a man, but as one who is lost and longs to be found and comforted.

'Meg, come to bed, sweetheart,' he begged and she knew the meaning in those words had nothing to do with desire.

'Let me just brush my hair.'

'I'll do it for you.'

She knelt in the bed, her back to him. He knelt behind her, his knees on either side of her body but there was no languorous tension, no delicious trembling, no heightened awareness, no soft laughter nor whispered kisses of what was to come. He brushed her hair, every stroke filled with his deep, deep love, a despairing love for the war had effectively emasculated Tom Fraser and as he grew stronger and more aware, his mind knew it and, as he did on so many nights he wept his frustration in her arms until he slept.

Will brought the Vauxhall round to the front of the house at eight o'clock the next morning and they all came out on to the gravel path to wave her off and for a moment she thought it was going to be alright. The puppies were there, jumping to Tom's hand and the other was clasped in Beth's. Will stood behind him and put a hand on his shoulder and Tom tried, he really tried to stop his head from shaking and his mouth from trembling, terrified beyond words to be without her, even for a few hours, but she felt her heart plunge in despair for how could she leave him . . . how . . . how? She had deliberately dovetailed the relationship between Will and himself, giving him a bond to which he could unite whilst she was away. He had accompanied Will in the fields and the gardens, about the stable yard, planting, digging, feeding the animals, walking the boundaries of the estate – which he had never left since the disastrous day at the airfield – and it had been for the sole purpose of getting Tom used to being without her, to relying, not just on her, but on the strong and gentle man who walked beside him each day. There were others in the house to watch over him. Annie, Edie Marshall, Sally Flash, no longer servants but friends now who loved him. She *must* work. Her inn and her hotel were gone but Martin's factories must be kept working, must be organised under her own firm leadership as they had been since Martin's death in 1914. Fred Knowsley, Peter Dobson the designer, all her other managers were excellent men, picked and trained, many of them, by Martin himself, but they needed a hand to guide them, someone to make decisions, to find a market for their product and to sell it when one was found. She had her investments, those she had made years ago. The war had created advantage for those willing to take a gamble and many businesses had been readily available to those with some cash to spare, as their owners marched off to war. Many were killed in the trenches and their widows were only too glad to be rid of the small workshops, the factories, the builders' yards, masons, cabinet makers, coach-builders and bootmakers, carried away on the tide of patriotic fervour which swept them to their deaths often left thriving concerns and Meg had speculated successfully in many of them, putting in men who could run them for her. They brought in a comfortable income on which to support her household but she could not let go unfinished what Martin had begun. There was not even a headstone to mark his place, where those who loved him could remember him, so this, what Meg did, must serve as his remembrance.

'My darling, what is it?' Meg's compassion for her husband was absolute. She took his hand. Will and Beth and Annie watched the familiar scene unfold itself as Tom was wrapped about in the comforting love of his wife. It enclosed them all, that love, touched them all, bound them together in this tragedy.

'What if I should . . .?' Tom's face was deathly afraid.

'What . . . tell me, sweetheart?'

'If I should . . .' He could not even speak the words to describe the dread he lived in. But Will Hardcastle, with the instinctive knowledge which is often given to those who are themselves damaged, was ready and Meg thanked God for the day she had met this man so many years ago.

'I was wondering if you could help me today, Tom. You see I'm not much good with tools . . .' which was untrue, 'and with you having worked with a carpenter in the past, I was wondering . . . well, I had this idea of setting up a small woodworking shop in the corner of the garage. I thought you could advise me on what wood to get. We could make things . . .' The vague wave of his hand gave the impression that whatever they were he and Tom would have themselves a wonderful time. He had the interest and enthusiasm of a boy of twelve and Meg could see Tom's eyes begin to clear and his own interest lifted the corners of his mouth in a half smile.

'A workshop . . .?'

'That's what we need, Tom. When the days are wet we could . . .'

'What a splendid idea, Will. We could make a . . . a . . .' He was confused then, unsure of what it was they would build, unsure of what he was about to say, his brain which had once been alive with humour and a willingness to take part in anything which sounded fun, awakened only momentarily, but Will finished the sentence for him.

'. . . a chair for the garden. How about that? For Mrs Fraser to sit on in the sunshine . . .'

'. . . and one for me as well, please, Daddy.' Beth looked up appealingly into Tom's face, absolutely without doubt that he could do it and Tom began to smile and Meg knew it would be alright . . . this time!

It was the first step and it was taken hesitantly by Meg Fraser but the day would come when she would be forced to attend full time to the growing needs of Martin's companies. The Royal Flying Corps and the Royal Naval Air Service had amalgamated in April 1918 to become the Royal Air Force. The government, under Lloyd George had no time for the newly formed service and the economies which were enforced lay over its grave. The 'war to end wars' was over and ahead was a bright new future with peace assured for generations to come so what did they want with the fledgeling air service, they asked. Economies *must* be made and the enormous number of men and women, the machines they flew and maintained were no longer needed. Major aircraft builders were finding themselves out of work but those who believed in the future of aviation were fighting for survival and Meg Fraser was one of them. She must at first revise the smaller factory to manufacture urgently needed consumer goods until civil aviation could find its feet since the demand for military craft was almost finished. Large, luxury motor cars, enormously expensive to tax were being built by some of the bigger companies but it was the lighter vehicle which would be the most popular. The twenties would see the appearance of a new type of motor car, the motor car for the man in the street and Meg meant to produce it. She had it in mind to develop a new company which would finance the start of the airline she intended to build, based on Martin's 'Wren', and its successor which Peter Dobson was already working on. She must run her young business alone now. Martin was gone and Tom as well. Like her daughter he must be loved and protected, given support and comfort when he was hurt and it was up to Meg alone to bear it.

She must do as Martin would have done had he come home to this bright future ahead of them.

Martin! It was almost five years since he had left her on a tide of promises which his death had left unfulfilled. It was not often she allowed herself the indulgence of deliberately bringing him back for the pain it caused her was more than she could stand but now she did. He had seemed to be about the hangar that day as Fred had taken her on a guided tour, just as though he was intent on seeing what was to be done with his 'Wren' and his Hunter automobile, and she had fancied his ghost would always haunt this place he had loved. And it was here that they had loved, here in this small sitting room with the fire playing on the pale walls, here where his child had been conceived. She let him slip in to her thoughts though she knew it would tear her apart. He came slowly, softly, like a shadow which has no menace, but is merely a hazed form with no substance. He took shape, stepping from the firelight with the same indolent grace, the same audacious smile, the familiar amused tilt to his dark eyebrows as though to say what the devil did Meggie Hughes imagine herself to be doing dreaming of a ghost. She smiled at him, knowing he would understand and held out her hands and he captured them swiftly, as he had captured her heart, her body, in a single dazzling moment. She had always loved him, but she had not known of it until that moment. He had held a place for her in his masculine heart, waiting for her to step into it, knowing before she did that it must happen, that it would take but a heartbeat when it did. He bent to lay his cheek against hers and she could feel the warmth of it, the smooth, just shaved texture of his flesh and smell the sharp, clean fragrance of lemon soap which lay about him. He grinned then, high-spirited, mettlesome, dangerous even, to those who would oppose him but *she* would not, his expression said, for she was his love. His eyebrows were thick and silken, black and fierce and she put out an enchanted finger to smooth them, then reached up to push back the tumble of his heavy straight hair from his brown forehead. His eyes were a deep, tobacco-leaf brown and she could see her own face in them, two tiny smiling Meg Hughes and she watched herself lift her lips for his kiss. She sighed and stretched her long body as it warmed to his. She waited for him to undo, one by leisurely one, the buttons of her silk blouse, sighing, dreaming, lingering over it and when she slipped, eager now as she had been then from the dainty lace of her bodice she heard him groan in the physical desire of wanting her, and she whispered his name . . .

'Martin . . . Martin . . . Martin . . . Martin.' She was weeping helplessly, her voice loud, desperate, *angry*! She had fallen to her knees and she clutched at the settee on which she and Tom had been sitting half an hour ago and the agony, the slashing pain cut

463

at her for she was alone . . . dear God, she was alone and her body agonised over it for it wanted Martin Hunter's and he was dead! She had deliberately let her mind play a vicious trick, bringing him back, putting his hands on her breasts and his lips about her eyes and throat and the female core of her had melted from the ice in which it had been preserved for five years and come savagely alive, devouring her and now . . . now she must quench it and go to the bed she shared with Tom. She sobbed helplessly, burying her face in the cushions to muffle the sound and for a while Martin Hunter's ghost stayed at her back, beseeching her to look round and see his smile but she dare not. *She dare not*!

They were alone, the next day she and Tom, the last of the short spring day gone with the skittish April clouds over the hillside and down into the Dovedale gorge. They had walked to the edge of the garden with the little girl, swinging her between them and after tea in the nursery had put her to bed together. Tom had bathed her first, watching her intently as she splashed her hands flat against the water, the spray she caused putting diamond water drops in her short tawny curls. Her skin was flushed, rosy with a child-like, breathless beauty and her huge, deep brown eyes laughed up into his.

'Mind, Daddy, or you'll get all wet,' she cried, beating the water more firmly so that Daddy, despite her warning, *would* get wet. They had played together as Meg watched impassively, still numbed with the pain she had suffered, by her own doing she was quick to acknowledge, the evening before and she barely heard, nor made the effort to capture the words he spoke as he lifted the child gently from the bath and began to rub her with a towel.

'Good girl,' he was saying. 'Stand still for Daddy, there's a good girl. You're like a little eel.' He was smiling, his blue eyes looking directly into her brown ones and his voice was soft with wonder. 'I don't know,' he said, 'you get more like me every day, you little imp.'

'Do I, Daddy?' The child looked trustingly up at him.

'You do indeed and lovely you are with it.' He kissed her rounded stomach and made the sound of a raspberry on it and she squealed with delight. 'Now stand still while I get your toes dry.'

They had gone, Meg and Tom, hand in hand from the nursery when Beth fell asleep and they sat in the fire-glowed peace of the sitting-room. He was calm, at peace in his love for the child. He lit his pipe and his long drawn out sigh was not of misery but of content.

'I can't get over it sometimes.' He smiled and his voice was wondering.

'Can't get over what, Tom?'

'Our Beth.'

'Our . . . our Beth?' It was the first time he had uttered the northcountryman's possessive use of a relative's name. In the old days he and Martin had always called her 'our Meg' as did Mrs Whitley and she had done the same with them. It was affectionate, unique and infinitely enduring especially in the vocabulary of a man or woman from Liverpool. She felt a pulse begin to beat in her neck and a tiny warning flashed behind her eyes.

'It's those eyes of hers,' he continued dreamily.

'Yes?' Dear God, what was coming her frantic heart had time to plead before he went on.

'Aye, they seem to get a deeper blue every day.'

'Blue . . .!'

'D'you remember mine, our Meg?' *Our Meg* now . . . '. . . when I was a lad? Mrs Whitley used to say they were as blue as speedwell. They're not now, of course. I suppose they fade as you get older but our Beth's certainly inherited them, that's for sure. They go with her lovely hair. That's from you, love, there's nothing more certain than that but those eyes of hers . . . well, there's no doubt where she got those from!'

He gave another small satisfied sigh then put his head on the back of the settee and drew contentedly on his pipe. 'Aye, she's a little beauty and no mistake and I reckon it's time we had us another, our Meg!'

The immaculately dressed gentleman with the cultured voice smiled at the startled farmer's wife as she shut the farm gate, bidding her a pleasant 'Good evening,' and raising his hat most politely.

She had turned away, ready to follow the dozen cows she had just brought in from the field, across the muddy, dung-spattered yard, and the dog who helped her lifted a delicate paw, waiting for her command.

'Excuse me, madame.'

She turned, astonished. *Madame!*

465

'I was wondering if you knew of a short cut to the "Hilltop Hotel" from here. I appear to have missed my way.'

'Well . . .' She hitched her shawl more warmly about her shoulders, eyeing him warily. 'I am a friend of Mrs Fraser, he went on. 'I had heard that Tom . . . Mr Fraser was returned from the war so I was on my way up to see him. How I got lost I do not know for I have been up here a dozen times.'

That was different, of course, if he knew the poor demented chap those here about had heard of, and no doubt a visit from a friend would perk him up a bit.

'Well . . . you go on a ways up here . . . see that lane, it'll bring you out at the back of the hotel and then . . .'

Chapter thirty-nine

She was at her desk trying to concentrate on the papers which were scattered upon it but the puppies' excited barking and the voice of her daughter bringing them peremptorily to 'heel', a command they both completely ignored, called to her and she stood up, going to the window to watch them. Will was there with Tom beside him, turning over the winter heavy soil ready for the planting of the zinnias, the begonias, marigolds, dahlias and lupins which would fill her garden with a rainbow of colour during the summer. Beth was dressed in scarlet, a bright woollen cap about her ears, a jumper and leggings knitted by Annie and all to match the lovely colour in her cheeks. Her eyes were alive with joy as the puppies carried her from one end of the large garden to the other, a swirling, leaping vortex of movement which brought a smile to Meg's lips.

It was Sunday and though she usually caught up with the many small tasks which were overlooked during her hectic week she was tempted to put on her coat and join the group in the garden. Over the sound of her child's laughter and the yapping of the dogs she could just make out the peaceful voices of Will and Tom as they discussed what should go where in the border which they were digging. The sun shone and when she opened the window she could hear a blackbird in the spinney beyond the garden wall lift his voice to the coming of summer, only weeks away now, and she filled her lungs with the sweet country air and felt her heart move in hopeful anticipation of good things to come, surely?

The two men turned as she leaned from the window and Tom smiled. His face was in repose, the pipe clenched between his teeth. His eyes, once so blue and vivid, were serene. He was doing what he loved best in the world. He was, in this moment, safe, content, his world peopled with those whom he loved and who loved him and he called out to Meg, his voice confidently strong.

'Come on out into the sunshine, sweetheart. Come and tell us where you want these lupins before me and Will come to blows over it!'

She laughed, shaking her head, then, on a whim, changed her mind.

'Alright, just for half an hour then. I could do with some fresh air to clear my head. I'll just go and get a coat.'

She was surprised when she rounded the corner of the house into the garden, surprised and faintly alarmed to see Will hurrying, his deformed leg swinging awkwardly, towards the far corner of the high-walled garden and the gate which Meg could see stood open. He held his garden fork in one hand but the other flailed the air as though he was trying desperately to cleave his way through some thickness which was doing its best to hold him back. Tom stood rooted to the spot where she had last seen him, watching Will stumble away from him, his face quite blank and staring with that awful expression she had come to dread, his pipe on the ground at his feet where it had fallen from his slack mouth.

She began to walk slowly towards him and alarm tip-toed stealthily into her mind and her heart-beat quickened. Her eyes darted about the garden, piercing through budding shrubs and bushes, behind massed rhododendrons and hydrangeas not yet in full leaf, searching for the splash of scarlet which would locate her daughter but there was nothing to be seen and as her gaze returned to Will she was just in time to see him vanish through the strong garden gate which he had erected when Beth started to walk. From somewhere distant she could hear the intoxicated yelping of the two puppies.

She began to run then for though there was nothing wrong – was there? – Will's urgency had transferred itself to her and she wanted to reassure herself that Beth was just beyond the open garden gate with the dogs. She had no time to stop to comfort the frightened confusion of her husband who had put out his hand to her as she went by him, his eyes begging her to tell him where his child was, to tell him she was safe and not gone with . . . with Andy, but flung herself down the green slope of the grass after Will, her only concern at the moment the safety of her daughter. She had time only to wonder at the strangeness of Will who was so careful of such things and of the child's safety, in leaving the garden gate open, and at herself for not noticing it as she looked from the window.

As she reached the swinging gate Will re-entered the garden, the two dogs dancing about his heels. His face was like paper, every vestige of colour drained away and he almost fell as he stumbled against her.

'She must have gone into the house.' His voice was no more than a thread of sound in his throat so desperately did he want to believe what he said and Meg turned again frantically, running past the pleading hand of her husband for the second time.

'Meggie . . .' he moaned as she went by but for the first time since he had come back from the war she had no time for him.

Annie turned peaceably as Meg flung herself into the kitchen, her face calm and relaxed as she fashioned the last of the lemon biscuits which Beth loved.

'You're in a hurry, lass,' she said. 'What's . . .'

'Where's Beth?'

Annie smiled, unperturbed in that last moment of peace but Meg gripped her arms with such violence Annie winced and tried to pull away as Meg hissed into her face for already her mother's heart knew and was terror-stricken.

'Where is she . . . where is she?'

'Nay love . . .' Annie's calm expression slipped away and though she was perfectly certain Beth was as safe as houses with her Will to protect her she could understand Meg's anxiety about her child in the face of what she herself now knew about the man who had menaced Meg for so long. Had she not seen it, the madness in his eyes when he had come to the house, and felt his evil but really there was no need to be so . . .

'Where is Beth . . .?' Meg was almost screaming, her hunted gaze raking the room as though Annie, and poor Edie who fell back before the force of her strange fury, had her hidden somewhere.

'She's out in the garden with Will and . . .' Annie began bravely, trying to place a comforting hand on Meg but she threw it off and ran from the kitchen, back towards the garden and the gate through which, in a moment her babbling mind begged, her little girl would surely re-appear.

Will had dropped his fork in the gateway. The puppies ran about unchecked, the heady excitement of being beyond the walls without supervision quite going to their silly heads, and Tom, his face like plaster, his eyes blank so great was his trepidation, had ventured to the brink of the gateway to peer hesitantly into the world which had taken his child from him.

469

'Beth...' he was crying, his confused terror driving him back and back into the madness she had thought was almost gone. Her own panic, and Will's, where Tom had known only calm and infinite comfort, drove him beyond reason and though he was aware that Beth had disappeared he could make no sense of it.

'Get out of my way, Tom.' Meg pushed him aside roughly, his need no longer mattering in the greater one of her child.

Will was just coming round the corner of the wall which surrounded the garden, his eyes darting frantically from tree to shrub to rock, to every conceivable bit of cover which might hide the little girl. He called her name again and again and the echoes of his voice leaped merrily across the hilltops and down into the valleys, coming back to him without her. His face was sweated now, and drawn with pain for in his haste he had fallen several times, savaging his crippled leg with more punishment than it could take.

'I can't find her, Meg ... bloody hell ... it's only been ten minutes ... I've looked in the yard and the workshop ... every place she could be hiding but there's no sign of her ... dear Christ ...' He pushed his soil-encrusted hand despairingly through his hair, turning his eyes away from her sudden awful stillness, for both of them had only one thought and neither dare speak of it to the other. 'I was talking to Tom ... you saw us. She was down by the gate ... the dogs had found something ... I don't know what. We hardly took our eyes off her ... we could hear her laughing and shouting to the dogs, you know how she does ... Jesus ... when it went quiet I turned round to see what mischief she was up to ...' he was near to tears '... and ... dear God, Meg ... the gate was open. I didn't even know she could reach the latch ... I thought it was locked ... I *know* I locked it. I know I did ... even then I thought she was playing ... hiding.' His voice broke in desolate appeal. He turned again to stare out across the Dovedale Valley and the springtime beauty of the hills flowed endlessly away into the distance. A trailing twist of cloud, like a knight's banner unfurled, drifted slowly in the eggshell blue of the sky and on the hills ewes called to their growing lambs and the peace was made all the more unbearable by the deafening thunder of the terror in Meg's heart.

'She's not in the kitchen,' she said baldly and her eyes clung to his, begging for something he could not give her.

470

'She *must* be somewhere in the house,' he proclaimed roughly, knowing it was not possible, praying it could be.

'I would have met her coming in as I was coming out.'

'Then where has she got to? The dogs were here, not far from the gate so it stands to reason she must be near. She's too small to have gone any distance . . .' His voice trailed away uncertainly and he put up a hand to shade his eyes from the sun. '*Beth . . . Beth . . .*' he called again and Meg stood mutely and watched him, paralysed by fear and the appalling conviction that . . . dear God, she dare not even think it!

Will's pale face had taken on a tinge of grey, like the colour of old cement. He began to move towards the plateau which overlooked the valley. The new grass was coming through, smooth and green, humped here and there with tussocky growth and scattered with grey pitted rock. It led gradually towards the stony path which was the only way down to the valley bottom and the fast flowing – at this time of year – river which ran there. A place so peaceful, so lovely and yet filled with peril for a small girl alone. She had been there a hundred times or more with himself and Tom, with Meg and the growing pups, but if she had gone out alone . . . dear God, let her be on her own . . . please . . . would not those same dogs have automatically followed her? They loved the water and the rough and tumble of climbing and jumping and racing with the child as she threw sticks for them.

He began to run, like a child with one leg in the gutter, his crippled limb slowing him, down the slope towards the path which led to the valley and when Meg would have followed him, mindless now and unable to think for herself he turned on her savagely.

'Not with me, you fool. Split our forces and we can cover more ground. I'll look down here and you go and circle the grounds. Look in the spinney and the fields and . . . for God's sake, woman, don't just stand there . . . go . . . go.'

They ran about frantically. Megan and Will, passing and re-passing Tom as he crouched at the garden gate calling for his baby in a plaintive voice. Annie and Edie, two elderly ladies, at first red in the face from their exertions and determination to find the child, then grey and terrified when they did not. Their old hearts pounded and their legs trembled with exhaustion as they climbed the stairs and searched attics and ran along hallways and into dust-sheeted bedrooms. They came outside when they had covered every nook and cranny in the house which could possibly hide a little girl and climbed over rocks and across pitilessly jagged paths and when the spring afternoon gradually faded into evening, whilst Meg put her face to the wall and wept, Will reached for the telephone.

The police constable could make neither top nor tail of the story Mrs Fraser babbled of a man who had intimidated her for years, and sent hastily for his sargeant, aware now that they were dealing with more than a child gone missing for an hour or two, and the sargeant, equally out of his depth telephoned headquarters for someone in higher authority to be summoned. The police Inspector was disbelieving though he did not show it, naturally. The poor woman was distraught, but surely, he thought privately, no one would put up with such things, if it were true, and if it was why had she not reported it to the proper authority? Certainly he would look up old police records, he told her but first would it not be more sensible to concentrate on the area about the house and grounds for surely that was a more likely place to find the little girl. Benjamin Harris, yes he had made a note of the name and he would certainly make enquiries as to his whereabouts but in the meanwhile ... No, they could not search the moor at night, he explained patiently for his men would not even find their own way, let alone a small child, in the dark. The vast, unchanging stretches of moorland and high hillside in which, though they were cut in a dozen places by stony tracks, a man could be lost within hours, perhaps never to be found, were not to be treated lightly but with respect and in an orderly manner, he said kindly and as soon as day break came they would begin. Not only his own men but all the scores of farmers and labourers who lived in the area and who knew it as well as anyone, and who had volunteered. Dogs were to be used he explained, those which searched for sheep when the winter snows fell. They were being assembled now and would beat a circle outwards from 'Hilltops' starting at dawn. It was, luckily, a mild night, he said comfortingly and the little lass would take no harm from cold. Dressed in scarlet wool, Mrs Fraser said, so she would be warm and easy to spot and she must try and get some sleep and see to her husband who was in a terrible state, poor chap.

But the doctor 'saw' to Tom, giving him such a massive sedative he fell into immediate and heavy sleep and Meg wished she might do the same for the pictures in her head were too terrible to contemplate.

Three days later the police called off their search of the area in a ten mile radius of the hotel. They had covered every square inch, looking behind and under each shrub and gorse bush and rock, every stretch of bracken and heather, in every hole and gully and cleft in which a small girl could slip, and found nothing, the Inspector pityingly told the frozen-faced woman who had once been the beautiful Mrs Fraser. His men were exhausted, he explained, having spent twenty hours in each twenty-four looking for her daughter, shifts of them working round the clock with the neighbouring farmers who had neglected their own duties to search for her. It was not that they were abandoning their search, far from it. Fresh men were to be drafted but the field of their enquiries must be widened for it was clear there was ... there was no more to be done around here. But Mrs Fraser was not to give up hope. No indeed. The police force of the country and of the whole of England had been alerted and if the child was to be found, they would find her. Mrs Fraser was aware, was she not, that they had done all they could in this area, he said, uncomfortable in the face of such anguish.

They sat, the four of them, stony-eyed and grey-faced, still in the same clothes they had worn three days ago and stared, not at each other for they could not bear the pain they saw there, hardly able to contain their own, but into the desolation of the future which could hold only the horror of knowing, quite positively that Benjamin Harris had gained the ultimate revenge.

They moved about the house in the next few days, unaware of the reporters at the gate or of the police constable who guarded them from their attentions. They moved from room to room, Will and Annie and Edie, mindless and staring, scarcely speaking, eating what was put before them by the kindly, damp-eyed women, farmers' wives and neighbours who slipped in with soup or a cooked chicken or an apple pie, for Annie was beyond cooking, or even caring. The doctor sedated Tom and anxiously watched them all slip away into the dream world which is the refuge of the badly hurt and those indifferent to the one about them. Of the man Benjamin Harris, no trace could be found, the Inspector told them. He had not been heard of since he had finished his prison sentence years ago. It was believed he consorted with the criminal fraternity but as far as the police were aware he had broken no law since. They would keep searching, of course, and put out bulletins to the force all over the country to be on the look-out for him. Mrs Fraser must get some rest and try not to worry.

On the first day of Beth's disappearance two of her pilots from the Hunter field had been up in their light aircraft, swooping dangerously low over the hills and peaks and moorland surrounding 'Hilltops' to a distance of twenty miles, looking for a splash of scarlet which might be her child, but it was as though she had vanished into the early morning mists which came before the sun, and the Inspector was of the private opinion that they were wasting their time. The little girl could not possibly have gone so far, not on her own, and if someone had taken her ... well ... his thoughts were black but he did not share them with the child's mother.

Will, so strong for Tom, so dependable and four-square when it was needed in the past, could not overcome the guilt which savaged him. He believed that if he had been more vigilant, less taken up with his own pride in Tom's recovery and the garden they were creating again for the summer, the child would still be alive. He knew she was dead, or worse, in the hands of that fiend Meg had told them about and his dreams, were filled with screams and Beth's small face and he knew he was going the way of the man he had once safeguarded. He was helplessly drifting in a nightmare in which he could do nothing but sit and wait ...

But Meg Fraser, her flying suit hanging about her painfully thin frame like an old sack, heedless of the chaos which prevailed in her home, driven by her own nightmares and not knowing what else to do, took off each day from the airfield, oblivious to the men of the press who surged about her at every appearance, flying her small airplane alone and for hours on end, day after day, only returning to re-fuel, criss-crossing systematically the skies above the Derbyshire peaks and moorland which surrounded her home, her eyes searching for that splash of scarlet among the rocks, the grey and green and brown of the empty stretches below her.

It was on the fifth day when she saw it. A speck, no more, tiny and unmoving on a steep crag, a mass of granite encircled by the sparse and tussocky grass which was all that would grow there. Sheep cropped close by and as the aircraft dropped even lower they scattered, running in waves of panic, mothers calling plaintively to their lambs to keep up. The small splash of red did not move as she put the aircraft almost onto the crag itself and for an anguished, desolate moment she knew it was nothing, no more than ... than ... dear God, what could it be so high on the peaks? No flowers of that colour grew up here. A piece of ... blanket, perhaps, a rug left by picnickers but no picnickers came to this desolate part of Derbyshire. It was almost inaccessible, even by men on foot, high and dangerously steep. So what ... what could it be?

Her heart was thudding in her throat, filling it, choking her as she swung her little craft round in a tight circle ready to fly over the rock again. She would go even lower this time since it no longer mattered if she smashed herself to pieces on the crags beneath. She did not care whether she lived or died without, first Martin and now Beth. When he had gone she had wanted to follow him then, but he had left her his child and from that child she had been given a new life. They had *been* her life, both of them. Not Tom, or her hotels, or the businesses she now controlled and if she died, who would grieve her and if she died *her* grief would die with her.

Putting the aircraft into a shallow dive she began her descent, aiming as slowly as she could for the crag on which the splash of colour could be seen. Down she went, closer and closer. She could feel the airplane begin to shudder in that familiar way just before a stall and she adjusted the controls slightly, feeling it respond. Nearer and nearer she got to the ground, watching, quite mesmerised, the tiny red patch come up to meet her, and when it moved and turned slightly to one side her mouth opened wide in a scream of joy and tears jetted from her eyes and her heart soared like the weightless bird she had become as she brought the aircraft out of its dive and into the incredibly beautiful blue of the skies.

Chapter forty

'I can walk it from here, thanks. It's only up at the top of this hill.'

'Are you sure? It'd be no trouble to take you up in the waggon. You look a bit done in!'

The carter looked anxiously at his passenger who had just climbed down and was standing now in the country lane which led nowhere but to the big house at the top of the hill. It was a winding lane, he knew, and long, steep too and this chap didn't look as though he could make it to it's beginning, never mind its end, but the man shook his head and smiled.

'No, thanks all the same. It was good of you to give me a lift from the station but I'll walk this last bit. I feel in need of some fresh air and this is the best I've breathed for a long time. And a bit of exercise won't hurt me, either.'

'Well, if you're sure.'

'No . . . thank you. You've been most kind.'

'Right-ho then. Good luck.'

'Thank you.'

The carter clucked at his horse and flicked the reins across his broad back and they moved off slowly in the pale spring sunshine. The man who had alighted watched them go, then listened for a long while until the sound of the horse's hooves had faded into the distance and were gone. There was nothing to be heard in the gentle warmth of the afternoon but the chatter of a bird in a nearby bush, the rustle of the breeze in the grasses and the high whinny of a pony from somewhere up the hill. His eyes were drawn to the flight of a darting bird with swept back wings, followed by another and he watched them go, something in his eyes and on his bemused face savouring their beauty and swiftness.

He was dressed in an assortment of clothes, a jacket and trousers which did not match, a long belted army greatcoat like that worn by officers, a checked cap of a rather foreign style and a pair of worn leather knee boots into which he had tucked the top of his trousers. He carried a soldier's knapsack. His face was thin, pale and weary with strain and his hair hung over the collar of his greatcoat, dark and streaked with grey, but when he turned his step was light and there was a strange glow deep in his brown eyes as he began the long climb to the house.

She was the first person he saw, as he knew she would be for had not his eyes hungered for the sight of her for nearly five years. She was alone, as he had dreamed of her, her hands busy at some plant, her head bent, and he stopped to watch her, holding this precious, precious moment to him. She wore an outfit the colour of amber. A fluted skirt with the hem eight inches from the ground showing the lovely turn of her slim ankles, and a knitted silk jumper of the same colour which fitted to just below her hips. Her hair caught the sun and the colours in it dazzled him. A rippling foxglow, the warmth of bronze, the tawny sheen of chestnut and with a shock he realised she had cut it short for it stood about her head like a puff-ball. She turned to pick up the trowel from the grass behind her and suddenly, as though aware that she was no longer alone, she became curiously still, wary almost, and, he thought, afraid. She lifted the gardening tool in front of her, holding it as though it was a weapon and he saw her glance about her, then over her shoulder.

'Will,' she called, 'are you there?' but there was no reply from Will, whoever he was. 'Will,' she called again and he had a moment to wonder at the guardedness in her, then he stepped from the shadow of the hedge into the sunlight.

They did not speak nor move then. She stood, a lovely frozen statue of gold and bronze and amber in her soft woollen outfit and every vestige of colour left her face and the blood drained from her brain and she thought she would faint. In her hand was the trowel and she gripped it so fiercely the fine bones of her hand threatened to break through the white skin which covered them. Her eyes, brilliant as golden crystal in her ashen face clung to his and she whispered his name, knowing of course that he was a figment of her imagination as he had been the last time and in that moment as the years and the experiences which occupied them slipped away, her love for him filled every cavity and hollow of her which had been emptied when he left, and she was in agony with it!

His lips, that beloved mouth moved to form her name but there was no sound and she knew it could not be him for he was dead.

Ghosts make no noise and this one was silent, but he *looked* so real. She could see the incredible glow of warmth, of *life* in the depths of his brown eyes, see the shadow about his chin where it was unshaven, the tiny scar he had retained from the crash at Brooklands. The ghost lifted his hand and removed the cap from his head and dark hair fell in an untidy, uncut tumble about his ears and in the darkness there was grey. He took a step towards her and for a moment her eyes fell from his face and moved down his body, taking in the rough clothing, the shabby boots, then swiftly rose to capture his again.

Across the years Meggie Hughes and Martin Hunter looked at one another and still Meg's brain would not accept it and yet her body, remembering the joy, registered with instant awareness who he was. But though her body knew, and her heart knew and rushed gladly to meet his in an ecstacy of reunion, her mind and her brain could not grasp it and lagged far behind.

'How lovely you are,' the ghost said and this time she heard the words and they frightened her for surely she was going mad. Twice now Martin Hunter's spirit had come to her, vividly, vibrantly, rousing her senses, hurting her senses, bruising her own hard won but often fragile courage. He had held out his hands to her last time, smiling as he had always done, looking as he had always done but ... but this time he did not smile, nor lift his eyebrows wryly in that humorous way he had, nor did he put his hands out to her. He was Martin's ghost for he had Martin's eyes but he looked nothing like the Martin she had known ... dear God ... oh sweet God!

'Meggie.' His voice was quite hoarse, his throat clogged with some great emotion and his eyes brimmed with tears. He said no more. He did not move. He seemed incapable of it now, just standing, his cap in one hand, the knapsack hanging awkwardly on one shoulder ... waiting!

Meg dropped the trowel and the trembling began in her hands, moving up through her wrists and arms and shoulders and on until the whole of her body shook violently and her teeth chattered. Tears began to run silently from the corners of her unblinking eyes and she moved her head from side to side, and her mouth opened in a great wail of grief, for if this ghost should go away and leave her alone again she would be desolate.

'Dear Lord ... dear God ... oh God, Martin ... I cannot, just cannot bear it if it is not you,' she cried. She put her clenched fists to her mouth and sank painfully to her knees on the grass and it was then he moved. There was no hesitating now, nor holding back. He dropped the cap and the knapsack and with a great joyous shout he was across the grass to her and she felt ... *could feel* his hands on her arms lifting her up and she stared into his wildly laughing face, not even daring to blink and then his arms were about her, holding her along the hard length of his body. She could feel the rough texture of his coat beneath her cheek and under her desperately clutching hands and she strained to get nearer to him, to get *inside* him where she belonged and the rippling shudders moved them both now as they wept. His breath was about her face and neck and the warmth of him unlocked the frozen, untouched heart of her and the pain was unendurably exquisite as life returned. They did not speak. They could not and for five whole minutes they did not look again into one another's face, just stood and rocked and wept and whispered the name each loved the best in all the world.

At last, though he did not let go of her he put six inches between them and she looked up into his face, then with the delicate touch of smoke on water he laid his lips on hers. They kissed reverently as though they had just exchanged marriage vows, then gripped one another fiercely again, kissed, and looked, and stood in a timeless, endless embrace, home again, both of them, where they truly belonged. Their cheeks were wet with their shared tears, of pain and regret, of anger at what could have been and of joy for what was!

'Meggie ...'

'Martin ... oh ... oh my darling ... Martin ... where?'

'Hush, hush ... there will be time ...'

'I am in a ... I have dreamed ...'

'I know, my sweet girl ... and I ...'

'But how ...?'

'Later ...'

'I love you so ... I have never stopped ... never.'

'I know ...'

'I thought I would die when they told me ...'

'Sweet Jesus, Meggie ... if I could ...'

They were smiling into one another's eyes, the pale sunshine capturing them in a shaft of golden beauty, their arms still about one another when Tom Fraser came round the corner of the house, his hand held in that of Martin Hunter's daughter. He was smiling. He had found the gardening fork Meg had sent him for, right at the back of the potting shed, just where he remembered putting it ... the other day ... last week was it ... no, longer than that ... when ... but his little girl, his lovely Beth had helped him and though he knew they had been gone a long time for they had seen many things to interest them, not only in the shed but along the path they had followed, he knew Meg would not mind. She had suggested they put a bed of bright peonies against the house wall and though it was a bit late, he said dubiously, to plant them, they could give it a try. He had helped Will propogate them from seed, in the cold frame and had been quite childishly delighted with his success.

She was there, just where he had left her, as he knew she would be for she never let him down but ... but there was someone with ... someone with her ... a man ... a tall man who ... a man who had his arms about and ... Oh God, Andy ... she was kissing him. She ... his wife ... his Meg was ... and the man was kissing her and rubbing his face against her cheek ... and ...

He stopped in his own garden and the flash of the exploding shell dazzled him and he couldn't see them any more and the little hand which held his ... not Andy ... no ... shook his ... and ...

'Daddy ... what's the matter, Daddy? Does your head hurt ...?' for Beth Fraser had become used to Daddy's headaches and knew that when he had one he went to bed until he was better. The small hand pulled on his and he held on to it with every ounce of strength he had for if he should leave go ... bloody hell ... he'd be lost forever, he knew he would. He must not leave go of Beth's hand, not for a minute or he would float away across the mud and the blood and the craters filled with ... filled with ... and there would be ... barbed wire and ... there was someone waiting there who ... oh God ... oh God, please don't ...

It was then that the miracle happened. It must be that for what else could you call the sight of the man who had been his brother and the sound of that familiar voice which long ago ... how long ... it must be ... and the strong arms which had held him and the fists, fierce and protective which had kept a frightened five-year-old from those who would hurt him. He had been a child then and now he was a man but still he knew Martin Hunter would always give him a hand.

'Martin! Is it you ... is it really you?' His voice was high with the incredible, unbelievable joy of it. Martin, *their* Martin, who they had thought to be dead, was come home to them . . . Martin! He let go of the little girl and on trembling legs began to run across the grass, reaching out with the hand she had recently held. 'Martin . . . bloody hell . . . where've you been . . . Martin . . . dear God! I can't believe it . . . Martin.'

They met, the three of them, in the centre of the lawn and their arms rose on either side of him and drew him into the circle of their love and they stood together, the three of them and wept. The little girl put her finger in her mouth and her own eyes filled with tears and her mouth trembled for Mummy and Daddy and the man frightened her, but Annie came to swoop her up and carry her into the kitchen where she had made gingerbread men and then she was held in the comfortable lap before the fire and she was allowed to eat *two* as a special treat.

He had bathed and shaved and changed into a pair of Tom's flannels and a warm sweater before he would tell them what had happened and the whole time he was from her sight Meg fidgeted about, longing to throw off Tom's trusting hand, longing to run after Martin, help him bathe, help him shave, help him . . . Oh dear God . . . she wanted to be with him, alone, in a room, *any* room, to peel away the jumble of old clothes he wore, to soothe his weary body, to cleanse it, caress it . . . to rest with him, hold him, *alone* . . . to lock the door and shut them all out, to listen to his voice as he explained what miracle had brought him back to her . . . what horror had kept him from her . . . to tell him about Beth . . . and Tom. *To be alone with him!*

They could not eat, any of them, though Annie put her best before them and they did *their* best. As she cleared away the table of their almost untouched plates she knew that Megan Fraser was as tight as a cork in a bottle and if she was not released soon, the bottle would shatter. She could hardly keep her hands off him, nor her eyes and they shone out from her face in two incredulous beams of love, lingering over his gaunt face, agonising over the slenderness of him, glowing and sighing and dreaming. Annie was afraid, for Tom, though as yet he had noticed nothing strange for he was himself in a delirium of joy over the return of his beloved friend, was not blind!

'I've been in a prisoner of war camp, Meg.' Martin's eyes were just for her as they sat before the fire when Annie had gone. The

481

curtains were drawn and Meg had switched on one lamp and the room was soft and lovely and so was she, his expression said.

'How . . .?'

'We went up that day . . . a lad . . . I can't remember his name . . . on a patrol. It was at the beginning of November and I hadn't been there long but I thought I would be home for Christmas, remember Meggie?' He stretched out his hand for hers and she took it and it was then he noticed she held Tom's with the other, but he thought nothing strange in it for were they not the three musketeers together again, drawn in that unbreakable circle.

'We'd only been up for half an hour or so when, for no reason, my engine stalled.'

'Oh Martin!' She knew the fear of that at first hand, did she not, her expression said, but she would tell him about that later. 'Could you not . . .'

'I couldn't get it started. There was no reason, none, why it should have happened. My speed and height were correct. My forward speed had not eased which is what often causes it. I was not pointed up beyond the maximum lifting angle but, there I was, in a stall and beginning to spin. I put all the controls at neutral and held them there. I pushed the stick forward until the wind began to whistle a bit, then pulled it back gently which should have enabled me to carry on but, nothing happened! I just . . . kept going down . . .'

'Dear God . . .' Meg let go of Tom's hand and both hers gripped Martin's and as she held them she felt the scar tissue which ridged across the back of each one and in the palms. She looked down and saw them then, for the first time. She had been so absorbed in his face, his eyes, the tall leanness of him, the grey in his hair, the paleness of his usually amber skin that she had not looked at his hands. Now she turned them over, running her finger tips tenderly across them and in a moment would have put her lips to them and his eyes said, 'Yes, go on,' but Tom's voice slipped through their total concentration in one another, like a child who cannot wait for the parent to continue the story.

'What happened then, Martin? You must have got out of it, but how . . . in hell's name?'

'I managed to glide in, don't ask me how, Tom but I did and as I hit the ground the bloody engine went . . .'

'On fire?' Meg's voice was no more than a thread of sound in the silence.

482

'Yes!' He put his hand to his eyes for a moment as he re-lived that appalling moment. 'But, as they say, the devil looks after his own,' he smiled, 'and I was thrown into a hedge. God only knows how. My suit was on fire, about the arms ... and ... and the front apparently, but I couldn't tell you what happened next, or for weeks after. I got a clout on the head. I was pretty badly burned about the hands and arms but when I came to I was in a hospital bed and the stupid thing was ... I couldn't speak! I didn't know French, or German, but it wouldn't have made any difference because I couldn't even speak my own bloody language. Shock, the doctor told me later, but of course, they had no idea who I was. The airplane was burnt out, along with its identification markings. They had stripped me naked when they put out the flames, the ones who brought me from the hedge and my papers, identity papers were all destroyed. And so I sat there, or lay there, week after bloody week trying desperately to tell them my name and my rank and all the other paraphernalia we are allowed to give them, and I couldn't even ask for the bloody bed-pan. My hands and arms were heavily bandaged so I was unable to write ...'

'Martin ...' He was visibly distressed and Meg put her hand to his face, cupping his cheek and it was then that the first gap in the drift of joy which enfolded Tom Fraser, allowed in a chink of understanding, of memory, of something which frightened him. It came and went so quickly he did not get a good look at it but he began to recognise the warning prickle at the back of his neck. It was very familiar, oh so very familiar and it had been fired on the battlefields of France, shaped and honed and sharpened and become so efficient it had saved his life, and that of those about him on a dozen occasions.

'I knew by the calendar that they would have told you by now that I was presumed killed ... it was May and still I was unable to say anything ... I realised that you would ... think me dead so I decided I must try to escape. By now I could talk again but *they* didn't know it. I thought it might help. If they thought I couldn't speak perhaps they wouldn't watch me so closely.' He paused and rubbed his lips across the back of Meg's hands and Tom Fraser sat up slowly. 'I tried four times, and managed it ... but, they brought me back. And still I didn't speak, except to you, Meg, and you Tom, in the dark when I was alone ... in solitary ... The three of us ... by God we had some good times, didn't

483

we?' He turned and put his arm about Tom's shoulders. '... and that's what I used to talk about to the pair of you ... those days ... in Great George Square ... the bicycles,' he turned back to Meg, 'but of course I kept the most intimate part of my life to my ...'

'Martin!'

His eyes had begun to glow about her, to run warmly across her face, lingering at her mouth. His face had become flushed and in it was the undeniable conviction that every dream he had had of her over the past five years was to be fulfilled this night. He seemed to have completely forgotten that then, five years ago, Tom Fraser had put his claim to her, had been engaged to her. All that was in the past, long ago and nothing to do with himself and Meg. He had a clear and treasured picture in his mind of what had happened the last time *they* had been together and surely it must create a stronger entitlement than Tom Fraser, or indeed any man, might make on Meggie Hughes. She had been his then and she was his now. Her eyes and her hands, her smile and the flush of her cheeks told him so and very soon, his eyes said with passionate certainty, they would leave this room and go somewhere ... to *hers* ... and shut the door on the rest and by God, if he had his way and he usually did, they would not come out until a week on Thursday. He had suffered privation and hunger, and in five years it had taken its toll of his strong and virile body, but he still had the vigour to love this woman, his hot eyes told her and Meg felt the ice cold dash of reality fling itself cruelly into her face.

'Martin ...' Her voice cracked on his name and she drew back from him.

'Yes, my ...?' His hands followed her and for some reason Tom stood up.

'Martin ...' Her voice became quite desperate and he looked surprised at her interruption. 'Martin ... tell us about ... why do you think the airplane crashed? Can it have been ...' What ... dear Christ, what could she say? She had, in her ecstasy and unheeding gladness, allowed her love for Martin Hunter to shine from her, to explode from her for how was she to contain the happiness, the most completely joyous moment of her life. She had thought him dead and he had risen from the grave quite miraculously and come back to her. She had mourned him grievously, a widow in her bereavement and not for one moment had her love diminished. She had suffered and thought never to

484

get over the loss of him, not just as a lover and her child's father but as the friend she had treasured for most of her life. But he had gone and she must go forward and leave him behind to live on only in her memory. She had built her life round her husband and her child, Martin's child who as yet he had not even noticed ... and around the companies Martin had left in her care. She had made it enough! She had given love and security and a small degree of hope to Tom, she had created a life for him and now, was she to take it from him? She must make a choice and the choice was simple. She must destroy Tom Fraser ... or she must fling back in his face the love Martin Hunter was so ardently, so trustingly offering to her.

'What?' he said, bewildered by the sudden change in direction.

'The "Wren"? She was a reliable craft. You built her yourself and would keep her well maintained, surely?'

'No!' He sounded mystified since he had no time to talk of these things, which, in any case could be gone over in the future. He could not concern himself with the past when he was aching to have Meg in his arms, in a bed, in the soft, lamp-lit, fire glow with no-one to interrupt what he meant for her.

'You did not maintain it then?' She knew she was babbling but how was she to ease that wary look from Tom's face, to get him to sit down again, to get him safely, *safely* from the room so that she might tell Martin ... Oh dear God!

'No, each aircraft had a mechanic.'

'A mechanic ...?'

'Yes, but you cannot be interested in that, surely. I don't know myself what caused the craft to go down though there was a moment when ...'

'Yes Martin ...'

'... when I heard a ... or thought I heard, just before the engine stalled, a crack ...'

His face had become thoughtful and though he still held her hand he had drawn back a little from the ardour which was frightening Tom Fraser. Tom could not say why really, he had this feeling of dread, for was he not here with the two people he loved best in all the world, with the exception of his little Beth, of course and he was completely aware that he had strange thoughts and feelings and fears, brought back with him from France, and for the most part, controlled now, but for some reason there was something, he could not remember what, which troubled

485

him, something from the far away past, which was often hazy. He was not awfully sure he cared for the way Martin held Meg's hand for so long, though of course that was silly for Meg and Martin were as close as *he* and Martin . . . still.

'A crack?' he heard Meg say and he sat down again just as suddenly as he had stood up.

'Yes . . . but the mechanic had checked everything so . . .'

His voice and his face and even the hand which held hers faded away into some swirling mist, black and grey and eddying, like the pictures she had seen once of a hurricane. The 'eye' of the hurricane she had heard it called, where there was absolute peace whilst all about was devastation and she floated in that peaceful eye whilst the hurricane of rage and bitterness swept about her, and she heard a voice, a thin, vicious voice and over and over it repeated the word Martin had just spoken.

Mechanic! *Mechanic*! *Mechanic*! 'Men of substance in the world of commerce, right down the social scale to one who was no more than a *mechanic*!' A mechanic! There it was in all its clear and horrendous exposure to her mind. The deed, the words, the intent and the completion of it!

So this was what he had done! And not content with the father he had tried also to kill his child. Though it had never been corroborated for what could a three-year-old tell of the scarcely remembered journey with a man who had given her a 'sweetie' and left her alone in the wastes of Derbyshire to die. The police had stepped up their search for Benjamin Harris to no avail. Now, a trick of memory brought back his words and what he had meant by them. She knew it just as surely as if he had walked into her sitting room, his presence thick with the black slime of evil and whispered it in her ear. He had gloated over it, triumphed over it, had laughed and sneered and wondered in his madness whether he should tell her, he said, and there was no doubt that when he was ready, or when he thought the time was right to administer another blow to Megan Hughes, the skivvy who had dared to challenge him, he would be back to tell her what he had done. What he *thought* he had done!

'Meg . . . are you alright, sweetheart?' Martin's hands were about hers and Tom hovered somewhere on the fringe of her returning consciousness. The room which had chilled was warm and familiar with her lovely things in it and Martin Hunter was here, here, safe and whole, alive warm, vital, smiling a little,

486

thinking her to be in a faint of enchantment perhaps because of his return and so she was. But in her rapture was fear, terror, hideous and almost more than she could stand for when he discovered that Martin was alive, that the man he had thought to be dead, the man Megan Hughes *loved*, Benjamin Harris' rage would be so savage it would be invincible. None of them would be safe . . . oh God . . . none of them! He would come back again and again until he had destroyed all those she loved, this man, Tom, her baby, Beth . . . aah, Beth.

As though her anguished thoughts had conjured up the spirit of the little girl there was a firm knock on the door and without waiting for an answer Annie entered the room. Her manner was anxious for what had gone on in this room during the past hour, her expression asked and what would she find here in the dreadful tangle that must surely be revealed, but whatever it was the child was not to suffer for it, that was certain. Not while Annie Hardcastle had breath in her body. Innocent and vulnerable, Beth Fraser, a fragile thread between these three whose exact relationship Annie was not awfully sure of, but whatever happened here this night, that thread must not be damaged!

Meg turned to the opened door and so did the two men, both smiling, one of them unaware that his hopes and dreams which had upheld him for five years were to be bludgeoned to death by this woman.

'I'm sorry, Meg, but . . . she won't go to sleep until you come, you or her . . . Tom.'

'Of course . . .' Meg stood up automatically and Tom did the same and his smile had become wider and as they both moved towards Annie, Martin leaned back in the settee and raised his eyebrows quizzically.

'What is it?' he said. 'Where are you two off to? Who won't go to sleep?' and Meg stood quite still, frozen and dying a little, her back to him, her eyes looking, anguished into Annie's.

Tom turned back, his whole manner one of simple joy, of achievement, of pride.

'Of course, you don't know, do you? God love us, in all the excitement we forgot to mention the most important thing in all the world. The most precious . . .' His face was wondering in his deep love for his daughter. 'Oh Martin, wait 'till you see her!'

'See who, for God's sake?' He was still smiling as Tom delivered the blow.

487

'Why, our little Beth! Our little girl! We have a daughter, me and Meg and though I say it myself, you've never seen a lovelier child, Martin. Just you wait! He'll love her, won't he, Meggie?'

And with a sweet and proudly rejoicing gesture Tom Fraser put his arm about his wife's shoulder and turned her to look into Martin Hunter's devastated face.

Chapter forty-one

'I can't stay!'

'Martin, please Martin . . .'

'I can't stay here now . . . with you and Tom . . .'

'But I can't let you go . . . Not when I've just found you again.'

'Found me! *Found* me! Jesus Christ, woman, did you ever look . . . did you even care that I was lost?' His pain was appalling. 'I've lived . . . lived for this . . . it kept me sane . . . I am not always strong, Meg, though you seem to think I am made of steel. I wept for you . . .'

'Oh Martin . . . don't . . . don't . . . let me tell you . . .'

'Tell me what? Surely what I see is self-explanatory. You are married to Tom . . . and you have a child. What is there to tell? It says it all and I can only repeat I cannot stay here and watch the pair of you play happy families. I'll . . . if Tom doesn't mind I'll borrow . . . these things and when I get settled somewhere . . .'

In his despair he had begun to shrug himself into the army greatcoat he had removed so joyously only hours before. His face worked pitifully for Martin Hunter was within a fraction of going, like Tom, into the totally dark world of the grievously wounded, the broken, the damaged, the world which the bloody war had created and in which so many existed. He turned away from her, evidently looking for his cap, his eyes quite wild but she stood up in front of him and gripped his flailing forearms and then, when he became still, took his face tenderly between her hands. She leaned forward and kissed him, her lips lingering on his, as soft and as sweet as warm honey and as her eyes looked steadfastly into his she felt him become less rigid under her hands.

Tom had gone to bed. Meg had postponed Martin's meeting with Tom's daughter, telling him she would be too tired for it tonight and reluctantly Tom had agreed though he promised Martin that first thing tomorrow, he would be introduced to his 'niece'. He had sat for an hour with Beth, watching over her as she slept, his hand hovering anxiously over her rosy cheek, his eyes never leaving her face, and Meg knew that this ritual that he went through each night, the gentle communion his damaged spirit formed with that of the innocence of the child, made him whole again for a small, peaceful space in time and he often went straight from the nursery to their bed, knowing he would sleep dreamlessly because of it. She had pulled the covers up round his neck and kissed him, in the same maternal way she did with Beth, switching out the light and creeping from the room as he fell asleep.

'Martin ... please ... look at me, *look at me*!' Her voice was controlled and she held herself back from falling, weeping, into his arms for he must be made to see, to realise the construction of her life, of Tom's life and she knew if she put her body against his she would be lost to everything but how desperately she wanted him.

'Martin, I love you.'

'Then why ...?'

'I was ... I had to ...'

'*Had* to! No-one has to do anything they don't want to do, Meg. I know that years ago you and Tom ... well, that Tom had this idea that you and he were to be married though God alone knows how he convinced himself of it. You had a ring ... Christ, I can remember in a letter I said ...' His face worked painfully and she knew he was trying to compose himself, to hang on to the tiny shred of control he had. 'But you said you loved *me*. You *did* love me, or have you forgotten that night?'

'No! Dear Heaven, Martin, how could I ever forget it?'

'Very easily, it seems, in another man's arms!' His voice was a snarl of torment and his ravaged face hated her for it and his pain was almost more than she could bear. There was visible menace in the bleak depths of his eyes and his fury at suffering it overwhelmed him. She was terrified of the destruction such pain and rage might unleash and that he would not be able to endure it. He was, or had been a strong and arrogant man but his vulnerability now weakened him and he could not bear her to see him as he was. Her kiss had calmed him, for a moment only, the sweetness, the unexpectedness of it taking him by surprise, but now he threw her off and turned his back on her, jerky, uncoordinated, malevolent in his jealous rage.

'My God, Megan, you are quite a woman, aren't you? Unnatural almost, one would say, really one would for Tom and I are

490

almost like brothers.' His voice was sneering. 'Did it give you a
kick to sleep with first one and then the other ... Goddammit, it
makes me want to vomit ... to ... to think of you ... in his bed,
to imagine you ... in his arms as ... as ... you must be insatiable,
my dear, not able to wait ... so why are you not with him now
... in the bed you share ... or perhaps...' His face became
contorted and she recoiled from the expression on it. 'Perhaps you
fancied a change ... a bit of new ...'

His face was quite unrecognisable and Meg knew he was, at
this moment, as deranged as Tom, but whereas Tom's danger was
directed only at himself, self-hurting and self-destructive, Martin's
was aimed at the one who had hurt him, herself!

'Is that it?' he went on, his breath hissing through his teeth. 'A
change from Tom, eeh and who better than Martin who hasn't
had any for so long he'll be famished for it! Well, madame, lets
be at it then ...'

'Martin ... aah, don't, don't, my love ... don't hurt yourself...'
Her heart was consumed with pity and as he came towards her
she did not step back this time, nor flinch, nor even show fear for
she felt none. She held out her arms to him and written on her
face was her deep and eternal love, strong, unquenched by time
and sorrow, undimmed by the foul words he spoke. He raised his
hand, his fist clenched as though he would strike her, then roughly
knocked her arms away. He was deep in frenzied confusion, she
could see it in his face, since what was in hers was undeniably the
truth and she knew, at last, that she must tell him about Tom.
Only then would he understand.

'Sit down, Martin, please.'

'What's the bloody use, Meg?' He pushed his trembling hand
through his shock of hair and let out his breath on a long, agonised
sigh. 'I might as well go now before Tom comes down to see where
the hell you've got to. If he does, I tell you, Meggie I can't
guarantee I won't knock him down.'

'He won't do that, Martin.'

'Why not? My God, if you were mine ...' his face spasmed and
his voice shook with emotion, '... I'd want to know why the hell
you weren't in *my* bed!'

'He won't come down tonight, Martin.'

'Oh, and why is that?'

'I put a sleeping pill in his drink. The ones his doctor gives me
for when they are ... needed.'

491

'A sleeping . . .? What in God's name are you saying?' He gripped her arms roughly and gave her a shake. 'Why should you give him sleeping pills, and for that matter what the devil is he doing in bed at this time of night. Bloody hell, it's only nine-thirty! His . . . his best friend, his old childhood mate is back from the bloody dead and he's in his bed and you've given him a *sleeping pill*. What the devil's going on here, Megan? What game are you playing? Jesus, if I didn't know you better . . .'

'Tom is ill, Martin.'

Martin stepped back and looked disbelievingly at her. He rubbed his hands over his face, pressing the palms into his eyes, then shook his head. He stood for several seconds, his eyes locked with hers, then he sighed and turned away. Taking off his greatcoat he threw it over the back of a chair before sinking tiredly into the depths of the settee, then in the manner of one who seriously doubts his ability to take any more he sighed again, softly, hopelessly.

'What is it, Meg? What are you keeping from me? What the hell has happened in the years I have been away? You'd better tell me . . . and lass, let it be the truth.'

'I have never lied to you in my life, Martin.'

'I know . . . I'm sorry. I don't often say that, Meggie, but tonight has been . . . somewhat strange . . . go on, tell me about Tom.'

'You have heard of shell-shock, Martin? The men in the trenches . . .'

'Yes. It took me a long time to get back here . . . through France and the field hospitals and on the way I saw sights . . . and when I got back to Blighty, in the hospital where they checked me out, I saw it . . . and Tom?'

'He cannot get over it. He . . . saw things . . . did things which will not let him alone. He'll . . . never recover . . . never, from his experiences. His friends . . . all of them in the 'Liverpool Pals' were killed and one in particular. I think his name was Andy though of course I can't ask Tom . . . I believe . . . I think . . . Tom killed him. Tom . . . has nightmares . . . he talks . . . the man was badly wounded . . . suffering, I suspect Tom put him out of his misery. He buries it beneath . . . other things, but . . . well, I have a man to look after him.'

'Jesus . . . to look *after him* . . . He seemed alright to me. Fitter than I am!'

'His mind is not . . . fit, Martin. That is why I cannot . . . I cannot destroy him further. If you and I, if I was to leave him he could not survive it. And then there is . . . my daughter. She is the light of his life. She *gives* him life, and, I think, hope for tomorrow. He sees tomorrow as her! There is nothing for him and the sad thing is he knows it, but through her, *he* has a future. I could not take it, nor her, from him and . . . I could not leave her. You know . . . you must know I love you. Tom is, has always been . . . my friend and I love him dearly but not in the way I love you, nevertheless, Martin, I must stay with him. You know I must.' Her voice broke on a thread of pain.

He was still then, quite fixed in the immutable truth and dread of what she had told him and in the knowledge of what it meant to *him*. For five minutes neither spoke, both encapsulated in the grief of the parting which was to come, to come *again* and Meg felt the numbness creep protectively over her because really she could not, *could not* bear it. She was torn apart, ripped from the enchantment, the delirium of joy she had been given, flung to the drowning depths of fresh sorrow, and for a dreadful moment she had it in her to wish that Martin . . . Dear God, forgive her . . . had not come back to her!

'How old is your child?'

'She is four this month. Her birthday is on the fifteenth . . .' She heard her voice trail away into an abyss of silence, a silence so complete and empty his triumph filled it, reverberated around it, drums beating, cymbals crashing, pipes piping and bugles sounding in the jubilation of the trap his quick mind had set for her and into which she had neatly fallen. When he turned her to him his face was alive again, the desolation gone, the jealousy gone, the anger gone and all that remained was understanding . . . and love, his strong, masculine, victorious love.

'She's mine, isn't she?' His eyes demanded the truth and when he saw it in hers he threw back his head and for a moment she thought he would shout his rejoicing to the ceiling, to the very room on the next floor where Tom slept. He sat like that for a long moment, his eyes closed, his face turned upwards, his lips parted in a sigh of thanksgiving, then slowly he lowered his chin and looked at her wonderingly, understandingly. Putting his hand beneath her chin, he lifted her face to look into his, then kissed her and his soul was in it.

'So that's why,' he said, never taking his eyes from hers, then he put his arms about her and drew her head to his shoulder and

held her to him and sighed in quiet, peaceful, contented acceptance. 'So that's why you married him. To give our child a name.
It's like Tom to do something like that! Well my love, my darling
Meg, we shall have to see what can be done for I am here to claim
and *protect* what is mine, *mine*, d'you hear, and no-one is going to
stop me. As for Tom . . . well . . . we must look for a solution and
we shall find one, never fear. I don't know what it is, sweetheart
but for every problem there is an answer. I am . . . sad, you know
that for like you, Tom is my friend and I do not relish the feeling
that I am to make him suffer but I will not let this illness of his
stand in the way of the happiness you and I deserve. Must we
sacrifice what is ours, our love, our life, our daughter in order
that Tom might have security. A place can be found for him,
near to us so that we can see him and he can watch the child . . .
our child, Meggie, grow up, but I cannot let him take what is
mine, my darling, *mine*! Tom is my brother, Meg and all my life
I have treated him as such but I will not allow him to destroy my
life. I have fought for this life of mine, for five bloody years. By
God, I have suffered too in the war and it is my turn to live now,
girl. You are my reason, the mainspring of my life, my hope and
ambition for the years we have ahead of us. I cannot give you up,
Meg, even for Tom. There must be a way out of this, there must.
Now, we will sit here for a while and I will hold you in my arms
for I have dreamed of this moment for five years. Of course in
my dreams the holding went on and on and the loving began and
in my dreams you loved me just as fiercely, but we cannot, not
under the same roof as Tom, but we will, my lass, we will. Dear
God, Meggie, I love you . . . I love you, d'you hear . . .'

The little girl was at the nursery table when Meg and Martin
entered the room the next morning and she looked up in quick
interest, her eyes, the tilt of her small head, the way her eyebrows
moved, even the quirk of humour at the corner of her mouth so
inexorably Martin Hunter's, Meg saw Sally Flash stare with open-
mouthed surprise, as she looked from him to the child. Beth
Fraser's face, so endearingly, eternally female, was, in spite of it,
a replica of her father's. Only the colour of her skin and hair were
different. She had the creamy silken flesh of Meg and her russet
tumble of curls, but in every other aspect she was Martin Hunter's
daughter.
    'Where's Daddy?' she demanded immediately, her brown eyes

accusingly on this stranger who had come in his stead. 'He said he would take me up to the paddock to see McGinty right after breakfast. I've eaten my egg, Mummy, see . . .' She held up the empty eggshell, 'And now I want to go and see McGinty!'

'Yes sweetheart, but this . . . this gentleman . . . has come to see you. He is an old friend of Mummy and Daddy's and I want you to . . .'

'But where's Daddy?' A sudden look of alarm, 'Has he got a heggate?'

'No darling, he hasn't got a headache and he will be here soon but . . .'

Sally Flash stood up nervously.

'I'll just go down to the kitchen for some more milk . . . there's none left in the . . .' She moved across the room and slipped diplomatically through the doorway leaving the disquieting recognition to hover in the nursery at the table where the handsome man had sat down beside Beth. She would just go and have a cup of tea in the kitchen and take comfort from Annie's stalwart presence, and pray to the God in whom she firmly believed that the stranger would take himself off again, for if he didn't she had the most curious feeling there would be trouble. Of what kind she was not awfully sure but Mr Tom had been going on for days about Beth's lovely *blue* eyes when all the world could see they were as brown as those in the face of the man who now knelt beside Mr Tom's daughter . . . oh Lord . . . perhaps Annie would know . . .

'This is Mr Hunter, Beth . . .'

'Please . . . not Mr Hunter. My name is Martin, Beth and . . .'

'Have you seen my new pony?'

Her eyes flashed brilliantly into his and Meg saw him blink, startled and onto his face came an expression she had never seen before, but then, until this moment, Martin Hunter had never looked into the inquisitive face of his daughter. His expression was guarded as yet, wary almost, as though he could not quite understand the emotion he felt, and he had yet to arrange it to his own satisfaction, in his methodical engineer's mind. Martin Hunter had come home to claim Meg Hughes and that, until now, was all he really wanted. Even during the night, in the room to which Meg had showed him, when he had known of the existence of his child she had really been nothing to him. A child, a girl, his, and so he would take her with him, and her mother, naturally for what was Martin Hunter's remained Martin Hunter's! But now, here she was, beautiful, bright, engaging and with a stubborn set to her chin which told him she had spirit. Her face was good-natured, appealing, but in it was something none of them, not even her mother had recognised. In her was the fledgeling challenge of Martin Hunter. He saw it in the face of his daughter and it was then his love was born.

'No,' he answered, 'but I would like to. I bet he's a beauty!' Like you, his eyes said and he grinned in delight.

The child's face lit up and she put her hand trustingly on his where it lay on the white tablecloth. 'Oh yes, and he's brave too and when I'm older I'm going to teach him to jump the fence but until then Daddy says I can learn to ride him in the paddock and . . .'

'But you are four years old, are you not?'

'Yes. My birthday is next week . . . er . . . Saturday . . .' She looked eagerly at her mother for confirmation and when Meg nodded, grinned back at him.

'Well, in that case I would say you are old enough to learn to ride right now, wouldn't you? If we put a long rein on him and I lifted you into the saddle I dare say you could ride him, don't you? Especially if I were to hold you, just until you were used to it. A big girl like you could . . .'

'Martin!' Meg's voice was sharp with warning but he did not hear, or chose not to, which was more likely and Meg was made aware, if last night had not confirmed it, that four years of imprisonment had not destroyed Martin Hunter's complete belief in his own judgement.

The child's face was a picture of enchantment and she jumped down from her chair and put her hand in Martin's.

'Oh can we, can we, Martin?' She looked up imploringly at Meg, 'Can we, Mummy, can we, please!'

The voice from the doorway was cold and even the little girl became quiet.

'Can we what, Meg? What is it she wants? You know I do not like her put in . . . in danger . . . she is so small.' Tom's hand on the doorknob fumbled to hold on to something and his face was clouded, uncertain, for his mind had taken that frightening turn again and he didn't quite know what to say, or do. Martin was there, talking to Beth and she had her hand in his which Tom

496

didn't like ... and he ... Andy ... no, no, it wasn't right ... it shouldn't be allowed ... she was his ... her ... oh Lord ...

With the mercurial mood of a child Beth flung off the friendly hand of the stranger and ran to her Daddy, putting her arms about him and holding him close to her. The top of her head came to just below his waist and his hands fell to her curls, thankfully, and he smiled in deep gratitude.

'What is it, my darling?' His voice still trembled and his head could not quite hold itself steady and the hand which caressed the bright copper curls of the child would not be still but he had control of himself and he would be alright for Beth was with him. She looked up at him now.

'Martin says I can ride McGinty, Daddy. He says it's easy so shall we go up to the paddock and ...'

'Oh no sweetheart, not yet. Perhaps when you are a big girl ...' He had not really wanted Meg to buy the animal in the first place for it was so ... so tall and his child was only ... only small and what if she fell off, he had said over and over again to Meg but she wouldn't listen and now look what had happened ...

'But Martin says I am a big girl now, Daddy.'

'Not yet, Beth, no darling, not yet ...' for if she fell those craters were deep and most had water in them and she could drown ... dear God ... that was close ... no ... no ... Andy ...

'But Daddy, if we put a ... what was it, Martin ... a rein on McGinty?' She let go of Tom, a little girl consumed with excitement and the need to do what she had been told she *could* do, and do it *now*. She turned away from him and moved appealingly towards Martin and the dreadful hole was there where she had been standing and without her to hold on to Tom fell right into it. Andy was there, grinning apologetically and ... and ...

'Beth, sweetheart ...' His cry raised the fine hairs on the back of Martin Hunter's neck and the hand he had been about to hold out persuasively to *his* daughter, hesitated, then fell to his side. The little girl turned back, away from him, to Tom. Martin saw the childish love there, the trust, the belief that he was her father, and he had called to her. She went to him at once.

'Oh Daddy, please ...' she begged but the demanding note had gone from her voice and as Tom fell to his knees before her she ran into his arms and put hers around his neck.

'Soon, darling, soon,' he said quite normally, then lifted her up in his arms. His shield, his protector, it seemed suddenly to Martin and he saw it then, the damage that had been done to his friend who must hide behind the love of a four-year-old child.

He put out an unsteady hand ready to lay it on Tom's shoulder. 'Your daughter and I were just introducing ourselves to one another, my old friend.' His voice was soft and compassionate and Meg turned away to hide the tears. 'She's a ... a little beauty, Tom. You've a right to be proud of her ...' and with these words Martin Hunter gave back his daughter, the one he had just met, and loved, ten minutes ago. 'We were talking about her pony. I'm afraid I was encouraging her to ride it, but then you know me, Tom, always a bit of a dare-devil ... remember the tricks I used to get up to on that bicycle?'

Tom's face opened up and became joyful. He held the child and moved towards his friend, his friend Martin.

'Could I ever forget? A circus performer had nothing on you! And that damned tandem you had me and Meg on, remember? I was the one who did all the work, pedalling for two whilst she sat back and smiled at all the lads. And they smiled back too, I'll not forget that, either, by God. Pretty! Pretty as a picture was my Meggie and still is, aren't you my darling, and now I've two of them! Two of them.' His voice was soft and proud. 'Can you believe my luck, Martin, can you?'

'No ...' Martin turned away, stumbling, almost running from the room. 'But I must be off ... really ... I wanted to get down to the factory ... and then ... there are ... I must find somewhere to live ... so you see ...'

'To live! But Martin, come back you daft beggar, where are you dashing off to? You must stay here with us, mustn't he, Meg? We've loads of room, a suite if you want it ... haven't we, Meg?'

'Daddy, can we go and see McGinty now?'

'Yes sweetheart, in a minute ... Martin ... where in hell are you dashing off to? Fetch him back, Meg,' but his wife was looking out of the window and her hand clutched the pretty flowered chintz of the nursery curtains and she did not seem to hear him and ... and when he put his hand on her shoulder she flinched away from him. What ... why did he ... he felt something frightful come at him from just over the top of the trench ... but it was alright because Andy ... no, not Andy ... Beth, his little Beth was here and he was safe. His blue-eyed Beth. His lovely girl.

498

Chapter forty-two

It was six weeks before she saw him again. She stayed at home with her husband and her child and her tired brain operated at a level which allowed her to make decisions about meals and what they should eat, about walks in the garden and what they should plant there, about visits to the nursery and which games to play with Beth and about the outfit she should wear on any particular day. The rest of the time it engrossed itself in the constant torment of longing for Martin. Quite simply she became again the woman who waited for Martin Hunter. Nothing else!

And in that dreadful wait which could have no ending, at the back of her tortured mind, struggling for a hearing since surely she could not ignore it, was the equally harrowing need to consider the danger of Benjamin Harris! She did not know where he was, or even if he was aware of Martin Hunter's survival, but somewhere out there, beyond the walls of 'Hilltops', he lived and schemed and waited, she assumed for the time to come round when he felt the need to torture Megan Fraser once more. Perhaps she should find some form of protection, perhaps she should tell Martin, warn him, tell him to be on his guard, for any man who would attempt the murder of a four-year-old child must surely be insane. A police constable had been put on duty patrolling the grounds of 'Hilltops' after Beth's abduction but that could not last forever and though the child was never allowed in the garden alone, Meg still had the wildest dreams of him returning to threaten them all with his evil. Perhaps . . . perhaps . . . if only . . . Martin would be sure to know what to do . . . dear God!

Her mind would turn despairingly in a nightmare of chaos and her suffering showed in the fine-boned hollows in her face and the delicate slenderness of her once well-rounded figure. Her eyes were haunted and in the night she would awaken in a sweat of panic, searching desperately for a haven, but there was only Tom! She moved about the empty, stagnant days blindly with nothing to stand protectively between her and her fears. Martin was the only one who could protect her but then if she allowed it, who would be left to protect Tom? She must forget Martin!

She had not tried to reach him in the six weeks since he had returned though it nearly drove her mad with pain, and he had kept away for both of them knew they were not strong enough to overcome what haunted them. She had gone to the factory to see Fred and tell him the incredible news that Martin had survived the war and would take over the factories again. Only when there was some emergency with which only she could deal in those first weeks – and this happened less and less frequently as Martin became familiar with the routine of managership – did she go to Camford and when she did, he stayed away. They spoke to each other through Fred, and if Fred had thoughts on the strangeness of it then he kept them to himself.

She tried to make plans for the re-opening of the hotel. The war was over. The nation was tired and dispirited for it had lost so many of its sons, brothers, husbands, a whole generation of young men who could never be replaced and it grieved badly for them. It had suffered hardship and privation and needed in some way to forget what it had gone through, it needed a break from the boredom of economies and doing without, the grinding routine of doing one's bit, something to take its mind from the problem of getting itself back into the strangeness of peace. A holiday, that was what they needed, they said, those who could afford it and there were many of them now for they had earned more money than they had ever imagined during the years of war. They went to Brighton and Blackpool and Skegness and those who required somewhat more – class, elegance, luxury and the peace and quiet in which to enjoy it, those who knew of its pre-war reputation – wrote to 'The Hilltop Hotel', to enquire of the discriminating Miss Hughes if she could 'put them up'. The telephone rang a dozen times a day and Annie said she was sick and tired of trudging up from the kitchen to answer it and would Meg be good enough to tell her what she was going to do! You can't keep putting people off, she told her, or they'd take their business elsewhere, but though her voice was sharp, the look she bestowed on Meg was soft for she, of them all, was the only one to know what Meg was suffering.

Meg watched Tom stride off each day with Will, a spade in one hand, the other in the hand of his daughter and the healthy colour in his cheeks denied the nightmare in which he had cried the night before, and she agonised on whether it would be possible to run the hotel, have guests, strangers about the place with Tom in his present state of mind. What might it do to him to have people he did not know and who did not know him, or his fits of silent strangeness – which could occur in the middle of a sentence – moving about in his safe world? Would it be safe any longer? He had improved, there was no doubt of it and the doctor, when she consulted him, was hopeful.

'Perhaps it might be possible if he were to be kept apart from the guests, Mrs Fraser.'

'You mean if we were to make part of the hotel into a private apartment for the family?'

'Yes, that might be the answer, and his work on the farm? Is there a path to it which might be kept separate from the rest of the grounds? That is all that is needed. Provided he is not alarmed by anything different, anything which is new and out of his own safe routine, I do not see why it could not be managed. I have said it so many times and I can only repeat it. Assuming he is not disturbed from the secure pattern you have created for him, from the things he does each day with Will and the people who make him feel ... unthreatened, then the fine balance he retains will not be weakened. The abduction of your daughter, fortunately, did little damage since he was heavily sedated most of the time and when he awakened she had returned, but any trauma can affect him if it is not correctly dealt with. In your capable hands though and with the care you give him there should be no problem, my dear.'

He thought he reassured her, the kindly doctor, but what he had done was to effectively close down the last fragile hope that Tom might, one day, recover enough to allow her to ... to ... to what? Leave him? Take Beth and all that he loved and simply walk away from him to Martin? Had she really believed it could happen? Had she? She had consulted Dr Carmichael on the subject of the re-opening of the hotel, but in her innermost secret heart she admitted to herself that she had hoped he might tell her that Tom was well enough to live his own life now. She had told herself she did not want to jeopardise Tom's health but in reality she had conjured up the make-believe nonsense, the dream, the fantasy for that was what it was, that she and Martin would one day be together but now she must put it away, drag herself from dreams and face the *real* world in which she lived. She must open the hotel. She could no longer work at the factories which had been her life for four years and she must *do something!* Perhaps if she were to begin again, take up the work which she had loved years ago it would bring her, if not happiness, then a purpose in life, an anchor to hold her steady until she could manage it alone.

For six weeks she held on to it, living again in the deep and slashing anguish she had known when they had told her Martin was dead, and agonised at the irony of realising that this time she grieved because he had come back. He had taken over his companies again, though a strained and painful note had been delivered to her telling her that she must still consider herself a partner and therefore entitled to a half share of any profit. Tom couldn't understand it, he said fretfully and wouldn't you have thought their Martin would have been over to tell them himself instead of sending notes. Four weeks, five, six and not a sign of him and why didn't Meg telephone him and ask him to come and visit them? After all, he was their oldest friend and really . . .

Meg, stung to despairing violence by his insistent voice, spoke harshly.

'*You* telephone him if you want him to come,' but Tom stepped back from that for the strange disembodied voice which came from the earpiece of the telephone reminded him too vividly of other voices he sometimes heard.

She did not know how it happened. There was some misunderstanding, a garbled message taken by Edie who was still none to happy with the telephone, passed on to Meg by Annie that there was some mishap at the factory, an order she had taken weeks ago, a mix-up, no-one could make head nor tail of it and Mr Hunter had asked . . . if she could spare an hour . . . he was to be away in . . . she couldn't remember where, but would Meg . . .?

Civil flying in Britain, halted by the war, was to be restarted on the 1st May and in the six weeks he had been back Martin had begun the design, completely new, for a commercial aircraft to carry passengers. Fred had told her he had constructed it in his head during the long, empty hours of his imprisonment and now it was on paper and the prototype ready for construction. Already companies were preparing for a regular civil air service in England and one, A. V. Roe and Company were to fly from Alexander Park in Manchester, to Southport and Blackpool, the cost of a one-way ticket to be four guineas, they had announced. 'Hunter Aviation' did not mean to be left behind in the race for domination of the new industry and as Meg entered the hangar

502

that day she was amazed at the progress already made on the three seat aircraft. She knew that Martin intended visiting the first post-war aviation event which was to be held at Hendon in June to see what *other* men were doing but the speed with which *his* industry was growing astounded her.

She looked about her with avid interest for this had been hers only a short time ago. Though it had never consumed her as the hotel business had, she had found the work stimulating, a challenge to her and she had missed it.

And there he was! She looked across the busy hangar and in that moment the fragile strength she had gathered about herself fell away leaving her exposed and defenceless as her eyes clung to the arrow straight back of the man she loved. She saw his glossy, well brushed hair catch the light from the overhead lamps and the grey in it was burnished to silver. She watched his hand lift as he made some remark to Fred and his teeth gleamed in his face as he smiled and glanced away, and in doing so – as she stood frozen by her longing in the doorway – he saw her.

It was too late then. It had always been too late, she said to herself in that last moment of sanity. This was inevitable for how could love such as theirs be buried. It was alive and should it be put beneath six feet of earth would it not claw its way to the surface and shout its message of hope and need and exultation to the very heavens!

He began to walk across the tumult of emerging aircraft, all in different stages of production, avoiding hurrying men and trolleys on which were the materials for their building. His step was springing and alert, his tread was sure, his confidence in himself here, in his own world, as substantial as the ground on which he walked. And yet there was a hesitancy in his deep brown eyes, as though, in his arrogance he was about to take a bold leap in the dark and was not absolutely sure where he would land.

She had removed the close fitting beret she wore for driving since some tiny, wilful, feminine part of her demanded she must be as beautiful for him as she could manage. She wore a military style leather greatcoat, made fashionable by the war, long and serviceable and extremely plain. It had an almost masculine style to it and, if she had tried she could not have contrived a more imaginative outfit to compel his attention. Its utter simplicity, meant for function rather than adornment served only to enhance her soft loveliness. Her hair, released from the confines of her beret, stood out defiantly about her head, and the vivid green of the scarf at her throat which Fred had given her years ago contrasted to light up her flawless skin and turned her incredible eyes to gold.

They looked at one another and their faces were identical in their expression of complete joy and the strong, deathless quality of their love.

'Meg.' Her name was a thread of sound on his lips and his eyes begged for compassion. She could not speak. There was a pain so great in her breast she could not breathe for it and yet there grew a lightness which threatened to pick her up and carry her on the wind, to wherever the wind would blow her.

He reached her at last and though three-quarters of the men who hammered and banged and whistled in the strange silence which came to envelop Martin and Meg, turned to stare she opened the door behind her and moving backwards, drew him inside the office.

'Meg,' he said again but made no move to touch her and in her fast fading reason she was glad, for if he had done so she would have fallen against him in an ecstacy of joy for all to see.

At last she could speak.

'I had no idea . . . I was told you were to be away . . . there was something . . .'

'It is tomorrow . . . There is a matter I must attend to in Birmingham. The order you took . . . Ashworths in Croydon . . . God, does it matter?'

'No.'

'How is . . .?'

'Who?'

'The child . . . my . . .'

'She is well . . . beautiful.'

'And Tom?'

'The same . . .'

'You are looking . . .'

He stopped then and the words, the polite, meaningless words dried up in his mouth to make way for the ones which were in his heart.

'I'm not awfully sure I can stay away from you for much longer, Meg.' His voice was harsh. 'Jesus, it's been five years. Five whole bloody years. To see you standing there with that . . . that ridiculous hair of yours all over the damn place. Meggie . . . I have . . .' He gave a short, agonised laugh. 'I have . . . played the game! Kept away from you these weeks so that you could look after Tom but do you think it's been easy? I'll be honest, Megan. I'm beginning to feel I don't give a damn about Tom any more, or indeed any man who keeps you from me and if you will come with me now I will take you from him without a qualm. I have tried to stay away from you . . . and our child. Sweet Jesus, I have tried but . . . Meg, Meg, help me!'

'Martin . . .'

'Let me . . .'

'What, my love?'

'Christ . . . I don't know!' He ran his hand through his hair and its shining smoothness fell into the familiar tumbled disarray she remembered from his boyhood. Her hand lifted of its own volition to brush it back from his forehead but he took it and beneath the interested, startled gaze of his own mechanics brought it reverently to his lips.

'Martin . . . please . . . I . . .' Her breath famed his cheek for somehow, dragged by invisible cords of unbreakable strength they were face to face, almost touching and in a moment might have been in one another's arms. An apprentice, goggle-eyed and grinning dropped a wrench, the sound echoing about the high-ceilinged hangar. Instantly Meg stepped back and in the fumbling fashion of a blind man marooned in an unfamiliar room, felt her way round the desk and sat down in the chair behind it. Her voice was cracked and desperate.

'For God's sake, Martin, sit. Sit in a chair and look as though . . .'

'What?' but his face was jubilant for she had just given him hope, a chance, it seemed to him and he was not a man to turn away from it.

'Pretend to . . . these are your men watching us. They were mine only a few weeks ago . . .'

'I don't give a damn. You came . . .'

'Stop it, stop it! We must act as though . . . can you not see what this could do? I am Mrs Tom Fraser and this is your business . . .'

'Come with me somewhere then . . .'

'For what, Martin?'

'I don't know,' but of course he did and his voice was filled with all the pent up longing of years and his eyes looked deep into hers and saw the same there.

505

'No . . . please . . . don't ask me. How can I? Tom is . . .'

Tom Fraser came into the office in that last frantic moment of his wife's conflict, his gentle, damaged presence putting its hand on her shoulder and with him was another, just as sweet and trusting, but Martin's eyes . . . no, Beth's eyes . . . no, no . . . Martin's . . . how could she say no? She had wanted him for so long . . . so long . . . dear God . . . help me . . . but it was no use and she knew now there was no other way for her. Right from the moment she had looked up in the garden and seen him standing there, the way had led to this. It was inevitable. Why had she imagined, she had time to wonder, dazedly, that she could fight it when all along she had known she had no wish to fight it! She was Meg Hughes who loved Martin Hunter. That's who she *was*! That's *all* she was! A feather in the wind, a leaf floating on the water, and with as much control of her own direction as they.

'Where?' Her lips formed the word silently.

'I have rooms in Camford.'

It had been five years but they did not fall upon one another in that first rapturous moment. They lingered tenderly, wordlessly, over cheek and mouth and throat, marvelling, dreaming, sighing in sweet content.

'I thought we would never know this again,' he breathed as he took her garments from her one by one. His lips and hands and eyes browsed about the soft curves and hollows, the secret crevices of her body and when he had fulfilled his need to etch the sight of her into his brain, the feel of her flesh against his own, the taste of her, the sound of her need in his ears and the musky woman's smell which was uniquely hers, and therefore, his, when they were both ready their bodies flowed, one into the other with the sweet fluid movement of honey and when it was finished they were still wrapped about in a reverie, dreaming, engrossed and lost to everything but each other. Mindlessly content, their separate worlds did not converge on this one.

'What is this magic?' he whispered, his cheek against the roundness of her breast, his mouth reaching once more for her nipple, and it began again. She lay naked beneath him, ready to receive him and her face looked directly up into his. The vigorous and lovely hours they had spent together . . . how long? It did not matter . . . what did? Hours of alternate gentle and fierce love-making had tossed her hair into a turbulent mass of curls about her head. She had the look of a wanton spirit and yet she still

506

retained that innocence which told him she was not familiar with the erotic arts of sensuality. Her eyes were soft with a glow which comes with love and the dreamy tingling of its aftermath and he was triumphant for he knew then that this was *his*, this joy he had given her, that she had known it with no-one but himself. She was his, *his* woman. *His*!

'Meg.' His voice was husky and she recognised the anguished need he had of her, the love, the adoration, admiration, even respect she compelled in him and her heart broke a little for that expression shone on another man's face and he was her husband.

He turned her to look at him and his face, so arrogant, stubborn, showing all the unyielding intractability which had made him what he was, had softened, become almost humbled. He was about to beg!

'My darling, will you ... will you allow me to see you? I promise ... I will make a vow that I will not interfere in ... in your marriage. How can I when I know what it would do to Tom.' His voice was drained of all emotion but it was there burning in his eyes. 'Could we not meet? I could take a house ... our own house. We could be alone ... do whatever you want or feel you should do ... be whatever you say. An hour or two ... I will ask no more ...' and he believed it.

Meg looked into his eyes and knew she could not resist. She had known from the moment their hands touched in the garden. Her heart had gentled and her mind, as strong and shining as new steel had given way to the enchantment of her re-awakened love. She had loved him, she would love him ... forever. There was no escape.

Taking his hand, his slender brown hand in hers she brought it to her lips and though her tears for Tom fell on it, they fell from eyes which were starred with happiness.

'Yes!'

They came from the house in which Martin Hunter had a suite of rooms. They were discreet, a man and a woman bidding one another farewell with a polite handclasp as each climbed into a separate automobile and drove away, and the well-dressed gentleman on the other side of the tree-lined avenue pressed back behind the trunk of a budding sycamore. He leaned against it for several minutes as though he was in acute distress and his face was grey and sweating. His mouth worked savagely and a line of white appeared at the edges of his lips and in his eyes was an expression so violent two ladies who were passing crossed hastily to the other side of the road.

Chapter forty-three

They met whenever they could. He took a small furnished house on the outskirts of Camford employing a woman to come in and clean for an hour each morning and in it he and Meg lived the half life of lovers, forced to hide their love, forced to fit their lives into the shape of other people's lives, forced to live by the hours of the clock, and the minutes of each hour as though every one was as precious and rare as the finest of gems. They must learn to fit into those hours every word, every tender look and gesture, every small and intimate expression of love which those who are together every day take for granted knowing they will be there the next day and the next and the next as long as life exists. Death can part, and does, but the young and those in love do not think of such things. Meg and Martin died a small death each time they parted, not knowing when they would see one another again. It was easier in some ways for Martin. Besides his renewed passion for the creating of what was to be the finest civil airplane in the country, he had no other life but Meg. He had no life but that in his factory where he was fast developing the form of 'mass production' designed by the American Henry Ford, and which would enable him to turn out by the dozen the small family car he had dreamed of years ago. He went to the factory in the morning and left it to come back to the house each evening and in between he was completely absorbed, completely happy. If Meg was there, waiting for him when he came home, which she was quite often in those first weeks, his day was made whole and he took her thankfully into his arms, holding her, leading her to the bedroom where the summer sunshine streamed across their naked bodies as they loved one another.

Afterwards they would sigh about the kitchen as she prepared a simple meal, more for the pleasure of eating together than because they were hungry, hands touching, lips touching, whispering in love and laughter, their bodies well content, their eyes speaking of love and the delight that had been, and would be again.

She wore a diaphanous drifting wrapper of misty blue, enchanting and daring, which he had bought her and he would untie the satin ribbons and pull it from her shoulders, holding her to him in the urgency, the sometimes frightened longing of a man who is desperate to claim what is really his but which eludes him. His body would shake and he would bury his face in her hair and only when she took him inside her, enfolding his strong yet vulnerable masculine body in the softness of her own, did he know peace. She gave him the certainty and hope, how he did not know, nor care, as he surged with her to the joyous fulfilment of their love, that one day this would be his, and only his, until eternity. He knew he did not share her body, *that* he could not have borne, with Tom Fraser. With quiet dignity and in no way detracting from Tom as a human being, a man who was lovable, she told him of Tom's inability to be a husband to her and did not blame him he knew it, for his own rejoicing. She understood for she loved him and knew the feeling of dread, sharing it with him when they were apart, of agonising on how he spent the time he was not at the factory and not with *her*!

Those were the bad times for him, she was aware of it. To come back to the house in which were a dozen reminders of her presence. Clothes, underwear, wisps of lingerie, a hairbrush, stockings, the perfume he had bought her, the scent plaguing his nostrils where only yesterday it had delighted them. The remains of a cake they had made together, helpless with laughter, two children again, the game of 'patience' she had begun then discarded when he teased her from it, kissing and sighing and slipping her blouse from her, and the dainty straps of her camisole off her shoulders until her breasts were in his hands and the rapture began again, there, on the rug before the fireplace.

She knew he brooded when he was alone, top heavy with menace since he was not a man to live by himself, nor to be denied what he wanted, needed and believed to be rightfully his. She was restless herself on such nights, more than she cared to count for Tom did not like to be left alone at the end of the day and there were only so many times when she could make the excuse that she had run out of petrol after shopping in Buxton, that the motor had broken down, that the solicitor who was disentangling the web of legalities brought about by Martin's return had held her

510

longer than expected, or that the preparations she was making for the re-opening of the hotel and which necessitated quite frequent trips here and there to consult decorators, furnishers and upholsterers, had taken longer than she had anticipated.

Annie knew, of course and probably Edie as well. They were not simpletons and the re-appearance of the man with Beth's brown eyes and Meg Fraser's sudden need to be elsewhere at strange times of the day and evening were soon calculated and the answer they arrived at was as plain as the nose on your face! Annie said nothing, and neither did Fred Knowsley when his employer simply vanished with no excuse given, for an hour sometimes two, with no concern apparently for the urgency of building 'Wren IV' which was to be shown at the next Olympia Show.

'Come with me to Hendon,' he demanded. 'Two days, thats all, three at the most and, my darling ... *nights*! Think of of it! Imagine it! To spend a whole night together without your having to scramble into your clothes and dash back to Tom! In a bed! To wake up in the morning and still be together ... Come with me, Meggie.' His voice was rough with urgency, needing to compel her to come, to *order* her for he found it hard to fit into the role of beggar. They had made love that afternoon, frightening themselves with their own desperation, hurting one another with nails and teeth, then, harrowed with sorrowing love, aching with tenderness for the pain they inflicted upon one another, and the need to declare the bottomless, endless enormity of it, holding one another voicelessly until it was time for her to leave.

She was the first to get out of the bed, her skin glowing with the heat which had coursed through her body but her eyes were flat, almost empty of expression. It became harder and harder as the weeks passed to force herself to leave, to desert this man who was her life. She felt guilt, a shameful resentment that it was for the sake of a man she did not love and a fear that if this was to continue she might let that resentment show, damaging further the fragile spirit of Tom Fraser. So many times in the past weeks she had felt herself wishing ... dear God ... she did not know what it was she wished, she only knew that the half thoughts and drifting hopes were contemptible. Her movements were listless as she shrugged into the pretty bed-gown – another present, another garment she could wear only for him – and moved to the darkening window.

'Come with me, my love,' he said again, striding challengingly from the bed towards her, holding her for a brief moment, then moving away across the room, excited by the idea, vigorous and confident that it could be done, that it must be done. He stood, completely naked, his body hard, brown again now, for very often if the small yard at the back of his house was sunny he would remove his shirt to tinker beneath the bonnet of his beloved motor. The 'Huntress' which had been moved from the factory to the outbuildings at the far side of the yard, and he was determined to return her to her former glory and the sun had coloured his chest and back and arms to a splendid nut brown. His long legs were the colour of amber, fluffed with dark hair which ran up his thighs to lie finely on his flat stomach and muscled chest. Though he was not a thick-set man, his shoulders were broad and the weight which he had lost in the prison camp was almost returned, and he was in almost as fine a physical shape as he had ever been. He was a man at the peak of his vigour, tireless in his energies, needing something to fill the lonely life he led, liking nothing better, when he was not behind the wheel of his motor car, or flying, to walk for miles on the Derbyshire fells.

Meg leaned against the window frame and watched him as he moved towards the bathroom and her eyes had taken on that look he remembered from a long time ago. A look which asked, 'dare she?' 'could she?' telling him she would not need a great deal of persuasion and his own gleamed though he was careful not to let her see it.

'Martin, you know I cannot . . .'

'I know of no such thing.'

'How can I leave? You know I cannot leave!'

'Why not?' He turned away from her intrigued face and going into the bathroom turned on the bath taps, still talking above the sound of the running water.

'You could tell . . . Tom and Annie you were . . . I don't know . . . what would be a legitimate excuse? Something to do with the hotel. You've told me Tom is quite happy as long as he has Beth and Will and he's become used to you being away during the day so what's to stop you?'

'Well, there's the night . . . He would not like to . . . You don't know what he is like sometimes, Martin . . . nightmares.'

'Could not that fellow Will share your . . . his room?' The subject was delicate and there was stilted coolness in Martin's voice. She heard him step into the bath with a long drawn out, hopeless sigh and she moved across the bedroom to the door which led into the bathroom. There was a contemplative expression on her face and her teeth worried her bottom lip. She watched him lie back in the water, admiring the shining golden brown of his wet body, then, taking the soap from the shelf beside the bath began to lather his chest and, back, smiling as he hunched his shoulders appreciatively. Her face was soft and beginning to glow again with that female appraisal which would lead to languor and the desire which Martin Hunter knew so well. Her hands smoothed and caressed, lingering over the strong arch of his neck, the silky curve of his shoulder, each small bone of his spine and his own desire took flame.

Her mouth fell to brush the pulse which beat at the base of his throat and her voice was soft and ragged.

'What could it be, d'you think . . . some exhibition . . .'

'Why not?'

'But where?'

'London, perhaps?'

'I would have to leave a telephone number where I could be reached . . .'

'Of course.'

'I could say I was . . .'

'What?'

'Let's think . . . of something.'

Her mouth had reached the hard strength of his stomach, just where the soapy bath water lapped but Martin Hunter's attention and interest in Meg's wonderings were slipping rapidly away on the sensuous tide created by her fingers and mouth. The sheer negligeé she wore was a pale, frosted grey, like silver in moonlight. It was of soft organdy, tied carelessly just below her breasts with a coral satin ribbon. It was simple and loose, falling from her shoulders in a graceful line to the floor where it cascaded into a score of narrow, coral-ribboned frills. The satin mules which exactly matched the ribbon had been kicked off. As she leaned over him he could see the twin, pearly crests of breasts and the amber tips of her nipples.

'You think . . .' he mumbled, '. . . for how you expect me to concentrate when you kneel there as beautiful as an angel and as wanton as a courtesan . . .'

'Wanton! Me! How can you say such things, Martin Hunter?' but she was laughing now.

'Because it's true and if by the time I count to five you have not removed that delectable bit of nonsense you call a bed-gown it will get rather damp for I mean to have you in this tub with me.'

'Martin ... stop it ... I want to discuss ...' but it was half-hearted and her eyes glowed into his and her lips parted moistly against her white teeth.

'One ... two ... three ...'

'Martin ... just one more thing. Shall we ...?'

'Four ... five ...'

The coral ribbon was twitched lazily aside and in a whisper of silvered mist the diaphanous gown fell about Meg's hips. The strong arms of her lover gripped her fiercely in a passion of love and as the water plunged wildly over the rim of the bathtub, Meg Fraser's white body was taken rapturously to lie against Martin Hunter's brown chest, the silken wet curves and valleys and peaks of her given the minute and assiduous scrutiny he vowed such beauty deserved. The explanation which Meg was to give her husband and those at the hotel as to why she must absent herself for several days at the end of June, was totally forgotten.

They travelled to Hendon in Martin's 'Huntress', leaving Meg's automobile discreetly parked at the rear of the house in Camford, and for three days and two nights they lived in a world which held just the two of them, the days filled with the excitement and wonder of the machines they both loved and the nights with the excitement and wonder of sharing, for the first time, the whole of the night together.

In the four years Meg had run 'Hunter Aviation', though she had not been involved with the design and building of the aircraft, leaving that to the experienced men she employed, she had come to love the aircraft which were manufactured under her guidance. She had flown whenever she could, going up at least once a month, trying out a new concept in design, she said, but if she were truthful, just for the sheer joy of flying.

Since the end of the war many aircraft of those belonging to the Royal Air Force had been sent to its salvage store at Croydon for everyone knew the peace of the world was assured and they were now no longer needed. Any man with £800 in his pocket might purchase a 'Bristol' two-seater fighter aircraft, a 'Sopwith Snipe' or even a 'Wren' for £100 less! There were even better bargains advertised in the *Aeroplane* including the one which offered an aircraft in exchange for a motorcycle! What use were these fighting machines now, they asked.

But at Hendon that first year after the war the men gathered who had the vision and shrewd intelligence to know that the aircraft industry was not finished. The war had given birth to an infant which had flourished and though it had not yet come to more than early childhood, it was certainly not to stop until it had achieved its full growth and these men were there to see what they might do to bring it to maturity. There were cross-country handicap races, putting man and machine through their partnered paces, in which Martin took part in a 'Wren III', winning a couple, much to his delight for he had four years to catch up on, he said. There were stunt men who looped and dived and flew so low their wheels almost brushed the ground, so recklessly, many of those who watched were of the opinion they cared neither whether they lived or died. They were fliers who had survived death in the skies above France and, having done so could not now adapt to civilian life. They were erratic, living for speed and adventure in their fast motor cars and any dare-devil job they could get in the air-circuses which were again becoming a crowd puller.

Meg was breathtakingly beautiful that weekend, clinging to Martin's arm in an ecstacy of joy. It was hot and sunny, the middle of what had been a perfect summer. She had dresses of georgette and voile and muslin, delicate and drifting with lace and embroidery, skirts made of yards of material gathered at the hip on a yoke. They were short, barely brushing her ankle bone, worn with long gloves and large, wide-brimmed hats like flower gardens. Colours of primrose, sky blue and apple green with a small handbag to match each one and no jewellery but the brilliant sparkle of happiness in her eyes. Martin was enchanted with her, swearing he was afraid to leave her alone whilst he went up since the moment he left her side the gentlemen would be round her like bees to the honey. Vital and glowing she was, in her love for the machines in which she herself was taken for a 'flip', and for the man who left her side only to go up himself.

They stayed in a small but splendidly appointed inn outside Hendon, sleeping in one another's arms, waking to the rapture of the other's nearness, to the knowledge that they need not wait, need not fret on what the other was doing, need only reach out to be loved!

'I would think I had died and gone to heaven, my darling,' he said lazily on the last morning, 'if it were not for the fact that we must get up in a short while and be on our way. It's a long journey from here to Camford and if we don't make a start soon you will not be back in the bosom of your family by nightfall.' There was a slight edge of bitterness in his voice.

Meg sat up in the sweet-scented sheets of the rumpled bed and shook back her hair. Martin watched her, putting a gentle hand to her cheek, his eyes bemused with his love for her. She was so soft and lovely, so comely, with all the attributes a man would ever need in a woman and yet, so strong! Her strength confounded him, her spirit warmed and delighted his and he would have given everything he owned to take her hand and slip away with her, vanishing forever from the responsibilities which sat heavily upon them both. She leaned now to look into his face, her own becoming sad. No matter how long they had, or what glorious moments they crammed into their times together it was never enough. She had lied to Tom and to Annie, Tom trusting and reassuring her that of course, she must go to see the latest designs of furniture and household gadgets which were on show, so necessary if they were to open up the hotel and that he would be fine with Will. Yes, a camp-bed could be brought into the room he usually shared with her and if he needed ... anything ... anything in the night when the demons often came to frighten him, Will would be there to exorcise them.

Annie had said nothing but in her eyes had been deep concern for this thing could only end in tragedy and surely Meg, who was an intelligent woman, must see it.

'Martin, you knew it had to end. We are lucky to have had this.'

'*Lucky*! Jesus, Meg ... we should ...'

'What?'

'Oh, never mind! You know how I feel! All these weeks of creeping about ... hiding.'

'What else *can* we do, Martin?' She tried to kiss his strained mouth but he turned away and the magical joy was gone in the desolation of having to part with her again.

'God knows ... nothing, I suppose,' he answered harshly.

'Then ... please darling ... don't spoil what we have by ...'

'But Meggie, can't you see what this is doing to us? Where it is leading ...'

'Leading?' Her voice had become wary for this was not the first time he had talked like this, as though he must worry and probe at the dark uncertainty of their future. He longed to see the child, his daughter, naturally and had been deeply offended when she would not allow him to come to the hotel to visit her, claiming that the dangerous situation it could create might only upset Tom's already precarious hold on normality. Martin was arrogant and menacing when he was denied what he thought of as rightfully his. Though, as yet, his pity for Tom was still strong she knew it would not be long before the picture he had carried of his friend the last time he had seen him, became hazed with time and he would not find it hard to convince himself that Tom was not nearly as bad as they made out!

'Yes, you know what I mean.' His voice was beset with peril. 'We cannot just drift on like this, getting nowhere, having no life beyond this ... this ...'

'What did you have in mind?' She asked coolly and the sadness swamped her for the joy had been so short-lived.

'I don't know. I have made no plans or even thought ... but surely, if Tom were approached ... told of the ...'

'Don't try it, Martin! It would not work and I will not have Tom ...'

'Tom! Tom! Tom! I hear nothing but what is right for *Tom*! I am sorry for the poor devil but would it hurt to bring my daughter to see me at ...'

'*She is not your daughter!* Can you not understand that though you fathered her she is Tom's child in *his* mind. He adores her and she loves him. She would ...'

'I am not asking you to ...'

'I don't give a damn *what* you are asking me to do. I will not let Tom and Beth be hurt by what *we* do. I love you Martin, more than anyone in this world ... oh yes, I admit it,' her voice was torn with pain, 'even more than Tom and Beth, but I care, *care* so desperately about them both I would walk from this room right this minute, turn my back on you and the few moments we steal from ... from others and never see you again before I would let you hurt them!'

The air was alive with the intense fever of two single-minded

517

wills determined upon their own course. Martin, in the coolness
of his mind and the fairness with which he judged and treated
others, had not intended to make the demand to be allowed access
to his daughter since he knew in his heart, if he was truthful, that
it could only cause disaster. He had been testing her, seeing how
far he could go, seeing how far *she* would go to protect her
husband. His jealousy drove him hard, making him careless of the
fragile fabric which made up his relationship with Tom Fraser's
wife. It was the very heart of his life and should he back her into
a corner on the subject of Tom and Beth he knew he could
endanger it. But that day, as Meg argued and fought with him
to safeguard her family, his stubborn impatience with what he
was beginning to consider in his recklessness to be her high-
handed rejection of him in favour of Tom Fraser put words in his
mouth which he had really no intention of speaking.

He sprang from the bed and began to stride about the room,
the enormity of his pride and the exacting strength which had
brought him through four years of imprisonment, forced reason,
compassion and even the love he felt for this woman to be thrown
furiously aside. He was a man who had been used, for most of his
adult life, to his own way and could be perilous when it was
blocked. He was a man who had the ordering of a hundred others,
only this woman being allowed to direct *him*!

'This obsession with what Tom Fraser must, or must not have
done to him is making me exceedingly impatient, Meg. Our very
lives are encompassed by his . . . his failure to function as a man.
Am I to blame for that? Am I to be made to pay for that?' His
jealous rage made him careless of what he said, his one desire
being to hurt her as she hurt him with her need to protect the
man he looked on as a competitor for her love. 'Must we all suffer
in order that *he* alone might know happiness. Even our daughter
is being brought up in the deluded belief that he is her father and
I will not have it. D'you hear?'

Caution was thrown to the wind as he mutinously began to
believe that were it not for Tom Fraser's shilly-shallying ways,
Martin Hunter would have not only his love to come and be with
him, but the child of that love! 'If it were not for this . . . this so-
called . . . illness of his which seems now to be safely contained
and catered to by that man you have to guard him, you and I
and Beth could . . .'

Meg flung herself before him, her face an inch from his.

'*You bastard*! How dare you? Tom is completely destroyed by . . .'

'Tom, Tom! Damnation woman, I'm up to my bloody gills with Tom.' He put his hard hands on her upper arms, forcing her away from him, holding her, shaking her, trying to bend her iron will with his.

'Take your hands off me, Martin, or I swear I will . . .'

'What? You will what, my fine lady?'

For a moment petrified in time they glared into one another's eyes, hating, loathing, detesting the very sight and sound and feel of one another. Martin's hands gripped her viciously then, slowly, imperceptibly they loosened and fell away and blazing golden eyes wavered from metallic brown, clouded, hazed with bewilderment and fear.

Martin was the first to speak, to break the rigid pose of horror into which both had fallen.

'Jesus . . . Meggie . . . I . . . I went mad.'

'No . . . you . . .'

'I was . . . insane with jealousy . . . I love you so I cannot bear to be put second.'

'Aah, don't . . . my love, my love . . .'

And all the anger drained away as hands which had longed to strike and hurt, lifted to touch and caress and soothe, and later, as they spent their last hour in the big bed before they began their journey back to their separate, hopeless lives, they clung together in the frantic desperation of those who know they must part and simply cannot bear it!

Chapter forty-four

The first motor car which did not belong to any of those who lived or worked at 'Hilltops', drew up to the hotel's freshly painted front door in the first week in August. It was a brand new 'Silver Ghost' Rolls-Royce with the distinctive 'Silver Lady' mascot, the 'Spirit of Ecstacy', as its designer had called it, on the front of the bonnet. It was chauffeur driven and when the splendidly uniformed young man who sprang nimbly down from its driving seat, opened the passenger door, from it stepped Nellie and Albert Marrington, looking exactly as they had done over five years ago. A little plumper perhaps, and decidedly more prosperous, but the same, even to the broad, 'take-me-as-I-am' north country accent with which Nellie greeted Meg.

'Miss Hughes . . . nay, it's Mrs Fraser now, isn't it, lass an' lookin' a treat an' all. It's right nice ter see yer after all these years an' the hotel looks grand . . . grand! Well, I said to my Albert if we're wantin' a quiet holiday on us own wi'out telephones ringin' and folk forever fetchin' him to sort out their problems which they should be able to do theirselves by now seein' as how he reckons he's retired, well there's nowt else to do but but get right away from it all an' where else can we find a bit of peace and quiet but at yon Miss Hughes' . . . eeh, sorry lass, Mrs Fraser's place. He's not one for cruises an' the like, my Albert. Don't care for foreigners, yer see, nor the food. We had us some good times up here afore the war and as I said to him, Albert, I said, if Miss Hughes's kept up the standard she had before t'war, she'll do fer us. We could a' done wi' you a few times in the last few years, I can tell yer! *Work*! He never stopped, my Albert! Well, he wouldn't, would he, bein' in textiles, like. All them uniforms, millions on 'em . . . but there, we musn't dwell on it, must we? It's all done with now and best get on wi' our lives . . . now . . . what lass? A cup o' tea, champion, champion, an' then we'll have us a look at yon suite yer promised us.'

It had taken the best part of two months to bring the 'Hilltop

Hotel' back to its former splendour and as Edie said, it reminded them of the days, nearly ten years ago now – my God, was it that long? – when she and Annie, Meg and poor Mr Tom, and old Zack – did they remember old Zack, old beggar must be on his grave now, surely ... had turned 'The Hawthorne Tree' from a ramshackle, run down old coaching inn, into the fine establishment Meg had made of it. Not that 'Hilltops' was ramshackle, far from it but five years of lying silently under dust covers with no more than a monthly inspection and a yearly 'going-over' had not done much for the lovely suites of rooms. They needed a good 'bottoming' in her opinion and when the army of decorators and painters had gone through them all and traipsed their careless feet all over Meg's lovely parquet flooring, and the carpets had been returned from the cleaners, that's what she meant to give them. The curtains had been washed and ironed, or specially cleaned in the case of velvet and brocades, and the upholsterers had mended fabric where the moth had got in, despite her efforts with the moth-balls, but she rolled up her sleeves ready for her mammoth and challenging task. She'd need some help, she told Meg for she wasn't as young as once she had been but two or three good girls should be enough for what she had in mind.

But two or three good – or otherwise – girls, or even *one* were not as easy to come by as once they had been. During the war the lot of women had improved noticeably. The men had gone to fight and the opportunities for their womenfolk to demonstrate what they could do were now readily available. They had become more critical of the conditions under which they worked, and of the work itself and were not really prepared to return to many of the forms of employment which had been theirs before 1914. One of these was the domestic drudge! Many of them, if they were over thirty, and subject to some educational and property qualifications, now had the vote and they were inclined to a growing independence and a reluctance to return to the injustices done to their pre-war selves.

'What are we going to do, Meg?' Edie wondered in despair when, in answer to the advertisement Meg had put in newspapers in Buxton and Ashbourne, and even as far away as Liverpool and Manchester, for several smart young ladies to work in the hotel trade, not one had put in an appearance!

'We'll just keep looking, Edie, and offer higher wages.' Meg, deep in the enchantment Martin Hunter weaved around her whenever she could get to the little house near Camford, the house they called their 'home', floated blithely through the days, nothing, it seemed, coming between her and the strange dream world in which she had existed since the day she had savagely threatened Martin that she would not see him again. It had badly frightened them both, that explosion of passionate rage in which they had fought one another, and in the weeks following it they had both been careful not to create a situation which might disturb the harmony of their love. It was as though it had been a violent and terrifying thunderstorm, brooding over them before its onslaught, pressing down on their unprotected heads, but now, with its might spent, its power diminished, the days of peaceful, blessed sunshine which followed gave her the strength to get through and overcome any difficulty – such as a lack of staff – with a calm which amazed even herself. She was not fool enough to believe it would go on forever, this acceptance of their fragile relationship but for the moment they were living it one day at a time, cherishing what they had.

'Come on, Annie, and you too, Edie. You both have cousins and second cousins and third cousins twice removed back in Great Merrydown. Don't tell me none of them have a strong and reliable fourteen-year-old we can train up to our standards. I need one good experienced girl for the dining room. Smart, ambitious and hardworking. The rest we can manage somehow. I will do the cooking, the reception and the bookwork and . . .'

'Give over, Meg! Three jobs *and* Tom to see to and then there's the child . . .'

'Will looks after Tom and Beth has Sally Flash and it will only be until we get firmly back on our feet. Now don't scowl at me like that, Annie Hardcastle. You know I can do it. I can do anything I put my mind to.'

She was invincible in her confidence, in her love and in the renewal of the strong will to succeed which Martin had put back into her with his own enthusiasm for his work. He was proud of her, he said, and there was nothing she could not do if she cared to and if she would just slip her hand . . . yes . . . just there and arrange her shoulders . . . my word, the light was superb as it rested in pale golden shadows on her, yes, yes, he knew they were speaking of the hotel . . . but really, whilst they were about it did she not think that if they were to lie on the . . .

Their love, and the laughter which appeared to go hand in

522

hand with it, the soft warmth of his approbation gave her something, some quality she found hard to describe but the vitality she now possessed reminded her of Megan Hughes of ten years ago. She knew she must work harder than she had ever done, and that her responsibilities were more than she had ever had but all she needed, she told herself, were some hardworking girls and perhaps an ex-soldier, if there was one who was not devastated by the war, to work in the bar and she could do it. If she had to work twenty-four hours a day herself, she would do it.

By the end of July she would re-open the 'Hilltop Hotel'!

'Well, my sister's husband's cousin has a couple of girls just left school. They're dying to get into what they call "office work" whatever that might be. Lady typewriters, I believe they call them but if they were told they were to be taught hotel management, which sounds more impressive than scrubbing floors,' Annie grinned, 'then I reckon they might be persuaded. If the wages were right!'

'Good, you write to them then . . . oh, and tell them they can use the typewriter in my office. That might fetch them!'

'You haven't got one.'

'That's easily remedied!'

The hardest part, of course, was dealing with Tom's fear at the sudden upheaval in the monotonous pattern which had been his life for over eight months and his utter terror at the spectre of meeting 'people'. He had become used to the two men who worked in the gardens and even the young lad who had been taken on to help *them*. He and Will planted and weeded the vegetable garden for though he had lost his peace of mind, his sure grip on the reality of life and the easy-going, smiling charm which had once been his, he had retained his gift for making things grow. Under Will's guidance he put in the seeds, not always sure what they were, and watched them come up and it was then, as the tiny green seedlings showed above the dark earth that his instinctive skill seemed to come to life as they did and he would nurture them, love them even until they grew to be the fine vegetables and the fruit which would be placed before the guests, who would one day seat themselves in Meg's refurbished dining-room. Whilst the prospect of this was in the future, whilst his garden and his life on what they called the 'farm' were filled with only Will and Beth, the gardeners, the dogs, he was perfectly certain that when the day came he would get through it quite unscathed.

523

They were guests, Meg explained to him as she held him in her arms one night, and he would have absolutely no need to even see them. They would keep to *their* part of the hotel and there was no way they could get through to *his*. To the apartment which he and Beth, Sally Flash and herself were to share. Yes, the dogs would be with him and Will would sleep in the attic room if Tom wanted him to. The gardens at the back of the house and the farm itself where his animals were housed, the cows and the goat, the pigs and the hens, would be out of bounds to anyone but himself and Will. Yes, of course Beth could go with them, until she went to school.

'To school?'

'Now you know she must go to school when she is five, Tom.' Meg was infinitely patient with him but sometimes she worried about the intense wall of protection Tom tried to erect about Beth ... his daughter. He still was not happy about the pony she was learning to ride and stood in a sweat of apprehension each time she was astride his back. Meg had bought a couple of sturdy mares, small and steady, believing that if she, and therefore Tom, could also learn to ride, going out on the quiet moor with Beth it might allay his fears but so far he had not been persuaded to get up on the mare's back. He would stand for hours stroking the soft nose of the animal, looking into the liquid eyes, soothed as he had always been by the contact he had with a creature he knew would not harm him but it seemed it was not in him to actually ride the mare.

'Why does she have to go to school, Meggie. Can't she have a governess. That way she needn't go out of the grounds. You know I don't like ...'

'Tom, she needs to be with other children. It's not good for her to be just with you and Will,' and Tom, the Tom who had onced romped with Meg and Martin, agreed, but the Tom who now lived in his body swore to himself that when the time came he would do everything to prevent his beloved daughter from going out into ... well ... there were shells ... and he had heard a whizz-bang the other day when he was in the meadow!

But as the day rapidly approached, as the constant and sudden appearance of strange men, the alarming banging of a workman's hammer, of saws cutting sharply through wood rattled his fragile nerves, Will was forced to take Tom to the furthest fields on the farm. Each evening when they returned, Tom would be more apprehensive at the sight of some new adjunct added to his familiar home, or worse still, some part of it taken away! Windows appeared where there had been none and a door which had been there when he left that morning was bricked up and plastered over when he returned and what would happen next, his wounded mind begged to know?

Meg was in Ashbourne, once again attending the solicitors who were still attempting to untangle the legal complexities caused by Martin's 'death', his will and his return to life which had made it null and void. She had spent an hour with them and her head was aching as she returned to her motor car and when the voice called her name her first reaction was annoyance for she had just been promising herself half an hour with Martin and the certainty that his clever and imaginative fingers would ease it away.

'Meg, Megan, is it you?' the voice asked.

Meg turned to stare at the woman who had called her name and though there was a certain familiarity about her eyes and the set of her mouth she could not for the life of her remember where she had known her.

The woman smiled and held out her hand.

'Eveline O'Hara.'

'Eveline . . .?'

'You don't remember me?'

'Well, yes, I know your face but . . .'

'The Adelphi Hotel. Miss O'Hara!'

Megan began to smile and through ten years of change and more change, of war and suffering, of happiness and grief, the memory of a young girl and this woman emerged – and she was Megan Hughes again, skivvy, kitchen-maid, chambermaid and finally assistant housekeeper.

'Miss O'Hara . . . why, of course . . . really, I don't know why I didn't recognise you. You are . . .'

'Older, Megan and . . . not quite so . . . strong.'

'No . . . we have all . . . the war took its toll.'

'Aye, it did . . .' and a shutter came down on the face of Eveline O'Hara as it did on a hundred thousand female faces all over the country at the mention of the war.

'Come and have a cup of tea, Miss O'Hara, and tell me all about yourself.'

'It's Mrs Coyle now, Megan, but call me Eveline, after all, I'm not that much older than you,' and Meg could see she was right.

She had always seemed to be middle-aged to the young Meg Hughes from her lowly position as kitchen-maid but now she realised she could be no more than thirty-five or six, though her hair was greying and her face was lined.

They sat in the small tea room for over an hour and at the end of it Meg Fraser had herself the 'experienced girl' she needed for her dining-room. Eveline Coyle was a widow now, her husband of two years gone with the very same 'Liverpool Pals' who had been mown down at Tom's side. She hadn't fancied going back to Liverpool where she had been so happy for such a short time with her Donny, she said sadly, so she was working in a local hotel as a glorified housekeeper-cum-receptionist-cum anything-else she was required to do but she wanted to settle somewhere, make a home for herself, put roots down, but there . . . that was enough about her. What had Megan been up to in the ten years since they had last met?

She drove home with Meg that evening, all her worldly posses-sions in the back of the Vauxhall, the recriminations of the hotel manager silenced by the month's wages Meg had stuffed into his greedy hand; and she wept a little when Meg showed her the small, sunny sitting-room and bedroom with which she was to do exactly as she liked for they were to be her 'home'.

'You put your roots down here, Eveline,' she said softly, 'for I mean to be here for a long while!'

And now they were here. The Marringtons first, as seemed only right and proper for they had been her first guests when she had opened 'Hilltops' before the war, and tomorrow their dear friends, Sir Joseph Hartley and his wife – 'made his brass in munitions, lass, and got a knighthood an' all, though my Albert said he bought it an' I say what's to stop Albert havin' one then? Lady Nelly, that'd be me,' and her good-natured laugh could be heard in every part of the hotel that week!

They came in their droves that lovely autumn, the private suites and bedrooms never empty. The newly rich who could now afford this luxury which the elegant Mrs Fraser offered, and the thoroughbred wealth which had not been earned but handed down. The war had to some extent drawn the classes together, or at least given the well-bred the tolerance to accept the well-feathered, for they were so exceedingly rich! The local gentry came to dine when a table could be found for them, careless and haughty but adding that touch of privileged class to Mrs Fraser's dining-room. They drank the excellent wines she served and ate the superb food she personally prepared – five years had not diminished her skills in the culinary arts, it seemed – and moved about her lovely, newly decorated, exquisitely furnished drawing-room and salon and the intimate and quite daring bar and grill room she had installed. They came in their motors, Rolls-Royces and Bentleys and Lanchesters, which gleamed in the soft lights falling across them from the windows, and no-one was ill-mannered enough to mention the shell of the man who was her husband and who, one heard, was locked up in a distant wing of the hotel with a man to guard him!

'When will you ever have time for me?' Martin asked her ominously, his pride in her not apparently foreseeing the cutting back of the hours they had spent together, little enough to start with, his expression saying. August had passed into September and then October and still the travellers came, their appetite for a long weekend, or a mid-week break or a few days away from it all scarcely abating. 'Does the bloody season never end?'

'It appears not, my love. The war seems to have introduced into everyone the desire to get away and have a holiday.'

'But it's been nearly a year since the war ended. Are they never going to forget it?'

'How can they? How can anyone?' and the silence would fall about them and Meg would feel the sharp-edged tension come between them and neither could remove it, nor even speak about it for both were afraid it might wound them so mortally they might never recover.

Beth Fraser, four-and-a-half years old and full of energy and charm and the bright beauty of her mother, raced across the springy turf of the slope which ran above the gorge of the Dovedale Valley. Though it was October, guests from the hotel still wandered lazily about the gardens and their well-bred voices begged one another to look at the darling child and was she not a replica of her mother, the superb Mrs Fraser, they said, and do come here, little girl so that they might pat her riotous curls. The child stopped, politely waiting but in her eyes was the rebellious look which, if they had known him they might have recognised in those of her father. She stood and submitted to having her rose-petalled cheeks admired and the length of her curling lashes, and when her mother's guests moved on, their interest turning to some

527

other topic of curiosity which they were certain Mrs Fraser arranged just for their entertainment, Beth sighed in childish exasperation for really it was very hard to have a *good* game without one or other of them interrupting it!

'Let's go down the path, Sally,' she begged her nursemaid. 'We could throw sticks in the river for Sidney.'

'Now you know Mummy doesn't like you to go out of the garden, Beth . . .'

'Oh just this once, Sally . . . please . . . we won't go far . . .'

'Well . . .' Sally Flash turned as though to search out Mrs Fraser and beg her permission but the only people about were hotel visitors, and all, she assumed about to bear down on her charge, and could you blame them for she was an extremely engaging little girl, but still, it was a nuisance!

'Alright then, but not too fast and *not too far!*'

It was cold and though the sun shone with the iced brilliance of winter it gave off no warmth. The summer and autumn, long and lovely, day after day with no intention, it seemed of ever ending had left overnight, turning the weather about so rapidly one day it was summer, the next deep winter and those who knew the ways of it in this high land of the Derbyshire peaks said it would snow soon and that the winter would be long and hard.

A yellow labrador puppy ran at Beth's heels, leaping and barking his excitement and delight at this escape from the confines of the garden, raising his nose to sniff the windless air, his bright, curious eye following the movement of the child.

'Sidney,' she called imperiously, showing him the stick she held in her hand, then, having caught his wandering attention, throwing it haphazardly a few yards along the path. 'Fetch Sidney,' she shouted, pointing to where the piece of wood had fallen but the puppy merely leaped to snatch at her hand before darting off again to follow some fascinating scent he had come upon.

Their concerted noise blasted crows from their cover to wheel about the thin blue sky and the man behind the grey pitted boulder smiled.

Shadows of the half naked trees made patterns through which the child and the dog romped and the vivid scarlet of her coat made a moving, rippling charge against the landscape which was already painted in winter colours of black and white. She wore no hat and her hair, cut short, sprang about her head in a flame of copper, moving in the still air like the russet coat of a running fox. The exertion had put poppy flags in her cheeks and the spangle of stars in the deep, chocolate brown of her eyes.

'Sidney, come here Sidney,' she called again and the puppy raced towards her, his eyes adoring, his expression resigned.

'Good boy, good old boy,' the child cried and bent to hug his head in a passion of love. 'See, fetch the stick. Go on, fetch the stick,' and the dog ran obligingly though he had scant idea of what they were doing.

Sally Flash walked slowly behind them, her eyes moving serenely from one lovely sight to another. A pussy willow bent towards the river, growing deep in fern and patches of moss. There was a coppice of hazelwood beneath which a dense layer of wood sorrel lay, climbing over fallen logs and the cut stumps of trees where they had been felled. There was a flicker in the roots of a beech tree and the bright eye of a water vole peeked out at her and she hoped the dog had not got its scent. She breathed in deeply, drawing the champagne like air into her lungs, pushing her hands further into the pockets of her coat as she followed her charge along the hard, frozen path beside the tumbling water of the Dove.

'Mind, sweetheart, those stones are slippery,' she called.

'Can Sidney go in, Sally?'

'He's already in!'

'Well of course! He is a gun dog, you know. It is part of his nature to take to the water.'

The old-fashioned phrasing made the nursemaid smile.

'Who told you that?' she called after the darting child.

'Will.'

'Of course . . . yes, he would know.'

The water flew about the ecstatic dog and the child shrieked with laughter and the man who crouched behind the boulder knelt and watched for a moment longer, then, as though he could not wait another minute he stood up and began to walk towards her.

'Good morning,' he called and the child stopped abruptly and backed away some hazed memory making her cautious, and the nursemaid hurried to catch up to her. Though she had been away up North visiting her own family when Beth was taken away she could still recall the terror with which Mrs Fraser had recounted it to her on her return. She put her arm protectively about Beth's shoulders, holding her to her side and the puppy ran back nervously, his tail ready to tuck itself between his legs. He leaned against the child and the three of them watched the man as he moved in their direction.

'It's a lovely day,' he said and his eyes never left the little girl and Sally Flash held her more firmly.

'Yes, indeed it is.'

'. . . and that's a fine dog you have there, Beth.' The small girl stared up at the tall stranger, her face assuming that guarded expression of a child who is not awfully sure she liked her name on the lips of a man she did not know.

'Thank you,' she said politely.

The man stopped then, aware that he had alarmed the child's nurse. He wore a pair of knee breeches with knee length socks and a good pair of stout walking boots. Under his serviceable tweed jacket was a warm woollen jumper with a polo neck and he wore a peaked cap. He carried a plain walking stick of cherrywood and had a small knapsack on his back.

'You don't remember me, do you?' he asked softly, almost sadly. His eyes looked directly at the child but the remark was addressed to Sally Flash.

'Well . . . I can't just . . .'

He turned to look at her then and the luminous softness in his deep, brown eyes fell warmly on her face, the residue of his feelings – for what, she wondered – still there.

'I'm Martin Hunter. You were with Beth on the morning I came to see her in the nursery, six months ago now. I've had a hair cut since then.' His smile flashed out humourously, then immediately he returned his gaze to the child as though he could not waste precious time on anyone else. He squatted down before her, holding out his hand and at once the puppy, all fears allayed, ran to him, fawning all over him in a delirium of joy.

'Don't you remember me, Beth?' He gave the appearance of being quite devastated if she did not. He held the puppy with a firm hand, looking humbly into the face of the little girl and Sally Flash let go of her, ready to allow her to go to him if she wished it.

'No.' The child was still suspicious and not at all sure she liked *her* Sidney, her own puppy and therefore allowed to love no-one but her, obviously delighted with his new friend.

'Can you ride McGinty yet?' he asked gently.

'Yes . . . well, nearly . . .'

'I thought to see you galloping all over the moor by now.'

'Daddy says I'm not big enough yet but . . .'

She moved a step nearer to him, her childish caution evaporating. There was something in this man which, now that his eyes were on a level with her own, she recognised, something which rang a bell in her young mind and it was to do with her pony.

'Of course, if Daddy says so.' His voice was solemn, then he winked.

'I know . . . I know . . .' Her face lit up and she hopped from one foot to the other in her excitement. 'You're the man who said I could ride McGinty 'cos I was a big girl, if we put a rein on him, and now Will lifts me on and holds the lead and I gallop and gallop round and round the paddock and when I get bigger Daddy says I can ride out . . .'

She came right up to him then and put her hand on his knee, looking delightedly up into his face, 'But I'm big enough now, aren't I . . . aren't I?'

'Well, perhaps if Mummy spoke to your Daddy . . .'

The child's face clouded and her mouth pouted rebelliously.

'No, she says we musn't make Daddy upset . . .', her face brightened, 'but if you asked him . . . could you . . . Mr . . . er.'

'My name is Martin.'

'Yes.'

'Had you forgotten?'

'Course not . . . but if you asked Mummy about McGinty . . . will you? Will you? I'm not frightened of falling off, like Daddy says.'

Martin Hunter's mouth tightened ominously and there was a hard gleam in his eyes. 'I'm sure you're not,' he said huskily. Somehow she had stepped between his knees, her small earnest face close to his and Sally Flash began to fidget for though this man had been to 'Hilltops' and was a friend of the Frasers, he had only been the once and now, here he was, out of sight of the house, practically embracing her employer's child.

'Do you know who it was who sent Sidney to you?' he was saying now, evidently trying to divert the little girl from the eternal argument which forever raged, Sally herself could vouch for that, over the riding of the pony, and the little girl pressed herself trustingly against his knee.

531

'He came in a basket, just for me, with my own name on it,' she said proudly.

'But do you know who sent him?'

'A friend, Mummy said.'

Martin Hunter put his arm about his daughter and Sally was quite frozen, unable to spoil this special moment which seemed suddenly to have been created between the man and the child. Surely . . . surely he could not really be?

'Yes, a friend. Can you guess who?' He grinned and raised his eyebrows comically and the child responded with a shout of delighted laughter.

'It was you . . . it was you!' and put her arms about his neck.

Chapter forty-five

'She told him she'd seen you. She never stopped talking about you and the bloody pony and the puppy, and how you said she was big enough to ride out on the moors and she had only to ask Mummy to speak to Daddy, and with no trouble at all she'd be off and away, up in the hills, the dog at her heels and you, I've no doubt, at her side. D'you know what it did to him, do you? Have you any conception of how he *really* is, Martin, have you, because if you have you are the cruellest man I know. God, I thought he was going to go right off his head, *right* off, not just partially as he is now. Do you know what it did to him, *and* to Beth? He terrified her, *terrified* her. Down in the corner of the nursery he was, his arms over his head, but worse still, he had *her* with him. Mind the shells, he was screaming, mind the bloody shells and calling her Andy. I had to get the doctor to *both* of them, Martin, and it was all I could do to stop him taking Tom away in a straight jacket. When I think of all the work, the care which I've put in, and Will and the others. Week after week, month after month, repairing his confidence, sheltering him, giving him a purpose, something . . . anything to hold his life together and then you . . .' her face was a mask of snarling venom, 'you have to ruin it, send him back into that hell, frighten my daughter just for your own bloody selfish needs. I'll not forgive you Martin . . . never . . . never . . .'

He stood like a rock, bleak, ashen-faced, appalled and at first could make no sense of what she was saying. He had tried to draw her eagerly into his arms as she came into the warm welcome of the room for it had been a week or more since he had seen her. It was a hostile day with the first early snow of the winter falling on the peaks, turning to sleet in the town and beads of it sparkled in the soft frame of her hair which spilled from beneath her beret and trailed icily across her cheeks in tiny, melting drops. Her face was blanched, strained to breaking point but her eyes were like newly fired copper and she was as steady as a rock as she put up warning hands to his chest.

'Don't touch me, Martin.'

'Sweetheart, what is it?' he had smiled at first, for though his brain told him instantly of her dangerous mood, even before she spoke, warned by the rigidity of her body and the way in which she held back from him, the muscles of his face had not yet had time to take her measure and had instinctively formed into an expression of glad welcome.

They were standing face to face in the comfortable sitting-room of the house in Camford, the flames of the fire in the grate turning the cream of the walls to rose and apricot. He had drawn the curtains when he heard her motor car in the drive, ready to turn the ordinary Sunday afternoon atmosphere in which he had been idly studying the newspapers into an enchanted, multi-coloured bower of warmth for his love. Surprised and delighted, since she was not often able to get away at the weekend, he had drawn her in, ready to take her beret, her long leather coat, her boots, indeed anything and everything which kept her lovely body from his.

'I shall not come here any more, Martin,' she whispered, 'and if you attempt to see me or Beth, I shall take her away, and Tom as well, as soon as he is able to be moved.' She was distraught, hardly aware of what she was saying, it seemed, incoherent almost, in her devastation. 'You must stay here,' she went on, 'because of your work but I can move to anywhere in the world a decent hotel is needed, and begin again, and I will if you come near me, or mine again. It will be hard for we have made a life for ourselves, a good life now ... the hotel is ... but by God, I'll give it all up to protect him. D'you hear? He is wounded, Martin Hunter – wounded, can't you see it? – and I cannot bear to watch him bleed again. The wound will heal if it is given a chance but you ... you bastard ... you've opened it up again ... and I helped you ...'

She began to weep. It had been seven days. A week of weary desolation in which Meg Fraser had fought the relentless certainty that she must remove Martin Hunter from her life at once, for if she did not she would kill Tom Fraser as surely as though she held a pistol to his head and fired it – and not only that, in the process she would destroy Beth's chance for the secure childhood which was her right

There was the other alternative, of course, which the doctor had pointed out to her of having Tom committed to one of the many institutions which had been created for the men who had returned with the same dreadful fears Tom carried about with him, but most of those, he said, had not the chance Tom had. The doctor had been astounded by his regression and had Mrs Fraser any idea what had caused it. Had he had a shock, or been frightened of something? He had been so sure that given time and the peace of the life he led, Tom could live a relatively normal existence but really, if this happened again he would seriously advise her to have him put away.

Put away! *Put away!* Tom, Tom the boy she had loved, the man she had loved and cared for . . . put away!

The doctor apologised hastily for his unthinking choice of words, saying he had not meant it as it sounded but if Mrs Fraser had seen as many men as he had in the same condition as her husband she would understand the strain, and anger, he felt. As Tom drifted restlessly into the deep sleep of the strong sedative, and Beth hiccoughed her childish bewilderment on her mother's knee before the nursery fire, Megan prepared herself for the process of killing her love for Martin Hunter.

It was hard. Night after night, as Tom slept fitfully against her back she slipped from their bed and going down to the sitting-room, stirred the dying fire to life and huddled before it with only Beth's puppy for company. The hotel had finally been closed since it was now the approach of the season for winter blizzards up in the Peak district of Derbyshire, and the roads around Buxton could be impassable for weeks at a time.

It was quiet in the dead of night and amidst the turbulence of her heart and mind and stomach, that quiet lapped around her. She knew she was in a state of shock, her own blank-eyed image in the mirror told her so. She existed in a pit of weariness on a level which allowed her to function as the mother, the comforter, the giver of orders, raw, hurting, blind but not deaf to the voices which begged her for direction. She had got through it. Tom was calm, frail but calm, deep still in the grip of sedatives. The child had been soothed and reassured that Daddy's 'headache' had gone, her trust in him restored, her childish fear overcome and the disaster, for that was what it had been, averted, and now she must put it all together, the shattered pieces of Tom's world, hedge it around with the only surety of permanence she possessed. Herself!

535

Meg Hughes, his wife, and with Beth, the one lasting quality in his fragile life.

'God in Heaven, woman, what the hell's the matter with you? You're looking at me as though I was a dog turd beneath your feet. What the devil are you screaming about? Jesus Christ, anyone would think I had told the child who her real father was, and could anyone blame me if I did . . . My God, all I did was greet my daughter.'

'*Will you stop calling her your daughter*!'

'Ten bloody minutes. Ten bloody minutes! I said nothing to upset her, or her nursemaid. In fact we spoke about her Daddy, for Christ's sake, though it was ashes in my mouth to say it.'

'Just the fact that you spoke to her at all shattered him. He does not connect you with the Martin he knew as a boy. Though he recognises the name you are just the enemy threatening his child almost in her own home. He's afraid of . . . of anything which . . .'

'And that's another thing, lady! Can you not see what that is doing to her. Oh not yet perhaps since she's still little more than a baby, but as she gets older. Jesus, she's longing to ride that pony of hers! She's not afraid and yet he's transferring *his* fears to *her*. He'll have her locked away in the same prison he's in and you're letting him do it! I was astounded to see her down in that gorge, I can tell you but I didn't arrange it, Meggie . . .'

His voice had become softer, not pleading, but asking for her understanding, her fair-minded recognition of the truth. 'I was walking but when I saw her coming down the path with the puppy I couldn't just turn away. There she was, bright and . . .' He smiled in remembrance, his face warm and Meg felt the lump in her chest swell and throb and threaten to choke her, and the dry-eyed pain deep in her skull stabbed further into her tortured brain.

'Don't blame me, Meggie. She's a grand kid. She reminds me of you when I first saw you. You weren't much older than she is now but you were the bravest little beggar I had ever seen. I was only eight years old but I could recognise spunk when I saw it. Some other girl was . . . I don't remember now . . . getting at you about something and you were ready to cry but . . .'

'Stop it, stop it, I won't have it! I won't let you do this to us. To *her*! To Tom! Don't you see, Martin, what we have, this . . . this between you and I, must *lead* somewhere or it will stagnate, but there is nowhere for it to go! You want it to move to its natural conclusion, as all relationships do, to a permanent commitment, marriage, family ... but *ours* cannot! I am married to Tom. I have a child, a commitment already, to both of them. I cannot give you what you want, what you need. I thought I could. I thought, in my naivety, that you and I could share something, *have* something which would be enough for us both but it is just not possible. I was fooling myself – I suppose in my heart I knew it – that we would be satisfied if we could be together even for just part of our lives. It was better than nothing. We ... I thought we would never ... have anything ... that you were gone forever but you came back and in my joy I allowed it ... allowed you and I to ... take the chance but it is not enough, for either of us. Are you willing to go on like this, living alone, sharing your life with someone who can spare but an hour or two from her own now and again? Watching Beth grow up ... from a distance ... waiting, hoping ... *for what*? Tom is a young man, healthy now in his body and would you really want him to *die* so that you and I can be together because that is what it would take. *Tom's death*! This will destroy us in the end, Martin. You know it will. You will come to resent ... my responsibilities ... to demand more and I will not be able to give it to you ... so ... you will find someone who can. You are a strong man, strong willed, you need ... your own ...'

She could not go on. Her killing rage had gone, drained away by the truth she had seen in his eyes and heard in his voice and Martin felt his own angry resentment slip from his taut body. He had not deliberately set out to waylay Beth and her nurse. His natural pride and concern for his daughter had put words in his mouth when he spoke to her which he had not, at the time, considered in any way to be harmful to Tom. He really did not know – no-one did, he supposed, except Meg and the doctor who cared for him – of Tom's true state of mind and he had no idea of the effect his meeting with his daughter would have on Tom, nor the terror which had apparently sent him back to relive those events in France which had destroyed him. Martin had been overjoyed to see the child and quite simply had gone to her as naturally as any creature will gravitate to its own young. He had wanted – longed – to ask her about the puppy he had sent her, to see her eyes light up and her small face glow, not in gratitude, but with that particular excitement which all children share when there are presents to be opened. He had merely wanted that joy, that natural joy of giving which all parents delight in.

'Sweetheart . . .' His voice was urgent and he reached out to his child's mother, to his love, his friend, his armour and shield for without her in his life he would be defenceless. 'Sweetheart, don't do this to us. Don't throw away what we have . . . Jesus, Meggie . . . what a waste . . . what a bloody waste . . . you cannot mean to . . .'

At that precise moment the telephone began to ring.

Tom Fraser straightened up and put his hand to his back. He let out a sigh of relief as he stretched his long body, then leaned on his fork, turning to look back at the long furrow of black soil which he had just turned over. He and Will had cleared the last of the seed potatoes, ready to store them carefully in sacks which would stand in the barn for the winter. When they were done they would prepare the ground for next season's sowing.

It was very cold and high up on the peaks there was already a lace cap of snow. Lower down the slopes the rich copper of the bracken made a startling contrast between the whiteness of the tops and the fields below which were still green. The sky was a heavy grey, patched with a strange feathered luminosity, threatening the blizzard which, Will said, would come in the next few days. There was already a smell of snow in the air and a thin, intermittent drift of sleet which settled on the men's shoulders, melting immediately it touched them. They wore warm jackets, stout cord trousers and heavy boots and each had a hand-knitted muffler wound about his neck. They both wore a cap and woollen gloves but the exercise moved their blood richly through their veins and they were not cold. They had the ruddy colour of outdoor men well used to being on the move.

Will lifted his head and squinted up into the sky, then tutted irritably. He stood for a moment considering the increasing heaviness of the clouds then turned to look at the heaped piles of potatoes which lay along the furrow.

'We'll have to move these spuds, Tom. I thought they could have been left till morning but I reckon the snow will come tonight and then we'll not be able to find them tomorrow. Damn it, if they're covered and then left to lie here they'll rot and all our work will have been for nowt.' He shook his head in annoyance. 'I would have brought the bloody wheelbarrow if I'd known. Well, there's nothing for it, lad, we'll have to go and fetch it. It'll not take long and the walk will do us good, stretch our legs a bit.'

'Shall I go, Will? You could be putting them together in one pile while I walk back to the barn. Save us a bit of time and we'll have the job done that much quicker.'

Will looked at him sharply, surprised and not a little wary. It was no more than a week since his employer's husband had thrown himself – taking his daughter with him – into the corner of the nursery, yelling of shells and snipers' bullets, he'd been told, and Mrs Fraser had asked Will to be especially careful of him as they moved about the grounds. True, the doctor had left him some medication which had quietened him considerably, saying he would keep him on it for a week or so until he had recovered his frail composure and since then Tom had been quiescent, standing when he was told, sitting, washing his hands, just like a child. He was like a becalmed sailing craft with no wind in its sails, one that has come through a storm at sea and finds itself at peace at last. His eyes were clear and steady, his face was serene and his manner patient, but Will was not awfully certain that it was not due more to the sedative than a natural peace of mind. He'd had these 'turns' before, of course, and recovered from them so perhaps his mind had buried the incident which had disturbed him, as it had all the others from his past.

They were on the east side of the estate about ten minutes walk from the house, just on the edge of a stretch of woodland known as Lawty Wood. It had been too cold for the child or even the dogs to come with them, and Will himself had wondered whether it might perhaps have been better to stay in the barn or the woodworking shop but this was the last of the potatoes and if they could get them in before the snows came he would be relieved. Besides with winter here they would be spending a lot of time indoors and this might be their last chance to work the ground before it became too hard. He had plenty to occupy Tom and himself in the workshop during the winter months. Plans to make some garden furniture and he had an idea in his mind which he was certain would interest Tom, to build a dolls' house for Beth. Her birthday was in April which would give them the whole of the winter to design and make, not only the house itself but the miniature furniture which would go in it. He was convinced the idea would delight Tom and keep him content and occupied in the long winter days ahead. Of course they would get out to feed the animals and clean out their winter shelter but this would be something special to keep Tom's thoughts from his fears. His own mother and Edie had agreed to help with the tiny curtains and bedcovers and when they had finished up here, he meant to get off home and discuss his idea with Tom in front of the cheerful fire in the kitchen.

He stood for a moment, studying Tom Fraser's quiet demeanour, considering what he should do. It would certainly save a lot of time if one of them went for the wheelbarrow whilst the other piled the potatoes in readiness for his return. Tom waited patiently to be told what he should do. It was very peaceful here inside his head today. His thoughts slipped painlessly in and out, nice thoughts about the warm, loving kiss Meg had given him this morning before she went to Ashbourne on business, thoughts about his little Beth and the comfort he had taken from the half hour he had spent with her as he read to her by the nursery fire. There had been no shelling for days, thank God, and it had been peaceful in the billet and Andy was fine now that the medics had taken him to the field hospital. He had really enjoyed the manual labour he had shared with Will this morning for it had sent the blood coursing vigorously through his veins and he had not had such a feeling of well-being since ... since ... since the days when he and Meggie and Martin had cycled to the Delamere forest.

He smiled, a sweet and gentle smile at Will, seeing no strangeness in the way his life now overlapped so effortlessly with that of the one he had once known. Martin, Meg, Beth, Will, mingled freely with Andy and Mrs Whitley, with Captain Holgate, his officer at Mons, with Edie and Mr Atkinson who had taught him all he knew about the earth and what he planted in it, and with Annie, and Emm who had died in the fire. They peopled his world, some more ghostly than others but today they were clear and happy, smiling behind Will's shoulder, even old Andy grinning in that lovely Irish way he had with him, all blarney and peat bogs, the 'Pals' used to say about him, and with a Liverpool accent despite his lineage, you could cut with a knife.

'I'll go, Will, I'll not be long.' His smile deepened. 'I'll not have to be with this lot coming down on us. It's going to blow up a blizzard before long,' and before Will could stop him he turned and began to walk steadily in the direction of the hotel which stood on the other side of the small wood. As he stepped between the trees he turned, lifting the fork he still carried and called to Will.

'I'll tell Annie to put the kettle on while I'm there. We'll be needing something hot inside us by the time we've got this lot shifted.'

Will Hardcastle was openly weeping, saying he shouldn't have let him go, the tears running unchecked through the lines of his suddenly old face, and the young lad who helped in the garden, his own a white mask of shock kept repeating again and again. 'I was only fetching them a drink . . . I was only fetching them a drink . . . I was only fetching them a drink . . .' as though some blame might be laid at his door.

Meg looked at the obscene shape which lay beneath the huge oak tree, her mind empty, her eyes sightlessly staring, her face white and quite expressionless and waited with all the patience in the world since what else was there left for her to do, for the police constable to reveal its horror. It was like a tent, she thought, the kind with which children play, a pole sticking up in the middle of it but beneath it lay something so dreadful she knew she would need every ounce of her fragile strength to bear it. She knew who it was, of course. She had known from the moment she had been told of it for who else could it be? It was the inevitable ending to ten years of torment but as the thought came to her she knew that the torment was not yet done with. Beneath that sheet in all its terror and dread lay the last chance Tom Fraser would ever have of a decent life and how was she to live with it, she asked herself in desperation.

The constable put out an unsteady hand to what lay on the ground for like them all, he was unused to violent death. The cover, one begged hastily from a white-faced Annie was stained with drying blood and dirt from the ground and was wet with the steadily falling snow, still sleet-like and not yet sticking, but getting thicker and more vicious with every hour.

'Are you ready now, Mrs Fraser?' the constable said and she nodded. She could feel Martin straining beside her, his face dark with anger, his shoulders hunched with the need to strike out at someone, *anyone*, in his fear for her, since he was convinced there was no need for Meg to see what was beneath the cover. Surely someone else could view what lay there and say if they knew who it was. There was absolutely no need, in his opinion, for her to be put through this damned charade but she herself had insisted upon it and there was nothing he could say to stop her, though he had tried.

'I have to see, Martin . . . what lies there.'

'Why? for God's sake!'

'I must know who . . .'

'Is it likely you would know . . . him?'

'Yes.'

'Because . . . of Tom?'

'Yes,' and he had taken her arm and turned her to him, quite dangerous in his bewilderment, and looked into her white face and strange clouded eyes, and his own, torn between his love and anxiety for her, and his need to protect her from something over which he had no control, had been wild.

'What the hell's been going on here, Meg? What has happened in the years I've been away? Who is this . . . person? Tell me . . .'

'I will, Martin . . . after . . .'

The constable drew back the sheet and those about pressed forward to see what he had revealed. Will was there, still weeping and there was another constable, as well as the police sargeant from the village anxiously awaiting the arrival of his superior officer from headquaters, for really he was not experienced in this sort of crime. Beyond them were the two men who, with Will and the lad, had covered up the body. The boy had gone, calling wildly for his mother, taken away by the doctor who had examined the body and pronounced it quite dead.

The face looked up at her from the pillow of rotting leaves. It was drawn into the familiar snarling expression of hatred with which he had greeted her on each of the occasions they had met. His eyes were open and staring at her and she had time to think before the grey mists of slipping consciousness tried to take her, that at last he had done what he had set out to do! She clung to Martin's arm, feeling its rock-like strength beneath her fingers and somehow held on to her anguished mind.

'Do you know him, Mrs Fraser?'

'Yes.'

'Can you give me his name?' The constable twitched the sheet and for a moment the gardening fork was revealed, its four prongs deeply embedded in the chest of the corpse and Meg felt the heaving murmur of her stomach become a roar as she began the long slide into unconsciousness.

'*Where is my husband?*' she screamed. 'Why is nobody looking for him?' Then the blackness came and Martin caught her as she fell into it.

He found the hiding place just as dark overtook him. It was no more than an overhang of rock surrounded on three sides by others, but it faced out into the bitter wind. The snow was thickening and he could barely see but he didn't mind. They wouldn't find him here, not in this. The space was fairly dry, lined with moss and dead fern and he settled his back to the rock and began to unwind the muffler from about his neck. He smiled peacefully. Annie had knitted it for him and one for Will, his to be blue to match his eyes, she said and Will's to be red to go with his nose! She was like that, was Annie, making a joke about her son's high colour but filled with love, she was, not just for Will but for him as well. She had wrapped that protective love around him, like they all had, trying to shelter him from what haunted him and though they tried, and had to some extent, succeeded, it was no good. That man today had proved it. He remembered him and his name, though he wasn't going to speak it now, and what he had done to their Meg, just as he remembered everything from the past and *all* their names. That was the trouble! They had jostled at his shoulder for years now, trying to attract his attention and he had run away, hidden behind Meg and Beth, sweet Beth who was Martin Hunter's child, but he could not hide any more behind those who tried so hard to protect him, even at the expense of their own happiness. Meg had loved him. Meg had loved Martin Hunter and now he would give them their rightful place in one another's lives, just as he was to take *his* rightful place beside his pals. He had tried to hang back, to let them go on, but it did no good. They waited for him and always would, patient and sad-eyed, telling him what he had always recognised but would not admit to until now, that he should have gone with them when they left.

He folded the muffler carefully, placing it on the ground beside him, then, shivering, though he did not feel the biting cold, one by one he removed every garment he wore until he was completely naked. He spread out his clothes, then lay down on his side, pillowing his head on his folded arm, his knees drawn up to his chest, looking out into the whirling, dancing joy of the snowflakes. His mind was very peaceful as he thought of them.

Meg and Martin. He had always known, of course he had, and had not needed what the man had said to remind him. It was true. He'd hidden it, just like he had tried to hide Andy and Johnny and Titch and Captain Holgate, under the debris of his broken mind, but now his mind was whole again and he could see into it and they were there waiting. Andy had his fags out and Titch had brewed up and across the devastation of the mud and blood and shattered waste of war he could see the poppies, and three children walked hand in hand through them towards him, laughing, he could hear them, and he smiled as he closed his eyes.